The baby, a naked boy child on a folded cloth, jerks his fists in the torch's glare and starts to whimper.

Nick feels a cool calm roll down from the top of his head. The baby is no more than three or four weeks old. He is badly dehydrated and in ketosis, his breath quick and faint and smelling of pear drops, his mouth and nose crusted with white matter. His skin is freckled with insect bites and his bottom smeared with dried, spicy orange baby-shit, but his pulse is firm, and no bones seem to be broken.

Nick lifts him up, and almost at the same moment gunfire starts up outside; rapid, sustained bursts interspersed with single shots. Nick and Isabel look at each other.

"Take him to the helicopter," Isabel says.

She turns and jogs out of the door into the sunlight, and something lithe and pale and quick smashes into her. Her assault rifle sprays a spasmodic burst into the red dirt as she falls under the weight of her attacker, which wraps its arms around its head and works its face between the rim of her helmet and the collar of her flak vest. As Nick runs forward, the white thing rears back to show him its bloody face, a chunk of meat caught between teeth like nails hammered into its wide lipless mouth, and Nick fires three quick shots, firing one-handed because he's holding the baby, no kick to the Glock at all, and the thing flies backwards, a bloody star blown into the keg of its chest.

By Paul McAuley from Tom Doherty Associates

The Secret of Life
Whole Wide World
White Devils

WHITE DEVILS

Paul McAuley

TOR®

A TOM DOHERTY ASSOCIATES BOOK
NEW YORK

NOTE: If you purchased this book without a cover, you should be aware that this book is stolen property. It was reported as "unsold and destroyed" to the publisher, and neither the author nor the publisher has received any payment for this "stripped book."

This is a work of fiction. All the characters and events portrayed in this book are either products of the author's imagination or are used fictitiously.

WHITE DEVILS

Copyright © 2004 by Paul McAuley

All rights reserved, including the right to reproduce this book, or portions thereof, in any form.

Edited by Ellen Datlow

A Tor Book
Published by Tom Doherty Associates, LLC
175 Fifth Avenue
New York, NY 10010

www.tor.com

Tor® is a registered trademark of Tom Doherty Associates, LLC.

ISBN 0-765-34679-6
EAN 978-0765-34679-7

First edition: February 2004
First mass market edition: April 2005

Printed in the United States of America

0 9 8 7 6 5 4 3 2 1

For Georgina, of course

Part One
THE ATROCITIES

Chapter 1

Nicholas Hyde is working late and alone when Tremaine Thompson comes up the hill to ask his question. The setting sun throws Tremaine's shadow ahead of him as he climbs through strip fields on the slope above the shallow tributary of the Congo River and the ruins of the village. The day's stored heat beats up from the red African dirt. Dry stubble crackles under his boots. In the gallery forest at the edge of the fields, mobs of butterflies, their wings printed with the blue, red, and white logo of a famous soft drink, are love-bombing flowering vines, as indifferent to what happened here as to what has been done to their genes.

Fourteen months ago, a ragged gang of armed men burst out of the forest and seized control of the village. They were soldiers loyal to Sergeant Samuel Nyibizo's military dictatorship, in headlong retreat from the victorious forces of a democratic coalition supported by Obligate, the biggest and brashest of the new wave of environmentally conscious transnationals. The soldiers shot two men who tried to resist, and rounded up the rest of the villagers and forced them to undress. They killed the village's pigs and chickens, set fire to the huts and the little tin-roofed schoolhouse, smashed the solar-powered water pump and the satellite dish. Then they marched the naked men, women, and children up into the fields.

A young woman who had been collecting wild ginger in the forest saw something of what the soldiers did before she lost her nerve and ran away. She said that they killed the women first, because they had been making the most noise—because they had been pleading for the lives of their children. She said that the soldiers raped the women and hacked them to death, and then they started to kill the men and the children.

"It was like they were butchering animals," she told one of the debriefing officers of the War Crimes Tribunal, in Brazzaville. "They took turns to kill. It was hard work."

Tremaine is in charge of the forensic team that is investigating the massacre on behalf of the humanitarian charity, Witness. The strip fields have been cleared of weeds and scrub, a grid of white tape has been strung from aluminium stakes, and little red flags on weighted wires mark the position of each scattering of bones. More than half the remains have been photographed, documented, and removed; those left are covered by sheets of green plastic. As he walks up the hill, Tremaine thinks that the red flags and pegged green rectangles scattered across the white grid have the look of a half-finished board game.

Nicholas Hyde is working near the top of the slope. Like Hell's own gardener, he's kneeling on a silicone pad, using the ceramic blade of his Emerson folding knife to tease up and cut away fibrous roots that have knitted themselves through the skull and ribcage and backbone of a woman's skeleton. He's so intent on his work that he does not look up until Tremaine Thompson's shadow falls across him.

"Man, how I hate that climb," Tremaine says, reaching into his day bag. He's seriously out of breath. Sweat maps dark continents across the front and back of his Philadelphia Police Department T-shirt. "Here you go. I thought I'd bring you a beer, seeing as it's the cocktail hour."

Nicholas Hyde fields the cold can and sits back on his heels and holds it against the back of his neck; Tremaine fishes out another, cracks it, and takes a long swallow. He's a heavy man with a broad, pleasant face and a shaved head. He has degrees in pathology and forensic anthropology, and took a leave of absence from the Chief Medical Examiner's Office in Philadelphia to work a tour as Witness Green Congo's Chief Forensic Investigator. He has three children and two grandchildren, a wife of thirty-one years he phones every night, a five-bedroom suburban house, and membership in two golf clubs: an ordinary life that's as far removed from what happened on this African hillside as the sunlit surface of the sea is from benthic trenches populated by pale, crawling flowers and transparent nightmares all maw and stomach.

"I see you're working up here without a gun," Tremaine says.

"It didn't seem necessary."

"As if you didn't carry one while you were doing your biodiversity work, way out there in the woods."

"Actually, we were usually escorted by soldiers."

"Mad dogs and Englishmen go out without a gun."

"Why is it that every American I meet has to prove that they can mangle the first line of that song?"

Nicholas Hyde says this without a trace of a smile. A lean, self-contained young man in running shorts, long-sleeved T-shirt, sneakers and Kevlar gloves, his complexion burnt nutbrown by the African sun. Giving Tremaine a deadpan stare, like Buster Keaton, or that little Japanese guy who used to make those weird gangster movies. He pressed hard to be transferred from lab to fieldwork, and has proven to be a good worker, dedicated, meticulous, and uncomplaining, although he's neither a mixer nor a team player. He always seems to be on the edge of things, quiet and watchful, the epitome of the infamous reserve Tremaine has consistently failed to detect in any of the other Brits, from irreverent journalists to sardonically weary aid workers, he's met out here. Perhaps that's why he keeps trying to get a rise out of the guy; perhaps that's why he's come up here now.

Tremaine says, trying to justify his little joke, "There are plenty of people who think we're the bad guys, Nick. Plenty who don't like that we're disturbing the dead, usually because they've got something to hide. They had themselves a nasty little civil war in the Congo. There were atrocities on both sides. Obligate tolerates what we do because it's good PR and even better politics—they believe that the atrocities we're documenting will eventually help indict Nyibizo and his Loyalists for war crimes. But that doesn't mean they feel they have to take care of us. Also, do I have to mention the wild animals? You're walking down some little jungle path and you come across a bull buffalo, you'll be sorry if you aren't carrying."

"I don't think you'd want to shoot at a forest buffalo with a handgun, Tre. They're pretty hard to kill."

"One shot through the eye will do it, or better still, between the front legs into the heart," Tremaine says, thumping his own chest and spilling a little beer on his sweat-soaked T-shirt. "No problem."

"Even if you do make the kill shot," Nicholas Hyde says, "forest buffalo generally travel in groups of three or four. And they're quick, too. They can easily run a man down. If you ever shoot one, Tre, you should make sure you're near a tree that you can climb, and get as high as you can before its friends come at you."

"I'll keep it in mind. But you know what we mostly have to worry about are bandits, gangsters, Loyalists . . . anyone who sees charity workers as easy targets, or wants to take us hostage, or blames us for the Black Flu, or wants to hack us open to get at our magic bullets. Twenty-five, thirty years ago, we wouldn't be having this conversation because we wouldn't have needed to carry guns, but now the world's in such a sorry state we can't afford not to."

"I'll be sure to bring a gun along with me next time," Nicholas Hyde says, and sets the unopened can of beer on the ground and turns back to the scatter of half-excavated bones.

"When you decide to work all alone up here, you have to remember to be super-careful." Tremaine Thompson finishes off his beer, suppresses a belch. "How's she coming?"

Nicholas Hyde is using his knife to scrape away the hard dirt that cups the face-down skull. He works with finicky care, his thumb close to the tip of the serrated blade; after a year in the sweltering rot of the swamp forest, the skull is porous and fragile, stained orange-brown by the iron-rich laterite clay. He says, "She had both her arms hacked off below the forearms, and there are deep cuts in her shoulder blades and arm bones."

"On the outer edges?"

"How did you know?"

"Defence marks. Someone swings at you with a machete, you lift your arms to protect yourself."

Tremaine demonstrates by wrapping his left arm over the top of his head. He has been in-country for five months, has worked two dozen sites like this. Body dumps on back roads; burnt-out buildings with walls bullet-pocked at heart height and floors ankle-deep in human ash; mass graves in churned fields; a church full of butchered skeletons; bones scattered in dry grass, in quiet forest clearings . . . And back in Philadelphia, of course, he has stood over more dead citizens than he cares to remember. But despite his intimate acquaintance with the dead, he still can't imagine what it must have been like to hack to death more than forty men, women, and children in one long, hot, bloody afternoon. *It was hard work.* The soldiers taking turns, making sure that they were all implicated in the atrocity. Taking no pleasure in the killing, working steadily until it was done. A grim but necessary job. Hard work. He catches between two fingers the wire planted beside the skeleton and squints at the number on its little red flag. "Gordy finished up the mitochondrial DNA comparisons just an hour ago. Twenty-three here was the mother of two small boys we found down where they killed the men and the children."

Nick doesn't look up from his work. "You came all the way up here to tell me that?"

"Don't forget that I also brought beer."

"We still don't know her name. We don't know any of their names."

"We've DNA-fingerprinted every one of them, and scans of the skulls will give us approximate facial reconstructions. Maybe the woman who survived the massacre will be able to recognize her family and friends. Or maybe some of the young men who were away at war when this happened are still alive. Maybe someone will come forward when we post everything we've found here."

"But that doesn't happen too often."

"You have to understand that things got pretty messed up

here. Two-thirds of the population died of the Black Flu, and half the survivors were killed by starvation, or by the military dictatorship, the civil war . . ."

"I've seen the mass graves," Nicholas Hyde says. Dry as a bone.

"Tens of thousands of people buried in them, no one knows how many, no one knows their names," Tremaine says, watching as the young Englishman jabs and scrapes at the hard red dirt around the skull. "Just like every town and city in Africa, all over what they used to call the developing world. We try to make sure that it doesn't happen again, that everyone who dies or was killed has someone who'll know who they were, who'll speak for them. Something like this, it might be a couple of years before we can put names to these poor people, find their relatives and let them know what happened. And yeah, there's always the possibility that we never will find out who they were. But we do what we can, and if you keep at this, Nick, you'll learn that's enough."

"You came to Africa because you think that's important."

"Sure. And I guess because I feel guilty because the States got off so lightly," Tremaine says, remembering people on the streets wearing all kinds of gas masks, drugstores rationing stocks of antibiotics, soldiers and National Guardsmen outside every public building, and lines waiting to pass through security checks. The media hysteria about bioterrorism, demonstrations outside research labs; the friend of a friend, a biochemist, who lost the fingers of her right hand to a letter bomb. The President addressing the nation the day after cruise missiles were launched at targets all around the world, making that speech about sterilizing the breeding grounds of evil, old enmities flaring into countless little wars and skirmishes all over the globe, and the self-perpetuating rounds of rumour, counter-rumour and black propaganda that ran on long after it was definitively proved that the Black Flu was not after all a bioweapon released by fanatics, but an entirely natural plague.

Tremaine says, "It wasn't the best of times, but it wasn't anything like as bad as it was here. Back in the States, there

were basically two kinds of reaction to what happened in
Africa and the rest of the Third World. The first, you saw on
the news a shot of bulldozers pushing hundreds of bodies
into a pit, and you thought, it's nothing to do with me, they're
just Africans, and you switched channels. The second, you
thought, those are human beings, someone's daughter, someone's son . . . You felt what the Germans call *Weltschmerz*."

"World sorrow."

"World sorrow. It touched you or it didn't touch you. I
guess it touched me. Hey, I think you've got it."

Nicholas Hyde lays down his knife and gently tugs the
skull from its matrix and turns it over in his gloved hands. Jaw
and cheekbones and eye sockets are stained black by tissue
decomposition. A fringe of hair still clings to the forehead.

"Take a look," he says, and Tremaine leans closer, the two
men caught up in this intimate moment.

There's a neat hole drilled into the brow of the skull, just
above the gaping nasal cleft.

"Someone took pity on her," Nicholas Hyde says.

"Probably with a .22 or some other small-calibre pistol,"
Tremaine says.

"There doesn't seem to be an exit wound. The bullet might
still be in there."

"This isn't a murder investigation," Tremaine says as
Nicholas Hyde sets the skull down and takes a series of photographs with a tiny camera. "We're not here to bring anyone
to justice. All we can do is speak for the dead. Document how
they were murdered, try to find out their names and their stories, and if nothing else give them a decent burial. Maybe
someone did take pity on her. Or maybe they were pissed off
because she was screaming too loudly, or because she spoke
back. Or maybe it was just an impulse. Someone had a pistol
in their hand, and here was this woman looking at them; they
shot her to see what would happen, or to cap a joke, or just
because they could. You can go crazy trying to figure out the
how and the why, Nick, and it isn't why we're here."

A beat of silence. The sun has gone down with its usual
lack of ceremony. The air is darkening all around the two

men. Insect orchestras are tuning up for their nightlong mass concert. Lights burn inside the half-dozen tents pitched at the river's edge; they look like a cluster of festival lanterns, like a brave little fleet of UFOs from a kinder, better world.

Tremaine says, "You've been with us something like six weeks?"

"Something like that."

If Nicholas Hyde resents Tremaine's little lecture, he doesn't show it. He tucks the camera in his shirt pocket and strips off his gloves, cracks the tab on his can of beer and daintily sips the spill of foam that wells up.

Tremaine says, "You like working out in the field?"

"I don't know if I *like* it. But it feels right. I feel as if I've found something I can do well. Something I didn't know I was looking for."

"You ever find yourself *liking* digging up the bones of murdered people, *liking* seeing what was done to them before they died, you know it's time to get out. Anyhow, the reason why I came up here," Tremaine says, "wasn't to give you a pep talk. I've got another job. A hot scene, just called in. We're the nearest team, and they're sending a helicopter to pick me up sometime tomorrow morning. I need an assistant, and I saw you working all alone up here and thought you might be interested."

"Why ask me, Tre? I don't have any forensic training. I'm just killing time until I get a new contract."

"Yeah, and have you applied for anything lately?"

"I've heard there's a job in Madagascar. Counting beetle species in second-growth forest."

"Shaking trees and counting the bugs that fall out of them? Forget about it, Nick. I know you've got a bad jones for this kind of work or you wouldn't be up here right now, taking the extra time to finish up this particular job. You have some medical training, you have your army training: it's about time I tried you out on a hot scene. If you don't come along, you'll be regretting it, believe me."

"What do you know about it?"

"It's a couple of hundred klicks north of here, an old oil

palm plantation on a tributary of the Likouala aux Herbes River. A light aircraft ferrying a group of aid workers reported smoke, the local army post sent a patrol to take a look, and they discovered a massacre so fresh the bodies were still bleeding."

"Loyalists killed them?"

"Obligate would like to think so, which is why they're grudgingly allowing us in as independent observers. I have to warn you that it's a hairy mission. There are plenty of Loyalists operating in the area; they killed a couple of people just yesterday, not forty klicks from the massacre site. Do you want to go for it?"

"Why not?"

Tremaine Thompson grins. "You're my man," he says.

Chapter 2

The helicopter comes in low over the trees, beating down through the air towards the river and the abandoned oil palm plantation and the dead. Nicholas Hyde, buckled into a seat by the open door of the cabin, sees a cluster of huts and a ruined brick building tucked into the river's sun-silvered bend, and a handful of narrow fields scratched along the edge of close-packed ranks of gengineered dwarf oil palms, the oil palms marching away towards a straight horizon made misty by the swamp-forest's exhalations, all this tilting into the sky as the helicopter swings around.

A shaft of sunlight sweeps through the cabin, dazzling Nick and lighting up the padded blue walls and the seats bolted along them, and the five Brazilian soldiers, the flight engineer, the government observer, the Witness photographer, and Tremaine Thompson. One of the soldiers is standing by the door, her left arm casually hooked through a strap; she grins at

Nick and points with her assault rifle at the long streamer of red smoke pouring from the plank-sided dugout canoe that's anchored in the middle of the river.

The helicopter hangs in the hot, wet air, its ceramic twin-turbine engines working hard as it turns through three hundred and sixty degrees. It's a twenty-year-old Bell 430i, with a fifteen-metre-diameter composite four-bladed rotor, auxiliary fuel tanks to extend its range, and an internal-load capacity of ten people or four thousand kilograms of cargo, leased by Obligate from the South African company that also supplied the two-person crew. When Nick asked why they were travelling to a hot scene in a helicopter with no armaments or surveillance gear, Tremaine Thompson told him that it was standard procedure: the Congolese Army has just two attack and six transport helicopters, all of them committed to patrolling areas still held by Loyalists, and in any case Obligate doesn't entirely trust the army—many units were formerly loyal to Sergeant Samuel Nyibizo, switching sides only when it became obvious that he was going to lose the civil war. "I won't deny the risk," Tremaine said, "but the local soldiers report that the area is clear, we have our boys from Brazil as back-up, and we'll do the job as quickly as possible, quick and dirty, in and out. You're going to learn a lot."

Nick watches as the red smoke is bent into a question mark by prop wash, wondering why the government soldiers who discovered the massacre are hanging about in the middle of the river. He's beginning to get a bad feeling about this quick-and-dirty in-and-out job. It's very hot inside the cabin. Sweat sheens his face, mats his close-cropped hair. He can feel sweat trickling down the skin of his chest and back, sweat soaking his feet and thin socks inside his neoprene boots. He's wearing an intercom headset and ear defenders, white nylon protective coveralls zipped tight over T-shirt and shorts and a spidersilk/fullerene flak vest, and an olive-drab webbing belt buckled over the coveralls, with a Glock-20 in a Rescomp secure holster behind his right hip. When he gave the Glock to Nick, Tremaine Thompson said that it was a nice weapon, accurate and virtually recoilless, with a floating breech that fires caseless seven-gram hollowpoints, twenty in the clip. Nick thought it was plasticky, underpowered, and a lot lighter than the Mark 4 Browning 9mm High-Power he'd been issued in the British Army, and said that he was amazed Tremaine was so enthusiastic about guns, because he must have seen any number of people killed by them when he was working in Philadelphia. Tremaine said, "Yeah, and that's exactly why I carry one back home, to make sure I don't end up on the slab with a ticket on my toe," which in Nick's opinion is the USA in a nutshell. He's uncomfortably aware of the weapon, as if it's a prop for a role he's been forced to play without adequate preparation. During his two years in the army, he'd never needed to use a gun in anger, and he certainly doesn't want to start using one now.

Kites and buzzards rise up from half a dozen points along the edge of the river, tilt away above the dwarf oil palms. A ragged posse of wild dogs snarl and nip at each other as they flee down a track between the huts and the fields. A brace of black, tassel-eared bushpigs trot into the thorny brush that has grown up along the edge of the oil palm plantation. The animals leaving behind dark shapes on red dirt in front of the huts, at the margin of the fields, on a path trampled through a meadow of elephant grass.

Something terrible has happened down there, but it's not clear precisely how bad it is. The only information about the massacre is a terse message sent out on shortwave radio by the army patrol, which claimed to have discovered half a dozen bodies but failed to identify them or give any details about the manner of their death. The obvious assumption is that the dead are refugees from the other side of the Congo River, innocents murdered by one of the roving gangs of Loyalist soldiers—since Obligate capped the wells of the Mboukou oilfield, the former boom town of Impfondo and the surrounding area in the north of the country has become a hotbed of pro-Loyalist sentiment and insurrection—but Nick has been in-country long enough to know that nothing in Africa is ever obvious or simple. The dead could just as easily be poachers or smugglers on the losing side of some gang war, or casualties of a skirmish between Loyalist factions, or victims of an outbreak of some kind of swamp fever or the plastic disease.

Lieutenant Gomes, the leader of the squad of Brazilian soldiers, has been using his radio to speak to the Congolese soldiers in the dugout. Now he switches to the helicopter's intercom and says, "We go in," and jabs down a thumb emphatically.

The helicopter sinks through the air, its prop wash beating circles of tarnished silver into muddy water. The untidy mopheads of a line of unmodified oil palms flail in its wake; long grass is blown flat in a wide circle as it settles towards the ground as gingerly as a dowager testing her bathwater.

Nick dry-swallows. He can't kid himself that the cold fist in his gut and the metallic taste in his mouth, like a penny laid on his tongue, are due to mere exhaustion. This is the real deal, a whole-body flinch, a crawling anticipation. The muscular hum of the helicopter's turbines resonates deep in his belly; the steel plates of the floor vibrate under the cleats of his boots. He feels unsteady, ghostly, not at all ready for this.

Tremaine Thompson leans at Nick's shoulder. A Phillie Phanatic cap jammed low on his shaved scalp, a bright glint in his eyes. He says, "You saw the soldiers?"

"I saw that they were in the middle of the river, nowhere near any of the bodies."

"My guess is, they camped on the other side of the river last night. Just in case the people who did this are lurking somewhere close."

"I also saw that they let dogs and birds get at the bodies," Nick says. "I don't think it's very likely they've done a full search."

"I don't think so either," Tremaine says. "Listen, Nick, we're going to work as fast as we can, but we're also going to do our best for these poor people. Stay frosty, okay?"

The helicopter touches down with a solid thump. The smell of baked dust is suddenly strong in the cabin. Lieutenant Gomes and his four soldiers pitch through the door, stubby assault rifles jerking this way and that as they fan out under the flickering shadow of the rotor blades. They're part of the contingent that Obligate hired from the Brazilian Army to manage its internal security. With their faces hidden by helmets and goggles, their jungle-camo flak vests strapped over segmented body armor that glistens black as beetle chitin, thick leather gloves, and harnesses and belts loaded with flares and grenades and spare clips, medipaks and water bottles, they look like science-fictional invaders. Bulky robots or half-man, half-ant starship troopers.

Nick unbuckles his harness and shucks the ear defenders and intercom headset, pulls up the hood of his coveralls, checks the seals and airways of his three-way respirator mask.

Grant Twentyman, the sturdy, cheerful New Zealander who's Witness Green Congo's official photographer, pauses at the door and tosses Nick a little canister. "Repellent," he says.

"Repellent?"

"Insect repellent. You'll need a double dose around fresh bodies."

Nick follows the photographer out of the helicopter. The soldiers break left and right. Two move towards the huts; Lieutenant Gomes leads the others at a brisk run around the tail boom of the helicopter, towards the river. Tremaine Thompson is climbing out of the helicopter's door ass-backwards. Grant Twentyman strolls away, taking a slow panoramic shot of the three intact huts and the charred circles where two more once stood, the brick building half-hidden by a secondary scrub of umbrella trees and straggly bushes, the fields and the edge of the oil palm plantation. The government observer, William Ndinga, trots after him, a nervous, wiry man in a black flak vest over jungle-camo blouse and trousers, the cuffs of his trousers tucked into his high-topped boots. His prized mirrorshades flash bright discs of sunlight as he looks around. His micropore mask hangs around his neck, vivid white against his matt-black skin.

There's a profound stillness in the hot air, broken only by the slowing throb of the helicopter's rotor blades.

Nick rubs lemon-scented insect repellent over his face and hands and wrists, then helps Tremaine Thompson carry a cool box down the narrow path cut through the elephant grass towards the river. Grant Twentyman and William Ndinga follow. Everyone treads carefully: Loyalists have been known to seed the area around a massacre with pop mines, deadly little things that, woken by the proximity of human-sized sources of heat, spring out of the ground and explode at waist height like the world's worst surprise. A hot breeze makes a sea noise in the tall dry grass. Insects chirp and sizzle and whine and saw. Somewhere in the distance, a bird is making a noise exactly like a hammer striking a metal pipe.

The grass abruptly gives way to a narrow track of trampled earth that wanders along the edge of the river to the strip of sand where the soldiers' dugout has been hauled halfway out of the water. Blue-backed swallows and ordinary house martins chase insects above the river's sunstruck silken slide. Four government soldiers in olive-drab fatigues, well-used Kalashnikovs slung across their backs, are smoking cigarettes and watching Lieutenant Gomes argue with their sergeant, a small man with a machine pistol in a plastic holster at his hip and a red beret folded under the shoulder tab of his blouse who shrugs sulkily as the lieutenant makes a short angry speech, jabbing a finger in the air for emphasis.

When Tremaine Thompson calls to Lieutenant Gomes, he stalks over, his goggles dangling under his unshaven chin, his black eyes flashing with contemptuous anger. He says, "These people are no help. They come here and they find one big group of dead. They take pictures, then they go across the river and they make camp. That's it, they have done their job. They do not secure a perimeter, they make no attempt to search the area properly."

Tremaine says, "How many bodies are we talking about?"

"I have found five that way," Lieutenant Gomes says, and jerks a thumb over his shoulder at the elephant grass. "My men are checking them for booby traps. Also, there are two by the huts, more in the fields. I do not know the exact number yet—my people have not finished their search. You have much work, I think."

Another trail through the elephant grass leads past the brick foundations of the plantation workers' barracks, where the red turrets of termite nests stand amongst sprawling cacti. The dead are a little way beyond these ruins, guarded by two of the Brazilian soldiers. An old man on his back, two women tumbled together, and two younger men who lie a couple of metres apart. Birds have been at their faces; they stare up at the sky with blind sockets black with dried blood.

The two soldiers talk briefly with Lieutenant Gomes, who says that it's safe to examine the bodies. Grant Twentyman straps on his respirator mask and begins to take full-length photographs of each body and close-ups of the faces and any visible wounds. William Ndinga kicks a stone in the direction of the body of the old man and says to no one in particular, "They come here, these people, they sneak into my country, they try to live where they are not allowed to live, and now they are punished for their trespasses."

"Stand well back, Mr. Ndinga," Tremaine says. "There's blood all over the ground, in case you haven't noticed. If these poor people *are* refugees from the Dead Zone, they could be carrying God knows what diseases. You get just one drop of blood on you, and I'll ask you to leave your clothes here; you'll have to ride bare-ass naked back to civilization."

William Ndinga's mirrorshades flash full of sunlight as he turns to look at Tremaine. "I have a magic bullet, just like you. Also, I know what I'm doing. I study biology in the university in Brazzaville, and I go to Cuba to do postdoctoral work with Professor Tomás Ortís at Hermanos Almeijeiras in Havana. My Ph.D. work was on the sequencing of the genetic code of the guinea worm, but I also worked on the wards. I have medical training. In Brazzaville, I helped nurse many afflicted with the Black Flu. I caught the plastic disease, but I cured myself. Anyway, I am not here to touch the bodies. I am an observer only. Touching the bodies, that's your job."

"He's absolutely goddamned right," Tremaine says to Nick. "Let's get to work."

They start with the women. They measure the bodies and estimate age and weight and distinguishing features, roll fingertips on plastic cards, map and measure bite marks and deep abdominal wounds, pry open mouths so that Grant Twentyman can photograph the teeth. One woman is much older than the other; they could be mother and daughter. They have both been shot in the head at close range by a small-calibre handgun. Nick suggests that they were executed, and Tremaine shrugs and says it's possible. "But whoever did it smashed in their skulls and scooped out most of the brains afterward, and tore out most of their livers, too."

"This is bad," William Ndinga says. He has picked up a stick and is using it to prod at the torn belly of one of the young men.

"Christ, man," Tremaine says with equal measures of dismay and disgust. "Don't mess up the evidence."

William Ndinga tosses the stick into the tall grass. "Your evidence is already very badly messed up. Look for yourself. His liver is gone, just like the others."

Grant Twentyman says, "Animals got at the bodies, right? Wild dogs, pigs, Christ knows what."

"Ordinary animals did not do this," William Ndinga says. "It was Loyalists. They eat their victims—*it's well known.* You must write this up and put it on your Web site, let the world know what the Loyalists do."

"These don't look like human bite marks," Tremaine Thompson says, as he roots in his equipment bag. "On the other hand, they don't look like they were made by dogs, either. Let's not assume anything until we know everything."

Nick helps Tremaine make casts of several of the bite marks with premixed dental plaster. They punch out little circles of skin for DNA sequencing, swipe the edges of wounds with sterile Q-tips, seal each set of samples in a Ziploc bag, set each bag in the rack inside the cool box. Nick feels a slight tremor in his fingers as he labels the bags, nothing to worry about. He's trying to think of this as a test, and he's determined to pass it, to fit in, but these bodies are very different from the waxy cadavers of the medical school anatomy room. They're still very much human. He can't help noticing pathetic details: the torn hem of the younger woman's red and yellow flower-print dress; the bracelet of coarse hair around the older woman's bony wrist. It's very hot, and his close-fitting respirator mask, with its tinted visor that gives everything a sepia tinge, the underwater sucking sound it makes with each breath, and the smell of spoiling human meat penetrating its micropore filters, gives him a touch of claustrophobia. The monotonous metallic sound of the bird calling somewhere in the brush comes and goes like the beginning of a headache. Despite Grant Twentyman's insect repellent, sweat bees, the small, black, stingless kind, cluster on the scant margin of skin between the mask's seal and the tightly cinched hood of his coveralls. Mosquitoes sing their Doppler whines. And this close to the river there will be plenty of blackflies, the kind that bite and then lay an egg in the wound. That these days can give you something far worse than a bad itch and maggots under your skin.

Tremaine finds a toy beneath the body of the younger woman, a doll crudely carved from a piece of soft wood. He shows it to Lieutenant Gomes, who agrees to search the immediate area in case the child who owned the doll is still alive and hiding close by.

"It was probably eaten," William Ndinga says, and Tremaine Thompson tells him to help Lieutenant Gomes if he has nothing better to do, and asks Nick how he's doing.

"I'm fine."

"Then let's take a look at the men."

The three men have been eviscerated and badly bitten, and there are. deep lacerations on their torsos and their arms. When Nick lifts the head of the old man, he feels pieces of bone move around beneath his fingers. The skull is like a broken vase held together by skin, and there's a ragged hole in the back where most of the brains have been scooped out.

Tremaine takes a look. "An animal didn't do this," he says.

"Someone pounded on him after he was down. Did you notice the wounds on their arms?"

"Defence cuts. You think they were killed with machetes?"

"I'm not sure. The wounds are pretty ragged, and machetes usually make deep, clean slices. They could have been made by some kind of club with nails or spikes sticking through it."

Half a dozen red, brass-capped double-o shotgun cartridges are scattered on the ground, and Nick finds a clutch of .32 long rounds in the back pocket of the old man.

"This guy had a rifle," he says, "but where is it now?"

"The Loyalists took it," William Ndinga says. He's affecting a bored, sulky attitude, but when Tremaine Thompson tosses him a pair of Kevlar gloves, he snaps them on and helps Nick and Tremaine and Grant Twentyman search along the edge of the tall dry grass. They turn up an ancient shotgun, its wooden stock freshly broken, and an empty clip from a .22 automatic, and find a trail smashed through the grass towards the edge of the plantation.

"That's where they took the child," William Ndinga says, turning a bent grass blade between finger and thumb. "You see here, the blood? It was already dead, I think."

Nick and Tremaine take samples of blood-spattered grass and finish documenting the men. They're packing up everything when Lieutenant Gomes comes back down the trail and tells them that he has found another body. "Something strange. Like, I do not know the English. Like a *macaco*."

Tremaine has unfastened his respirator mask. He smiles at Nick, and says to Lieutenant Gomes, "You want us to take a look at a monkey?"

"A monkey, yes. A big monkey. A very strange monkey," Lieutenant Gomes says, very serious, anxious to convince them of the importance of his find. "It was shot dead. This way, come and see."

It's sprawled on its back in the long grass to one side of the trail, its arms and legs casually askew, like a pale starfish stranded by some strange tide. Most of the head has been vaporized by a close-range shotgun blast. Swarms of flies and ants are feeding on the long scatter of congealed blood and shreds of tissue.

"*Un diable blanc*," William Ndinga says and crosses himself.

"It looks like a chimpanzee," Grant Twentyman says. His mask dangles at his neck, and now he pushes back the hood of his coveralls and rakes his fingers through his sweat-soaked blond hair. There's a swipe of green sunblock across his forehead, another down the blade of his nose. "A shaved albino chimpanzee someone took a serious dislike to."

"Chimpanzees are extinct in the wild," William Ndinga says. "Chimpanzees and gorillas, they catch our diseases and die. This thing is a monster, a white devil, probably made by gene hackers across the river."

"Bullshit," Grant Twentyman says. "People still poach chimps. I saw one just three months ago in a market in Burundi, skinned and butchered. Bush meat for some rich family's wedding."

"If it was butchered," William Ndinga says, "how do you know it was a chimpanzee? Maybe it was a child, did you think of that? Burundi is a very bad place. There are men that kill orphans and sell them as bush meat. *It's well known*."

"Bullshit," Grant Twentyman says again, but far less forcefully.

Tremaine Thompson looks at Nick. "You're the biologist. What do you think?"

Another of Tremaine's little challenges.

Nick says, "I'm pretty sure it isn't a chimpanzee."

"I think so too," Tremaine says. "I don't know much about apes, but this looks plain wrong."

The headless corpse is the size of an eight- or nine-year-old child, with child-sized male genitals but well-developed muscles, big, flat hands and feet, and strong black claws instead of nails. It is quite hairless. There's a gristly ridged growth around its barrel chest and irregular bony or cartilaginous plates under the pale skin of its arms and legs, slabs which slide around a little when Tremaine probes them.

Nick finds a half-dozen broken teeth in the bloody detritus in the grass. Tremaine picks them over and says, "They all seem to be incisors or canines."

"That's what I thought."

They both get down on their knees and do a close search, collecting plenty of fragments of sharp-edged teeth but failing to find any flat-topped molars or premolars. Tremaine sits back and looks up at the soldiers and says, "It has claws, a lot of sharp teeth, and a kind of internal body armour. Very definitely a shoo-in for weirdest corpse of the month."

"It was not alone," William Ndinga says. "Its friends killed those people and ate their livers and their brains. They took away a child, and ate it too."

"It's possible," Tremaine says. "When we get back I can see if any of the teeth we found make a match with the casts of the bite marks on the corpses."

"Strange things come across the big river," Lieutenant Gomes says.

"He's right," William Ndinga says. "It is very bad, on the other side of the Congo. Half their country is destroyed by rogue biotechnology, but they are so greedy that they let transnats come in and build more laboratories. There is much perverted science, many crimes against Nature. This is a very good example, if you want my opinion."

"Whatever it is," Tremaine says, "I want it zipped into a body bag. It's coming back with us."

Lieutenant Gomes snaps an order; one of the soldiers trots off towards the helicopter. As Grant Twentyman videos the pale, headless corpse, stepping carefully around it, Nick says, "What about the other bodies?"

There's a moment of silence while the other men look at each other. Then Tremaine Thompson says, "We can't risk it, Nick. They could have been refugees from across the Congo, from the Dead Zone. The chance they could be carrying some kind of biowar disease is too great."

"But we're taking this thing back with us."

"Because we want to find out what it is," Tremaine says.

"Perhaps the government soldiers will bury the bodies," Lieutenant Gomes says, looking at William Ndinga.

"You know there is no time," the government observer says. Sweat beading along the edge of his hairline is attended by a dozen small, industrious black bees. "When you go, they go too."

"Bullshit," Nick says. "If you give me a shovel, I'll do it myself. It can't take long to dig a shallow grave."

"A shallow grave is no good," Tremaine Thompson says. "Animals will soon dig it up. And we don't even have time for that, Nick. We have to document the other bodies and scram."

"So that's what you meant by quick and dirty," Nick says. He can feel spots of angry heat burning on his cheeks.

"That's exactly what I meant," Tremaine says. "It's not good, it's not right, but there it is. Meanwhile, we're here to find out how these poor people died, and we still have to document the other bodies."

William Ndinga says, "This white devil was not alone. Its friends could be nearby. In my opinion, we should forget the other bodies and get on the helicopter and leave at once."

Lieutenant Gomes says, "For once he is right. This area, it is not secured. We do not know what is out there. We must finish very quickly."

"Listen to the man, Nick," Grant Twentyman says, taking one handle of the cool box as Tremaine takes the other. "The clock is ticking."

William Ndinga catches up with Nick as they walk back along the path through the tall elephant grass. "You are angry because you think we are not civilized," he says.

"Not at all," Nick says. It's true. He's more ashamed than angry; he knows that he should have kept quiet because he's the outsider here, because in Africa doing the right thing is never as simple as it seems.

William Ndinga is anxious to explain. "Leaving bodies to be eaten by animals isn't something civilized men should do," he says, "but sometimes it is not possible to be civilized, you understand? Maybe the soldiers come back in a few days, when they know the area is safe. But you cannot expect them to risk their lives."

"We don't even know if they were refugees," Nick says.

"Of course they were refugees," the government observer says. "You say, how does William Ndinga know this? I say, because of where they chose to live. Listen, you're a biologist, just like me. You know that two thousand years ago, when the climate was much drier, this was all grass plains, with forest only in the valleys and around the rivers. You know that two thousand years ago many people lived here."

"They grew oil palms. When I was working on the biodiversity surveys, we often found husks of *Elaeis guineensis* in streambeds deep in the forest."

"Exactly! Before the forest came, people could live here, they cultivated this land. You can still find raised terraces in the forest, places where people once grew crops. You can find pottery in sandbanks along the river. All of this is true, scientifically proven. But the climate changed, the rains came again, and the forests spread and the people vanished. One theory is that they simply moved somewhere else, but I think that they stayed and tried to make a living, until some kind of forest disease caused a catastrophic depopulation. It's well known that many forest animals harbour diseases that can spread to people. It's well known that haemorrhagic influenza, the Black Flu, came from a river valley in this very forest, just five hundred kilometres to the west, over the border in Gabon. A Japanese logging company started to cut down the trees there, and the workers got sick. They were taken to hospital, and the nurses and doctors and other patients got sick too, and very soon millions of people were dying, in Africa, everywhere in the world . . . How many people died from the Black Flu, in England?"

"A hundred and fifty thousand. Not as many, I know, as here."

"In my country, two million died. It was more than seventy percent of the population. And in all of Africa, half a billion people died. People fled the cities because that was where the Black Flu was spreading fastest, but most of them ended up in refugee camps, and the Black Flu spread through the camps, too. And because a whole farming season was lost in most countries, many more died of famine, and of typhoid and plague and measles, and then there were the riots and the wars . . . All because people tried to exploit the forest. Because they went where they were not supposed to go. The only good in all this misery," William Ndinga says, repeating with relish a mordant observation that Nick has heard too many times before, "was that the Black Flu ended the Aids epidemic, because it killed almost everyone whose immune system was compromised by the HIV virus. But now we are at the beginning of a new age. We will rebuild our country in harmony with Nature. We will use science to understand Nature, not to subdue her. We will build good hospitals and provide clean water, and educate the people. We will control our population growth, we will use sustainable technology, we will live where we are meant to live, and we will conserve the forests for the good of all the world, as agreed with UNESCO."

There isn't any polite way for Nick to respond to this sudden, fierce outburst of naked propaganda. There's the sentiment, never overtly expressed but lurking just beneath the surface of Obligate's pro-Gaian philosophy, that haemorrhagic influenza was a blessing in disguise, a natural mechanism that in Africa has winnowed the human race to a sustainable level.

William Ndinga says, "That's why I know those people were refugees—because only refugees and other criminals would try to live in a place so full of diseases. And not just natural diseases. Before the Black Flu, gene hackers came to Africa from all over the world, because weak governments were easily bribed to allow laboratories to work without any regulation. They created all kinds of problems we must now live with. The plastic disease, for instance, is very bad in the forest. If you live in here, and if you have no protection, you are certain to catch it. Even if you have a magic bullet, there is a ten percent chance of infection."

"I know."

Nick's biosurvey team once stumbled across an old pygmy encampment in the deep forest where the remains of several victims of the plastic disease lay intermingled under a collapsed shelter overgrown with flowering vines. All the flesh had rotted away, leaving bones cased in smooth chunks and tattered sheets of blackened polymer. The plastic disease is caused by a species of bacteria, transmitted by blackfly bites, that has acquired a gengineered plasmid, a little circlet of DNA carrying genes originally designed to make complex long-chain hydrocarbons in plant cells. The bacteria multiply avidly in human soft tissue, and in the last stages of the disease the victims are turned into grotesque living statues, paralysed by hard, knotty strings and lumps of polymer under their skin and muscles.

"It is everywhere in the forests," William Ndinga says, "and it is very bad in the farming country just now. I myself caught it. A nodule began to grow on my chest. A hard little lump, like a canker. I cut out the infected tissue and burned the wound with flaming alcohol. Then I gave myself a course of Floxapen. The real stuff, made in France, not the shit sold on the black market. I was lucky—most strains of the plastic disease are resistant to antibiotics now."

Nick is impressed in spite of himself. He says, "You're a survivor."

"I'm the head man of my family. I have to survive. I have to work hard. I have many people to support, and now it is possible to make money again I want to buy magic bullets for all my family. I want to buy a Mercedes Benz. A cabriolet with a hydrogen cell and an electric motor driving each wheel. The latest model," William Ndinga says, and stops.

Nick and everyone else have stopped too. They have heard the sound of automatic gunfire, a small but distinct popping in the distance. A shared instinct makes them all crouch low. Nick reaches for the Glock holstered at his hip, then realizes that no one else has drawn their gun. There is nothing to see but the blank sky above the tall dry elephant grass on either side of the path, and the gunfire has already stopped.

Lieutenant Gomes speaks quickly into the microphone of his headset, then says, "One of my men saw something in the trees. They go to check it out."

"More white devils," William Ndinga says. "We should go, right away."

Grant Twentyman takes a packet of cigarettes from the breast pocket of his coveralls, shakes one loose, and bites on the filter. He says, "I bet it's wild dogs, waiting to get back to their meal," and flicks his lighter, touches the flame to the end of the cigarette.

Tremaine Thompson says, "We're here to do a job. I'd like to finish it."

Lieutenant Gomes takes off his helmet, blots sweat from his brow with the heel of his glove, puts the helmet back on. He says, "I think it is okay if you can do it very quickly. My men see nothing. This is just a scare, nothing more."

"We'll work fast," Tremaine says.

They load the cool box full of samples onto the helicopter. Nick drinks a litre of water straight down, pours another litre over his head.

Tremaine says, "We're halfway there, gentlemen," and asks Nick to document the two bodies by the huts while he and Grant Twentyman check out the bodies in the fields.

"No problem," Nick says.

"Good man," Tremaine says, and lays a hand on Nick's arm and lowers his voice. "This is pretty bad. I'm not surprised everyone is so jumpy."

"I think they were trying to get away," Nick says. "I think that when they knew they weren't going to make it, the men shot the women; perhaps they shot the kid too. To save them from something worse."

"We can't be sure of that," Tremaine says.

"We both saw what they were running away from. What do you think that thing is?"

"I don't know."

"Do you think it's gengineered?"

Tremaine Thompson passes the flat of his hand over his shaved scalp. "I don't think we've stumbled on some undiscovered species. I'm looking forward to seeing Bridget's expression when I ask her to autopsy it."

"They were brave people," Nick says. "I don't like leaving them here like this."

"Someone will come back to bury them, I'll make sure of it. Meanwhile, we'll document the rest of the bodies, do the best we can for them. Okay?"

"Okay."

"Good man," Tremaine says again.

The two soldiers return, a green body bag sagging heavily between them. Tremaine fastens a biohazard seal around the double zip, and Nick helps him stow the bag in the helicopter's cabin. Then Tremaine and Grant Twentyman pull out another cool box and head past the huts, followed by William Ndinga and Lieutenant Gomes and one of the soldiers, all of them moving briskly, anxious to get the job done, while Nick and the other soldier, the young woman who smiled at him in the helicopter, carry a cool box over to the huts.

Two bodies lie on pounded red earth near the charred circles of the burnt-out huts, so close together that their heads are almost touching. Both corpses are those of young men; both are badly mutilated. Nick pulls on his respirator mask and a fresh pair of gloves, and sets to work. The same bite marks, the same severe damage to the heads. He finds a broken bone nearby, the thigh bone of some large animal. Its ball joint matches depressions in the skulls. No sign of knife or machete lacerations, no sign of gunshot wounds. These men were beaten and bitten to death. He thinks of the headless body, wonders how many friends it had.

When Nick has finished, he bums a cigarette from the soldier. She is standing upwind of the bodies, half watching a little solar-powered TV set on a stump outside the doorway of one of the huts. The TV, connected to a mesh aerial pegged to the wattle-and-daub wall of the hut, is showing an episode of a hospital soap. A woman in a smart suit is telling a woman in a nurse's uniform about the benefits of having a career instead of a baby. The military dictatorship distributed tens of thousands of these TVs, tuned exclusively to the official station; now Obligate pumps its own propaganda through them.

Nick pulls down his mask, scratches vigorously under his chin and behind his ears, and lights his cigarette, maybe the fiftieth or the hundredth since he gave up after his heart attack. The young woman has some English, and asks him if he's from London.

"All my life, I want to visit London."

She's stocky but cute, with heavy black eyebrows that almost meet above her lustrous brown eyes, and Nick is pretty sure that she's flirting with him. "London is nice," he says, "but I actually grew up in the country. If you want to see the real England, that's where you should go."

"Maybe you take me there," the soldier says, "some time when this is over."

Her name is Isabel Fonesca. She is from Sao Paulo, the youngest daughter of a middle-class family, her father a manager of a textile mill in one of the city's industrial satellites. She tells Nick that she is the rebel of the family; she joined the army because she did not want to follow the same path as her three sisters—university, marriage, children. Like many young people, the Black Flu made her aware of how lightly she held on to life, and therefore how precious it was. She does not want to take anything for granted, she says. She wants adventure; she wants to see the world.

Nick tells her that he joined up for much the same reasons as she did, and Isabel says, "You were in the English Army?"

"The British Army, sure."

"Where did you see action?"

"I wasn't a rough tough straight-shooting front-line infantry soldier like you. I had two years' medical training before I joined up, so naturally they put me to work in an ordnance depot. I was one of the guys who make sure you get the weapons, the right calibre ammunition, spare parts . . ."

A year in the big depot outside Reading, off the M4. First

running one of the electric forklifts in a brightly lit warehouse full of guns and ammunition and the smell of gun oil; then, after he got his corporal's stripe, working in the logistical section. Taking one day off each week to work towards the electronics qualification that would get him out of there.

Nick says, "One time I was in Albania with the peacekeeping force for a couple of months. That was the closest to any action that I ever got."

"Until now."

"Good point."

"But you are not now in the army. Why did you leave? You were unhappy because you thought you should have been a medic?"

"Actually, I think they should have put me in the regimental band. I played flute in the school orchestra, and in combat, band members become stretcher-bearers. As for why I left, I caught a heart attack. It was a viral infection, a terrorist weapon."

The well-used lie, a close cousin to the truth, comes easily to him, but still he feels a tiny pang of guilt.

"You like the army," Isabel says. "You miss it."

"Yeah, I liked it. You knew exactly who you had to be, what you had to do . . ." The conversation has definitely veered in the wrong direction. Nick drops his cigarette butt, grinds it under his heel. "It was a long time ago. I like here, too. I like it a lot."

Isabel says, "You like Brazzaville? So do I. Plenty bars, plenty good music . . . And they like soldiers. They like us. I get plenty free drinks in those bars. You too, if I tell them you are English soldier. Sammy's Bar, I go there a lot. Stop by and ask for Isabel Fonesca—you might not recognize me without combat gear."

She's a soldier; she's sounding him out, looking for some action to fill the time when she isn't being a soldier. It doesn't mean anything more than that.

Nick says, "Maybe I will. But right now I think I should check the huts."

"Already we look. Nothing there."

"I guess they all tried to run. Did you find out how the fire started?"

"They have a thing for making strong drink . . ."

"A still."

"For sure, a still. So, they are boiling up palm wine or whatever to make it stronger, it gets knocked over, and boom!" Isabel flicks up a hand. Her fingernails are trimmed close, but painted silver. "It sets fire to the hut. We look in the ashes, we look in the huts, we don't find any bodies. We are almost finished here, I think. This evening I will be drinking cold beer in Sammy's."

"What about the brick building?" Nick says. "Did you look in there?"

It's a long shed much obscured by ferns that have prospered in its courses of rotten mortar. A dead woman lies just inside the doorway, a bloody wedge bitten out of her throat. Isabel Fonesca watches quietly as Nick documents the body. When he has finished, she steps over the dead woman and leads the way into the ruined building.

Half a dozen shafts of sunlight swarming with dust motes slant through holes in the plastic sheeting of the roof. Nick and Isabel shine their flashlights into shadowy corners. Bats hanging upside down from the roof girders shift the bony membranes of their wings, just as children, disturbed in their sleep, will stir and pull blankets over their heads. Candy-coloured cockroaches as big as mice scatter across soft heaps of guano. A gecko clings to the rough brick wall above a wooden workbench brittle with rot and termites. A broken sheet of corrugated plastic leans against the workbench, and Nick hears something moving behind it.

"Probably a rat," Isabel says, but holds her rifle steady while Nick eases back the plastic sheet and shines his torch under the bench.

The baby, a naked boy child on a folded cloth, jerks his fists in the torch's glare and starts to whimper.

Nick feels a cool calm roll down from the top of his

head. The baby is no more than three or four weeks old. He is badly dehydrated and in ketosis, his breath quick and faint and smelling of pear drops, his mouth and nose crusted with white matter. His skin is freckled with insect bites and his bottom smeared with dried, spicy orange baby-shit, but his pulse is firm and no bones seem to be broken.

Nick lifts him up, and almost at the same moment gunfire starts up outside: rapid, sustained bursts interspersed with single shots. Nick and Isabel look at each other.

"Take him to the helicopter," Isabel says.

She turns and jogs out of the door into the sunlight, and something lithe and pale and quick smashes into her. Her assault rifle sprays a spasmodic burst into the red dirt as she falls under the weight of her attacker, which wraps its arms around her head and works its face between the rim of her helmet and the collar of her flak vest. As Nick runs forward, the white thing rears back to show him its bloody face, a chunk of meat caught between teeth like nails hammered into its wide lipless mouth, and Nick fires three quick shots, firing one-handed because he's holding the baby, no kick to the Glock at all, and the thing flies backwards, a bloody star blown into the keg of its chest. Nick steps towards it through the drift of blue gunsmoke, the Glock extended in one hand, the other cradling the baby to his chest, his heart pounding, thinking that it's as if one of the gargoyles from the square tower of the Saxon church next to his mother's house has come to life. It's still moving: three rounds to the chest, and it's still alive. It glares at Nick and pushes up in a sudden smooth rush, and he shoots it in the face and shoots it again as it collapses at his feet, blood and brains spattering him to the waist.

The baby starts to cry, a feeble whining hiccough, his face like a clenched fist against the white nylon of Nick's coveralls. In one direction, the helicopter's rotor blades are beginning to turn above the tall elephant grass; in the other, several hundred metres away, figures are moving out of the scrub along the edge of the oil palms, pale figures smaller than men, moving very quickly. Nick sees a little knot of them all over someone struggling on the ground, sees Grant Twentyman swing his video camera in a desperate attempt to keep two more at bay. One of the soldiers is firing quick, controlled bursts as he steps backwards. An orange muzzle flash flickers under the dense-knit canopy of the dwarf oil palms—something is shooting back.

Isabel Fonesca lies facedown and still. Her helmet has come off and her lustrous black hair has spilled free of its net. Blood is pooling rapidly around her head and shoulders. It is soaking into her flak vest. When Nick rolls her over, her head tips back to show the massive wound in her neck. Nick gets blood all over his hand when he brushes back her hair and tries and fails to find her pulse behind her ear.

Something is running headlong towards him, and he jerks up and then lowers the pistol because it is William Ndinga, blouse pulled from his belt, mirrorshades gone.

"All dead," he yells and runs straight past, towards the helicopter.

Nick sees that he is right. Grant Twentyman is down, the soldier is down, and quick, pale-skinned figures are scampering towards him, not pausing at all when he fires off three quick shots. One of them is dragging an assault rifle. Nick turns and runs, clamping the baby tightly to his chest, forcing himself not to look back, chasing after William Ndinga through air so packed with wet heat it's like running in the bad dream everyone has. Running headlong towards the throbbing noise of the helicopter. Screaming because he sees its tail boom tip up as it begins to rise. A hurricane full of dust and chaff blows around him. The flight engineer squats at the open door in his orange flight suit and white helmet, one hand clutching a strap, the other reaching for the baby as Nick holds it above his head, making a grab for it and missing as for a heart-stopping moment the helicopter rises higher. Then it settles back with a solid thump, and Nick can hand the baby to the flight engineer and haul himself through the door and collapse against the hot steel plates of the floor. He lies there, gasping with relief, clutching the Glock in a death grip, as the helicopter goes straight up, faster than an express elevator.

After a few moments, Nick manages to sit up and brace himself against a seat. He sees figures dancing in triumph or rage on the flattened circle the helicopter has left in the elephant grass, pale figures running towards the river, where the outboard motor of the government soldiers' dugout canoe is making a wide creamy wake in brown water. Then the helicopter makes a steep turn, and sky and sunlight fill the door.

While Nick settles the baby on clean towels folded on one of the seats, the flight engineer checks the pictures he took with his phone. He's pleased that he had the presence of mind to keep taking pictures as the government observer and Nick ran for the helicopter. He has half a dozen dubiously fuzzy long-range shots of the soldiers going down, but far better than any of those is the good, clear picture he took after hauling William Ndinga aboard, the picture of Nicholas Hyde standing resolute amidst whirling dust, offering the baby to the sky.

Chapter 3

The pilot of the helicopter, badly spooked and convinced that at any moment someone under the treetops will launch a ground-to-air missile, aims his bird straight at Brazzaville, and refuses to change course when Nick suggests that they head for the nearby town of Liranga, where there's a Catholic mission that can take care of the baby. They have a brief, fierce argument, Nick squashes an impulse to put his gun to the son of a bitch's head and retreats to the cabin, where the flight engineer is fiddling with the biohazard seal of the body bag that contains the corpse of the decapitated white devil.

Nick pushes him away, hard enough to send him sprawling, stands over him, and gives him chapter and verse about the risk of contamination. The man gives him a sullen look before picking up his phone and stepping into the cockpit, leaving Nick and William Ndinga alone in the noisy cabin with the baby and the body bag and the cool box stuffed with grisly trophies.

Nick is trembling with fatigue and spent adrenalin, but manages to clean the baby with alcohol and distilled water from the helicopter's medical kit, dab antiseptic on his insect bites, and feed him sterile rehydrating solution drop by drop. William Ndinga watches from the other side of the cabin as Nick improvises diapers with gauze and paper towels, and at last steps over and asks, "Is he going to live?"

"He's going to need medical attention, but I think so." Nick is cradling the baby in his lap. He has exchanged his claustrophobic respirator mask for a lightweight micropore face mask and has sealed the belt and holstered gun in a Ziploc bag which he's stowed in his day bag, but he's still wearing gloves and his blood-spattered coveralls.

William Ndinga pulls up his face mask and sits next to Nick. "You know that he must go into quarantine," he says, leaning close and shouting to make himself heard over the roar of the helicopter's turbines.

"I know."

"I will radio ahead and arrange it. In any case, I must make a report right away."

"I wasn't going to leave him behind."

"Of course." William Ndinga puts a hand on Nick's shoulder and says, "The others are dead."

"Yes. Yes, they are."

"I was right," William Ndinga says. "We should have left straightaway."

The baby stirs and solemnly squints up at the two men. Nick gently rocks him, says, "You were right about there being other white devils. Where did they come from?"

"I did not see anything," William Ndinga says with an emphatic shake of his head. "It happened very quickly."

"You went to look at the other bodies," Nick says. "What happened then?"

"There were two bodies on the path, and it looked as if another had been dragged into a stand of maize. The lieutenant and one of the soldiers went in to search for it, there were gunshots, and then those things were everywhere. That is all I know."

"They were hiding in the field."

"They came out of the fields, out of the trees . . . They were everywhere. That is when I ran. I think everyone tried to run. I was running for the helicopter, and I did not see anything." William Ndinga nods slowly, thinking things through, getting his story straight. He says, "I did not see anything. And it would be better for you if *you* did not see anything, either."

It takes the helicopter—sometimes flying over the broad, blood-red flood of the Congo River, sometimes over the endless green forest—three hours to reach Brazzaville. When Nick's mobile phone at last picks up a signal, he gets through to Dan Cooper, the director of Witness's operations in Green Congo, and tells him bluntly, no other way to do it, that Tremaine Thompson and Grant Twentyman are dead.

"We were ambushed, Mr. Cooper. Things came at us out of the trees. Gengineered things like gargoyle apes. White devils."

He's hunched in his seat, the phone's headset plugged into one ear, his finger in the other. Shouting into the headset's bead microphone to make himself heard above the steady roar of the helicopter. Dan Cooper wants to know where he is, where the bodies are, and he says, "We had to leave them behind, Mr. Cooper, but I have the body of one of the things that killed them. I'm bringing it back to Brazzaville. And I have a survivor of the massacre, too—a baby."

There's a pause, and then Dan Cooper says, "This isn't a safe connection, Nick. We'll talk when you get back. Hang in there."

* * *

It's dark when the helicopter, tanks almost dry, finally lands at Maya Maya Airport, settling into the glare of a circle of floodlights. Soldiers are lined up in front of half a dozen jeeps and a pair of ambulances. There's no sign of Dan Cooper or anyone else from Witness. When Nick carries the baby down the steps, a doctor in hooded coveralls and a respirator mask steps forward.

Beyond the perimeter wire of the airport, a stringer for CNN, sprawled on the roof of his Nissan Pilgrim and using a light-hungry telephoto lens a metre long, gets some grainy but good footage of the exchange.

Nick tries to follow the doctor, but two soldiers intercept him. They spray him with biocidal agent before asking him to strip off his coveralls, flak vest, boots, and gloves. They allow him to retrieve his day bag, then wrap a silvery blanket around his shoulders, bundle him into a jeep, and drive him at high speed to the decontamination shed.

He takes a long shower in one of the cubicles, hot water smelling strongly of disinfectant spraying hard from three directions in the white-tiled stall as he scrubs himself over and over with handfuls of pink, gritty soap. He is very tired, tired beyond fear of the quick lithe shapes he can imagine swarming everywhere he is not looking.

Dan Cooper is waiting for him when at last he comes out of the cubicle. He has stuffed his sweat-soaked T-shirt and shorts into his day bag and is wearing a clean tracksuit and plastic shower sandals. His short black hair sticks up in wet tufts.

"This is a hell of a thing, Nick," Dan Cooper says. "Has a doctor seen you?"

"They had a paramedic check me over, but actually I'm fine. Not even a scratch." Nick feels tired but alert. There's a chill beneath his skin that the shower hasn't touched. The bright light bouncing off the white tiles of the corridor hurts his eyes; perhaps that's why they're tearing up. He asks about the baby, and Dan Cooper tells him that it was taken straight to Tangalai Hospital.

"I'd like to see him."

"I'm sure he's getting the very best care."

They're talking in low voices. At the far end of the brightly lit corridor, two soldiers and a paramedic in green scrubs have turned to watch them.

"Let's get you out of here," Dan Cooper says.

Dan Cooper is a tall, sandy, fiftysomething American whose amiable authority reminds Nick of his housemaster at Rugby. He knows when to talk and when to listen, and lets Nick tell his story as they walk through the close, warm African night to the ghostly white Range Rover.

"They all died, Mr. Cooper. Tremaine Thompson and Grant Twentyman and the Brazilian soldiers . . . These things came out of the trees; they must have been laying up after they killed those poor people. They killed them and took parts of them to eat. I think they took at least one kid, too. They must have been concealed close by, and when we came along, they ambushed us."

Dan Cooper fires up the Range Rover and drives past shuttered hangars towards the main road, and Nick tells him about the decapitated creature they found in the grass, the badly mutilated bodies, the dead woman in front of the ruined factory building.

"I think she was the mother. She hid the baby and distracted those things. Some birds, when a hawk or a rat or some other predator gets near their nest, will drag a wing on the ground and pretend to be wounded to draw the predator away. That's what she did, Mr. Cooper. They killed her, but she saved her baby. You said he'd been taken to Tangalai. Is he okay?"

"They have a good paediatric section, Nick. I'm sure they'll do everything they can."

"The body I brought back—I want to be there when it's cut. I want to see."

"This is the dead animal you found at the site."

"The Brazilian soldiers found it. It had been shot at point-blank range, probably with a shotgun. The head is mostly gone, but the rest of it is intact. It's in a body bag in the helicopter. There's a cool box full of samples too. We swabbed the wounds for saliva, made casts . . . No one told you about that?"

"I'll look into it," Dan Cooper says.

"There were four or five squads of soldiers waiting when the helicopter landed. They took the baby, hustled me straight off . . . I bet they took the body and the sample, too."

"Don't be hard on yourself, Nick," Dan Cooper says. "It's a hell of a thing you did."

"Where are we going?" Nick says. "This isn't the way to the hotel."

Nick and most of the Witness staff have rooms in a hotel in the old French Quarter at the heart of Brazzaville, but the Range Rover is heading in the opposite direction, swaying on its sturdy suspension like a big boat in a rough sea as it speeds along an unlit, deeply rutted road, bushes pressing out of the darkness on either side.

"I found you a room at the UNHCR mission," Dan Cooper says. "I stopped by the hotel, though, before I came here, and got a change of clothes from your room. You'll get the stuff you left at the camp in a few days."

"It's mostly dirty laundry. What's wrong with the hotel, Mr. Cooper?"

"I'm given to understand that it's too exposed."

Nick is sensitive to revealing nuances of speech. He says, "You're given to understand? This isn't your idea?"

"Not altogether. Tink Glazer suggested it."

Tink Glazer is the Obligate official who oversees the work of all non-governmental organizations in Green Congo.

Dan Cooper says, "It's a good idea, Nick. The BBC crew are staying at the hotel, and every correspondent and stringer in Brazzaville hangs out in the bar. You don't need that kind of hassle right now. We'll get you squared away somewhere quiet, so you can rest up and recover, okay?"

Nicholas Hyde, staring through the Range Rover's windshield into the unfathomable African night, doesn't reply.

Chapter 4

It's early morning, just after dawn, when Matthew Faber discovers that he is standing on an outcrop of dead coral, watching the Gentle People amble down the scrub-covered slope towards the beach. He's naked except for his tool belt, and out of breath and slippery with sweat, his pulse thumping in his head, his feet cut and bruised—he's been running. The nail of the small toe of his left foot has been torn off; under a scab of black blood, the raw wound hurts like hell. And his hands hurt too; the knuckles are scraped and stiffly swollen, as if he's been using a boulder as a punching bag. Physically (he twists to examine his flanks, palpates his shoulders, his back), he's gotten off lightly this time, and the feeling of sick claustrophobic dread, the fear that is a large part of his other self, the dark half that possessed him last night, is fading fast. He remembers an octopus he once disturbed in a tidal pool, a bag of bruise-coloured flesh and a knot of writhing tentacles sliding backwards into a crevice, and shudders once, all over.

The bright new sun slants low over the sea. Waves breaking on the outer reef crest boom like siege cannon, a long line of foam renewing itself between the blue lagoon and the green, deep water beyond. The Gentle People are moving slowly between wind-bent thorny bushes and outcrops of weathered coral heads. Small, gracile figures turning as one to investigate a solitary fig tree whose fruits are not yet quite ripe, turning as one to move on.

Three, five, seven: all of them together this morning, everything as it should be. The small childish part of Matthew's mind that loves lists is reciting their names, although the names he has given them are not their true names;

those are songs that cannot be properly rendered into ordinary human speech, the mingled songs he hears now, coming and going on the breeze.

Dr. Peltzer, the psychologist who treated him in Nairobi, warned Matthew that he shouldn't think that the songs which bind the Gentle People could in any way help him devise a technique or strategy to bind the satellite cores of his shattered mind. He should not fetishize them. He should not make them into a model of how his mind works after what he likes to call his "laboratory accident." But despite Dr. Peltzer's sound advice, Matthew Faber believes that when the Gentle People's individual songs rise towards a single harmony, he can begin to feel the oceanic sense of reintegration that the psychologist was able to briefly evoke with certain passages of music—Mozart most particularly. He believes that the Gentle People's songs are to them as the great Gloria of the Mass in C Minor, the *Riconosci in questo amplesso* sextet of *The Marriage of Figaro*, or the Adagio of the Clarinet Concerto are to him: thought and world knitted together in a glorious extended moment of precise and ecstatic unity.

The sea breeze moves gently over his bare skin; sunlight warms his right flank. Matthew is giving himself up to the moment, the air and the sun and the sound of the sea and the songs of his children, and the shattered pieces of his mind, engrams and satellite cores, are beginning to dissolve into each other, when his phone rings.

A momentary pang of anxiety, but it's all right, it's Elspeth. She says, "Don't tell me she didn't call you too, Daddy."

Part of him reluctantly comes forward, like a schoolboy thrust out of a crowd of its peers. "Last night, yes."

"It was half past two in the morning when she called me."

"Well, yes, but I suppose it's earlier where she is."

"I tried to phone you straight after."

"I was . . ."

"You were frightened. Did Dr. Dave come out?"

That's Elspeth's nickname for Matthew's dark half, taken from a bug-eyed, fright-wigged mad scientist from one of the

Saturday-morning cartoons of her childhood. Its true name is
cd2, the engram he erased from the minds of the Gentle People, the engram that in primates mediates the capacity for
anger and physical violence. Cd2 is an opportunist. Set free
by his "accident," it has become more powerful, more perva-
sive. In times of stress, it does more than colour the emotional weather of his primary core, the irreducible node of
self: it takes over.

He says, "I'm fine," and his wounded little toe sharply
throbs as if in recrimination.

"Do you remember what she said to you?"

"A little. She was upset. She didn't mean half the things
she said."

"If she meant only *half* of what she said to me, it's still bad
enough."

"Teryl always had poor impulse control. When she feels
threatened, when she feels she needs to protect herself—"

"She lashes out. She threatens murder. I haven't heard
from her in three years. I thought we'd never hear from her
again, she really was going to leave us alone . . . I should
come out and see you. It's been a while."

"You have your work."

"I can always spare a few days."

"How is it?"

"Never mind about my work, that's not the point."

"Worry about your bones and stones, not your poor mad
father."

"Daddy, you have to take this seriously."

He loses sight of the Gentle People as they move into the
shadows beneath the belt of palms that lean over the beach,
but he can still hear their songs, blown to him on the sunstruck salt breeze.

"Talk to me, Daddy," Elspeth says in his ear. "We have to
deal with this."

That familiar note of loving exasperation in her voice.
Matthew remembers how she used to dance ahead of him
along the icy path when he took her for a ride on the Swan
Boats on Boston Common, her impatient expression when

she turned and saw her poor distracted father plodding far behind, lost as usual in the intricate coils of his thoughts.

Elspeth says, "You know I never asked about anything you did when you and Teryl were involved with Danny Lovegrave and Pleistocene Park, but right now it's important that I ask this one question."

His heart trips. What did Teryl tell Elspeth? After all this time, did she finally break the long, fragile stalemate and tell Elspeth the truth about the Gentle People? Surely she wouldn't dare. She's just as guilty. But she was so very angry, and when she gets angry, she becomes irrational, loses control . . .

Elspeth says, "This thing that was brought back from wherever it was in the Congo. Could it be anything to do with Danny Lovegrave's work?"

"It's possible."

"It's possible?"

"I don't know for sure. There's a lot toward the end that I don't really remember."

"The reason I ask is that I don't think Teryl would have made those threats unless she thought you had something to do with it."

Coming and going, a harmony building from individual voices. And the salt sea breeze, and the growing heat of the sun . . .

Elspeth says, "Daddy? Are you still there?"

"I don't remember," he says.

It's the truth. After the "accident," Matthew really doesn't remember what else he might have done with Danny Lovegrave, what Danny Lovegrave might have forced him to do. He and Elspeth have been through this so many times before, he really has tried to remember, but there are gaps, blank spaces on the map of his memory, *terrae incognitae* where monsters lurk. And if he thinks too hard about what might be hiding in the gaps he gets angry and frustrated, and his dark half comes out.

Elspeth says, "Anything at all, Daddy. Anything that comes to mind."

"A lot of people worked for us. Teryl took some of them with her when she moved to Obligate, and I suppose some of the rest of them might be alive, despite the Black Flu and the Dead Zone and all the rest."

"Do you think Danny Lovegrave might still be alive?"

"If he is, I think we would have heard from him, don't you?"

He hears Elspeth take in a breath and let it out. She says, "Well, we're going to have to deal with this. It isn't going to go away. Did you see the coverage of that charity worker who rescued the baby?"

"No. No, I didn't."

"I'm going to dump the files in your phone's memory. You can choose to look at them or not, but they all basically make this guy into a hero. The only good thing is that it looks like Obligate has already put some spin on it. The papers and news channels are saying that his friends were killed by some kind of rebel soldiers."

"Then we don't have to worry about it. It's what Teryl would call containable."

But poor Teryl, feeling exposed because she has risen so high in Obligate and now the past is suddenly clawing at her ankles, obviously feels that it isn't at all containable. She either strongly believes or has discovered that these things in the Congo, these white devils, are the brothers and sisters of the Gentle People; she threatened him because she's scared that someone will discover the secret which even now he can't bring himself to confess to his daughter, the unforgivable act of hubris that still binds him to Teryl, and Teryl to him, and both of them to the shade of Danny Lovegrave. Perhaps Danny held back some embryos, he thinks. Perhaps he escaped from the Dead Zone, carried on with his work somewhere or other . . .

Elspeth says, "Daddy, the point is that even if it *is* containable, it isn't just about you and Teryl. She's part of Obligate, and they own a whole country now. They could cause us serious trouble if they wanted to."

Matthew scratches the grey thatch on his bare chest. He says, "Okay. Hmmm, what shall we do?"

"The first thing is to change your phone number and set up

a firewall, make sure she can't hack you again. Then I'm going to find out if it's possible to beef up security."

"I'm an island," he says. "I mean, I'm *on* an island."

I'm not an island; I'm an archipelago.

"Teryl has a lot of resources, Daddy."

I'm poor Ben Gunn. I'm Prospero. My books are drowned, my staff is broken, and my island is full of noises, sounds, and sweet airs that give delight . . .

Elspeth says, "I'm going to ask for some soldiers to back up Sergeant Mbau."

"I don't know if that's necessary."

"There's some part of you that knows it is. Listen to it, Daddy, okay?"

The Gentle People have reached the spring that spills over the rocks at the far end of the beach. His heart catches for a moment when he sees Cassius and Caesar cuff at each other, teeth bared, but then Cassius retreats, and the others are jostling around Caesar to get at the spring, and the brief spat seems to be forgotten. The Gentle People are still discovering their capabilities and limitations. They use a greater range of tools than any species of ape, they have a definite Theory of Mind, and while they do not seem to have a language capable of expressing abstract concepts, they do have their songs. And despite the lack of the cd2 engram, they're beginning to exhibit aggressive behaviour—squabbles and spats and confrontations associated with the establishment of a social hierarchy. Well, even sheep establish an order of rank; perhaps it's one of the fundamental behaviours hardwired into mammalian brains, it could be associated with parasympathetic flight-or-fight reactions . . .

"Daddy? You'll be okay for now?"

"I'll be fine."

Cassius squats on his haunches, watching the rest of the Gentle People scoop up water with their palms. The song comes and goes, sometimes sustained by only a single voice, sometimes picked up by all of them, an emergent harmony that's beginning to mesh precisely with the harmony inside his head . . .

Elspeth says, "I'll talk with David about security and the rest. I love you, Daddy."

"I love you too."

Matthew Faber switches off his phone, closes his eyes. And gives himself up to the sublime.

Chapter 5

The villa rented by the United Nations High Commissioner for Refugees in Brazzaville stands on the brow of a low hill east of Maya Maya Airport. It's a rambling, single-storey whitewashed building with a steeply pitched roof of terracotta tiles sprayed with a lumpy coat of black solar-cell paint and a long terrace that overlooks a lush green lawn with island beds of banana plants and bamboos and canna lilies. Most of the UNHCR personnel quit Green Congo after Obligate took over the refugee programme, and Nick is alone on the terrace, drinking a cup of coffee, when Captain Jean Badiledi finds him.

It's almost noon, the air hot and heavy, but it's pleasant to sit in the shade of one of the big canvas umbrellas. An ancient bougainvillea is inextricably entwined around the terrace's latticework iron rail, and its pink flowers scent the air. A pied crow keeps watch over this peaceful spot from its perch on top of a pole-mounted security camera at the corner of the terrace, stirring every time a plane or a helicopter passes overhead, ruffling its wings indignantly, settling down again.

Nick has been watching the crow for a while. He envies it: envies the circumscribed order of its life. His phone has been screening calls all morning; several of the local journalists have left handwritten notes with the concierge of the villa, offering Nick the chance to tell his side of the story; Lucy

Stewart, the famous English PR guru, has volunteered her services at a greatly reduced fee "in consideration of the humanitarian aspects of your amazing story"; and now here's this slim man in a green, neatly pressed army uniform that seems one size too big coming across the lawn and up the stairs to the terrace. He introduces himself and holds out his hand, takes it away sharply when Nick makes no move to shake it, draws up a chair and sits down on the other side of the little round table, fastidiously plucking at the thighs of his trousers to preserve their crease. His face masked by metal-framed sunglasses with square, amber-tinted lenses, his tightly curled hair razored close, a skinny moustache clinging to the line of his upper lip. He takes a little brushed-aluminium recorder from his jacket pocket, looks at Nick, and says, his finger touching the *on* button, "You understand this is not an interrogation."

"Yeah, I noticed you didn't bring your thumbscrews and electrodes." When Captain Badiledi does not smile, Nick says, "I was told a debriefing."

Dan Cooper phoned first thing this morning to warn Nick that the army wanted to talk to him and offered to sit in on it himself or to arrange for a lawyer to be present. Nick said it wasn't a problem, he wanted to talk. He said, "Isn't that why we're here, to tell the truth about the dead?" Dan Cooper hesitated, then said that the truth was already getting muddied, and told Nick that the flight engineer of the helicopter had an arrangement with a news agency in Brazzaville, that the man had taken pictures and uploaded them to the agency's office, that the agency had sold them on. "I'm very much afraid they're all over the media by now. But don't worry, Nick, you come out of it well, and Obligate is dealing with the flight engineer."

Nick used his Wizard, his customized AI help service, to work up a selection of brief one- or two-paragraph articles culled from a dozen epapers and news channels. It found a short video sequence taken by a CNN stringer at the airport: a fuzzy shot of the helicopter touching down on concrete starkly lit by blazing lights; an even fuzzier shot of the brief tug-of-war between the doctor and Nick over the baby; a cut-away to the reporter speaking direct to the camera, high on speculation and low on facts. And it found the photographs taken by the little camera in the flight engineer's phone. The one that shows Nick holding up the baby in a swirl of flying leaves and bent grass is not so bad, but the grainy sequence showing, at the very edge of visibility and distorted by glare and heat haze, an indistinct struggle between pale and dark figures, is far worse, because it forces Nick's imagination to flesh it out.

Fortunately, none of the news channels or epapers have made much of the story; even on CNN, with its exclusive footage, it's no more than a ninety-second human-interest item trailing way behind the headline stories, a "daring rescue" carried out under "heavy fire" from "rebel troops loyal to the former dictator," no mention at all of mutilated bodies or white devils. Nick takes that as a good sign, believes that all he has to do is stay cool and do what he is told, and it will blow over and he can get back to work. Telling himself now that this thing with Captain Badiledi isn't going to be a problem, just the two of them having a friendly, civilized talk about a massacre.

Captain Badiledi switches on the recorder and sets it on the table, leans back in his chair and looks through the tinted lenses of his sunglasses at Nick and asks why an Englishman is working for an American charity.

Nick says, "We have Kenyans, Ugandans, Canadians, some Norwegians . . . It's pretty much an international operation."

"And before that you were working for Obligate, I believe on the biodiversity program. So, you are a biologist."

Nick takes a sip of coffee—weak instant stuff boiled up in an urn. He says, "I guess you could say I'm a kind of gypsy ecologist. Before I came here, I worked on various surveys and reclamation projects in the EU. All short-term contracts, not much different from the one I had when I was working for Obligate."

"And when your contract with Obligate was finished, you joined Witness."

"I hoped to renew my contract, but by then Obligate had already brought in its own people."

"You stayed in Green Congo, even though you did not have any work."

"Well, I like it here. I was looking for a new contract, and a friend told me about Witness. I started out as a volunteer, and then they signed me up to work in the field." Nick, beginning to distrust Badiledi's disingenuously casual manner, says, "What has my employment record got to do with anything, Captain?"

"We're having a general talk, establishing background . . . The work you do for Witness, I should think it is very different from the work you did for Obligate."

"The fieldwork? You'd think so, but the mechanics of it are much the same. Doing grid surveys, taking samples . . . Also, I think it helps that I took a premed course. I was studying to become a doctor, until I decided that medicine wasn't for me." He's tired, or he wouldn't have let that slip out. It had been his mother's idea, of course, that he should follow in Christopher's footsteps. And of course she'd made sure that he'd gone to the same university . . . He says, "I started out doing volunteer work in the lab. Bottle-washing, isolating mitochondrial DNA from tissue samples—"

"Mitochondrial? I do not know this word."

"You know what DNA is."

"Of course. It is what genes are made of."

"Human cells have two kinds of DNA. Genomic DNA, found in the cell nucleus, and mitochondrial DNA. Mitochondria are tiny compartments where energy-generating reactions take place; they're like the cell's batteries. They each contain a circlet of DNA, and each cell contains hundreds or even thousands of mitochondria. Because there are many more copies of mitochondrial DNA than of genomic DNA, mitochondrial DNA can be extracted from highly degraded tissue samples, and that makes it very useful in identifying bodies that have been lying in the open for a year or two. Witness runs mitochondrial DNA comparisons to find out if bodies found in the same place were related to each other, and to try and tie them in with living relatives."

"So, you do laboratory work. Why then were you sent to the illegal settlement on the Likouala aux Herbes River?"

"I started out in the labs, but I have a lot of fieldwork experience, so I ended up working with one of the field teams. I was working on a site near Massaka when Tremaine Thompson, he's the chief forensic investigator for Witness—*was* the chief forensic investigator—asked me to help out at what he called a hot scene. I guess he thought I would benefit from the experience." It's weird and unsettling to be talking in the past tense about someone who was alive just yesterday. "Tremaine was killed. So was the photographer who came with us, Grant Twentyman. He was a New Zealander; I didn't know him that well. And five Brazilian soldiers. Can we get into that now, Captain? I really do want to tell you what happened. And when I'm done, perhaps you can answer some of *my* questions."

"There is actually very little to discuss," Captain Badiledi says. "You were sent to investigate a recent massacre, and you were ambushed by Loyalist rebels."

Nick feels a prickle of alarm, says, "They weren't Loyalists."

"Monsieur Hyde, I have read the transcript of a verbal report made by the sergeant in charge of the army patrol that was sent to the scene. He said that you were attacked by a large force of Loyalist troops. I have talked with the helicopter crew, and also the government observer, and they are all in agreement."

I did not see anything. And it would be better for you if you did not see anything, either.

"With respect, Captain Badiledi, your guys didn't exactly do a good job out there. They didn't make a proper sweep of the area, let alone secure a perimeter. They didn't even find all of the bodies of the people who had been massacred. When we went in the next day, we were ambushed, yes, but not by Loyalists." Nick leans in, speaking to the recorder on the little table, its winking red light. "The things that attacked us weren't human, and your soldiers didn't even know they were there, let alone get a good look at them. I did. They were naked, with

white skin. Not white like mine, but grainy, translucent. A few
of them had guns, but most of them used their claws or teeth, or
clubs. Bone clubs, like out of the Stone Age."

"You say these soldiers were not human? What were they,
then? Apes? Apes with guns?"

Captain Badiledi touching the corner of his skinny moustache with a thumbnail. Letting some amusement show in his
face.

Nick says, "They had gargoyle faces, devil faces. Wide
strong jaws full of fangs, big nonretractable claws, pale skin
with bony plates underneath. They moved very quickly, and
yes, some of them knew how to use guns. I think they took a
rifle from the people they had killed. And after they killed the
soldiers, they took their rifles too. They came out of the trees.
Ran straight at the soldiers, showed absolutely no fear. I
guess the soldiers shot some of them, but they kept coming . . . And I shot one. It attacked one of the soldiers right in
front of me, and I shot it."

He remembers for a moment the way the soldier, Isabel
Fonesca, looked at him when it started, when she told him to
take the baby to the helicopter. He says, "Let me tell you exactly what happened." And he does, from the moment Isabel
Fonesca was attacked to his escape with the baby.

"Sometimes the more extreme groups of Loyalists will
paint themselves," Captain Badiledi says when Nick has finished. "They strip naked and paint themselves and take drugs
that make them crazy, without fear. I myself have seen this
many times, in the war of liberation. They also mutilate themselves with implants, with animal teeth and animal claws, to
make themselves seem more fearsome. It is easy, in the heat
of combat, to mistake them for animals or even monsters, and
it must have been very confusing for you. You were carrying
a baby, you shot someone for the first time . . . That's correct,
isn't it? You have never killed someone before."

"I got a very good look at what I shot, Captain, and I certainly wouldn't ever mistake it for a soldier daubed with
whitewash. It had a face like a gargoyle ape, and it was small,

too, not much more than a metre in height. Small and strong and very fierce."

"Then it was almost certainly a child," Captain Badiledi says. "It's well known that Loyalists kidnap children and make them into *kidogos*—child soldiers. I am not surprised that you are upset because you had to shoot it, but I understand why you had to do it. *Kidogos* are not ordinary children. The Loyalists brainwash them, turn them into ruthless killers. They are more obedient than adults and less afraid, so the Loyalists like to use them on the front line. In the heat of combat, it is easy for an untrained person to become confused. There is no disgrace in that."

Nick says, "I know that after I shot it three times in the chest, it got right back up and came at me again. It had some kind of internal armor. I had to shoot it in the head to put it down."

"It was a child made crazy by drugs," Captain Badiledi says. "You had to kill it, I quite understand, but knowing that you killed a child is a hard thing to deal with. You make excuses to yourself, yes?"

"I know what I shot," Nick says, "and I'm sure you know about the body I brought back. I believe it went to the Obligate research centre, along with a cool box full of samples from the people who had been massacred. I'll be happy to go along to the research centre with you, and find out what the people there have made of it."

"But I know already what they found," Captain Badiledi says. "It was, I understand, a chimpanzee. It had suffered a disease that had caused hair loss and changes in its skin pigmentation. Also, it had been treated with a strong solution of common bleach. No doubt it died and was washed before burial, just as anyone would do with a dead person."

"This was before or after someone shot it in the head?"

Captain Badiledi shrugs.

Nick says, "If the people at the research centre have finished with it, they can release it to Witness. We can take a look at it, make some tests."

Captain Badiledi says, with the sly smile of a poker player

trumping someone's unimprovable hand, "Unfortunately, I believe that it was disposed of."

Nick's anger is a swelling heat in his chest. "Friends of that thing killed at least fourteen people, they took down five armed soldiers, and you *disposed* of it?"

"That's my understanding, Monsieur Hyde. Because, I would think, of the disease that killed it. And in any case, as I have explained, your friends and the soldiers were killed by Loyalists."

"Those things weren't Loyalists, Captain, and you know it."

Captain Badiledi switches off the recorder and puts it in his pocket and stands, saying briskly, "You were caught in the middle of a firefight, Monsieur Hyde. I'm not surprised that you were mistaken about what you saw. You are upset, perhaps in shock. Your judgement—it has been affected. We will talk again when you are feeling better, when you are able to understand what really happened. Meanwhile, you must rest, sit in the sunshine, enjoy the seclusion of this place."

"Am I under arrest, Captain Badiledi?"

Captain Badiledi smiles his sly, untrustworthy smile and says, "Under arrest? Of course not. I know you want to help me, Monsieur Hyde, and as long as you stay here, in this quiet, safe place, why should I need to arrest you?"

Nick phones Dan Cooper, gives him a summary of the conversation. "He more or less warned me that I'd be sorry if I didn't come around to the official viewpoint. He told me that I couldn't leave the country until I agreed with his story. He told me that the body I brought back had been, I quote, 'disposed of.' Because of a disease he said it had, the same imaginary disease that was supposed to have made it lose all its hair. He told me to think about my story, think about how I could have become confused in the heat of combat. Those were his exact words, Mr. Cooper: 'the heat of combat.' We should go back there right now. Go back to the massacre site and retrieve the bodies of the refugees, and the bodies of Tremaine and Grant Twentyman and the soldiers. Document them thoroughly, prove that they couldn't possibly have been killed by Loyalists. There's Grant's video camera, too, and the body of the white devil that I shot."

"White devil?"

"That's what the government observer called it. This army captain wants me to believe that they were Loyalist troops, child soldiers, but I know what I saw. And those things were so fast—it was like they were in a different movie, one running twice the speed of ordinary reality. That implies changes in the way their nerves fire, in the fibres of their muscles . . . They had some serious gengineering done to them, and the Congolese Army and Obligate are trying to cover it up, Mr. Cooper, I know it."

"Why would they want to do that, Nick? Obligate would love to get some evidence that Nyibizo's Loyalists are using gengineered animals to commit atrocities against civilians. There's nothing they'd like better than to find a smoking gun; they'd run with it to the International Court at The Hague and ask the UN to drag Nyibizo from his luxury villa in Gabon, arrest him for war crimes. It would be a tremendous publicity coup."

A plane goes over, a Green Congo Air Force Starlifter, its four engines making black smoke as it gains altitude. The pied crow fluffs its wings and voices an indignant protest at this threat to its sense of propriety.

Nick says, "Then let's get that evidence for them, Mr. Cooper. I'm ready to go right now."

"We're guests in this country, Nick," Dan Cooper says. "There's a certain protocol to be followed. I'm pressing very hard for return of the bodies of Tre Thompson and Grant Twentyman, but it's the usual thing, Obligate blaming the army for not going in to retrieve the bodies, and the army command in Brazzaville blaming the local commander in Liranga."

"And you don't think that's suspicious, Mr. Cooper?"

"I'm going to do all I can. Hang in there, Nick. Try to relax, okay? Try not to worry. Can you do that?"

Chapter 6

Nick does his best. He phones Tangalai Hospital and gets through to a nurse in the paediatric unit who tells him that the baby is doing fine. He sifts through a new batch of emails and phone messages. Most are from journalists. CNN wants to record an interview with him. Lucy Stewart wants him to know that she has already secured two highly attractive offers on his behalf, and if he would like to call her . . .

Nick deletes everything and switches off his phone, reads with careless inattention a hundred pages of a buckled twenty-year-old legal thriller someone left behind in the villa's small library. He goes for a long run, two hundred laps of the villa's garden, alternately sprinting and jogging. He takes a long shower. The face in the mirror over the rust-stained sink in the bathroom is the face of his dead brother. "If you really wanted to hide from yourself," he tells it, "you would have had plastic surgery."

He has a restless night, despite taking two of the Percocets that Dan Cooper gave him. Again and again, he wakes in the grip of helpless terror, and then the memories come back in a vivid rush. The young Brazilian soldier, Isabel Fonesca, going down under the sudden impact of the white devil. Grant Twentyman's desperate scream as he tried to bat away his attackers with his video camera. Pale creatures scampering towards him through scrubby grass like malevolent ghosts. The thought of the baby helps: sleepless and sweating on the hard, unfamiliar bed in the sweltering dark, Nick clings to the clear memory of how at one point during the long, thrumming helicopter ride back to Brazzaville, the baby stirred from sleep and gripped his thumb with small hot fingers and an absolute, unconditional trust.

He is eating breakfast, trying his best to make small talk with the half-dozen UNHCR staffers without revealing anything at all about why he's staying there, when his phone rings. It's Dan Cooper. He says that he has bad news. He says that the site of the massacre has been napalmed.

Nick excuses himself and steps through the French windows onto the sunlit terrace. Dan Cooper says in his ear, "I'm told there was renewed Loyalist activity in the area. The Congolese Army sent in a couple of attack helicopters to retrieve the bodies yesterday morning. Someone aimed a ground-to-air missile at them, and they responded by dropping a stick of napalm bombs."

Nick feels as if his blood has suddenly become carbonated. "That's bullshit, Mr. Cooper. If there had been any Loyalists, and if they'd had a ground-to-air missile, they would have used it against us. The army didn't napalm the area because they were attacked; they did it because they wanted to destroy the evidence."

"The army has already held a briefing, Nick. The reason I've told you is because I didn't want you to find it out from some journalist, not so you can make trouble."

"I appreciate that you told me, Mr. Cooper. Do you have any news about the body I brought back?"

"I'll keep asking questions, of course. I'll press Tink Glazer for a formal report. But I'm not in a position to demand anything, Nick. I hope you realize that."

"We both know the army is going to do its best to cover up what happened, Mr. Cooper. And we owe a duty to Tremaine Thompson and Grant Twentyman to get at the truth."

There's a pause. Nick is aware of the buzz of insects in the garden, the chink of silverware on china, and the murmur of conversation coming through the French windows. Dan Cooper says in his ear, "I'm going to do all I can. I know you feel you should do something, but right now the best thing you can do is stay where you are, and try to get some rest.

And Nick, if any journalist tries to talk to you, I don't want you to say anything other than 'no comment.'"

"Is that an order, Mr. Cooper?"

"It's good advice, Nick. Saying the wrong thing to a journalist in this country could get you in a whole heap of trouble."

Nick cuts the connection, thinking that this isn't going to blow over after all, thinking that maybe it's time to get out, move on. Maybe even change his identity again . . . Yeah, but that means leaving the country, and that means agreeing with Captain Badiledi's fantasy about Loyalist soldiers and drug-crazed *kidogos*. Besides, he's been Nicholas Hyde for four years now. He likes being Nicholas Hyde, is comfortable in his skin. And Nicholas Hyde has the duty of speaking for his dead.

His phone rings again, and his Wizard asks if he wants to speak with William Ndinga. Nick accepts the call, says, "Monsieur Ndinga. How did you find me?"

"I have a satellite dish. I get Pan-Afrique. I get all the major African channels. Also the BBC, Canal Plus, CNN, NBC, CBS. You are big news. You're famous."

"I still have to wonder how you found me."

Nick seeing the government observer for a moment: his proud, strutting walk, his neatly pressed jungle-camo blouse and trousers, his mirrorshades.

"Everyone knows everyone else in Brazzaville, Nicholas," William Ndinga says, enunciating with the exaggerated care of the profoundly drunk. Drunk at, Jesus, half-past eight in the morning. "Tell me, please, how is the baby?"

"It's fine. How about you?"

"I miss Grant. We worked together many times. He was a good man. What happened to him—he didn't deserve it."

"None of them deserved it," Nick says, thinking of Tremaine Thompson. *I need an assistant, and I saw you working all alone up here and thought you might be interested.* "The official line seems to be that they were killed by Loyalist soldiers. I understand you agreed with it."

"Nicholas, Nicholas. You are English, a European. You think that there is such a thing as absolute truth. But here— here there are many truths. I tell the army what I saw, and the army tells me, no, William Ndinga, *this* is what you really saw. And that is what I must see, do you understand?"

"Who talked to you? Was it a captain, by any chance? A sly son of a bitch by the name of Badiledi?"

"I tell him, what if monsters exist? He said that the monsters are only in my head."

"The white devils are real," Nick says. He feels an intimate chill creep over every centimetre of his skin. He says, "We both went through a bad time, William. We're probably not thinking straight. But we know what we saw."

"*It doesn't matter what we saw.*" William Ndinga's breath rasps in Nick's ear. He says, more quietly, "Listen, Nicholas, you are a famous man now."

"I don't think so. I'm no more than a fifteen-minute wonder."

"People will want to talk to you. Be careful what you say."

"Or what, William? Obligate took the body we found. They napalmed the area, too—did you hear about that? What else are they going to do?"

"He came to see me again. With another man, a magistrate. I had to give a sworn deposition, Nicholas. Do you understand?"

"What did you say, William? Did you say that we were attacked by Loyalists? If you did, I know that you know it isn't true."

"I know I am a dead man," William Ndinga says, and rings off.

The pied crow is at its post on top of the security camera. Nick looks at it and says, "It's all right for you. You know exactly what you are."

Then he goes to look for the concierge, to order a taxi.

During the civil war that deposed Sergeant Samuel Nyibizo's military dictatorship, Tangalai Hospital was destroyed by a third-hand Indian cruise missile with a bug in the software of its navigation system. Obligate rebuilt the wrecked

building to the design of an award-winning retrofuturist
South African architect, and now its polychrome sails and
domes rise from the centre of Brazzaville's main refugee
camp like a prop from a twentieth-century science fiction
movie. The camp is such a wonderful advertisement for
Obligate's philanthropy that there are rumours it will be
made permanent. It sprawls on either side of the road to the
hospital, row upon row upon row of grey emergency-shelter
igloos stretching into the distance under a heat haze thickened by the smoke from thousands of cooking fires, a
refugee suburbia interrupted only by the occasional mango
or palm tree. The igloos are one-piece units blown from recycled plastic, complete with bunk beds, solar-powered lights,
and composting toilets, designed to provide instant emergency accommodation anywhere between the Arctic Circle
and the equator. Some have extensions ingeniously patched
from scrap metal and plastic sheeting; others have been
transformed by entrepreneurs into shops, bars, bicycle-repair
workshops, and laundries. There are eight schools, each pro-
viding their pupils with a daily, nutritious vegetarian meal as
a reward for attendance, four food markets, an open-air cinema, and two warehouse-sized churches. A free-trade zone
of anonymous prefab factory units where many of the
refugees work for a guaranteed minimum wage, stitching
Obligate's Lotek sneakers and clothing, assembling slates
and phones, carving Rainforest toys and masks, and rolling
Rainforest cigarettes. A media company staffed entirely by
refugees produces a daily newspaper for the camp and inspi-
rational documentaries and video diaries about the lives of
the inhabitants for Obligate's corporate channel, and a daily
guided bus tour is laid on for journalists and VIP visitors. The
camp provides everything but the dignity of self-
determination for its inhabitants; none of the video diaries or
documentaries mention the crippling rates of alcoholism,
abortion, and suicide, the skirmishes between rival gangs, or
the occasional, brutally suppressed, riots.

On the way to the hospital, Nick's taxi passes billboards
advertising Rainforest products that no one in the refugee

camp can afford, billboards with slogans exhorting people to use their free contraceptives, billboards extolling the happiness of two-parent, single-child families, billboards publicizing rewards for those who volunteer to be sterilized. It passes a cadre of Obligate volunteers working on a new spur road, cheerful young men and women in green dungarees and identical short haircuts who are levelling and tamping down the gravel roadbed. It passes small children shepherded fore and aft by their teachers as they walk in single file along the shoulder of the road carrying butterfly nets and plastic bags full of dead and dying butterflies, the boys in green short-sleeved shirts and black shorts, the girls in green dresses, their bare arms dappled with fragments of polychrome logos. The children are paid one cent for every hundred gengineered butterflies they collect; Obligate, with a touching faith in the industry of the children and a grievous ignorance of insect reproductive capacity, boasts that in five years similar programmes will eliminate every gengineered butterfly and cockroach in Green Congo.

Nick tips the taxi driver an extra five dollars, asks him to wait. The doctor in charge of the paediatric unit is a stocky man with a harassed air, a stethoscope draped around his neck, and a row of diagnostic pens in the breast pocket of his green short-sleeved surgeon's tunic. He says, "I can give you just two minutes," and leads Nick between walls of translucent blue plastic that lean together four metres overhead. Air plants grow on narrow ledges and in little niches; children's artless, affecting drawings and finger paintings are tacked to noticeboards and screens. The cool air smells of antiseptic and ozone.

Nick says, "If there's a problem, I can come back another time."

The doctor's smile is quick and shy. "The only problem is that we are always very busy. We must deal with people already in the camp and with people coming in from the countryside, perhaps fifty or sixty every day. The Pan-African Red Cross, Médecins du Monde, and Médecins Sans Frontières, they all have field clinics out there, but still many people make their way to Brazzaville. A lot of them with the plastic disease. In the last month, we are seeing a new strain with a very rapid conversion rate, more and more cases of it in the north. People travel downriver to bring us their infected babies and children, but by the time they get here there's not much we can do—too much of the body mass has been converted. We put them on fluids, and we try to keep them cool because badly infected individuals lose control of their core temperature, and we watch them die. Your baby, though, you don't have to worry about him. He is fine. Very strong, a real little fighter."

The intensive-care section of the paediatric wing is a quiet, red-lit bubble containing half a dozen rows of tiny cots elevated to waist height. The baby Nick saved lies naked on a waffle-weave blanket inside an isolation tent. A line connected to a bag of straw-coloured fluid is taped just above the chubby crease of his elbow. Nick puts his hand on the tent's clear plastic by the baby's head and feels something move through him.

"We gave him the standard battery of tests, and he came up clean," the doctor says. His face softens as he looks down at the baby. "He's doing very well, considering."

"He was badly dehydrated when I found him," Nick says. "He'd been left alone for at least twenty-four hours."

The doctor nods. "His blood was thickened; he showed poor skin turgor and a markedly sunken fontanelle. That is the soft spot—"

"On top of the skull. I know."

"You have medical training?"

"Just a little. Enough to know that he was dehydrated."

"The dehydration was not severe. Young babies are surprisingly resilient—they have a pad of fat between the shoulder blades, in function much like the hump of a camel, but you did well to begin to rehydrate him as quickly as possible. We have tested for kidney damage, and he is fine, and there was no bleeding from the intestinal tract."

"He's still in containment."

"In Class Two containment, yes, but soon we move him

out. All he seems to have is hookworm, but that's not unusual, and we're treating it with a five-day course of Filoxin. Do you want to give him a name? The nurses are calling him Moses, but as you saved his life, you should have the honour."

"Moses is just fine," Nick says. "Where's your cashier's office? I want to make a donation in his name."

As Nick walks towards his taxi, a tall young man in a white shirt and brand-new blue jeans slides off the hood of a little yellow Fiat parked on the shoulder of the road and jogs over, calling his name.

"Nicholas Hyde! Monsieur Hyde! A moment, sir. Please, just a moment!"

The young man reaches the taxi just as Nick shuts the door, and taps on the window with the tips of his fingers.

"Monsieur Hyde, please, just a moment of your time! I know about the massacre!"

Nick cranks down the window a scant centimetre.

"Thank you, Monsieur Hyde," the man says, and flattens a laminated card on the glass. It's a media pass: HARMONY BONIFACE: CONGO REAL TIME, printed under the man's photograph and DNA patch. "My credentials. As you can see, I have the honour of representing *Congo Real Time*, a very important voice of the people in our brave new democracy. Perhaps you can tell me, Monsieur Hyde, why you are visiting the hospital today."

"You said that you have some information about the massacre."

Harmony Boniface has a nice, unforced smile. The tight curls of his hair are cut short and dyed bright red. "Perhaps you have a comment about the search for so-called mutant apes."

"Where did you hear that?"

"Units of the army close to the Likouala aux Herbes River, in the north of the country, have been sent out to look for white, hairless apes. I have good contacts in that region. It's where you rescued the baby, I believe, and where your comrades were killed. Perhaps you have some comment."

"I wish the soldiers the best of luck."

"Then these things, they're real?"

"I really can't talk to the media," Nick says, and tells the taxi driver to get going. He watches the young man sprint back to the little yellow Fiat as the taxi pulls away, and adds, "Ten American dollars if you can lose that guy."

The taxi driver is a teenager with mirrorshades and long dreadlocks. He looks at Nick in the rearview mirror, grins, and says, "Just tell me where you want to go, boss man."

"It's such a nice day, I feel like going to the zoo."

Like Tangalai Hospital, the Brazzaville zoo was one of the first construction projects inaugurated by Obligate after it bought up the debts and assumed control of Green Congo. Officially, it's the Green Congo Biodiversity Research Centre, the heart of a commercial project to collect and analyse for potential exploitation every plant and animal in Green Congo's swamp-forests, but everyone in Brazzaville calls it the zoo because its centrepiece is a recreation of a bai, an edaphic forest clearing, filled with animals that are mostly extinct in the wild.

Nick pays off the taxi at the staff entrance. When he came here just a week ago, to walk the new survey team through the data he had collected, his retinal pattern was still on file, but when he stares into the black lens of the camera now, the light above it stays red, and the gate doesn't unlock. He presses the buzzer and tells the security guard on the other end of the intercom that he's here to see Conway Wydler, the man in charge of the field teams, and is told that Mr. Wydler is unavailable and asked what his business is. "Never mind," Nick says, because he sees on the far side of the parking lot one of the technicians, a local guy, Louis something, humping a yellow hazardous-waste bag towards the incinerator.

Nick calls to him, and they talk through the chain-link security fence. Louis tells Nick that they sealed off a whole lab block when they brought in the body of the *kidogo*.

"They said it was infected with a biowar agent," Louis says, hooking his fingers through the fence's mesh. He's a skinny man in baggy orange coveralls. "The block, it is still sealed off. Major trouble all around."

"And is the body still in there?"

"Come on, Nicholas, they don't tell people like me what they do. But I do know that Professor Meade came here to see it."

"Teryl Meade?"

"The boss lady herself. You have met her while you were working here?"

"I've been reading about her, but I've never met her. I was just one of the hired hands, like you."

"They say she did something to her mind," Louis says. "They say she can look into your eyes and read your thoughts. She came here with some of those Brazilian soldiers in the middle of the night, and when we all come to work the next day, we have to wait outside the gate for two, three hours in the sun before we are given clearance."

"I guess that's when they lost my retinal pattern. Louis, do you think you can buzz me through?"

"I'd like to, Nicholas, but I can't. I should not even be talking to you—we were told, don't talk to outsiders."

"I'm not an outsider, Louis; I used to work here."

Louis shakes his head.

"Perhaps you can find my old boss, Dr. Wydler, and tell him I'd like to talk to him."

"This is going to get me into trouble. I know it."

"Tell him I'll be waiting in the zoo, at the bai."

Nick has his phone, and his phone has a camera. All he needs to blow Captain Badiledi's story out of the water is just one picture of the decapitated body that's lying somewhere in the lab complex—all he has to do is persuade Conway Wydler to give him access for thirty seconds. Conway's a contract worker, just like Nick was, and a stand-up guy. Nick reckons that as long as Louis passes on his message, he has about a fifty percent chance of swinging it. If Conway Wydler doesn't turn up, he plans to buttonhole him when he leaves work, ask him some pertinent questions. Meanwhile, he has a little research to do.

He walks all the way around the lab complex to the public entrance of the zoo, buys a Rainforest power bar and a tall cup of Rainforest mango juice from the concession stand, and wanders along a path of polymer-stabilized red dirt that winds through a rim of carefully planted forest trees to one of the observation platforms at the edge of the bai.

It's a wide basin of lush grass patched with salt-rich muddy swamp, divided into two unequal segments by a deep, fenced trench. The larger segment houses fifteen species of bird, a small herd of forest elephants, forest buffalo, a troop of red colobus monkeys and a troop of grey-cheeked mangabeys, tortoises, aardvarks and two species of pangolin, bongo antelope with vivid white stripes like bar codes down their chestnut flanks, small, brown-red bay duiker antelopes and even smaller water chevrotain, and red river hogs that trot through the vivid green grass and black mud on hooves as elegant as couturière shoes, rooting through balls of elephant dung for undigested morsels. The larger segment is where most of the visitors congregate because that's where most of the action is, but Nick is interested in the smaller segment, the kingdom of a little tribe of chimpanzees.

He leans at the rail of the observation platform and chews his way through the cardboardy power bar and sips warm, sweet mango juice and looks down at the sunlit patch of trampled grass where several chimpanzees are squabbling over a pile of fruit. He sees at once that no one could mistake these compact, muscular animals for the quick, lithe things that killed Tre Thompson and Isabel Fonesca and the others. It is not just because of their coats of dusty black hair, the shape of their small heads, or their mournfully expressive faces. The proportions of their bodies are all wrong, and they rarely walk very far on two legs—and then with the awkward staggering gait of a novice toddler, their big feet with gripping toes turned slightly inwards. They prefer to knuckle-walk over any distance, and Nick twice sees the dominant male make quick dashes on all fours to drive his subordinates away from the fresh delivery of pineapples and bananas that he has not yet finished picking through. If the white devils were gengineered from chimpanzee stock, someone would have had to do some serious splicing and dicing.

He's been standing at the rail of the observation platform for only a little while when a young woman leans next to him, looks sideways into his face, and asks if she can help him.

"I'm just here to look at the chimps."

"If you would like it, I can tell you about them, Monsieur Hyde. I am Florence Bague. I am a primatologist. The chimpanzees, they are my work."

Florence Bague wears a red-and-yellow wraparound and a skintight T-shirt, printed with the Obligate logo of the cloud-wrapped planet Earth on a green field, that's lifted in front by her breasts to reveal her navel. Her hair is done up in tight braids that show off her shapely skull, reminding Nick of an Egyptian sculpture of Nefertiti he once saw in the British Museum.

"Have we met before, Ms. Bague? I'm pretty sure not, because I would certainly have remembered you."

"You are the famous man who rescued the baby. Also, I believe you once worked here."

Louis didn't pass on the message, Nick thinks. He got scared and went to his boss instead. He says, "I was mostly in the field, but yeah, we had a lab around the back. Maybe you can tell me if Conway Wydler is about. I came to tie up some loose ends, but it seems that my retinal pattern is no longer on the security system's database."

"Perhaps that's because you're no longer working for us, Monsieur Hyde. And I believe Monsieur Wydler is in the field."

"He is, huh? What about his assistant, Ellen Broussard? Or Jack McFee, the fellow in charge of the biodiversity database?"

"Perhaps they are working in the field too."

"If everyone is in the field, whose idea was it for you to come out and find what I want?"

"I'm sorry?"

When Florence Bague smiles, she shows an endearing gap in her front teeth. She's leaning so close to Nick that he can feel the heat of her body. She has a clean, wholesome smell: soap and shampoo, no perfume.

Nick says, "I understand that Teryl Meade is very interested in the body that I brought back, so I think it must have been her idea to send a pretty girl to find out what I want, perhaps give me a quiet warning to keep away. The question is, was it her idea or yours to not wear a bra?"

Florence Bague laughs. "This is how I always dress. You don't like it?"

"It's very becoming."

"Are you interested in chimpanzees, Nicholas? If you like, I can tell you something about them."

"It just occurred to me that they might have been cloned. I ask because I believe they're extinct in the wild."

Florence Bague puts her hand on his. "You are teasing me, Nicholas, because I'm sure you know that Obligate does not use cloning or gengineering. We have fifteen chimpanzees. Five adult males, eight females, and two infants. The infants were born here; the adults were all bought from a zoo in Japan just a year ago, and already they have started to breed. They are very happy here."

Nick takes his hand away. "Why are they fighting if they're so very happy?"

"That's not really fighting," Florence Bague says, her smile deepening. "For chimpanzees, it's what passes for ordinary social intercourse. The one doing all the chasing, he's called Noah. He is the dominant male, the Big Man. The other males keep challenging him, but he always drives them off. These skirmishes are not just about food, of course— Noah must constantly prove his physical prowess. If he lost just one fight, he would also lose his status. He would be driven away from the group, or even killed. Of course, we wouldn't permit that here."

Florence Bague seems genuinely happy to be telling Nick about the animals she loves, and although she must certainly be subject to the subtle and continuous brainwashing that's part of Obligate's corporate culture, she doesn't have the shiny-eyed evangelical fervour of the Obligate employees with whom Nick had to deal when he was working on the biodiversity survey team. Obligate doesn't call it brainwashing, of course: it's Emotional Reorientation, a staged process that leads ever upwards to the ultimate goal of becoming a lucid freethinker. There are Obligate clinics in the main shopping streets of every large European city, staffed by happy, good-looking young people offering free assessments of Emotional Intelligence, bait to draw in the unwary, the unhappy, the lonely. Nick once had a date with a woman who'd just started a course of treatment; she explained that what he thinks of as his self, an observer securely seated in the theatre of his mind, is in fact an unstable, dynamic core that's in a continual state of flux as it integrates experience and sensation. According to the ideology she expounded at some length in the little bar in Soho where they'd agreed to meet, we are never exactly the same person from one moment to the next. She explained that Emotional Reorientation deals with the self-sustaining knots and whirlpools that our dynamic core sometimes spawns. These dense little packages of intense emotion—engrams—can be accidentally subsumed into the dynamic core at inappropriate moments, and ER uses neuromagnetic imaging to identify and erase them, and to amplify useful functional states—happiness, empathy, ambition, creativity, self-confidence, and so on. Nick's date told him that she'd only had two treatments so far, but she already felt so much better about herself. "More focused, more positive. Not so cluttered. *Cleaner*. You really should give it a try," she said, which was about where the date ended, because the last thing Nick needed was another woman trying to change his mind.

He wonders now how far along the curve of ER's modification program Florence Bague has progressed, wonders if her happiness is unearned or the real thing, and if it really matters.

In the grass arena below the observation platform, Noah makes another dash, screaming angrily as he scatters the two males who were sneaking up on his left. The third scampers in on the unguarded right flank, snatches a hand of bananas and hastily retreats. The female chimpanzees, companionably plucking reeds from the edge of a swampy pool and washing the plump white roots in the water before eating them, don't bother looking up. They've heard it all before: the energetic male screeching and hooting is for them ordinary everyday background noise. A tiny baby, all head and legs and arms, clings spiderlike beneath the largest female.

"You see how clever they are," Florence Bague says fondly. "That male, the one who took the bananas, he is Japhet. He is one very smart chimpanzee. He rarely challenges Noah. He lets the others take the risks, then exploits the openings they create."

"Aggression is a normal way of life for them," Nick says, remembering the way the white devils danced in a kind of furious spasm around the bodies of Tremaine Thompson and Grant Twentyman and the soldiers.

Florence Bague leans a little closer, pressing the warm, soft length of her body against his. She says, "Chimpanzees live in small groups dominated by an alpha male. He bullies the subordinate males and controls the reproductive lives of the females. If the other males want to mate, they must either depose the alpha male, or they must trick him—sneak off with a receptive female. What they're doing now, it is not serious. This is an artificial environment, they are always together, they have plentiful food, so they have a lot of time and energy for this kind of low-level squabbling. Like humans, chimpanzees exhibit male-dominated fission-fusion behaviour; the alpha-male tyranny is not absolute. In times when food is difficult to find, he accepts that the group must split up so that it can search a wider area, and conversely, the smaller groups accept his domination once more when they get back together."

She points at the forest elephants wallowing in the other segment of the clearing. Polished wooden bangles clatter on her slim, fine-boned wrist. "Elephants are also male-dominated. The big alpha male keeps his rivals away from the best food and the tastiest part of the salt lick; he even chases off the buffalo. But he would never allow his group to split up, even when they were starving. Elephant tyranny is absolute."

"But elephants don't kill each other, and I believe that chimpanzees do."

"Chimpanzees are very much like people. Many of the engrams that trouble people who have not yet enjoyed Emotional Reorientation have their origin in chimpanzee behaviour. For instance, chimpanzees are very intolerant of outsiders. Males, especially adolescent males, will gang up in hunting bands and attack lone females from rival groups. If they find a receptive female, the males will abduct her and force her to mate with them. And if she is not receptive, they will kill her."

Noah has turned towards the sound of Florence Bague's voice, is looking up at the observation platform. His gaze meets and holds Nick's, and Nick feels an unexpected spark of contact. That moment of looking into another's eyes and experiencing the presence of another mind.

"Look away," Florence Bague says softly. Her hand still lightly rests on Nick's arm. "A direct stare, it can be a threat. You'll upset him."

"You can feel their intelligence," Nick says, oddly moved.

"Chimpanzees are like us in many ways," Florence Bague says. "There is still much debate about the quality of their intelligence, but what is certain is that like us they can make models of others in their heads. They have a Theory of Mind. We recognize that reciprocal comprehension at some level. That's why their cruelty is so terrible—when chimpanzees kill, they know that they are killing other living creatures. Chimpanzees are not innocents, as some Western sentimentalists insist. They do not murder simply because of Darwinian imperative, to maximize their reproductive potential. They share with untreated human beings many engrams that encode corrupt behavioural patterns."

Noah is ripping off the top of a pineapple that he holds between his feet. The other males approach the remaining fruit, hooting softly.

Nick says, "I'd be very disappointed if this turns into a sales pitch for ER."

"You're an unbeliever, Nicholas, but I can assure you that engrams are quite real. They are the cause of much human misery and conflict. I'm sure that in your work with Witness you've seen many horrors created by people with nonlucid minds."

"I've always thought that evil was a lot more complicated than a few bad thoughts floating around inside our heads."

"Engrams are not thoughts. They are behavioural paradigms. The science is very well established."

A sudden frosty edge to her manner now. Florence Bague thinks he's dissing Obligate, which to her is not merely an employer but a way of life. Better thinking through mind-washing.

"Thinking about thinking," Nick says, "isn't really my thing. Tell me some more about the chimpanzees. What's the most interesting thing about them?"

"The most interesting thing? Apart from the fact that in the forests they were hunted to extinction by men infested with unsocial engrams?"

"Yeah, I know, men like me. Unreconstructed brutes."

"We could test you, Nicholas," Florence Bague says. "Discover which engrams are currently troubling you. Help you come to terms with the terrible event that you were so lucky to survive."

"I guess you were briefed on that. Are you going to tell me that I brought back the body of a diseased chimp? That my friends were killed by child soldiers high on drugs?"

"We are not your enemy, Nicholas."

"You want to co-opt me."

"We want to help you."

"Thanks for the talk, Florence. Really. It was very enlightening. And be sure to thank Teryl Meade, too."

Chapter 7

Captain Jean Badiledi is asked—it's really an order, softened by the usual flourishes of protocol meant to disguise the uncomfortable fact that, like every other arm of government, the Congolese Army is directly controlled by Obligate—to meet Professor Teryl Meade in the Green Congo Biodiversity Research Centre at six p.m. He isn't told why she wants to talk to him, but he knows that it must be about either the fuss over the napalm or his failure to convince the Englishman, Nicholas Hyde, to agree to the official story about the massacre. In any case, he's almost certainly in serious trouble, and it doesn't help that, although he arrives exactly on time, he's left to kick his heels for more than thirty minutes outside Professor Meade's office door. Her secretary—almost certainly a queer, Jean Badiledi thinks, for why would a real man work for a woman?—is a bloodless son of a bitch who stonewalls every one of his questions. This queer sits behind a glass desk shaped like a puddle, wearing a baggy, single-piece beige suit that looks like it's been woven from well-used sacking, his manicured fingers pecking the air, his wire-rimmed glasses filmed over like mirrors. One-way mirrors: when Jean Badiledi takes out his cigarettes, the secretary says sharply that there is no smoking in the building.

They're on a kind of platform or balcony above the atrium of the research centre's administration building, with its pale pink sandstone floor, polished black fossils laid into a random third of the flagstones, and clusters of tall palms set amongst sand and white rocks—a sort of beach effect, Jean Badiledi supposes. He sits straight-backed on one of the squashy cubes that seem to grow out of the floor of the platform like forest fungi, their fabric exactly matching the floor's streaky grey-and-white rubber but with the prickly texture of some kind of animal hide. Increasingly pissed off as time ticks by, but also increasingly worried. Professor Meade is a powerful woman, the third or fourth most powerful person in the country, and this is the centre of her power, an anthill of Obligate employees, clean-cut, energetic young men and women in cheap wraparounds or green dungarees or baggy natural-fibre clothing dyed every possible variation of rust or beige by lichen or berry pigments, some of them barefoot, others wearing sandals cut from old tires or slippers woven from some kind of grass, all of them purposefully scurrying about on mysterious errands. Everyone in the army calls them zombies; there are rumours that they are linked together in a common mind, that if they hold on to your hands and look right into your eyes they can read your mind like a book, that their courses of Emotional Reorientation are really a powerful magic that can suck out men's souls. One story has it that the basement of their big blue building, locally called the Electric Pickle, contains a stainless steel tank in which all those stolen souls writhe in torment, a psychic nuclear reactor that's the source of Obligate's power. Jean Badiledi is an educated man and doesn't believe any of this superstitious nonsense, but there's definitely something creepy and forced about the cheerful energy of the people who hurry past in their dreadful no-fashion clothing, and there's something shiny about their eyes, as if they've been glazed with a thin film of plastic.

Jean keeps on his sunglasses, taking them off only when he's finally shown into Teryl Meade's office by the baggy-suited queer, who announces in a tone of weary disdain that Captain Badiledi is here for his six o'clock, as if the late start is entirely Jean's fault.

The office is sparely furnished. A freestanding workstation with a skinny metal stool behind it, actual books crowded into slots carved at random in the walls, a lucite shelf with animal skulls lined up along it, the skulls growing bigger and rounder from left to right, all this lit by reddish sunlight piped through thousands of fibre-optic wires set in the ceiling. Teryl Meade stands dead centre, smoking some kind of cigarette that's loosely wrapped in what looks like a dried leaf and smells of cloves and burning grass—the no-smoking rule doesn't apply to her, of course. Very thin in a sheath of red silk, her skin so white that it might well be powdered with flour, a ghost's skin, hair red as blood standing up stiffly like a clump of grass and cropped so that it slants oddly from front to back, left to right, like a kind of slouched, flat-topped beret. She offers one of her funny cigarettes to Jean, explaining that they're Rainforest cigarillos, Obligate Green Congo's very latest product, made entirely from herbs native to the swamp-forest; he refuses politely, instead takes the opportunity to light up one of his expensively imported Camels, drawing the harsh smoke deep into his lungs and feeling it calm his heart.

"I read your report about the interviews with the witnesses," Teryl Meade says.

Getting right down to it, the same direct manner with which she offered him the job in the first place.

Jean says, "I was very happy to do the work for you, Professor."

"Perhaps you can convince me that you persuaded all of the people involved in this unfortunate affair to agree to the official version."

Teryl Meade turns away before Jean can answer, steps over to the slit window that runs along the curve of the office's outer wall at head-height, dents a blade of the silvery blinds and squints out. She's like a bundle of twigs, Jean thinks, the kind of thing a *féticheuse* might sell you to put a curse on your enemy. Standing two paces in front of the closed door, sweating into his beautifully tailored uniform, he can feel the power coming off her in cold waves.

He says, "If you have read my report, you know that I had useful conversations with all the witnesses. I hope you have also seen the report made by the local commander; a copy was hand-delivered to your office. I myself flew to Liranga early this morning to personally convince him of the importance of the matter." And to pay the man to sterilize the area, but if Teryl Meade isn't going to mention that, neither will he. "I also believe that the coverage in the media has been very favourable."

"The money was satisfactory?"

"As I said, I am happy to have been of service, Professor. Of course, if there is anything else—"

"I paid you ten thousand dollars. You could at least say thank you." Teryl Meade turns from the window. "Relax, Captain. No one has ever managed to plant a bug in this office. I sweep it myself, twice a day; you can speak frankly here. I know the commander was happy to cooperate. What about the soldiers who discovered the massacre? Can they be trusted?"

"Absolutely. In any case, they saw very little."

"And the helicopter crew?"

"The pilot also saw very little, and is not interested in making trouble. As for the flight engineer, I had him arrested yesterday afternoon, over those photographs he sold. He is in solitary confinement in the military prison, and will say anything in exchange for his freedom."

Teryl Meade considers this, then says, "I think he should stay in prison for now, but not in solitary confinement. He can mix with the other prisoners. Perhaps there will be an accident, a fight . . ."

"I am sure that he will not talk."

"He is too close to the media."

"I understand. Well, then, perhaps he will be involved in an argument with one of the guards. He grabs for the man's weapon—"

"I don't need to know the details. What about the government observer?"

Jean says, not liking where this is going, "Let's say that after only a brief discussion, he was extremely eager to be of help."

"And what about Nicholas Hyde?"

There it is.

"I was able to find him, and to put him at his ease. He was very open with me."

"And?"

"He is well-educated, but naive. A quiet manner, but forceful. He was still in shock, and also angry, but for the most part he was able to contain his anger. I would also say stubborn," Jean says, thinking of the young white man's steady gaze, the flash in his eyes as he leaned across the table to speak loudly into the recorder.

"I would say so, too."

Jean decides that he can lose nothing by being candid. What kind of miracle does she expect, after she told him that he was to be discreet, that he was not to use any of his usual methods of persuasion?

"You said that I could speak frankly, Professor. Frankly, Monsieur Hyde is both naive and headstrong, which in my experience is an unfortunate combination. Also, he is English, and quite young, and so cannot imagine that there are circumstances where telling the truth can be dangerous. He expressed very firm opinions about what he saw, and given his attitude and his medical training, I think it is understandable that I could not persuade him otherwise. He told me that he shot one of his attackers, and that he had a very clear look at the body that was brought back. I myself was present at the autopsy. I am no expert, you understand, and no one gave me the courtesy of an explanation, but even I could see that it was something unnatural."

"Like your cigarettes."

"I am sorry?"

"They're from the States, aren't they? You people, you love your alpha-male status symbols, even if it means that you have to break the law to get them. In fact, breaking the law is part of the point. Your cigarettes are manufactured using genetically modified tobacco—cancer-free, in common parlance. You must be very confident of your position, Captain, to smoke one in my presence."

You people. You Africans; you poor ignorant blacks.

Jean holds Teryl Meade's gaze and pinches out the glowing tip of his half-smoked Camel between thumb and forefinger, ignoring the nip of pain. He says, "I was sent to put the official version to Nicholas Hyde, but I was also told to do nothing more than talk to him. I was told, do not arrest this man, be very polite to him. Because, I must assume, he is a white man, because he works for an American charity, and because he has rescued an African baby. And for this very ordinary act, because he is a white man in Africa, he is suddenly famous, and if he disappears or is found dead there will be trouble. So, I talk to him in a polite way, a friendly way, exactly as I am instructed, and you should not be surprised that he refuses to cooperate."

Captain Jean Badiledi, sweating in the silence that follows his speech, wonders if he has gone too far.

At last, Teryl Meade says, "You are in the Intelligence Section of the People's Army, Captain. A very sensitive position, a position of great responsibility. But, if you'll excuse the expression, you seem to have risen without trace."

"I see that you checked my background before employing me. I am not insulted, of course, because I understand the necessity. Well, many records were lost in the war. As for me, before the war, before I joined the democratic revolution against Nyibizo's dictatorship, I was the manager of a bank. I was educated at the Sorbonne, in Paris, France, and I returned to my country to work hard."

All of which is partly true, like all the best lies. Jean believes that the successful man must know how to reinvent himself, that he must always be ready to grasp an opportunity. His great role model is Colonel Denis Sassou-Nguesso, who in the late twentieth century came to power after the unfortunate assassination of President Ngouabi; Colonel Denis Sassou-Nguesso had breakfast alone with the president one morning, and only he came out of the room. Later, after Denis Sassou-Nguesso's Marxist government collapsed and he had been driven into exile, he managed to reinvent himself and return to power. Jean Badiledi believes that the successful man must be as flexible as Colonel Denis Sassou-Nguesso, must always be ready to seize an opportunity to strike at his enemies.

"Many records were lost, but you didn't manage to erase *all* of your past, Captain," Teryl Meade says. She steps across the room, her legs flashing in the reddish gloom like scissor blades, and touches the skulls lined on the shelf as another woman might touch an arrangement of flowers. "I was able to uncover quite a few interesting facts. I know that your degree is from the University of Lyons, and that it is a very ordinary baccalaureate in accountancy, not the first-class degree in Political Science and Economics that you would have people think. I know all about the petty scams that keep you in your imported cigarettes, your handmade shoes and tailored uniforms, the Mercedes, and your three mistresses, including that twelve-year-old girl. I know about your debts, and I know about the six murders for which you were personally responsible, including those of your predecessor and of the manager of the bank where you worked before the war of liberation." She looks at him and says, "None of that need concern us, I hope, except that it proves that you are a resourceful and ambitious man with few scruples, which is why I hired you in the first place."

Jean feels as if his blood is suddenly full of snakes.

Teryl Meade picks up one of the skulls, cradling it in hands like pale spiders. She says, "Do you know what this is?"

It is dark brown, and as cracked and crazed as a piece of old porcelain, its lower jaw and most of the teeth in the upper jaw missing. It is clearly very important to the woman. Jean says, "It is a very unusual keepsake. A trophy, perhaps?"

"It's the skull of a female *Australopithecus afarensis,*" Teryl Meade says. "A cast of the original, of course—even I can't afford the real thing. *Australopithecus afarensis* was a relatively small bipedal hominid with a protruding face and a brain about a third the size of ours. It lived in eastern and southern Africa from about four million to three million years ago. Modern humans, who like to think of themselves as the most successful animals on the planet, have been in existence for only a tenth as long. *Australopithecus afarensis* was little more than an upright ape, but it is part of our lineage. You could say that this skull is the cradle of our minds.

"Some years ago, I was involved with my former husband in a famous and very misguided attempt to recreate as closely as possible this very species from chimpanzee stock. It was not entirely successful, as you might imagine. In fact, it was a prime example of nemesis clobbering hubris. In the aftermath, I completely renounced what seemed to me at the time, and seems to me still, a breathtakingly arrogant stunt. I divorced my husband, and Obligate bought what remained of our company at a knockdown price. Immediately after I moved to Obligate, I was at the forefront of the research that led to the development of Emotional Reorientation, but now I find myself plumb in the middle of the asshole of the world, in charge of a research laboratory that's mostly concerned with developing cosmetics and soft drinks. And I'm told to be *grateful*, Captain, I'm told to *move with the times*, I'm told that screening jungle plants for the ingredients of a better face mask is the hot new direction in scientific research. And this from a man who wears a crystal around his neck, in which he fondly believes is a digitalized representation of his soul. I am mocked," Teryl Meade says, with a fine bitter fury, the skull creaking in her grip. "I am not trusted, simply because I am a scientist. And now . . ."

Jean Badiledi says, "I understand completely. You think that these monsters are connected with the research you abandoned. You are worried that it will put an end to your career. That's why you hired me to talk to the witnesses; you couldn't use one of your many employees here in Obligate because this problem is personal, and it's well known that employees of Obligate are loyal first and foremost to their company. And that's why you paid such a considerable sum of money to have the army clean up the site of the massacre—"

"That's none of your fucking business, Captain."

"Of course not, Professor. In that matter, I was simply your bagman." Jean Badiledi is beginning to enjoy himself. "You are worried that Nicholas Hyde may make trouble for you because he insists on telling the truth. He is a loose end, and you need to deal with him. I will be happy to oblige. I promise you that it will cause you much less trouble than the affair with the napalm."

"When did you talk to him?"

"Yesterday afternoon, after I discovered where Witness had tried to hide him."

"He came here today. *Here*, Captain. He was snooping around, trying to get in, trying to get at that body. I sent out one of my assistants to talk some sense into him, but he wouldn't listen."

"He is the kind of man," Jean Badiledi says, "who'll listen politely when you try and reason with him, and then go his own way. That was his attitude when he and I had our little conversation. But this business with your ex-husband—you said that it was years ago. What does it have to do with the monsters that killed the Brazilian soldiers and Monsieur Hyde's friends?"

Teryl Meade places the skull back on the shelf. "You can leave my ex-husband to me. I want you to deal with Nicholas Hyde. He can't be killed; it would cause unnecessary complications. But I'm sure that a resourceful man like you can find some way to demolish his credibility. Find out who he is, if he has anything to hide, his weaknesses . . . Let's say another ten thousand for your trouble?"

"This may take much of my time. And there will be expenses. Research, a bribe here, a bribe there—"

"*Twenty* thousand, then, as long as you also make sure that the other survivor of the massacre, the government observer, will also stay quiet."

"Unlike Monsieur Hyde, he was most eager to cooperate."

"Nevertheless, I don't think there will be a problem if you—how do you Army Intelligence guys put it?—promote him out of the game."

"If we're still being frank with each other, Professor, the price for that—"

"All things considered, I think I'm owed a discount, don't you?"

Captain Jean Badiledi tells his driver to take him to the bungalow where he keeps the oldest of his three mistresses, and as the big car moves off relaxes into the embrace of the Mercedes's virgin leather upholstery.

Jean Badiledi is an ardent disciple of Sun Tzu's *The Art of War* and has made the mistake common to armchair soldiers of applying that slim volume's principles to his own career. He knows that the witch has given him only a few crumbs of the truth, that she is hiding much more than she's letting on, and remembers what the old Chinese general had to say about the use of spies and the divine manipulation of the threads. A little research is in order, and then perhaps he can begin to turn this affair to his advantage. Meanwhile, he's already thought of an obvious way of discrediting Nicholas Hyde—it will be the easiest twenty thousand he's ever earned—and he feels that he deserves a little relaxation at the end of a difficult day.

Chapter 8

A phone wakes Nick from a dream about the library of his old school, except that for some reason it is crammed full of computers and people working away at them. He knows that one of the people is his Wizard, whom he needs urgently to find, but as he walks up and down the aisles they all keep their backs to him, and anyway, he doesn't know what his Wizard looks like . . .

His mind still scattered by sleep, he thinks that his Wizard is calling him, it must have uncovered some more information about Pleistocene Park, or perhaps it has finally found Matthew Faber's phone number, and it's time he gave it a skin-job so he can talk to it face to face instead of relying on the basic voice package . . . Disconnected thoughts blowing through his mind without taking hold as he rolls over on the hard, narrow bed, gropes through the mosquito netting and switches on the light, picks up his phone and presses the *yes* button to stop the muffled trill, remembering at the same moment that he's blocked all incoming calls because so many journalists have gotten hold of his number.

The Ziploc bag containing the gun and the holster and the webbing belt lies where he left them on the bedside table. He should have given them to Dan Cooper, asked him to take them away for sterilization . . .

His phone is buzzing in his ear, and another phone is still ringing somewhere in the room. After a moment's thought, Nick pulls open the drawer of the bedside table and discovers an old-fashioned push-button telephone inside; an amber light is flashing on the cradled handset, in synch with the insistent mechanical peal. He picks up the handset and holds it to the side of his face, and his mother's voice says, "Is that you, Christopher? What *have* you been doing?"

Instantly, he is back in the half-timbered Elizabethan manor house, with its uneven floors of ancient, black oak as hard as iron, the exhausted sofas on either side of the huge fireplace in the living room and the faces of the dead looking down from paintings or caught in the crowd of silver frames on the wing of the piano, the arthritic tick of the grandfather clock in the hall doling out time second by second. And his bedroom with its view of crooked brick chimneys rising above a swayback tile roof like an illustration from a book of fairy stories, and the line of two-hundred-year-old yews half-hiding the square-towered Saxon church standing in the neat graveyard on the other side of the tall boundary wall (one of the graves, the grave of his brother, killed with his father in a road accident, always gave him a spooky feeling, because it had his own exact name on it, incised above the dates of birth and of death—the latter almost exactly a year before the date of his own birth).

And the swimming pool with its oval of unquiet green water and surround of slippery slate tiles enclosed in clipped box hedges, and the gravel walk and wide flower borders of the Long Garden, designed by Gertrude Jekyll, and the Great Lawn dropping in two sweeping steps to the little river, and the meadow rising beyond with cows grazing around the ornamental faux-Greek shrine that his great-great-great-grandfather had built . . . And the stables with the clock tower, the clock stopped for over a century at a quarter to three, and house martins and bats swooping after insects in the darkening air of a summer's night, the smell of grass and petrol after the lawn had been mown, his mother's scent of *L'Air du Temps* and gin and tonic, her bright expectant look as he dutifully unwrapped the refurbished old-fashioned toys and computer games each birthday and Christmas, and always an air of brittle hush, the house a chilly shrine to the brother he had never known, in whose exact footsteps (although he did not know it then) he was supposed to follow.

He says, "How did you find me?"

"Darling Christopher, it's so good to talk to you, too, after all this time."

The sharpness of the rebuke softened by perhaps her fourth or fifth gin and tonic of the evening.

"That isn't my name. Not any more."

"Of course it is, darling. Nicholas Hyde, what kind of name is that? A very nice young woman helped me find you, if you must know. Very highly recommended by Tony Ryder."

Who is the family lawyer, and once upon a time his mother's lover.

His mother saying now, "I'm very proud of you of course, Christopher, but I must say I'm shocked too. I had absolutely no idea you were in Africa. It's been two years, Christopher, and not so much as a phone call, or even a postcard. I've been so worried about you, darling. I thought you were dead . . ."

"That's the idea," Nick says, and slams the handset onto the ancient phone's cradle, gropes in the back of the drawer, rips out the telephone's wire, and slams the drawer shut. But this isn't enough to quench his anger, and he picks up the Glock-20 in the Ziploc bag and smashes it down on his phone, the phone's plastic shell cracking as he hammers it again and again with the polycarbonate grip of the Glock, the screen separating from the face plate, and soot-black fragments of fullerene circuit board flying away, carbon micrometeorites crammed with suddenly meaningless strings of zeroes and ones.

He rolls over and lies still, wide awake in the middle of the hot black African night, his entire skin slick with sweat, his pulse pumping in his head. His phone is as intelligent as a cat, and he's just given it a fatal lobotomy, and it isn't even his, it's rented from Obligate Green Congo Information Services. He is clutching the Ziploc bag containing the belt and the holster and the gun to his chest. And there it is, like some-

thing he knew all the time but until now didn't understand, a
way of getting some hard evidence about the monsters that
killed Tremaine Thompson and Grant Twentyman, the soldiers and the refugees.

Chapter 9

Shalynne comes down the steep slope crabwise and un-
handily, slipping and sliding between thorn bushes, setting
off little runs of loose stones. A heavy African-American girl
in hiking boots, acid yellow cycling shorts and a loose pink
T-shirt, a cloud of frizzy hair dyed the colour of straw framing her plump round face. Halfway down, she stops for a moment and cups her hands to her mouth and shouts, "They're
coming!"

Cody Corbin is sitting on the steps of the rear door of the
camper van parked at the foot of the slope, bending plaintive
chords from the flat-board slide guitar in his lap. He looks up
at the girl for a moment, then sets down the guitar and stalks
to the edge of the steep drop. He's shaven-headed and bare-
chested, his skin so deeply tanned it's hard to make out the
tattoo spread across his muscular back. He lifts his field
glasses to his eyes and scans the switchback road that snakes
between the ochre bluffs below, the bluffs tumbling towards a
wide plain cross-hatched with huge square fields that stretch
away under a darkening sky that threatens rain. Poisoned sky,
poisoned land, poisoned fields of poison wheat, poison soy,
poison potatoes. Poison spread by evil minds that mock
God's creation and dare to rewrite His sacred texts: profanity
upon profanity heaped over His good Earth.

The Zeiss glasses, cased in yellow rubber, are equipped
with power focusing and face- and object-recognition software, and have enough magnification to pick out the red-

rimmed eye of the buzzard that side-slips through sheer air. Cody quickly spots the motorcycle, headlight on, moving fast, leaning into the curves of the steep, winding road. Even though it's still a couple of klicks away, he can see that Rusty is riding pillion behind Erefaan.

"They're coming," Shalynne says breathlessly, at his shoulder.

Cody lowers his field glasses but does not turn around. He can smell the girl's barnyard odour. He asked her once why rich kids never seemed to wash, and she talked for ten straight minutes about the importance of preserving the microbial ecology of the human body. Shalynne is stuffed full of idealism, no shortage of that, but she doesn't have any notion about what she's getting into, and she's been nothing but trouble ever since he allowed Rusty to bring her along. She stole her father's credit cards, and although Cody made her cut them up into tiny pieces and eat them, that wasn't the end of it, because now the police are looking for her.

"You just earned yourself another demerit," Cody says, and adds, when Shalynne starts to protest, "You should have stayed put and used the walkie-talkie, like I told you. Get on back, and think about how you messed up. Maybe try prayin' for enlightenment."

"There are scorpions up there, Cody. Big black ones." Precisely hitting the wheedling whine of a self-righteous five-year-old, no doubt the same tone she used on her parents whenever she wanted to get her own way.

"Get on back up there, and stay there until I tell you otherwise. Keep your boots on, don't turn over any rocks, you'll be okay. I wanta know if anyone's following them. You see anything, use the walkie-talkie."

Cody keeps his back to the girl as she walks away. He knows that without rules we're no more than animals. He honours with burning fervour the principles and iron discipline his father beat into him. Moran Lee Corbin taught his son hard lessons about temptation and evil. Cody knows that evil is very real. He knows that there are devils going to and fro in the world and walking up and down in it. When he was nine, a demon drilled a hole in his head and filled him up with evil thoughts. His father did the exorcism himself: three nights of praying and fasting. At the end of it, Cody had a fit, damn near swallowed his tongue, and saw the demon leave him. It took the form of a cartoon dog, a Snoopy demon dressed all in black, its eyes like burning coals.

Moran Lee Corbin was a preacher from a long line of Kentucky stump preachers and snake-handlers. He toured county fairs with an old-fashioned tent show until he managed to parlay a spot on a local cable TV station to a full three-hour spectacular, syndicated to fourteen stations across the South. Moran Lee promised cures and heart's ease to any who pressed their hands to their TV screen while he prayed with a living necklace of rattlesnakes and water moccasins around his neck, and pretty soon had to employ twenty women to take credit-card donations and open the envelopes containing widows' mites. He got up a Web site and cut half a dozen CDs, rapping hellfire and redemption over the wail of a steel guitar played in the style of Sonny Treadway and Aubrey Ghent. He tapped into the apocalyptic zeitgeist of the new century, kept a stock of canned goods and an impressive arsenal in a dry basement beneath his hilltop house. He refused to render unto Caesar, and because he paid no taxes, and none of his vehicles had licence plates, the FBI and the Bureau of Alcohol, Tobacco and Firearms came after him. At the end of the long siege, Moran Lee Corbin was shot dead, his wife was badly wounded and died in hospital a day later, and his only child, Cody, just twelve years old, shot and wounded an FBI agent with his .22 rifle when the man broke down the door of his bedroom.

The Feds confiscated the house in lieu of fines and unpaid taxes, and Cody spent six years in the Hardin County Juvenile Detention Center. Two days after he was released, fresh from setting fire to the Elizabethtown field office of the Department of Public Advocacy, Cody broke into his father's house, which had stood empty all that time because everyone in the area knew its history, opened the safe buried in the cellar, and took the musty roll of dollar bills, the small, soft leather bag that contained thirty-eight gold Krugerrands, and the box that contained his father's favourite gun.

Cody was eighteen. He burned with the carefully hoarded hatred he'd easily managed to conceal from the inept psychologist at the Detention Center. He bought a van, paid a spray-gun artist to paint on the offside panel a dark angel in blue denim and black leather crushing a devil snake beneath his motorcycle boot, and went out into the world.

The times were with him. It seemed that all the debts for the sins of the last century were finally being paid off. Two presidents were assassinated within a year of each other. The war against terrorism flared up again. The weather turned strange. Millions of people starved to death in Africa and Asia as droughts and floods ravaged arable land. Countries clashed over water rights and fishing rights. Ragged armies of refugees fought each other. The Australian Navy sank a supertanker hijacked by refugees fleeing a vast forest fire in Indonesia. Europe closed its borders.

Cody nearly crashed his van when thousands of frogs fell out of the sky near Oxford, Mississippi. In Athens, Georgia, in the middle of August, it snowed for three days and nights. Three weeks later, Cody arrived in the aftermath of the super-hurricane that razed Atlanta, and stayed to work as a volunteer in one of the tent cities. He also firebombed three FBI regional offices and shot and killed the Atlanta section head of the Bureau of Alcohol, Tobacco and Firearms. The murder was blamed on looters; Cody moved on. He had his van resprayed black to hide the mural, a necessity he regretted so much that two weeks later, just before he crossed the border into Mexico, he had a reproduction tattooed on his back, a dedication in pain and ink and blood.

He hooked up with a group of Radical Greens and in the next few years helped burn down or blow up more maquiladoras and university and private research laboratories than he cared to remember. When the group was at last betrayed by a government spy, he moved to Africa, where most US biotech companies had relocated their research facilities to escape federal restrictions and public disapproval.

Two years later, the Black Flu swept the world like God's final judgement; within six months, plague and famine and war killed a billion people.

Cody prospered. He fought in three civil wars, discovering he could do God's work *and* turn a profit. He stands now in African stormlight at the edge of the precipice, head shaven to a greasy black stubble, the great tattoo of the Archangel Michael slaying the Serpent across his broad back, his brown-and-white camo trousers neatly pressed, his black combat boots spit-polished to a mirror shine. One hand on his hip, the other holding the yellow field glasses to his eyes as he watches Erefaan and Rusty come home and thinks about the hard task ahead of them.

As the motorcycle climbs the last bend, the exhaust beat of its 1,000cc engine striking hard echoes off red rock, Cody strides into the centre of the road. Erefaan slides to a halt and kicks down the stand and sits there, leaning on the handlebars and giving Cody a hard stare. "This had better be good," he says, "because we were about ready to take him."

Rusty climbs awkwardly from the pillion seat. "We had his routine nailed," he says. "Alternate routes, bodyguards, we had it all down."

"My man Rusty here was ready to pull the trigger on the bodyguards," Erefaan says.

"I would have done it, too," Rusty says.

This tall, skinny, light-skinned young Kenyan who knows nothing but is always trying to assert himself, staring at Cody through orange wraparound spex that probably cost more than the fee from any one of the hits that Cody and Erefaan pulled off in the past couple of years. He stands with his arms crossed over his chest, a petulant kid trying to look tough, in a black denim jacket and combat trousers and new hiking boots—the same brand as Shalynne's, the fools probably bought them in the same shop—the bush of red-brown hair that gave him his nickname tied in a black do-rag.

Cody says, "I know you're pissed, 'cause of all the good work you put in. But when it comes down to it, that guy is just your average lab rat, and this was just your average kidnap.

This new thing, I can promise you you're goin' to like it a whole lot better."

"He's a key worker," Rusty says stubbornly. "The government would have paid anything to get him back."

"He's a mid-level team-leader working in an out-of-the-way agricultural department lab," Cody says, "with but a single ten-year-old patent to his name. Which is why it would have been easy to take him, with or without your so-called inside information. The hot guys, the guys worth real money, the *real* gene wizards, they're guarded twenty-four–seven by small armies; you need a crew of dedicated, experienced men to get within spitting distance. This guy, we wouldn't have gotten much more than enough to pay for a couple of months' worth of gas and food. But now something better's come along, so instead of sulking I want you to smarten up and listen, you hear?"

"I gave you everything you needed for the job," the boy says. "And I was ready to waste the bodyguards, I really was."

These rich kids. Rusty's parents are both senior civil servants; Cody recruited him from the cell of Radical Greens in Nairobi because he knows computers, and because he'd stolen the access codes for the government intranet from his father's slate. But Rusty is unblooded, he insisted on bringing along Shalynne, and he has ideas way above his station. Cody steps up close and catches the boy under his chin, his thumb on the boy's pussy beard, pushes his head up so he can't avoid his stare, and tells him, "You need to learn that sometimes you have to leave a good target alone when a better one presents itself. That's why I aborted this job, you hear? Look in my eyes and tell me now you hear what I'm tellin' you."

"Sure, whatever." Rusty trying and failing to put a note of defiance in his voice.

Cody pushes the boy away. Erefaan says, "The kid's okay. He's just pumped up, is all."

"Go fetch Shalynne," Cody tells Rusty.

"Yeah," Erefaan says, raising his voice as Rusty trudges

off, "where's that Shalynne at? I got something she needs to pay attention to."

Erefaan is still sitting on his hog, leaning cross-armed on the handlebars. A rangy, loose-limbed man with the kind of deep black skin you only find in Africa and a laid-back attitude that disguises his quick mind. His blue jeans are spattered with red mud; the sleeves of his denim jacket have been ripped off to display his jailyard muscles; a crocodile tooth hangs on a leather thong against his bare chest. Erefaan likes to tell a story about how he killed the croc with a knife, one blow square between the eyes, but Cody is pretty sure that the story is just that, a story, that Erefaan stole the tooth somewhere or other. He's a good soldier, with an impeccable history of Radical Green activism, but he's given to vanity.

"We need to think about what to do with Shalynne," Cody says.

Erefaan nods. "'Cause of this police thing."

"Her parents just hired a public relations guy, brought him in from the States. Can you believe it? He was on three TV channels this morning, talkin' about how their precious African-American daughter was abducted by African terrorists no better than animals."

Erefaan laughs. "He really say that?"

"Not in so many words, but his meaning was clear."

"I was thinking," Erefaan says, "that we could get a ransom from her parents. Maybe we should get in touch with this PR guy."

"I was thinkin' that, too, until I got this new deal."

"It really is sweet, huh?"

"Remember I told you about this client I did a bunch of jobs for, right after the plague year?"

"Your fairy godmother."

"She called me up this morning. Wanting me to hit someone for her, like it hadn't been three years since I last worked for her. It's good money, my man, but we'll be needing Rusty's computer skills, and we need to do something about Shalynne."

"You've got a plan," Erefaan says.

"If I told you there's a way of giving Rusty his chops and solving the problem of the girl all in one, would you have a problem with it?"

"Shit, Cody, you know we can always find more girls like Shalynne. And she just won't wash herself, no matter what I tell her. I say, girl, you stink so bad you got vultures coming to check out how long you been dead, and she says how she's spent a lot of time developing a natural balance of bacteria, she's not going to destroy it with unnatural chemicals. By which, see, she means soap."

"I know it. The police lookin' for her won't need tracker dogs, they can just follow their own noses."

"Tell me about this new thing," Erefaan says. "This contract from your fairy godmother."

"Somebody's been making monsters," Cody Corbin says.

Chapter 10

Witness Green Congo is housed in a two-storey office building in an unremarkable commercial street of small factory units and empty lots. The white concrete of its windowless frontage, half-hidden by stands of yellow-leaved banana plants slowly dying from a mosaic virus, is badly pockmarked by bullet holes from the civil war. The ground floor contains an autopsy suite and long aisles of steel shelving packed with evidence boxes, one box for each of the unclaimed dead, each box containing documentary material—identity cards, ration cards, passports, photographs, and letters—and clothes and fragments of clothes carefully washed and ironed and folded into insecticide-treated paper bags; the first floor is a warren of offices and labs behind a reception area where people searching for missing relatives and friends can tell their stories to counsellors, donate cheek-cell scrapings for DNA comparison, and use computers to examine files containing photographs of facial reconstructions and clothing and personal possessions.

Although death is the everyday business of Witness, its people are not used to dealing with the deaths of their own, and when Nick arrives early in the morning, the greetings he receives are mostly muted and embarrassed. No one is using the little lab space where he ran mitochondrial DNA comparisons until he persuaded Tre Thompson to let him try his hand at fieldwork. He passes the Glock through the airlock of the safety cabinet and methodically swabs it with BloodOff, a blue, thixotropic gel guaranteed to cook the DNA of every known virus and bacterium. He wipes the gun down, takes it out of the cabinet, drips thin oil into its action and dry-fires it before burying it in the bottom of his day bag. Then he steals a couple of cartons of Coke from the refrigerator in the reception area and goes downstairs to the autopsy suite.

Inside the big, brightly lit positive-pressure tent, Bridget Nzube is examining a body laid out on one of the two stainless steel autopsy tables, pointing to wounds and talking into the bead microphone of her headset as her assistant takes close-up video shots. When she finally notices that Nick is watching her through the tent's thick plastic, she says something to the assistant, shoots her surgeon's gloves into the bucket under the autopsy table, and pushes through a flap that seals shut behind her like a heart valve. She is wearing a green gown over a yellow T-shirt and blue jeans, her short grey dreadlocks are done up under a brightly printed scarf, and she brings with her a faint whiff of the sweet, disgusting smell of death.

"There was bad trouble in the refugee camp last night," she says. "Fighting between two gangs, the usual nonsense. Six unidentified bodies have just arrived, and they're going to keep me busy all day."

"It's nice to see you too, Bridget."

Bridget Nzube strips off her headset, looks him up and down. She's in her early fifties, on secondment from her work as a pathologist at Kenyatta National Hospital in

Nairobi. Nick met her after his contract with Obligate ended and he moved into the hotel where most of Witness's staff live. She suggested that if he had nothing better to do while he was looking for a new job, he might as well wash bottles in the Witness labs, and he said, why not?

She says, "I've been meaning to come and see you. But the bodies are piling up, and Dan Cooper said you needed peace and quiet . . . So, how are you?"

"I didn't get so much as a scratch."

"I don't mean physically. Forget your famous English reserve for a moment. Tell me how you've been coping."

"I'm fine. Really. Here, I brought you a Coke."

"I suppose that means you want something."

"Can we go somewhere and talk about it?"

Bridget's office is a tiny cubicle behind the refrigerated freight container where tissue samples are stored. It's noisy and hot, with just enough room for a small metal desk and a couple of plastic chairs. Bridget and Nick sit knee-to-knee and sip Coke and talk about the massacre and the ambush. She questions him closely about mutilations and bite marks and the decapitated body, listens while he tells her how Tremaine Thompson and Grant Twentyman and the Brazilian soldiers died. He speaks quietly, tries not to leave anything out. Bridget asks more questions, says, "You're certain that Tre and the others weren't killed by *kidogos*?"

Nick has sweated through his shirt. It sticks to his back, clammy in the close heat of the little room. He says, "You're not the first to make that suggestion."

"I've seen the terrible things that children can do, Nicholas. They're kidnapped, brutalized, drugged . . . The boys I'm cutting right now were hacked to death with machetes and homemade spears over some silly territorial dispute. The oldest is no more than twelve or thirteen, and the boys who killed them are about the same age. All of them orphans, and I bet most of them fought in the civil war."

"They weren't children," Nick says. "They weren't painted white; they weren't wearing animal masks. That story is part of Obligate's attempt to cover up the truth. That's why they napalmed the area. That's why they seized the body I brought back and locked it away in the Obligate Biodiversity Research Centre. I went there yesterday to try and find out what had happened to it, but I couldn't get in. Someone, I'm pretty sure it was Teryl Meade, had removed my details from the security system."

"Teryl Meade? The woman in charge of the Research Centre?"

Nick sees a way of telling Bridget about his research. "She formulated the principles of Obligate's famous Emotional Reorientation. She and her former husband used to own a biotech company, Qualia, that specialized in neuronal feedback techniques—"

"Matthew Faber," Bridget says. "Her husband is Matthew Faber."

"He *was* her husband. He's retired, living in some backwater in Kenya. He doesn't even have a phone number."

"You tried to get in contact with him?"

"Tried and failed. Do you know him?"

"I know *of* him. His family was very wealthy in the good old, bad old colonial days, and it's still pretty influential. His father was in charge of the administration of the National Parks, his mother was on the board of the hospital where I did my medical training. Matthew Faber worked there too, years ago, in the neuroscience department. His first wife died, I believe she was murdered, and then he was poached by Harvard Medical School and went to America."

Nick says, "Teryl Meade and Matthew Faber set up a biotech company together, ended up working at Pleistocene Park, in the Democratic Republic of the Congo."

"The place that recreated extinct species, like in the movie?"

"Saber-toothed cats, giant sloths, some kind of car-sized armadillo, mammoths, all kinds of animals. They were going to build a series of what they called biomes. Big domes, each with a different climate, different kinds of extinct animals. The country was being rebuilt after years of civil war, and Pleistocene Park was one of the flagship projects; it was going to be the biggest theme park in the world. It had Korean money, South African money, European Union money, Japanese money . . . Teryl Meade and Matthew Faber were working with a biotech company led by one of their former colleagues at Harvard, Daniel Lovegrave. According to an article I found in the *Scientific American* archives, they were going to reverse-engineer chimpanzees into an approximation of some kind of man-ape. One of our ancestors."

"They weren't apes," Bridget says, "they were hominids. And only one species of hominid evolved into modern humans. The rest, and there were a lot of species, more than a dozen, died out."

"If you want me to be impressed, I'm impressed."

"Kenya is one of the key locations for hominid research. It has the best collection of hominid fossils in the world."

"Whatever they were, they were supposed to be the centrepiece of Pleistocene Park."

"And you think someone used the same kind of reverse-engineering techniques to make the things that killed Tre and Grant and the others."

"Perhaps. Or perhaps the original experiments went badly wrong. Pleistocene Park's research labs were right in the middle of what became the Dead Zone, Bridget, and they were bombed by the Americans in the war against bioterrorism. Some of the animals could have escaped."

Bridget sips her Coke, thinking about this. "So Teryl Meade is trying to cover up the existence of some kind of gengineered monsters. Monsters that she helped make before she joined Obligate and saw the light."

"I know what I saw, Bridget. I shot and killed one of them, the one that killed Isabel Fonesca. I can still see it when I shut my eyes. It was as close to me as you are, and there was blowback; I got its blood on me. I dumped the coveralls in the decontamination shed, I wasn't thinking straight, but I kept this, and I was hoping you could do me a favour," Nick says, and pulls out the Ziploc bag containing the webbing belt.

Bridget gives him a cool but not unsympathetic look. "Nicholas, I understand why you want to find out about these things—these monsters, if that's what they are. But tell me, what will you do when you have found out the truth? Go to the media?"

Nick thinks of Lucy Stewart's message, thinks of his mother's phone call, says, "Something like that."

"Nicholas, this is Africa. Do you think the media cares any more about what happens in Africa?"

"I know what you're going to tell me, Bridget. It doesn't make any difference."

"You say you know—but do you truly understand? Let's suppose you're right. Let's suppose that these things really are the result of some kind of crazy biotech project. So what? In Africa, in the last five years, millions of people died of the Black Flu and war and starvation. In the Western mind, Africa, after the Black Flu, has returned to the nineteenth century. It has become a place where white men can make little empires and have adventures without having to worry about offending the people who live there, a place where they can impose their will over horror, savagery, and endless atrocity. It has become a place where people *expect* to find monsters."

"I'm not looking for adventure," Nick says. "I'm looking for the truth."

"You aren't looking for adventure? Isn't that why you came here in the first place?"

"I came here to help Obligate cheat the Congolese out of their birthright, until you made me see the error of my ways," Nick says, deadpan, and holds up the Ziploc bag. "Will you help me?"

"You want me to prove that the things which killed Tre and the others were some kind of gengineered chimp."

"I want to find out what they are."

"From a few specks of blood."

"One thing I learned here, you can find out all kinds of things from a speck of blood."

"Even if you're right, what good will it do? This massacre may have tickled the interest of the media for a moment, but only because there was a good picture in it—a white man rescuing a black baby. Beyond that, no one cares."

"There's more to it than the massacre," Nick says, "or Obligate wouldn't be trying to cover up the truth."

Bridget's phone rings. She listens, staring at Nick, says, "Yes, he's here. Yes, yes, I will," and folds the phone away and tells Nick, "Dan Cooper wants to talk to you right away. Something has happened to the baby you rescued."

Chapter 11

Eight thousand kilometres north and east of Brazzaville, Matthew Faber is half-asleep in the shade of his favourite tree, a big salvadora that grows just below the summit of the little island. His broad-brimmed hat tilted to shade his face, his spex showing nine different views of the Gentle People, a three-by-three grid. When Elspeth phones him, the grid shifts to the left and her picture comes up on the right. She's sitting with her elbows splayed either side of her slate, chin propped on her hands, his sweet, smart, brown-skinned girl.

"How are you, Daddy? Were you asleep?"

"I was working," he says, and calls up the phone's menu on his spex and patches in the feed from the camera spiked to one of the salvadora's branches.

"Daddy," Elspeth says, "you'll fry out there. Or scorpions will sting you to death."

He gives the camera a little wave, says, "Nonsense. It's too hot for scorpions."

It is. A brisk dry wind is blowing off the shore, and even in the shade of the big tree it's more than forty degrees centigrade. Air shimmers over bone-white outcrops, the stony slope. Matthew realizes that his mouth is as parched as the brittle tufts of grass that thrust between cracks in the coral pavement, takes a swig from his water bottle, and says, as he takes off his hat and pours a little water into it and sets it back on his head, "I hope you haven't been fretting about me."

"Listen, Daddy, I've been talking with David."

David Oloitip, the Minister for Wildlife Conservation and one of his oldest friends, conspired with Elspeth to find this refuge.

"I suppose you asked about extra security. I appreciate the thought, but it isn't necessary."

"David agrees with me, Daddy. The soldiers will arrive in a couple of days."

Anger and fear and uncertainty spark in different parts of his head. "I won't let anyone take them away from me," unexpectedly pops out of his turmoil, like a watermelon pip squeezed between two fingers.

"The soldiers won't go near the island. They'll patrol the road and the mangrove swamps and help Sergeant Mbau and the other rangers set up a new surveillance system. Hopefully, it'll only be for a little while. Also, David has offered to talk to Teryl, to try and mediate between the two of you and get this settled as quickly as possible. Daddy, are you listening to me?"

He's watching the nine different views of the People while wondering how to turn down Elspeth's well-meaning interference. They're resting in the shade of a stand of acacia trees on the other side of the island. Small, lithe, black people sprawled on stony ground that they've carefully swept clean, even though their hides are pretty much thorn-proof.

Matthew says, "Of course I am. A new surveillance system. Mediation."

Elspeth says, "It'll take David two or three days to make the arrangements. Meanwhile, I still think I should come visit."

The two oldest males, Caesar and Cassius, sit side by side, looking in different directions. Cassius is using a bundle of leafy twigs to flick away the flies that buzz around him. Hannibal is picking nits and salt flakes from the head of his younger sister, Bianca, who sprawls bonelessly between his thighs with a look of utter content. Bianca's twin, Emilia, squats by the trunk of a dead tree knocked flat by last summer's storms, digging for beetle grubs in the rotten wood.

He says, "There's no need for this fuss, Elspeth. Really. Nothing is going to happen."

"I haven't achieved satori, Daddy. I can't sit like the Buddha under the bo tree and let the world work things out. We need to talk about what to do in the long term. And anyway, I haven't seen you for more than six months, and the dig is winding up . . . It all works out quite nicely."

"There's no need for all this fuss," he says, while in another part of the wood, Brutus desultorily tosses pebbles in the white dust, and Isabella, the oldest female, scrubs her square yellow teeth with bark peeled from a twig. "Teryl divorced me, she repudiated the work we did together, she made a clean break. She's known about the Gentle People and me for a long time, and she has never bothered us until now. This thing out in the Congo upset her, she said some things she probably regrets, but if she really was worried that this silly old man and his little tribe could hurt her career, she would have done something about us long ago. It's a stalemate, sweetheart. We're safe as long as she keeps quiet, and vice versa."

"Things have changed," Elspeth says.

"You said yourself it will blow over. And it *will* blow over."

"It isn't just you and Teryl, Daddy. If the media get their teeth into the story, if someone finds out that David helped me find a hiding place for you and the Gentle People, his career will be ruined. You know what they'll say. Genetically engineered monsters hidden away. A government conspiracy . . . David thinks that we should think about finding a more secure home for you and the Gentle People, and I think that he might be right."

"Are you really worried about us? Or is it that you're worried about yourself? Your reputation?"

Words as slippery and hard to hold as pips.

"Are you really pissed off at me," Elspeth says, "or are you afraid of change?"

His grown-up little girl, staring calmly into the camera of her slate.

"I'll have to put it to the vote."

There's a silence.

He says, "I didn't mean it, sweetheart. You deserve your reputation. I'm very proud of you."

Elspeth looks away at something off camera for a moment, then says, "I have to get back to work. But I really do want you to start thinking about the possibility of moving somewhere else. Don't just shake your head, Daddy. Don't dismiss it out of hand."

"They've been on this island for three and a half years. They're happy here. They've settled down. They've grown into the place. It's their home."

Matthew knows what she's thinking—that the Gentle People can never really be at home anywhere in the world, that he's being selfish, that he's more worried about disrupting his long, carefully documented, unpublished and unpublishable study of the Gentle People than about Teryl's threat. He also knows that these thoughts are unworthy, bubbling up from the claustrophobic basement where his dark half lurks. He tries to tell himself that Elspeth's concern is genuine—after all, she took almost a year out of her career to help him set up this place, to help him make a home for the Gentle People— but in the end, fear wins out over rationalization. Fear is the strongest of all emotions, with unmediated pathways that short-circuit the parliament of the higher cortex by transmitting stimuli directly from the sensory thalamus to the amygdala, and right now his satellite cores must be swarming around these reentrant circuits like moths around candle flames, filling his mind with *post hoc* justifications for the fear and anger fuelled by the secret that he and Teryl share— the truth about their strange children.

He says, "They have developed behaviours uniquely their own. Not modifications of what I gave them, or what they learned from the chimpanzees they grew up with, but things all their own."

"I know, Daddy."

"Not just the vocalizations, although that's the most obvious example." He's talking very quickly: he needs to keep talking, to keep thinking. His dark half, Dr. Dave, the cd2 engram, feeds on unreason, on the unmediated pathways of reflexive fear; thinking about the things that make him afraid, assimilating them into his primary core, keeps Dr. Dave at bay. He says, "They are developing a culture here. A lot of it is site-specific. They have more than fifty distinct tool-using behavioural activities. They no longer make cutting tools by randomly smashing cobbles, but chip at broken edges to lengthen them. They—"

"I know, Daddy. I know."

"It's their *home*."

The dark half is squeezing his thoughts, drawing in more and more satellite cores. His hands are working independently, jerking in front of his chest like the paws of a palsied boxer.

Elspeth has witnessed this kind of conflicted spasm many times before. She leans towards the camera of her slate and says, "Hush, Daddy. Hush now. Take a breath, that's it, and another. Nothing's going to happen right now."

Matthew takes a deep breath. Another. After a little while, he says, "I'm fine."

"I don't blame you for getting worked up. When you feel a little calmer, will you think seriously about the possibility that you might have to move?"

He remembers the way she would hold on to his thumb when they went for a walk, the surprisingly strong proprietorial grip of her small, hot, sticky fist, remembers how his heart would well over at this sign of her love, the love that drives her present concern. He says, "This will blow over, sweetheart. You'll see."

"I want you to think about it when you're calmer," she says.

"It won't come to that."

"Daddy, sooner or later someone will make the connection between the white devils and Pleistocene Park. What will you do when they come looking for you?"

"Perhaps I'm tired of hiding. Perhaps I'm tired of making excuses for what I did. Perhaps it's time the truth came out. I'll be all right. Really. Go back to your work, sweetheart, and I'll get on with mine."

"Daddy—"

Matthew cuts the connection, switches off the phone when it rings a few seconds later, and gets up and starts to walk along the broken-backed ridge of the island towards his children.

Chapter 12

Dan Cooper volunteers to take Nick back to the UNHCR villa in his Range Rover. When they drive up to the security gate of the parking lot of the Witness building, the half-dozen journalists who have been waiting for them scramble out of their vans and 4×4s. Cameras and directional mikes are aimed like firing-squad rifles at the Range Rover; men and women call out questions, shout Nick's name to try and get a reaction.

"Are you going to be deported, Nick?"

"Have you been charged?"

"Nick, do you have any comment about biowar contamination?"

"Hey, Nick, what killed the baby?"

Dan Cooper says, "Someone must have tipped them off," and leans on the horn until the guard ambles out of his hut.

Nick sees a battered yellow Fiat parked on the other side of the street, a tall young red-haired man leaning against it. He says, " 'What killed the baby?' It's a good question, Mr. Cooper."

The guard takes his time unlocking the gate. Nick catches the gaze of the BBC's correspondent and puts the palm of his right hand against the side window, holding it there as the guard hauls back the gate and the Range Rover shoots forward with a screech of tires, scattering the little pack of journalists as it speeds away from the Witness building.

Dan Cooper made him promise not to talk to the media; Nick thinks that the two words he carefully printed on the palm of his right hand don't violate the literal interpretation of that pledge.

None of the journalists give chase, but Dan Cooper pushes the Range Rover hard as he drives through the dusty avenues of the French Quarter, sounding his horn as he races through every intersection, taking no notice of the squawks of the proximity alarm or the admonitions that the vehicle's computer keeps flashing up on the windshield.

"Someone at the hospital must have told them that the baby died," he says.

"They knew I've been served a deportation order, too. That's nothing to do with the hospital, Mr. Cooper, and everything to do with Obligate. They've made up some bullshit about a biowar disease to get me out of the country. I wouldn't cooperate with Captain Badiledi, I wouldn't agree to fall in line with the official version, so they used poor Moses against me."

"Moses?"

"The baby. That's what the nurses named him, at the hospital. I saw him yesterday, Mr. Cooper. He looked as healthy as you or me, and the doctor in charge of the paediatric unit said that apart from a dose of hookworm he was fine. He didn't die of any biowar disease. He was spirited away to the military hospital, and then he was murdered."

"We don't know that, Nick. The military hospital is the only place with Class Four isolation facilities, after all. I think you should know that I had a pungent conversation with Tink Glazer. He's very unhappy about the affair. He says that the helicopter was not properly equipped to deal with the return of a live, infected body. He says that lives were put at risk."

"I tended Moses myself," Nick says. "I wore appropriate barrier clothing and a micropore face mask, and no one else on that helicopter had any contact with him. Not the pilot, not the snap-happy flight engineer, not the government observer. If they're so worried about infection, they should put me in quarantine. Or should at least insist on checking my magic bullet to see if I've been exposed to any pathogens. In fact, I'll be happy to submit to any medical test you care to give me, Mr. Cooper. And you should talk to the doctor who treated Moses. Get a statement, a sworn deposition, something we can use against this."

"I don't have that authority, Nick. The bottom line is that we have to work with the people who run this country. If we piss them off, they can ask us to leave. I don't like it any more than you do, but sometimes the best thing to do is walk away. I'll keep working on Tink Glazer, of course, and I promise I'll let you know if I find out anything about that poor little baby. But that's the best I can do."

The avenue drops away downhill, and Brazzaville is suddenly spread out before them, a grid of white buildings and dusty streets skewed around the long, tree-lined boulevards of the Avenue du Djoué and Avenue de Gaulle, its low skyline dominated by the blue upright clamshell of the Obligate headquarters. Built on the site of the old Elf tower, it rises twenty storeys above the circular park, open-plan offices like a stack of in-trays wrapped in an envelope of quilted, self-cleaning blue plastic, immaculate and orderly and utterly alien.

Nick says, "The government observer, William Ndinga, was with Tremaine Thompson and Grant Twentyman when they were attacked." The thorn that hooks his heart every time he says the names of the dead hooks it now. "William Ndinga saw what I saw, Mr. Cooper, but I think that the fellow from the army, Captain Badiledi, leaned on him. William phoned me yesterday, told me that it was dangerous to contradict the official position; reading between the lines, I think he was ashamed that he'd been forced to keep quiet. If you're going to talk to anyone, you should talk to him."

"That's the last thing I should do. You've been here long enough to know how bad it is. Two million people died of war and plagues, and despite Obligate's PR bullshit about restoring democracy and investing in the future, the country is still under martial law. Anyone can disappear, and no one would ask why. Everyone is afraid, and the worst thing is, it's healthy to be afraid. If William Ndinga saw you coming down the street, do you think he would stop for one second to talk to you? Give it up, Nick. Let it go. Don't make it into something personal."

At the bottom of the hill, the Range Rover bounces hard over the weed-grown single-track railway line and turns onto the only paved street that runs through the ruins of Poto-Poto. Once the poorest quarter of Brazzaville, it's now a huge boneyard, the place where the bodies of three hundred thousand people killed by Black Flu and civil war were burned on mass pyres. On either side of the road, low mounds of red earth stretch away like regiments of sand dunes, each crowned by a numbered plaque on a steel post, the only monuments to all the dead who have left nothing behind, not even their names.

Nick says, "I understand your position, Mr. Cooper, but surely you understand why I can't leave this alone."

Dan Cooper turns to look at him, and for the first time since they left the Witness building, the Range Rover's speed drops below eighty kilometres per hour. "I had to talk to Tre's wife last night. I had to tell her how her husband died, and what happened to his body. I had to persuade her not to come out here. I don't want any more conversations like that, Nick, so promise me that you won't get into any more trouble."

"I've been given a ticket for the ten a.m. flight to Brussels, Mr. Cooper, and I'm pretty sure the police or army security will make sure I'm on it. What kind of trouble can I get into in less than a day?"

After Dan Cooper leaves him at the UNHCR villa, Nick borrows the concierge's phone. He gets through to someone at the National Museum in Nairobi and is told that Elspeth

Faber is working in the field; and he leaves a message on her voicemail service asking her to call back—he has a couple of questions about her father's research. It's a long shot, but he feels that he needs to do something. He's buzzing with fight-or-flight adrenalin. He's boxed in, out-thought and outmanoeuvred on all flanks, and the clock is ticking. He's certain that the journalists will mention the deportation order in the reports they file; if his mother finds out, she'll be waiting at Brussels Airport tomorrow, to reclaim her long-lost son.

He picks at his lunch, pulls on the tracksuit he was given at the decontamination shed, and for a couple of hours runs a circuit around and around the villa's neat lawns. He showers, finds an ancient computer, checks his emails and voicemails. Lucy Stewart, the PR guru, still wants to speak to him. So do the *New York Times*, *Le Monde*, the *Guardian*, the *Telegraph* . . . He asks his Wizard to do some research into the price of changing his identity again, telling himself that it's just a precaution. He asks it about Obligate, and Daniel Lovegrave and Matthew Faber and Teryl Meade, and when Bridget Nzube comes across the lawn, followed by a soldier carrying Nick's olive drab kitbag across his shoulders, he's sitting on the terrace, trying to puzzle his way through the hard copy of a review paper on remotely induced firing of neurons that Matthew Faber published fifteen years ago.

"I thought you'd want help packing, so I went to the hotel," Bridget says after she has dismissed the soldier and sat down and refused Nick's offer of something to drink. "It looks like someone has been through your stuff. I couldn't tell if anything was missing, but this was the only thing that was broken. I won't ask why you keep a picture of yourself."

The glass has fallen out of the black plastic frame she hands to him, and someone's boot has printed cleat marks across the face in the photograph.

"It's my brother," Nick says. "He was killed in a road accident."

Bridget's take-no-prisoners attitude briefly softens. "I'm sorry."

"It's okay. It was before I was born. Bridget, you didn't come all this way to deliver my dirty laundry."

She studies him for a moment, then says, "I'll work up those bloodstains, but I want you to understand that I'm doing it for Tre and Grant. This is about them, not about anything that Obligate is trying to do with you."

"Absolutely."

"I looked at that *Scientific American* article you mentioned, did a search. I think I have a good idea of how Daniel Lovegrave planned to construct an approximation of an early and very famous form of hominid, *Australopithecus africanus*."

"Lovegrave called it the rewind and replay technique," Nick says. "He said he was going to de-evolve chimpanzees to a simpler form and then somehow evolve them in a different direction."

"He planned to split the difference between the human genome and the genome of the common ancestor of hominids and chimpanzees—the extinct animal that gave rise to both separate lineages. An American team had already reconstructed the common-ancestor genome using a sophisticated comparison between the genomes of humans and the big primates, chimpanzees and pygmy chimpanzees and gorillas. To get his australopithecine approximation from chimpanzee ova, Lovegrave was going to remove genes unique to chimpanzees and add an artificial chromosome containing a mix of appropriate primate and human genes."

"But basically they would still be chimpanzees."

"If that's all you want to prove, it should be easy enough. Chimpanzees have forty-eight chromosomes, and humans forty-six, so the hybrid, derived from a chimpanzee ovum with an added artificial chromosome, should have a total of forty-nine. In fact, I did stain up a couple of samples and look for dividing immature white blood cells, but outside the bone marrow and the lymph nodes where they normally reproduce they are very rare, and I had no luck. That's why I'm going to have to do some DNA sequencing."

Bridget smiles as she explains all this, lit up, using her hands a lot.

Nick smiles, too, says, "You're having fun."

"Most of the time, I'm either looking at long-dead bodies cut up with machetes or shot to death, or looking at fresh bodies cut up or shot. It's good work, it's necessary work, but it isn't rocket science."

"So what will you do? Look at the mitochondrial DNA?"

Bridget shakes her head. "All that would prove is whether or not this creature was derived from a chimpanzee ovum."

"Because mitochondria are inherited maternally, and if this thing was grown from a chimpanzee ovum, all the cells would contain chimpanzee mitochondria."

"Very good," Bridget says.

"I picked up a few things working in the lab. So you're going to look at the genomic DNA."

"We share ninety-five percent of our DNA with chimpanzees, and that five percent difference, roughly one hundred and fifty million nucleotide bases out of a total of three billion, is fairly evenly distributed across the entire genome. I'd only need to sequence a relatively short length of the DNA isolated from the blood on your belt, say a million bases or so, to prove whether or not it is human or chimpanzee."

Nick says, "And if the thing I shot was a hybrid, the difference will be even smaller."

"Not exactly. The problem is that if it is a hybrid, I don't know what was added and what was taken away. So what I'm going to do is run a complete DNA sequence, the kind every baby in the USA and Europe gets at birth, that babies of the privileged and employees of Obligate get here. I have a contact who'll let me run a sample on the sequencing machine in the Obligate clinic. I'll stitch it together and compare it with human and chimpanzee gene maps in the GenBank database. If it *is* a gengineered hybrid, I should be able to pick up terminator sequences added to any genes that have been suppressed. And if there's an artificial chromosome in the mix, the capping sequences at either end will be very easy to spot."

"How long will all this take?"

Nick is thinking of weeks, months, but Bridget says, "The

sequence will run overnight; the analysis may take a little longer. It's a brute-force method, but it will work, no problem."

"Thanks, Bridget. I owe you."

"I'll be honest with you, Nicholas. When I first heard your story, from what Dan Cooper told me of it, I thought you were crazy with anger and grief and shell shock. But when you told me about the mutilations those poor people had suffered, I remembered the animal attack that came in five days ago, and I thought perhaps you weren't so crazy after all."

"What kind of animal? Where was it?"

"It happened at an old oil-pumping station near the Likouala aux Herbes River, about forty kilometres from the place where your team was attacked. A plane went to pick up two biosurvey workers and found them dead, and then there was some kind of firelight, and the co-pilot of the rescue plane was killed. Obligate claimed it was a Loyalist atrocity and wanted the usual impartial documentation. Bill Parks cut the bodies, and I went over the autopsy file with him. They were badly clawed and bitten, partially eviscerated, and their skulls had been smashed and brain tissue was missing. Bill says that the bites didn't match any of the charts, so he wrote them up as an animal attack, species unknown."

"They definitely weren't human?"

"Every pathologist knows what human bite marks look like. You would be surprised how often people bite each other in fights. We are fierce animals, and it is a reflex action."

"What about the bodies? Do you still have them? We can swab the wounds, run antibody comparisons with the blood—"

Bridget laughs. "Please, Nicholas, slow down! The bodies are gone. Obligate claimed them, and I suppose they were either buried here or sent back to America. But I do have this," she says, and digs into her purse and pulls out a data needle.

"Is that what I think it is?"

"Promise me that you won't do anything stupid. Obligate owns this country, Nicholas. It owns the police. It owns the army."

"I've been given my marching orders. By the time you've run that DNA sequence, I'll be on a plane to Brussels."

They talk about what Bridget plans to do after she finishes her tour with Witness. She tells him to look her up if he ever visits Kenya, says that she has to get back to the last of the murdered kids. They hug. Bridget says, "You're a nice guy, Nick, and a terrible liar. Whatever it is that you're planning to do, please be careful."

Nick skims the autopsy file and borrows the concierge's phone again, uses its directory function to find the number of the mobile phone that Theodore Yssel, the pilot who brought back the bodies of the biosurvey workers, is renting from Green Congo's telecommunications company. The voicemail service clicks in on the fourth ring, and Nick cuts the connection. What's he going to do, give the concierge's number and wait around the villa? And even if he leases a new phone to replace the one he broke, and leaves a message with his new number, he'll still have to wait for this guy, Theodore Yssel, to call him back . . .

While working for the biodiversity project, Nick was ferried to and from survey sites in a variety of light planes, their pilots working for different companies that in turn worked for Obligate. He makes a few calls, and one of his contacts gives him the name of a restaurant where Theodore Yssel spends most of his evenings, saying that she doubts whether Nick will get much sense out of him. "The man always liked a drink, but from what I've heard, he's been drinking all day, every day ever since his friend was killed."

Nick signs out a battered Peugeot from the villa's car pool and drives into the centre of Brazzaville, and after two hours queuing in a crowded, swelteringly hot currency-exchange office draws out against his credit cards as much cash in American dollars as he can. As he walks towards the Peugeot, a big man in camouflage fatigues falls in step beside him and says that Captain Badiledi would like to talk with him.

"I'll be happy to make an appointment," Nick says. Trying to keep it light, although apprehension is already gripping his heart.

"He is here," the big man says, and steers Nick to a black Mercedes double-parked on the busy street. The gull-wing door lifts up and there's Captain Jean Badiledi in his crisply pressed uniform and amber sunglasses, tucked in the far corner of the tan leather backseat like a scorpion in a shoe.

Nick climbs inside, the door swings down, and Captain Badiledi says, "You are a busy man, Monsieur Hyde. Yesterday you went to the Biodiversity Research Centre, and also to Tangalai Hospital. Today you go to the Witness offices, and now here you are. It is a great worry to me."

The Mercedes's air-conditioning is icy; Nick shivers in his short-sleeved shirt. He's sitting as far away from Captain Badiledi as he can, the bolster of an armrest pressed against his spine. He says, "Why are you following me? Is it army business, or is it something to do with Teryl Meade?"

Captain Badiledi studies Nick for a few moments. Smiling, stroking his skinny moustache with his forefinger, saying at last, "I don't want you to get into trouble, Monsieur Hyde. You should go back to the UNHCR villa until it is time for you to leave."

"You're not the first to express that opinion."

"Believe me, it would be much better for you if you took notice of all this good advice."

"Or what? Would you arrest me?"

"Would you like me to arrest you?"

"What happened to the baby?"

"I understand that it was infected with a biowar disease. It was moved into Class Four isolation, but unfortunately it died. These things happen."

"What kind of disease?"

"A fatal one. No doubt there will be a report. If you have discovered something, Monsieur Hyde, you should tell me."

"If I do find anything, Captain Badiledi, I'm sure you'll hear about it."

"It would be better for you if you told me first. It might help my investigation."

"I'll be on a plane tomorrow. You won't have to worry about me any more."

"But I am worried about you, Monsieur Hyde. You do not believe me, but it's true. Let me tell you something, and then perhaps you will tell me something in return. Do we have a deal?"

"That depends on what you tell me."

"It concerns Professor Meade and Pleistocene Park. You have been doing some research into Pleistocene Park, have you not? Please don't bother denying it: Obligate owns everything in Green Congo, including the telecommunications company. When I learnt of your interest, I did some research of my own. I discovered that the death rate amongst Professor Meade's former colleagues was abnormally high. Many disappeared, of course, when the Pleistocene Park facility was destroyed during the troubles. But many others found new work in other countries, and quite a few of them suffered fatal car accidents, fatal robberies, unexplained shootings. Not just in Africa, but also in the United States. And in Europe, Singapore . . ."

"She's trying to cover something up," Nick says.

"Do you really think she'll let you persist in your investigations, Monsieur Hyde?"

"I'm not investigating anything, Captain. I'm getting ready to leave."

"To return to your mother, perhaps?" Captain Badiledi looks out of the smoked-glass window, looks back at Nick, says, "Why does she call you Christopher, by the way?"

It isn't just the icy air-con that's making Nick shiver now. He says, "I don't see what my mother has to do with any of this."

"She is rich, is she not?"

"Not exactly."

"She has a large house, a pension from the bank at which her husband worked. No doubt other assets too."

"We're estranged. I don't have anything to do with her any more."

"I understand. You have a quarrel, a big argument. You come to Africa because you believe you can make a new life here, like so many white men. You even change your name.

Nicholas Hyde isn't your real name, is it? But I think that your mother must still love you very much. She sees you on the news—her lost son, suddenly a hero. She pays someone to trace you, and she calls you, wants to make amends . . . No doubt, if you asked, she would be happy to give you any help she can."

Nick says, "You want me to get money from her to pay you. For what?"

"Suppose I find out the truth about your white devils. That is what you want, isn't it?"

"And what about you? Aren't you worried what Teryl Meade will do, if she finds out that you have been helping me?"

"I have been frank with you, Monsieur Hyde. And frankly, I am already worried. Obligate owns everything in this country, and Professor Meade has a great deal of power in Obligate. I will admit it, she has a great deal of power over me. But if there was a scandal . . . You understand?"

"You're thinking of selling her out to save yourself."

Captain Badiledi smiles, shrugs. "You could let the world know the truth, Monsieur Hyde. What is the problem with that?"

"The problem is that I no longer have anything to do with my mother, Captain. I left that part of my life behind."

"I know that it will be difficult for you to go back, that it will be hard on your pride to ask such a favour. But I strongly advise you to think about it, because we will talk again about this before you leave."

The gull-wing door rises up behind Nick. Sunlight and hot, sticky air roll over him.

Nick spends thirty minutes driving aimlessly around the avenues and side streets of the centre of Brazzaville. He tries not to think about last night's phone call. He tries to believe that his mother doesn't already have people looking for him right here in Brazzaville—the so-called reporter who ambushed him outside the hospital, for instance. He tries to convince himself that Captain Badiledi can't have discovered why he broke with his mother; if the man knew the truth, he would be attempting blackmail rather than offering help.

He pulls over and stops several times, watches cars and trucks and crowded buses go by. He gets out and walks up and down a busy shopping street, watching windows for the reflections of people who might be following him, the way you do in movies. Two young soldiers walking hand in hand. A stately matron wearing a silk wraparound and a nation's ransom in gold jewellery, escorted by two thugs in black one-piece Armani suits. A very tall, very thin Sikh in a white turban and a white frock coat. A businessman in an electric blue collarless African suit. A noisy swarm of teenagers in tracksuits and expensive spex. An Obligate cadre sweating into his sackcloth suit as he hands out free condoms. Nick buys a cup of coffee from a pavement merchant, a shrunken old man in an Obligate T-shirt that reaches to his knees who conjures a potent brew using a hand-grinder, a spirit lamp, and a tiny copper saucepan and serves it in a foamed-plastic thimble. He drives some more. Brassy sunlight pours through the dusty windshield, but the chill of the Mercedes's air-con seems to have crept into his bones. At last, when he's as sure as he can be that he isn't being followed, he writes into the slate on the Peugeot's dash the restaurant name that he was given and follows its directions south and west, towards the river.

The sun has been swallowed by the horizon, but red light lingers in long, thin clouds stretched above the rooftops and trees. A freight airship making its way high above the city glistens like a drop of fresh blood in the darkening sky.

The restaurant is a whitewashed single-storey building on the bank of a tributary of the Congo. As Nick climbs out of the Peugeot, a hologram of a cocktail shaker tilted to an old-fashioned Martini glass blinks on in the dark air above the restaurant's steeply pitched roof of red-painted corrugated iron. The shadows skittering away beneath the raffia palms at the edge of the parking lot are nothing but shadows.

Nick gives the maître d' ten dollars and the pilot's name,

and the man leads him through a long, glassed-in terrace full of wicker chairs and round tables laid with white linen. The place is already half-full. Waiters in collarless white jackets carry trays of food and drink shoulder-high. Three American businessmen around a table cluttered with papers, slates, and beer bottles give Nick frank stares as he follows the maître d' to the man who sits alone at the far end of the terrace, his chair turned around so that he can look out at the river.

"Theodore Yssel, I presume," Nick says.

The man looks up at Nick and says, "I know who you are. You're the guy who rescued the baby."

"Guilty as charged."

"Nicholas something."

"Nicholas Hyde."

"You were on CNN."

"If you saw that, maybe you can guess why I'm here."

Theodore Yssel is in his early thirties, only a few years older than Nick, with a whisky bloom on his cheeks and a cap of blond hair as dry as straw. A chunky mechanical watch with a steel strap hangs on his thick wrist. The collar of his white jacket is stained with the salt of dried sweat; sweat shines on his broad, sunburnt forehead. He half-closes one eye as he looks at Nick, opens it, half-closes the other. He says, "That massacre you escaped from, people are saying it was Loyalists, drug-crazed *kidogos* . . . But I bet you don't think it was *kidogos* killed your friends, do you?"

"Can we talk about that?"

There's a square plastic container on the table in front of Theodore Yssel, grainy white, a snap-top lid. He pats it with his fingers, then says, "You must want to talk to me pretty badly, you came looking for me. Do you drink beer?"

"Absolutely."

Theodore Yssel crooks a finger in the air and says loudly, before the waiter has reached the table, "Two more Primuses, Abel, and a shot of Johnnie Walker Black. Don't give me that look; it's gone six. Sunset. *Cocktail hour*, my friend."

His voice and gestures are slightly blurred. He drains his glass of beer, looks at Nick, and says, "How did you hear about me? Did you get hold of the police report?"

"The bodies of the two biosurvey workers you brought back were autopsied by a Witness pathologist. You were mentioned in the autopsy file."

"I don't know how they died. They were dead when we found them. All we did was bring them back."

"They were badly mutilated."

"I've seen worse. A guy I knew once walked into a live prop blade; from the knees up, he pretty much went everywhere."

"The person who did the autopsy thinks that they were killed by an unknown species of animal; Obligate claims that it was a Loyalist atrocity. I'm trying to find out who is right."

"The report says Loyalists, yah? *I* told them that I didn't get a clear look at what killed Johnny. My friend, Johnny Grundlingh."

Nick says, "Wait a minute. You *saw* them?"

"The army officer who debriefed me said they could have been pygmies. I said, as if there are still pygmies alive anywhere at all. So the guy said, perhaps they could have been *kidogos*, child soldiers, and I guess that's how it got written up."

"This army officer, was he a captain, by the name of Badiledi?"

"He was a lieutenant. I don't remember his name."

"It's just that the man who debriefed me, Captain Badiledi, made the same suggestion."

Theodore Yssel looks at Nick, does the thing with his eyes again. "If they weren't *kidogos*, what do you think they really were?"

"That's what I'm trying to find out."

Floodlights come on beyond the terrace, lighting the river's swift, dark flow. What Nick at first thinks are logs or baulks of timber stranded on a bar of pale sand in midstream begin to stir; a few slide smoothly into the water.

Theodore Yssel points with his thumb at the American businessmen at the table next door. "See those people? They come into the country for two days, three days. They do their business, and they come here for the show. The owner of this place is a nice guy, but he's a businessman also. He had the idea for the show, and it's about the most popular tourist attraction in Brazzaville. What they do here every night is throw an antelope into the river so people can watch the crocs feed while they eat their four-course dinners. It's very popular. People take photographs. They video it. They call up their families and hold their phones or their spex to the windows, so the folks back home can watch the show too. A glimpse of the local colour. A genuine bit of horror from the heart of darkness. They do it three times a night. If you stick around, you can catch the first show. Does that sound like your kind of fun, Mr. Hyde?"

"Not really. Is that why you come here, Mr. Yssel?"

"Johnny and me, we did a little business on the side with the guy who owns this place. Who'd probably shit himself if he knew I was talking with you. Anyway, a lot of businesswomen pass through, and plenty of them are game for a fling with a bush pilot. What I'm doing now is trying to remember those good times. Maybe that's what you should do, too."

A waiter sets a shot glass of whisky and two bottles of beer and two frosted glasses on the table. Theodore Yssel lifts the brimming shot glass, says, "To absent friends," and knocks the whisky back in one.

"Absolutely." Nick takes a swallow of tooth-jarringly cold beer straight from the bottle, says, "I was helping to investigate a massacre. More than half a dozen people had been killed and mutilated. The things that did it, the white devils, came back while we were documenting the scene. Two of my co-workers were killed, Mr. Yssel, and five soldiers. I was lucky—I got away."

"And you're here because you feel guilty, eh? You want to make amends."

"One of the men who was killed, Tremaine Thompson, told me something that stayed with me. He said that the best we could do, working for Witness, was to speak for the dead. To discover the truth about how they died, to tell their last story. If you don't want to talk to me, I'll respect your decision, but I do think you can help me speak for the dead, Mr. Yssel."

"White devils." Theodore Yssel tastes the words in his mouth, clearly liking them, as he carefully pours his beer into a frosted glass. He says, "You got a good look, but you were told that you saw something else, and no one is interested in what you actually saw. And now you're wondering if I saw the same thing. Well, I'm sorry to disappoint you, Mr. Hyde, but I really didn't see anything at all."

"We found a body—it wasn't like anything any of us had seen before. I brought it back, but Obligate took charge of it. It was taken to the Biodiversity Research Centre, and it just so happens that the director, Teryl Meade, was once involved with a project to recreate extinct hominids by reverse engineering chimpanzees."

"These creatures, these white devils—you think they were gengineered chimpanzees?"

"They certainly weren't ordinary chimps. Have you heard of the Pleistocene Park project?"

Theodore Yssel smiles. "Sure. It was some kind of safari park full of extinct animals, across the big river in the DRC."

Nick tells Theodore Yssel what he's learned about Pleistocene Park and Qualia, the work of Teryl Meade and Matthew Faber and Daniel Lovegrave. "I think the white devils are something to do with the gengineering work that Teryl Meade was involved with at Pleistocene Park. I think that's why she is trying to cover up the truth."

"What do you want from me?"

"Mr. Yssel, I believe that the white devils killed the biosurvey workers you went to pick up. I want to find out what they are. I want to find out where they came from, and I want to find out why Obligate is so eager to hide the truth. I'd like to know what you saw. Frankly, I'd like to know that I'm not going crazy."

Theodore Yssel takes a sip of beer, meditates for a moment, then takes another, larger sip. "You're from England, I think."

"You got it in one. Most people here think I'm from Canada. Or New Zealand."

"I was in London one time. I don't suppose I'll ever go back there again. How long have you been in Africa, Mr. Hyde?"

"Nine months, more or less."

"Just nine months. Me, I'm a tenth-generation South African Afrikaner. My grandmother was a liberal, she married a native African when it was still more or less illegal in my country, and as a result I'm something like one-sixteenth Zulu. I wish it was more—Zulus, they're hard fuckers. They might have lost at Blood River, but they beat the fuck out of us before that, and they beat the fuck out of the English, too. Also, it would have meant a much happier childhood. I'm very proud of my country, Mr. Hyde, and I love Africa, but I am also mostly white, and I know what Europeans did to this continent. Some of my recent ancestors were absolute bastards, but it was even worse here, in West Africa. There was the ivory trade in the nineteenth century, there was the rubber trade . . . Slaves and slaughter. Atrocity upon atrocity. That's what our people did to Africa, and now the Europeans are here again, pretending that they have the highest of humanitarian motives when what they're actually doing is recolonizing the place. Obligate forced out French interests by supporting the so-called democratic uprising against Samuel Nyibizo, and now the French are supplying Nyibizo and his Loyalist guerrillas through Gabon, because they hope to win back the Mboukou oilfield. Round and round it goes, atrocity upon atrocity. What happened to us, it's nothing compared to all that, is it? My advice is that you should forget it. You should go back to England. Drink warm beer and watch nuns playing cricket in the fog."

"If you don't want to talk because you're scared of the way things are here, I understand. All you have to do is ask me to leave, and I'll walk away."

Yssel finishes his beer, signals to the waiter for another round. He says, "Coming here, coming to talk to me, it was your idea? No one else knows about it?"

"I'm not working for Witness any more. This is between you and me."

"You said that you saw them. You said that you brought back a body. You said that they definitely weren't pygmies or *kidogos*."

"They were about the size of eight- or nine-year-old kids, but they were very quick and very strong. They had chalky white skin, mouths full of sharp teeth. The soldiers shot at them, but they kept coming, and they were so very quick."

"You don't know what they were."

"I know they weren't human."

The waiter sets down another shot glass of whisky, two more beers, two more frosted glasses.

Theodore Yssel says, "Johnny and me, we grew up together. We got out together. We got our pilot licenses together. We stuck together ever since. Our last job, it was a routine pick-up near the Likouala aux Herbes. You know where that is?"

"Absolutely."

Yssel knocks back his whisky, pours out his beer. The mouth of the beer bottle rattles against the edge of the glass. He watches the disc of foam rise, says, "These people were part of a team doing some kind of survey in the swamp-forest. Obligate people, full of that goofy confidence they have. One of them managed to get himself a broken leg, and his team left him with someone to look after him at this pumping station. It was abandoned, but the airstrip was still usable. We were going to pick him up on our way back from a job in Liranga, an absolutely routine bit of bush flying, but when we got there, the sick guy and his friend were dead. Their bodies were pretty badly torn up—I thought they had been mauled by an animal, perhaps a leopard. A leopard will creep up on a sleeping man, crush his skull. That's what I thought. Johnny wasn't so sure, but anyway, we wrapped the bodies in groundsheets and loaded them onto the plane, and I got on the radio while Johnny went back to get their stuff."

Theodore Yssel is staring out at the floodlit river moving

past the terrace, the beer bottle in his hand forgotten. "I was still on the radio when Johnny came running back out of the bush towards the plane. The place had been abandoned for more than a year, and it was pretty overgrown. The airstrip had been laid with concrete, but there was grass two, three metres high growing out of cracks, there was bamboo and elephant grass on either side . . . I didn't see what was chasing Johnny right away; I didn't do anything until he scrambled into the cabin, started shouting at me to get the plane started and get out of there. He was frantic. We'd been in some pretty hairy spots, and I never before saw him so scared. I fired up the engine, and just as we started rolling, a bunch of these little fuckers came chasing after us out of the bushes and grass. That's when the bullet went past me. It punched a hole in the door, about a centimetre in front of my nose. When we got into the air, I looked around at Johnny, and he was dead. The bullet that missed me hit him square in the head." Theodore Yssel takes a swig of beer. "I can't help thinking that if I hadn't sat there on my dumb ass trying to see what Johnny was running from, if I'd started moving straightaway, it would have made a difference."

Nick says, "We had five Brazilian Army soldiers with us. They were in combat gear, they had assault rifles, and the white devils ambushed them, took them out and killed my colleagues, all in about five minutes."

The two of them speaking in hushed voices about their dead with the clatter and chatter of diners all around them.

Theodore Yssel says, "They were small, like you said, white as a dead fish's eye, and very ugly. That's what I told the army lieutenant, and he told me they were probably *kidogos*, and I went along with it." He looks at Nick. His eyes are pale blue, with fine, almost invisible lashes. "When I get back to Nairobi, I don't know, give me a call. Maybe I can see a lawyer, make a deposition."

"I appreciate the offer, Mr. Yssel. I really do. And thank you, for telling me what happened to you. I was beginning to believe that I was going crazy."

"Don't do anything until you get out of here. I mean it. While you're still in this country, you won't want to do anything that will piss off Obligate."

"It's good advice, but it's a little too late. Obligate has served a deportation order on me. I'm supposed to be on the plane to Brussels tomorrow morning."

"And you're seriously thinking of not going?"

"If Obligate wants to get rid of me, it must mean that they've got something to hide. And it isn't as if they're the mafia."

"Listen, my friend, they want someone to leave the country who refuses to go, they ask the army to deal with it. You know what a helicopter ride is?" Theodore Yssel doesn't wait for Nick to answer. "It's something the army used to do before the civil war. If they didn't like you, for whatever reason, they'd take you for a ride above the Malebo Pool, two, three hundred metres up, kick you out of the cargo door with your arms tied behind your back. Award you points for how you hit the water. If the fall didn't kill you, you'd drown, and in any case, the crocs would deal with your body. I always think of that when I see someone here eating crocodile steak."

"That was in the bad old days," Nick says.

"Some of the same guys are still in the army. If you ask me, a flight to Brussels sounds a lot better."

"What are you going to do?"

Theodore Yssel squares his hands around the plastic box. "I'm leaving this fucking country tomorrow. I had Johnny cremated. You know how hard that was to do in this country? The fuckers want to bury everyone in one of those green cemeteries they have, where you say a prayer and plant a tree and pretend you're saving the environment. I told them I was taking Johnny back to Kenya, had to fill in about ten thousand forms and pay hard cash to get him cremated. Tomorrow, I'm taking him back to Nairobi, and then I'm going to fly out along the edge of the Mau Escarpment and open the window and crack this box and let his ashes ride the slipstream. Tonight, I'm going to sit here and have a few cocktails with him."

"And watch them feed the crocodiles?"

Yssel shakes his head. "They tie up the antelope, to make

sure it doesn't escape and spoil the show. That's not my idea of fun. I'm going to have a few drinks with Johnny, and while the people are watching the crocodiles feed, I'll be watching their goddamned faces."

Chapter 13

Shalynne is digging in pouring rain in the middle of a field of maize, lit by the camper van's high beams. Her blond hair hangs limply around her dark round face; her T-shirt and shorts are soaked through and cling to her body. She stands knee-deep in the oblong hole she's excavating from thick red clay, working clumsily with a long-handled shovel, rooting with its blunt blade, throwing a thin spit of water and clay to one side, wiping rain from her eyes, bending with weary stoicism to root up more mud.

Rain falls all around, heavy drops seeming to slow and drift as they slant through the converging shafts of yellow light, pattering on the long leaves of the tall dark green maize plants that crowd either side of the track. Erefaan stands over Shalynne, wearing a black slicker that sheds a kind of shimmering hem of water. An assault rifle as blunt as a baseball bat is cradled in his arms, and his face is half-hidden by a black slouch hat. Whenever Shalynne stops digging, he makes an abrupt gesture with the rifle and she gives him a sullen, hopeless look and sets to work again, shivering not with cold but violent, barely suppressed emotion. Clay washes back down into the shallow pit, the grave she is slowly deepening.

Rain makes a noise like radio static on the roof of the van, just a few inches above Cody's head. He's leaning against the steering wheel, staring through the streaming windshield. He has a terrible headache, and now and then takes a slug from

an unlabelled bottle of oily white rum as he watches Shalynne dig.

Rusty sobs in the back of the van, steady as the rain.

That goddam boy is nothing but tears and piss, Cody
thinks. The iron band around his skull clamps a notch tighter;
he takes another sip of rum. Fields of poison corn and poison
potato stretch all around. Once this is done, Cody plans to
drive on past the ruined town of Meru and find some clean
land where they can make camp, and then tomorrow they will
begin the long drive across the eastern plains to the coast.

Outside, in the pouring rain, in the glare of the van's high
beams, Shalynne has fallen to her knees and is trying to get
up, slipping in flooded clay and using the long handle of the
shovel as a crutch. Her sodden T-shirt is streaked with red dirt.
Erefaan steps to the edge of the pit, shouting at her, putting the
rifle in her face; when Shalynne looks up at him with mute,
hopeless exhaustion, Erefaan shakes his head and grabs her
arm and hauls her bodily from the pit. She falls to her knees
again, hair dangling in wet strings around her face. Erefaan
prods her with the rifle, then looks back at the van, squinting
in the dazzle of the headlights, and shakes his head a fraction.

"She's about done," Cody says to no one in particular, and
heaves himself out of the seat. The drumming rain seems
even louder in the stale darkness in the back of the van. Rusty
sits on the edge of the wide bench, head in his hands as he
sobs steadily. Cody feels a tender welling of pity, lays his
hand on the boy's shock of springy hair and says, "I know. I
know."

A sigh, a gulp. Rusty turns his head to look up at Cody, his
eyes dark smudges in his shining face. He shivers under Cody's
palm and says, as if it explains everything, "This fucking rain."

" 'Thou sendest rain into the little valleys thereof: thou
makest it soft with the drops of rain, and blessest the increase
of it.' You know the rest of it?"

A sob, a sigh, a shrug, dry curly hair moving under Cody's
palm.

" 'Thou crownest the year with Thy goodness: and Thy
clouds drop fatness. They shall drop upon the dwellings in

the wilderness'—that's us, here in the wilderness—'and the little hills shall rejoice on every side.' You don't know it? It's a psalm, a good one."

"I don't know the Bible that well."

"You'll find it in *The Book of Common Prayer*. Nowhere near as old as the Bible, and not God's direct word, but it has plenty of good thoughts in it. 'Blessest the increase of it,' but not here, not amongst these unnatural plants. This increase, it's cursed. It's cursed because it's against the natural order that proceeds from God's greatness. In the Garden of Eden, listen to this: 'out of the ground made the Lord God to grow every tree that is pleasant to the sight, and good for food.'" Cody's voice unconsciously shades a mite deeper, the words thrilling in his blood, the blood of the son of a preacher man. "*He* made them, see, not man. He made them in His perfect creation. Man has made evil from God's goodness by tampering with that perfection, and that's why we're here, to drive that evil from the land."

"She's just a dumb little rich girl," Rusty says. "I let her come along just to shut her up. We could let her go, let her find her own way back home to her mother and the stepfather she hates so much. She'd call them, and they'd come—"

"Uh-uh. Letting her go isn't an option."

"She wouldn't say anything. She'd keep quiet."

Rusty speaking with a low hopelessness, addressing a point somewhere around Cody's knees.

"No, son, she would not. She's a disobedient creature, and you know it."

"I told her what she had to do when she wanted to come along. And she promised. She promised that she'd do exactly as she was told."

"If she did make any kind of promise like that, you know that her word isn't worth anything. She stole her stepdaddy's credit cards, didn't she? Brought them right along, and if she'd used any one of them just once it would have put the police right on our tails. And who knows what else she did, who she might have told about this thing of ours? That's why we have to do this. That's why you have to be strong. This isn't any kind of punishment, son. It's a way of making things right."

* * *

Afterwards, Cody hands the shovel to Rusty and tells him to finish the work. The boy takes it without a word and starts scraping wet clay into the grave. Rain falls all around, falling through the headlights of the van, falling on the rustling maize plants, falling on the slickers of Cody and Erefaan as they watch Rusty dig.

"Man," Erefaan says, scarcely moving his lips, "this is all fucked up. We should have done the two of them together, wham bam, move on."

"Unless you've suddenly got a whole lot more technical, we still need the boy," Cody says. "We have to fix those surveillance cameras, and then there's the video."

"And that's another thing. Doing these killings on camera, don't you think that's kind of strange? Posting photos of our jobs on the Web, that's one thing. But making a movie . . ." When Erefaan shakes his head, water flies left and right from the brim of his black slouch hat.

"You read the clippings, you saw the pictures of those things. The client wants video footage of their dispatch, that's what we do."

A curl of clay spatters on the ruin of Shalynne's upturned face; Rusty turns away and bends over and spits a mouthful of taupe stew between his feet.

Erefaan says, "You think you can get the kid to do that, after he just shot his girlfriend? Man, but you're cold."

"I'm goin' to talk to him," Cody says. His voice is muffled by the micropore mask over his mouth and nose. "In the end, this will make him stronger."

The boy hadn't done so bad. Shalynne was so exhausted that she made no protest when Erefaan made her kneel. Cody was holding his Colt Python under his slicker when Erefaan handed Rusty his automatic, one hollowpoint round in the chamber, no clip, but there was no problem. The boy tremblingly extended his arm until the muzzle of the automatic almost touched the back of Shalynne's head. Her mouth was moving, but no one heard what she said. Cody wanted to think it was a prayer, but knowing the girl it was as likely some line from a pop song. Rusty closed his eyes when he pulled the trigger, and Erefaan roundly cursed him when he afterwards dropped the automatic in the mud, but on the whole, his first kill and in circumstances like this, the boy did just fine.

Erefaan says, "You okay, man? You look, I don't know, sort of *pinched*."

"It's these plants," Cody says. "We're right down amongst all these plants. The air—it's full of their poison. You can smell it."

"It's what they call the G8 strain," Erefaan says. "The one with the fungus gene that pumps out growth hormone, makes them grow fast. At least the rain keeps the pollen down. And we have the filters in the van's air-conditioning. Once we get going you'll be okay."

By the shallow grave, Rusty spits a string of phlegm to one side and picks up the shovel from the wet clay and starts to work again, glancing back every now and then at Cody. Erefaan knows and understands that look because he's seen it so many times in jail. It's the look of someone pushed beyond caring about himself, the look before a shank flashes in the canteen, in the yard, in a cell after lock-up time. "You're going to make this right with this boy, you're going to have to talk *hard*," he says, but he says it softly, and because of the noise of the rain falling all around Cody doesn't hear him.

Chapter 14

It's raining at the Hominid Gang's camp by Lake Turkana in northeastern Kenya, a fine rain that warps and twists in the salty wind that blows out of the darkness. It beads the sides of the tents pitched amongst a stand of acacias above the

winding channel of a sand river, sets a blurry halo around
each of the little constellations of electric lanterns that hang
from the lowest branches of the crooked little trees.

Elspeth Faber is out on the salt flats beyond the old shoreline of the lake, helping half a dozen workers stretch plastic
sheeting over a scaffold framework to protect the dig from
the unexpected rain. Working in the glare of a rack of lights
on top of their Land Rover, they clip flapping sheets of thick
transparent plastic to the steel poles, tape seams, weigh down
the edges with flat stones. When Elspeth tries to fling the last
sheet over the frame, a sharp gust of wind throws it back at
her and she sits down on her butt, tangled in wet, flapping
plastic, laughing at the wretched stupidity of it all, the workers laughing too as they unwrap her and help her haul the
sheet into place.

"That's a great job," Elspeth says. She's soaked through,
covered in mud, quite out of breath. "Give me ten minutes to
check it."

The workers tramp off to share a couple of illicit spliffs in
the Land Rover; Elspeth walks around the big oblong tent
they've made, carefully shining her torch along every one of
the taped seams. The rain is falling harder, drumming on the
plastic sheeting. The water pump burbles, spits a spray of
muddy water. Raindrops prick Elspeth's face, glitter in the
short, tight braids that make a kind of helmet around her
face, on her blue Helly Hansen windbreaker. She carries a
pistol holstered at her right hip; leopards prowl the stony
shore of Lake Turkana, and although most know enough to
keep away from people, there are always a few crazed or
desperate enough to take up the ancient trade of hunting hominids.

There's a lot of sheeting to check—the trench is thirty metres long and six metres wide. When at last she is satisfied
that the dig is waterproofed, Elspeth squats down and shines
the flashlight through rain-slick plastic, tracing the neatly terraced contours of the trench, bidding farewell to four
months' work.

A family of manlike creatures set up camp on a sandbank on this very spot just under one and a half million years ago, where a small river made a sharp curve. They were members of the *Homo ergaster* species of hominid, tall, slender people with small heads and the heavy brows and prognathous jaws of cartoon prizefighters. Evidence from the interleaving of layers of litter and flood deposits suggests that they used this place as a seasonal camp for at least forty years, returning year after year until their family group died out or moved away from the area or changed its wandering habit. They used fern fronds to line the depressions in the sand in which they slept, chipped lava pebbles into tools, made spears from the branches of young thorn trees. The men brought back animals that they trapped or scavenged on the lava slopes above the river; the women and children gathered berries and insects, dug up tubers and fat beetle grubs, and speared catfish and hunted for crayfish and freshwater mussels in the shallows of the little river. They left behind more than a hundred of the flat, teardrop-shaped stone hand axes characteristic of the Palaeolithic period, as well as a litter of sharp-edged stone flakes and robust choppers, many unfinished, and animal bones shaped into digging tools. One corner of the camp, at the downstream edge of the sandbank, was used as a midden, a dumping ground for bones, mussel shells, and the hulls of nuts. Much of the rubbish was washed away when the river flooded in the rainy season, but some was not. The stones remain, and so do the bones, hundreds of them. Hippo bones, the bones of extinct species of antelopes and giraffes. Catfish bones, monkey bones, the bones of a kind of giant pig. And other bones, too, bones that hint at something terrible and dark at the dawn of consciousness.

As she squats in the darkness above the site of the ancient camp, rain gusting around her, the beam of her flashlight softly diffused by the plastic sheeting as it shines on neat, sharp-edged terraces that step down to the ancient killing floor, Elspeth can clearly imagine the lives of the people who lived here each summer. A million and a half years ago, the area around Lake Turkana was a vast flood plain, with seasonal rivers curling down from the mountains to feed shallow, brackish lagoons and a system of lakes that drained eastward, into the Indian Ocean. There were crocodiles and three species of hippo, giant warthogs, antelopes, two species of leopard, hyenas and saber-toothed cats. There were giant elephants with two pairs of tusks, and herds of zebras and three-toed horses. Huge flocks of flamingos fed on blooms of algae in the shallows of the lakes and lagoons. And there were also three species of hominid: *Paranthropus boisei*, a robust, small-brained vegetarian species of australopithecine, with massive jaws armed with millstonelike grinding teeth; *Homo habilis*, a gracile, ape-faced toolmaker; and *Homo ergaster*.

Elspeth can see the bank of coarse white sand fitted like a parenthesis into the bend of the slow river, can see two dark-skinned creatures that are not quite human sitting in bright sunlight, chipping from lava cobbles the sharp-edged flakes they'll need to butcher the small antelope that they have brought back to their camp. One woman is using fibrous material stripped from the inner surface of bark to clean her teeth; another is breaking open mussels with her strong fingers. A group of children watches the gleaming muscle of a freshly caught catfish flop on the sand. All of them are naked, but some wear grass-twine loops around their waists or upper arms. A toddler staggers about on bow legs until its mother scoops it up and feeds its mouth to the dark nipple of her flat breast, one leathery hand cupping its head and the other supporting its buttocks as she looks around, her brown eyes wary under the massive ridge of her brow.

All this fleshed out from bones and stones, brought to life in the theatre of Elspeth's mind.

Finally, the boldest of the workers toots the horn of the Land Rover. Elspeth switches off her flashlight and walks past spoil heaps and upturned wheelbarrows to the Land Rover, allows herself to be driven up the long, shallow slope to the camp. Loud laughter comes from the square blue mess tent—as usual, the Americans from George Washington University are sitting around the table after supper, drinking beer and talking about the day's finds. She hears Harry Brenner's nasal voice rise above the others. A sharp white light shines under the raised flap in front of another tent, where Mary Ekalale, a plump young woman in jeans and a chunky fleece vest, sits on a camp chair at a rickety wooden table, peering through a big magnifying glass that depends from an articulated stand, using a pair of flat-ended tweezers to push fragments of bone around a plastic tray.

Mary is Elspeth's graduate student. With her nimble fingers and uncanny ability to discern in a handful of fragments the three-dimensional shape from which they were shattered, she can reconstruct bones faster than anyone else in the Hominid Gang; she prefers to work without the assistance of the FastFit AI, which uses raw processing power to parse millions of configurations of virtual, wire-frame models of laser-scanned fragments. She looks up as Elspeth approaches; Elspeth returns her smile and says, "How's it going?"

"This one is very hard work," Mary says, "but I think I almost have it."

She is making a temporary assembly of a split and crushed femur, using an acrylic glue that turns to harmless powder when exposed to strong ultraviolet light. The familiar sharp smell of the glue is strong in the damp night air. In the white tray, under the big magnifying lens, more than twenty pieces of glistening dark brown mineralized bone, carefully washed and cleaned, have been fitted together in a solid curve that's recognizably part of the head of the femur.

Mary points with her tweezers. "It isn't quite finished, but you can see where they used a stone to smash it apart to get at the marrow. And here, look, there are hack marks where they cut away muscle and tendon."

"Like the others."

"This one's from a child, almost certainly habilis, but I need to finish the preparation before I can be sure."

"It makes five habilines," Harry Brenner says. He ducks under the raised flap, cradling three bottles of Tusker beer against his grubby Georgetown University T-shirt. Drops of water glisten in his beard, his elf-locked curls. "How's the site, Elspeth? Safely tucked up for the night?"

Elspeth takes one of the bottles. "What are we celebrating?"

Harry says, "Take one, too, Mary; we couldn't have done it without you." He's grinning like a brand-new, first-time father. He says, "Our paper's been accepted. And, here's the sweet part, Phil Rees is going to make it a lead article when it comes out."

Philip Rees is the editor of the electronic science journal, *Nature*. Elspeth and Harry Brenner emailed him a draft of their paper six weeks ago, and she has tried to put it out of her mind ever since. Most scientific journals are aimed at small, highly specialized audiences; *Nature* publishes the most important papers in every scientific field, and is read by everyone. A paper in *Nature* is a big tick mark; a lead article means you've truly arrived on the international circuit.

Elspeth says stupidly, "A *lead* article?" Harry is grinning at her, and they embrace and pound each other's backs and clink their bottles and drink.

"I should have thought to lay up a bottle of champagne," Harry says.

"The beer's just as good," Elspeth says.

"You're going to be famous," Mary says.

"So are you," Elspeth says. Although Mary hasn't yet won her PhD, Elspeth insisted that she should be listed as one of the paper's dozen co-authors.

"We're all going to be famous," Harry Brenner says.

Elspeth takes a sip of beer. "What about the referees? What did they say? What do we need to change?"

"It's nothing much more than fine-tuning. Mary, why don't you put down your tools, go have a drink with the others? You come along, too, Elspeth. We're putting this dig to sleep for the season, and we're going to publish a landmark paper. We deserve a little party."

But Harry Brenner doesn't lead Elspeth towards the mess tent. Instead, he takes her arm and leads her through lamplit rain to the shelter of the grandfather acacia that leans out over the sand river.

Elspeth is giddy with the beer and the flush of sudden happiness. She says, "What is this, Harry, a tryst? Or is there a problem with one of the referees? Please don't tell me one of them was Dana Hotchkiss. That woman won't ever believe anything that comes out of this site."

"Phil knows all about her; she's overplayed her hand once too often. This time, she didn't get a look-in."

Elspeth takes a deep breath, lets it out. "I'm amazed."

"We have evidence for types of damage on bones of at least five habilines and two ergasters that are identical to damage on animal bones from the same midden. We have long bone fragments with hack and scrape marks, and we have three-dimensional analyses that strongly indicate that the narrow stone flakes we recovered could have caused that damage. We have evidence that long bones were split apart or crushed at their ends to remove marrow. We have evidence that the spongy tissues at the ends of metatarsal bones were crushed to remove fat. We have the partly reconstructed ergaster skull with evidence of hammering damage. What's to argue about?"

"What do the referees say?"

"We've got to deal with a few minor queries about dating, do some toning-down in the conclusions, cut a couple of sentences someone feels are too speculative. That's about it. We'll go over it together, in the morning. Listen, Elspeth. We're about to publish what has to be the most important paper on hominids for a decade. There's going to be a lot of media interest."

Harry is giving her a serious, concerned look. Above them, rain makes a dropping sound in the leaves.

Elspeth thinks she understands what this is about. She says, "And we still have to finish off that secondary midden and put the site to bed, and I'm about to take off for a couple of days. I know I could have picked a better moment, but I can't put it off."

"Did you talk to him today? How is he?"

Elspeth's cover story is that her father has suffered what might be a minor stroke. She says, "He's going to be fine. Harry, you know that I'll be back as soon as I can."

"But you want to be sure. I understand completely." Harry tries to look suitably solemn, but can't suppress his glee. "Man, this is going to be as important as Don Johanson's First Family, or Leakey and Walker's Turkana Boy, or Wilson and Sarich's Mitochondrial Eve. 'Preliminary evidence for interspecies predation and cannibalism in Lake Turkana *Homo ergaster.*' If only Raymond Dart was still alive!"

"You're drunk, Harry."

"Maybe just a little." Harry's grin takes years off his age, exposing for a moment the preternaturally bright kid who, while growing up in Lawrence, Kansas, amassed a huge collection of arrowheads and pottery shards, who spent his university vacations helping to excavate dinosaur fossils in the badlands of Montana. He says, "I deserve to let rip a little. And so do you. This is one of those life-changing moments. Just to begin with, it's going to guarantee funds for another season's work."

Elspeth nods, waiting to see where he's going with this.

"And the great thing is, it's good science, Elspeth. Underneath all the bullshit media conferences and sexy PR and dubious reconstructions, the science is solid."

"We're doing good work here, Harry."

"I know it. And we'd do *extraordinary* work if we had the time. But we have to rush to press, grab the headlines, use anything we can in the Darwinian struggle for funding . . ." Harry knocks his bottle against hers, says, "Here's to the good old days, when research wasn't run like a beauty contest," and takes a long swallow of beer.

"We already have enough hard data to prove our hypothesis," Elspeth says. "That's what counts. And once we've processed the rest of the finds, we can work up the population data. The science is as good as anything in the good old days."

"I get maudlin when I'm drunk, don't I?"

"Just a little. Come out with it, Harry. What else do you want to tell me?"

Harry steps a little closer and says, "It might not come to anything, but Phil Rees says that *Newsweek* has been sniffing around."

"And how did *Newsweek* find out?"

Harry shrugs, as guileless as a cartoon cat with canary feathers caught between its teeth. "You know how these things go. Maybe a leak at the *Nature* office. Maybe one of the referees, or even one of the workers . . . Well, anyway, the news is out." Harry tilts the bottle to his mouth to get the last swallow of beer, and says, "We probably should think about a media conference."

"Right."

"It's actually a fantastic opportunity."

"Of course it is."

"I thought you'd be mad."

"Harry, African scientists have been scuffling for funds forever. We've never had access to the kind of research grants Americans got in the good old days. I know better than you that we need all the publicity we can get, because we need all the *money* we can get. But have you really thought this through? The politics are going to be horribly tricky. These are some of the first Kenyans. We're going to have to be very careful not to present them as bone-through-the-nose, missionary-in-a-pot cannibals. We're going to have to think very hard about how to make sure that the science doesn't get buried by the sensation."

Harry grins around the lip of his beer bottle. "Then you agree to a media conference? Because we need to have our say, Elspeth, before the rumours start multiplying."

"You get this circus safely back to Nairobi, I'll meet you there, and we'll work out how to survive our fifteen minutes in the spotlight."

"The hell with fifteen minutes. Everyone on the planet gets fifteen minutes if they stick around long enough." Harry toasts the rainy night with his beer bottle. "Mary's right. We

really are going to be famous, Elspeth. Murder and cannibalism in the Early Palaeolithic? Forget funding for next year's
season. We'll get enough money from this to set up our own
museum."

Chapter 15

Nick has to drive around Maya Maya Airport to get to the exclusive residential estate where William Ndinga lives. Under
the dark sky, long lanes of red and green lights and the distilled glare of racks of floodlights make a kind of luminous
tent over the skewed crucifix of the runways, like a slice of a
more advanced planet intruding from another dimension, like
one of those perfect science-fiction futures so often promised
but never delivered. The terminal building and a fringe of
hangars glow like a scatter of radioactive bones. A trio of air-
ships are tethered in front of the biggest of the hangars like
an improbable haul of skyfish.

When Nick hears the roar of an approaching plane, he
pulls the Peugeot over and gets out and climbs onto the hood.
A boxy white Seraph goes past, its red taillights growing
closer together, sinking into the darkness. The main runway
stretches away beyond the double fence and razor-wire tangles. A Starlifter is falling towards it by ponderous degrees,
dragging the howl of its four turbofan engines out of the black
sky, underlit by floodlights that come on in a long line beyond the other side of the road.

We are children of nature: at times of heightened emotion
we seek out the pathetic fallacy—a stormy sea, a lonely lake,
an orchard laden with blossom. Nick, making do with what
he can find, stands on the dented hood of the Peugeot and
screams happily into the catastrophic howl as the belly and
wide wings and clusters of black-tired wheels of the giant

plane skim above him. He empties his lungs and draws another breath and screams again as the howl drags past and
changes in pitch, screams as the Starlifter thumps down with
a squeal of tires and its engines reverse thrust and spit four
tongues of blue flame.

In the aftermath, the night suddenly seems so very quiet.
Insects essay their chirps and whistles as Nick, grinning like
a fool, his blood fizzing with exhilaration, climbs down. The
sharp whir of the Peugeot's electric motor is shockingly loud.
The man who has tailed him from the restaurant starts his
Seraph when Nick drives past, and pulls out after him.

The residential estate was carved out of the gentle slopes of
the hills to the south of Brazzaville during the oil boom to
house Elf-Aquitaine executives and senior engineers. It's
centred around a string of artificial lakes and a country club
with a full-size golf course. The clubhouse, supermarket, cinema, school, and state-of-the-art hospital were looted and
burned to the ground during the civil war, and Obligate is
symbolically replanting the golf course with native trees to
create a bird sanctuary—as if there aren't already enough
birds in the seventy percent of Green Congo that's still
swamp-forest—but it's still the most desirable place to live in
Brazzaville. Most of the rambling villas have been appropri-
ated and refurbished by senior members of the new government, and are sealed behind high walls and razor- and
smart-wire barricades. CCTV cameras monitor every square
metre of their grounds, and armed guards are posted outside
their gates. Following the directions given by the Peugeot's
slate, Nick drives past these mini-fortresses to a more modest
street of tile-roofed bungalows half-hidden from the road by
bougainvillea hedges and stands of fan palms, big satellite
dishes on tile roofs, SUVs and runabouts nose-to-tail on
poured-concrete drives—a chunk of a Florida housing tract
dropped into the heart of Africa.

The uncurtained windows of William Ndinga's house
blaze with light. The little crowd gathered in front is watch-

ing six men unload from a pickup truck a coffin got up to look like a Mercedes stretch limo. When the crowd parts to let the men carry the coffin across the lawn to the house, a woman cries out as if pierced to the heart.

Nick parks the Peugeot under the canopy of a huge cedar-like tree. He came here because he wanted to confront the government observer with Theodore Yssel's story, but now he has a taste like a copper penny in his mouth, a queasy chill in his stomach.

A small, chubby boy in a yellow T-shirt wanders into the centre of the road, the fingers of one hand crammed into his mouth as he stares boldly at Nick. A woman rushes out of the crowd and snatches up the child, and a moment later two men walk quickly towards the Peugeot, shouting in Lingala. One bangs on the roof, and Nick slams the door open so they have to step back as he gets out of the car. He shows them his empty hands and smiles and asks them what's going on. The air is hot and close. He's sweating through his shirt. His heart is hammering. It's the first time since he arrived in Africa that he has been in a place where he is the only white man. This is their country, not his; he's a clueless intruder on a foolish mission. The larger of the two men jabs his finger at Nick and makes a short angry speech.

"Wait a minute," Nick says. "I know William Ndinga. I'm his friend! *Je suis un ami!*"

Other men are drifting across the road. One of them is the young red-haired reporter who tried to talk to Nick at Tangalai Hospital. He pushes through the gathering crowd, his white shirt glimmering in the dark, and shouts, "Get in your car! Start the motor!"

Nick steps backwards, climbs inside the Peugeot, and watches in the rearview mirror as the reporter backs around the passenger side, talking to the men. They answer him angrily; the big man kicks at the side of the Peugeot and shouts, kicks the car again. The reporter folds himself into the passenger seat and tells Nick, "Drive quickly."

Nick pulls away before the reporter has time to close the

door. Some of the men run after the car. One throws a stone that stars the rear window.

The young reporter twists in his seat to watch the lighted house dwindle. He says, "Why are you here?"

"I wanted to talk to William Ndinga."

"So did I. Unfortunately, we are both too late."

"I saw the coffin," Nick says, thinking that William Ndinga finally got his Mercedes. "What happened?"

The reporter holds out a hand. "First, you must give me your phone. It is not well known, but the phones here can be used as listening devices, even when they are turned off."

"I don't have one any more. It had an accident. Tell me about William Ndinga."

The reporter studies Nick for a moment, then says, "There was a traffic accident. He lost control of his car and it ran into a wall and its hydrogen cell exploded: *boum!*" He makes a fist with his right hand and smacks it into the palm of the left, then flicks the air with his fingers. They are very long, with neat, oval nails that glimmer palely in the dark.

Nick says, "I didn't know hydrogen cells could explode."

"Exactly. William Ndinga's family claims that it was sabotage—something to do with the Loyalists. They say he was important in the government, and that's why he was killed. Do you believe that?"

"Was there an autopsy?"

"This is not Europe or the United States. Tonight his family and friends have the wake, and tomorrow they bury him."

"What about the car?"

"It will have been stripped for spare parts by now. The gendarmes wrote it up as an accident, so no magistrate will be involved—there will be no investigation. You should not have come here, Monsieur Hyde. Everyone will think that you are a spy, you might cause more trouble for these poor people. Still, I am pleased that we finally have a chance to talk."

Nick pulls over to the side of the road and looks at the young man. "Thanks for your help back there. I'm grateful, I really am, but I really can't talk to you about this. I don't even know who you work for."

The reporter holds out his hand, shrugs when Nick doesn't take it. "I represent *Congo Real Time*, Monsieur Hyde. I am—"

"Harmony Boniface. I remember you from the hospital. Who told you I would be here?"

"It was luck. I was investigating William Ndinga's 'accident.'"

"You just happened to be here. Just like at the hospital, or outside the Witness building this morning."

"Most of the reporters in Brazzaville were there, I believe."

"Who are you really working for? If it's for Tony Ryder, you can tell him I'm not coming back."

"I don't know any Tony Ryder. We are both interested in the same thing, Monsieur Hyde. That's why I'm here."

"Believe me, this is not something you want to ask questions about. I think William Ndinga was killed because of it."

"I am already asking many questions. Listen to me, Monsieur Hyde. I understand why you are reluctant to talk, but I think we can help each other."

"With respect, Monsieur Boniface, I've never heard of *Congo Real Time*."

"It is a clandestine webzine. It tells the stories behind the stories put out by Obligate's public relations machine."

"If it's clandestine, where did you get that media pass you showed me?"

"Obligate says that it recognizes and supports all forms of internal discussion. It says that it supports freedom of speech. I take it at its word. I publish *Congo Real Time* on the Green Congo intranet, and I also sell stories to news agencies."

"Stories like my story."

"Never before as important as your story. Monsieur Hyde, I believe we share the same interest. We want to find out why Obligate is trying to cover up the truth about what happened at the oil palm plantation. So, perhaps we can help each other."

"I don't think so," Nick says, and reaches across to open the passenger door.

"I know things you need to know," Harmony Boniface says quickly. "About the barge, for instance."

Nick hesitates. "What barge?"

"A river barge was found stranded on a sandbank thirty kilometres upstream of Liranga, just ten days ago. It was unregistered, its three crew dead and badly mutilated. The army thought that they had been murdered by Loyalists—Loyalists sometimes cut out and eat the hearts of their victims; they believe it gives them strength and protection. The army also thought that the barge could have come from across the river, from the DRC. Perhaps from the Dead Zone. So it was towed into the centre of the river and firebombed and sunk, with the bodies still on board."

"How were they mutilated?"

"Their heads were smashed in, they were eviscerated . . . Just like the poor refugees who were massacred at the oil palm plantation, yes?"

"Wait a minute," Nick says. He doesn't trust this plausible young man, thinks that he could be an Obligate hireling who's trying to win his trust by feeding him a few inconsequential facts. "How do you know about the refugees?"

"I have many friends, Monsieur Hyde," Harmony Boniface says. "When I heard about your heroic adventure, I hoped to find some background to it, some local colour I could sell to the news agencies. One of my friends in Liranga reached out to one of the soldiers who discovered the massacre. He saw very little of what attacked you—he and the other soldiers were waiting near the river when the shooting started, and when the helicopter took off, they took to their boat—but he did see what had been done to the bodies of the refugees. It's a strange thing, but today I learn from my friend that these very same soldiers have disappeared. They have been reassigned, but no one knows where. I fear they met the same fate as the flight engineer of your helicopter, the man who took the photograph that made you famous."

"What happened to him?"

Harmony Boniface smiles his nice smile. He is very young—at least a couple of years younger than Nick. "He died. He was being held in the military prison, on charges arising from the sale of that photograph. Apparently, he attacked two of the guards, and they had to shoot him."

"Someone is tidying up the loose ends."

"I think so too. I think you are in great danger, Monsieur Hyde, and I risk my own life to help you. I have another friend, a man who has something I know will be of great interest to you. I will take you to him."

"Is he the owner of your webzine?"

"Not at all. I have the honour of being the owner, the chief reporter and photographer, and the designer too." Harmony Boniface has turned away from Nick to look at the guard sitting in a booth outside a pair of wrought-iron gates in a tall white wall. He says, "I think we should move on. We have attracted attention."

Nick says, "Who are you really working for?"

"I am a reporter, Monsieur Hyde, chasing after a very big story. This really is not a safe place to talk. The people who live in these big houses—they are important. Politicians, civil servants, army officers . . ."

The guard is sauntering across the road towards the Peugeot. He wears a black flak vest under his denim jacket. The strap of an assault rifle is slung over his right shoulder, its butt snug under his armpit. A CCTV camera on a tall pole beside the gate swivels to track him.

"Tell me about this friend of yours," Nick says.

"I really think we should go before that fellow begins to ask awkward questions," Harmony Boniface says, and flinches when the guard raps on the roof.

"We'll go as soon as you tell me what your friend has that might interest me," Nick says.

The guard leans in at the window, says loudly that they can't park there.

Nick smiles at him and shakes his head, says to Harmony Boniface, "Are you going to tell me, or do you want to get out and explain things to this guy?"

Harmony Boniface digs into his shirt pocket, pulls out a

piece of paper, and unfolds it: it's a fax, a blurry reproduction of a close-up photograph of a pale nightmare face.

The guard raps on the roof again, and this time it's Nick who flinches. He somehow engages the Peugeot's selector, and moves off.

Harmony Boniface blots sweat from his forehead with the sleeve of his shirt. "You are a brave man or a crazy fool, Monsieur Hyde, I am not certain which. Where are we going?"

"I'll give you a lift into town. We can talk on the way. Did you get that picture from your friend? Where did he get it?"

"He took it himself, just yesterday. You recognize the creature, I think. I believe you would call it a white devil. Robin Ellis, the BBC reporter, said you had written that on your hand when you were driven away from the Witness building this morning. Everyone is trying to find out what it means, but I think so far my exclusive is safe."

"Where is it? How did your friend capture it?"

"I believe some hunters found it. They recognized it from a description Obligate agents have been circulating to local army units. Apparently," Harmony Boniface says, deadpan, "the Green Congo Biodiversity Research Centre is offering a reward for the bodies or heads of an unusual species of hairless, white-skinned ape."

Nick laughs.

"Yes, I know. They think that the region is so remote that they can do anything they like there. Obliterate an area with napalm, disappear soldiers, offer rewards for white devil . . ."

"These hunters must have caught it somewhere near the Likouala aux Herbes River," Nick says. "And your friend must live in or near Liranga, because I can't think of anywhere else in the area where you could find a fax machine."

"That's very clever," Harmony Boniface says. "What happened is that the hunters went directly to a Big Man in their village. They wanted him to broker the deal for them, and he thought I might know something to help him make a better deal. I will be very happy to take you to him."

"And how much would that cost me?"

Nick drives through the ruined security gate, accelerates onto the main highway. A big truck sounds its horn, although its headlights are already diminishing in the rearview mirror.

Harmony Boniface says, "You pay me nothing. But if you want to see the white devil, perhaps buy rights to take photographs and video footage, perhaps even buy the body, you must talk with my friend."

"I pay him, and he pays you."

"A man must live, Monsieur Hyde. But I think the story you want to tell is important. Obligate does not want the world to know about it. They kill a government official, they kidnap and kill a baby, they make you leave the country . . . I know this must be a big story. I will write it, and make us both famous."

"Let's pretend I'm interested. How would I go about meeting your friend?"

"First," Harmony Boniface says, looking in the mirror on the passenger side, "we must lose this fellow who is following you."

Nick looks in the rearview mirror and sees that the truck's lights have apparently doubled: a white Seraph is overtaking it.

Harmony Boniface says, "It's okay. Do what I say, Monsieur Hyde. Because I know you will be followed, I have made an arrangement."

The white Seraph stays a safe hundred metres behind the Peugeot, speeding up when Nick speeds up, slowing down when he slows down.

Nick says, "You knew I was being followed because you were following me; it's no coincidence that we both happened to be at William Ndinga's house at the same time."

Harmony Boniface shrugs.

Nick says, "You took a big risk. What would you have done if they caught you?"

"I would have told them the truth. I would have told them that I was trying to get a story."

"You aren't frightened that they might disappear you, or stage an accident like William Ndinga's?"

"Obligate is at the leading edge of open-source, late-stage capitalism. It makes available a detailed breakdown of the environmental costs of manufacturing every one of its products. It claims that it encourages a plurality of expression here in Green Congo. It donates ten percent of its profits to charity. It would be very embarrassing if it arrested or assassinated a genuine accredited journalist. It would be very bad public relations."

"And you think I might be crazy," Nick says.

The Seraph draws up to the Peugeot's bumper when they join the end of a short queue waiting at a traffic light, its headlights filling the Peugeot's interior with their harsh white glare. A billboard stands in front of a parking lot on the other side of the road, *Remaking the World Together* written in an artfully childish scrawl across Obligate's logo of a green planet in a blue square. Nick recognizes the name of the bar on the huge holographic sign that floats in the black air beyond the billboard and the parking lot.

"Sometimes this is how it happens," Harmony Boniface says. There's a tightness in his voice; he's genuinely scared. "They stop you at a traffic light or an army checkpoint. When they are finished, they dump guns and grenades on your body, and they claim they have shot a rebel spy. But don't worry, I have a plan to lose them."

Nick polarizes the rearview mirror to cut the glare. "There's only one man. Maybe we should talk to him."

"Turn left at this light," Harmony Boniface says. "It is all arranged."

An army truck growls past the queue of traffic, blasting its horn as it runs the red light. Nick pulls out and sharply accelerates, chasing the truck across the intersection and then braking hard and pulling into the crowded parking lot. As the Peugeot bumps over the curb, Harmony Boniface says, "What are you doing? This isn't the plan!"

"It's *my* plan," Nick says, and brakes and reaches behind his seat for his day bag.

"You think perhaps they will not kill you, because you are white, a foreigner, a charity worker. That's a mistake. They can kill anyone they like."

"Except reporters, right?"

"I have a *plan*. We go to the M'Bamou Palace Hotel, where all the journalists stay. We walk through the kitchen—"

"Harmony, look at me. If you think you're getting into something too dangerous for your blood, you can walk away."

"It is too late. They have already seen me with you."

"So are you ready to come with me? Take a deep breath, and let it out slowly before you answer."

"I am not a child or a coward," Harmony Boniface says. "If you knew exactly what was happening, you would have great fear too. You don't even know where you are going!"

"You can tell me once I've fixed our tail."

They climb out into sweltering air tainted with a faint smell of sewage. Nick tells Harmony Boniface to leave his door open.

"He will see the car. It is blocking the aisle."

"That's the idea."

Rows of 4×4s and SUVs and runabouts gleam in the harsh glare of a clutch of floodlights raised high on a steel pole in the middle of the parking lot. The long, low bar squats under the holographic sign floating above its flat roof, *Sammy's Bar* in flowing red letters two storeys high. Nick hears music pulsing from its open door, remembers with a sharp pang Isabel Fonesca's invitation. *This evening I will be drinking cold beer in Sammy's.* A kilometre away, the blue Obligate building stands against the night, neat lines of lights outlining the floors inside its plastic envelope. Nick thinks that it looks like some giant, luminous deep-sea creature, improbable and weirdly beautiful, and wonders if the rumour is true, that the place is full of high-resolution CCTV cameras trained on every part of the city, some of them even now watching this parking lot.

Harmony Boniface is looking all around, as if expecting to see a hundred soldiers suddenly jump up from behind the rows of parked vehicles. He says, "If you think to lose him by going through the bar, my plan is much better."

Nick sees the white Seraph turn off the road into the parking lot. He grabs the reporter's arm and drags him into the gap between a Land Cruiser and a battered Nissan Simba. Tells him to crouch low and stay still, looking him right in the face when he starts to protest, telling him again. The Seraph comes slowly down the aisle, stops ten metres behind the Peugeot. Nick works his way around the back of the Land Cruiser, ducks down to look beneath it, sees someone step down—polished black boots, camouflage trousers. He finds the roll of dollars inside his pocket and works off the top two notes with finger and thumb, then frees the Glock and takes a breath and steps around the front of the Land Cruiser.

The big man who intercepted Nick outside the bank is standing by the open door of the Seraph, holding a phone to his ear, a gold puffa jacket over his fatigues. Turning as Nick walks up to him, looking at the Glock, looking at him. He has a shaven head and a broad face with round cheeks nicked by acne scars, and is wearing spex with small, oval lenses.

When Nick tells him to raise his hands, he immediately puts them above his head and says, "You are making a mistake."

Nick is pointing the Glock at the man's midsection, hoping he isn't wearing any protection under the fatigues. He says, "Switch off your phone and drop it on the ground. Then take off your spex. Just in case you're making some kind of movie for Captain Badiledi."

The man opens his fingers; the little phone clatters on the concrete. As he folds his spex into the inside pocket of his puffa jacket, he says, with a friendly smile that reveals a gap between his front teeth, "That's a nice little gun. Ever use it?"

"Just a couple of days ago," Nick says. "I'm pretty sure you've got a gun, too."

"Of course."

The man is amused, or is doing a good job of pretending to be amused, watching Nick's face and not the Glock.

Nick says, "Here's what we're going to do. With your left hand, bring out your gun."

The man shakes his head. "I think we should talk about this, Monsieur Hyde. I am here to protect you, not harm you."

"Keep your hands up," Nick says. "I don't want any misunderstandings. You're a soldier, but right now you're working in a private capacity for Captain Badiledi. Am I right?"

The man makes a very small movement of his shoulders that could be a shrug.

"I was in the army, too, once upon a time. I know how it goes. You're sent out to do a job, but you aren't given all the information, you aren't given the right equipment. And when you screw up, guess who gets the blame? Always the poor bloody infantry, never the people who give the orders. You were sent to keep an eye on me, but Captain Badiledi didn't give you any back-up."

"That's not true. The others, they will be here pretty soon."

"You have help, but you're all alone in the chase car? I don't think so."

"Perhaps you want to talk to Captain Badiledi. I can take you there, right now. Or take you home, and we both forget this happened."

"Captain Badiledi paid you to follow me. Probably didn't pay you too much, so you decided to go it alone rather than share the money. All you had to do was follow some charity worker, how hard could it be? But Captain Badiledi forgot to tell you that I was in the British Army before I signed up with Witness, didn't he?" The man makes another small movement of his shoulders, and Nick says, "What's your name? You know mine, and we might as well be on a first-name basis while we try and work out what to do."

The man thinks it over, then says, "Leroy. Magne Leroy."

"You have a family, Magne?"

"Of course."

"Children to look after, relatives too, I bet," Nick says, remembering something that William Ndinga said to him. "All those people relying on you because you're the head man, it must stretch that army wage thin. No wonder you're taking work on the side. But Badiledi gives you just a few lousy dollars for a night's work, expects you to split it with whoever else you need to get the job done, and doesn't even brief you properly."

Magne says, "What you try to say?"

"It's Badiledi's fault that we're in this situation, Magne. I think I know how to get us out of it, and to begin with you're going to have to show me your gun. Show me a little trust, okay?"

The big man says, "I have to reach around, under my jacket."

"Just do it slowly. Use your thumb and forefinger."

The stainless steel automatic dangling in the big man's grip looks as small as a toy.

"Now drop the clip," Nick says, "that's right, and get rid of the round in the chamber, too."

The ejected round catches the light for a moment, clatters onto the roof of the Seraph.

"Now drop the gun and kick it towards me."

Magne Leroy lets the automatic swing between thumb and forefinger, then shrugs and lets it fall.

"Kick the gun to me."

The big man gives Nick a sad, patient look and with the side of his boot sweeps the automatic under the Seraph.

"I guess that'll do," Nick says, and takes a deep breath. He still isn't sure what he would have done if the man had called his bluff.

Magne Leroy says, "Perhaps you put away your gun now. We can talk how to fix this thing."

Nick glances through the smoked glass of the Seraph's window, sees that the ignition card is in its slot. He says, "I'm going to get something out of my pocket. Before I do, I want you to know that it's nothing to get alarmed about."

"You already have a gun on me, my friend. How much more alarmed can I get?"

Nick digs out the two bills, wads them up and tosses them underhand. They strike Magne Leroy in the chest and fall between his boots. "A hundred American dollars," Nick says.

"You're bribing me?"

"I bet it's more than Captain Badiledi paid."

"You want me to let you go."

"One way or another, you know you're going to have to let me go. But if you do it my way, you won't get into trouble. I want you to tell Captain Badiledi that I came straight here to this bar. I was alone. I had a few drinks, I saw you watching me, I made a run for it, and you lost me."

"You left your car here."

"Right. I left on foot."

"Or caught a taxi," Magne Leroy says. "There are always taxis waiting outside the bar."

"There you go."

Magne Leroy smiles. "It's not bad. But why couldn't I follow you in the Seraph?"

"Maybe it was stolen, or maybe it wouldn't start, or you were blocked in. You and the friend, remember, that you were supposed to have along."

"This will get me in trouble."

"If you don't mind me saying so, you're already in trouble."

"You don't want me to say you went to William Ndinga's house. You don't want me to talk about the reporter."

"That's up to you. But if you tell Captain Badiledi about those things, it doesn't give us enough time at the bar for the rest of the story to make sense."

"Okay, I understand. So, now you put the gun away, and I drive off."

"No. Now I want you to step back from your vehicle, sit down on the ground, put your hands on your head."

"Why not," the big man says, and steps back and suddenly turns and dodges away between parked vehicles towards the road, moving quickly and lightly for someone his size, his gold jacket flashing. Nick tracks him for a second, then scoops up the clip and the two bills, calls to Harmony Boniface, asks him if there's any place nearby where they can get a taxi.

"Of course. There are always taxis waiting outside the bar."

Nick pulls the card from the Seraph's ignition and pockets it, then finds his Emerson folding knife and jabs its blade into the front tire, twisting it until hot air hisses out over his hand.

"You make a bad mistake," Harmony Boniface says as they hurry across the parking lot towards the bar. "You make the security people angry, and for what? You still have to trust me. You still need me to help you find the white devils."

"Yeah," Nick says. "But this way I get to see them on my own terms."

Chapter 16

Bridget Nzube phones Nick early the next morning. The sequencer worked through the night on the half-dozen samples of DNA she isolated from the spatters of blood on his belt, and it took her only five minutes to run a comparison against the primate-genome databases stored on the GenBank website. She was astonished by the results, and is anxious to tell Nick the results of her investigation.

When the call is diverted to the voicemail service, she thinks for a moment, tapping the tip of her pen against her teeth, then gives a brief summary of what she has found, and hangs up. She is disappointed that she could not discuss what she found with Nick, and hopes that he will stop by the Witness building before his plane leaves. It would be nice to see him just one more time, and ask him a couple of pertinent questions about his white devils.

Bridget Nzube does not know that the unsleeping electronic watchdogs of the army security service are monitoring Nick's mobile-phone account. Thirty seconds after she hangs up, an AI phones Captain Badiledi and plays him the message. Jean Badiledi listens to it twice, then calls Magne Leroy into his office and tells the big soldier that he wants a certain Witness worker brought here as soon as possible.

"Make sure no one sees you take her," he says. "And Leroy, I promise you that if you fuck up *this* time, you will lose a lot more than your fee."

Chapter 17

Erefaan has been in some broke-down, bombed-out, burnt-up places in his time, but this has to be the poorest excuse for a town he's ever seen. A corrugated dirt road, a mission that's no more than a couple of cinder block sheds and a scaffolding tower topped with a big black cross, and a scatter of knee-high ruins left over from some short, sharp engagement during the border war with Somalia. Blackened steel shell casings are stacked like cords of wood along the wall of one of the mission's sheds. A string of shallow craters bites the edge of the road. A burnt-out army truck squats on its axles, half a dozen graves in a row beside it. The place looks deserted, but when Cody gets it into his head to make a stop outside the mission, a ragged gang of kids runs to the van, and a few men wearing threadbare desert-camo gear and armed with battered Kalashnikovs slouch over as Cody and Erefaan set up the sound system.

Before getting into his rant about the end times, Cody warms up the little crowd with a couple of hymns. He's got up like a death crow in black T-shirt and black jeans and black biker boots and his wide-brimmed black preacher's hat, perched on the edge of his picnic chair and hunched over the strung plank in his lap. The crowd swaying along to the riffs he wrenches from the guitar, clapping the long, bent notes that punctuate his sermon like the howls of heartbroken angels: Cody sanctifying himself for the killing that's coming in a couple of days.

Erefaan sits it out in the shade of the van, squatting with his back against a hot, dusty tire and sipping from an ice-cold bottle of flat-tasting filtered water. He has no time for Cody's preaching, but has to admit the man has a sweet touch on the

slide guitar. The early-afternoon sun bleaches the land white.
The heat is brutal. A few puffball clouds hang high in the hot,
blue sky and a reef of darker clouds hugs the eastern horizon:
more rain on the way. Cody manages about an hour's preaching in the furnace heat and when he's finished starts up an intense conversation with the mission's priest, a tubby man in
blue jeans and a San Francisco 49ers shirt. Erefaan snags a
couple more bottles of water from the van's refrigerator and
slips away, following a path that winds through the pockmarked ruins of a safari lodge. Someone has leaned a couple
of Russian mortars against a broken wall, something Erefaan
might have a use for if only he had a launcher, and if he could
trust armaments that have been cooking in the equatorial sun
for a couple of years.

Rusty is sitting on a low wall in the shade of a doum palm,
tossing stones into the cracked basin of what was once a
swimming pool. He's bare-chested, in combat trousers and
high-top boots and his orange wraparound spex. He takes one
of the bottles of water and cracks it and takes a long swallow
without once looking at Erefaan, who sits beside him and
holds the other bottle against the side of his neck to chill his
blood.

A couple of small kids watch them from a distance, one
wearing only a red string around his waist, the other not even
that, both shaven-headed and painfully skinny. Beyond them,
nothing but stretches of sand and outcrops of vivid green
grass, a few arthritic thorn trees hunched against the long, flat
horizon. Some town, all right.

"Cody would have liked it if you helped out at the sermon," Erefaan says after a while.

"I don't believe in that stuff," Rusty says.

"I don't either, brother, but number one, it keeps Cody
calmed down, and number two, it's our cover. Right now
Cody is bending the ear of the mission priest, digging up all
kinds of information. And if we meet any army patrols on our
way to the coast, they'll have heard about this on the bush
telegraph, you see what I mean? They'll think we're just a
bunch of harmless travelling gospellers spreading the good

word, and the best thing about it is that it's more than halfway genuine. Cody truly does believe in all that shit."

Rusty shrugs. He's locked into himself like a punk after his first time, helpless and hurting and angry.

Erefaan says, "Everything's got its reason, is what I'm saying."

"Cody told you to come and tell me that?"

"Hell no. Cody expects you to do your part, brother. He wouldn't have let you ride along in the first place if he didn't think that. Once he's chosen you, that's it. He puts his trust in you, and he expects you to put your trust in him."

"You don't think I'm committed?" Rusty says with a defiant stare.

Erefaan shrugs, thinking that he doesn't really know this kid at all. Cody recruited Rusty as a replacement for Iban while they were resting up in the safe house outside Nairobi, took him on several long walks to sound him out, that way Cody has of giving you his full attention, like looking into your soul, and decided that the kid was okay. And that was it, no discussion, Rusty was coming along. Erefaan got a chance to talk with the kid while they were scouting the abortive kidnap, but he has a reserve Erefaan couldn't break down, not even with ripe stories about other jobs and prison life, and like many Radical Greens, he also has this air of moral superiority, an assumption that because he has dedicated himself to a higher purpose, his virtue is unquestionable. He doesn't seem to understand that to serve the cause you sometimes have to get on the wrong side of things, have to get down in the dirt and blood like a car mechanic or a surgeon, get that bad stuff in your skin, under your fingernails. Killing Shalynne should have been a lesson to him in the hard choices that sometimes have to be made, but it seems to have locked him up even tighter.

Erefaan thinks that once upon a time, back in university at Jo'burg, he might have been a little like Rusty, although Rusty has a genuine belief in the cause, while Erefaan has to admit that he fell in with the Greens and anti-capitalists because he liked to mix it up, and there was no better place for it than at one of their demos. The stunning volume of the crowd's chants and songs, the police in their black body armour drumming their riot sticks against their Perspex shields, sunlight flashing from shields and visors, rocks and bottles soaring through the red and green smoke of flares and white billows of gas blowing across the strip of no-man's land between protesters and police. The pure adrenalin blast he got whenever he dodged out of the safety of the crowd to grab one of the hissing, red-hot canisters of CS or tear gas and sling it back into the police line, so pumped up that he hardly noticed the snot and stinging tears running from his nose and eyes—this was before he had the sense to get hold of an army-surplus gas mask, and wore only a wetted handkerchief, and that mostly to disguise himself in front of the police video cameras. The tension building until at last the police made their charge. Erefaan always knew when it was about to come, always managed to get out of the way before the main body of protesters turned tail and ran, their unity broken by snatch squads and high-pressure electrified blasts from water cannon. The feeling Erefaan got from a good demonstration was almost better than sex, although there was usually sex to be had afterwards, after the post-mortem in a bar or someone's room, his eyes tender and his clothes stinking of garlicky gas, beer, and reefer slowly mellowing his combat high.

Erefaan was noticed—his coolness under fire, his willingness to mix it up at the front, to get right in the teeth of the police. A word in passing one day from a girl he'd met at one of the post-riot gatherings, an off-campus rendezvous with an older couple, questions about his dedication to the cause of cutting out the cancer of global capitalism and getting rid of the neocolonialist pollution of African genes and the African ecology. Erefaan answering yes to everything, quiet and serious, knowing that this was his chance to get into some real action.

First, there were long discussion meetings to endure, and study of Marxist and Radical Green and anti-colonialist literature not much more boring than his engineering course. He helped to plaster posters and slogans over the campus, passed on plans of university buildings, once put up in his room a comrade passing through on the underground railroad, a taciturn man who slept for twelve hours straight and left without saying more than a dozen words. Erefaan didn't even know why he was on the run, and knew better than to ask. By this time, he was no longer attending any of his classes, and a month later he went on his first raid, a night infiltration of an experimental farm sixty kilometres outside Jo'burg. Nothing difficult—cutting wire fences, slapping parasitic feeds on CCTV cameras, and taking down two ill-equipped security guards with sticky foam and ether-soaked rags, dropping fused incendiaries through the ventilation slots of the long, brightly lit greenhouses. When the explosions lit up the horizon two hours later, Erefaan felt as if he'd been sanctified by holy fire. Damage estimated at thirty million rand, a twenty-second spot on the national news, big kudos to everyone involved.

Then a long stretch of routine action: leafleting outside shops and cinemas and fast-food restaurants owned by multinationals; attaching viral patches to the software of electronic billboards, turning the happy faces of the young couple sharing a bottle of a famous soft drink into grinning death skulls; picketing the homes of engineers working at an opencast mine. The next real job came six months later, a raid on a commercial genetics laboratory where things quickly went wrong. A security guard had a pistol no one knew about, one of Erefaan's comrades was wounded in the stomach, and the police cornered Erefaan and two others as they were trying to lift the wounded girl into the van.

Erefaan fell hard: life in the labour camps. He was put to work cutting down one of the forests his comrades were campaigning to preserve. He built up his muscles and kept out of the way of the real criminals and their Number gangs. Then, a year into his sentence, the Black Flu swept the world and the madness began. Erefaan was sent to work at a trash incinerator converted by army engineers into a huge gas-fired crematorium. He loaded bodies in green body bags onto the conveyor belt, raked out ashes full of bone fragments and teeth. The labour gangs were issued respirator masks and coveralls, and everyone scrubbed down with disinfectant at the end of every shift, but the body bags leaked and sickness spread quickly. Every man in one of the dormitory huts died in a single night, and they all went into the incinerator the next day. A priest who said prayers over the dead as they were fed into the furnace, a man Erefaan liked, one day coughed a pint of rich red blood into his hands and died an hour later; he went into the incinerator too. Rumours swept through the dormitory huts faster than any virus. Out in the World, enemies were accusing each other of bioterrorism, were settling old scores and reviving old hatreds. Israel nuked Cairo and Amman and Damascus after suicide bombers blew up a van packed with spent nuclear reactor rods in the centre of Tel Aviv. The Saudi kingdom fell to Islamic fundamentalists, and America and Europe were drawn into the jihad. Every day for a month, the sky over the crematorium was scratched by the high, white contrails of B-52s heading across the heart of Africa. Pakistan nuked India, and India nuked Pakistan. The President of South Africa was assassinated and the military took control; dozens of political prisoners were soon working alongside Erefaan, and most of them got sick and died. Six months of this, and then one day Erefaan and two dozen other prisoners were loaded onto a truck and driven to a township where some kind of accelerated elephantiasis had killed almost everyone. They dug deep trenches and bulldozed hideously bloated bodies into them and burned the bodies with kerosene. The worst three weeks of Erefaan's life; he will never forget the stench of the great reefs of greasy smoke rising from the trenches, the sight of what was left as he helped cover over the remains. After a week's quarantine, he was sent to a holding camp, then reassigned to a labour gang, back in the forest where he had started out; two years later, the military made way for a civilian government, and his sentence was commuted.

When Erefaan came out of prison, he was a forgotten and unwanted martyr-hero for a radical cause that was now a respectable political entity, with two MPs in Parliament and representatives on just about every city council. He spent a couple of months in a labouring job in a bakery, and then, bored out of his mind, hooked up with Cody. Perhaps he sees in Rusty a more idealistic version of his younger self; perhaps that's why he can't be as hard on the kid as Cody would like him to be. Cody believes that Shalynne's murder was an initiation trial that should have purged Rusty of every trace of bourgeois sentiment, but Erefaan knows that the kid resents what he was made to do, feels used, feels soiled, feels angry. Sometimes Erefaan has felt exactly the same way.

He reaches out now, with a mix of tenderness and pity, but stops a couple of inches from the curve of Rusty's back, where the knobs of his spine are visible under freckled brown skin, then snatches his hand away when the kid looks around.

Rusty says, "I was thinking about the job."

"Best not to think about it at all," Erefaan says, "until you're on the edge of it. What you should be doing now is kicking back, enjoying all this spectacular scenery."

"I was wondering," Rusty says, his gaze steady and solemn behind the orange-tinted spex, "about this client of yours. The fairy godmother."

"I never had anything to do with her before, but Cody did some work for her before we hooked up. Earned some good money hunting down a couple of scientists from one of those grey labs they had out in the Congo. You don't have to worry about her. Whoever she is, she's solid."

"That's what Cody told me."

"There you are. Listen, brother, don't be worrying about the job. You've seen the information we've been given. It'll be an easy in-and-out; we could walk through it blindfolded. Maybe you're thinking, what bullshit, they recruited me to replace a comrade they lost in Uganda, and this is going to be another fuck-up just like it. But see, that wasn't one of our own jobs, it was a stupid little action dreamed up by a bunch of local activists. We were passing through, and these kids got excited by these big bad ecotagers in their midst and wanted to show us what they could do. It was a dumb, nothing piece of shit, we went in for the fun of it, and what happens? Someone had tipped off the farmer, and he and his boys were waiting for us when we came to burn his fields. All of them armed, and those kids had nothing but cans of gas and electric torches. Iban went to save a couple of girls and got cut off when we were making a retreat, and a lucky shot took him down. A dumb piece of shit, like I said, nothing at all like the job we have now. We know where we're going, we know the target, we have maps and photographs, information on the security gear right down to the serial numbers on the cameras. This job, you don't have to worry about it at all."

"You don't ever feel used, doing a job like this? I mean, this guy, whoever he is, is calling all the shots. He has his own agenda, and you go in and do whatever he tells you to do. You follow his orders."

"You should talk to Cody about this, you really should. Especially if you have a problem following orders. This is a war, in case you hadn't noticed. We're on the front line. We're soldiers. And soldiers follow orders, damn right they do. When I go in, I want to know that the people with me are going to follow the plan and do what has to be done, no more and no less."

"We decided amongst ourselves what to do and how to do it," Rusty says. "We discussed it, we took a vote. Everyone had a say in what we did. Our last campaign was against the sale of logging rights in Kikuyuland to a Korean company. The usual story of government cronyism and corruption. We organized against it. We were spiking trees and sabotaging machinery, and we were also issuing statements to the media, helping the local people to bring a court action. And everything we did was decided democratically."

Erefaan fingers his crocodile tooth. "What did you like more? The sabotage or the court action?" The boy looks sideways at him, and he says, "You don't need to answer that, because I *know* what it was, or you wouldn't be here. We heard you were hot stuff, and that's why we came to you."

"What I didn't know, when I agreed to come along, is that you're work-for-hire."

"We need to make money so we can do the other stuff.

What's wrong with you, Rusty, you have trouble following this? It's simple enough. Go ask Cody if you don't get it, he'll put you straight."

He'll put a cap in your ass, Erefaan thinks, and then, brother, you won't be a problem any more.

"I'd rather ask you," Rusty says, "because we have something in common. South African, Kenyan, we're brothers in blood."

"What are you saying? That you don't like a white man giving you orders?"

"Do you?"

"What kind of question is that? You think I'm like some old-time apartheid kaffir saying yes baas, no baas? Man, you're crazy. It isn't like that at all."

"I think he uses people, Erefaan, and he finds it easier to use us because he doesn't quite see us as people. You know why he made me kill Shalynne? It wasn't anything to do with blooding me. It was to show me he's the boss."

"You got to get over that," Erefaan says. "It's hard, I know, but she won't be the last person you have to kill. This isn't about setting fire to a couple of bulldozers or banging spikes into trees to mess up chainsaw blades. This is the front line."

"I know this is a war; I know there are going to be casualties. But Shalynne was just a silly little rich girl who wanted to spite her stepfather any way she could—that's why she slept with just about everyone in my group. I didn't want her to come along, but I guess Cody saw her as some kind of comfort woman."

Erefaan says, "You have to admit that she had a sweet ass." And adds, when he sees Rusty's expression change, "Don't take it so hard, man. You said it yourself: she was just some dumb rich American girl, looking for some action with us bad Africans."

"She was dumb, but she didn't deserve to die. Those silly punishments Cody handed out, they were his way of showing he had power over her, and when he made me kill her . . . that was his way of showing he had power over *me*."

Erefaan looks over at Rusty, thinking from the catch in his

voice that he is crying—he was crying hard enough when he finally got up the nerve to put a bullet in Shalynne's head—but the kid's gaze is dry-eyed and steady. Erefaan says, "What are you saying here? That I shouldn't trust Cody because he's white, and I should trust you because we're both Africans?"

"He had you out in the rain making Shalynne dig her own grave," Rusty says. "He got rid of her without a qualm, you think he won't think twice if he has to get rid of you?"

"I think you should be careful what you're saying," Erefaan says. "You think we're having a cosy little conversation here? You think we're bonding? How do you know that I'm not going to tell Cody all about this?"

"I don't," Rusty says. "But after what he made me do, I don't give a shit."

"It made you feel bad when you did her," Erefaan says. "I understand that. You believed you had ideals to live up to, but now you're as dirty as the rest of us."

"Who did Cody make you kill, to be part of this thing of his?"

"It was no big deal. Like you said, there are always going to be casualties."

"How did it happen?"

"It was an animal-house technician at a medical research centre. We tossed flashbang grenades into the room where the night workers had a habit of taking a break around midnight. Down they went, all except this one man. He came walking out of all the smoke and kept on walking, hands up, bleeding from the ears, a dazed look in his eyes and this stupid grin on his face. There was no time to get him out of the way, so I capped him. It was no big deal."

The poor guy had no fight in him whatsoever, they could have bundled him down and tied him up, but Cody had told Erefaan to shoot him. Got right in his face and yelled at him while the guy was smiling and shuffling towards them, and Erefaan panicked and did it, one quick burst. The guy so out of it, he probably didn't even know he was dead when he hit the ground.

Rusty says, "The man Cody made you kill, he was black, wasn't he?"

"Yeah, he was black. This was in Jo'burg, my first action with Cody. If you don't know, ninety percent of the people in Jo'burg are black."

"And if it had been a white man," Rusty says, "do you think it would have happened in exactly the same way?"

"Yeah, I do. And I also think it's time we were getting along."

But as Erefaan walks back through the burnt-out ruins towards the road, he can't help remembering the way Cody had glanced at him when Rusty shot Shalynne, the little spark of satisfaction in the man's eyes.

Chapter 18

Elspeth Faber's plane is a single-engine Cessna older than the century. Before she's ready to leave, she methodically checks the flaps on its wings and tail, its fuel and hydraulic lines, tire pressure, and the radio. She hugs Mary Ekalale and tells her to make sure that the site is put to bed properly. She shakes hands with Harry Brenner, and he tells her that they're going to knock them dead in Nairobi.

"I'm not going to miss it."

"I hope not." Harry points his chin at the plane. He's wearing his sweat-stained bush hat; a vulture's flight feather is tucked into its band. "You okay flying that thing on your own?"

"How many times have you flown with me, Harry?"

"It's a long way to fly solo. I don't want to hear you've done an Amelia Earhart; I need you to face the media with me."

"I'll see you in Nairobi," Elspeth says. "When you've nailed down a date for the media conference, and if you have any thoughts about what we're going to say, be sure to email me."

The Cessna barrels down the bush airstrip, splashing through puddles from last night's rain, makes its sudden lifting leap and cuts quickly through the low clouds, climbs into sunlight and blue sky above a white cloud deck that stretches away in every direction, broken only by mountain peaks to the north. Elspeth flies southeast, sometimes above the clouds, sometimes below. When she skims over the southern end of the lake, flamingos that have been feeding on soupy green algal blooms in the interlocking rings of grey-white salt deposits take wing below her, thousands of them pinkly tiling the air, every bird straining to outrace its own flickering shadow. This glorious sight lifts Elspeth out of herself. She has always loved flying, loves looking around at the land spread below. Checkerboards of cultivation, rumpled green forests, rocky deserts, lion-coloured plains: the ridiculous abundance of Kenya's landscapes never ceases to amaze her.

Elspeth Faber, just turned twenty-seven (the Hominid Gang held a birthday party for her at the dig: vodka cocktails and a chunk of chocolate-chip ice cream that the cook had kept hidden in the freezer for two months, stuck at random with birthday candles that kept relighting themselves when she tried to blow them out), feels that she's far too young to take charge of her father's life but knows that she can't pass the responsibility to anyone else. It's going to be hard to reconcile Matthew to the arrival of David Oloitip's soldiers, and it's going to be even harder doing what she should have done long ago, telling him that she knows what the Gentle People really are. It has to be done: if they're going to get through this thing with Teryl they have to be one hundred percent honest with each other, no more secrets, no more evasions, but she gets a cold little cramp of anxiety every time she thinks about it. She tells herself that they'll get past it. They'll go for walks. They'll snorkel over the reef, catch a fish and barbecue it, sit on the beach in the shade of the palm trees and drink beer. She'll talk about her stones and bones, and he'll talk about the Gentle People. She tells herself that it will be good to see him again, but the truth is that she can hardly bear to see what he's become after his accident (if it had been an accident). His baffled distraction and abrupt mood swings, the inarticulate agitation and rage when Dr. Dave manifests itself, are horribly like the early symptoms of Alzheimer's. There are still flashes of his old brilliance, but much of the time he's like a crazy old beach bum shambling along and arguing out loud with the devils inside his head. The man from her childhood, that strong, tender, sheltering presence, fizzing with good-humoured energy, full of unqualified love, the man who could turn anything into an adventure, even a trip to the supermarket or the orthodontist (for two years, Elspeth had wires and screws clamped into her mouth to straighten her teeth into the even white arc of the American ideal), is gone forever. She remembers that he ran a lot back then, pounding the streets of Cambridge, loping through the park beside the Charles. He ran fifteen kilometres a day. He said that running helped him think about thinking. At the end of every day, he would come thumping up the stairs and burst into their apartment and pick her up and whirl her around until she was breathless and giddy with laughter, and then they'd decide what they were going to cook together.

Elspeth was three years old when her mother died, four when she and her father moved from Kenya to America; she has no real memories of her early childhood in Nairobi, or of the young woman whose photographs her father kept in a drawer in his bedroom. As far as she is concerned, her childhood was idyllic and wholly American. She put her hand over her heart and recited the Pledge of Allegiance every school day. She had sleepovers and makeovers with her girlfriends. She had her own cellphone and TV, a five-speed bicycle with a banana seat. She might have lived in America for the rest of her life if her father hadn't married Teryl Meade.

Matthew had a string of casual girlfriends after he moved to the States, never anything serious—and then there was Teryl. Teryl Meade was one of Matthew's colleagues at Harvard Medical School, and Elspeth knew that they had been working closely together, but she had no idea what was really going on until she came home from school one day to find them waiting in the apartment, eager to spring their surprise.

A double surprise, really. They were quitting the medical school to set up their own biotech company; and they were going to get married.

That her father was genuinely happy helped soften the shock, but although Elspeth tried to make herself like her stepmother, Teryl wasn't the kind of woman who let anyone get close to her. And it seemed to Elspeth that after he and Teryl married, Matthew's natural ebullience was diminished. Teryl took charge of everything, and Matthew followed her lead with a kind of dazed, amiable helplessness. It was Teryl's idea, for instance, to move from their comfortable apartment and the leafy neighbourhood with its buckled brick sidewalks and Chinese laundry and family-run Italian deli, to a cold, minimalist house that stood in a twenty-acre lot on a pine-covered ridge north of Boston. Elspeth hated the house almost as much as she had come to hate Teryl. When she finally escaped to college, she supported herself with a grinding series of McJobs so that she wouldn't have to ever go back, would never again have to endure Teryl's bright, brittle dinnertime conversations, the tense, headachy silences that filled the house after one of their rows, the way Teryl stalked from room to room when she came home, her gaze bird-bright as she looked for misplaced toys and scuff marks—she once lectured Elspeth for ten straight minutes about fingerprints on the door of the stainless steel refrigerator. Teryl constantly complained about the time she had to spend looking after Elspeth, but Elspeth remembers that it was mostly a string of housekeepers, none with English as their first language, none lasting more than six months before Teryl found some excuse to fire them, who prepared her supper and ran her baths, turned down her bed, and made sure she did her homework and brushed her teeth. Matthew and Teryl were working long hours at Qualia's laboratory and in their offices at home, but Elspeth remembers that the door to her father's office was always open, and the door to Teryl's office was always closed. Her father was doing his best work then, so engaged with the humming hive of his thoughts that he hardly noticed the world around him; if he knew that Elspeth was unhappy, he never mentioned it. But he was always pleased to see her, no matter how distracted he might be by his work, and sometimes she fell asleep in his lap while he tapped away at his computer into the small hours of the morning. She remembers at age fourteen standing outside the door of Teryl and Matthew's bedroom while they argued about sending her away to private school. For once, her father prevailed, but Teryl took it out on him for months afterwards, and Elspeth resolved to get out as soon as she could. By the time Matthew and Teryl started work at the Pleistocene Park research facility in the Democratic Republic of the Congo, she was back in Kenya, working at Nairobi University towards her Ph.D.

She flies over the stony desert of the Sagererua Plateau, the symmetrical volcanic cones of Marsabit printed against the horizon with the simplicity of a child's drawing, each cone wearing a cap of fleecy white clouds. The deep burr of the Cessna's engine fills the hot cabin. Sunlight splinters on the scratched Perspex of the windshield. She flies over the vast emptiness of eastern Tsavo, plains of grey-brown scrub stretching away towards distant table mountains. Flying a dogleg to the south because there are too many warlords and bandits in the north these days; there's a rumour that some Somali *shifta* have gotten hold of a batch of Chinese-made hand-held ground-to-air missiles. After she crosses the equator, she picks up the course of the Tana River and follows it for more than a hundred kilometres before turning east towards the Indian Ocean. She checks in with Mombasa air traffic control and turns south, flying parallel to the shore in hot, buffeting air under fleets of fast-moving clouds, mangrove swamps and white beaches and blue ocean with breakers creaming over brown reefs on her right, on her left huge fields of sisal broken by big, silver-grey baobab trees, and then flat green marshes between dry brown hills.

At last, five hours after she left Lake Turkana, Elspeth spots the familiar triangle of her father's island in the wide blue bite of the shallow lagoon, the dock and long shed of the old marine research station tucked into the fringe of mangrove swamp. She makes a wide turn, the yoke of the harness cutting into her shoulders, the sea behind her and the sun on her left, the stall warning beeping urgently as the dense, dark green ribbon of mangroves unravels under the plane's wheels. A red-dirt airstrip cut into dry brush on a low rise rushes towards her, and then she's down with a hard thump and a puff of dust, the engine roaring into reverse as she fishtails to a halt.

Hot, soggy air heavy with the smell of salt and decay envelops her when she cracks the door. Three men in olive-drab tunics and shorts are jogging towards the plane, rifles slung over their shoulders. One of them—it's Sergeant Mbau— waves to her.

As she steps down to meet him, Elspeth tells herself that everything is going to be fine, and at first nothing seems to have changed, except that the three rangers are curiously protective of their charge and try their best to convince her to put off visiting the island.

"He is like a child," Sergeant Mbau says. "As long as every day is more or less the same, he does not make a fuss. But if something happens when he does not expect it . . ."

"He makes a very big fuss," Christopher Githongo, the youngest ranger, says.

They're sitting at a table in the shade of the salt-silvered veranda of the laboratory building, with a view of the lagoon and the little island. There's a pitcher of lemonade, freshly baked oatmeal cookies. On the far side of the wide, neatly trimmed lawn, the Kenyan flag snaps above the tin roof of the rangers' whitewashed bungalow.

"He is more and more inside his head," Sergeant Mbau says, and taps his forehead with a finger. "Except for the Gentle People, he does not pay attention to the world."

Sergeant Mbau is a stocky man in his late sixties, with a pleasant, pockmarked face and an easygoing manner. Elspeth has known him for most of her life. He helped Matthew Faber with the fieldwork for his Ph.D. thesis on territoriality in Rift Valley baboons, kept in touch after Elspeth and Matthew moved to the United States, and took them on camping trips whenever they visited Kenya. Elspeth is deeply grateful that he came out of retirement to help his old friend, and she always pays attention to his advice, but she feels that for the first time he isn't being entirely straightforward with her.

"He is like a sleepwalker," Meji Mills, the third ranger, says. He's a lanky man with a lazy, raffish air, sprawling in his chair and boldly gazing at Elspeth through the round, blue-tinted lenses of his sunglasses. His lower front teeth have been extracted in the Masai fashion. His tunic is unbuttoned, showing the bead necklaces and thin silver chains looped on his smooth chest.

"He doesn't see anything he doesn't want to see," Christopher Githongo says with a wide, nervous smile, "and he doesn't hear anything he doesn't want to hear. You can be standing right next to him, and it is as if you are invisible."

Meji Mills nods. "And if you try and disturb him, his dark half can come out. There's no dealing with him then. He's like a dervish!"

"The Gentle People do not like disturbance either," Sergeant Mbau says. "We mostly keep away from the island now, Miss Elspeth."

"He knows I'm here, and he knows I've come to talk to him," Elspeth says. "I know he isn't happy about it, and I know he doesn't like to be disturbed. I know just how protective he is toward the Gentle People. But he knows that something needs to be done. He knows that we have to talk about it."

The three rangers exchange glances. Sergeant Mbau says, "Well now, the thing is that there's a little problem with the Gentle People."

"They're growing up," Meji Mills says. "Becoming interested in each other, if you know what I mean."

"But they're only six years old," Elspeth says.

"Chimpanzees grow up faster than that," Sergeant Mbau says. "I know you will say that the Gentle People are not really chimpanzees, but they are not people either."

Sergeant Mbau doesn't know the truth about the Gentle

People; only Elspeth and David Oloitip know. And her father, and Teryl . . .

Elspeth says, "Are you trying to tell me that my father will become upset if I find out that they're growing up?"

The men look at each other again.

"It's not exactly that they're growing up," Sergeant Mbau says at last. "It's *how* they're growing up."

He won't explain further; says that Elspeth should see for herself.

"Why not right now?" Elspeth says.

Her father is waiting for her on the little beach. When she cuts the motor of the inflatable dinghy and slides over the side, he wades out to her and they embrace in warm, thigh-deep water before hauling the dinghy onto the sugary white coral sand.

"You look good," Elspeth says.

And even though he has only shaved one half of his face that morning, he *does* look good. A little stooped perhaps, his face a little more lined, but he's deeply tanned, and his lean runner's frame doesn't hold a gram of spare weight. He's wearing only a pair of ragged shorts, a canvas tool-belt hung with a Boy's Own collection of gadgets, and a floppy cloth hat once bright red but now a washed-out, salt-stained pink. His spex hang from a loop of string around his neck.

Matthew Faber lifts his hat and runs a hand over his sparse tufts of white hair, gives her a rueful smile, and says, "A little older, a little balder. You look good too, Elspeth. Healthy. Happy."

"I haven't seen you for so long, of course I'm happy." She hesitates, then says, "Where are the Gentle People?"

"Oh, out foraging somewhere . . ."

He doesn't seem to be upset by her question, but she can't tell if he's being his usual vague self or deliberately evasive, and decides not to press it. Take it easy. Take it step by step.

Elspeth has brought a cool box of food with her; her father

insists on carrying it up the steep, narrow stairway cut into
the ridge of the raised coral reef. They sit in the shade of a
coconut palm at the edge of the little cliff that overlooks the
sea and drink iced coffee and talk about their family—the
cousin who just got married, a new baby, the twins who will
graduate from university this year, Uncle Dickie and his
drink problem and his plan to sue the city council for failure
to deliver public services to the affluent suburb where he
lives, the money problems everyone is having in the economic slowdown.

"Poor old Dickie," her father says. "He lost his business,
he lost his wife and children, he's living off the charity of his
relatives, and he always thought he deserved more than most
Kenyans just because he's white. If anyone ever wants to
make a statue of a typical *wazunga*, Dickie's their man to
model for it."

Sometimes Matthew has a touch of Teryl's acid sharpness. His clinical psychiatrist, Dr. Peltzer, once told Elspeth
that the models of other people we all construct in our
minds, so that we can anticipate what they might do, work
out strategies to please or trick them, have in her father become unbound and can sometimes express themselves as co-
gently as the primary core of his consciousness. So
Teryl—or at least, Matthew's model of Teryl—is loose in his
head, and, although she has never detected anything of her
own self in his behaviour or his speech, so, she must suppose, is Elspeth.

He asks about her work, and she tells him about the *Nature* article and the press conference she's due to give with
Harry Brenner. He listens carefully as she gives a précis of
their work and tells him about the evidence that suggests that
the habiline bones were processed for meat: cut marks at
joints, which show that the bones had been disarticulated;
hack marks and scrape marks where muscle was removed;
long bones split on anvils by stone hammers to remove the
marrow.

Matthew thinks about this, squinting off at the sea's bright horizon, his hands aimlessly plucking at the coarse turf. There are deep lines etched into the skin around his eyes, a freckling of shiny little scars on his nose where benign cancers have been removed. He says, "These bones are from how many individuals?"

"At least five *Homo habilis* and two *Homo ergaster*, although we don't know if they were all killed together. The site was in use for around twenty years."

"You're certain that the *Homo ergaster* specimens were processed in the same way? That it wasn't the result of some kind of mortuary rite?"

"If it was a mortuary rite, it still would be an amazing discovery, the earliest by a million years. The ergaster bones were processed exactly like animal and habiline bones, and we have a partial reconstruction of an ergaster skull that was hammered apart."

"To get at the brains."

"Possibly, yes. It's speculative, but it's backed up by the other evidence of methodical butchery."

Matthew nods. "If these individuals were butchered, how do you know they were prey for your ergaster family, and not just carrion?"

"We can't know that for sure, but the bones are from juveniles and infants, which certainly suggests prey selection. It could be that over the years there were many incidents of leopard predation on the local habiline population, and our ergasters scavenged the bodies, brought the long bones back and cracked them open to get at the marrow. But there are no leopard-tooth marks on the bones—no tooth marks of any animal—and they were processed in the same way as animal bones. Also, *Paranthropus boisei* shared the same habitat as the two *Homo* species, but so far we haven't found any of their bones at the campsite."

"Because your gracile ergasters would find the robust *Paranthropus* more difficult to kill."

Elspeth nods, happy to be sitting in the shade looking out over the sparkling blue sea, talking to her father as scientist to scientist, happy that he seems more focused in person than on the phone. She should try and see him more often; it would help both of them.

"It's possible," she says, "although *Paranthropus* juveniles would have been vulnerable to predation. But Harry and I think the most likely explanation is that *Homo habilis* and *Homo ergaster* not only shared the same habitat, but were in competition for the same resources. They interacted more frequently and more strongly with each other than with *Paranthropus*, and *Homo ergaster* won out. One of Harry's postgrad students ran a computer simulation based on established models of the effect of human predation on extinction rates of large North American mammals. It shows that *Homo ergaster* predation could have wiped out local populations of *Homo habilis* in five thousand years."

"That won't be an important part of your presentation at this press conference, I hope. Computer models are vulnerable to criticism because they multiply approximation and speculation."

"We won't be making any wild claims, Daddy. The models are well established. The only novelty is that we're applying them to early hominids."

"Hmm . . . Still, I have the feeling that Dr. Brenner likes to speculate a little too much."

"We all do. We sit around the campfire, tossing ideas back and forth . . . But it doesn't mean they're going to creep into publication."

"It's good work, Elspeth. A fantastic discovery." Her father toasts her with his empty coffee glass. "My little girl, the soon-to-be-famous palaeoanthropologist. I'm very proud of you, even though you didn't think to share it with me until now."

"That's because we've only just finished the work, Daddy, and we had to do it in a rush."

Elspeth tells Matthew that it started when she and Harry discovered a couple of habiline bones at the end of last season's fieldwork; on the basis of that find, they were able to scrape together enough funding for a full excavation. She tells him how she spent the last three months shuttling back

and forth between Lake Turkana and Nairobi so that specimens could be cleaned and processed as quickly as possible;
she tells him how she and Harry wrote the paper on site.

"In the good old days we could have taken our time, but
the money's very tight. We can't do any more work until
we've raised some more funds, so we had to scramble to get
into press."

"But you're pleased with the work."

"You bet."

"It's going to make you famous, sweetheart. The oldest
murders on the planet. Older than Cain and Abel."

"It's hardly murder. Just one species of hominid killing another for food. The way chimps will kill monkeys, if they get
the chance."

"Still, it helps disprove Raymond Dart's contention that
we're fallen creatures, inherently more violent than our, what
did he call them?"

"I believe it was our anthropoid ancestors. And Dart's theories were disproved a long time ago anyway, by Hiraiwa-
Hasewaga's studies of xenophobic killings and infanticide in
chimpanzees. And by you, Daddy, when you proved that
chimpanzees possess a version of the cd2 engram."

"All higher primates have cd2, but bonobos and gorillas have
social behaviours that suppress it. Bonobos reinforce social co-
hesion with sex; gorillas live in groups dominated by a single
sexually active male. You'll never know if cd2 was expressed in
your ergasters, but they certainly possessed it, because the ancestral species we shared with other primates must have had it
too." Her father's smile is lopsided. "Of course, that won't stop
people speculating. They'll be reprinting Robert Ardrey."

Elspeth smiles too. "That poetaster."

"And the Social Darwinists, who still like to think that violence is all the fault of the male hunting urge, who think that
cd2 is only expressed in males despite all the evidence to the
contrary, they'll be delighted."

"Harry dislikes Social Darwinists as much as you do,
Daddy. He's lining up his counterarguments already."

"Hah! I hope not like ducks in a row."

The remark is pure Teryl. Elspeth remembers that Teryl was in her element at faculty parties, always the centre of a group of mostly male admirers, a cigarette (an expensive imported brand with violet paper and a scarlet filter) held at an elegant angle while she demolished reputations with judicious bon mots. Perhaps, Elspeth thinks, he can't believe that Teryl means him harm because his version of her is closer to him than his own skin, one of the many voices shouting at each other in the noisy cave of his skull.

She says, "There's no evidence that male ergasters did the hunting, as with chimpanzees. It could just as easily have been the females, or males and females together."

Her father hums to himself for a while. At last he says, "Chimpanzees do what they must to survive. Humans choose. That's the essential difference. *Homo ergaster*, now, could they choose? Were they self-conscious?"

He often says *humans* instead of *people* now. As if they're a separate species that he's able to observe dispassionately from his unique perspective.

"We're still arguing about self-consciousness in chimpanzees. We'll never know about fossil hominids."

Matthew blows air through his nose.

"The Gentle People aren't fossils, Daddy. And even if they were exact reconstructions of australopithecines, which they're not, they're in the wrong context."

"That was never the point, Elspeth, and you know it. The point was that producing creatures with traits intermediate between humans and the rest of the primates would yield immensely useful ethical benefits. The ridiculous absolutist idea that humans are special, that they should be venerated because they possess some kind of specious moral worth that distances them from the rest of the animal kingdom, has been able to flourish only because the intermediates between modern humans and the common ancestor we share with chimpanzees and bonobos are all conveniently dead."

He's talking faster and faster, his words slewing together.

"If we'd been able to finish our work and open Pleistocene Park, Elspeth, the Gentle People would have shown up absolutism for what it is: incoherent, illogical, and based upon un-reasoning prejudice. They would have changed public attitudes towards other species, would have demonstrated the insignificance of the racial and cultural differences that have caused so much human suffering. It could still happen, Elspeth, if the hysteria about gengineering recedes. Perhaps humans will realize that the Gentle People aren't monstrous freaks spawned by perverted and misguided science; they'll be treated as individuals with individual worth . . ."

Tears are leaking from his right eye, and he looks away in shame and confusion.

She covers his right hand with hers, presses down against its agitated tremor. She says, "It's all right, Daddy. I know why you're upset. Sergeant Mbau told me a little about what's been happening to the Gentle People. You know that you can talk about it with me."

"I don't think I want to talk about anything right now." Matthew's left hand makes a fist and thumps against the ground. He shudders all over, like a cat that's come in out of the rain, and gives her a funny lopsided grin. The pupil of his left eye is much bigger than that of his right. "Go away, Elspeth," he says. "I think Dr. Dave is coming out, and I don't want you to be here when he does."

Chapter 19

Harmony Boniface's father studied aboriculture at the School of Forestry in Bordeaux, and after returning to the Republic of the Congo worked for the Congolaise Industrielle des Bois, where he developed a fast-growing strain of bemba, a species of hardwood tree native to the swamp-forest. Wood harvested from the plantations of his gengineered bemba became one of the country's most valuable exports, and he was rewarded by promotion to the position of Secretary to the Cabinet for the Ministry of Scientific Research. Three years later, in the aftermath of the Black Flu pandemic, the mercenary army of Sergeant Samuel Nyibizo overthrew the government. Harmony's father was one of several dozen high-ranking civil servants hanged in a public ceremony in the football stadium; unlike most of his colleagues, he refused to sign the preprinted "confession," and was beaten unconscious when he tried to make a speech. Many people remember him with respect and affection, and by evoking those memories and offering a bribe of three bottles of Johnnie Walker Black Label whisky, his son is able to hitch a ride on a tug to what had once been the biggest timber mill in the country, two hundred kilometres upstream of Brazzaville.

The tug's AI navigation system, equipped with three-hundred-and-sixty-degree high-resolution sonar and radar, drives it steadily through the darkness, passing M'Bamou Island at the eastern end of the Malebo Pool and ploughing through the deep, swift currents of the wide gorge beyond. The captain, a gloomy man with deep furrows scored into his cheeks, insists on sharing the whisky with Nick and Harmony and his two-man crew in the hot, noisy bridge. They turn up the volume of a battered radio tuned to a Cameroon station that's playing plangent sub-Saharan pop, drink whisky, and bitch about Obligate. Nick learns that the tug was part of a fleet that before the Black Flu and the civil war had towed rafts of logs to the railhead below Brazzaville. It was good work, the captain says, and well paid; in addition to his first wife, comfortably established in Brazzaville, he had wives in four villages along the river, and planned to buy his own speedboat ("For smuggling," Harmony whispers to Nick). But the railway was wrecked in the civil war, Obligate has shut down most of the forestry industry, and now the tug is running errands instead of doing proper work; the captain expects it to be decommissioned before the end of the year. "We drink to the end of an era," he says mordantly, splashing more whisky into the glasses on the chart table.

One of the crew wakes Nick just after dawn, and he climbs

on deck half-blinded by a headache that pulses to the rhythm of the tug's powerful engines. Harmony Boniface, obscenely amused by Nick's condition, tells him that they're about to dock at the timber mill. Empty, half-collapsed jetties slide past. Elephant grass and bushes have colonized the burnt-out ruins of long, low storage sheds. One of the dockside cranes has toppled into the water. Giant yellow bulldozers which once grappled forest giants are rusting in a long line. The sky is grey with smoke, and there is a taste of burning in the air.

Nick and Harmony eat breakfast in the trim bungalow of the timber mill's manager. Fried bananas, manioc paste, and coffee. The bananas have been cooked in palm oil and taste of burnt sugar and axle grease, and the manioc paste is the usual inedible grey sludge, but the coffee isn't bad and takes the edge off Nick's headache. He drinks several cups loaded with sugar while the manager, a trim, energetic man with a massive tic in one eye, explains that because Obligate wants the vast plantations of bemba and limba and okoume to return to the native state, men formerly employed by the Congolaise Industrielle des Bois are felling and burning several million dollars worth of timber.

"Obligate come to Africa and pretends to want to help us rebuild our lives," the manager says, his left eye twitching, "but in fact its people are neocolonialists. They tell us that they know what is best for our own country. They tell us not to cut down our forests. They tell us not to make plantations of gengineered trees. They tell us it is bad to use the oil we have under our feet. They tell us not to have too many children. But listen: we are not stupid. We were an independent country for more than fifty years. We had many problems, it's true, but before the Black Flu we had peace, a democratic government, and a slow but steady improvement in living standards. And despite what Obligate says, we also worked to conserve our forests, for tourism and for sustainable exploitation."

"They destroy my father's strain of bemba," Harmony Boniface says.

"It's true," the manager says. "Obligate has dismantled what is left of the laboratories of the Congolaise Industrielle des Bois and stolen all the research. They say that we do not need it—that we will make a living by harvesting wild fruit and nuts for their Rainforest brands. They tell highly trained scientists and technicians that they must live like pygmies, but what can you do? This is their country now. Everything in it is theirs. The river is theirs, the forest is theirs, the government is theirs."

His peppery mix of indignation and resignation is very French. He tells Nick that they have been felling and burning the trees for a year; it will take at least another year to clear the plantations. "And for what? It will take centuries for the natural forest to return, because the soil is no longer suitable for it, and meanwhile all this valuable land will grow nothing but kaka. You know what that is?"

"Crappy forest," Nick says. His stomach is cramping from too much coffee.

The manager winks violently. "Exactly."

"I worked on the biodiversity surveys. We saw a lot of kaka around abandoned villages and towns."

The manager says, "Obligate trades our carbon tax for political influence. But we don't need to influence other governments; we need money to rebuild our country."

"He's right," Harmony Boniface says. "Obligate is worse than the tyrants it says it wants to save us from. At least those old tyrants were Africans, but these are white men, and white men, I hope you don't mind me saying this, Nicholas, are the worst of all. They steal our country's wealth, they oppress us, they establish a cult of personality, just like any other tyrant. They do what they want, and no one can stop them. After the Black Flu, it is the same in many poor countries. They cede power to transnats in exchange for investment, and the transnats are happy to do it because they get many benefits from owning a country. They can make their own laws. They have access to high levels of credit and to development loans, and they don't have to pay taxes. Best of all, they have *diplomatic immunity*. I wrote an article about this last year. It was published in *Le Monde*, in France."

Nick says, "And no one in Obligate did anything about it?"

Harmony grins. "Of course not! In fact, publishing that article made me safer, because it raised my profile. It would cause a scandal if I was disappeared by Obligate, because it claims to have re-established a democratic government here. Of course, it is no such thing, it owns the ruling party *and* the opposition, but it would not be good publicity if a reporter was silenced."

The manager puts his arm around Harmony's shoulders, as if posing for a photograph. "He is his father's son," he says, his smile twitching as his left eye spasms. "He will do great good with this story, Monsieur Hyde, and I am proud to be of help. Our plane, it is the best, very well maintained, very reliable. The only problem is the fuel. A few years ago, it would not be a problem, of course. The government had a big share in the oil production. But now there is no more oil, and we are strictly rationed for diesel and aviation fuel, so for extra flights we must purchase fuel on the black market. You can understand that it is a very great expense . . ."

The flight from the timber mill to Liranga costs Nick five hundred American dollars. When the Beechcraft gains altitude, he sees threads of smoke from dozens of pyres rising into the sky, blurring into a general haze that spreads from horizon to horizon. All because, Harmony says, of a few changes made in the genomes of the trees. "It's exactly like burning books," he says, "because they contain an idea you don't like."

The Beechcraft flies high and level over undulating forest cut by winding rivers and swathes of blue-green swamp. The vast landscape, dwindling away in every direction towards the circle of its misty horizon, seems utterly without habitation or history. Innocent of thought, neither good nor evil but simply itself, where a myriad of acts of violence—the blood of a deer torn apart by a leopard, a crowned eagle falling upon a monkey, a crocodile clamping its interlocking teeth around the leg of a bushpig—pass unwitnessed. Two hours out, the plane crosses a loop of the Congo, a broad plain of blood-red water speckled with forested islands and white sandbanks, and drops towards the little airstrip at Liranga.

Liranga is a brand-new frontier settlement built on the ruins of an old fishing town. Muddy streets lined with oil palms and umbrella trees; cinder block bungalows and wattle-and-daub thatched huts; a squat, bunkerlike row of shops, a bank, and an army barracks; a new brick-built church next to the mission hospital; and an airstrip of polymer-sealed dirt, where Harmony Boniface's contact, Xavier Emmanuel, is waiting beside his ancient Renault truck.

After paying their guide his fee, Nick insists on stopping at one of the shops, where he buys two long-sleeved T-shirts and a pair of light running shoes, a straight-bladed machete, a flashlight, binoculars, and a water bottle with an integral micropore filter. Harmony says that he won't need any of these things, that they will spend only a little time in the forest and will be back in Liranga that very night, drinking Primus beer and eating fish soup and bushpig and saka-saka in its best restaurant, but Nick feels better after he has changed into one of the clean T-shirts and put on the running shoes, which he knows from experience are far better than hiking boots for walking in the forest.

An old woman presides over a public phone at the back of the shop. Nick buys a card from her and calls Bridget Nzube, but a mechanical voice tells him that her mobile is unavailable, and when he tries her office, her assistant says that Dr. Nzube hasn't yet turned up for work. Perhaps she's at the university, Nick thinks, working up the DNA from the blood spatters on his belt. He thanks the assistant and hangs up, and the phone promptly rings, like a petulant child demanding attention. The old woman snatches it up, listens for a moment, then hands it back to him.

Captain Badiledi's voice says, "Apart from missing your flight to Brussels, what are you doing in Liranga, Monsieur Hyde?"

Nick slams down the phone, picks up his purchases and walks quickly out of the shop into blinding sunlight and superheated air. He feels like he's been punched in the stomach. On the other side of the deeply gullied road, two soldiers are sharing a cigarette beside a muddy 4×4. One of them looks towards Nick, mirrorshades flashing. Captain Badiledi phoning the commander of the barracks. His picture extruding from a printer. Roadblocks.

Harmony leans against the Renault truck, drinking a can of Coke. He stares at Nick and says, "You look like you have just seen a ghost."

"It's time to go," Nick says.

Xavier Emmanuel puts pedal to metal and aims his old truck at a bone-rattling eighty kilometres per hour down the badly patched two-lane blacktop to Youmba and the Likouala aux Herbes River. Past the remains of the oil-storage facility (a long-tailed hawk perches with regal indifference on the rusting spar of a canted electricity pole), past an abandoned construction site where flowering vines grow over a rusting framework of steel girders, into the deep shade of the forest.

Xavier is a short, bow-legged man with the bombproof serenity of someone who has survived the worst thing in the world. He lost his entire family to the Black Flu, he tells Nick, and nothing else will ever hurt him as much as that. He wears a green army jacket with its sleeves torn off, ragged shorts, and fraying sneakers. An orange beret is perched at a jaunty angle on the clipped white wool of his hair; a generic 9mm automatic, its grip wrapped in duct tape, dangles by a piece of twine from the belt of his shorts. He was a forest guard before the civil war, employed by the Ministry for the Conservation of Water and Forests in the war against elephant poaching. The beret is all that's left of his uniform, but he is still a man of influence in the area, and that's why the men who captured the white devil asked for his advice.

"They didn't know if they had caught some sorcerer's familiar, in which case they were all dead men, or if they had something truly valuable," he tells Nick. "They were too frightened to bring it to me, and too frightened to try and sell it in the market, so I had to go to their camp to see what it was. I confess that I was nervous. I am not superstitious, I was trained at the university in Brazzaville, but this forest is one of the last wild places. No one knows all its secrets. For instance, foreigners believe that a dinosaur species, the last of its kind, lives a couple of hundred kilometres north of this place, at Lake Télé. Japanese television came here to look for it, and the British Broadcasting Corporation, too."

Harmony says scornfully that someone proved from the forest pygmies' descriptions that this mythical beast was probably a folktale memory of rhinoceroses, from the time long ago when the forest was drier and more open, and Xavier shrugs.

"Perhaps that's what the pygmies thought those people wanted to believe," he says. "Certainly, something large lives there. I have seen tracks bigger than anything left by elephants. I have heard strange noises. The foreigners think it is a dinosaur, but who can say what Mokélé-mbembé really is? So when these men said they had caught a ghost, it was possible that they were right. Even when I saw it, I could not tell if it was an animal or a human being. But I knew that it looked like the thing you were looking for, Harmony Boniface, and I went to Liranga and straightaway sent you the picture I had taken."

Nick listens to Xavier's story with less than half his attention. He's leaning at the open window, hot wind parching his face, wondering where Bridget Nzube is. Wondering if she is in jail or being interrogated in some airless, windowless room. Wondering if she is still alive. Perhaps Dan Cooper has already got her out, or perhaps the Kenyan Embassy made a formal protest; right now she could be on a plane, on her way back to Nairobi and her family. But how likely is that, he thinks, and a sick, scalding guilt sweeps through him. He shouldn't have run out of the shop. He shouldn't be in this truck, heading into the swamp-forest on a fool's errand. He should have phoned Dan Cooper; he should have let him know what had happened to Bridget, and why . . .

Xavier explains that the men caught the white devil in the forest to the north just two days ago, two days after the white devils attacked the soldiers and the Witness team. The white devil had been drinking at the edge of a sandbar, and when the men's dugout went past, it ran into the water and tried to attack them. They let off a panicky volley, one shot hit the white devil in the shoulder and knocked it down, and they tangled it in their heavy nets and battered it into unconsciousness before hauling it aboard. When Xavier saw it the next day, he knew that it didn't have long to live. Its shoulder was badly infected, and it had a broken arm and two half-healed gunshot wounds besides. The men wanted to kill and skin it before it died, but Xavier persuaded them that it was worth more alive.

Because he'll go mad if all he can do is think about Bridget, Nick asks what the men had been doing in the forest, and Xavier shrugs and says that they were probably hunting.

"They're poachers," Nick says.

"No, not poachers," Xavier says. "Poachers come across the border, from Gabon and Cameroon and the Central African Republic. Poachers hunt elephants for ivory and the bush-meat trade, but these men hunt for meat to feed their families. Because they are proud, you see. They do not want to live on the food they have to buy from Obligate."

"Still," Nick says, "your friends wanted you to pretend that you had caught the white devil, so that they wouldn't get into trouble."

Xavier Emmanuel shrugs again.

Harmony says, "It is more complicated than that, Nicholas. These are uneducated men, and they are also very traditional. A transaction like this, it's very important. They wouldn't think of doing it themselves. Ordinarily, they would present the white devil to the chief, but the war and the Black Flu have destroyed the tribal system, and there are very few villages with chiefs now. Anyway, Youmba has been settled by Obligate with a mix of refugees from different parts of the country. They don't have anyone in authority except the Obligate agent. So they ask my friend Xavier Emmanuel, who is the Big Man of the village. They trust him to make the deal for them."

"I make two deals out of this animal," Xavier says. "You pay me to take you to it, and I will get a share of the money you will pay the men to take pictures of it."

* * *

They drive past Youmba to an inlet where Xavier has hidden a plank-sided dugout and head up a tributary of the Likouala aux Herbes River towards the camp of the men who caught the white devil. Nick and Harmony Boniface sit cross-legged one in front of the other in the dugout's narrow well, and Xavier perches on a pad of tightly folded cloth at the stern, one arm resting lightly on the tiller of the brand-new reaction motor, which pumps a muscular swell astern as it pushes against the sluggish current. An ancient bolt-action rifle is propped at his feet. Harmony Boniface breaks out his video camera and takes shots of Nick, of the trees that crowd down to the water on either side of the river, long reaches of water hyacinth and water lilies and reeds, floating rafts of vegetation that spin past, a family of black-and-white colobus monkeys that sit at different levels in a sturdy tree laden with pink fruit, a cloud of butterflies that blows across the water, emphatic black swooshes on their orange wings. They are establishing shots, Harmony says with blithe optimism, for the documentary he'll make and sell all over the world.

Nick is tired and irritable and sick with guilt. When Harmony turns around to point the camera at him for the sixth or tenth time, he says, "You'll use that thing up before you really need it."

"It has a terabyte of memory," Harmony says. "I could keep it running a hundred hours and it still would not be used up. Also, it has a satellite uplink. Whenever it gets in range of a mobile-phone network, it squirts watermarked footage straight to my storage site on the Web. *Don't worry.* I'm a good reporter. The best."

The silvery camera is not much bigger than a pack of cigarettes, with a smooth, irregular shape, like a water-smoothed pebble or a cyborg's internal organ, that precisely fits into Harmony's hand. He points it at Xavier Emmanuel and says he'll make him the most famous *pinacier* in Green Congo, and the old man tells him not to be so stupid.

"If you show my face in your movie, I throw you in the

river and make you swim all the way behind us. Or maybe I just leave you here and make the movie myself."

"And how would you make it known to the world? For that you need *Congo Real Time*. You need me."

"I'm doing this because I knew your father, Harmony Boniface, and because you said this white man will pay me well. I am not interested in your funny little newspaper, and I have no desire to be famous—it's very dangerous to be famous in this country."

"He's absolutely right," Nick says.

"Of course he is," Harmony says. "But for you it's too late. You're already famous. And when I sell this to the networks you will be very famous indeed."

"I know," Nick says. He thinks for the fiftieth or hundredth time of Bridget, and his skin prickles.

Harmony aims his little camera at a bird that's standing on a branch of a dead, half-submerged tree and stretching its black wings like a heraldic sunbather. "There, Nicholas, what is that one?"

"A long-tailed cormorant. They're as common here as herons are on the Thames. You must have seen hundreds of them when you were living in your mother's village."

Harmony says, "I didn't pay any attention to the wildlife, Nicholas. I was too busy dreaming of what I would do when I returned to Brazzaville."

Just before her husband's execution, Harmony's mother and her children escaped from Brazzaville and went back to the village on the Congo River where she had been born. They lived there for three years, and Harmony claims to have hated every minute of his exile, but he's been behaving like a kid in a sweetshop ever since they climbed aboard the dugout. Nick wonders if the reporter has dropped a few mikes of something to kick up his mood, or if it's no more than relief that so far the trip has gone exactly as planned. Pretty soon, Nick will have to put a crimp in his day and tell him about Bridget Nzube and the phone call from Captain Badiledi.

The river seems endless and utterly deserted, its black

channel pressed narrowly between trees that crowd down to the edge of the water. It's the middle of the afternoon, and stiflingly hot. Incandescent sunlight shatters into thousands of bright shards on the water. They pass the remains of a village—a line of oil palms, a couple of rotting dugouts on a narrow sandbar, a few huts collapsing under smothering blankets of flowering lianas—and then the river makes a wide bend, and its sluggish stream splits around a tangle of sandbars overgrown with grey reeds. A forested ridge climbs up from the river, and at its crest Nick sees a slim fretwork tower standing sharply against the sky.

Harmony says that it's a microwave mast, part of a network that before the war linked this remote region with the rest of the world. "The oil companies did survey work here. They wanted to extend the Mboukou oilfield. Masts like this carried some civilian traffic, but mostly they were for the convenience of the oil workers."

The reaction motor idles throatily as Xavier Emmanuel steers the dugout between the sandbars. A broad reach of water opens up, choked with the dark green, dinnerplate-sized leaves of water lilies. A big dugout is drawn up in the centre of a long, narrow ridge of white sand that curves beneath the overhang of the forest. Xavier switches off the reaction motor and, as the dugout slides to a halt amongst a thick press of lily pads, stands up, cups his hands to his mouth, and gives a high, piercing, ululating cry. He waits a whole minute, watching the edge of the forest, then calls again.

Harmony says, "Where are they? What's wrong?"

Xavier doesn't reply, but catches at the pistol that dangles from his belt, raises it, and fires into the air. The shockingly loud gunshot is instantly swallowed by the darkness under the trees. A flock of grey parrots takes flight from the tree line, dipping low and screeching to each other as they scatter across the reedy sandbars. The old man sits down, picks up his rifle, and lays it across his lap. Nick feels cold fingers walk up his spine, and reaches into his day pack and finds the hard angular shape of the Glock and pulls it out, all the while watching the trees along the shoreline.

"Something has happened," Harmony says. "They should be here. They should be waiting for us. Something has happened—something bad. I can feel it in the air. I can smell it, really I can."

Xavier looks up at the sky, craning around as he searches its four quarters, looks at the mechanical watch fastened to his left wrist by a strip of plaited grass. He says, "Perhaps they moved up to the ridge after I came here yesterday. They can see for many kilometres from up there."

"They would have seen us on the river," Harmony says. "And if they saw us, they should have come to meet us. But they're not here."

"Their boat is here," Xavier says. He takes up a long-handled paddle with a leaf-shaped blade and starts to drive the dugout towards the shore.

They drop over the side into knee-deep water and haul the dugout onto the sand. Xavier picks up his rifle and says that he will go and find the men, and when Nick insists on coming along, Harmony says that he won't be left behind. They walk in single file into the shade of the trees, along a path that wanders between prop roots and stands of fern. A slough of black mud is partially bridged with slippery logs that have been rolled into it; they scramble up the other side and push through the big, glossy leaves of a clump of phyrniums into a tongue of tall, pale grass, still and silent in the hot sunlight.

A path leads through the grass to a clearing of trampled red earth and a crude shelter built from green bamboo poles and palm leaves, with a blackened fire pit in front of it. Xavier sifts a handful of ashes, straightens, and stalks across the little clearing and picks up a length of stout bamboo that's badly splintered at one end. Xavier sniffs it, tosses it aside.

"They took the white devil," he says.

"Or it got free and killed your friends," Harmony says. The silvery blob of the camera dangles by its yellow strap from his right hand, and he's looking all around in quick, nervy jerks, as if expecting that at any moment something will jump at him out of the shadows under the trees.

Xavier sucks his teeth. "It was very sick, very weak. They

had tied a rope around its body so that it could not move its arms and fastened one end of the rope to this stake. When I saw it, it was lying on its side, its legs drawn up, looking very miserable. There were insects crawling in its wounds. It snapped at me when I took its photograph, but it did not try to do any more than that. No, I think it was too sick to have got free. I think my friends took it up to the ridge. That is where we should go now."

The hot, wet air pressing against every square centimetre of Nick's body, the silent shadows under the trees on either side, the shimmering volumes of air above the tongue of man-high grass, fill him with a primitive dread. He wants to run. He wants to climb into the dugout and fire up the reaction motor and power out of there as fast as possible. He says, "Let's do a proper search. Quarter the area, see if we can find any sign of where they went."

Xavier points at the trees behind the shelter. "The path to the top of the ridge is that way."

"We'll look around here first," Nick says. "I have a bad feeling about your friends."

Harmony finds the body almost immediately. He calls to Nick and Xavier and stands back as they examine it. The slim young man lies on his back in a circle of crushed grass at the edge of the trees, face tilted to the sky. Little black bees crawl busily over his dull eyes, his parted lips, the deep mouths of the wounds on his arms and on his belly.

"You'll find that his head has been smashed in," Nick tells Xavier. He's turning in a slow circle, but there's nothing to see except the trees along at the edge of the tall grass and a few electric blue butterflies tumbling around each other in the shimmering heat haze. "That's what they do: smash in the skull and eat the brains."

Xavier wipes his bloody hands on the front of his sleeveless jacket and looks up at Nick. "It could have been a leopard," he says. "Perhaps that is why the others aren't here."

"You must listen to Nicholas!" Harmony says. "He's seen men killed by white devils before. *He knows what he's talking about!*"

"There are many leopards in this part of the forest," Xavier says, and slowly gets to his feet.

The dead man looks up at the sky, slyly oblivious, with nothing to care about, nothing to fear.

Nick says, "We must be very careful. After they feed, they lie up somewhere close. That's why we were attacked when we came to investigate the massacre. They were resting after their feast, and along came a fresh batch of food. I bet they couldn't believe their luck."

"We should get back to the boat," Harmony says.

"There are two men missing. I will go up to the ridge to look for them," Xavier says, and turns and pushes through the grass towards the crude shelter and the path through the trees that lies beyond.

"We should wait by the boat," Harmony says to Nick, "and if the old man doesn't come back, we should take it and go back down the river."

"We came here to do something," Nick says. "The biggest story of your career, remember?"

"Do you really think that white devils killed this man?"

"Yes."

"And you think they are somewhere close by?"

"Yes. Yes, I do."

Harmony flaps a hand at the bees circling around his head. "So if we stay here, we're sure to die."

"We should stick together," Nick says, and starts through the grass after Xavier Emmanuel.

"You're as crazy as the old man," Harmony says.

The path climbs steeply through the deep green heat beneath the tall trees, but it is dry and easy to follow. Nick twitches the Glock at shadows that are only shadows and tries to move as silently as he can. Harmony makes a lot of noise behind him. "I brought you here to die," the reporter says. He's out of breath, and sweat has darkened the front of his shirt.

"I came because I wanted to. So did you."

"I trusted this crazy old man. That was my mistake. He was a good friend of my father's, and I thought that meant he was also a friend of mine."

They come out of the trees into reddening sunlight at the edge of the scrubby clearing around the microwave mast. It's a slim pencil of white-painted fretwork thirty metres high, partly overgrown with vines that form a kind of tent at its base. The ring of black solar panels around its waist has been badly shot up. A variety of dish aerials point in different directions. A concrete hut stands near its base, its gaping doorway smoke-blackened, its roof collapsed, its walls pockmarked by bullets. Xavier is squatting in front of this little ruin with his rifle laid across his knees, and he stands up as Harmony and Nick walk towards him.

"They aren't here," Harmony says.

"We will wait a little while," Xavier says.

"Your friends are all dead," Harmony says. "The white devils came to free their comrade, and they killed your friends, and they dragged the bodies away and ate them."

"Perhaps," Xavier says, "perhaps not."

"If your friends are alive," Harmony says, "why didn't they take their boat and run away? That's what I'd do! And if they were stupid enough to stay here, why didn't they come when you called? You tell me why, and perhaps I'll think about staying, but otherwise I am going back to the boat. I am going as far away from here as fast as possible."

Xavier consults his watch again, says, "We will wait just a little while," and takes out a crumpled pack of cigarettes from the pocket of his jacket and begins to pick through it.

"We will die if we stay here! Didn't you listen to Nicholas?"

Harmony's voice is screwed high by fear and frustration. He stares at Xavier, trembling from head to foot. Nick thinks for a moment that he is going to attack the old man, but then he swings around and stalks away to the top of a rise beyond the microwave tower.

Nick says, "He's right. I'm sorry to say it, but your friends are dead."

Xavier picks a leaf from one of the skinny vines that criss-cross the cracked clay around the burnt-out hut, wraps it around one end of a crumpled cigarette butt, and sets fire to the other end with a flick of his lighter. He takes in a lungful of smoke and slowly breathes it out and says, "They were good men. They were good hunters. Perhaps one was caught, but the others could have run away into the forest."

"The white devils are very fast," Nick says. "Very quick, and very fierce and fearless."

Xavier draws on his cigarette and shrugs. "Perhaps this time the white devils went away. Things do not always happen the same way."

"In my experience they do," Nick says, thinking of the story that the pilot, Theodore Yssel, told him. The dead bodies of the survey workers all torn up, the white devils chasing his friend through the bush, fearlessly charging at his plane.

Xavier says, "We have guns. If they come for us, we can shoot them."

"The white devils have guns too," Nick says. "They have guns they took from the soldiers that they killed, and probably from your friends too, and they know how to use them. It's a mistake to think of them as animals, Xavier. If we're going to wait, let's do it out on the water. We'll be able to see them coming, if they do come. Harmony will be able to take pictures of them, and we'll be able to make a run for it."

Xavier shakes his head. "We'll wait here," he says.

When Nick walks up to Harmony Boniface, the tall young man says, without looking around, "I don't think Xavier is interested in his friends. He hopes the white devils will attack us. He wants to shoot one, so you will pay him the rest of the money."

"He was right about the view," Nick says. He can see the bend that the river makes, and the forest stretching away on either side, a green blanket punctuated here and there by giant trees that rise above the general canopy.

Harmony says, "What's he doing now?"

Xavier has walked to the other end of the clearing and is looking up at the darkening sky. After a minute, Nick hears the low throb of an engine. Xavier lights a flare with his cigarette and waves it above his head. Red, sweet-smelling smoke drifts across the ridge, and Nick suddenly sees a small black helicopter with a pair of fat floats make a tight turn above the river and skim up the slope of trees towards them.

When the helicopter settles on the high end of the ridge, Nick expects it to disgorge either Teryl Meade and a cadre of Obligate staffers in sackcloth suits or a platoon of soldiers led by Captain Badiledi. Instead, two thugs in brightly coloured shirts and blue jeans jump down, pistols flicking in Nick's direction, followed by four huge, lion-coloured dogs barely restrained by chains held by two skinny men in ragged, many-pocketed jungle-camo trousers and jackets, with well-used carbines slung over their shoulders. One of the thugs strolls towards Nick and Harmony; the other helps down a stupendously overweight black man dressed in a white silk flying jacket over a pink silk shirt, his sharply creased white trousers fastened by a gold-link Versace belt, a riding crop in his hand.

"I don't know," Harmony says, when Nick asks him who these people are. "But I think we are in big trouble."

The thugs pat Nick and Harmony down quickly and expertly, smilingly relieving Nick of Glock, machete, and Emerson folding knife, while Xavier talks in French to the fat man, a pleading note in his voice. The fat man shakes his head, obviously displeased, and makes a short speech, slapping his palm with the riding crop for punctuation. Now Xavier is shaking his head, and the fat man suddenly dances forward and slashes Xavier across the face with his riding crop, slashes him again as the old man drops to his knees with his arms wrapped around his head.

One of the thugs disarms Xavier while the fat man shouts orders to the two men with the dogs, who unclip the leashes of their animals and run after them as they bound away down the trail towards the clearing. The fat man watches them go, hands on saddlebag hips; when they have disappeared into the darkness under the trees, he turns, suddenly all smiles, and struts over to Nick and Harmony. He looks, Nick thinks, like a minor politician daring a brief visit to the front line to gain some much-needed combat credibility.

"I am honoured to meet you," the fat man says to Nick. "It is not often one meets a genuine hero. And this must be Harmony Boniface, the famous journalist."

His shaven scalp shines like oiled teak. Leopardskin implants make narrow parentheses over his ears. Gold flashes on his fingers, in his smile. With his broad face, flat nose and bulging, bloodshot eyes, he looks like a startled bullfrog, but he wears his ugliness without apology, with the ease of someone used to power. He's a type Nick recognizes from his duty in Albania—a fixer, a middleman, a ruthless but fastidious power broker swollen on bribes and fifty percent cuts.

"You seem to think that you know who I am," Nick says, "but I don't know you."

"I am Raphael." The fat man waits a beat, then says, his smile just a shade less wide, "At the moment I suppose I am more famous on the other side of the big river. But with your help, Monsieur Hyde, that will change."

"You seem to have made some kind of arrangement with Xavier, so I guess you know about the white devils."

"I am very angry with Xavier Emmanuel," Raphael says. "Because of him, I have to fly my very expensive helicopter all the way out here. He makes me wait on this miserable river in the middle of the fucking forest instead of telling me at once where his ragged-arsed hunters are keeping their white devil. I wait all fucking day, and now I find it has escaped."

"I brought you Nicholas Hyde," Xavier says, and cringes when Raphael swipes at him again with the riding crop.

"Cretin! What good is he without the white devil? You should have told those hunters to come back with you to Youmba, instead of letting them squat out here in the asshole of the world."

"I did not have an arrangement with you until I came back to Youmba," Xavier says stubbornly. "Besides, there is an Obligate agent there. And soldiers too. They would have taken the white devil. That's why I left it here."

"Yes, and where is it now? I have to spend a day in this mosquito-ridden backwater, waiting for you to come back and tell me where to meet you. And for what? The fucking thing has escaped, so now I personally must waste more time looking for it."

"Its friends came for it," Nick says. "They killed the men who had captured it and made their escape."

"Really? Is this true, Xavier Emmanuel?"

"It's true that one of them is dead," Xavier says. "But he could have been killed by a leopard."

The fat man looks up at the sky and asks theatrically, "Can you believe this cretin? Well, Xavier Emmanuel, perhaps you are lucky. Perhaps the white devils are nearby, digesting the meal they made of their former captors. Perhaps my men find them quickly, so I can go back to my ranch tonight. In which case, perhaps I will find it in my heart to forgive you. Otherwise . . ." He swipes at the old man again.

The thug with steroid-abuse acne and a row of stout thorns grafted to his forehead is squatting on his heels, cleaning his nails with a gravity knife and affecting indifference, obviously used to Raphael's performance. The other man, Nick thinks, is the one to watch; he's serious and alert, with a microphone-headset clamped over his shaven scalp, and he's taken up a position that gives him a good line-of-sight on both Nick and Harmony.

Nick says to Raphael, "I don't think you realize how dangerous—"

"Of course I do! That's why I'm here! That's why I brought the dogs, and my skilled hunters, and a shitload of expensive equipment! Listen, my friend, I deal in danger every day. That's how I make my money. That's why I have this helicopter, my ranch, my beautiful house, my beautiful wives . . . Human beings thrive on danger, because it was once a large part of our lives. We were hunters, and we were hunted, too. We are built for fight and flight, it's in our brains," the fat man says, tapping the side of his head with his riding crop, "and it's in our hearts. If we don't find an outlet for it, our blood chokes up. We get heart attacks. We get brain seizures. We get the diseases of white men."

Nick says, "If you do capture one of the white devils, what will you do with it?"

The fat man smiles and says, "What were *you* planning to do?"

"Take photographs. Bring back the body."

"Show the world what killed your friends."

"Something like that."

Raphael taps his cheek with the riding crop, pretending to think about this. "You are a famous man, Monsieur Hyde. You have an enviable media profile. Perhaps it's only for a little while, but at the moment you can get the attention of the world. Isn't that right, Monsieur Boniface?"

"I hope so," Harmony says.

"I hope so too. Also, Monsieur Hyde, Obligate is scared of you. They pretend that the baby you rescued was infected with some biowar disease. They want to throw you out of the country. I admit that I find that very interesting."

Nick says, "What do you want to do with the white devil?"

"Oh, there's so much. For instance, I have a client who will be very disappointed to learn of the escape of the specimen captured by those poor friends of Xavier Emmanuel. He was greatly looking forward to fighting it barehanded."

"Xavier said that it was badly hurt," Nick says.

"Yes, and my client was going to handicap himself appropriately. He was very keen for the experience, and now I am embarrassed, because I must return and tell him the sad news. But if I could promise him another specimen, I cannot tell you how happy he would be! And there are many more like him. Listen, suppose that I get the white devils, you get your revenge, and Harmony Boniface gets his story?"

Nick thinks about this. He says, "You don't just want the white devils. You also want publicity."

"I already have an excellent client list, of course, but I hope to expand. Something like this should get a lot of interest, don't you think? Monsieur Boniface's little newssheet, with all respect, it isn't much, but it is a genuine newssheet, and he has a certain reputation. And the story, I can guarantee that if you are involved, it will be a grave embarrassment to Obligate."

"You don't like Obligate."

"They try and stop my business, and they confiscate property I legitimately hold in Brazzaville. Before the recent troubles, I was building a beautiful hotel, very modern, very luxurious, on a wonderful site overlooking the cataracts at the western end of the Malebo Pool. When the dictatorship was deposed, I thought, now I can go back and finish my work, make a contribution to the economy of that poor country. Instead, I find that my property has been confiscated! Obligate are thieves, Monsieur Hyde, thieves and liars and hypocrites."

Nick says, "You think that Obligate made these things?"

Raphael puts his riding crop to his lips, then says, "Why is it important who made them?"

The alert thug touches the earpiece of his headset, then steps forward and whispers something in Raphael's ear. The fat man nods, and says to Nick, "I told you that my men are good. In the few minutes we have spent getting to know each other, they have found the body of one of Xavier's friends, and a trail leading west, into the forest. Now, Monsieur Hyde, you must give me your word that you won't cause any trouble."

"I wouldn't dream of it," Nick says.

"That's good, because I have Michel and Adolphe here, and my two hunters, and their dogs, and I don't think you could fight them all, could you? And I also want you to give your word that when the white devils are caught, you will stand in front of them and give an interview with Harmony Boniface."

"That's why I'm here," Nick says, knowing that he's a fool to trust this man, that he will probably be killed when he's no longer of any use, but at that moment not caring very much.

"That's settled, then," Raphael says, and turns to Harmony Boniface. "This will be quite a story for you."

Harmony Boniface has sweated through the front of his shirt. His smile is very wide and his eyes are very frightened, but he says with great conviction, "I hope so."

"It will be. A world exclusive that will make you famous, almost as famous as me. Now, I want to see for myself what these white devils can do. Adolphe, make sure that Xavier Emmanuel doesn't try and run away. I don't want any unpleasantness."

It's growing dark under the trees. The alert thug leads the way. Xavier, handcuffed to the thug with the thorns, Adolphe, is pushed ahead of Nick and Harmony and Raphael. Raphael picks his way down the path with surprising ease, slashing at leaves with his riding crop, ignoring the mosquitoes that have quickly found the group of men.

Nick says, "If Obligate made these things, what are they for? Are they some kind of terror weapon?"

Raphael smiles. He likes this idea. "Yes, why not? A terror weapon against the Loyalists."

"Killer apes. Obligate must be desperate."

"Of course they are desperate. It is obvious. The Loyalists, they are very embarrassing to Obligate. They are doing very well in the north, and Obligate, it does not want to be seen to fight a war. It wants to be seen as friends of Africans so that it can expand its interests. Harmony Boniface," Raphael says, "you must write all this down. This is all good material for your story."

Yes, Nick thinks, but it isn't the truth. Because if Obligate had known about the white devils in the first place, it wouldn't have let Witness near the massacre site. It would have buried the bodies there and then, instead of trying to cover everything up afterwards. He says, "What makes you think that you can find the white devils before Obligate does? I mean, Obligate must know about their habits, how they think, all the rest. And the white devils aren't like ordinary animals. They're smart. I saw them use rifles. I saw them ambush trained soldiers."

"Do not worry about what Obligate knows. All that, I know it, too."

"You have spies."

"Why not?"

"What else do they tell you about the white devils?"

Raphael laughs. "They are my spies, not yours."

They come out into the clearing. The long tongue of tall grass is like a ghostly white pool in the twilight, the green stars of fireflies winking here and there above it. The older of the two hunters is waiting for them by the hut, and shows Raphael the body in the grass, the broken bamboo stake, and the bitten pieces of rope. Raphael insists that Harmony video all this, giving him loud, impatient instructions, telling him not to be afraid, telling him that as long as he does good work, he isn't going to die here. The hunter's dogs watch with black, intelligent eyes. They have heavy leather collars with ten-centimetre spikes, and leather harnesses with little video cameras fastened on top of their heads. Their shoulders and flanks are armoured with warty, armadillo-like plates, and their claws are long and curved and sharp, digging deep into the hard dirt.

Raphael sees Nick looking at them, and says, "You like my dogs?"

"They're pretty serious dogs."

"I design them myself. Their sires were Zimbabwean Ridgebacks. Lion killers. My dogs are even stronger—two of them can bring down an elephant. My men say they get a good scent from the rope. We can also use it to prime the drones. Is it true that you shot and killed a white devil? What gun did you use?"

"A Glock-20. Your man has it, and I wouldn't mind having it back."

"Not much of a gun. You were very lucky, I think, although there's nothing wrong with being lucky." Raphael snaps his fingers, and the alert thug tugs something from his waistband and hands it to him. "This," Raphael says, showing Nick the sleek little handgun, "is made by Heckler and Koch; I just buy a dozen of them. It is gas-powered, fires flechettes clipped from a strip of memory plastic, two hundred a second on full automatic. Adolphe, *s'il vous plaît*."

The thug steps away from Xavier, who starts speaking quickly in French. Nick sees what's about to happen, and says, "Don't—" as Raphael negligently twitches his hand in the old man's direction. The little gun makes a sound like a zipper torn apart, and Xavier is knocked backwards into the long grass.

"Now that," Raphael says, "is what I call a gun."

Nick's pulse is loud in his ears. He says, "You could have let him go. He was too scared to have said anything."

"Forget about the old man. He's not important. Besides, he betrayed you, he sold you out to me. So you should be glad that I got rid of him. Also, he should not have left those poor men here with their prize. If he had taken it downriver, they would still be alive, and we would be on our way home. Forget about him. What's important now is what you can do for me."

Nick takes a breath. He says, "All right. When do we start?"

Calling the man's bluff.

Raphael grins. "I think we should wait until morning, don't you? It will be night soon, and I don't think that even a crazy white man like you would want to hunt white devils in the dark."

Chapter 20

The van is the latest in a long series that in Cody Corbin's mind merges into a kind of tunnel of plastic trim and self-cleaning carpet, air-con chill and the odour of stale cooking and chemical toilets, stretching way back to the Eden of his very first van, consecrated by the blood of his murdered parents and marked by the sign of the avenging angel. This one isn't the best he's ever used—he had to dump the last and find a replacement as quickly as possible after the debacle in

Uganda—but it's by no means the worst. It has six independent axles with infinitely variable gears running off a
computer-controlled flywheel drive that uses liquid petro-
leum gas supplemented by power from solar-cell paintwork.
When fully fuelled, it has a range of fifteen hundred kilometres and a top speed pushing a hundred and ninety k.p.h. on a
good road; on solar power, it can limp along indefinitely at
walking pace. It has a satellite navigation system, a satellite
dish and a shortwave aerial, full climate control that can flush
internal air through military-grade .22 micron filters and carbon dioxide scrubbers at two hundred litres per minute, four
bunks and the big fold-down bed in back, a serviceable
kitchen, a shower and a chemical toilet that needs constant attention and gives off a nasty swamp odour: Cody has never
yet owned one that works properly. Two motorcycles on the
rear racks—the Harley-Davidson hog and a 125cc dirt bike.
Caches in the hollow spaces between the chassis and the car-
peted floor hide four Chinese AK-47s—you can't argue with
a classic design—and twenty spare magazines, an M-23 and
five hundred NATO rounds, two short-shanked Mossbauer
shotguns and a weird fat-barrelled rifle that fires thumb-sized
armour-piercing rocket grenades, an Uzi with a wraparound
stock, a Russian single-shot ground-to-air missile launcher
he bought in a moment of foolishness, flashbang grenades
and shrapnel grenades and three kinds of gas grenade, thin
strips of Semtex explosive and fuse wire and mercury-tilt and
timer and phone-chip detonators, monomolecular diamond
wire and the diamond mesh gloves to handle it, a pack of
blank credit chips and a black-box register, thirty thousand
dollars in new twenty-dollar bills and two hundred gold
Krugerrands. And in a separate compartment that no one but
Cody knows about is his dirty little secret: a bioreactor containing a culture of gengineered yeast that thrives on almost
any kind of organic carbon (Cody always plumbs it into the
toilets of his vans, which is why they never work too well)
and excretes a polymer that simple reduction with nitric acid
turns into Semtex every bit as good as the classic "magic
marble" made by the fabled Explosia factory in the Czech

Republic. Cody shot the gene hacker who sold him the original culture in an attempt to make amends with his conscience, but he still feels a queasy touch of guilt whenever he has to make use of the explosive produced by the poison bugs.

All things considered, Cody thinks, it's a pretty good van; it'll be a damn shame if he has to dump it after this job. He drives at a steady, cautious sixty k.p.h. over the rough road, heading east towards the coast through dry bush, one of the places God put on Earth to remind men, by its absence, of the bounty of His creation. Cody reckons that as long as the van doesn't break down or get stuck in some slough, they'll reach the coast by no later than noon tomorrow. He drives for most of the day, using uppers to stay sharp, drives straight through a couple of brief, fierce thunderstorms, and doesn't stop until the light begins to go from the sky.

Erefaan brews up coffee and microwaves a stack of army rations while Cody folds back the carpet, unscrews a floor panel, and starts pulling out the weaponry that they'll need tomorrow: guns greased and wrapped with spare clips in cauls of black plastic; grenades nested in layers of form-fitting foam rubber like hundred-year-old eggs. Cody strips out and rebuilds the actions of two of the AK-47s. Erefaan checks out the Uzi and one of the Mossbauers, earphones buzzing with the Jo'burg *kwaito* he likes so much, and the boy sulks around in the back until Cody gets on his case, tells him that he can fix up some supper.

After they've eaten, Cody suggests a little target practice. He's still tightly wired by crank and long hours of driving and thinks it'll be a good idea to kick up some, it steadies the nerves. And he wants to see how Rusty handles a gun; it'll help him decide how best to get rid of the boy when the time comes.

Cody has parked the van at the mouth of a narrow, steep-sided draw that cuts through a long bluff that looms above the road. Its flat, sandy floor is littered with big boulders that have cracked off and rolled down the sides. The air is very hot and still. Low grey clouds press down like a headache from horizon to horizon.

"It's like being on the Moon," Erefaan says, looking around. He's still wearing his earphones and has put on a pair of black wraparound shades. While he and Rusty get into a little skeet shooting with the piece-of-shit Russian 9mm automatics, one tossing flat rocks into the air while the other takes shots at them, turn and turn about, Cody stalks along the edge of a wide fan of scree, kicking over likely looking stones. When he hears Erefaan come over to see what he's doing, he says, "There are snakes here. I know it."

"Man, I wish you hadn't told me that. I hate snakes."

"Most people do. I was thinking scorpions, but a snake might be a whole lot better."

"I was wondering when you were going to start talking about how we're going to do this thing."

They walk slowly in the heavy, blood-hot air. Cody kicks over a stone, glances at Erefaan. "Maybe we drive right up to the rangers' post, and when they come out to see who we are, I toss a fat old snake in their faces. Think it would work?"

"I think you need to sleep off those uppers you been munching all day," Erefaan says.

"What were you and Rusty talkin' about this morning?"

"This morning?"

Erefaan trying and failing to sound casual.

"You wandered off while I was establishin' our credentials as a hard-working missionary group. Came back maybe an hour later with Rusty. The two of you all of a sudden like best friends."

"You need to ease up on the kid," Erefaan says. "We've got a tough job ahead of us, and he's still new to this."

"That's not what he told me back in Nairobi. Way he talked, you'd think he was God's newly appointed angel of death."

"Yeah, but it was hard, what you made him do. All I'm saying is ease up on him, let him get his head straight about what he has to do. It won't help any of us if he fucks up."

"He was bitchin' to you about that girl, uh? You know we had to get rid of her, and that's what we did. Or are you takin' his side now?"

"Shit, Cody, it isn't like that. I know Shalynne was nothing but trouble."

"Exactly. And that's why we had to do her."

"That's why we shouldn't have brought her along in the first place."

"We didn't know this sweet little job would come up. Oh my. Look at that." Cody has knocked over a flat red rock as big as a family Bible, exposing a coil of brown, muscular rope. "You leave this to me," he tells Erefaan.

"I intend to," Erefaan says.

"Know what it is?"

"I know it looks about twice as ugly as any of my warders."

"It's a carpet viper. Has a nasty bite to it."

The snake lies in the hollow it's made in the sand, its tongue flicking from side to side as it tastes the air. Still trying to work out what happened to its shelter, alarmed but not yet angry. Cody grins at Erefaan, flexes his fingers. His father taught him how to handle snakes. He knows that a snake will only strike when it absolutely has to, that all things being equal a man can always make up his mind to move before a snake, and that as long as you move before the snake does you'll be okay. He feints with his left hand and pounces with his right, catching the end of the snake's tail. The snake throws a couple of sinuous waves in the sand as it tries to get away, finds itself anchored, and doubles back on itself. Cody lets go when it makes a half-hearted strike, grabs its tail again when it tries again to move on. Playing this game a dozen times, Cody each time gripping the snake higher and higher up the length of its body, until at last it is exhausted and submissive. He gets a good two-handed grip, right hand near its head and left hand on its mid-section, lifts its limp, heavy length and brings its yellow eyes level with his.

"Shit," Erefaan says, his eyes widening behind the black band of his shades.

" 'And God said, Let us make man in our image, after our likeness: and let them have dominion over every creeping thing that creepeth upon the earth,' " Cody says, his face so close to the snake that he can see his reflection, upside down, in the milky drop of venom that hangs from its fangs. He feels the slow pulse of its blood under his thumb where it rests on the top of its skull, the answering pulse in the scars of the old snake bites on his arms, and twists his arm and hand, deftly coiling the snake's loose, heavy length around his forearm. Feeling the muscular strength of its body as it flexes, the weight and power of this reptile, nourished in the dry dust of the desert, becoming one with his own potency.

"I'll let it go now," he says, "and catch it again first thing tomorrow. It, or another just like it."

Down the boulder-littered length of the draw, Rusty calls to them, points at the heavy brow of rimrock that looms above him. There's still some light up there, and the little boy looking down at them is sharply printed against the grey sky. He's eight or nine years old, and quite naked.

Cody pulls his Colt Python in an awkward left-handed grip, aims, and snaps off three quick shots, the noise like thunder between the rock walls. A cloud of dust hangs where the boy was standing. Erefaan says, his voice sounding odd and hollow in the echo of the gunshots, "You gone crazy?"

"Go on up there," Cody says, cold and calm, strength from the snake he holds flowing over him. "Go on up there and check it out."

"And do what? Shoot the kid if he isn't already dead?"

Rusty is walking towards them, not quickly, but not slowly either, the pistol held down by his thigh.

"Well exactly," Cody says. "My left hand ain't so good as my right. I have a feeling I coulda missed him."

He's staring into Erefaan's face, the snake in one hand, the Colt Python in the other. It was his father's favourite gun, hidden with the Krugerrands and the dollar bills in the safe buried in the cellar.

"You certainly scared the piss out of him," Erefaan says. "And if he wasn't hit, he'll be long gone by the time I get up there. Then what you want me to do? Track him to his home and shoot him there, along with anyone else I find?"

"It's an idea," Cody says, keeping his gaze right on Erefaan's face.

"I told you," Rusty says.

"You better keep out of this," Erefaan says, without looking around.

"He didn't have any reason to shoot at the boy," Rusty says.

"He was watching us," Cody says. "He saw you two fooling around with your guns. What else was I supposed to do?"

"Shit," Erefaan says, his face twisting with disgust. "This is fucked up. I'll go see what's what, but when I come back I think you and me better have a talk about this." He spits on the ground, turns on his heel, and starts up the slope.

Cody looks at Rusty. "Just you and me now," he says, speaking out of the immense calm that sings in his head like a piece of glass about to shatter under some immense pressure. "Maybe you can tell me what you and Erefaan were talking about this morning. Erefaan ain't been the same since, and I don't care for it."

"I'm not scared of you," Rusty says, but his hand is clamped so tightly around the plastic grip of the pistol that his whole arm is trembling.

"I don't care for it," Cody says, "because Erefaan seems to have gotten mixed up about what to do and what not to do. So I reckon we should get it into the open."

"You won't like it."

"Try me."

The boy meets Cody's stare, defiance sparking in his eyes. He says, "I told him you like to kill black people. And I was right. You do."

"I don't like to kill *anyone* unless it's strictly necessary," Cody says. He feels as if he's floating somewhere in the calm, singing darkness inside his head, watching and considering with cold detachment while the snake strength that flows through him like God's own judgement gets ready to strike.

Perhaps Rusty sees it, because he raises his pistol, puts it right in Cody's face, and says in a tight, choked voice, "You made me kill Shalynne, you tried to kill that boy, and you'll kill me too, won't you?"

Cody laughs. "You might only have shot that poor little rich girl in the back of her head because I told you to, but it still makes you as much a killer as me. The man you were so set on kidnapping, the scientist from that research centre, what colour was his skin, huh? And that boy, anywhere else he could be a goatherd, but out here? I don't think so. More likely he's workin' for a gang of bandits. Plenty of bandits out here, if you didn't know it."

Rusty is still staring at Cody. "You'll shoot anyone who's black and not care, isn't that right? Just say it. Tell me it's true."

For a moment, Cody thinks of throwing the snake in the boy's face. But then Rusty's gaze wavers, and Cody lets the snake slide from his hand instead; Rusty steps back hastily as it coils over itself and flows away over the sand.

"You save your anger for the job," Cody says.

Rusty tries to give him another hard look, but his anger is gone, and he can't meet Cody's gaze again. He turns away, clumsily shoving the pistol in the waistband of his shorts. Erefaan is coming back down the slope ahead of a cloud of red dust. He sees Cody looking at him and spreads his hands wide.

"Looks like the boy got away," Cody tells Rusty. "Well, we had our fun here. We'll drive on a ways, just in case he comes back with his friends. We don't have the time to get into any kind of argument with a bunch of ragged-assed bandits."

They walk back through the draw towards the van. Cody lets Rusty and Erefaan get ahead of him. Rusty talks a mile a minute, waving his hands around; Erefaan listens, nodding now and then, once glancing back at Cody. Cody feels cold and strong. He needs Rusty to hack the surveillance system, and he needs Erefaan to help him take care of the rangers, but this little dust-up has helped him make up his mind to deal with both of them as soon as they've done their part.

Chapter 21

Nick wakes at dawn, rolls over in the shallow trough he's made in the sand. Michel, the more intelligent and capable of Raphael's two thugs, sits on a camp stool a few metres away, scooping food from a ration carton with his fingers. The other thug, Adolphe, is taking a leak at the edge of the sandbar. Mist hangs in layers above the lily-choked reach of water, turning the trees on the far side into ghosts of themselves. Nick's thin blanket is silvered with dew; the T-shirt he'd folded into a pillow smells musty and clings damply to his skin as he pulls it on. The black helicopter, which Raphael flew down from the ridge yesterday, squats under its shroud of camouflage netting. The two hunters are buckling harnesses over the armoured flanks of their dogs, and Harmony is videoing them.

Breakfast is an army ration pack pulled at random from a plastic crate. Nick gets pineapple curry and a square of starchy rice soaked in a creamy oil that tastes of burnt coconut, a cracker and a slice of rock-hard cheese, a lemon-scented wipe. As he sips industrial-strength coffee from a self-heating carton, Raphael lifts up an edge of the netting draped over the helicopter, ducks under it, and swaggers over, dapper as a movie star in a clean white silk shirt and khaki jodhpurs, smelling strongly of crisp aftershave and carrying in one hand a bag of clear, heat-sealed plastic stuffed with bloody ground meat. He slept last night in a hammock in the helicopter while everyone else camped on the mosquito-infested sandbar and took turns keeping watch. He squats like a sumo wrestler beside Nick and asks him if he's ready for the hunt.

"Absolutely."

Nick slept surprisingly well last night, lulled by a piping chorus of frogs. His spell in the army taught him that when there's nothing else to do, you might as well catch up on your sleep.

"You have a long day ahead of you," Raphael says. "Walking through this forest, it isn't easy, especially for a white man."

"I'm looking forward to it. Really. What about your guys?"

Last night, the two hunters, father and son, retrieved a TV lodged high in a tree; now they sit side by side on the sand, eating their rations and watching the soap that plays endlessly on the TV's only channel. The harnessed dogs sprawl in a companionable tangle at their feet. Adolphe squats nearby, his head bopping to the beat of the music from a recorder plugged into his ears as he strips down and reassembles a rifle. Michel is thumbing red-fletched darts into the fat breech of an air rifle, keeping an eye on Nick.

Raphael says, "My men are experts. You don't need to worry about them."

"That's good, because the white devils are very smart."

Raphael smiles. "You keep saying this. I think because it would hurt your pride to admit that your friends were killed by dumb animals."

"They laid up after the massacre at the oil palm plantation, which is how we came to be ambushed, and they laid up after they killed the two men from the survey team, too. But this time they didn't hang around, even though they'd killed Xavier's friends."

"They had their wounded comrade to think about."

"That's true, and let's hope that slows them down, because from the timing of the various incidents, I estimate that they're capable of making at least twenty kilometres a day through the forest. Maybe more. But I think they moved on because after they killed my friends and the Brazilian soldiers, their bivouac was napalmed, and they don't want to be caught out again. They're fierce, but they're not dumb. They learn quickly."

Raphael smiles, showing half a dozen gold teeth. "Hunting

them—I think it will be as dangerous as hunting men. So it will be a lot of fun. My clients will love it. It'll be a whole new experience, and only Raphael will be able to supply it."

"They're fierce and smart, and they have guns," Nick says. "And they know how to use them."

"It's true they are very smart," Raphael says, tossing the meat-stuffed plastic bag from one hand to the other. "But it is also true that they need to eat. They have a high metabolism. They get hungry very quickly. They need to eat every day, and what they like to eat best is man-flesh. Not only that, but there is a chemical they need, too."

Nick understands. "Because they were gengineered. They were deliberately given a metabolic deficiency."

"They will be needing this chemical very badly now, because they have been without it for a week. And without it they get sick. They die. It is like we need salt. They can smell it from a long distance. Here," Raphael says, and tosses the bag of meat to Nick. "This is what we will use as bait."

The thick, taut plastic gives off a rich, bloody smell when Nick runs a thumb over it.

"The plastic is strong," Raphael says. "It won't break when I drop the packages from the helicopter, but there are thousands of tiny, tiny pores in it, so the white devils will be able to get the scent."

"The meat is salted with the chemical they need?"

"Better than that, the meat is very much like human meat," Raphael says, and laughs when Nick drops the heavy bag and wipes his hands on his thighs. "Do not worry—it is not real human meat. It is from pharm goats, the kind that make human proteins for medicine in their blood. So their blood and meat smell like human blood and meat. It will make the white devils very hungry, and it is laced with taglets—little radio transmitters that start working when they are bathed in stomach acid." Raphael picks up the bag and stands. "I will fly ahead of you, drop clumps of these in a broad band across the forest, and then I will set down somewhere and wait. The white devils may be smart, but, as you can see, Raphael is smarter."

While Raphael's men pack up their gear, Nick goes down to the water's edge and fills his water bottle with the hand pump and filter, then strips off his T-shirt and splashes muddy water on his chest and under his sticky armpits. The mist is boiling away in the growing heat. Mosquitoes whine about his head; despite the little zapper that sizzled and hummed near the ashes of the campfire last night, he has lumpy bites on his eyelids and around the rims of his ears, and more worryingly—because his magic bullet is almost completely effective against malaria but much less so against the plastic disease—he has an all-over itch from blackfly bites.

Harmony Boniface wanders over, squats beside Nick and splashes water on his face. When Nick asks the reporter how it's going, he says, "How it is going, I am stuck in the forest with a bunch of crazy men. And you, Nicholas, are as crazy as them, because you seem to actually like this place. I was awake most of the night, listening to the screeches and the howls and imagining the worst. But every time I looked at you, you were sleeping like a baby."

"Well, I worked in the forest before I joined up with Witness. I guess I'm used to it."

"It's like being trapped in a sweatbox," Harmony says, "with a bad hangover that never goes away."

"Sometimes you have to suffer to get your story."

"It's more than just a story to me," Harmony says. "And after what you told me, more than that to you, I think."

Last night, Nick was able to snatch a few moments alone with Harmony Boniface and told him about Captain Badiledi's mocking phone call and his fears for Bridget Nzube's safety. When Harmony said that it wasn't certain that she was dead, that perhaps Captain Badiledi had merely put a tap on her mobile phone, Nick said, "Why would he do that, unless he knew that she'd found out something about the blood? And if he knew she'd found something, he'd have to silence her. I shouldn't have asked her to do it," he said, and then Michel came over and told them it was time to sleep.

Harmony says now, "Listen, Nicholas, I don't think

Raphael will let us live, so I want to tell you this. When my father was disappeared, but before we knew he was dead, my mother called a family meeting. She said that the thugs who had taken over the country were crazy and scared. She said that we should leave Brazzaville because they might kill all of us, in case we tried to get revenge for my father's death. She is a very strong woman. She won the argument, and we left Brazzaville and went back to her family's village. I hated it, but she was right to do it, because most of the families of government officials who didn't leave, they were wiped out. I had been studying journalism in the university before it was closed, and my mother found a man in the next village, a refugee like us, who had worked for one of the newspapers. She paid him to tutor me. We did not have a computer, or any books—we did not even have paper. I learned mark-up language by watching him write in the dirt. I learned it by heart. Then, when the dictatorship was finished, and Obligate took over the country, my family gave me money to set up *Congo Real Time.* So you see, this is all for my family, and for what happened to my father."

"I'm sorry," Nick says. "I didn't realize—"

"You white men don't understand how strong the family is in Africa. It's the one thing that works, Nicholas. The government, the economy, the education system, everything, it's shit. You can't rely on it. But you can always rely on your family." Harmony glances over his shoulder, then leans closer to Nick and says, "If Raphael does take us across the big river, and we get inside the footprint of the phone network, I'm going to squirt all my footage to my storage site. If we are disappeared, at least the story will get out. Maybe people will even work out that Raphael murdered us."

"I don't think he wants to kill us, Harmony."

"We're fucked, Nicholas. We're still walking around, but we're as dead as Xavier and his friends."

"He needs us alive. We're his validation. It wouldn't be good publicity if we disappeared."

Harmony shrugs. "Do you think we have a chance of finding these things?"

"Raphael's pretty smart, under that swagger and bluster, and those two hunters seem pretty competent. Michel too, I guess. Adolphe . . . it's hard to know about Adolphe; he spends most of his time listening to his music. And Raphael seems to know an awful lot about the white devils. I'm fairly sure that he has some kind of connection with the people who made them."

"No, Nicholas, it is very simple. Raphael lets it be known that he wants to find something, what he will pay for information, and people like Xavier Emmanuel come to him. This isn't the West, with its conspiracies and secret societies and government cover-ups. Trying to stop the truth escaping here, it is like the story of the little Russian boy and the dam."

"I think you mean the Dutch boy and the dike."

"No, this is a true story," Harmony says. "I am talking about something that happened, I think in Tanzania. The Russians built a dam, and the little son of one of the engineers was playing one day and found a stream squirting out from one side—a leak, you know? Of course, he told his father, and his father beat him and said that he mustn't tell such lies, this was a Russian dam, no such thing could happen. And the boy said, yes, it's a Russian dam all right, but it is African water."

"Raphael told me that the white devils had been without a metabolic supplement they need for a week. How could he know something like that if someone who'd helped make the white devils hadn't told him?"

Harmony shrugs.

"I should ask him," Nick says. But when he starts to get to his feet, Harmony puts a hand on his arm and says, "Raphael is enjoying a game with you, teasing you by telling you some things, keeping other things from you. I think he likes his games very much, and it would be dangerous to spoil them."

The helicopter dusts off in a storm of sand, leaving Nick and Harmony Boniface, and the two thugs and the two hunters, to follow the trail left by the white devils. It runs parallel to a stream that snakes into the forest. At first, the four big dogs run quickly and eagerly through the margin of swamp between the stream and the trees, and the men have no trouble following them in Xavier Emmanuel's dugout. Then the swamp narrows and vanishes, the trees crowd in, and the going is harder. The stream threads between dense vegetation and the prop roots of big trees, and the dogs spread out through the undergrowth as they search for the scent trail left by the white devils and are frequently lost from sight.

The forest canopy filters most of the sunlight, and the dim air beneath this high green roof is hot and humid and utterly still. The stream grows shallower and more sluggish. Sometimes it's necessary to get out of the dugout and push it over ridges of white sand on which the small black hulls of oil palm nut kernels are scattered. Nick remembers talking to William Ndinga about the time when the Congo basin was drier and the forest had retreated to the folds of land around the river, and many people lived here, cutting terraced fields into the grasslands, growing oil palms, boiling the nuts for palm oil and leaving the hard kernels everywhere. William Ndinga, dead now, in his Mercedes coffin. Tre and Grant Twentyman dead, Bridget Nzube almost certainly dead . . .

Nick's thoughts keep returning to Bridget as the dugout putters through the hot green shade of the forest; it's like trying not to touch an aching tooth with his tongue. If he'd surrendered to Captain Badiledi, would she have been released? Probably not. Almost certainly not. Besides, she was probably dead. After Badiledi finished questioning her, he would have taken her for what Theodore Yssel had called a helicopter ride. *You won't want to do anything that will piss off Obligate,* the pilot had said. Absolutely goddamn right, Nick thinks. It's right up there with "Always filter your water," "Keep your gun cocked and locked," and "Never get off the boat." Bridget had warned him, too. She'd known that helping him was dangerous and had accepted the risk. But Nick knows there's no absolution in that thought, knows that he has to find some way of living with the fact that if he hadn't asked his friend to analyse the white devil's blood, she would still be alive.

At last, the trail bends away from the stream. While Nick and Harmony help Adolphe drag the dugout from the water, the hunters and Michel take turns looking through a pair of spex that shows pictures transmitted by cameras on the dogs' harnesses. Michel notices that Nick is watching them, and says, "What do you think?"

"I'm impressed."

"I bet you think we hunt with spears and nets."

"The dog-cams are pretty good toys, if you like toys."

Michel lights a small black cheroot. "The dogs and the tagged meat, that's how we'll catch them."

The older of the two hunters, Jean Nkala, says, "We must be careful, Michel. These are not natural animals. They do not belong in the forest, so they are very unpredictable. It is not enough to know about how they were made, because that does not tell you how they will behave in the forest."

"Don't pay attention to this mystical shit," Michel says to Nick, and blows out a stream of smoke. "There's nothing magic about these animals. They can be shot like anything else."

Nick says, "So why hasn't the Congolese Army found them?"

"That's easy. First of all, the army is scared to go into the swamp-forest—the soldiers are more scared of it than you, Harmony Boniface," Michel says, jabbing his cheroot at the reporter, "if such a thing is possible. The army in this country, frankly, it is shit."

"I don't know about that," Nick says. "And the Brazilians are pretty well equipped."

"The ones you were with," Michel says, "they got killed, didn't they?" Looking at Nick very calmly. The air rifle slung over his muscular shoulder. A black automatic shoved down the front of his camouflage pants, its cross-hatched grip denting the broad muscular band of his belly.

"Yes," Nick says, "they were killed. But I survived, and all I had was the Glock you took off me. Which I'd like back, by the way."

"I don't think so."

"The gun is mine, and when it comes to it, I can't be sure that you'll shoot straight."

Michel rolls the cigarillo from one side of his smile to the other. "You're a tough guy. I like that. Adolphe, what are we going to do with this tough guy?"

Adolphe walks over. "He isn't so tough. When his friends were killed, he ran away. And when we are done here," he says, pushing his thumb into Nick's chest, "maybe I'll kill him and take his magic bullet."

Nick feels the man's hatred fizzing like crazy electricity behind that touch and thinks that this isn't so different from the army, when some moron decides to prove just how hard he is and you have to stand up and take it or ever afterwards be bait to anyone and everyone. He says, "Is this before we've made the video piece about the white devils, or after?"

"Maybe I'll cut it out of your chest while you're still alive," Adolphe says. He pushes his face into Nick's, trying to give him a serious stare but failing to bring it off because he's slightly cross-eyed. His breath smells of the cinnamon gum he's mechanically chewing.

Nick says, "Do you know how a magic bullet works?"

"I know how to get one out," Adolphe says. He thumbs Nick's chest again, this time turning his nail in the flesh, and Nick knows that Adolphe will go all the way, that he can't back down, and grabs the man's wrist and twists hard, forcing him down on one knee.

"It isn't implanted in my chest," Nick says, maintaining pressure, feeling as if he's holding down a writhing eel of electric rage, "but under my left armpit, and how it works is very important. Are you listening?"

"Let me go, you fucker."

"I'm telling you something useful," Nick says, wrenching the man's arm when he tries to get up. He's suddenly no longer afraid, but wide awake, feeling as electric and crazy as Adolphe. He says, "I'm telling you something that might save your life. Magic bullets are infinitely programmable antigen factories. *Listen to me.* They boost their hosts' immune systems by producing artificial antibody proteins against specific infective agents. But every magic bullet has to be specifically tailored so that the antibodies it produces won't be attacked by the host's own immune system. Are you following this, Adolphe? If it wasn't tailored, those antibodies would produce a massive inflammatory immune response, and the host would die in a couple of hours. If you took my magic bullet and stuck it inside you, it would poison you."

Adolphe tries to twist away again, teeth bared as he bites down on his pain, and the pistol holstered at his left hip brushes against Nick's leg. Nick sees that Michel sees this, sees too that Michel has taken a sideways step so that he has a clear shot, and he plants a foot in Adolphe's chest, and shoves hard and sends the man sprawling.

The others watch as Adolphe gets up, glaring at Nick as he rubs his wrist. Nick glares back, ready to fight if he has to.

Michel is the first to turn away, clapping his hands and saying loudly, "Let's get on with our business."

Harmony sidles up to Nick and says, "I am impressed, Nicholas. You're a tough guy. But now you will have to kill Adolphe before he kills you. And then Michel will have to kill you."

Nick still feels the jolt of electric anger. It makes everything immediate and vivid and clear. He says, "First we have to survive the white devils. Then I'll worry about Adolphe and Michel."

Chapter 22

Elspeth's father isn't waiting for her on the beach this time. She grounds the dinghy, lifts out the thermos flask, and climbs the narrow flight of steps to his hut, but he isn't there either, although he knew that she was coming across to the island. She phones him, standing in the doorway of the hut as the phone rings and rings, looking at the overturned bed and chair, the clothes, books, food cartons, bedding, and wadded papers strewn over the floor. She's relieved to see that there's no real damage, and no blood, no sign that he has hurt himself; it's no worse than the trashed bedroom of a tantrum-prone teenager. Last night, heartsick and hopeless, she sat at the end of the research station's jetty, listening to the wordless screams and howls coming and going on the warm breeze across the water, listening to the silence afterwards and finding it hard not to imagine the worst, until at last Sergeant Mbau, who'd been using the network of cameras to keep an eye on Matthew, came to tell her that it was over, her father was sleeping.

She redials and listens to the phone ring out again, a needle of anxiety pricking her heart when he doesn't pick up, although he'd seemed cheerful enough when she called him an hour ago, and Sergeant Mbau said that he'd been up and about since dawn. She tells herself that it doesn't mean anything; he's growing more and more absent-minded, and probably switched off his phone by mistake. She could call Sergeant Mbau, ask him if her father is anywhere near one of the cameras, but she's pretty sure she knows where he will be, decides to go look before she asks for help, and sets off towards the steep, stony slope of the island's central ridge.

It's the middle of the morning. Heat and light beat down from a brilliant blue sky. Insects sing in the grey scrub. When Elspeth reaches the top of the ridge, she stands there for several minutes, getting back her breath and revelling in the beautiful view—the brown shapes of corals under the clear water of the lagoon, like the scrambled pieces of a giant jigsaw, the line of white surf along the edge of the outer reef flat, the sea glittering out to chains of fluffy white cumulus at the horizon—before crabbing down a steep path that switchbacks between stony outcrops towards the stand of acacia trees where, as she knows from previous, happier visits, the Gentle People like to doze during the heat of the day.

Her father is sitting in the shade of a big white boulder on the slope above the acacia trees. Wearing the same pair of ragged shorts as yesterday, the same floppy cloth hat. He does not look at her when she sits down beside him and sets the thermos flask between her knees, but he squinches over a little to make room. The ground drops sharply to a little arena of white sand and the grove of wind-stunted acacias where the Gentle People sprawl in sun-speckled shade.

After a little while, Elspeth says, "How are you feeling?"

The Gentle People stir; perhaps it's the sound of her voice; perhaps a warp in the hot breeze has brought her scent to them. Caesar, the oldest and biggest male, scrambles to his feet and slowly comes forward into the sunlight, looking up at Elspeth and Matthew. Behind him, the two young males, Hannibal and Brutus, squat side by side, sort of leaning on long crooked sticks, the butts caught between their callused heels, the splintered tips higher than their heads. Spears, Elspeth realizes. They've made spears. One of the twins, she's pretty sure it's Bianca, sits half-asleep in the sun with her back against a boulder. The other two females are hooting softly somewhere in the shadows under the low, twisted trees.

Elspeth says quietly, "Have I spooked them?"

Matthew doesn't reply.

"I thought they would remember me. Make some kind of fuss."

Cassius ambles out of the other side of the grove and starts picking up and discarding stones. Hannibal and Brutus grow a little agitated, softly stamping the sand, and Bianca stirs and half-opens her eyes, but Caesar seems to be making a point of not looking at Cassius. He squats on his heels and thoughtfully snuffles the air, staring up at Elspeth and her father with soulful intensity. No one could mistake him for a chimpanzee, Elspeth thinks. His long arms and short legs are similarly proportioned, coarse black hair is brushed straight back from his low-browed, large-jawed face, and hair grows thickly on his legs and arms and back, but his chest and abdomen are a muscular shield of bare black skin, and he is taller and more slightly built than any ape, and has a true bipedal gait. On the other hand, to the experienced eye he doesn't look much like what he's supposed to be, the gracile species of early man-ape, *Australopithecus afarensis*. The proportions of his limbs aren't quite right; his brow is a little too high; his dental pattern is too modern, and the enamel of his teeth isn't thick enough.

Cassius is collecting nicely rounded cobbles—good for throwing. Every so often he pauses and stares long and hard at Caesar, who's still making a point of ignoring him. Elspeth says, "When did they become interested in stones, Daddy? And spears, too. That's new, isn't it?"

"They use the spears for surf-fishing. They're not very good—they tend to stab at random, instead of taking aim—but they catch quite a few fish. These days, you know, they're almost self-sufficient."

Matthew's voice is soft and hoarse. There are bruises and fresh, crescent-shaped cuts on his face.

Elspeth says, "I was wondering about Cassius's stones."

"They're about as good at throwing as chimpanzees—not very good at all. They'll never make the cricket team."

"They learnt all this by themselves?"

"I suppose you'd like to think that it's innate. That some kind of stone-throwing gene evolved deep in our past, the progenitor of spears and rifles and nuclear missiles. That they started to use stones as weapons because some kind of innate, hardwired behaviour kicked in. Well, it wasn't anything like that, not at all. It was because of the crabs."

"They threw stones at crabs?"

"They've become very good at finding crabs. They can't swim, of course, but they wade out into the lagoon, feel around with their toes . . . They crunch up the smaller crabs whole, but have to crack the shells and claws of the bigger ones to get at the meat. At first, they just dropped crabs onto rocks. Then they worked out that it was better to drop a rock onto the crab. As for the spears, Brutus and Hannibal started out using branches for support on slippery rocks, discovered that they could use them to hook out crabs from under rocks, went on from there to select straighter branches, strip them of leaves . . . I have it all documented, if you're interested. It is learned behaviour, like food-washing in Satsue Mito's macaques."

"I still remember the film of old Imo squatting in the sea, washing her sweet potatoes, from my comparative anthropology course. She was one smart monkey."

It's all right to talk about this, she thinks, as long as they can talk about it like two sensible scientists, as long as her father doesn't become angry or defensive.

"Bianca worked it out first," Matthew says, "and soon the other females and Hannibal and Brutus were copying her. Caesar and Cassius took longer. At first, they just stole crabs smashed by the others, but eventually they caught on, too. Now they all use stones to hammer crabs open, and they've extended the technique to sea urchins. It's given them access to a whole range of new foods. So you see, weapon-making isn't in their genes, it's just another example of male appropriation of female kitchen culture. I suppose your American colleague would be disappointed, if he knew."

"Are you mad at me because of my work, Daddy? Do you feel that what Harry and I found threatens you somehow?"

Caesar looks up and yawns, showing blunt yellow canines, looks away. Cassius wanders towards the shade of the thorn trees, hugging half a dozen stones to his chest.

"I brought you something," Elspeth says, and opens the thermos flask and shakes out a sparkling cascade of ice and ice-water and a slim bar of Cadbury's Dairy Milk chocolate.

Matthew greedily breaks off a chunk of chocolate and feeds it to his mouth. "Sergeant Mbau doles it out piece by piece. He makes me feel like a lab rat rewarded for good behaviour. Do you want some?"

Elspeth shakes her head. "He cares for you very much."

"He's a good man. A good friend. He hates nothing in the world. Except, perhaps, the goats. I'll accept the soldiers, Elspeth, but you can tell David that I'm not going to move. I can't move, because the People can't move. This is their home now."

Well, he brought it up on his own. Elspeth thinks it's a hopeful sign, and listens as he tells her about the Gentle People's foraging techniques, about how they venture onto the reef flats at low tide to harvest seaweed, sometimes using shells to scrape tasty crusts of red algae from coral boulders. She's heard most of it many times before, but is happy to let him talk because it makes him happy.

"They've learned how to survive here," Elspeth says after a long silence, "but they can't protect themselves from the outside world, and David can't keep the soldiers here forever. At some point, we'll have to think about what to do next."

Matthew wipes a chocolate smear from the corner of his mouth with his forefinger, sticks the finger in his mouth and says around it, "I don't mind the soldiers coming here, because they aren't really necessary. You and David shouldn't take Teryl so seriously, Elspeth. She says something, then she's sorry for it. She says she'll do something, but it doesn't mean she will. David is a good man, but he starts to panic at the first whiff of scandal."

"So does Teryl, with good reason."

Matthew hunches up, chin almost resting on his knees, arms wrapped around his shins. At last he says, "You've always hated Teryl."

Teryl made them move into that cold house and tried to send Elspeth away; it was Teryl's idea to take the contract with the Pleistocene Park project and to move to the Democratic Republic of the Congo to complete the work; it was Teryl who ran from the consequences of that decision, who abandoned Elspeth's father and sold to Obligate the engram research she had stolen from him; it was Teryl who, Elspeth suspects, was responsible for the shattering of her father's mind. Of course she hates Teryl, but that isn't the point.

She says, "This isn't about ancient history. This is about what's happening here and now. It's about what's still between you and Teryl."

"There's nothing between us. The divorce was final, and I got custody of the children, as it were. End of story."

Elspeth feels a twinge of alarm. He's shutting down, turning away from her. Just like yesterday. Caesar stands up, and Hannibal and Brutus stand too, leaning on their long sticks. Are they sensitive to her father's mood, to his tone of voice? What will happen if they think she's attacking him? She says,

"Teryl stole your research, Daddy. She took all the engrams you defined and sold the lot to Obligate."

"It's only money, Elspeth."

"You're right, the money's not important. But it was your work, Daddy, and she stole it and stuck her name on it."

After she discovered what Teryl had done, Elspeth wanted to set a pack of patent lawyers on her, but Matthew would have none of it. He says now what he always says when she raises the subject. "No one owns knowledge, not really. Anyway, what's done is done. It's all in the past. It's best not to think about it."

"I don't think it's over as far as Teryl is concerned. Rightly or wrongly, she blames you for whatever is going on in Green Congo. And she's a power in Obligate—she could hurt you badly if she wanted to."

"I'll take my chances."

"And what about the Gentle People?"

"I'll look after them!"

Not quite a shout, but loud enough to raise echoes.

The Gentle People screech and hoot and stamp their feet, and Cassius charges out from beneath the trees, running with an awkward sailor's roll, and launches a stone towards Caesar with a quick, scooping overhand toss. It falls short, smacking into deep dry sand, but Cassius has already thrown another, and this one bounces off Caesar's muscular, hairy back. The big male whirls around, hair bristling all over his body, and raises his arms and stamps from side to side, a classic primate threat posture, but Cassius stands his ground. Hannibal and Brutus clutch each other, making soft hooting sounds; Bianca has scrambled to her feet and is standing very still, eyes wide; someone begins to scream and thrash branches in the middle of the stand of acacia trees.

Elspeth is utterly unnerved. She's never seen the Gentle People behave like this before.

Caesar suddenly charges at Cassius, who drops the rest of his stones and flees. The others hoot and screech as the two big males chase into the trees. Hannibal and Brutus pound the ground with the butts of their sticks.

Matthew squints at her. One eye open, one eye closed. "They get pissed off sometimes, just like us. They'll be squabbling over a tasty bit of crab, they have their kitchen implements in their hands . . . It doesn't mean anything."

"Cassius is challenging Caesar's dominance," Elspeth says. So this is what Sergeant Mbau and the other rangers think her father is upset about: the Gentle People have started to use aggressive behaviour to determine their social ranking.

Matthew says, "If I thought it meant anything, I would have told you. But it isn't anything, really it isn't. Not much more than horseplay."

Elspeth takes a breath, now or never, and says, "There's something else we have to get into the open. Something we should have talked about a long time ago. Something a lot more important than a bit of horseplay." Her blood is tingling. She says, "Daddy, I know what they really are."

Matthew looks at her, looks away, shrugs.

"Daddy, look at me. I have to tell you this. Look at me, please, this is very important. I know what they really are. I know why Teryl is so scared. I know what she's trying to hide."

Her father still won't look at her, even when she puts a hand on his shoulder. He's hunched into himself, rocking to and fro.

Elspeth says, "I've known ever since the medical tests we had done when I brought you all back."

"The medical tests . . ."

"As soon as the blood tests came through, I knew that the Gentle People weren't what the Pleistocene Park publicity claimed. I knew they weren't derived from chimpanzee ova."

"We tried," Matthew said. "We tried everything, but what we wanted to do turned out to be too difficult. It was Danny's idea, not mine, but God help me, I went along with it . . ."

When it's clear that he isn't going to continue, Elspeth says, "I think that you knew I knew, didn't you? I'm not angry, Daddy. If I was angry, I would never have helped you."

Matthew takes a deep breath. He still won't look at her. "Who else knows?"

"Just David."

"Not Sergeant Mbau?"

"Just me and David. The medical technician who did the blood tests and so on didn't know where the samples came from. I told him that there had been a mix-up. It was more or less the truth."

Matthew is still rocking gently back and forth, his arms wrapped around himself.

"Daddy? Please don't go into a fugue. Not now. We really do have to talk."

But he turns his head when she touches his cheek, and although she spends twenty minutes trying to draw him out, he doesn't say another word.

Elspeth ties up the dinghy at the jetty, gets a Coke from the ancient refrigerator that murmurs gently to itself in the shade of the veranda of the old laboratory building, and walks across the lawn to the picnic table in the shade of a clump of date palms, where Sergeant Mbau is reassembling his ancient M16 rifle.

He looks up when Elspeth's shadow falls across him and says, "I see that you had no luck."

"That depends on what you mean."

Elspeth is tired and frustrated, but is relieved that at least it's out in the open now. That there won't be any more secrets between her and Matthew.

"He won't agree to move," Sergeant Mbau says. "About the Gentle People, he is a very stubborn man."

"How long have they been fighting?"

"For about six months. Was it Cassius and Caesar?"

"Cassius threw stones at Caesar. He has a strong arm, but his aim isn't very good."

"What did your father say?"

"He was with them when I arrived." Elspeth sits in the chair on the other side of the table and pops the tab on her can of Coke. "I think he wanted me to see how they'd changed, or he would have done what he did yesterday, met me on the beach and asked me not to go any farther. But when it came to it, he wouldn't or couldn't talk about what we have to do. He didn't get angry; he just sort of shut down."

Sergeant Mbau slots the bolt into the M16's breech, works it to and fro. Sweat glitters on the bald spot that crowns his head. He says, "I've seen it many times. He turns away from you inside his head. He is ashamed, I think, that his idea has gone so badly wrong."

The Coke is so cold that it makes Elspeth's teeth hurt. She says, "The fighting really isn't a big deal. They're adolescents working out from scratch how to interact with each other, how to deal with the hormones surging through their blood. They squabble and bicker, play dominance games . . ."

"Do you remember," Sergeant Mbau says, "how they used to be? They were always hugging and grooming each other. Kissing. Always touching."

Elspeth smiles. "Making that communal noise that Daddy claims is singing."

"That horrible screeching! I do not find it musical either, yet your father listens to it for hours with a fond smile on his face. But as they grow up, they no longer sing as much as they used to. The patterns your father put in their heads, the way he shaped their minds, it is all changing."

"Poor Daddy. Teryl threatens him, I come here to tell him that he has to face up to the fact that things can't stay as they are, and his children are misbehaving."

"As all children do," Sergeant Mbau says, and thumbs steel bullets into a magazine.

If only it was as simple as that, Elspeth thinks. If only that was the only secret her father wants to hide from the world. She changes the subject, says, "Are you expecting trouble?"

"Christopher and me, we're going to hunt goats. You know that I am not happy unless I kill at least one every day."

Sergeant Mbau's war against the goats is legendary. Most of the people of the local tribes died in the Black Flu pandemic, but their goats survived and multiplied and are now overgrazing the bush and the fringes of the marshes.

Elspeth says, "Those bloody soldiers should be here by now."

"There is a lot of trouble with *shifta*. The military is badly stretched by it. But don't worry, they will be here in a day, two days. Meanwhile, Meji will stay here with you. Also, we can keep watch while we hunt. Christopher is very good at using the camera network. He wears those glasses, so he can see what the cameras see. If anyone comes down the road, we'll spot them three kilometres away."

"If they come down the road."

"We have many cameras, Miss Elspeth," Sergeant Mbau says. He shoves the magazine into his rifle and stands up. "And the soldiers will be here soon, making noise, causing trouble, trampling about everywhere . . ." He sucks air through his teeth, making a sharp noise of disgust.

"Maybe they can help you," Elspeth says, "with the goats."

Oppressive afternoon heat settles over the little station after Sergeant Mbau and Christopher have driven off in the 4×4. Every movement is an effort. Meji Mills sits on a chair in the shade of the veranda of the old laboratory building, where a little breeze comes off the water, listening on a headset radio to a football game in Nairobi. Elspeth locks the door of her little room in the bungalow and dozes for a couple of hours in her hammock, wakes with a headache. She puts on her swimsuit and takes the spear gun from the rack under the locked gun cupboard in the bungalow. The exercise will help her to think, and she's determined that there'll be fish, not goat, on the menu tonight. She walks out of the bungalow into bright sunlight, the spear gun in one hand and her fins in the other, and sees the young man, a stranger in shorts and a T-shirt and orange wraparound shades, crouching amongst the flowering bougainvillea planted at the corner of the bungalow's porch.

It's all quiet, and Rusty is just planting the second of Cody's little packages—a piece of crap with the electronics taped to the outside and no tamper wire; add a blinking red light to indicate it's armed and a counter running back to zero, and you'd have the perfect Hollywood spoof of a suspect device—when this girl comes out of the bungalow. Slim and long-legged in a black one-piece swimsuit, some kind of gun in her hand, looking straight at him.

As Rusty scrambles to his feet, she says, "Who are you? How did you get here?" and then he runs, the shoulder bag banging against his hip as he dodges through a little stand of scruffy palm trees. He hears her call out behind him, but he doesn't look back, runs straight down the raised road that cuts through the strip of mangroves, runs out into brilliant sunlight and swerves off the road, his heart pounding behind his eyes, running hard through the dry brush until a root tangles one of his feet and the ground flips past the sky and slams into the length of his body.

He rolls over at once, very aware of the long, hard shapes in the shoulder bag underneath him. His mouth is full of dust and all his breath has been knocked from him. His pulse is pounding in his head. He reaches into the bag and pulls out the automatic and racks the slide and crouches there, spitting dryly, sweat all over his body, watching the line of dark green mangroves. No one seems to have followed him. The girl probably went to fetch the ranger, he thinks, the one dozing on the veranda of that old shed down by the water. Who by now could be calling his two friends—there's no way of checking, because the virus he inserted into the surveillance system is feeding loops of the last twenty minutes of recorded footage through the cameras.

Rusty stands and walks quickly back towards the van, trying to get his story straight. The girl just walked out of the bungalow, a gun in her hand, and he couldn't get at his own gun because he was holding the piece-of-crap pipe bomb. So he dropped it and ran before she could do anything. What else could he do? He rehearses this excuse as he walks back to the van through the hot, dry scrub. This girl no one knew about walked out of the bungalow and put a gun in his face and told him to stay where he was, but he was too quick for her, he dodged around the side of the bungalow and got away. That's what he'll tell Cody, and then he'll put his own gun right in the *wazunga*'s face, see how he likes it. The one time Rusty was in jail, before his father's lawyers paid his bail, he shared a cell with a made member of a Nairobi street gang who told him there was nothing to it, all you did was walk up behind the guy, put the gun between the two tendons at the back of the skull, and pull the trigger. Angle it up, you take off the top of the guy's head. That's the way he'll do it: the way he did it when he killed Shalynne. He closed his eyes when he pulled the trigger, the rain falling all around and Shalynne saying something softly, hopelessly, and he told her it was okay, it wouldn't hurt. Closed his eyes and squeezed the trigger so hard he bruised his finger. This time he'll keep his eyes open, Rusty thinks, watch Cody's expression change when he tells him to turn around. Maybe make him kneel down, tell him, see, just like Shalynne. After the talk they had, he's pretty sure Erefaan will let him do it, but shit, he'll be the one with the gun, why would Erefaan risk his life to save Cody, even if he wanted to?

He sees the long black shape of the van through the scrub, wonders if maybe he should just wait for Cody to turn his back on him and do it then, but knows he'll lose his nerve if he doesn't do it quickly. Put the gun in the man's face and do it.

"Bullshit," Cody says, after Rusty has said his piece.

"She was about as far from me as you are," Rusty says. "Just a couple of paces. She walked out and pointed her gun at me."

"Bullshit," Cody says again, his mean little eyes glittering under the wide brim of his shapeless black hat. For some reason, he's holding a cardboard box against his chest. "Ain't no one there but those three rangers, and two of them are off in the bush somewhere, which if you remember is why we sent you in. You were supposed to sneak in, plant the stuff, kill the one guy left behind if you had to, sneak back out. Real simple, but what did you do instead?"

"There wasn't *supposed* to be anyone else," Rusty says, "but there she was. With a big fucking gun."

Although, saying it again, he isn't so sure that it was a regular gun; he only got a glimpse.

Cody picks up on his uncertainty. "We took a good look around using their very own surveillance cameras before we slipped that virus into the system. Did you see a girl then? If you did, I'm amazed, because you didn't say a word. How about you, Erefaan? You see her? I was looking over this scudder's shoulder while he hacked the system, and I surely didn't. The one ranger asleep on the job, that was it."

"Ease up, man," Erefaan says. "Whatever happened, the kid is seriously spooked."

"She was there," Rusty says, hating the whine he can hear in his voice. He's sweating hard. Sweat stings his eyes; a tender heat inflames his face. "Maybe she came in the plane. There wasn't supposed to be a plane here, but there it is, at the end of the fucking airstrip. So why not a girl?"

"And where was she when you checked the cameras this morning? Where was she when you checked them an hour ago? She stepped out of thin air? This is bullshit," Cody says, his face so close that Rusty feels specks of his spittle freckle his cheeks. "You fucked up. Fine. We can deal with it. But don't lie to me. I can't abide lies."

"I don't know *where* she was this morning," Rusty says, "but twenty minutes ago she was definitely in the bungalow, and you know there aren't any cameras in there."

"The kid's got a point," Erefaan says. He's leaning against the van, stroking with his thumb the crocodile tooth hanging against his chest, trying to look cool.

"He fucked up," Cody says, without taking his gaze from Rusty's face.

"I did the plane," Rusty says. "I was doing the bungalow when she walked right into me, almost."

"And she had a gun, I already heard you. But you have a gun too. Why didn't you use it?" Cody cocks his head, a little smile on his face. That same little smile he was wearing when Rusty looked around after he shot Shalynne. Cody says, "Don't tell me, she was a little black girl, and the guard, he was black too, and I'm the only one here wants to shoot people of colour."

Rusty's anger surges up, solid and strong and hot and red. He shoves his gun in Cody's face, says, "Let's walk back there, see how real she is."

Cody's expression doesn't change. He says, "You want to shoot me, you should take off the safety first. It's that little button, there by your thumb."

Rusty knows enough not to look down, lets his thumb feel for it, and Cody flips the box and, oh shit, a fat brown snake flies out. Rusty screams and steps back, and Cody takes the pistol from him, just like that.

Cody sticks the automatic in his belt, gives Rusty the full benefit of his stare, and tells the boy to go unstrap the bikes. "We have to get movin'. Those rangers'll be back any minute now."

After Rusty has slouched sulkily around the side of the van, Erefaan says quietly, "Man, you really wanted him to go for it."

"He angers up good, don't he? His problem is, he can't follow through."

Erefaan gives him a cool look. "You want to shoot him, you should have shot him after he fixed the cameras, instead of sending him in there, wait for him to fuck up. Now look at it, both plans are fucked. Plan A, with the explosives, and Plan B, with the snake."

"The snake, you happen to see where it went?" Thinking of the back-up plan he would have used if Rusty hadn't been able to fix the surveillance system: drive up to the rangers, pretend Rusty got bit, and when they go look at him, throw the snake in their faces and draw down on them.

"Went off under the van," Erefaan says. "You want to fetch it out, you're on your own."

"We don't need it now. We'll see if Rusty managed to fix up the plane and go right in, take care of that fucking girl and the one ranger they left behind. Then you wait for the other

two while Rusty and I go over, do what we came to do. Me
with the gun, him with the camera."

"I can handle the camera as well as he can," Erefaan says.

"Yeah, but someone has to stay behind, see to those other
two rangers, and you know it can't be Rusty. You do them
quick, you can have some fun helping me hunt down those
monstrosities."

"Yeah? What about Rusty?"

"Let me worry about him. Meanwhile, I reckon we better
give him a hand with the bikes, before he gets himself a
rupture."

Chapter 23

Jean and Joseph Nkala and their dogs lead the way as the
hunting party follows the trail of the white devils. Low hum-
mocks of dry ground are interlaced with swampy seeps
where smoky clouds of mosquitoes and blackflies twist over
shallow, stagnant pools. Trees stand in every direction like
the close-packed columns of an endless greenhouse. Their
trunks all sizes, from pencil-thin saplings to mature giants
that rise straight up for twenty or thirty metres before split-
ting into dense interlaced crowns of leaf-laden branches.
Lianas sag and dangle like an unravelling net under the leafy
canopy, and some trees are smothered from base to crown by
the intertwined arm-thick cords and glossy green leaves of
strangler vines. Creepers and briars and surface roots tangle
across the ground between the man-high stalagmites of termite mounds, and scrawny bushes and saplings grow everywhere between the trees, the thin screen of their scanty leaves
thickening in every direction like a green fog.

The swamp-forest is not quiet: the sharp whistles and hys-
terical laughter of birds, the constant sizzle of insects. When

something starts up a horrible, heartrending shrieking, Adolphe unslings his assault rifle and says, "Tell me that was an animal."

"Of course it was an animal," Nick says. "A tree hyrax."

"He is right," Michel says. "They usually call at night, but this one—something must have found its nest."

Adolphe notices that Harmony is videoing the exchange, says, "Motherfucker," and halfheartedly cuffs at the reporter. His shirt is dark with sweat from neck to waist, and he sways a little as he tries to get his breath, like a boxer trying to summon his last scraps of energy to go the distance. A drop of sweat hangs from each of the line of black thorns that prick his forehead.

As they walk on, Michel tells Nick, "When it comes to it, I won't let Adolphe kill you. He wants to play with you, take his time, but I will make it quick and clean. One shot, you won't know a thing. Or maybe we have a duel, like in your Western movies. What do you think?"

"I think we have a job to do."

"You need to lighten up," Michel says. "You have this grim, squinty-eyed look, *exactly* like Clint Eastwood. Like you don't like anything you see."

"I made a deal with your boss, Michel. That doesn't mean I have to like him, or the people who work for him. When we're done here, you can come and talk to me if you still have a problem with that."

"Hey, Adolphe," Michel says, "what are we going to do with this tough Englishman?"

Adolphe's sullen expression doesn't change as he looks at Nick and touches a finger to the side of his head. "*Boum!*"

Michel says, "I give you your Glock, we take our positions, we draw and shoot. Or if you don't like that, we can take turns. I even let you go first. Seriously."

"You're a fan of Westerns?"

That's what the Brit troops used to watch, in Albania. Westerns, and movies about the Gulf Wars and Afghanistan. The Finns built a sauna; the Germans played volleyball; the

Brits watched movies and drank alcohol-free lager and black-market whisky, a hundred euros a bottle.

Michel says, "I'm the biggest fan they have. Especially the Italian Westerns. They show it like it should be, you understand?"

"That's why you like Clint Eastwood."

"Clint's pretty good, but the bad guy, Lee Van Cleef," Michel says, sucking in his cheeks and narrowing his eyes, "he's better. He has all the tricks, he never takes any side but his own, and he has no sorrow about anyone he kills."

"I believe Clint shot him in *The Good, The Bad and The Ugly.*"

"Sure, but Van Cleef came back. He kicked all kinds of ass as Sabata. You and me, we redo the end of *The Good, The Bad and the Ugly*, we see who wins out this time."

The two hunters and their dogs set a fast pace. Nick quickly falls into the familiar rhythm of forest walking. Michel keeps up with him, but Adolphe and Harmony are soon trailing behind, ploughing grimly through the hot, heavy air, stumbling over prop roots, snagging their clothes on creepers and briars, splashing flat-footed through leaf-covered sloughs. Every half-hour or so, the hunters stop and wait for the others to catch up, the dogs casting impatiently through the undergrowth around them, and they all drink from their water bottles and set off again.

"You walk well, for a white man," Michel says, after the fifth or sixth water break.

"It was my job," Nick says. "I did long transects through the forest, studying biodiversity. I'd run out six-kilometre-long lines from a Topofil, using satellite fixes to set the end points, then I'd walk back along the line, recording every plant the line intersected. I'd throw random quadrats at five-hundred-metre intervals, too, and count all the plant species in them."

"I once work for something like that," Michel says.

"You did? Across the river?"

"*D'accord*, before the Black Flu and the Dead Zone. It was

where I learn my good English. I was a bodyguard for scientists who collected material in the forests. Many of the forests were already destroyed, you understand. They were logged, or people burnt them down to make farms, but there was still a lot left. The scientists took samples of *everything*. Plants and insects and animals. They even took cores of the dirt and froze them."

"In liquid nitrogen. We did some of that too. If you want to be able to recreate the whole ecology, you don't just need the plants and animals, but all the microbes, too—the fungi and bacteria and whatnot in the ground. Nematodes, for instance—microscopic, very simple wormlike creatures. There are more species of nematode than of all other kinds of animal on Earth."

"They froze the dirt in big flasks, and it went to America."

"Gaia Two," Nick says. "In Arizona. Obligate bought it from the U.S. government three years ago. It has the biggest collection of genetic material on Earth, and Obligate just sits on it. I suppose the point is to stop biotech companies using it."

All this time they are walking around trees, ducking under branches and loops of lianas and creepers, avoiding tripwires of briar and vine, and roots that stick up through the leaf litter like admonitory fingers—breather roots supplying air to the roots that anchor the trees in soil sodden with oxygen-poor water.

"Across the river, you are either very rich or very poor," Michel says, "but at least you are not ruled by crazy people. You can make your own destiny."

"Just like the Westerns."

"Yes, just like them! But here, in this country, the people were almost ruined by the Communists in the last century, until they threw them out. And then Samuel Nyibizo took over and finished off what the Communists started. That's why Obligate could buy the place. They say they want to help the people, but they break the spirits of men, hypnotize them to make them want to live only in cities, to work in factories for very little money. In the last century, white people came here to steal our diamonds and ivory and rubber; in the century before that they took our young men and women for slaves. Now they want our souls."

Michel stops, and Nick stops too, and hears the dogs barking in the distance.

Adolphe puts his hand on his rifle, says, "*Qu'est-ce-que?*"

Michel shakes his head slightly, cupping a hand over the earpiece of his headset. After a moment, he grins and says, "They have found a white devil."

Harmony makes Nick do his speech to the camera twice. "Don't worry about doing it the same. I take the best bits from both, make you into a superstar."

So Nick does it all over again, his gorge rising as he squats next to the white devil's body and tries not to breathe in its stink, tries to ignore the sweat bees and flies crawling over his face as he concentrates on the black lens of Harmony's little camera. He manages to make it to the end, and then stumbles to his feet, steps around the finlike buttress roots of the big tree, and spews half-digested pineapple curry and coffee.

Michel was talking with Raphael on his shortwave radio while Nick said his piece to the camera. Now he comes over and says, "You did good. You kept mentioning Obligate—Raphael will like that."

Nick rinses his mouth with warm water from his canteen, spits it out. "What's the plan? Is Raphael coming to pick up the body?"

He finds that he can look at the white devil now. It's propped in a sitting position between the buttress roots. Harmony is stepping around its splayed legs, taking brief shots from different angles. Its head lolls sideways and its white-filmed eyes stare vacantly at its right hand, which lies limply, palm up, on vivid green moss. Its tongue is a swollen black maggot pushing against the thorns and nails of its teeth. It is very dead, a loose-limbed doll leached of significance.

Michel grins around the cheroot plugged into his mouth

and says, "We need a fresh body. This one, it's been dead at least twelve hours, maybe more. Raphael says it's probably no good, but we'll tag it anyway, come back if we can't get anything else."

With a cold little shock, Nick suddenly understands something. He says, "Raphael wants to clone them."

"A live one will be better," Michel says. "We have a client who very much wants to hunt one. He is willing to pay a lot of money."

"You should have brought him along instead of me."

"He's a crazy man, even crazier than you. He wants to use a bow and arrow; he wants to try and track them by himself. Crazy. No, we do this scientifically, with the dogs and the tagged meat. A female will be best—we harvest the eggs from the ovaries. But a male will be okay too. Raphael has all kinds of hackers working for him. So we get one, the helicopter comes, and we get out of here. We go back across the river, we go home."

"As easy as that, huh? How is the helicopter going to land in the middle of the forest?"

Michel shifts the unlit cheroot from one corner of his mouth to the other. "It doesn't need to land. Don't worry— we've thought of everything."

Adolphe is clowning with the body of the white devil, putting an arm around its shoulders, patting it on top of its head, telling Harmony to take a good picture of him and his new friend. The two hunters squat side by side a little way off, flanked by their dogs, making a show of being unimpressed.

Nick says, "If Raphael manages to make more of these things, Obligate will try and take them from him. And Obligate has an army."

"And we'll be on the other side of the big river. I don't think Obligate will want to start a war."

"I wouldn't be so sure of that."

"I hear you talking with Raphael last night," Michel says. "You tell your story, you tell him how the white devils killed your friends, then you plead with him. But he wouldn't listen, so now you're pleading with me. But listen, do you think I will help you when my boss won't?"

"The difference is that Raphael is crazy, and I don't think you are."

"All you have to do is tell the world about how Obligate made the white devils. You tell the world that Obligate tries to suppress the truth—the lies they told about the massacre. You do what you agree to, and maybe you and that silly reporter get to go home. Maybe Raphael even pays you something for your troubles. What's so hard about that?"

Nick says, "Why I'm here—it isn't about money."

"I understand," Michel says. "You want to kill the white devils because they killed your friends."

"That's not exactly—"

"Maybe we let you kill one. You can fight it. A small one, I think, and perhaps we cripple it first, so it does not kill you straightaway." Michel takes off his baseball cap and uses it to wipe his forehead, sets it square on his head. "Adolphe, unless you're going to fuck him, you leave your friend alone. Let's get going. We find a white devil and Monsieur Hyde can fight it, one on one. We make bets who wins, eh?"

Adolphe pats the cheek of the white devil as he stands up, smiles at Nick. "Maybe we use him as bait," he says. "He'll be better than the goat meat."

The ground begins to rise in a gentle slope and becomes drier. The trees are more widely spaced, and it is possible to see for a hundred yards or more in any direction and to walk freely and easily. Sunlight splashes across cracked clay almost bare of ground cover and deeply gullied by runoff. Then there are no more living trees. They have reached the edge of a necropolis of giant bleached trees whose massive layers of leafless branches are hung with ragged grey sheets and streamers that sway in the slight, hot breeze like a vast abandoned laundry. Bits of dead wood crackle underfoot, and a thin layer of freshly fallen dry white dust coats the crazed clay hardpan. Even the termite mounds that stand amongst the trees look dead; their red clay pinnacles, hard as fired brick and dusted with white ash, are leached and gullied like candles melting into the ground, and tangles of thin black laces are woven through them. Hot light glares on the dead white trees and the white, ashy ground. A faint but pungent smell hangs in the hot, clammy air, a cellar smell of rot and mould.

"They are all the same kind of tree," Harmony says to Nick when they stop for a water break. He turns slowly, taking a wide panoramic shot.

"I've seen this before," Nick says. "These big trees are *Gilbertiodendron dewevrei*. They have deep roots and a symbiotic relationship with a fungus that lives on sugars secreted by the roots. The fungus is very efficient at extracting any nutrients released into the soil from decaying leaves and so on, so other trees can't grow near them. But a biowar fungus escaped or was released from some lab in the aftermath of the Dead Zone, and it displaced the symbiotic fungus, killed the trees, and overgrew them."

"This is nothing," Michel says. "I've seen far worse across the river. There are places there where the forest glows at night. And in the Dead Zone, all the leaves and grasses turned into plastic, and the plastic flooded the ground."

Jean Nkala takes a long pull from his water bottle. His fingers are shaking as he screws the cap back on. Three dogs are tangled around him; his son is walking behind the fourth as it casts about. "This is a place of the dead," he says. "A place of ghosts."

Michel glares at him. "Don't talk such nonsense. Scientists made the things we are hunting, not sorcerers."

They walk on in single file, creeping through the dead, white forest like ants crossing a spill of flour. Nick is at the end of the line, behind Adolphe, who turns now to give him a hard look. Everyone is keyed up, anxious and excited. Fine powder coats Nick's running shoes and whitens his trousers to the knee. A peppery smell like dry spoiled bread is strong in his nose, parches his mouth. It's very quiet: no birdsong, no insects. Mirages shimmer above the baked white ground. Ragged sheets hung from bone-white branches creak and sway, releasing siftings of white dust; it's easy to imagine quick pale things dropping out of this restless drapery onto his back or suddenly scrambling out of the huge, grey-white folds of parchment that are thrown up around the bases of the trees like heaps of flayed elephant hide. Once, Nick is startled by a splash of colour on the white ground ahead of him, but what looks like a bloody hand thrust up from the dusty clay is only some kind of parasitic plant, a cluster of blood-red fleshy flowers on top of a thick pale stem looking just like what all flowers really are—sexual organs. Harmony stops to point his video camera at it, and Adolphe cuffs him and pushes him forward.

Nick plods on, head bowed, sweat dropping from the tip of his nose and his chin. Dust stirs knee-high with every step. The dogs and the hunters draw ahead, the dogs stopping now and then to cast around before setting off again, jiggling motes in the white glare, disappearing between the shrouded trees.

Ten or twenty minutes later, Adolphe shouts, and Nick looks up and sees someone running towards them. His heart trips. The man is running very quickly under the heavy canopy of the dead trees, bent low, jinking this way and that through shimmering layers of hot air. Then Nick realizes that it isn't a man at all, but an animal, a duiker antelope not much bigger than a labrador racing flat out across the bleached ground, dusted white all over, its black eyes rolling as with a graceful leap it twists away from the men. Adolphe unslings his rifle and fires a short, quick burst, shattering dead branches and sending up a great cloud of white dust where the antelope had been a moment before. As if in answer, shots sound in the distance, dull pops muffled between the hot white ground and the sky's blank glare. Michel shades his eyes as he stares into the shimmering glare and speaks urgently into the bead microphone of his headset, asking Jean Nkala over and over to talk to him.

Something else is running towards them out of the layers of

heat haze, a jiggling black dot growing in mass and definition. Adolphe raises his rifle, but Michel steps up to him and knocks it aside as the dot resolves into one of the dogs, coated in white dust from head to tail, a splash of blood vivid on its flank.

Chapter 24

"He came around the corner of the bungalow," Elspeth says into her phone. "He looked at me and took off. I was carrying the spear gun, and I guess he thought it was a rifle."

"Don't go after him, Miss Elspeth," Sergeant Mbau's voice says in her ear. "Stay there with Meji. We come straight back and look for him."

"You didn't see him on the cameras?"

A pause. Then Sergeant Mbau says, "You are standing outside the bungalow?"

"Right in front. Me and Meji."

Who, scared of what she has picked up, is actually standing in the middle of the lawn, half-watching the road through the mangroves, half-watching her. His gaze grabby behind the blue lenses of his sunglasses, travelling over her bare legs, the contours of her hips and her breasts in her swimsuit. He might be a ranger, Elspeth thinks, but he's also a strange man with a gun; she should have put on a wraparound before she left the bungalow.

Sergeant Mbau says, "There may be a problem with the cameras. Christopher says he can see the bungalow, but he cannot see you."

"The boy left something behind, under one of the bushes along the wall of the bungalow. A paper bag, an ordinary shopping bag."

"Walk away, Miss Elspeth. Don't touch it. Don't look into it. Just walk away."

"I already looked. There's a piece of grey plastic pipe, capped at both ends, a battery and some circuitry taped to the side. I—"

"That's a bomb, Miss Elspeth. Probably what they call a telephone bomb, with a detonator connected to a phone chip. They call it up, it fires the detonator and sets off the main charge."

"Meji said it was a bomb, too."

Meji looking straight at her when she mentions his name, the pink tip of his tongue touching his upper lip.

Sergeant Mbau says, "You walk away from there right now, Miss Elspeth. Don't touch it, do you understand? Just walk away."

"I pulled out the battery wires," Elspeth says. "I'm wondering now, what should I do with this thing? I'm standing here with it in my left hand."

There's another pause, then Sergeant Mbau says in her ear, "Put it down very carefully. It is probably full of homemade explosive, and not very stable."

"I could throw it in the water."

"And if it does not go off," Sergeant Mbau says, "one of us will have to retrieve it. Put it down and walk away. There may be other bombs, so I think you should get away from the buildings. I will call your father, Miss Elspeth, and also Mombasa. Meanwhile, I suggest that you walk out to the road and wait for us."

"That's where the boy went."

"Okay. Then ask Meji to take you to a place of safety at once, and wait there until we arrive."

"Right," Elspeth says. She switches off her phone and clips it to the neck of her swimsuit, carefully sets the short length of grey plastic pipe on the grass, and picks up her spear gun.

Meji says, as Elspeth walks towards him, "What does he want us to do?"

Elspeth is filled with nervous energy. She doesn't want to crouch somewhere in the mangroves or the bush in her swimsuit, with this man staring at her tits through his playboy sunglasses. She says, "I'm going over to the island."

"That isn't a good idea," the ranger says, trailing after her as she walks towards the jetty.

"This is all about my father," Elspeth says. "I have to tell him what happened. I have to make him understand that he is in danger."

Hot sun on her bare arms and legs, coarse blades of grass tickling the soles of her feet—she has the airy feeling that anyone could be watching from the shadows under the belt of mangroves that embraces the old marine station.

"He is safe on his island," Meji says. "We should find a safe place, too, I think."

"That boy won't be alone. There must be others out there, and they could have a boat. If you want to do something useful, Meji, go get me a rifle or a pistol. This spear gun is good for fish, but not much else."

"I don't think so," the ranger says. "Sergeant Mbau has the key for the gun cupboard."

"You have a perfectly good rifle, Meji. You could shoot off the lock."

"I cannot damage government property," Meji says, with a nervous smile that shows his protruding front teeth. "Besides, there may be other bombs. We will wait here, Miss Elspeth, for Sergeant Mbau. He will know what to do."

"I tell you what, Meji. You wait here, and tell Sergeant Mbau where I've gone."

Meji doesn't try to stop her when she clambers into the orange inflatable. He stands at the edge of the jetty, watching as she presses the starter button of the Yamaha motor. As it sputters into life, there's a distant thump, like a giant door closing, and a cloud of black smoke rolls into the sky above the mangroves.

Elspeth stands up in the pliant well of the inflatable dinghy, shading her eyes. It has to be her plane, she thinks. The boy or someone else blew up her plane. She hears the roar of overdriven engines coming down the road, and Meji says, "That's the sergeant," but instead of the 4×4, two motorcycles come flying along the track through the belt of mangroves. A big black Harley-Davidson, two men on it, and a smaller, stud-tired dirt bike ridden by the boy that Elspeth surprised. The Harley skids to a halt, ripping a long slide in the manicured lawn, and the white man riding pillion points something at Meji, a stubby black gun sort of wrapped around his forearm. Elspeth hears its harsh bark, sees its stuttering muzzle-flash, sees splinters fly in a ragged line down the planks of the jetty. Meji spins around, his sunglasses flying away, as if to show Elspeth the wet red stain spreading over his tunic, and there's another stutter of gunfire and red strings burst from Meji's torso and he pitches forward and kicks once and lies still.

Elspeth grabs her spear gun, lets herself fall backwards into warm water and scissors away from the jetty, swimming as strongly as she can over white sand and ribbons of green weed. When she comes up for air, she sees across a width of sun-dazzled water that two men are standing at the end of the dock, and takes a deep breath and dives under again, swimming parallel to the shore, her whole body flinching in anticipation. She comes up again by a picket fence of prop roots at the beginning of the belt of mangrove trees, loops an arm around the smooth bend of a root and hangs there chin-deep in the water, her heart hammering and salt water burning in her eyes, thankful that it's high tide.

The jetty is two hundred metres away. Just one man standing at the end now, and the inflatable dinghy is aiming itself towards the island, two men in it. She should have taken it—no, they could have picked her off easily. Stuck her knife in it, then. Easy to think that now she isn't being shot at. She grabs for her phone, can't find it, gets a mouthful of water and spits it out as she pats the neckline of her swimsuit.

The phone is gone.

Think, Elspeth. These men have been sent by Teryl, no doubt about it. Either she paid them or she put the word out to Radical Green terrorists. They've blown up the plane; two of them are on their way to the island; the third—she can't see if it's the boy or not—is walking back down the jetty now, walking past the two bikes leaning on their kickstands. Waiting for Sergeant Mbau and Christopher Githongo to turn up. He knows I'm around somewhere, Elspeth thinks, but the sun is in his eyes, he can't spot me. Lucky, lucky. I don't have a phone, but I have the spear gun, I have (she bends down to check the sheath strapped to her calf) my diving knife.

She moves through the belt of mangrove swamp, planting her bare feet carefully in silky mud, mindful of what might be hiding under the surface of the waist-deep brown water—one wrong step, and the sharp hard tip of a breather root could pry open one of her kneecaps. Mosquitoes find her. As a child, she prided herself that she was never bitten by mosquitoes; now she knows that she's bitten as much as everyone else, she just doesn't react to their bites. It's hot and sticky under the dense canopy of glossy green leaves. The air is thick with the smell of decay. The prop roots are fringed at the water line with seaweed like coarse brown hair. There are barnacles and strings of little black mussels. Yellow crabs skitter away from her as she wades through tide water and sucking mud; she tries not to think of water snakes.

When she reaches dry land at the edge of the mangroves, Elspeth can see the back of the bungalow, the generator shed, and a cluster of oil drums. Beyond the green lawn and the old lab building, the calm silver skin of the lagoon stretches under the high sun towards the white hump of the island. It's barely ten minutes since her plane was blown up and the motorcycle passenger shot Meji Mills. The ranger's body lies on the jetty, but Elspeth can't see if his rifle is lying there too. She crouches amongst stiff green leaves, swamp mud drying on her calves and thighs, tells herself to think. Sergeant Mbau is coming, but she has to find a phone right away so that she can warn him about the third man, and warn her father about the two men in the inflatable. Meji Mills must have had a phone, she'll have to run straight across the lawn to reach his body and she can't see the third man, he might be searching the bungalow or the lab building, he might be waiting for her to show herself . . .

She hefts the spear gun, runs in an awkward half-crouch

past the generator shed and creeps along the side of the bungalow, her entire skin tingling. No one on the veranda, no one on the sun-drenched green slope of the lawn. She's nerving herself to make a run for the jetty when a hard noise cracks across the lagoon, and she sees smoke rising from the northern end of the island—oh shit, where her father has his hut—and sees someone walk out from behind the old laboratory building. A tall man in blue jeans and a denim vest, an assault rifle with a skeletal stock cradled in his arms, walking purposefully across the lawn towards the road that cuts through the mangroves.

She's too far away to shoot at him with the spear gun, but there's something else she can use, lying in the grass near the bungalow. Probably homemade, Sergeant Mbau said, probably unstable.

The big man stops halfway across the lawn, head to one side, listening. Elspeth hears it too: the rangers' 4×4 coming fast along the road beyond the belt of mangroves.

The man unclips something from his belt, a phone. He flips it open, stands there in a hip-cocked pose, and Elspeth realizes what he is going to do just as the 4×4 speeds out into the sunlight and the string of bombs planted in the road goes off, a dull thump and a blossom of red flame and black smoke that flips the 4×4 on its side and sets it on fire. The big man walks forward, firing from the hip, firing short hard bursts into the burning wreck.

Elspeth played a lot of softball with the Americans at the dig. They played most evenings in the bed of the sand river, under floodlights rigged in the trees. It was hard work running in the soft sand, but Elspeth discovered she had a killer instinct for scooping up fly balls and throwing them to the shortstop. She uses those muscles now as she dashes forward and scoops up the length of pipe. The big man turns around just as she throws it as hard as she can at the burning 4×4. He rolls his head to track the pipe as it drops into the burning vehicle. Nothing happens. He turns, smiling, raising his assault rifle, and a ball of flame blasts out and blows him off his feet, blows scalding air over Elspeth. She feels her hair crackle, the skin of her naked arms and legs wither.

The man is down on his belly, beating at his smouldering hair. Elspeth steps amongst burning patches of grass, cocks the spear gun, and points it at him as he rolls over and looks up at her and says, "You nearly set me on fire, girl. What were you thinking?"

He sounds petulant, not frightened at all. His eyes are calm, looking up past the spear gun at her face. He has a South African accent.

Elspeth remembers how the soldiers once dealt with a couple of villagers who thought they could rob the Hominid Gang's camp, says, "I want you to sit up. Sit up and sit on your hands."

And steps back when he scrambles to his feet, hands loose and easy at his sides. He's big, at least thirty centimetres taller than her. He says, "You're no park ranger."

"Perhaps you didn't hear me. I want you down on your knees, right now."

"Yeah?" The man's tongue pokes out his cheek while he considers this; his gaze slides sideways for a moment. Measuring the distance to the assault rifle on the grass. He says, "You want to play a game?"

"Just do it, okay?"

"Or what? You shoot me with that thing? I don't think so." Reaching behind himself, coming out with something, a black automatic pistol, and yelping and dropping it as he goes down on one knee, because Elspeth has shot him in the leg with the spear gun.

The aluminium shaft sticks up from his thigh; blood is darkening the leg of his blue jeans. "You shot me," he says, looking at his leg, looking at her, all the playfulness gone from his voice now, his face tight with pain and amazement.

Elspeth picks up the automatic he dropped, straight-arms it in his face and says, "You stay right where you are, you son of a bitch, and I won't have to do it again."

Chapter 25

Michel is pumped up and exuberant, striding about the sun-drenched glade and talking in rapid French into his headset as he points the camera he took from the harness of one of the dead dogs this way and that. The bodies of the three dogs and two white devils sprawl on a kind of lawn of thousands of black, thumb-sized nubs of fungus that stud the ashy crust. The white devils have been shot in the head and chest at close range and lie on their backs in wide circles of blood-soaked dust like a brace of murdered sunbathers; the dogs are so badly battered and slashed that they seem to have exploded. The packs that Jean and Joseph Nkala carried have been torn open and their contents strewn all over the dusty clearing, but there's no other sign of the two hunters apart from a bloodstained jacket and Jean's broken spex.

Michel points the camera at the bloody heap of one of the dogs and says into the microphone, "Those things really wanted them dead." He cocks his head, listening to something, then says, "Harmony Boniface, Raphael says be sure to get good close-ups of the dogs as well as the white devils. It will be a good advertisement."

Nick is squatting in the shade of a big tree that spreads tiers of thick, bone-white branches high above. He's watching the shadows under the dead trees around the edge of the glade, their leafless branches draped with a thick weave of grey, brittle cords like the webs of monstrous spiders. The hot, still silence of the dead forest seems as deep as an ocean. When Michel walks over to him, he says, "It's time you gave me back my gun."

Michel shrugs. "We will be gone soon. Meanwhile, I promise I look after you."

"Michel, have you asked yourself why they took the bodies of Jean and Joseph, and not the dogs?"

"Maybe they like only the taste of men."

"I think they took the bodies because they hope we'll go looking for them. They're waiting for us right now, probably not very far away. And if we don't come after them, they'll come after us."

"I hope they do," Michel says. "Because then, I shoot them all. Those two ragged-assed locals had a lot of fight in them, but you better believe I have a lot more."

Adolphe is kneeling beside the surviving dog, speaking softly and tenderly to it, rubbing his knuckles over the leathery armour of its flanks. He looks up and says, "The bonus, Michel Aloue. Don't forget the bonus Raphael will pay for a live white devil. Maybe these things are eating now. We can sneak up on them."

"This isn't one of your cowboy-and-Indian movies," Nick says to Michel. "They could be watching us right now, have you thought of that? They could be anywhere under the trees and the fungus. We might never see them until they opened fire, and then it would be too late."

Michel shades his eyes and looks at the trees. "They don't watch," he says. "They attack. That's their nature."

"Raphael told you that, did he? Did he also tell you they have guns? You didn't find Jean and Joseph's rifles, did you?"

"If they want us to find them, we *should* follow them," Adolphe says, standing up. "The dog helps us, we shoot them with the tranquillizer darts."

"They want us to follow them all right," Nick says. "And that's exactly why we should stay here."

"You don't know anything," Adolphe says. "When you saw the white devils, you ran away."

Michel reaches into his pack. "Raphael is right now in the air, heading straight for us. Ten minutes, fifteen at the outside, we are gone, and when we go," Michel says, holding out the Glock to Nick, "you must promise that you give this back to me."

Nick stands up and takes the gun. "Scout's honour."

"Maybe Raphael can drop his sleeping gas," Adolphe says. "Then there is no problem."

"Absolutely," Nick says. "We don't know where these things are, but we can drop gas on them. And of course they'll all be standing in one place, and they'll stay asleep until we find them."

"Maybe the gas doesn't get all of them," Adolphe says, "but we only need to bring back one alive to earn the bonus."

Michel walks over to Adolphe and squats down beside him and lays an arm around his shoulders. "How about this crazy guy?" he says, grinning at Nick. "These things are like the worst kind of ghost, and he wants to chase them."

Adolphe says, "I'm serious, Michel Aloue. You shouldn't make fun of me."

Nick says, "They ambushed Jean and Joseph. They killed them, and they killed three of Raphael's dogs, all in about two minutes." He's worried that Adolphe will do something stupid and draw the white devils down on them. He says, "If you think they're just some kind of animal, you're making a bad mistake."

"But they *are* animals," Adolphe says. "Very fierce, but that's all. We find them and bring them back alive, and we get the bonus."

"All this man thinks about is money," Michel says, giving Adolphe a playful shake. "What do you think, Monsieur Hyde? You want to help Adolphe hunt down the rest of these things?"

"I think we should get out of here as quickly as possible," Nick says. "We've lost two men, we don't know exactly how many are out there, and this isn't a defensible position."

Michel shakes Adolphe again. "You hear the Englishman, Adolphe? He's right. We've done our job. We take these two bodies and we go home. *We forget about the bonus,*" Michel says, thrusting his face close to Adolphe's and locking gazes until the other man looks away. "That's settled, then," Michel says, and stands up. "Harmony Boniface, why are you staring at me? You have your famous documentary to make."

Nick walks over as Harmony starts videoing one of the white devils. It was shot twice in the chest, and the back of its head is blown away. Harmony says, "Did you ever think that whoever made these may have made many more? And maybe they made other kinds of monsters, too."

"I expect Raphael has had the same idea." Nick pushes the Glock into the waistband of his trousers, kneels by the body and probes the mess of one of the ragged chest wounds, feels something hard slide around and digs it out and shows it to Harmony.

"It's a bullet." Harmony's cap of red hair is matted with sweat, and his face is coated with a thin, cracked mask of white dust.

"A flattened bullet. These things have internal body armour, something like Kevlar or spidersilk. The one I killed got up after it took three shots to the chest. They're not just fierce animals. Someone has done some serious gengineering on them. They've been designed."

"Raphael wants to make more of them."

"I think so."

"And what will he do to us, now that he has his bodies and his little documentary?"

"You'll be okay, Harmony. You're a declared opponent of Obligate. You're useful to him. Hell, he might even pay you."

"He is not really the kind of sponsor that *Congo Real Time* prefers. Here," Harmony says, squatting down beside Nick and looking around before pressing something into his palm. "This is the spare memory stick for the camera. All the footage I shot of you is stored on it. I make a copy of it—just in case."

"Just in case," Nick says, closing his fingers over the sliver of plastic. "Absolutely."

He retreats to the shade of the tree, drinks from his water bottle, splashes a little water on his face, and wills himself to stay still. Michel and Adolphe pose with the bodies of the white devils and Harmony videos them and takes filler shots and records ambient sound to lay over close-ups. At last, Nick hears the steady burr of the helicopter. He stands up as the black machine skims the tops of the dead trees, raising clouds of fine white dust as it makes a tight turn and comes back, the beat of its rotors tremendously noisy, a bundle of green netting hanging limply from its belly. Everyone turns away and hunches down as dust blows out in a circle, and the dog breaks free and Adolphe chases after it, smashing through the web of fungus between two trees. Nick sees the grainy red flare of a muzzle flash somewhere deep in blowing clouds of dust, and throws himself flat. The helicopter rears up, dragging the net out of reach, and he has a sudden sick feeling of *déjà vu*.

Michel is kneeling beside the body of one of the white devils, looking up through the swirls of blowing dust and shouting into the microphone of his headset. Nick stands up and pulls the Glock from his waistband and runs towards Michel, throwing himself flat again when another burst of gunfire crackles from somewhere under the dead trees, crawling the rest of the way on elbows and knees, rubbery nubs snagging his shirt and trousers, dry dust blowing into his nose and eyes. "Tell him to come back," he says, shouting to be heard over the roar of the helicopter, which has risen a hundred metres above the crown of the big tree. "Harmony and I will load the bodies! You lay down suppressing fire!"

"I'm not leaving without Adolphe," Michel says.

"He's already dead!"

"He's my little brother," Michel says, and turns away and speaks into his headset, pressing his hand over the earpiece as he listens to Raphael's reply, then sprinting towards the trees. Nick looks up at the helicopter again, realizes that he can't contact it without Michel's headset, yells at Harmony to stay where she is, and chases after the big man.

A dense briar patch of brittle ropes is strung everywhere between the trees. There are stiff curtains and convoluted labial folds and tall stands of black whips, all looming out of thick billows of dust. Nick loses sight of Michel, then hears a burst of gunfire and turns towards it, leading with the Glock, his hand sweating on its polycarbonate grip as he ducks under a rigid brown sheet as dry as scorched paper. Michel is looking at something lying at the foot of a tree. It's Adolphe, blood all over his face and his throat and his shirt, runnels of blood running bright red through white dust, dust settling on top of the blood as it creeps around his legs, the smell of blood and the peppery smell of the dust thick in the air. Something crashes through a thicket of grey briars and Nick turns, the Glock extended, sees Harmony's cap of red hair as the reporter ducks under a tangle of fungal cords, the little video camera held up by his shoulder. Drops of sweat leave dark lines as they run down his dust-covered face.

Michel is pointing his black automatic at a heavily draped clump of trees. "It went in there," he says. He takes a deep breath, lets it out. "It was on top of Adolphe. It saw me and ran. I think maybe I hit it, but the motherfucker was as fast as a cockroach."

"This is a bad place," Harmony says. "We should get back to the helicopter."

"These motherfuckers are mine," Michel says. His head moving from left to right, right to left, as he scans the frayed latticework of fungus looped between dry white trunks, the sheets hung from dry white branches.

"It's a classic fire-and-fall-back ploy," Nick says. His mouth is very dry. "They draw us in, then they ambush us."

"Let them try," Michel says, and empties the automatic into the trees. Dead wood splinters; sheets shiver and shatter and drop. Michel lets the empty clip fall to the ground, slams in a fresh one.

"They'll be waiting for us farther in," Nick says. "Tell Raphael to drop down and pick us up. We can get out before they come back."

Harmony says, "I'm taking Adolphe's gun," and as he pulls the assault rifle from the dead man's lax fingers something child-sized drops onto him from above and buries its face in his neck. He turns under the weight of the thing, a burst from the assault rifle ripping into the trunk of the tree, ripping into the ground in a wide arc that nearly reaches Nick and Michel. Harmony drops the rifle and batters at the white devil's head with his fists, but it twists sideways and its spike-filled mouth closes around his wrist like a trap.

Nick sees his shot and fires. The thing's head snaps back, a spray of blood and bloody fragments dashes across the white tree trunk, and Harmony pitches forward under the dead weight. Nick scoops up Adolphe's rifle and sprays what's left of the clip into the trees, screaming as he fires, screaming until the clip runs out. He drops the rifle and kicks the body of the white devil out of the way and hauls up Harmony Boniface in a firefighter's lift. The reporter's head lolls, his eyes half-closed. His shirt is drenched in blood; blood drips from his mangled hand.

Michel follows Nick towards the clearing, carrying the body of his brother and shouting into his microphone, telling Raphael that the white devils are dead, that they're coming in, shouting to Nick, "He wants us to load the bodies first!"

"Fuck that!"

Shots pop in the near distance: the white devils are closing in on them. Michel lays Adolphe on the ground and reaches into the pocket of his olive-drab jacket, takes out a dark plastic oblong the size of a packet of cigarettes, pulls the pin with his teeth, and tosses it in a hard, flat arc into the trees. A dull thump, a sudden blink of orange amongst the white tree trunks and folds of fungus, a rolling cloud of dust and papery fragments. "Fuckers!" Michel yells, and throws another grenade.

The noise of the helicopter is right overhead now. The limp bundle of the net drops towards them out of swirling dust. Michel rolls Adolphe's body into it, helps Nick settle Harmony. The reporter's skin is clammy, his pulse thready. Nick pulls off his T-shirt and rips it in half, uses one half as a tourniquet around Harmony's wrist, presses the other into the gaping wound in his neck. Harmony opens his eyes and says, "Don't let those things kill me."

Nick puts his head next to Harmony's, says, "Absolutely not."

The cloth packing Harmony's neck wound is bright red and sopping wet. He coughs a little spray of blood, says, "I lost my camera."

A fire has taken hold amongst the trees, burning fiercely inside a rolling shroud of black smoke. Michel suddenly drops the white devil he has been dragging towards the net and runs, shouting into the microphone of his headset, telling Raphael to get going *right now*, diving inside the tangle of the net as the helicopter jerks upwards. Plastic mesh flexes under Nick's feet; it's like trying to stand in a hammock. He falls to knees and hands, shoulder to shoulder with Michel. Looking down through green mesh as the cage swings off the ground, its taut teardrop bob tightening against him as he sees white devils—two, three, five of them—race out of a billow of black smoke. Coming so very fast, one jumping high and grabbing hold of the bottom of the net and swinging up like an acrobat, clinging with hands and feet as the net rises between the bare crooked branches of two trees. Nick snatches his hand away as a lipless mouth crammed with nails and spikes rips at the mesh. The white devil's fierce, close-set black eyes glare at him; it breathes a vile stink into his face. Then Michel reaches over calmly and presses the muzzle of his automatic against its forehead. The white devil's head snaps back with the shot, and its clawed fingers relax, but Nick manages to grab its skinny wrist as the net swings through smoke and dust and the spidery crowns of the dead trees, rising higher under the helicopter's roar into the hot sunlight.

Chapter 26

The Gentle People's song is a ragged chorus that peters out, starts up again uncertainly, fails voice by voice by voice. The brief scrap between Cassius and Caesar has unsettled them, and they are foraging only within the immediate area around the acacia trees, stripping back the bark of the dead tree for grubs, poking through dry grass for grasshoppers, venturing a little way up the slope to pick bright red fruit from a big clump of prickly pear. Caesar restlessly patrols the edges of the group, cuffing anyone who wanders too far from the rest. There's a lot of anxious hugging and grooming, smooching, and perfunctory genital contacts.

On the other side of the island, Cassius sprawls on one of the branches of the big salvadora tree, staring out to sea. Planning his next move or consumed by shame or unable to comprehend the reason for his exile: it's impossible to say.

Matthew Faber keeps an eye on them all as he goes about his chores in the hot, bright whip of the onshore wind. Replenishing the salt licks with the amino-acid supplement required by the Gentle People's tweaked metabolisms. Checking and cleaning the lenses of the network of little cameras. Collecting dung for analysis. Running the filter pump to top up his water reservoir.

He's bone tired, a feeble old man with a head full of tangled string, resolutely not thinking about Elspeth and Teryl—the only advantage of his split mind is that he *can* not think of the white rhinoceros while turning boiling water to gold. He takes a siesta in the hammock strung between two of the palms outside his hut and reads a little and falls asleep while Mrs. Clennam interrogates Little Dorrit about Mr. Panck's intentions, and is woken by his phone, the mesh of the ham-

mock biting into his bare skin and sunlight flashing through
the notched palm leaves above, so befuddled by sleep that
he's no one in particular, dismissing the phone's bright trill
by reflex.

Sergeant Mbau's voice buzzes in his ear, telling him that
they may have a little trouble on the way. "Nothing to worry
about, Matthew, but you should keep a lookout, I think."

A sudden sharpening, like turning the focusing screw of a
microscope and seeing a whole hidden world swim into
sight.

"What am I looking for?"

Matthew Faber swings his legs over the side of the hammock (the woven edge cutting into his thighs, the BookMan
falling face down on the threadbare grass) and places his feet
in his sandals. He feels a clear, sharp vigilance, almost every
part of him integrated into a single core for the first time
since . . . when? He can't remember. Since the accident, certainly. Only his dark half remains separate, lurking just out of
sight like a shark patrolling the deep water beyond the reef's
drop-off.

"I don't know yet." Sergeant Mbau sounds a little breathless. There's a lot of background noise—a vehicle driving at
high speed over rough ground. "Miss Elspeth disturbed an intruder, and the camera system isn't working. That's all I
know."

"Elspeth saw someone? Who was it? Is she all right?"

Matthew steps inside the hut and with his right hand lifts
up the spear that has leaned beside the door, waiting for this
very moment with the obdurate patience of the inanimate,
while his left eye focuses on the menu of his spex. A line of
virtual icons scrolls down, and he tries and fails to bring up
views from random cameras, every one giving the same error
message.

"My cameras aren't working either," he says, but Sergeant
Mbau doesn't reply. The local phone net has died. Across
the lagoon, beyond the ribbon of mangrove swamp, a column of black smoke leans into the sky. He feels a sharp spur
of adrenalin, there's a brief dark blink, and he's walking

with brisk purpose along the path past his shower and toilet, using the spear to help him climb to the top of the outcrop. He tries to shake off the feeling that someone is standing right behind him, and shades his eyes to get a better view of the shore.

The orange inflatable is accelerating away from the jetty. He watches as it draws a white wake across the sunlit mirror of the lagoon, watches it slow, drift sideways, as someone stands up in it. He waves, thinking that it must be Sergeant Mbau or perhaps Elspeth, and there's a flash and something small and dark screams through the air towards the island, and a hundred metres away his hut vanishes in a flash of fire. A solid blast of hot air knocks him flat on his ass; coral chips and pieces of wood rain down all around him.

The dinghy is picking up speed, making a long, wide turn around the point of the island, where water creams over the reef flats, and he can feel his dark half rising like a shark closing on a shoal of fish, but he won't have it, not again. Focusing on the world with his newfound clarity, he sets the butt of his spear firmly on the ground and uses it to climb to his feet, then sets off past the burning ruin of the hut towards the top of the island's ridge.

He tries to phone Elspeth as he gimps up the steep path, but the local net is still out of action. He switches the phone to *memo*: he'll leave a message and hide it somewhere, just in case. He says, "I just wanted to tell you that I think it might be Danny Lovegrave. Those devils, I mean. He was sick when I left, I don't know if he's still alive, but do you remember how he was always pushing things to extremes? I know my memory isn't all it should be, there are gaps, but I remember very clearly he said once that if you can eliminate violence in self-aware minds, maybe you can go the other way. Anyway, I thought—"

He stops: he can hear a distant popping beyond the ridge of the island. Gunshots.

"I thought you should know." He wants to tell Elspeth more, to tell her everything, but he can't get the words out, and says instead, "I love you, darling. Please don't think badly of me."

More gunshots, and an eerie noise rising, half a dozen voices keening on the same note. It's the Gentle People, but he's never heard them make any sound like that before. It freezes his heart. He feels a ghostly expansion as every hair on his skin tries to stand away from every other. Then his dark half surges through every part of him, and he drops the phone and starts to run up the long, dry slope, heedless, head-long, howling.

Get it done, Rusty thinks, all the way across the mirror-bright stretch of water to the island. Get it done as soon as they're out of sight of Erefaan. Get it done because this man will kill you when he's finished here. Trying and failing to nerve himself up while Cody drives the inflatable dinghy at full throttle across the lagoon, its blunt nose tipped up, its motor digging a wide white wake. Cody sitting in the stern with his arm draped casually over the tiller, barechested in brown-and-white–camo trousers tucked into the black combat boots that last night he spent two hours spit-polishing to a mirror finish, his head freshly shaven, his hard blue eyes hidden behind mirrorshades, his unfeasibly large handgun holstered on his left hip, the biggest combat knife Rusty has ever seen in a sheath on his right. At his feet are two plastic jerrycans of gasoline mixed with palm oil to make a crude kind of na-palm, an assault rifle, and a black plastic tube. Cody looks every centimetre the Radical Green warrior—fierce, commit-ted, invincible—and all Rusty has is the video camera and a piece-of-shit 9mm automatic.

Cody cuts back on the throttle and, as the inflatable begins to drift, its motor throatily idling, stands and picks up the plastic tube. He flips down a cap at the front, unfolds and locks a pistol grip at the back, flips up a square sight, and Rusty sees that, Christ, it's a shoulder rocket, and throws himself into the well of the inflatable as Cody squints through the sight and fires without warning. Flame flares out the back of the tube and the rocket trails white smoke as it draws a perfect straight line above the lagoon and smacks into a ridge above the island's palm-lined beach. The hard noise of the explosion echoes out across the water as stuff tumbles out of an expanding cloud of smoke, some of it striking through the fronds of the palm trees that line the beach, some of it splashing into the sea.

Rusty is so astonished that only now does he realize that he missed an easy shot when Cody was busy aiming, but shit, who would try to shoot a man armed with a *rocket*?

"That'll give him something to think about," Cody says, and sits down and throttles up the motor again.

Rusty grabs for the nylon cord looped inside the inflatable's fat rim as it makes a hard, fast turn, heading around the point of the island. He has to shout above the roar of the motor to ask who Cody is talking about.

"The scudder who made the things we're goin' to kill. Remember?"

"Sure." The mad old scientist and his monsters. Rusty hardly cares about them any more.

Cody's mouth is set in a grim line. "Get your shit in order, boy. This is serious work."

The thunder of waves breaking in a white line at the crest of the outer reef flat is much louder beyond the point. This side of the island slopes steeply down to the sea. Dabs of white water mark the flat tops of coral micro-atolls. Cody steers into a channel floored with white sand. Colourful fish flick away on either side of the inflatable as he drives it towards a notch in the shore of big, tumbled boulders, a spring dripping amongst green-slimed rocks and a steep path leading up the slope.

There's another moment when Cody steps out of the inflatable into knee-deep water, holding the assault rifle with its weird stock above his head and his back turned to Rusty, showing the big tattoo of a muscular angel holding down with one foot the big snake he's spearing. *Do it now.* Rusty pulls the automatic from his belt, says, "Hey, Cody . . ."

Cody looks around, a weird grin crimping his mouth, and says, "Leave the shooting to me. You're here to make a movie for our client, show the good work we're about to do here."

As he wades away, Rusty has to hurry after him, holding the video camera at his shoulder so it isn't splashed by salt water. When they have clambered onto the shore, Cody catches hold of Rusty's elbow and says that they need to say a prayer, and that's what they do, kneeling side by side on a flat-topped boulder, Cody asking God to help him deal swift mercy to the things that mock His glorious creation, standing up as Rusty mumbles *amen*, striding away up the steep path.

Do him now, Rusty thinks, but Cody moves like a mountain goat; he's already a good way off, too far for a sure shot, so Rusty picks up the video camera and, the sun burning at his back, follows him up the path between dead-looking bushes that clutch with wiry roots at friable white coral. This isn't at all like the times Rusty went into action with his friends, everyone quiet on the way in because they were all feeling the same sick jangling funk, but drawing strength from a shared sense of purpose. What Rusty feels now, trudging up the steep path in the full glare and heat of the sun, Cody getting farther and farther ahead, is a deep, dismal sense that things have gone very badly wrong. Cody is as crazy as a snake, it's as simple as that. He draws his strength from his craziness, and he's so strong that he pulls people along with him, but he never lets them get close. People aren't people to Cody; they're things to be used and discarded. Fuck it, Rusty thinks—he should have shot the man when he was getting out of the boat, not said anything but just done it, put the gun to the back of his head and blown his brains into the water for the reef fish to feed on. Told him afterwards, How do you like it in Hell, motherfucker?

Cody has stopped on a patch of stony ground in the shade of a big, sprawling tree, the assault rifle slung on one shoulder, his arms folded as he stares down the path and waits for Rusty to catch up. Rusty's gut twists—suppose the man can read his mind? But when Rusty reaches him, out of breath and drenched in sweat, all Cody says is, "Listen."

Rusty hears it: a strange screeching sustained by several voices, blown to them on the hot wind. He remembers that old play he studied at school. An island with a wizard and a

monster and the wizard's beautiful daughter—that must be
who the girl is, he thinks, the girl who walked out onto the
porch of the bungalow slim and imperious and beautiful in
her swimsuit, so cool when she looked at him and asked him
what he was doing there. He'll kill Cody and save her father,
and she'll fall into his arms.

A stone bounces off the rocky slope; Rusty looks up as another strikes a tree branch, knocking a drift of leaves into the
air. Cody is running up the path towards a dark little figure silhouetted against the blue sky. He dodges a badly aimed stone,
shouts, "Get a good picture of this!" and unslings his assault
rifle and fires a quick hard burst that kicks dust along the crest
of the ridge. The figure drops from sight and Cody chases after it, whooping with glee. Sick with fear and disgust, Rusty
remembers the kid in the draw, and thinks, Fuck it.

Just like that. Fuck it. Cody will probably come looking
for him after he's killed the monsters and the wizard, but
Rusty doesn't care. He doesn't want to be part of the man's
craziness any more, wants nothing more than to get away. He
walks around the big tree and finds a narrow path that kinks
sharply past an outcrop of white boulders. And there's a man
coming towards him, a skinny white-haired old guy, naked
except for a pair of shorts and a pair of chunky spex, using
some kind of staff as he gimps up the slope. The wizard.

Rusty walks towards him, the video camera dangling from
his wrist by its strap, and the man stops and points his staff
at him.

"It's okay," Rusty says. "It's okay, I'm not going to hurt
you," and sees that there's blood all around the old man's
mouth, blood dribbling down his chin. His jaw is moving, it
looks like he's chewing on his tongue, and behind the lenses
of his spex his eyes are wide and wild, white showing all
around the irises.

"Wait," Rusty says, but with a little jinking prance the man
rushes forward and slashes at him with the staff. Rusty steps
back because, Christ, there's a knife lashed to the end—it
isn't a staff at all, it's a crude kind of spear. Seeing this bright
and clear as he dodges another swipe, and then the edge of

the path crumbles and his left foot twists and gives way as the old guy whips the spear back. The tip of the knife slices Rusty's chest and belly as he sits down flat, his left leg folded awkwardly beneath him, the sharp burning slash hurting less than his twisted ankle until he puts a hand to it and feels hot, sticky blood soaking through his T-shirt.

The old guy dances in, pulls Rusty's gun from the belt of his combat trousers, and dances back, his face working as it tries out and rejects half a dozen different expressions, his mouth still chewing, spraying blood and spittle as he makes a kind of furious fizzing noise.

"You cut me," Rusty says. "I was going to help you and you cut me." Looking at his bloody hand, full of amazement and disbelief. He wants to lift up the blood-soaked T-shirt but doesn't dare. He can feel the edge of the cut under the slashed cloth. It doesn't seem too deep, but it's bleeding hard and hurts horribly. He presses his palm across the lower part, scared that if he tries to get up his guts will spill out. The old man's hand is shaking, but he has a good grip on the automatic and he's pointing it right at Rusty's head. The pupils of his stary eyes are growing and shrinking independently of each other.

Rusty says, "Dr. Faber? That's who you are, right?"

Getting the man's attention now. He squints at Rusty and says, "You came in the boat."

His voice is wet and rasping.

"Yes, sir, that's right, I did."

"You blew up my home."

"No, that was this other guy. Cody Corbin. A white man, an American. You saw him?"

"You came in the boat."

"Listen to me, okay? Cody is crazy; he came here to kill you. I know where the boat is. I can get you away."

Get them both away. Where? Somewhere in the mangroves, hide out until Cody gives up and goes away. Maybe the girl has called for help, she can bandage his wound while he tells her how he rescued her father.

The old man turns to squint up the steep slope. Rusty hears the faint pop-pop-pop of gunshots, spaced, deliberate. Cody doing the Good Lord's work up there, killing devils. He says, "That's the guy I was telling you about. Hey! Dr. Faber, please, you have to listen to me. We have to get away before he comes to find you."

But the old man is moving away up the path, and Rusty sees someone running very fast down the slope ahead of a cloud of dust. A child, Rusty thinks, and then realizes that it's one of the things they came here to kill, not a child at all but some kind of woman, a small, naked, hairy woman with flat, large-nippled breasts and a face like an ape's. The old man spreads his arms wide, the staff in one hand and Rusty's automatic in the other, and the ape-woman flings herself at him, wrapping her long arms around his neck and her legs around his waist, exactly like a frightened child, nuzzling the old man's neck and making a high keening noise as he looks up at the slope and points the gun at, oh shit, Cody. Who is crabbing down the slope towards them, one hand holding his assault rifle, the other grabbing at bunches of dry grass as stones slide out from beneath his boots.

Rusty starts to get up, pressing his bloody T-shirt over the burning gash in his belly. Blood spills over the waistband of his trousers, his ankle stabs fire up his shin and gives way again, and he's down on his knees, shouting at the old man to shoot Cody. "He's the crazy man I told you about. Shoot him! Shoot him now!"

The old man drops his staff and sets down the hairy ape-woman (she promptly flings her arms around his hips) and extends the automatic in Cody's direction and starts firing. He fires as steadily as punctuation, the muzzle of the gun jerking high with each shot, and Cody keeps coming, grinning under his mirrorshades, not flinching at all as the old man fires until the automatic clicks dry. Eighteen shots, every one of them a miss, or no, Rusty thinks, they were blanks. Cody knew what he was thinking and gave him a gun loaded with blanks. And now Cody pulls his Colt Python from its holster and fires once, a chest shot that knocks the old man off the path, so quickly dead he doesn't even have time for a last breath.

The ape-woman screams, high and shrill, scampers off a few metres down the path and then creeps back, making a kind of soft hooting noise under her breath as she reaches out to the old man's body, touching his mouth, his cheek. Tears swell in her brown, human eyes, spill down her cheeks, catch in the black fur on either side of her wide mouth. She doesn't look up as Cody comes down the rest of the way and steps onto the path. He glances at the ape-woman, then looks down at Rusty, and says, "You're a grave disappointment to me, boy."

Rusty says, "Wait," but Cody brings up the Colt Python, and something as big as a car slams into Rusty's chest, and he's on his back looking up at the sky . . .

Cody shoots the boy, pow, right in the chest, and Rusty is knocked onto his back and tries and fails to take a ragged breath, his eyes rolled back in his head. Cody's pretty sure the boy's gone, but shoots him in the head just to make sure, shoots him again through what's left of one eye. There's a coppery taste in his mouth that reminds him of the time when the demon came in, the Snoopy demon with eyes like burning coals that his father at last exorcized. It's back, or something like it. Maybe it came in through the snake, insinuating itself through that flow of smooth cold strength. He takes a breath all the way down to the bottom of his lungs, lets it go, and feels a bracing calm roll over him.

Rusty's more-or-less headless corpse is splayed on bloody dirt like the aftermath of some dreadful heathen sacrifice. Cody frees the strap of the video camera from the boy's limp wrist, wipes blood from its lens with his thumb, and turns it on the atrocity, which is cradling its maker's head in a vile parody of love and making an annoying keening noise. It takes just a few moments to sight the Colt Python alongside the camera: one clean shot in the atrocity's head, another just to make sure. Nothing to it, Cody thinks, he doesn't need the boy after all. He circles the two bodies, pointing the video camera at creation and creator united in death, at the rich red delta of their blood running together, soaking into the white dust. A ringing in his head—no, it's his phone.

Cody unhooks it and presses the *yes* button, and a girl's voice says in his ear, "Who am I speaking with?"

"Maybe you'd like to tell me who *I'm* speaking with."

"I have your friend," the girl says. "I shot him with a spear gun. Right now he's trying to bandage his leg."

There's a trembling defiance in her voice that makes Cody believe her. "You shot Erefaan? Well, ma'am, you can keep him."

"I'll be waiting here for you. With some soldiers who'll be here any minute."

"Even if they're coming by helicopter, I reckon I still have plenty of time," Cody says, and switches off the phone and walks on down the path towards the inflatable. He has to get the jerrycans of napalm mix up to where he left the bodies, and then he'll have to come back for the atrocity that nearly got away, but like he told the girl, there's plenty of time to get the job done.

Part Two
THINK BETTER

Chapter **27**

The day after the video clip of Nicholas Hyde and the corpse of the white devil is released onto the Web, Teryl Meade is summoned to Freddy Layne's office suite in the Hilton Hotel for what he calls a friendly little situation update.

"We'll just talk this through, figure out what kind of fix you've got yourself in," he says on the phone, and Teryl, well aware of the hard edge Freddy Layne hides behind his affable good ol' boy act, pays a king's ransom to ensure that her personal lawyer is on the next flight from New York to Brazzaville.

The Hilton is a twelve-storey glass and steel tower block built on Brazzaville's riverfront fifteen years ago, during the minor economic boom fuelled by development of the Mboukou oilfield. Obligate Green Congo commandeered and refurbished it after the civil war, and Freddy Layne, CEO and principal shareholder, has bagged the penthouse suite as a temporary base of operations while waiting for the completion of his high-tech, low-impact mansion. One of the Hilton's elevators is permanently reserved for Freddy Layne's use and is screened off from the rest of the lobby by the solid concrete wedges of anti-blast barriers. Two Brazilian soldiers check the IDs of Teryl and her lawyer, and they must pass through a scanning frame and allow the soldiers to run the snouts of bio-agent sniffers over them before they're allowed to ride up to the twelfth floor, where another pair of soldiers recheck their IDs, and a secretary ushers them into the penthouse.

The big reception room is a stuffy greenhouse with hummingbirds and butterflies flying free and peahens pecking around luxuriant stands of bamboos, aroids, ferns, and castor

oil plants set in a floor of white gravel. Window-walls give
views over Brazzaville in one direction and across twenty-
four kilometres of water in the other, to the shore of the
Democratic Republic of the Congo and the high-rises of Kinshasa, glittering like little knives in the late afternoon sunlight. Right now, Teryl thinks, Nicholas Hyde is busily
plotting with his new ally somewhere in Kinshasa, but as far
as she's concerned, he might as well be on the Moon. The stiflingly hot, steamy air is thick with the smell of growing
things. Teryl's lawyer, Sherman Cates, is already wilting inside his raw linen suit, loosening the knot of his silk tie as the
secretary, a muscular ex-Navy SEAL stuffed into a pale yellow suit cut from a lumpily woven natural fibre, leads them
through the mini-jungle to a kind of glade at the far side,
where in the deep green, undersea shade of tree ferns and palmettos Freddy Layne and his executive officer, Evangeline
Wisdom, sit amongst cushions on a huge Persian rug laid
over silver sand.

Freddy Layne is an eightysomething baby-boomer with
the bloom and vitality of a man half his age. He wears only a
sarong and his famous soul-casket, a multifaceted, teardrop-
shaped crystal with a core of flickering green neon hung on a
red string around his neck and nestling in his vigorous grey
chest hair. Innumerable bouts of cosmetic surgery, his white,
perfect smile, California tan, and swept-back wave of blond
hair give him the look of a bland, computer-designed composite of half a dozen movie stars. He was a hippy and a session musician in the nineteen-sixties, a record producer in the
seventies, and a movie producer in the eighties and nineties,
was almost bankrupted after he diversified into dotcoms at
the beginning of the century, and made his current fortune by
catching the wave of Gaian capitalism before almost everyone else. He's had more religious conversions than most people have had marriages, and currently belongs to a libertarian
Jainist sect that believes in personal immortality through the
application of technology and in the eternal existence of the
material world. He affects an amiable, avuncular air that
Teryl finds intensely patronizing, and when he offers his

guests refreshments from the samples of forthcoming Rainforest products scattered on the rug, she takes out her cigarillos and innocently asks if she can smoke, and is gratified to
see him flinch.

"They're blended from herbs one hundred percent natural
to the forest," she says, "but if you'd rather I didn't . . ."

"We have to think of the butterflies and bees," Freddy
Layne says, "not to mention the poor little hummingbirds.
We can't have them hacking up their lungs from the effects
of secondary smoke as they flit from flower to flower, can
we?" He's twinkling at Sherman Cates now, pulling the tab
from a cardboard carton shaped and printed to resemble a
section of bamboo. "Do try this, Mr. Cates. There's a type of
hollow liana growing in the deep forest that provides natural
refreshment to the natives when they go walkabout. Our laboratories here in Obligate Green Congo—perhaps I should
say Professor Meade's laboratories—have used that liana-
water as a basis for this soft drink. It's chock-full of minerals
and vitamins and amino acids, comes in three different
flavours. This one, I believe, is mango-guava, very lightly
carbonated, exceptionally tasty."

"I didn't bring Sherman all the way here to act as a product
tester," Teryl says.

Freddy Layne awards her a dazzling smile. He seems to
have about a hundred snowy white teeth, all exactly the same
size. "That's my girl. Always fearlessly direct, absolutely no
bullshit. Qualities necessary in a scientist, of course, and
don't think I don't appreciate that. But forgive me, Teryl,
sometimes that attitude can give the impression that you're
not proud of what we're doing here." He turns his smile on
Sherman Cates. "Know why we gave our enterprise the name
'Obligate'? In the biological sense, obligate means being
able to exist under only one set of environmental conditions.
As a species, humans are obligate—absolutely dependent—
on the biosphere of good old planet Earth: if we destroy her
ecosystems, we sentence ourselves to death. That's why we
do everything we can to spread the word about the wonderful
diversity of our planet, including marketing products derived

from plant species unique to threatened ecosystems. It in-
creases environmental awareness and feeds back funds into
local communities through sustainable use of local products.
And besides, this liana-water is tasty stuff. Enjoy."

Sherman reaches across the table to accept the carton. Wet
spots are spreading under the arms of his linen jacket. His
florid face shines with a film of sweat, and sweat has pasted
the fringe of his fine blond hair into little points. He says, "I
think my client is anxious to get to the point of this meeting."

"I can see that you're suffering from the climate, Sherman," Freddy Layne says. "It's something else, isn't it?
We're only in April, and it's already fiercer than a Texas summer. I'll send you a gift basket of our best Rainforest body-
care products to help you get adjusted. All of them developed
right here in our Brazzaville labs, of course. Also, it'll help
you appreciate Teryl's input to our company, both as pioneer-
ing scientist *and* director of the Biodiversity Research Centre. There's an Elephant Mud face pack that I know you'll
enjoy. A rich clay packed full of natural salts and minerals—
elephants travel for miles to find it, isn't that right, Teryl?"

Teryl says, "Are you ready to talk about Nicholas Hyde,
Freddy?"

"Have it your way," Freddy Layne says. "Roll her, Evangeline."

Evangeline Wisdom flicks a remote control; the infamous
video clip begins to play on a big screen that stands behind a
wooden trough packed with blood red orchids. Teryl has seen
the clip far too many times already and watches Freddy Layne
pretend to study it, the old fake pressing his hands together and
touching the tips of his fingers to his lips, nodding thoughtfully.
When Evangeline Wisdom freezes with a careless flick of the
remote the final image of the fright-mask of the dead white devil, Freddy says, "My Uncle Vernon owned an old-style travelling show—dog-headed boy, bearded lady, thinnest man in the
world, dancing chickens, a cabinet of medical curiosities . . .
He would have paid good money for one of these. I know," he
says, favouring Teryl with another smile. "I'm not getting to
the point as quickly as you would like. Well, as I see it, the point

is not whether any or all of this is true. The point is, Teryl, fig-
uring out what we have to do to help you out of this jam."

"I can deal with it," Teryl says. Obviously, Freddy knows
about the white devils and her attempts to destroy all evidence
of their existence, but she doesn't know what else he knows—
what the white devils really are, for instance; why she had to
have Matthew Faber and the Gentle People eliminated.

"With respect," Sherman Cates says, "the first thing we
must establish is that the present unfortunate media attention
is based on nothing more than unsubstantiated accusations
made by a man whose mental stability has clearly been affected by the unfortunate incident in which he was involved.
He has made a libellous attack on the professional reputation
of my client. I will be pursuing it with all vigour in the courts,
and we have come here to seek your support. I believe," the
lawyer says, flicking up the titanium catches of his zebrahide
briefcase, taking out a sheet of paper, and skimming it across
the rug to Evangeline Wisdom, "that the first response should
be a clear and strong denial of all Nicholas Hyde's claims.
I'm very happy to supply you with a draft statement, and I'm
also very happy to offer my client's full cooperation in its release to the media, up to and including an unscripted press
conference for immediate release to all relevant media."

"Oh, I wouldn't worry about PR," Evangeline Wisdom
says. She's an imposing African-American in a brightly patterned wraparound, her noble head topped by a tower of
scarf-wrapped dreadlocks. She has a calm, no-nonsense
manner and a fanatic loyalty to her boss. "We're already putting our own spin on this thing, and we have some information that we believe will completely demolish this silly young
man's credibility."

Teryl says, "What information?"

"You came here ready for battle, Teryl," Freddy Layne
says. "But don't you worry, it's all in hand. It's containable.
All you have to do is put your trust in Freddy."

Sherman Cates looks like he's swallowed a mouthful of
battery acid. "I hope that we will be allowed access to this information before it's released."

"You bet," Freddy Layne says. "We're here to help. We're all partners in this thing of ours, after all."

"What we do need to know," Evangeline Wisdom says, giving Teryl a look as serious as a heart attack, "is whether Nicholas Hyde's accusations are true."

Sherman Cates closes the locks of his briefcase with a loud snap. "With respect, I don't believe that this is an appropriate venue for that kind of discussion."

Freddy Layne looks at Evangeline Wisdom, who says, "Let's cut the legal crap, Mr. Cates. The plain truth is that Teryl fucked up. She went out on a limb to cover up this thing, and she sawed the damn limb off behind her. This meeting is about how to pick up the pieces, not to hand out blame or engage in a dick-measuring contest. Which is not something you want to get into, by the way. We're idealists, and we're proud of the fact, but don't think we're naive. Obligate is engaged in the reconstruction of an entire country, to make it the first properly self-sustaining low-impact economy on the planet. It's a big, difficult task, and we're in for the long term. We know the score in the real world, Mr. Cates, and believe me, if you're thinking of going to the courts, you'll regret it. You really don't want to tangle with our lawyers."

"It's true," Freddy Layne says. "We keep 'em chained up in a pit and feed 'em on swamp water and live alligators. When we let 'em go to work there's not usually a whole lot left of the opposition afterward. You'll do far better, son, talking with us, man to man."

Sherman Cates listens to this good cop/bad cop bullshit with a tight-lipped, solemn expression, but Teryl can't help laughing. She says, "What exactly do you want to discuss?" and shrugs off Sherman's damp hand when he places it over hers.

Evangeline Wisdom ticks the points off on her fingers. "The disappearance of the body retrieved from the massacre site on the Likouala aux Herbes River. The improper authorization of the napalming of the site. The disappearance of the baby rescued by the Witness worker, Nicholas Hyde."

"We also know most of what you got up to with Captain Jean Badiledi of the Congolese Army," Freddy Layne says. "You found him to be a very helpful fellow, I believe. And by golly, he was certainly very helpful to us—very eager to explain his side of things. But it's the baby that most concerns me, Teryl. Dead babies are bad ju-ju, PR-wise. What were you thinking?"

"It was infected with a biowar virus," Teryl says. "It was taken to a Class Four isolation facility for treatment, but it died there, and its body was disposed of in an appropriate manner. The body retrieved from the massacre site was disposed of in the same manner for the same reason. The site was napalmed—"

"To contain a possible outbreak of a biowar virus spread by Loyalist guerrillas. It's not a bad story," Evangeline Wisdom says, "except that we have Nicholas Hyde displaying the body of one of these so-called white devils on a video clip and saying that you napalmed the plantation to cover up their existence. That's why we need to know the truth about Pleistocene Park, Teryl, and all the rest."

"You know exactly what I did there," Teryl says.

"I know what you *told* us you did," Evangeline Wisdom says. "Is there anything else you think we should know?"

Teryl forces herself to meet the woman's hard gaze and says, "I didn't have anything to do with the creation of those . . . things."

Freddy Layne says, "But it's likely that whoever *did* make 'em used the methods you helped develop for the Pleistocene Park project. And that's what's got you so stirred up that you haven't been thinking straight."

Getting right to the heart of the matter, giving her a bright, inquiring look that reminds her for a freezing instant that his bullshit good ol' boy act hides a sharp, dangerous mind.

"If you want to supply my client with documentation that substantiates your accusations of misconduct against her," Sherman Cates says, "we'll take it away and study it, and then we'll be happy to discuss it at a properly convened meeting. But I'm not prepared to allow Professor Meade to be subjected to some kind of kangaroo court."

Freddy Layne ignores him. "How about it, Teryl? You think someone bootlegged your research?"

Sherman Cates says, "You don't have to answer that, Teryl."

Teryl says, "It's all right, Sherman. I want to. Freddy, you know very well that my work at Pleistocene Park and earlier, at Qualia, is used right here in Green Congo. It's the basis of Emotional Reorientation, which is the basis for Obligate's corporate structure. I suppose it's possible that it was used to pattern the behaviour of those things, but as far as I'm aware, there's absolutely no evidence to support that hypothesis."

"But you thought that you'd save Obligate some embarrassment by trying to cover up their existence," Evangeline Wisdom says.

Teryl doesn't deny this. So far this is going much better than she hoped. Freddy Layne and Evangeline Wisdom don't seem to know what the white devils really are, don't seem to know anything about the elimination of Matthew and his so-called Gentle People. They haven't even mentioned the unfortunate coincidence of Matthew's death, something that she should have arranged years ago, as soon as she learnt that he was still alive, that against all the odds he had escaped the Dead Zone. Pity and sentiment weakened her; she won't make that kind of mistake again.

"My client's history was well known to Obligate when she was hired," Sherman Cates says. "Professor Meade made a full disclosure at the time, and I don't think it would be helpful to her or to Obligate to bring it up now."

"She portrayed herself as a dedicated scientist who quit her job because she was shocked and disgusted by the unethical behaviour of her colleagues," Evangeline Wisdom says. "But if she was in the right then, why has she worked so hard to fabricate some kind of cover-up now? Is she afraid that the existence of these white devils will somehow prove that she hasn't told us the full story?"

"That's pure speculation," Sherman Cates says, tugging

the knot of his tie down still farther, "based entirely on a prejudiced reading of my client's motivations."

"You look as if you're about to suffer some kind of meltdown there, Sherman," Freddy Layne says. "Take off your tie and jacket, why don't you? And slip that rod out of your butt while you're at it. We're in Africa. It's okay to relax. Sip some of that refreshing forest-water, kick back some, and Evangeline will tell you what we plan to do about this little ol' mess, and what we want Teryl to do for us."

In the elevator, Sherman Cates shakes out a linen handkerchief, mops his face, and says, "That could have gone a lot worse."

"Let's not talk here," Teryl says.

Sherman looks at the security camera in a corner of the elevator's ceiling, looks at Teryl.

"The limo too," Teryl says. "I'll take us to a restaurant I know. You deserve a cocktail after your performance, and I think you'll enjoy the cabaret."

Sherman keeps up a flow of inconsequential talk in the limo. Teryl learns far more than she cares to about his children, his new wife, the summer home he's building on the South Carolina shore, but it's an excellent smoke screen, the human equivalent of white noise, guaranteed to bore the socks off anyone listening in. At the restaurant, she tells him to leave his phone behind, explaining, as they walk through the gathering dusk and the pink light of the restaurant's hologram sign, "We completely control the local network. That's why you had to hire a phone when you arrived. Only the phones we manufacture work here, and satellite phones are not only illegal, we do our best to jam them. We can track anyone in the network's footprint, listen in to any conversation, follow every click trail and read every email and text message; we can even activate phones remotely and use them as listening devices. Obligate effectively owns this country, Sherman, and like any colonial power, it's being changed by what it owns. Freddy Layne's going native, and the main ingredients of local politics are paranoia and mistrust."

"If I didn't know you better, Teryl, I'd think that you were going native too."

"I've been in Africa too long, that's for sure."

They're given one of the best tables in the glassed-in veranda, with a ringside view of the floodlit river. Teryl points out the crocodiles on the sandbank and tells Sherman that they are part of the cabaret.

"They're on the menu too, I see."

"It's not bad. Like a fishy steak."

"I've eaten alligator. What's this, saka-saka?"

"Greens. What's your opinion, Sherman? How much trouble am I in?"

"It isn't as bad as it could be. Exceeding your authority, misuse of Obligate facilities in pursuit of a private agenda . . ." Sherman takes a sip of his gin and tonic, ice cubes rattling in the big square glass. "They're misdemeanours, Teryl, not capital offences."

"If Freddy finds out that Nicholas Hyde has allied himself with this Raphael character, if he finds out that Raphael is trying to blackmail me—"

"Well, he hasn't, and we'll make sure that he doesn't. Look, Teryl, it's clear that the Obligate board is as anxious to cover up this episode as you are. They could fire you, but the importance of your research is well known, and a hasty action like that would have a negative effect on the share price. I'm very confident that we can negotiate a slap on the wrist at a closed session of the board, followed by a discreet resignation in, say, six months' time. Your contract is pretty watertight when it comes to provision for compensation, so as far as the financial side of things is concerned, you won't have anything to worry about. You could retire, start independent research . . . The world will be your oyster. What's the manioc like?"

"Like grits cooked in disinfectant. So, I get my contractual severance package, you get your twenty percent, and they keep the ER research. I'm not certain that's a good bargain."

"Obligate retains the intellectual property rights of any research you did while employed by them, but you still control the original patents. You and your ex-husband. His daughter now, I suppose. I was sorry to hear about your loss, by the way."

"Matthew had been ill for years; the stroke wasn't unexpected. And I hadn't talked to him ever since . . ."

"The unpleasantness over Pleistocene Park."

Teryl looks at Sherman, wondering exactly how much he knows. She had to tell him about Nicholas Hyde, Raphael, and the blackmail attempt in case it came up at the meeting with Freddy Layne, trying to pass it off as a minor nuisance, telling him that Raphael was offering to sell the body of the white devil to her. But that's only part of the truth. Raphael has done some rudimentary analysis of the corpse's DNA, and is threatening to tell the world what the white devils really are unless she pays him a round ten million American dollars. Sherman has found a contact in the American Embassy in Kinshasa who is willing to act as a go-between, but Teryl is pretty sure that trying to buy the man's silence won't be good enough.

"What you have to decide now," Sherman says, "is whether you want to take this in the direction that I've outlined."

"Will I take the opportunity to quit, lose the ER research in exchange for a good pay-off and no stain on my character? Of course I will. You don't know what it's like here. There's no possibility of doing any real research. Elephant Mud face packs and Rainforest 'Heart-of-Sap' water—those are the pinnacles of our so-called scientific program. That, and the obsessive cataloguing of every bug and weed. Obligate really is going native, Sherman. Freddy consults a *féticheuse* before every board meeting now, some illiterate three-hundred-pound, sixty-year-old charlatan he's installed in a luxury mansion in the best part of Brazzaville. A couple of weeks ago, he held a rally in one of the airport hangars. A Texan Swing Band and some kind of horrible native music, all jungle drums and electric guitars. We had to dress in native costume, dance on stage with members of the puppet government, drink palm wine, and pretend we liked it. And Freddy did some kind of rap routine. For a whole hour, Sherman, I kid you not. He loved every minute of it, and the zombies lapped it up. You bet I want out."

"Layne's a smart operator, and he has a ferocious team of lawyers. He's letting you off lightly, Teryl. I think in a year's time you'll know you've made the right decision."

"Meanwhile, I want you to free up as much of my money as possible. Keep my shares in Obligate, of course; I don't want to give Freddy any more ammunition than he already has, but I need liquidity to pay off Raphael and get hold of that body."

And deal with Raphael and Nicholas Hyde, but there's no reason to tell Sherman.

Sherman looks at her over the top of the menu and says, "Are you sure that's what you want to do? Blackmailers rarely stop at one bite of the pie, Teryl."

"All you have to do is have your contact in the embassy over there make contact with Raphael, let him know that I'm willing to pay for the specimen. And then, when this is all over, I can start thinking about my new project. That's what I'll need most of the money for."

As she hoped, Sherman brightens at once. He says, "This is a new line of research, perhaps?"

"It's still very much in the golden vapourware stage. Maybe nothing will come of it, but you never know."

There's no such project, of course, but the hope that she is developing a new cash cow will keep Sherman sweet for as long as she needs his help. After that, well, it's probably just as easy to have someone killed in the States as in Africa—just more expensive.

Sherman says, "You want to set up on your own. Well, it's not an ideal time, but the climate is changing. The economy is recovering, people are growing less wary of scientific research now that the memory of the Black Flu is healing over, and of course investment in medical research is greater than ever . . ." He is looking around for a waiter. "This is good, Teryl. I'm pleased for you. How about we discuss it over dinner?"

She says, "How about we try and relax, enjoy our meal, enjoy the show. This place is famous for it. They tie up an antelope—"

Someone in army uniform is walking between the tables towards them.

"What is it, Teryl?"

A skinny man with amber-tinted sunglasses and a razor-cut moustache and an untrustworthy smile—Captain Jean Badiledi.

Chapter 28

Although it's the middle of the afternoon, it's raining so hard that it's as dark as midnight. The headlights of the Toyota Ahisma that takes Elspeth Faber to her father's funeral make yellow tunnels through the rain; rain hammers on the roof; raindrops flick away like spit off a hot griddle from the ultra-slick windscreen. Elspeth sits in the backseat, behind the driver and his assistant, two large, painfully polite men in black suits, black ties, white shirts, and expensive spex. A police radio mutters to itself under the luminous circles and stars in the smoked-glass dash. Scattered lights in the half-empty office buildings and apartment blocks of central Nairobi swing away to the right as the Ahisma crosses Uhuru Highway and drives past Uhuru Park, over the hill to the little white chapel of the crematorium, where a small pack of reporters and TV crews is penned behind yellow sawhorses and a line of police in green raincapes. Camera lights burn like little suns behind the rain as, under an umbrella held by one of her minders, Elspeth hurries into the chapel, trying not to hear the shouted questions about her father, about Teryl Meade, about Pleistocene Park and the white devils.

Only a few of Elspeth's relations have turned up. The Fabers, once one of Colonial Kenya's first families, have been much reduced by plague and emigration, and the scandal surrounding Matthew Faber's death has kept away most of those who still live in Nairobi. Uncle Dickie, her father's younger brother, gives Elspeth a shaky hug, enveloping her in a cloud that's one part whisky, two parts aftershave; Tim Walker, one of her cousins, says that some of them will be meeting at Papa Loca's afterwards, to drink to her father's memory. Elspeth shakes hands with her father's former colleagues at the university. She has a brief conversation with Richard McRae, the family's lawyer, fabulously ancient and possessed of immaculate courtesy, about the reading of her father's will—McRae assures her that it's a mere formality, as her father owned no property, and half the money earned by his patents will come to her and the rest will go into a trust fund to promote research into neuroscience at Kenyatta National Hospital. She makes polite talk, thanks people she scarcely knows for their condolences, and feels as if she is standing slightly outside everything until Mary Ekalale, splendid in a black-and-gold wraparound and matching turban, envelops her in a heartfelt hug, presses a scrap of paper into her hand, and says in her ear that if there's anything else she can do . . .

"I'm doing fine, Mary. Really I am." Elspeth, moved by the woman's human warmth, is suddenly on the brink of tears. She discovers that the black dress she bought just this morning from one of the shopping channels doesn't have any pockets, and tucks the scrap of paper into the strap of her black bra.

Mary looks around and says in a stagy whisper, "You just go up to the check-in desk and give them that number."

Elspeth sniffs, swallows something the size of an oyster. "I owe you, Mary."

"I owe *you*, Dr. Faber. You're going to make me famous."

"About the other thing we discussed yesterday . . ."

"I am still okay with it. Very nervous, of course," Mary says. "I hardly slept all night, thinking about it. But it is a great honour."

"I won't pretend it'll be easy, what with the media madness and everything, but I know you'll do me proud."

Mary's unselfconscious smile dimples her cheeks. "Someone from a British news channel rang my doorbell this morning, offered me ten thousand shillings for my story. I talked about my work, and he stood on my step the longest time in the rain before he realized that I didn't want to say anything about you. They've been at the museum too, of course, but the police keep them out of the building."

"Don't let the bastards grind you down," Harry Brenner says, coming up behind them. He has trimmed his hair and beard, wears a neatly pressed navy-blue short-sleeved shirt, a black tie, and black slacks. He hugs Elspeth, says in her ear, "Let's have a few minutes afterward," and then stands aside so that the rest of the Hominid Gang can offer their condolences.

Elspeth sits alone at the front during the brief service, sitting upright and very still through the minister's stumbling homily, watching the coffin slide through the black curtain to the accompaniment of something by Bach that seems to be played at half-speed, thinking how much her father would have hated this. She thanks the minister, shakes the same set of hands all over again, and there's Harry Brenner, laying a hand on her arm and steering her behind a big display of lilies.

"I'm as sorry as hell about this," he says.

"You seem to be bearing up, Harry. I'm sorry you had to put the dig to bed by yourself."

"Hey, the least I could do. It's all squared away, no problem." There are beads of sweat in Harry's hairline. He's embarrassed and anxious because of what he needs to ask her. "The thing I was wondering, the media conference? You remember it's in exactly one week?"

"I hadn't forgotten, despite everything," Elspeth says. "But you don't have to worry about the media paying attention to me, because that's why I don't think I should attend."

Harry nods, trying to look serious, trying not to show his relief. "I'll do us proud, I promise."

"I know you will. And in my place, Harry, I know you won't mind, I want Mary Ekalale."

"With all respect, I don't think Mary has the experience—"

"I know that she doesn't quite have her PhD, but she's

been working with me for three years, she knows as much about the site as I do, and she did most of the work putting the bones together. Also, what's most important, she's Kenyan."

"You know there'll be a lot of media attention even if you don't turn up. We're presenting something tremendously important, and tremendously controversial. One wrong word, one botched answer, and there'll be blood in the water. People have already heard rumours about our find—I've been fending off some pretty hostile questions from Dana Hotchkiss, and she's almost certain to have primed someone to question the dating, which is your area of expertise. If you're not there, we can skate over that, but if Mary is standing in for you, she'll have to come up with the answers. She might be good at putting together bone fragments, but what does she know about the spin-resonance data and the work you did on sorting out the horizons?"

Elspeth feels suddenly tired, and a little impatient with Harry, who probably thinks that he means well by trying to protect her. Because that's what men do, protect women even when they don't want to be protected. She says, "Mary knows what I know. I want her there, Harry. There's no question that the Museum won't be represented. This is a Kenyan project, carried out in Kenya, partly funded by the Kenyan government. I don't think it's too much to ask that a Kenyan takes part in the presentation of the results. Mary will be fine."

"Well, she has a good teacher," Harry says, "one of the best. You're a cool lady, Elspeth."

Is she? What she mostly feels, riding in the back of the Ahisma, a stainless-steel urn containing about two kilograms of bone fragments still warm from the crematorium's furnace on the seat next to her, is a numb detachment, a kind of emotional amputation. She's finally and irrevocably lost her father, but his death has become public property, she's on the run from the media, and there's no time for her to stop and grieve.

The Ahisma makes a hard left through red traffic lights

onto Uhuru Road, and then turns right, passing through the security barriers in front of the new Parliament Building, driving into the underground car park and coming to a stop beside a long black limo. The man riding shotgun hops out and opens the passenger's door and ushers Elspeth inside the limo, where David Oloitip is waiting for her.

He offers her a drink from the little bar after she's settled beside him on the soft leather bench; she says she's okay, and thanks him for his help.

"I hope you understand why I couldn't come to the service," he says. Solemn but relaxed in his high-collared African suit, brown silk with a fine sheen, polished black shoes, a heavy gold Rolex on his right wrist, a bracelet of braided elephant hair on his left. Sitting half-turned in the corner, his right arm resting along the top of the deep, comfortable seat, his kind, ugly face intent on hers, his brown eyes grave behind a pair of spex with thick black frames.

"It was something of a circus, but the police managed to keep the media at bay."

"And your house? The police are taking good care of you?"

"I'm under siege, but I'm coping."

"I wish I could have been at the funeral. Matthew was a good man. A good Kenyan and a great scientist, and one of my best and oldest friends. I knew him, dare I say it, before you were born, and I know that I will miss him very much."

"You were a good friend to him, David. And to me. You did so much for us in the last four years that I hardly know where to begin to thank you."

David Oloitip smiles. "We fall back on platitudes at times like this, don't we? And it's a politician's habit to say nothing and spend a long time doing it. But if I may be permitted one more cliché, please believe me when I say that this will pass. The media will soon find something else to tickle the public's fancy. The circus will take down its tents and move on."

"Not for a while, I think. Not while that video is still getting heavy rotation on the news channels."

Elspeth has watched it over and over. Raw, unedited

footage beginning with a tracking shot that moves past men and dogs in the deep rainforest to close in on a white, naked body sprawled amongst spindly saplings; an abrupt cut to the same body propped against a tree trunk; a close-up of its slack face, the small, deep-set, death-filmed eyes, the wide mouth crammed with ivory needles; close-ups of bullet wounds, of a hand lying palm-up on moss, fingers tipped with black thorns. Then another cut, the camera zooming in and steadying on a man squatting beside the body, a white man in a blue T-shirt, slim and deeply tanned, black hair close-cropped. Nicholas Hyde, the man briefly famous for having rescued a baby from a massacre, looking at someone out of view, then speaking directly to the camera. His expression grim and determined as he explains that this is the body of one of the white devils that were responsible for the massacre of refugees and the deaths of soldiers and Witness volunteers, that the truth about this massacre was suppressed by Teryl Meade, director of Obligate's research programme in Green Congo and formerly one of the scientists who worked on the gengineering of extinct animal species for the Pleistocene Park project.

News channels have linked the video clip to Teryl's carefully scripted statement, in which she denies all knowledge of the so-called white devils, reiterates her famous recantation of gengineering, and expresses sorrow at the death of her former husband. There are links to stock footage of Obligate's research facilities in Brazzaville, to archival material about Pleistocene Park (supplemented with recent satellite pictures of the drowned ruins), to an on-line library page containing links to sites and articles about Daniel Lovegrave, to various interviews in which Matthew Faber speculates about hominid intelligence. Most news reports are pegged to the obvious deduction: Matthew Faber, with or without the help of his former wife, created or helped to create the white devils, and the official story that he died of a stroke hides the truth that he committed suicide in remorse after he learned that they had escaped. One of the more assiduous scandal sheets has unearthed a brief, long-buried news item about the arrival at a refugee camp of Matthew Faber and a group of "experimental chimpanzees," and promises its readers that it will do everything in its power to find out just what these so-called chimpanzees really were.

Elspeth should hate Nicholas Hyde: he brought back the body that frightened Teryl so very badly in the first place; he seems determined to uncover the truth at any cost. But in the video clip he seems neither proud nor triumphant about having tracked down one of the white devils, and although barely suppressed anger burns behind his solemn gaze and awkward speech, there's a weary fatalism too, as if he knows that revealing the truth to the world will cost him dearly. Elspeth has played and replayed the clip, fascinated by this enigmatic man, wondering what he would say, how he would react, if he knew what the poor creature he killed really was.

"The video is an unfortunate development," David Oloitip says, "but in many ways we have been lucky. There is no mention of the Gentle People, and media speculation about the connection between the white devils and Matthew's death is inevitable; we live in an age in which conspiracies and cover-ups are believed to be the norm. As long as we keep our heads, we can put this behind us."

David's concern is genuine, but for the first time in her life, Elspeth is aware that he's holding back from her, possessed by a politician's wary reticence. He hasn't looked at the stainless steel urn that she has placed between them. She says, "I'm sorry, David. This must be hurting you badly. How much trouble have I made for you?"

"Even though I was aware of the risk of discovery," David Oloitip says, "I was always happy to help your father. Of course, I could not anticipate something as dreadful as these white devils . . . Well, so far, the President is behind me. Also, and this is very good news, he has approved a brief statement to be released later today, an appreciation of your father's work. And I have some news concerning Erefaan Williams, the man you so bravely captured, but perhaps you do not want to hear that now."

"He helped murder my father, David." Amazing herself that she can say this so calmly. "Of course I want to hear it."

"Mr. Williams has been very cooperative. It seems that the leader of the gang was an American with deep links to many Radical Green organizations. His name is Cody Corbin. Here," David Oloitip says, reaching into his jacket, unfolding a piece of paper, "I have a photograph."

Elspeth looks at it, looks away. "It's him."

"You are sure?"

"I'm sure. He rode up on the big motorbike, the Harley, with Erefaan Williams behind him."

"Mr. Corbin is a very bad man. His father was a libertarian preacher who was killed resisting an FBI raid on his property. His mother was killed in the same raid, and Corbin shot an FBI agent. He was just twelve years old at the time. After he was released, he disappeared for a while. There is an outstanding warrant in the U.S. concerning an arson attempt on a government building, and he is also wanted in Mexico for involvement in numerous acts of sabotage against factories and research laboratories. We believe he fled to South Africa after the Radical Greens he was involved with were arrested, and that is where he met the fellow you caught. Erefaan Williams is a known terrorist who went to prison after he was caught breaking into a genetics laboratory. He was released two years ago, and it seems that he and Mr. Corbin have been working together ever since. There are reports of their involvement in various acts of kidnapping, sabotage, and arson in South Africa, Uganda, Zambia, Tanzania . . . Also, Mr. Corbin is suspected of involvement in the murder of at least four scientists who once worked for the Pleistocene Park project."

"If he's so well known, why has no one ever arrested him?"

"All this is based on intelligence reports, rumours circulating in the Radical Green community, and so on. But until Mr. Williams's confession, nothing useful. It seems that Cody Corbin and Erefaan Williams entered Kenya using false passports two months ago and were sheltered by known Radical

Greens in Nairobi. Christopher Kassam, the boy who was found shot dead with your father, was a student in economics at the university here in Nairobi. His parents both work for the Kenya Commercial Bank. The body of an American girl associated with the same group, Shalynne Thomas, was found two days ago in a field near Meru. I understand that when Erefaan Williams was told that Cody Corbin had shot and killed Christopher Kassam, he said, 'Of course he did.' He said that Mr. Corbin was a racist so-and-so who killed people of colour without a thought."

"I bet he didn't really say 'so-and-so.' Has he said where Cody Corbin is likely to be now?"

"If Mr. Erefaan Williams is telling the truth, he and Cody Corbin planned to escape across the border into Somalia. We have a description of the camper van they were using, we are making inquiries, but I can't pretend that it will be easy."

"It's a pity the soldiers didn't think to look for him when they finally arrived."

They'd turned up five hours after Elspeth put out the distress call, four men in a 4×4. By then, she had trussed up Erefaan Williams and had crossed to the island, and found her father's body, the body of Christopher Kassam, and the funeral pyre.

David Oloitip says, "The soldiers had to secure the area around the marine station against further attack, they had to search the island . . . The soldiers did what they could, Elspeth, and the army and the police and the security service are doing all they can now. Believe me, I will be as happy as you if we find Cody Corbin. Given the kind of man he is, he'll resurface sooner or later, and I pray that it will be within reach of our police or security service."

"He pulled the trigger, David, and I hate him for it, but he was doing it because Teryl paid him to do it."

Elspeth is certain that Teryl examined the body brought back by Nicholas Hyde from the site of the massacre in the Congolese jungle, that she discovered that the white devils were created by the same methods as the Gentle People. That's why Teryl had Matthew Faber murdered; that's why she had the Gentle People killed and cremated. Any true Radical Green terrorists would have videoed the bodies, taken samples, denounced the crime to the world, but Teryl made sure that her accomplices got rid of the evidence, made sure they burned the bodies of the Gentle People so that they couldn't be autopsied. Elspeth has already put her case against Teryl as forcefully as she could to David Oloitip, and all he would say then is more or less what he says now.

"We both know about the terrible crime your father and your stepmother and Daniel Lovegrave committed in the name of science when they created the Gentle People, but we have no evidence that she was directly involved in your father's murder. Surely, for the sake of his memory, it is best to let this affair die away."

"What about Erefaan Williams? What will happen to him? How are you going to keep all this from coming out at his trail?"

"You spent a significant portion of your childhood in America, Elspeth. Circumstances are very different here."

"There won't be a trial? Erefaan Williams will fall out of a window trying to escape, something like that?"

David Oloitip shrugs.

"And Teryl gets away."

"Believe me, we are anxious to question her. But she is in Green Congo, she is a senior executive in the company that owns the country, and so far there is nothing to link her with Cody Corbin and Erefaan Williams. However, the video clip has badly blemished her reputation, and I doubt that she can remain with Obligate much longer."

"She kills my father, and I have to be thankful that she might lose her job."

"Elspeth, I think you need to find somewhere away from all this, the media circus, all the rest. Somewhere you can rest. I have a villa in the South of France, an apartment in Switzerland, another in New York. All are at your disposal."

"Is that a bribe, David?"

"It is an offer from an old family friend. Please do consider it."

"Of course I will."

But Elspeth has other plans. There's the message her father left on his phone: *I just wanted to tell you that I think it might be Danny Lovegrave. Those devils, I mean. He was sick when I left, I don't know if he's still alive, but do you remember how he was always pushing things to extremes?* If Danny Lovegrave is still alive and working, he must be somewhere in Africa, somewhere near the place in Green Congo where the white devils massacred those poor people. And the same scandal sheet that uncovered the four-year-old story about her father and the "experimental chimpanzees" also traced the origin of Nicholas Hyde's video clip to a server in Kinshasa, in the Democratic Republic of the Congo, a straight shot across the Congo River to Brazzaville and Teryl Meade. As soon as Elspeth realized that the Kenyan government wasn't going to pursue Teryl, she asked Mary Ekalale to buy her a ticket on the weekly flight between Nairobi and Kinshasa; it leaves tomorrow afternoon.

Chapter 29

"Of course I told them that I was working for you," Jean Badiledi says to Teryl. "I was sure they knew all of it already, so what else could I do? But although I tell them the truth, I am in much trouble. I am in trouble because of what I do for you, Professor."

"You're in trouble because you had a baby killed," Teryl says. "According to Freddy Layne, it's bad ju-ju. He's very unhappy about it, and so am I, because I certainly did not order you to do it."

They're leaning close to each other in the middle of the crowded restaurant's clatter. At Teryl's request, Sherman Cates has taken his drink to the bar. He's perched on a tall stool at the counter, watching them through the veranda's wide doorway.

"I do what I have to do to help you out," Captain Badiledi says, "and now I am told my commission is suspended. I can no longer work. I have no work and no money, Professor Meade, and I have a family to look after. I have a wife and two little babies. I have my mother and father. I have my wife's brother and his family. How will they live now? How will *I* live?"

"I paid you a fair price for your work, Captain. Or have you already spent that on your mistresses?"

"They have frozen my bank account. They say they must investigate where the money comes from." Captain Jean Badiledi studies Teryl through his sunglasses. "You were happy, I think, with the work I did for you."

"I'm not happy about the dead baby. It's going to cause me a lot of trouble."

"Forget about the baby. He would have grown up as an orphan, with no father to teach him how to behave, how to learn a trade . . . If he lived, he would have become a thief or a beggar. And most orphans don't live long. They don't know who they really are, so they die of shame."

"Freddy Layne knows that the baby didn't die of a biowar disease, and if that bit of black propaganda was supposed to destroy Nicholas Hyde's reputation, it didn't really work, did it? Also, he took no notice of the warnings you gave him, and he escaped from Brazzaville and went on to cause me all kinds of trouble. On the whole, I'd say that you created more problems than you solved. I'd say that you didn't really earn the money I paid you. Yet here you are, with your hand out for more."

"You think my problems are nothing to do with you," Captain Badiledi says. "You think that you and I, we are finished. But you are wrong. Because, you see, I told them about the work I do for you, but I do not tell them everything I know." Pausing, waiting for her to ask what he didn't tell them, running a thumbnail along the thin line of his moustache as Teryl lets the silence stretch, saying at last, "Nicholas Hyde threw away his phone, but his answering service was still working. I diverted all the calls to my office. Just after he disappeared, someone working at Witness called him." He leans forward and says close to Teryl's ear, "Dr. Bridget Nzube. Perhaps you heard that she disappeared."

"If you were responsible, I don't want to know."

"It was to help you, of course."

The man leaning back in his chair and smiling with self-satisfaction, as if expecting her to pay him off there and then.

Teryl says, "If you're trying to blackmail me over another of your murders, Captain Badiledi, I can tell you now that I'm not interested."

"I had her disappeared because of what she found out. This woman was a pathologist. She was in charge of the laboratory where they test DNA samples of dead people. It seems that Nicholas Hyde found the blood of a white devil on his clothing, and this woman had the results of a genetic sequence she had done on the blood. As you can see from her confession." He places a sheet of paper on the table and says, as Teryl scans it, "I think you see she did very thorough work. I have her interrogation on video, of course, and also the raw data."

Teryl thinks that it wouldn't be difficult to get rid of this foolish, greedy man. Tell him they needed to talk in absolute privacy, ask him to drive her somewhere quiet, out of the way. Grab his gun and shoot him, tip his body in the river and leave it for the crocodiles . . . She crumples the piece of paper and thrusts it in the pocket of her red leather jacket, says, "Let me get this straight. You murdered a woman to obtain this information, and now you want to be paid for it."

"It is not easy, to make a woman disappear. It is much harder than a baby. But I think you agree it was necessary, because of what she found. And what she found—frankly, I am shocked by it, Professor Meade. I can see why you are so anxious to hide the truth."

The people at the tables around them stir, turning to look through the glass wall of the veranda. Two men in fatigues and rubber boots are carrying a live, hobbled antelope through the glare of spotlights towards the riverbank. The cabaret is about to begin.

"I don't think you've thought this through," Teryl says. Her hand is still closed around the piece of paper in her pocket. She can feel the edges biting her skin.

"I have thought about it very carefully," Captain Badiledi says, watching her through the amber-tinted lenses of his sunglasses. "This information, it could cause you much trouble. I think it is why you destroyed the body that Nicholas Hyde brought back; it is why you bribed the army to napalm the oil palm plantation. And now just a few spots of blood could undo all that. But I can save you. Already I have stopped Nicholas Hyde finding out about this, and if you want, I can make it disappear. Just like poor Bridget Nzube."

The two men lay the antelope a few metres from the edge of the water. One of them displays an enormous saw-edged hunting knife to the audience and slowly and carefully makes half a dozen long, shallow slits in the antelope's flanks. As the two men walk away into the darkness beyond the glare of the floodlights, long shapes slide off the sandbank in the middle of the river. Some of the people behind Teryl and Captain Badiledi push back their chairs and stand to get a better view. A man holds a video camera to the glass. Sherman Cates is leaning in the doorway, his square glass of gin and tonic in his hand.

"It's a very silly show," Captain Badiledi says, "but it teaches a useful lesson. Just a little blood in the water, and the feeding frenzy starts."

He's a loathsome creature, Teryl thinks, but he could still be useful to her—he could help tie up a loose end in her plan to eliminate Raphael and Nicholas Hyde that's been worrying her. She says, "It isn't the blood. That's just theatrics. There's a bell in the water—when they feel it vibrate, the crocodiles know that there's food waiting for them. You see, Captain, you don't have all the facts. If you'd come to me yesterday I might have given serious thought to paying you—or getting rid of you. But now I know that Nicholas Hyde has the body of one of these so-called white devils, not just a few spots of blood."

"I saw the video clip. But he does not know what you and I

know. He does not know what the white devils really are. If he did, he would have said so."

"He knows," Teryl says, "and he and his confederate are trying to blackmail me about it. So if you expect to be paid off, I'm sorry, you're too late."

Captain Badiledi stands up. "If you do not wish to buy this information," he says loudly, "then perhaps Obligate will be interested. Or perhaps one of the foreign journalists."

Luckily, everyone is watching the crocodiles tear the antelope apart.

"And if you did, what do you think will happen to your women and your two little babies and the rest of your family? Sit down, Captain," Teryl says, and beckons to Sherman Cates. "I don't pay for botched jobs, and I don't give in to blackmail, but now that you're no longer employed by the army, I think I might have a little job for you. A very well-paid little job."

She watches the man try to hide a variety of emotions. As she suspected, greed wins out. With men like him it usually does. He sits down. He says, "What kind of job?"

"To begin with, I need you to take a message to someone. Let's talk with my lawyer here, and work out how you would prefer to be paid."

Chapter 30

Before she checks in, Elspeth Faber makes two circuits of the concourse of Nairobi International Airport, walking under big screens showing ads and infomercials and arrival and departure times, walking past people waiting for other people, past a suitcase on mesh rollers following a businesswoman like an obedient dog, past a pair of bored soldiers with sleek little submachine guns slung under their arms, past a man in orange coveralls, gloves, and a respirator mask who sets an *Out of Service* cone in front of the men's restroom and wheels a silvery tank of anti-bioagent inside. Although no one seems to be following her or loitering suspiciously, she has the hyperalert feeling of being watched. An hour ago, she told the two men from the security service that she was going to take a nap and climbed out of her bedroom window with her prepacked day bag, slipped through the gate to the service alley, and walked five blocks in the pouring rain to the local supermarket, where she found a taxi to take her to the airport. As easy as that—her bodyguards were supposed to stop people getting too close to her house, not to stop her walking away from it. She thinks that she has at least another hour before they check on her and hopes that she hasn't got them into trouble.

Standing in line at the Kenya Airways counter, she briefly entertains the thought that she could fly to just about anywhere in the world. Fly away from all this, fly away from her life. She could even go back to the States. And then what? Pretend none of this has happened? Try and forget whose daughter she is? Change her name, become a fugitive from her own life?

She checks in, passes through the sniffers and scanners into the Departures Lounge, finds a bar, and slowly drinks a glass of Tusker beer, quenching the anxiety burning in her empty stomach. The bar is decorated like a mid-twentieth century safari lodge, with fake animal heads and animalskin shields and crossed spears around the walls, and fake zebraskin upholstering the seats of the booths and the cushions of the wrought-iron stools at the bar, which is framed with plastic vines and bamboo. A group of Chinese businessmen are celebrating a successful deal, making elaborate toasts and knocking back thimbles of Braveheart whisky. A few couples hunch like conspirators, their carry-on luggage at their feet. The only other solitary drinker, a raffishly dishevelled man in a white jacket, stares at Elspeth and at last picks up his glass and comes over. She's about to tell him that she isn't interested, that she's just here to enjoy a quiet drink, when he says, "Dr. Faber, I believe. Let me guess, you're going to Kinshasa too."

She stares at him, pierced cleanly through by shock. He's about her age, a cigarette drooping in the corner of his mouth, mild, washed-out blue eyes in a face prematurely aged by tropical sun, a cap of blond hair as disarrayed as a little boy's. The kind of guy who, if you don't know the type, seems to possess a romantic, world-weary familiarity with exotic adventure.

He smiles and says, "I met Nicholas Hyde in Brazzaville. He told me all about your father and your stepmother and Pleistocene Park."

"Nicholas Hyde?" It occurs to Elspeth that this raffish man could be some kind of journalist. "I'm sorry, I don't know him. You must have mistaken me for someone else."

"I saw you on the news yesterday—at your father's funeral? Imagine my surprise when you walked in here. I'm Theodore Yssel," the man says, and holds out his hand, shrugs when she doesn't take it, and sits uninvited and a little unsteadily on the stool next to hers. Giving her a quick, lopsided smile that no doubt helps charm gullible tourists into bed, but that makes Elspeth even warier, ready to distrust everything he wants to tell her. He sucks down what's left of his drink, ice cubes rattling against his teeth, says, "The least I can do is buy you a drink," and snags the bartender's attention, asks him for another Johnnie Walker Black over ice, asks Elspeth if she wants something stronger than beer.

"I'm fine with this."

"I used to have this sunset rule," Theodore Yssel says, "but I've been sort of breaking it since I got back."

"From Green Congo, where you met Nicholas Hyde."

"Yah, and not by chance. As a matter of fact, he came looking for me."

Leaving it hanging there as he pays for his whisky and takes a thirsty sip, the moment stretching until Elspeth takes the hook and asks why Nicholas Hyde wanted to see him.

"We had a common experience he wanted to discuss," Theodore Yssel says, looking straight at her. "We both lost good friends to the white devils."

He tells the story, taking his time. Explains that he was working as a bush pilot in Green Congo with his friend Johnny Grundlingh, describes how they were ambushed when they went to pick up a survey worker who had injured himself in the forest, how they found the badly mutilated bodies of the injured man and his companion, how he and Johnny Grundlingh had to flee for their lives, how a stray bullet missed him by a centimetre and killed his friend.

"I can see it now," he says, "the way they came running out of the bushes and grass like savages in one of those old Tarzan movies. The army turned the bodies of the biosurvey workers over to Witness because they thought they'd been killed by Loyalist guerillas. They wanted the world to know about the latest atrocity, you understand. Later on, Nicholas Hyde read the autopsy report and knew at once that they had been killed by the same things that killed his colleagues. You remember the photograph? Him and the baby?"

"Of course."

"He was part of a team that went in to investigate a massacre just a few days after Johnny was killed. Those same white devils had massacred some refugees, and they killed Nicholas Hyde's friends and some Brazilian soldiers, too. Ambushed them, killed seven of them just like that," Theodore Yssel says, snapping his fingers. "Nicholas Hyde and one other guy and the helicopter crew escaped, brought back a baby who had survived the massacre, and the body of one of the white devils. Nicholas Hyde told me that the army confiscated the body and a set of samples from the people who had been massacred, that they claimed the whole thing was a Loyalist atrocity. And they disappeared the baby. They suppressed the truth. That's why he came to me."

"What does this have to do with my father?"

"Nicholas Hyde thought that the white devils had something to do with the Pleistocene Park project, which your father and Teryl Meade were part of, once upon a time. They were making apemen there, right?" When Elspeth does not answer, Theodore Yssel says, "One of the news channels mentioned you dig up hominid bones for a living. Where do you work? Lake Turkana, Olduvai? I don't suppose anyone has started up the digs over in Ethiopia again, things being what they are."

"Mostly Lake Turkana."

Theodore Yssel nods. "I've done a lot of flying around there. Lodwar, Loyangalani, Eliye Springs. . . . It used to be a popular tourist destination."

"Most of my work is on the east shore, about seventy, eighty kilometres north of Loyangalani. The lake has been shrinking for the last fifty years; we're working on a site exposed by the receding shoreline."

"It's nice country. Even after the troubles. Maybe I flew in supplies to one of your camps, once upon a time."

"I doubt it. We usually bring in our own."

"I guess the season is just about finished now, uh?"

"Just about."

"But I don't think you're flying to Kinshasa for a well-deserved rest. That is where you're going, isn't it?"

"Where I'm going is none of your business, Mr. Yssel."

Theodore Yssel shrugs. "The weekly flight between Nairobi and Kinshasa leaves in an hour. My guess is that we'll both be on it."

"And why are you going there?"

"I saw that video, like I bet you did. And like you, I worked out where Nicholas Hyde is. I think he's fallen in with some unpleasant people, and I want to help him. After Johnny was killed, the army persuaded me I was mistaken, that what I'd seen were Loyalist soldiers in ghost-paint. It's true, you know, that some of the Loyalists paint themselves white— they think that it makes them immune to bullets, biowar agents . . ."

Theodore Yssel has a habit of drifting off, developing a thousand-metre stare. Elspeth prompts, "You know differently."

"I know what I saw, but I was persuaded to go along with what the army wanted me to have seen. I thought, fuck it, I'm leaving the country anyway, you understand?"

"You didn't want any trouble."

"Exactly. And then Nicholas Hyde found me—"

Elspeth's phone rings. She takes it out of her day bag and switches it off and says, "It's probably the people who are supposed to be protecting me. I'm sort of on the run."

"They can track you with that thing, you know, even when it's switched off."

Elspeth realizes that he's as jumpy as she is. She says, "It's not like I was under arrest, Mr. Yssel. They were just protecting me from the attention of the media."

"I bet."

"You were telling me why you're going to Kinshasa."

Theodore Yssel lights a fresh cigarette. The thumb and forefinger of his right hand are the exact colour of the brittle pages of the old journals down in the university library stacks. "I left Green Congo right after I met Nicholas Hyde. Came back here, scattered Johnny's ashes over a place he always loved, had a little wake for him. So, then I was in a bar, and saw Nicholas Hyde on the news. I saw you, too, heard your father had died. And I realized that I had some unfinished business, and here I am. And I guess you're here because you saw that video of Nicholas Hyde and the white devil, worked out he is in Kinshasa. . . ."

"I did some research," Elspeth says. "One of those 'zines that deals in conspiracies discovered that the video had been released onto the Web via a server in Kinshasa."

"That's a pretty slender clue. You must want to talk to him pretty badly."

"How do you know where he is?"

"In my line of work, you hear that all kinds of weird shit is going on over in the north and east of the DRC, in the Dead Zone. You have all those warlords, gangsters, rogue units from half a dozen armies . . . Then there's this guy, Daniel Lovegrave, the gene wizard who was working with your father and stepmother. I never met him, but I met plenty of people who claimed they had."

"You think he's alive?" Elspeth says, remembering her father's last message.

"You hear all kinds of things. That he was dying of cancer

and cloned himself, imprinted his own mind on the clone. That he's dead, but this fanatical cadre of followers is carrying on with his work . . . But on the whole, yah, I think he's alive and that he took the genetic blueprints of the apemen your stepmother and father were helping to make and messed around with them, came up with the white devils." Theodore Yssel draws on his cigarette, gives her his cute grin. "I can see you like the idea."

Elspeth says, "You want to ask me about my father, if I think he had anything to do with making those things. Well, he didn't."

Theodore Yssel says, "But you think someone gengineered the white devils using the same techniques. A little chimp, maybe a little hyena . . ."

"It really doesn't work like that."

"You don't think so? Gene wizards, biopunks, gene hackers, they've done all kinds of strange things in Africa, and most people never get to hear of them. Nicholas Hyde said that Teryl Meade definitely thought that the white devils were something to do with Pleistocene Park, which is why she wanted to cover up the whole affair. He told me she went out of her way to let him know that Obligate has no kind of gengineering programme, just like she did in that statement they keep showing."

"And you think he's right."

"Where I was brought up, the more you said you were innocent, that you'd done nothing wrong, the less you were believed. Only the guilty feel that they need to proclaim their innocence. I told you that Nicholas Hyde brought the body of one of those things back after the massacre, and the army took it away, and took away the baby he had rescued too, and murdered it. That's when I think he started to get mad."

"Is that how he seemed, when he talked to you? Mad?" She's thinking of the grim, determined look Nicholas Hyde gave the camera as he crouched next to the body of the white devil and talked about a conspiracy to hide the truth.

Theodore Yssel drains his glass, wiggles it at the bartender. "How did he seem? Angry, but cool with it. He said that he wanted to speak for his dead, to make sure that their story was heard. Are you sure you don't want another drink? We've got at least thirty minutes before they start boarding."

"I don't think so. It was very generous of you to share your story with me, Mr. Yssel, but I don't think we're after the same thing at all."

Theodore Yssel tells the bartender to hit him one more time, and says to Elspeth, "You know Nicholas Hyde is in the Democratic Republic of the Congo, you know he's probably in Kinshasa, but I bet you don't know exactly *where* he is."

"And you do?"

"I have a very good idea. Those two men he was with? Not the two guys with the dogs, but the one in the cowboy boots, and the one with the little thorns in his head. I happen to know who they work for. So, are you interested in coming along with me?"

Chapter 31

Cody and the woman are praying together, kneeling by the double bed in the back of the camper van, when Rudy Kaufmann knocks on the window. "Your friend's plane, it has arrived," Rudy says when Cody opens the door. "I have someone driving him from the airstrip, and I came to ask if you want him brought here."

The grizzled old man, in his usual filthy desert-camo fatigues, grey hair brushed back from his bald spot and hanging in greasy rat's-tails to his shoulders, his eyes blanked by sunglasses with little silvery lenses, is trying to look around Cody to catch a glimpse of the woman, who is unhurriedly wrapping a wide strip of red cotton printed with yellow birds around her hips, over her breasts. He's a devious old scudder who claims to have served time in the French Foreign Legion before becoming a mercenary and fighting in just about every civil war you care to mention, now self-appointed king of this desert shithole, and about as trustworthy as a weasel in an egg factory.

"Your bar will do fine," Cody says, gripping the top of the door frame, pulling himself up and swinging to and fro, forcing Rudy to take a step backwards. Cody is wearing only his combat pants, the Colt Python shoved into the waistband. The air is hot and close, feeling as always like a thunderstorm's on the way. Apocalyptic afternoon sunlight bleaches the land white. A few puffball clouds hang in the hot blue sky, and a line of darker clouds hugs the eastern horizon, out towards the coast.

The old man's smile shows snaggly teeth stained black and orange by *khat* juice. He says, "I have your friend driven here from the landing strip, I let you use my bar for your business . . . It's a lot of trouble for me."

"The man's no friend of mine," Cody says. "He can pay for his own ride."

"He's not your friend? So it could be he comes here to make trouble. Perhaps he wants to collect that reward they offer for you. For only a small cost, I can arrange for someone to keep watch on him, someone who will step in and help you if he tries anything."

"One of those *mooryans* stand outside your bar all day, chewing *khat*?"

"Why not? They are good fighters."

"All I see them do is get wired on *khat*, pick fights with each other in the afternoon, crash out in the evening. I don't know what else they can do," Cody says, standing aside for the woman, "and I don't care to find out. If anyone is plannin' any trouble, they can answer to me."

Rudy turns to watch the woman sashay past the gaggle of mostly naked children who dog any action in the little settlement like a Greek chorus. "She's a good ride," he says. "Nice and roomy. When you picked her out, I thought, there's a man, he might be a preacher, but he likes his home comforts."

"I take what I can find."

"You think your friend might want some entertainment, after he's finished his business with you?"

"You can ask him," Cody says. "Now, if you don't mind, I'm gonna move this van out of sight of the road."

"You don't want this man who's not your friend to know your disposition, eh?" Rudy nods judiciously, one soldier to another, says, "While you talk to him, I can for a small extra fee arrange to have someone guard your vehicle."

The man just won't give up. Cody knows that if he stays here for much longer, Rudy will get up the courage to try and collect that reward himself, and then he's going to have to kill the old scudder. He says, "I believe I already told you. Anyone tries to mess with my stuff, they'll learn a hard lesson."

Cody drives slowly down the main road, past the burnt-out remains of the mission compound, past the crater where a gas station once stood, past the row of one- and two-storey concrete buildings that, blackened by the soot of old fires and pockmarked by bullets, is just about all there's left of this place, which before the Black Flu was a truck stop on the transcontinental highway, with over a hundred working girls, twelve bars, three hotels, and two VD clinics. Rudy Kaufmann's bar is the only establishment still operating, its flat roof patched with corrugated iron scavenged from other buildings. Loud Zimbabwean funk-metal thumps out of its open windows and door. Young men in pick-and-mix military clothing lounge outside, their jaws rhythmically moving as they chew wads of *khat*, killing time at the fraying end of another long, hot afternoon. Several are sitting on the hood of a jeep that has a .50-calibre machine gun bolted to the back, what they call a technical. Rudy pays them in rice and *khat*; his own private army. They watch as Cody's van turns off the deeply rutted road, crosses the stony ford laid through a riverbed that contains no more than a string of muddy pools fringed by green reeds, bumps up the bank on the far side, and disappears into the belt of doum palms.

Cody locks up, walks back through the palm trees, and

squats on the litter of dry fronds at the edge of their shade,
patiently scanning the shimmering road with his field
glasses. Pretty soon, a small black dot appears, jittering behind shimmering volumes of furnace air, growing larger,
turning into a 4×4 dragging a rooster-tail of red dust that
blows past it when it draws up beside the bar. Cody watches
as Rudy talks with the two men who climb down, watches as
they disappear inside, waits exactly thirty minutes before
walking back into the ruined little town, gathering a little procession of excited children along the way. The young men
outside the bar make way for him, touching fingers to their
foreheads, respectful of this killer priest with the angel and
serpent on his back. Cody preached to them yesterday, made
a point of catching a couple of snakes and handling them the
way his father taught him; he's pretty sure that if it comes to
it, these *mooryans* would rather take his side than Rudy's.

The new arrivals are sitting at a table with the old mercenary, one a slim man in a short-sleeved white shirt and tan
pants, the other shaven-headed, wearing olive-drab pants
tucked into combat boots and a pocket-vest that leaves his
muscular arms bare. All three men look at Cody when he
steps inside, and the slim man stands up and extends a hand
when Rudy explains unnecessarily that here is the famous
Cody Corbin. Cody inclines his head towards Mr. Muscles,
says, "Who's this scudder?"

"He's my driver," the slim man says, lifting his hand away.
He's wearing amber-tinted shades, has a skinny moustache
above his smile. "I am Captain Jean Badiledi. It is a pleasure to
meet you, Monsieur Corbin. Your reputation goes before you."

"I was told there'd be just one of you," Cody says.

"Magne can wait outside," Captain Badiledi says, "if he is
making you nervous."

Mr. Muscles, Magne, slowly gets to his feet, and Cody
says, "Hold it there," and pats the guy down, telling him to
put one foot and then the other on the seat of the chair so he
can check for an ankle holster or maybe a knife. Magne sub-
mits with good grace, a faint smile lifting one corner of his
mouth.

"You can leave us," Captain Badiledi tells Magne when Cody is finished, and Rudy says, "Now we all know who we are, we can sit down and talk."

Cody slaps a five-dollar bill on the table and says, "What you can do is go get me a Coke. Shut off that heathen noise you call music while you're about it, and then make yourself scarce. I want to talk with this man in peace."

"I think you forget that this is my bar," Rudy says with a show of affronted dignity.

"Way you keep havin' to mention it, I'm not likely to forget," Cody says, and takes the Colt Python from his waistband, sets it on the table, and sits down. "When you bring that Coke, I want it cold and unopened, okay?"

The Coke comes in an old-fashioned wasp-waisted bottle. Cody twists off the cap, drinks down the sweet dark liquid in one swallow, belches. "I have to tell you," he says to Captain Badiledi, "that I don't like this at all."

"It is an extraordinary situation," Captain Badiledi says, "and extraordinary situations call for extraordinary remedies."

Cody says, "They teach you that in military school, uh?"

"My military education has been entirely practical," Captain Badiledi says. He's calm and poised, making a point of meeting Cody's gaze and not looking at the big pistol lying on the table between them.

"There's a couple of things we need to get clear straightaway," Cody says. "First, I waited two whole days in this shithole to talk with you, I haven't been paid for the job I've already done, and I'm not minded to stay here any longer than necessary. Second, this is not how I usually do business. I like to keep my distance from my clients, and so far that's worked just fine. I don't need face-to-face briefings to get the job done. I don't even need to know who I'm workin' for. I do my work, I get paid, everyone's happy. So, what I have to ask is, how do I know you're who you claim to be? Because it's possible someone hacked my line of communication to set up this meeting, and I wasn't told you were bringing a friend."

"I have been told by our mutual employer that if I express my appreciation about your work with such people as Parker

Adams, Marc Szkopiak, Josiane Levy, and Amandio Collar, then your doubts will be eased."

They are all targets Cody has eliminated at the request of his fairy godmother. He says, "Let's say I believe you're who you're supposed to be, and cut to the chase. If you've come to pay me for work already done, and deliver information so I can get on with this new job, all you have to do is hand everything over, and we can both be on our separate ways."

"Deliver information? No, it is quite the reverse. I have in fact come to take you away."

"Yeah? And just where are you supposed to be takin' me?"

"You are a very suspicious man, Monsieur Corbin."

"I'm careful. That's how I stayed in the game so long."

"You want to know the details of this job. I understand completely. Listen, then: we are going to Kinshasa, in the Democratic Republic of the Congo, to deal with a man who has caused our employer much embarrassment." Captain Badiledi mentions a name and says that Cody may have seen him on the news channels, watching through his sunglasses for a reaction and not getting one.

Cody says, "I don't have much time for the news. Aside from the fact that news channels peddle lies and propaganda, it's well known that they're crammed full of subliminal messages."

"It is of no matter. He is involved with another man, who calls himself Raphael, a small-time criminal with an inflated opinion of himself who runs a freak-show safari ranch. I can bring you up to speed on this place, provide maps and satellite photographs and so on, as we travel."

"Wait a minute. You want to come along with me?"

"Of course."

"And your boyfriend is part of the plan too?"

"He's part of *my* plan," Captain Badiledi says. He's still smiling, but something is hardening in his gaze.

"You have your own particular personal reasons for going after these two scudders, uh? Now why do you think I'd want to help someone like you?"

"You've been a loyal worker," Captain Badiledi says, "but

you don't even know who you've been working for, or why. Have you ever wondered if you're on the right side?"

"I know I've been doin' the Good Lord's work. That I've been riddin' the world of people who believe they can set themselves above His creation. People you mentioned, and plenty more besides."

"But this man, Nicholas Hyde, he is no scientist or gene hacker. You escaped from Kenya after eliminating gengineered creatures and assassinating their creator, yes? Well, Nicholas Hyde has been chasing the origin of another kind of gengineered creature, so-called white devils that were let loose in a remote part of my country. In doing so, he has become involved with the other target, Raphael. They have captured and killed a white devil, and now they are attempting to blackmail our employer."

Cody feels a tug of interest. "How so?"

"It is quite simple. She herself was once involved in gengineering. In fact, she helped to create those creatures you eliminated; the man you killed was both her collaborator and her husband. I believe that these white devils were created with the same techniques, and that is why she wants Nicholas Hyde and Raphael eliminated and the body of the white devil destroyed—she does not want the truth to be known. As for those names that I mentioned to establish my credibility, they were scientists, yes, but they also once worked with her. You claim to be doing God's work, Monsieur Corbin, but I must say that God's work is strangely close to the personal interests of our employer."

"Why are you tellin' me all this? What's your interest?"

"I am supposed to accompany you on this job, but not just to help you. After you eliminate these men, instead of paying you I am supposed to eliminate you too. That is what our employer asked me to do, Monsieur Corbin. However, I have other ideas."

Cody grins. "You think you and your boyfriend can take me down, uh?"

"I do not want to kill you, Monsieur Corbin, because I believe that our employer plans to kill *me*, on my return. Also, she has made threats against my wives and my children. That is why I am telling you this. Otherwise, I would do what I was asked to do, and walk away without a thought."

"Maybe you *should* just walk away."

"If I left you here, how long would it be, I wonder, before the unsavoury character who runs this place decided that you were more valuable dead than alive? I am sure that he knows of the reward offered by the Kenyan government, and I know that he is very interested in the weapons he believes you have stored inside your van. He talked much about what they might be. Or, on the other hand, perhaps we can work together." The man stares at Cody through his sunglasses, trying hard to sound casual as he makes his pitch. "We kill Raphael, but we keep Nicholas Hyde alive. He's a hero—our employer knows people will believe what he has to say. Also, we try to get hold of the body of the white devil, and we tell our employer that unless she pays us, we'll sell it to the highest bidder, let some TV company find out what it really is."

"You want to blackmail her."

"She has threatened me, she has threatened my family, and she wants to kill you. And besides all this, why should she profit from her crimes against Nature?"

Cody thinks about shooting the man through the heart. He thinks about shooting Rudy Kaufmann. And then, what? Set up as the new shithole king? Drive off, try to make it solo across bandit territory to some place where his face isn't known, where no one knows about the price on his head?

"Okay," he says. "Let's talk."

An hour later, Cody locks the door of his camper van, picks up his stuff, and tells Jean Badiledi, "Let's go."

"That is all you bring?"

"Guns, a guitar, and a change of clothes—what else does a man need in this world of sorrow? You take good care of my vehicle," Cody says to Rudy Kaufmann. "I'll be back for it in a couple of days, just as soon as I've done this little job, so don't go pokin' around. You might learn a lesson you won't like."

The old scudder touches two fingers to his temple in a loose salute, shows off his bad dentistry, and says, "I'll look after it like one of my own."

They're halfway to the bush airstrip when the sound of the explosion cracks across the desert. Cody turns in the back seat of the 4×4 to look at the little column of black smoke rising against the bleached sky, says to Jean Badiledi, "Looks like Rudy's curiosity got the better of him."

Jean Badiledi turns to look at the smoke too. "What did you use?"

"A motion detector rigged to spark a couple of kilos of Semtex. They're gonna be hard put to find much of ol' Rudy." Cody meets the driver's gaze in the rearview mirror, says, "Do we have a problem?"

The driver looks away, shakes his head.

Cody tells Jean Badiledi, "Those *mooryans* hanging around outside the bar might come after us in their technical, but I doubt it. I don't think they liked Rudy any more than I did."

Jean Badiledi smiles. "You teach a harsh lesson."

"Like my daddy used to say, what other kind is worthwhile?"

Chapter 32

The plane, a decrepit 767 with most of its seats stripped out, is carrying fifteen tons of tobacco leaves in tightly wrapped aromatic bales and just eight passengers. Elspeth Faber and Teddy Yssel get a row of seats to themselves. Teddy settles at a window with a bottle of Johnnie Walker Black Label and Elspeth stretches out in the centre row and tries to rest, but her nerves are rubbed thin, the plane is cold and noisy, and level shafts of brilliant sunlight pierce the windows, so she soon gives up on sleep and tries once more to find out exactly how Teddy knows where Nicholas Hyde is. But Teddy will only give annoyingly elliptical answers, and turns the conversation around and asks her about her father; Elspeth gives him a carefully edited portion of the truth, watches him lose interest as she tells him about her research.

"I thought *all* those apemen were cannibals," he says, and recounts the plot of some dumb teenage-caveman movie he once saw, the warm-up for a handful of well-polished anecdotes about the adventures he shared with his poor dead friend Johnny Grundlingh, stories he's no doubt told a hundred times before to potential pick-ups in bars. At last, whisky-maudlin, he begins to talk about his strange childhood in Riebeecksland, the fundamentalist Afrikaner homeland in Tanzania, and the real Teddy Yssel begins to show through the macho bullshit.

"It was a terrible place," he says. "A theme park set in the eighteenth century. No electricity or TV, no Web access, no cars or trucks except the self-defence force's Land Rovers, just ox-carts and horses. Christian National Education at school, hours of propaganda every day about the peaceful, oppressed, misunderstood Boers. God, race, and land. Divine intervention at the Battle of Blood River. The murder of Boers in British concentration camps. The Great Betrayal. The international conspiracy against apartheid. The Second Great Trek. That was our education—that, and farm work. If you got to be a blacksmith or a store owner, you were a big man in the community. It was a concentration camp, you understand, of our own making. The self-defence force, it was there not to keep our enemies out, but to keep us in. But we escaped, Johnny and me. We got out. We were both eight years old when the Second Great Trek got started. We were old enough to remember the rest of the world as we grew up. We knew what we were missing, and we wanted it back. We used to watch aeroplanes, you know? We didn't have planes in Riebeecksland, of course, but you could see the contrails of commercial airliners and Tanzanian military planes. We used to lie out in the pasture, Johnny and me, watch these tiny silver beads drag white contrails across the wide blue sky and wonder who was in them and where they were going. I made a glider once, a little toy glider. My father found it and made me burn it, and then he took off his belt. A rawhide belt it was, with an iron buckle. I remember the way he always took it off when he was going to punish me. Staring at me and slowly pulling that damned belt out loop by loop, doubling it over in his hands . . . Yah, Johnny and me, as soon as we could, we got out. Damn right we got out."

Just before they were due to begin ten years' compulsory service in the self-defence force, Teddy Yssel and Johnny Grundlingh decided to escape from Riebeecksland. They set out on the Day of the Covenant holiday, walking due south. They evaded patrols by travelling only at night. They navigated by the stars, used the survival techniques they had been taught at school to walk across three hundred miles of desert to freedom.

"We worked all kinds of crappy jobs until at last, two long years later, we got our pilot licences. It was like a fairy tale. We had done what we dreamed of. We had escaped, and we had become pilots." Teddy Yssel laughs. "Oh man, we were so young. We thought we were going to live forever." He offers Elspeth the bottle of whisky, and when she refuses it says, "To our dead," takes a big slug and without shifting in his seat somehow makes himself remote from her, staring through the window at the atomic light of the gorgeous sunset that's dismantling itself beyond the darkening horizon.

The plane lands at N'Djili Airport an hour after sundown, taxis past the gleaming brand-new passenger terminal to the cargo area. The black air is hot and stifling, and stinks of burnt alcohol from the exhausts of noisy trucks idling as they wait to be loaded. Elspeth feels that she's pushing through heavy, wet blankets as she shoulders her day bag and follows Teddy Yssel down the rickety aluminium ladder and across a veldt of concrete slab towards the feeble orange lights that burn outside the long, low customs shed.

A tall man in a white T-shirt and pressed blue jeans pushes

through the crowd of passengers and officials at the baggage-reclamation area and slaps palms with Teddy Yssel. "Dieudonné will take us through immigration," Teddy tells Elspeth. "He works for this old friend of mine. She'll put us up for the night."

"I take care of everything," Dieudonné says. He has a craggy, shaven head and a theatrical presence. Silver wire is sewn in tight little loops along the rims of his ears. His thumbnails are painted with bright red nail polish. "Do you have American dollars? The Congolese franc is no good for bribes."

He takes Elspeth's and Teddy Yssel's passports and sandwiches a salad of dollar bills between the pages, winks at Elspeth. "All you do is stay very close to me, there will be no problem. Teddy, my old friend, I hope you do not bring anything doubtful with you."

"Those were the good old bad old days," Teddy Yssel says. "We're here on a moral mission. I'm here for Johnny, and I guess Elspeth is here for her father. We're going to find out the truth and bust everything wide open."

"Sure thing," Elspeth says, wishing she had one tenth of Teddy's whisky-fuelled confidence. She picks up her day bag and follows the two men to the far end of the noisy shed. Dieudonné hands the passports to two uniformed officials behind a buckled plywood counter, talks with them in rapid French. The dollar bills disappear; the passports are stamped with temporary visas; they are waved through.

Outside, a tribe of ragged barefoot children materializes from the darkness, pleading for sweets, for money, for antibiotics. Dieudonné throws a scatter of small coins at them and walks quickly through the hot, humid darkness to a battered thirty-year-old Isuzu Trooper that at his command disarms and unlocks itself with a long sequence of beeps and clicks and whirs. "We go at once," he tells Elspeth and Teddy, "before the soldiers see us and decide they deserve a bribe."

Teddy Yssel collapses into the shotgun seat, saying, "It's still as bad, yah?"

Dieudonné starts the Trooper and eases away from the

sheds, switching on the headlights only when he reaches the exit road. "If you work for the Five," he says, inclining his head to speak to Elspeth, "or if you come here to do business with any of them, you arrive at that nice new passenger terminal, there is no problem. One time I was there to pick up someone, I saw a poodle some executive had brought from the United States of America carried straight through. It was sitting on a silk pillow in a basket, like a little king. But if you are an ordinary person, you need a man like me to get you past customs and immigration, and even then there are difficulties. The Five give money to pay the army and the police, but somehow the money disappears." Dieudonné laughs, bangs the steering wheel with his palms. "It is very mysterious how money vanishes in this country! There have been investigations, but no one can find out where it goes. So the soldiers and gendarmes, because they are not paid, they take what they need from the people. They behave like a conquering army."

Teddy and Dieudonné talk about Johnny Grundlingh as they drive past kilometre after kilometre of bulldozed mounds of rubble humped either side of the wide highway. Uneven swales colonized by bushes and grasses stretch into the darkness, mysterious fires twinkling here and there. Dieudonné tells Elspeth that this was once *La Cité*, a vast slum district established when Belgian colonialists kept Africans from the centre of their own capital city, and is now, after the Black Flu, the mass grave of two million people.

"I suppose you have something similar in Nairobi," he says.

"Something similar," Elspeth says, thinking of the white memorial stones that stretch, row on row on row, across three square kilometres of Nairobi National Park. Although the stones are set above portions of ash taken from the mingled remains of dozens or hundreds of bodies burned on hasty pyres, the vast cemetery is carefully divided into Christian and Muslim plots, and every stone has been decorated by grieving relatives with flowers and photographs and keepsakes. But this dreary place, where the uncommemorated dead are mixed with the rubble of their houses, is more like a garbage dump than a necropolis, and Elspeth realizes with a little pang of dismay that she's now more than two thousand kilometres from home, in a country where things are done very differently. Although she has no sense of danger in the company of these two strange men in this strange city, in her mind she is still travelling to an ideal destination where the knotted mystery of her father and Teryl and the Gentle People and the white devils will unravel at a touch.

They pass single-storey mudbrick houses set amongst palms and mango trees, a huge covered market that occupies an entire city block, dark and shuttered at this hour. They pass an old man who walks slowly along the shoulder of the road, a tall stack of torn pieces of cardboard balanced on his head. They pass through a checkpoint that chokes traffic down to a single lane between ten-metre-high coils of trophic wire garnished with the corpses of birds snared by the restless razor-sharp tendrils. They drive through the wide, tree-lined boulevards of central Kinshasa, where the streetlights are working and the roads are newly surfaced, crowded with scooters and white taxis, SUVs and 4×4s. A busy, brightly lit shopping street is lined with stores selling discount electronics and bolts of cloth. The shops and high-rise office and apartment buildings lift into the night. People are strolling about, eating at open-air cafés and restaurants, drinking in noisy open-air bars; there's an air of prosperous normalcy.

Dieudonné keeps up a running commentary. He's one of those charming, cheerful, competent fixers who grease the wheels of commerce in Africa. Elspeth tells him that she hasn't seen so many white people in an African city since the Black Flu, and he says that the Kinshasa Free Zone is under heavy manners. He points to the white-gloved policemen directing traffic at every intersection, the armed guards outside the restaurants and bars. Tanks are drawn up on the wide lawns outside the spotlit Parliament building. Half a dozen armoured personnel carriers and squads of soldiers guard a twenty-storey glass and steel office building—the headquarters of Cytex, one of the five transnats that more or less own what's left of the Democratic Republic of the Congo.

"We let them in because they said they would help the reconstruction," Dieudonné says. "But they are as bad as the Belgians."

"Don't ask him about the Belgians," Teddy Yssel says. "He can talk for six hours straight about the Belgians. They were a terror here. Worse than the Boers, if you can believe it."

"The Five pay off the government and the army," Dieudonné says, "and in return they can do their research without restrictions, they have a cheap, docile workforce, they pay no taxes . . ."

"And fellows like you get a cut of the action," Teddy says. He takes a sip from his bottle of Johnnie Walker Black Label, offers it to Elspeth, and says, when she refuses with a shake of her head, "I don't have any disease. I'm as clean as you. We have a wonderful health service in South Africa. After Johnny and me escaped from Riebeecksland, the authorities fixed us up at once with magic bullets."

"I don't want a drink, that's all."

"You need to relax a little. And it's way past six, the sun has set. Cocktail hour."

"Maybe later," Elspeth says, thinking that Teddy has been drinking ever since she met him, seven hours ago.

Dieudonné says, "Our problem is that our country is stuffed with riches, but we can't stop people stealing them. In the last century, after Mobutu lost power, our neighbours fought to gain control of the east, because that's where the diamonds and minerals are. Politicians and soldiers in Uganda and Rwanda and Zimbabwe grew very rich at our expense. Sergeant Samuel Nyibizo is a Rwandan who made his fortune as a middleman in the coltan trade—that's how he could pay for the army that took Brazzaville after the Black Flu. I remember how happy we were when peace was finally brokered by the Pan-Africa Congress and the Five offered to help in the reconstruction of our country. Because the world was at last taking notice of our troubles, our country was united, we would benefit from our own wealth. But ordinary people saw little of the Five's aid, the peace lasted only a few years before the Black Flu struck, and now there are again many difficulties. We have lost control of much of the country, and here in Kinshasa we have given up our independence to the Five, but we do not benefit from the profits they make. Much is taken from us, little is given. It is the usual story."

"You don't have to lecture her," Teddy says. "Her father, the famous mind-bender, worked here, before the Black Flu." He takes another swig, a big one; bubbles float up through the amber liquid to the sliding pyramid of air at the end of the flat-sided bottle. He glances back at Elspeth and says, "You think I'm a drunk, but I'm not. The difference is that while I *like* to drink, I don't *need* to drink. I don't drink when I'm flying—but, the point is, I'm not flying now."

Elspeth wonders how often he's used that line on prospective dates.

Dieudonné says, "I know about your father, Dr. Faber. He was working with the famous Daniel Lovegrave, in one of the big research stations in the north. I heard they were making monsters."

"Not exactly," Elspeth says.

"The man we've come to find," Teddy Yssel says, "he's the one who knows all about monsters."

The road splits right and left. The right fork swings towards the science park, where giant scallop shells, flying saucers, glass and steel domes, and bone-white ziggurats stand in hectares of sculptured parkland, everything floodlit and standing against the African night with hyperreal particularity, floating away in the distance as Dieudonné takes the left fork, driving into a grim industrial estate of long, low warehouse units. Only a few streetlights are working here. Walls are scribbled with garish gang-tags. Dieudonné draws up in front of a gate in a high wall around one of the warehouses and sounds the horn. After a couple of minutes an old man with a submachine gun slung over his shoulder drags the gate open, and Dieudonné drives through.

The warehouse is a single-storey, prefabricated shed that has been turned into a low-budget hostel. Its large compound is crammed with brightly painted minibuses and camper vans and 4×4s. Old-fashioned solar panels are tilted this way and that on its flat roof; in one corner, windmill generators roar and rattle in the hot, dry wind. Inside, people of two dozen nationalities are eating at long communal tables, playing ping-pong and table football, wigging out on the Web, talking in clusters on nests of beanbags and cushions. They're mostly in their twenties, and mostly what Teddy Yssel calls workers in the slipstream economy—this is one of the few countries where gene hackers and biopunks can still find employment. A couple of tall, skinny boys wear traditional red tribal robes and bead necklaces, with strings of beads wound around the distended lobes of their ears, and one girl is wrapped from head to toe in layers of black mesh, only her startlingly green eyes showing, but most are dressed in no-label T-shirts and baggy shorts, or surplus jackets and pants from a dozen different armies, and everyone has some kind of body mod. Eyes seem to be the most popular, perhaps because it's through the eyes that we first make contact with strangers and so the unexpected is immediately arresting. As she follows Dieudonné and Teddy through this exotic crowd, Elspeth sees lizard eyes, cat eyes, goat eyes, eyes like crushed jewels. One person of indeterminate sex has the large black eyes and polished ashen skin of an alien grey. There are people with crests of brightly coloured feathers on top of their heads, people with bands of glimmering scales on cheeks and foreheads, people with animated tattoos rippling with busy, colourful detail across their chests and backs. Elspeth thinks that the whole bunch looks like a crowd of extras from some cheap science-fiction show.

The hostel is run by Teddy Yssel's old friend, Darlajane B., a small, spiky old woman in a red jumpsuit, her elfin, lined face as white as a Pierrot's, with kohled eyes and bright red lipstick, hair shaved to a stubble dyed arterial crimson. From their easy familiarity, Elspeth suspects that Darlajane B. and Teddy Yssel go back a long way. They settle in the old woman's office, a freight container elevated on scaffolding above the canteen. One side has been cut out and glazed with thick panels of Perspex. There are cushions scattered over dusty Persian carpets, ferns growing in brass pots, low tables strewn with tools and electronics and trinkets. A metre-high figure crudely hacked from black, splintery wood stands in one corner; a rack of old-fashioned cathode-ray TVs flickers quietly in another.

Darlajane B. clasps Teddy's hands in hers and says that she is so sorry to hear about Johnny Grundlingh, and they share gossip and a fat joint while Elspeth nurses a bottle of Tusker beer. Her dismay is biting deep now. She feels that her life has somehow taken a wrong turn, that she's become entangled in something that she wants no part of. It doesn't help that Darlajane B. soon wants to talk about her father and Teryl.

"I used to follow their work," Darlajane B. says, "back when neural enhancement was the hot topic. There was a rumour that your father had some sort of laboratory accident. He used a new technique on himself and it went wrong." She gives Elspeth a sharp look. "But I suppose you will not want to talk about it, so soon after your tragedy."

Teddy says, "The man we're hoping to find thinks the things that killed Johnny had something to do with Pleistocene Park."

"I doubt it," Darlajane B. says. "The place was destroyed during the so-called war on bioterrorism, and I believe the whole area is now under water. Several of its scientists passed through here on their way out of the country, but that was some time ago."

"I've heard a rumour," Elspeth says, "that Daniel Lovegrave is still alive."

I think it might be Danny Lovegrave.

"I hear all kinds of things, and most of them are not true. Don't bogart that joint, darling," Darlajane B. tells Teddy, and draws a deep toke that lights crackling sparks in the joint's smouldering end. "These science-fiction killer monstrosities that this man, Nicholas Hyde, was hunting. They have something to do with the work of your father?"

Elspeth shrugs.

"It's obvious," Teddy says with the owl-eyed solemnity of the profoundly drunk. "Elspeth's father and her stepmother owned this company called Qualia. Qualia and Daniel Lovegrave had a contract with Pleistocene Park to re-create extinct apemen—"

"Hominids," Elspeth says. "*Australopithecus africanus.*"

The Gentle People. Murdered, and burnt to ashes.

Teddy ignores her, caught up in his crazy theory. "And Obligate bought Qualia, and now Elspeth's stepmother is head of Obligate's research centre across the river in Brazzaville. It is well known that Obligate has a big store of genetic material. Who's to say what uses they might have for it? Perhaps they made killer apes to try and end the war in the north. This is beautiful stuff, don't you think? We're going to wrap it all up in one neat parcel and shove it as far up Obligate's ass as it'll go."

Elspeth says to Darlajane B., "Teddy told me that he knows where Nicholas Hyde is. He thinks that you can help us make contact with him."

"It will be expensive. The man he stays with likes money," Darlajane B. says, rubbing thumb and forefinger together, "and will want a big dash to arrange an introduction."

Of course it will be expensive, Elspeth thinks, her dismay suddenly bottomless. They'll take my money, and that's the last I'll know.

"I don't need any introduction," Teddy says. "I've worked for this guy before."

"I heard you were fired," Darlajane B. says, winking at Elspeth. "He did not tell you that?"

"It was a while ago," Teddy says. "And it was no big deal."

"Perhaps it's time you told me exactly who this man is," Elspeth says.

Teddy smiles, shrugs.

"Teddy likes his secrets," Darlajane B. says.

"Hey, fuck you."

"Fuck you too, darling," Darlajane B. says with a sweet smile, and tells Elspeth, "The man calls himself Raphael. He has a big-game ranch east of Kinshasa. He clones animals, and rich people shoot them. Some of my kids have worked for him."

"My guess is," Teddy says, "he wants those white devils for his menagerie."

Elspeth says, "People would want to hunt those things?"

"Sure," Teddy says. "Why not?"

"Raphael has two kinds of clients," Darlajane B. says. "Most of them, they are executives of the Five who buy into the white-hunter thing as a status symbol. They want trophies for their den or their office. So they are driven out into the bush or the forest, and, what a surprise, here is a rhino or a lion or whatever, just waiting to be shot with their brand-new Holland & Holland rifle. Every kill is guaranteed because these poor animals are doped to the eyeballs, taken to the spot by truck, and staked out. And most of them are sick, too, because Raphael does not use the highest standards when he's cloning. So, that is what most of his clients are like. But the rest, they are more dangerous. They want the real thing. They want the thrill of the hunt. They want to test themselves against their prey. They go out into the bush with perhaps just a spear, to kill a lion the way the Masai do it, or perhaps with a bow and arrow. Those people, they will love the white devils."

Elspeth laughs.

"You think it sounds strange," Darlajane B. says.

"I think it sounds like a ridiculous fantasy. I think this guy sounds like a James Bond villain."

"He cultivates a flamboyant style. Also, he offers his clients very exotic animals to hunt. Just a few months ago he bought a saber-toothed tiger from someone. He is right now trying to clone it."

"A saber-toothed cat," Elspeth says, her blood prickling.

"I think it was from Pleistocene Park originally, and I see that you think that too."

"Danny Lovegrave had three of them," Elspeth says. "I saw them when I went to visit my father."

Darlajane B. says, "Raphael has a story about how he

hunted it down in the Dead Zone. I think it is a piece of non-sense—just one of the colourful tales with which he enter-tains his clients. Some warlord took it for a trophy or totem, perhaps—or maybe a jackal, one of the men who scavenge in the Dead Zone, trapped it. But there is a chance that if you can find the man who sold it to Raphael, he will know if Daniel Lovegrave is still alive."

"Here's another idea," Teddy says with a sloppy grin, clearly in love with his own cleverness. "Suppose Raphael collaborated with Elspeth's stepmother in the first place? They made the white devils, and the white devils got free."

"If Raphael helped make these white devils," Darlajane B. says, "he could easily make more—he would not need to hunt them. Besides, I would have heard of it. Raphael likes to boast. He is very bad at keeping secrets."

"The thing I still don't understand," Elspeth says, "is why Nicholas Hyde has fallen in with this man."

"Maybe Raphael doesn't want to work with Teryl Meade any more," Teddy says. "He gets this hero to denounce her, to tell his story about monsters and a conspiracy, so that she'll get in trouble with Obligate. Who are so very much against gengineering."

But so is Teryl, and Elspeth has never doubted the veracity of her stepmother's Damascene conversion. Once Teryl changes her mind, it stays changed.

Elspeth says, "Another thing—if these white devils did es-cape from Raphael's ranch, how did they get from one side of the Congo to the other? If this ranch or whatever it is is east of Kinshasa, it isn't even *on* the Congo."

Teddy Yssel shrugs. He's too in love with his own story to be interested in annoying details. "They got out, got across the river, wandered around until Nicholas Hyde and those Brazilian soldiers stumbled on them. Who knows how long it's been since they escaped?"

"It can't have been too long. They're not exactly incon-spicuous."

"Hey, I don't hear any ideas from you." Teddy twiddles his fingers for a turn with the joint.

"That's because I don't have enough facts," Elspeth says.

"Dr. Faber thinks you make too much from very little," Darlajane B. says to him. She's pretty sharp, for a stoned little old lady. "Listen, Dr. Faber, I will help you, if you want it. I liked your father's work, and I do not very much like Obligate, or the other transnats for that matter." She takes another toke, and starts searching under the cushions on which she sprawls. "So, my hospitality I give free, my help at cost price. Many people pass through here; I hear all kinds of things. Much of it is rumour and fantasy of course, but there is also much hard information. Also, I spend far too much time on the Web. I have very many contacts there."

Teddy says, "Listen to her, Elspeth. She knows all kinds of people."

Elspeth says, "So you're, what, an information broker? A data miner?"

"That's part of what I do." Darlajane B. finds a roach clip and fits it to the stub of the joint and hands it across to Teddy Yssel. "There you are, darling. Knock yourself out."

Teddy takes a big hit and says in a small, choked voice, "Whatever Obligate is trying to hide, my good friend Darlajane B. can find it out."

Darlajane B. says, "If you think like Obligate, of secrets and compartmentalization, then you will lose. They are better than you at that kind of thing, and they have very much more resources. You have to think around them. Sideways, up, down, around. Fortunately, the world is not a tidy place any more. There is no neat cause and effect. Plots like yours, Teddy, exist only in the minds of paranoids in possession of too few or too many facts. Rationalization, like science, is dead."

Elspeth says, "Science isn't dead." She still feels deep misgivings about these people, but it's no longer scary, more like a kind of existential vertigo. Perhaps she's getting a secondary high from the drifting layers of sweet smoke that fill the room.

Darlajane B.'s smile shows small, spaced teeth like nubs of corn. "You do not think so?"

Elspeth takes a swallow of beer. "Perhaps there's no such

thing as good old-fashioned curiosity-motivated inquiry any more, but there's still plenty of good science being done."

Darlajane B. says, "I don't disagree with your ideals, Dr. Faber, but to me, people like you are very much a relict species, like the coelacanth. You exist in a marginal environment. Always you must struggle for funds, scraps of endowments, sponsorship, and always you must work harder for less and less, because the world cannot any longer afford such work. The nineteenth-century culture of science's Golden Age, which flourished only when ideas could be exchanged freely, was destroyed when scientists became obsessed with making money, and so also with secrecy, because to make a profit they must hide their ideas from their rivals. All the best researchers left the universities to make obscene amounts of money from their little area of speciality in government research facilities and the public sector, and in short order scientific culture consumed itself because there was no one left to generate the basic unprofitable work on which the high-flyers depended. It was like an ecosystem that removes its primary producers."

"It was destroyed," Elspeth says, "by people like you. By people who recklessly misused half-understood technology, without any thought about the consequences."

"People like me?"

"And your friends down there, with the feathers and scales and the funny eyes."

Darlajane B. sticks another monster joint in her mouth, lights it with an ancient Zippo, and draws smoke deep down into her chest with a rattling sigh. "Biopunks did not create the Black Flu. They did not design the virus that created the Dead Zone. In fact, the biopunk culture, it is very like the culture of traditional, old-fashioned science. It depends upon the free exchange of information. Those kids down there are employed by companies like Cytex on a casual basis, like the old software companies, with no career structure, no rights to the intellectual properties they generate ... They work in huge teams on six-month contracts, one-year contracts, to keep eighty- and ninety-year-old baby boomers healthy. They will never have papers in *Science* or *Nature*, so they show what they can do by experimenting on themselves. Their mods are advertisements for their skills. They are habitual braggarts because their standing depends on letting everyone know what they have done; their entire culture is based on the idea of open source, from pirated genomes placed on black servers, to DNA sequences and gene hacks disseminated in philes and ezines. The only difference between biopunks and your kind of science, Dr. Faber, is that their work stands or falls not by peer review prior to publication but by its utility. By the number of downloads it receives. By word of mouth. Biopunks and gene hackers are not wild-eyed fanatics; they are idealistic kids who love science. Some of them have to work for the transnats to make a living, but they all believe that research and information and exchange of ideas should be free and unregulated, not locked up by copyright and litigation. They are, I suppose, old-fashioned romantics. It was biopunks who got together with staff at the research hospital in this city and developed and grew in vast amounts a vaccine for the Black Flu. It was only thirty percent effective, not as good as magic bullets, but still they are seen as heroes."

"Man," Teddy Yssel says admiringly. His pupils are the size of dimes. "You sure talk a lot when you get stoned."

Darlajane B. passes him the joint. Its end is printed with red lipstick. "I am not stoned. Or not too much. I am passionate. I have done many things, always on the margin. I was a rock star in Communist Berlin when it was more or less illegal. I was in prison a year because of it, and let out just in time for the fall of the Berlin Wall. Somewhere I have a video clip, it shows me dancing on top of the Wall. The one moment when my life and history came together. After that, I sell pieces of the Wall to tourists, I sell surplus Red Army equipment. I move to the Czech Republic and make money running clubs and bars—even a launderette. I get involved in the freeware scene, this in Holland, and with gene hackers. Then I move to Africa with my boyfriend when things for gene hackers become too difficult in Europe. He died of the plastic disease, poor fellow. Now I have this place."

Elspeth says, "So that's why you defend the gene hackers.

It isn't anything to do with ideology—you were one of them."

Darlajane B. says, "And you defend old-fashioned science because you're an old-fashioned scientist. We choose our ideologies because of what we are, and you may not agree, but I think we are very much alike. We are on the same side. That is why I am happy to arrange for you an introduction to Raphael."

"Darlajane B. knows everyone who is anyone in Kinshasa," Teddy says.

"Not exactly," Darlajane B. says. "But it is true that all sorts of people pass through here."

"She is famous for her tolerance," Teddy says.

"That I am not," Darlajane B. says sharply. "Just last week, I threw out these people who wanted to hold some kind of revivalist meeting here. Not because they were Christians—these days you have to feel sorry for Christians. But because they insisted on their right to take over the place for their meeting, that is why I tell them to move on. I tell them I am a godless old Communist who does not want anyone imposing their beliefs on anyone else. One of them, all jail muscles and tattoos, made threats. So when they leave, I have a bad thought for them and bang a nail in Smoky Joe."

She points to the statue that squats in a corner, radiating a louring menace like the psychic equivalent of an exposed fission pile. It grins mirthlessly, its wide frog mouth crowded with real human teeth, hundreds of nails and iron spikes hammered through its chest and head. Darlajane B. explains that it's a nail fetish she took in trade, a thing once owned by a village sorcerer; if you wanted something to happen to someone, good or bad, the sorcerer took your money and your nail, and knocked it into the fetish to make your wish come true.

"If I bang in a nail for you," Darlajane B. tells Elspeth, "I will do it with a good thought. But those fucking Christians are due for some deeply bad luck. They don't believe, but it doesn't matter. Now we will go and eat. This weed is making me hungry. Then tomorrow morning, first thing, I phone

Raphael, okay? It should not be difficult. He likes white women, likes to bring them to his parties."

"I've got a better idea," Elspeth says. "Raphael seems to have a thing about Pleistocene Park. I think you should phone him now and tell him that Matthew Faber's daughter wants to talk with him."

Chapter 33

Casey Chrisafis flexes his arm to show off the four parallel furrows that run from elbow to wrist and tells Nick, "These here are from a leopard. I hit it with an arrow, a four-hundred-fifty-grain bulletpoint, just below its ear. Ninety-nine times out of a hundred it would have been a surefire kill shot, but this cat was one mean motherfucker, and it took off into the bush with the arrow sticking straight through its neck. I followed the blood trail, convinced that I'd find its body a hundred, two hundred yards in. But the fucking thing had managed to haul itself into a tree, and when I went underneath, it dropped on me like a rug. Landed right on my back, hooking in with its claws here, when I raised my arm to push it off, and on my scalp. Check it out."

Casey Chrisafis bends over the breakfast table, parting his virile black hair at his forehead to show Nick a vee-shaped ridge of scar tissue.

"It must have hurt," Nick says.

"I didn't feel a thing at the time," Casey Chrisafis says as he sits back. "Just this weight on my shoulders, hot breath in my ear, and something wet and warm suddenly running into my eyes. So, I twisted, the leopard dropped off, by this time barely hanging on to its life, and I wiped my own blood from my eyes and finished the job with my knife. Cut its throat, one pass. I was so pumped, I didn't realize that half my scalp was hanging off—I didn't even wonder about where all the blood was coming from. I managed to take the skin and the head, wrap it all up, and carry it back to camp. Came in, humping my trophy and covered in my own blood, and wondering why people were looking at me so strangely. I asked for a cognac, and then I fainted. I lost three pints of blood that time. Had my scalp stapled together right there in the field. My barber hates it, says the scar makes my hair lie all wrong. Know what I say to him, Nick? I say: deal with it. My belief is that getting rid of a scar is like getting rid of part of your life."

Having made his point, Casey Chrisafis sits back and takes a sip of his coffee, slurping it with noisy satisfaction through his strong white teeth. He's sixty-eight, but has the muscle tone and easy vigour of a man half his age, is wearing a white, short-sleeved linen shirt and khaki shorts. He came in last night after three days in the bush stalking some kind of extinct wolf, and now he's regaling Nick with his stories of boyish derring-do while they eat breakfast on one of the terraces of the main house of Raphael's safari ranch. Rows of sprinklers have come on across the wide, lush lawns, amongst the stands of palms, banana plants, magnolias, bamboo, and palmettos that hide the guest cabins. The air smells of wet earth and grass. Somewhere in the paddocks, beyond the airstrip and the laboratories and the roundhouse byre where cows pregnant with cloned or gengineered animals are quartered, an elephant trumpets plaintively.

Casey Chrisafis is the man who wanted to fight the white devil—the wolf hunt was meant to compensate him for his disappointment. He believes that he's a genuine wildman, a natural-born hunter, the pure quill. For the past hour, over a leisurely brunch of fruit and scrambled ostrich egg, he has told Nick about stalking black bear in Alaska, armed with just a spear and a knife, about deep-ocean shark fishing, about living off the land while following the songlines in Australia, about the two years and three million dollars he spent trying to catch live specimens of giant squid in the benthic trenches of the Pacific off New Zealand. He says that in this world of sorrows, after Black Flu and the subsequent wars and famines levelled more than two-thirds of the Earth's poorest people, you have only two choices: either cocoon yourself in a deeply buried Level Four shelter, or realize that death no longer has any power over you and go out into the world to test yourself against its extremes. He's a self-made multimillionaire, a former TV producer who grinned when Nick told him he hadn't heard of any of his shows and virtualities, and said that he'd put that part of his life behind him.

"I lost an ex-wife and two children to the Black Flu. She refused to have a magic bullet fitted, thought it would turn her into a cyborg or some such nonsense. Well, Nick, I didn't care about what *she* did—it was her choice—but she wouldn't let the kids be fitted with them either. I was dragging her through the courts for child abuse when the Black Flu took them. After that, I figure that everything else is gravy. That you might as well enjoy life to the max. I tell you, Nick, you don't know what you have, you can't begin to appreciate it, until you come close to losing it. I may be my insurance broker's worst nightmare, but as long as the doctors can patch me up and keep coming up with new ways of stopping me from getting old, I'm going to be hanging it out beyond the edge as far as humanly possible."

Casey Chrisafis takes out a cigar now, clips one end with the little diamond-bladed cutter hung around his neck, and lights the other, grinning at Nick through smoke he slowly and luxuriously exhales through his nostrils. He has a noble Roman nose, twice broken in bare-knuckle fighting.

He says, "You sure you won't try one? They're some of the last Romeo y Juliettas; there won't be any more after that virus wiped out the tobacco plantations in Cuba. I have two hundred gross stored in a special vault back home, and I always bring a few along with me for occasions like this."

"The coffee is too good to spoil," Nick says.

As a matter of fact, it's the best he's ever tasted: a sweet, mellow blend from a tiny village in the north of Ethiopia where, according to Raphael, they grow a strain of coffee bushes with a thousand-year-old pedigree. "I buy the entire crop," he told Nick, "because I believe that my guests should have the finest of everything. But the secret of brewing fantastic coffee is not just in the beans, my friend; it is to add a pinch of graveyard dirt to every pot." He said it with a wink—as with so much he said, it was impossible to know if he was joking or not. Probably even he doesn't know half the time, for Raphael is his own most fabulous construct. The ranch, with its absurdly over-the-top decor and exotic menagerie (Raphael's pride and joy is a saber-toothed cat, which he claims to have trapped himself in the Dead Zone), is merely a stage set for his self-aggrandizing performance.

For the past four days, Nick has felt a weird sense of calm, as if he's living in the echo of some great bell. One minute he's in the swamp-forest, fighting for his life; the next, he's lifted out of there at the end of a rope with a dying man in his lap and a monster snapping at his heels and dropped here, where silent servants in white tunics pad soundlessly about, refreshing your drink before you need to ask, laying out your clothes, drawing your bath, turning down your bed. Where women surgically altered to look like virtual actors lounge around the swimming pool in nothing but their smiles and suntan lotion, not quite whores, but definitely available. Where you can spend your mornings dawdling over brunch and listening to the empty boasts of a pampered pedagogue. Raphael's ranch, formerly the hobby farm of a minister of the regime that collapsed during the Black Flu pandemic, is a cross between an exclusive hotel, a research laboratory, and a dude ranch. The main house is built along the edge of a low rise, a series of glass and steel and concrete boxes crammed with gold-leaf murals and gold-plated plumbing, satin-panelled walls, intricately inlaid hardwood floors, crystal light fittings, and antique furniture. There's a library, a fully equipped gymnasium, an Olympic-sized swimming pool laid with lapis lazuli tiles and fed by a series of artificial water-falls. After his escape from the swamp-forest, Nick slept in an eighteenth-century *lit bâteau* with Harmony Boniface's blood still under his fingernails and was woken by a servant who pulled back the watered-silk drapes before offering breakfast on a silver tray.

The first thing Nick did that morning was send Harmony Boniface's raw footage to the BBC's correspondent in Brazzaville. The second was to find Raphael, and confess. He expected to be shot or thrown into some dank subterranean cell, but after a long, dramatic pause, Raphael started to laugh, and said that it would add to the authenticity of the material. He seems very pleased by the attention the video clip has received. Over dinner last night, he told Nick that the scandal was already damaging Obligate's stock price, smiling serenely when Nick asked him if it had forced Teryl Meade to resign, saying that it was only a matter of time, just as it was only a matter of time before they were in business with the white devils.

"I am forced to be patient, and so must you."

"Fortunately, patience is all that we need," Andrew Królicki said. He is Raphael's chief scientist, a cadaverous Polish gentleman with iron-grey hair and a high-collared black suit, a devout Catholic who recited from memory the service for the dead when Harmony Boniface was laid to rest in the shade of a giant tree in a corner of a remote pasture.

They were sitting on Raphael's private terrace, at a table laid with starched linen and set with ivory-handled gold cutlery and Florentine silver chafing dishes, and bowls and plates and coffee cups that were part of a complete set of SS tableware—their first meal together, Raphael turned over a plate to proudly show Nick the stamping: a thick black swastika inside a red circle.

"And I am amazed," Raphael said now to his chief scientist, "because usually I must spend a week, a month, even a year, waiting for you to solve some tiny little problem." He was very cheerful, mopping sauce from his plate with half a cinnamon roll and folding it into his mouth, saying around it, "But this time, the details of chromosomal folding, gene activation, and all the rest, none of that presents a problem. Usually it's the same old mantra. More time, more money. This once—we are blessed."

Smiling at Nick, who wished the man would swallow his mouthful.

"We are lucky," Andrew Królicki said.

"In more ways than we can tell," Raphael said.

The two men were amused by some shared secret.

"You can clone them?" Nick had believed—had fervently hoped—that it wouldn't be possible. Certainly not in just three days.

"I *have* cloned them," Andrew Królicki said. "I completed the cell-fusion treatment this afternoon. At this moment, I have more than one hundred embryos about to enter the four-cell stage. In four days, God willing, some of them will have become blastocysts, ready to begin implantation into suitable hosts."

"I am amazed, Nicholas," Raphael said, "and I see that you are, too. I only employ the best people, but this, it is a miracle. I have struck a serious blow against Obligate. I am the proud father of many new children. I am blessed."

"Many *potential* new children," Andrew Królicki said. "We do not know what the post-implantation survival rate will be."

"Enough will survive," Raphael said. "All is well with the world."

"And even if some survive implantation," Królicki said, "we do not know how long they will take to become adult. We have been lucky so far, yes, but there are still many problems."

Raphael slurped down a heroic draught of champagne, wiped his mouth with the back of his hand, and said, "Listen to him, Nicholas. Always the spectre at the feast. They will be useful in only a few years, which is still too long, but I am sanguine. In the short term, the white devils will destroy my enemy. In the long term they will make me much money." He saluted Nick with his glass, drained the dregs. "I owe you more than I can tell you."

Right. But Nick is no nearer to discovering who made the white devils, and for all its luxury, the safari ranch is still a prison. He tried walking away from the main house in several directions, each time encountering exceedingly polite armed guards who told him that he was entering a restricted area, and perhaps he would like to turn around . . . ? The third time, the guards called Michel, who told Nick that if he tried it again, he'd be injected with a spinal tap that would shock him senseless if he strayed more than a hundred metres from the house. "It will be for your own good," Michel said. "Raphael likes you, and he likes to think you like him. You don't want him getting mad at you. Be nice to him, be nice to his guests, and you'll get along just fine."

Now, Casey Chrisafis is pulling up the left leg of his khaki shorts, showing Nick a scar the size and shape of a thumbprint on his inner thigh, asking him to guess what kind of animal did it.

"I'd say it was a person, not an animal," Nick says, weary of playing straight man, "as it looks very much like a bullet wound."

"Absolutely damned right. There's a story to it—a good one." Casey Chrisafis gestures to a waiter, tells him to bring more coffee. "You'll appreciate this," he tells Nick, "after your own little adventure. A good friend of mine organizes war tourism, maybe you've heard of it? A very simple idea, like all the best. He has someone on the ground, ex-Delta Force, ex-French Foreign Legion, ex-SAS, ex-whatever, co-operating with local people on one side or another of some pissant civil war. They make an arrangement to bring in mercenaries to help out, only the mercenaries are customers of my friend, you understand? They go through a couple of weeks of basic training, learn weapon-handling and a few useful phrases of the local language, and are inserted right in the middle of the war with a specific goal. You get a week of combat, and then you're airlifted straight out. Expensive? You better believe it. But you'd be surprised how many go for it. Because war, Nick, that's the greatest sport of all. My father fought in Vietnam, my grandfather in the Second World War—he was actually waiting to invade the Japanese archipelago when the atomic bombs were dropped. I always regret that I didn't follow them into the army—I could have fought in the last great, good war, in the Stan, Iraq, wherever. I could have been a Ranger or a Night Stalker, you heard of them? Very tough guys, specialize in infiltrating enemy territory, fly ground-hugging helicopters at night or parachute in from a plane up near the stratosphere. Two miles free fall before you open your parachute: completely undetectable.

"Well, I got my turn in some little town in Turkmenistan a couple of years ago, fighting on the side of the locals. It was going good, too, until we walked straight into an ambush. Our guide was shot dead, we were pinned down, and I got this"—Casey Chrisafis says, fingering the silvery oval on his thigh—"when my buddy and I tried to do a flanking move, get around the cocksuckers who had ambushed us. Who, by the way, turned out to be the same people we were supposed to be helping—you can bet my pal didn't send any more aid in *their* direction. It was some kid with a homemade Kalashnikov who did me. He popped up out of the rubble, squeezed off a burst before my buddy took him down. I was lucky. Only one bullet hit me. Shattered the ball of my thigh bone, missed my femoral artery by a hair. The joint is some kind of plastic now, works better than ever. Still, at the time, even with three Syrettes of morphine, you can bet it hurt. Anyway, our support people came in with a couple of gunships and shot the shit out of the unfriendly friendlies, and I was medevacked straight out. But before it went toes-up? It was the best fucking three days of my life."

Casey Chrisafis toasts the memory with a slurp of coffee, then holds out his cup for a refill from the impassive waiter, who has padded up with a tall silver pot on a silver tray.

"Pitting yourself against an animal in its natural habitat," he says, "with no support, armed with just a knife and a hunting bow, you can't deny that's something. But pitting yourself against your fellow human beings? That's something else. You ever heard of the most dangerous game? Now *that* is the ultimate hunting experience, going one on one against someone as experienced as you. I tell Raphael, clone me, train up my clone, set us against each other . . . how can I lose?"

Casey Chrisafis shows all his teeth when he laughs, then plugs his cigar into his mouth and leans forward.

"You know what I'm talking about, Nick, because you've been there. Those white devils: hunting them must have been the best thrill in the world. I was sorely disappointed when Raphael failed to bring back a live one."

Now they're coming down to it: the reason why this blowhard has come to find Nick on this quiet sunny morning.

"From what Raphael was saying, one or two of them must still be out there," Casey Chrisafis says. "Here's a proposition. Don't say anything, just hear me out. You're kind of an unwilling guest of Raphael's, aren't you? I mean, you were out there on your own mission before his people co-opted you, and you were brought here when as far as you're concerned the job's still unfinished. All Raphael wanted was to bring back one of those white devils, dead or alive, but you want to kill all of them. What would you say if I could help you out?"

"You want to hunt them."

Casey Chrisafis glances at the waiter, who has retreated to the far end of the terrace. "You bet."

"With what? Bows and arrows?"

"With anything you want. I mean, they had rifles, didn't they? So we can take rifles, too. The way I see it, it's more like war than hunting. These things are smart, they're fierce, they have an inbred hatred of human beings. It's them against us, and if we don't root them out now, they could start breeding out there in the jungle."

"This isn't some sci-fi movie, Mr. Chrisafis."

"We can go tonight. I'll sneak you out; I have a helicopter standing by in Kinshasa. We'll be in the forest before Raphael realizes you're missing. What do you say?"

"I'd say that you and the white devils were made for each other. I also think that when you told me that you don't care about your own life, it's really an excuse not to care for other people."

Michel is walking towards them, the big man looking serious, a toothpick cocked between his lips.

"You can bring your man here along," Casey Chrisafis says. "I hear he's pretty cool under fire."

"He isn't my man. What's the problem, Michel?"

Michel uses his tongue to roll the toothpick from one side of his mouth to the other, says, "There's something I think you should see on the TV."

The library has deep leather armchairs, thick carpets, a pool table, very few books on the mahogany shelves that stretch across one wall from floor to ceiling, and a cinema-screen–sized plasma TV. Michel finds the remote and turns the TV on and flicks to CNN.

And there's Nick's mother, standing at the five-bar gate at the end of her gravel drive, smiling vaguely at a semicircle of journalists, explaining that she doesn't regret it at all, she brought back her lost son and that's all that matters to her.

Michel says, "Can I ask one question?"

Nick marches across the room and switches off the TV. He feels both cold and calm, and as transparent and fragile as one of the crystal light fittings. "If you want to know whether it's true, yes, it's true."

Michel is perched on the arm of one of the deep leather armchairs, looking at him with a not-unfriendly expression, the toothpick stuck in one corner of his mouth. "Let me see if I have got it right. Your brother died. And your mother—"

"My father and my brother died in a car accident. My mother paid to have some of my brother's stem cells harvested from the marrow of his long bones, had the rest done at an Italian clinic. My father was a stockbroker who specialized in cutting-edge biotech companies, and my mother used his contacts to get what she wanted. They harvested her eggs, enucleated them, injected treated nuclei from my brother's stem cells . . ."

"She wanted to clone him, bring him back from the dead. And you're the result."

Nick wanders around the big, airy room, Michel turning to watch him as he runs a finger along one of the empty bookshelves, rolls the white ball across the red baize of the pool table.

"They got thirty-eight viable foetuses. I was the only one that survived until term. I found all this out after my heart attack. It turned out that I had a congenital problem with one of my arteries, the kind of thing that's very common in clones."

Telling his story with a growing sense of lightness and relief, not even flinching at the word.

"The nucleus of the egg is derived from an adult cell, so certain genes can get switched on in the wrong sequence during development of the foetus, or not get switched on at all. In my case, there was a problem with the development of my circumflex artery—a kink in the blood supply to my heart that eventually caused a full-blown heart attack. I had to leave the army because of it, and I went back to live at home while I was recuperating. And when I was fit enough to think about looking for a new job, when I told my mother that I was leaving, we had this fantastic row. She wanted me to stay at home for the rest of my life; she said that she didn't want to lose me again . . . And that's when it all came out. I already knew some of it, I suppose. The date on my father's grave, for instance. He died almost a full year before I was born. I always supposed that my mother became pregnant with me because of some kind of fertility treatment using stored sperm, or that I was the result of some fling . . . In England, I know you'll find this hard to believe, but we don't always talk about these things. Anyway, my mother was always very controlling, and it wasn't until I learned the truth that I realized why. She wanted me to be just like her dead son, she tried to give me exactly the same childhood . . ."

Nick takes a deep breath, lets it go. "Well, there it is. And I don't see that it changes anything."

"I admire your balls," Michel says. "You must have known that someone would take a long, hard look at your background after you released that video, but man, you did it anyway."

"I've been living with it for so long . . ." Nick shrugs, rolls the white ball across the width of the pool table, catches it on the rebound. "I thought it might come out after the massacre, because of the fuss over saving the baby. I could have run away from it, changed my identity, but I'd already done that once, and I felt that I had to tell the truth about what happened. About the white devils. And I'm glad I did, because it's a relief, really, to have it out in the open."

"You must realize that this is very bad for you, Nicholas."

"Who broke the story? How did they find out?"

"Because, you see, Monsieur Raphael is very angry about it."

"He clones lions and tigers and elephants. He was very pleased, yesterday evening, when he let me know that he's cloned the white devil we brought back. I don't think he's averse to the concept. How did the media find out, Michel? My mother's spent the last twenty-five years living in a fantasy world, fondly believing that she'd brought her dead son back to life. I don't think she would have confessed to those reporters on her own initiative. Someone led them to her."

"Nicholas, listen to me. You are in very big trouble, do you understand?"

"It was Obligate, wasn't it?"

"It does not matter who found out, Nicholas. What matters is that cloning human beings is against the law, even in the Free Zone. That is why you kept it secret, I understand absolutely. But you should have told Monsieur Raphael about it before you put out the video clip. Now, you understand, he feels that he has no choice. He is very angry because suddenly the video is not good news. It is instead very bad publicity for what he plans to do. It is a threat to all the money he wants to make."

"It has to be Obligate. Obligate, or Teryl Meade."

"Raphael told me to kill you, Nicholas. He told me: go and kill the son of a whore. You understand that?"

"I'll talk to him, Michel. Get this ironed out."

Michel holds up a hand. It's big enough to wrap most of the way around a basketball. Or a man's head. "Monsieur Raphael wants you dead, Nicholas. He sent me to do the job, which is lucky for you, because I have a better idea. What I will do, I will let you go."

"Let me walk out of here, when for the last four days that's just what you've been stopping me from doing?"

"Things have changed."

Nick smiles. "How do I know you won't just shoot me in the back?"

Michel smiles too. "How do you know? You do not know. But that is not my style, Nicholas; if I wanted you dead, I could have done it already, without telling you the bad news."

"Maybe we could get into something here, just you and me."

"Another time it might be fun."

"That guy who likes killing so much, Casey Chrisafis, can be our referee. We stand back to back, walk away from each other, ten paces, turn and fire, one shot each."

"And you turn around after step one and shoot me in the back? No," Michel says, "I prefer the Wild West style of shoot-out. I will stare you down, your nerve will break, you will go for your gun first. Then we see who has the fast hand."

"I'll talk to Raphael," Nick says. "This can be fixed."

"You lied to him," Michel says. "Raphael does not take that well. He likes to think that he inspires trust. Man, you didn't even tell him your right name!"

"What will he do when he finds out what you've done?"

"He'll be very angry. But when he calms down he will realize that I am right. You are famous, Nicholas, and people are looking for you. Better the trail doesn't lead here. Besides, I do not want to kill you. We saved each other's lives in the forest. It would not be civilized to shoot you now. You have your passport and your money on you, I think."

Nick hesitates, then says, "Sure."

"In case you see a way of escaping," Michel says. "Well, my friend, this is it."

"I'll go," Nick says, "if you'll answer just one simple question."

"Right now, Raphael is busy with a visitor, but we do not have all morning to play games. You should go home, Nicholas. You have done what you wanted to do. The world knows about the white devils."

"But it knows about me, too. And I think Raphael could be right. I think the two things cancel each other out." With a flick of his wrist, Nick sends the white ball scooting into the pyramid of coloured balls. They break apart, colliding and recolliding with a dry clatter like so many bones. One—the black—drops into a corner pocket. Nick looks at Michel and says, "See that? Do you think it's an omen?"

"If it means will you be killed if you stay here, then it's a pretty good one."

"Just one question, Michel. One thing I need to know."

"It will give you power over me," Michel says, as if to himself.

"I need to know, Michel. Because this thing isn't finished, and I can't walk away from it."

"If I can answer this one question, will you leave?"

"If it will help me find out who made the white devils? Absolutely. You'll never see me again, I swear it. Just tell me this: where did Raphael get that saber-toothed cat he's so proud of?"

"He has, I believe, already told you his story. It escaped from Pleistocene Park when the place was bombed, and he hunted it down."

"Yeah, but I don't think it has been wandering around in the Dead Zone for four years. It's gengineered; it needs a special food supplement, just like the white devils. It came from Pleistocene Park originally, but who sold it to him?"

Michel takes out the toothpick, examines it, and says, "It was from a mission in the Dead Zone."

"A mission? Like a Catholic mission? Where was this, exactly?"

But Michel won't answer any more questions. He says that's all he knows. He says, "Are you coming, or do I shoot you down here, like a dog?"

A dusty red Isuzu Trooper is drawn up near the wide marble steps of the main entrance. A man in a clean white T-shirt and blue jeans leans against the hood, smoking a cigarette. One of the ranch's Range Rovers, striped black and white like a zebra, is parked beyond, its rear door cocked. Two servants in safari suits are dragging a khaki kitbag the size of a coffin from the back, watched by a big man with a shaven head and spex with small, oval lenses. Michel tells the servants to hurry up, he needs the Range Rover; the big man picks up a canvas carry-all and follows them as, carrying the kitbag between them, they stagger away down the path that leads to the guest cabins.

Nick has the feeling that he's seen the big man before. It nags at him like a mislaid word as Michel drives away from the ranch. They've gone several kilometres down the long dirt track, past dry grassland studded with thorn trees, and Nick is beginning to relax and think about what he will do when he gets to Kinshasa, when Michel suddenly swears and brakes sharply, throwing the Range Rover into an expert skid that turns it through a hundred and eighty degrees.

A column of smoke is rising beyond the low, tree-clad rise where Raphael's house shines in the sun.

As the Range Rover accelerates back the way they've just come, Michel steering with one hand as he talks quickly and urgently into his phone, Nick remembers seeing the big man standing in a parking lot at night in a gold puffa jacket, a phone in one hand and a gun in the other. Magne Leroy. The man paid by Captain Jean Badiledi to follow him, back in Brazzaville.

Chapter 34

The guest cabin has a round double bed with a genuine ze-braskin throw over snowy linen, wicker furniture with leopardskin-print upholstery, tall-stemmed bird-of-paradise flowers in the big brass vase by the French doors that look out onto the blue eye of a swimming pool and three other cabins set around it amidst palm trees and flowering bushes. Jean Badiledi tips the two men who carry in Prosper Kwezi's kit-bag with twenty-dollar bills peeled off the roll he found in Prosper Kwezi's wallet. When they have gone, Magne Leroy, leaning against the jamb of the French doors, the bag of pipe bombs at his feet, says, "I saw him."

"You did? Very good. Where is he?"

"He was getting into one of those stripy Range Rovers with someone who looked like he works around here."

"And?"

"And they drove away."

"Did he recognize you? Did you try and speak with him?"

Magne Leroy shrugs. "Surely that is not so important now."

Before this is over, Jean thinks, he will give the man a short, sharp lesson to remind him of his place. He says, "Who are you working for? Me, or Corbin?"

"Besides," Magne Leroy says, ignoring the question, "there was, as I said, a man with him. And this man had a pistol at his hip, openly displayed. So no, I did not talk with him."

"He drove away with this man. Where were they going?"

"It looked like they were leaving. Maybe this Raphael is not so happy with Nicholas Hyde, either."

Jean's phone rings. He looks at the call ID and tells Magne Leroy, "Make yourself useful. Ask around after Nicholas Hyde. Find out where he has gone. Find out when he is coming back. And be discreet."

"I know how to do my job," Magne Leroy says, and saunters away.

Jean locks the French doors, goes into the bathroom, turns on the shower, and answers the phone.

Cody Corbin says, "It sounds like you're in the rain, but how can that be?"

"I'm running the shower. In case there are listening devices."

"If they have an AI, they can tune in on our phones and

break their encryption," Cody Corbin says. "But it doesn't matter now. Things have changed."

"Things are going just as I said they would," Jean says, feeling a prickle of alarm. "Already, we have seen Nicholas Hyde."

"I already told you, he's no use to us now. Or didn't you believe what you saw on TV?"

Cody Corbin phoned Prosper Kwezi's hotel room early that morning, asked Jean if he was watching TV.

"As a matter of fact, I was about to take a shower," Jean said. "What do you want?"

"Turn on your TV," Cody Corbin said, "and you'll see why Nicholas Hyde is now worth precisely zero to us."

It took Jean just a minute to order the TV to locate any item about Nicholas Hyde. The clip was playing on the BBC World News channel. Jean watched for thirty seconds, then picked up the phone and told Cody Corbin that it didn't change anything.

"Were you watchin' the same thing I saw?" Cody Corbin said. "He's a monster, *mon ami*, same as the white devils. Anything he says is worth nothin' now, so he's worth nothin' to us. Best thing we can do is put him out of his misery."

"Whatever he is, he will still be worth something to Teryl Meade," Jean said, speaking quickly and urgently. "I tell you, as long as we have him, she won't want to kill us, and she won't dare harm my family. I know the woman. It doesn't matter what the TV news says about him. He has hurt her pride; she will want to see him die, so we can use him to get close to her. Listen to me: *we must stick to the plan.*"

Jean's plan was very simple. Get hold of Nicholas Hyde or the body of the white devil, preferably both, take them back to Brazzaville, and tell Teryl Meade to come and deal with them herself, and to bring a fat upfront fee while she was at it. She would certainly have some kind of protection with her, but Jean was counting on Cody Corbin to spring a surprise. Maybe they wouldn't kill her straightaway; maybe they'd take her prisoner, ransack her house, force her to tell them where she kept her valuables. Show her how blackmail was really done, show her that she couldn't get away with threatening a man's family. Then kill her. It was a simple plan, a good plan, but Cody Corbin made it clear that he didn't like it, and he was like an ox—stubborn, inflexible, plodding. Once he was set on a course of action, you had to beat him about the shoulders just to make him look around.

In the two days they spent together in Kinshasa, he more or less ignored Jean and Magne Leroy completely, padding about the suite in the Inter-Continental Hotel, mumbling to himself or grimly working through his rigorous sets of push-ups and sit-ups, or stomping off into his bedroom to play his slide guitar or pray. He prayed for an hour, two hours straight, kneeling at the foot of his bed like a penitent little boy, hunched over his clasped hands to display the great tattoo spread across his naked back, his whole body trembling like a clenched muscle, as if prayer was a kind of agony to him. Magne Leroy didn't seem to mind; he spent most of his time watching South African league football on the big TV, but Jean was unnerved by Cody Corbin's intense brooding presence, and revolted by the way the man absentmindedly shovelled food into his mouth, the way he pissed noisily and at length without bothering to close the bathroom door, by his strong odour of ancient sweat and musk. Jean once suggested that they should get separate rooms, but Cody Corbin said that he liked to keep close to his partners. Meaning, of course, that he didn't trust them.

Magne Leroy was no help at all. "You find this amusing," Jean said, and Magne Leroy shrugged, said that Cody Corbin was a strange man all right, but he was an American, what do you expect?

That was certainly true, but even for an American, Cody Corbin was uncommunicative, surly, short-tempered, equally immune to flattery or threats. A loner. Yesterday morning, when they all drove out to the perimeter of Raphael's ranch, Cody Corbin vanished for six hours, came back after dusk and woke Jean by leaning through the window and pressing the muzzle of his big revolver to Jean's temple, his twisted idea of a joke. Jean pushed the gun away, saw Magne Leroy watching in the rearview mirror. The big man's face was carefully neutral, but he was in on the joke, all right, or he would have given some kind of warning.

"I had a good look around," Cody Corbin said, sliding into the back of the car next to Jean. "Saw everything I needed to see. Once you get inside the perimeter, you can pretty much roam around at will. This is the kind of guy who relies on his reputation to keep people away. A place like this, I don't know why it hasn't been taken down already. It's wide open."

Jean said, "Did you see Nicholas Hyde? Did you see the body of the white devil?"

"We don't even know whether they brought it back. But if they did, it has to be in the lab building, and I didn't have any reason to go inside." Cody Corbin was using tissues and a bottle of mineral water to scrub the green and black tiger stripes from his face. After a few beats of silence, he said, "Why are we still here, Magne? You take us back to the hotel now. You can rest up, watch your soccer. And you can catch yourself some more beauty sleep, captain. We have a big day tomorrow."

As they drove along the well-made road towards Kinshasa, Jean tried to get some idea of what Cody Corbin had found out, tried to draw him into discussing how they could extract Nicholas Hyde. But the mercenary was more interested in talking about the atrocities that Raphael was manufacturing in his laboratory.

"I could take it all out," he said. "The lab building is just a prefab block with only two ways in, the main entrance and a loading dock, and the place where they grow up their monsters isn't much more than a big barn raised on concrete blocks. Half a dozen charges and a man with a rifle could take out the buildings and the people working in them, sweet as you like. If I had my man Erefaan with me, we could have done it already."

"You can take Magne with you tomorrow, with my blessing."

"I think I'll work alone. No offence, Magne."

"No problem," Magne Leroy said.

The two men working together, Jean thought, working against him. He asked Cody Corbin if he had found out where Nicholas Hyde was being kept, but the man didn't even try to answer the question, and that was when Jean decided to take the initiative. Show Cody Corbin and Magne Leroy who was really in charge.

He called up the Intelligence Service in Brazzaville, had them find out the names of all the guests currently at the ranch and the names of those booked to arrive in the next few days. A party of three was due to depart early tomorrow morning, and two more guests were expected to arrive sometime on the same day: one an American, a white woman; the other a Nigerian oil-futures broker, Prosper Kwezi, who had once spent a week in Brazzaville, who was right now staying at the Memling Palace Hotel in Kinshasa, whose photograph was on file.

Jean told Cody Corbin that he was going for a drink, took a taxi to the Memling Palace Hotel, and after several hours saw, through the glass frontage of the lobby, his target climb out of a limousine. The man leaning down to shake hands with someone inside the limo, then walking unsteadily through the sliding glass doors, towards the bank of elevators. As he went past the sofa where Jean was pretending to work at his slate, a cup of coffee untouched by his side, Jean jumped up and introduced himself and told Prosper Kwezi they'd met in Brazzaville, what a fantastic coincidence to see him here.

The man, half-drunk, clearly trying to work out who Jean was, allowed himself to be steered into the bar. Jean bought him a large whisky and got him talking about Brazzaville. Prosper Kwezi relaxed, was soon enthusing about the fantastic deal he had just done with the government of the DRC, about the little holiday he had given himself as a reward, hunting a trophy leopard. Jean let the man buy another round, learnt that he was here alone, that he had enjoyed at the government's expense the hospitality of several whores, that he was a crack shot but he was going to hunt the leopard in the traditional way, stalking with a spear, three or four days alone in the bush, the safari ranch was sending someone to pick him up early tomorrow morning and he couldn't wait. The man refusing the offer of another drink, shaking Jean's hand, telling him that if he was ever in Lagos . . .

Jean had already bribed one of the desk clerks to give him the number of Prosper Kwezi's room. Five minutes after they parted, he was knocking at the door. As soon as it started to open, he kicked it in, the edge smashing into Prosper Kwezi's face and knocking him backwards, and Jean stepped inside and planted his Nemesis switchblade against the man's chest and pressed the button. Prosper Kwezi shuddered when the Nemesis's front-opening ten-centimetre blade punched through his heart, and Jean caught and held his dead weight, and laid him on the floor, the Nemesis's black handle sticking up from his white shirt in the centre of a widening circle of blood. Jean closed the door, called the suite in the Inter-Continental and told Cody Corbin what he had done, told him that he planned to pose as Prosper Kwezi, get inside the safari ranch, and get close to Nicholas Hyde.

Cody Corbin, remarkably unruffled by Jean's initiative, said that he'd see him in the morning, and rang off before Jean could ask him to send Magne Leroy over to help with the body. So Jean dealt with it himself, wrapping Prosper Kwezi in a groundsheet, dumping camping equipment out of a kitbag, and stuffing the oil broker's body inside. He hung the DO NOT DISTURB sign on the door of Prosper Kwezi's room and spent a wonderful night sound asleep in Prosper Kwezi's bed.

And then, first thing the next morning, Cody Corbin telephoned him with his bombshell.

Jean said that it changed nothing. He said that they must stick to the plan, said that either Cody Corbin followed him in, or he could forget about sharing any of the money they were going to make from Teryl Meade.

"I'll help you, *mon ami*," Cody Corbin said, "but only because I want to take out those labs and the man who owns them."

"You'll find the body of the white devil first. Don't forget that."

"I'll send Magne over to your hotel. I figure you need him more than I do."

"We need Nicholas Hyde and the body of the white devil," Jean said, but Cody Corbin had already rung off.

When the front desk called an hour later, and told him that the Range Rover from Raphael's safari ranch had arrived, Jean took Prosper Kwezi's body with him, still stuffed into the kitbag and bulked out now with clothing and a sleeping bag—he couldn't leave it for one of the maids to find, and it would nicely muddy the waters if he dumped it at the safari ranch. He also decided to try to find some way of driving off with Nicholas Hyde, leave Cody Corbin and Magne Leroy to take their chances, see how they liked it when the tables were turned on them.

But now, barely ten minutes after Jean has arrived at the safari ranch, Nicholas Hyde has gone missing and Cody Corbin is once more telling Jean to forget about him. Saying, "You're still fixated on that sorry scudder, after what you saw? You didn't believe me when I told you things had changed, but you better believe me now. I've found us a different target, *mon ami*. I've put us back on track."

"No, no, no. Wait. I'm in. I'm ready to make contact with him. Listen to me, if he gets away or is killed, we'll have done Teryl Meade a favour, and we'll have no way of getting to her. You must wait until I have made inquiries. Perhaps in an hour, perhaps two, we will be ready to move."

"I'm in position now," Cody Corbin says, "by the place where they make their monsters. I've planted my surprises, I'm squattin' here in the bush with about a zillion insects doing their best to drain every drop of my blood, and then, well, I bet you can't guess who turns up."

"This is no time to play games."

"That means you have no idea, right? Well, I'll tell you. It's the daughter of the man I assassinated, the woman who took down my good friend Erefaan Williams. I recognize her from TV coverage of her father's funeral. Her daddy and Teryl

Meade made monsters," Cody Corbin says, "and here she is with some guy, lookin' at this sorry mutant tiger they have in a cage right by the airstrip. I can see the fat scudder who owns this place drivin' up to meet her. Maybe she and him were connected all along, or maybe she's lookin' to start up something new in the line of monster-making, is lookin' for technical support. Whatever it is, I can't help but think that she has to know at least as much about the white devils as your good friend Nicholas Hyde, and maybe a whole lot more. So what I want you to do is go find a vehicle and head this way. You and Magne are going to help me pick her up."

"This is because this woman caught your friend? Listen, Monsieur Corbin, that is not my affair."

"It's because she might know something we can use against Teryl Meade, you sorry scudder. I'm going to provide a diversion, so you and Magne better get ready to snatch her."

"We are here to extract Nicholas Hyde, to take the body of the white devil, nothing else. That is our plan."

"Plus, I saw on TV she comes from one of those old families made a lot of money in Africa in the colonial days; I bet they'd pay a good ransom for her. Bring those packages I gave Magne; I don't want to waste them. And don't spend too long gettin' here; I'm ready to make my move. When I do, I want you and Magne to be in place, ready to come in. I kill the men, you snatch the woman. You understand?"

"Listen to me," Jean says, his hand sweating on the phone.

"Kill the men, snatch the woman. It's pretty simple. You don't back me on this, *mon ami*, I'll come lookin' for your sorry ass when I'm done," Cody Corbin says, and hangs up.

Jean resists the temptation to throw the phone against the tiled wall of the bathroom. He calls Magne Leroy and tells him to meet up in front of the house. He picks up the canvas carryall that contains the pipe bombs, puts his automatic and two spare clips inside, and walks straight out.

The zebra-striped Range Rover has gone, but the dusty red Isuzu Trooper is still parked at the foot of the wide, white marble steps that lead up to the main entrance of the rambling glass-and-steel house. No sign of Magne Leroy, no time to wait for him. Jean palms his Nemesis switchblade in his right hand, wraps one of Prosper Kwezi's twenty-dollar bills around the middle and index fingers of his left hand, and walks up to the driver, who is leaning against the Isuzu's hood, arms crossed over his clean white T-shirt.

Jean waves the bill in front of the man's face, says, "Perhaps you can do me a favour . . ."

The man looks at the money for just a moment, all Jean needs. He punches the Nemesis into the man's chest and the blade pops straight through his breastbone. The man collapses just as someone, Magne Leroy, appears at the top of the steps. Jean puts his foot on the dead man's head for leverage and pulls out the Nemesis's blade, wipes it on the dead man's T-shirt, finds, *voilà*, the Isuzu's ignition card in his pocket.

Magne Leroy canters down the steps, saying, "Where are we going?"

"Tell me again which way Nicholas Hyde went."

Chapter 35

The saber-toothed cat sprawls in the middle of the dusty enclosure, in the shadow of a flat-topped acacia tree. It has the muscular, shoulder-heavy build of a bear and a lion's tawny hide, mottled with dark spots on its hindquarters. Every now and then its stubby tail flips back and forth, disturbing a cloud of flies that soon resettles around the crusted sores on its flanks, but otherwise it does not move. Its mouth hangs open and its pink tongue lolls between the pair of upper canines that curve like ivory daggers past either side of its lower jaw. Its sleepy eyes are capped with white cataracts.

Elspeth is certain that it is one of the three sabertooths that Daniel Lovegrave reverse-engineered from pumas, tweaking regulatory genes controlling body growth and jaw development, implanting tooth-buds to produce those massive fangs, manufacturing a disneyfied approximation or pastiche of the species of saber-toothed cat, *Smilodon fatalis*, that until about ten thousand years ago hunted in the grasslands of the Pacific Coast of North America.

"The thing is," Elspeth tells Teddy Yssel, "that they all had problems with their spines and pelvises from birth, because of the *in utero* growth-hormone treatments. They could hardly walk, let alone run down anything. Also, their metabolisms were tweaked; they had an absolute requirement for a specific dietary supplement."

"What are you saying?" Teddy Yssel stands a little too close to her, his fingers hooked in the wire mesh of the fence, as he stares at the sabertooth. She can smell on his breath the shot of whisky that he had with his breakfast.

"I'm saying that the story that Raphael caught this animal in the Dead Zone is pure nonsense. That if it had escaped from Pleistocene Park, it would have starved to death in a few weeks."

A cow lows in the distance, and the sabertooth lifts its head for a moment, ears cocked. Flies hang like clusters of black grapes below its rheumy, frosted eyes. Elspeth feels a pang of sorrow, remembering the three oversized kittens that she helped feed on her first and only visit to the Pleistocene Park laboratory complex, remembering the arguments that she had with her father about the morality of the project; they fell out so badly that she didn't see him or talk to him again until she found him in the refugee camp at the border between the Democratic Republic of the Congo and Uganda.

She says, "Don't you see what this means, Teddy? Someone must have looked after this poor animal. Someone must have kept it alive all this time."

Teddy puts a finger to his lips and rolls his eyes at the security camera canted on top of a tall steel pole at one corner of the enclosure's steel-mesh fence.

Elspeth says, "We're being watched?"

"Raphael will let us cook until we're good and nervous, and use anything we say against us."

Elspeth leans close to him and says quietly, "The poor thing is a long way from home. We have to find out where Raphael got it."

"Elspeth, you must listen to me," Teddy says. He speaks softly but urgently, keeping his eyes on the saber-toothed cat. "Raphael is a vain man. He had us brought here not just to cook in the sun but also to show off his prize. You must pretend to believe whatever nonsense he tells us. It is important that you do not try to make him look foolish."

"We have to find out where the sabertooth came from, Teddy, because I think it came from the same place as the white devils."

"Darlajane B. is probably right," Teddy says. "A warlord took it for a trophy or totem, and Raphael found out about it and made an offer. Or perhaps Teryl Meade has something to do with this—maybe she's been selling him the frozen eggs of all kinds of gengineered animals, and he's been raising them. But if you ask him about it, he'll get angry, and you'll never find out."

"This is one of Danny Lovegrave's originals, Teddy. I know it."

"We'll find out," Teddy says, "by making ourselves seem useful to Raphael. Not by calling him a liar."

They wait more than half an hour in the pitiless glare and heat, long enough for Elspeth to walk slowly five times around the tennis-court–sized enclosure. The saber-toothed cat raises its heavy head and snuffles the air, and she remembers Danny Lovegrave's little trick. Teddy Yssel sits next to their bags on the hump of earth at the edge of the dry ditch that runs beside the road, his cap of blond hair pasted down by sweat, a dark sweat stain growing across the back of his cheap, brightly patterned shirt as he smokes cigarette after cigarette and with casual irritation slaps at the big, bronze-winged flies that settle on his face and his bare arms. At last a horn toots, bright and cheerful as a cartoon. Teddy stubs his cigarette in the dirt and stands; Elspeth shades her eyes with her forearm and sees a zebra-striped jeep speeding along the dirt road, past the line of young eucalyptus trees that half-hides the prefab block of the ranch's laboratory, past a kind of huge, circular shed in the middle of a labyrinth of steel-pipe cattle pens, past the small airstrip where a black helicopter squats beside a pair of steel fuel tanks that shimmer in a glassy shroud of their own reflected heat. A zebra-striped single-engine Beechcraft is cocked at the far end of the long ribbon of red earth.

A large ugly man in a white suit and a white Stetson sits beside the jeep's driver; Teddy needlessly tells Elspeth that this is Raphael, and after the jeep brakes in a cloud of red dust, steps over the ditch to greet him. The fat man, Raphael, climbs out of the jeep and fussily smacks dust from his white jacket and trousers with a fly whisk, ignoring Teddy's outstretched hand.

"Theodore Yssel," he says when he has finally dusted himself off. "You have come back to me. Where have you been?"

"Here, there," Teddy says. "You know how it is."

"You found someone who would allow you to fly again, eh? I am amazed." Raphael swaggers past Teddy towards Elspeth. A ruffled pink silk shirt is slashed open under his white jacket to display the swell of his belly. His feet are shod in honey-coloured waffle-weave loafers. He says, "You have been admiring my prize possession, the symbol of my great power. I was once offered half a million American dollars for him, but I will never sell him or allow him to be hunted. What do you think? Give me your honest opinion."

"I think you should take better care of him," Elspeth says.

Raphael dismisses this with a flick of his fat, gold-ringed fingers. "The skin problem is congenital. We have tried antibiotics, we have tried topical steroids, we have even tried gene therapy. In fact, I have an appointment with a veterinary doctor any moment now, which is why I asked Wamos to bring you here."

"And what about the arthritis, and the cataracts? What he really needs," Elspeth says, "is to be put out of his misery."

"We have been trying to clone him," Raphael says. "Of

course, the big cats are always difficult, and a delicate construct like him, he's *very* difficult. Inserted genes fail to express themselves; suppressed genes are activated . . . No doubt you know something of this?"

Looking at her slyly under the brim of his white Stetson.

"I know he's suffering."

Teddy Yssel says briskly, trying to regain the initiative, "Raphael, this is my friend, Dr. Elspeth Faber. I am sure that you have heard of her father, Matthew Faber, of Pleistocene Park fame. Elspeth, this pirate is the very man you need to talk to. He produces all kinds of monsters, and he isn't ashamed of it."

"So," Raphael says, "she is what? Your girlfriend? Congratulations, Teddy, your taste has greatly improved. But alas, I already have all the hostesses I need, and besides, my guests' requirements generally do not run to the, let us say, natural look."

Teddy's smile is weak. "Dr. Faber is my business partner."

"You are in business now? What kind of business? Darlajane B. was very vague, so be quick to explain. I am eager to talk with the veterinary doctor—as I said, he will be here in just a few minutes."

"She heard of your interest in the exotic," Teddy says. "She was in town and asked to meet you."

Raphael smiles at Elspeth, displaying vampiric incisors. "This man is trouble," he says. "He charms you, he loves you, and he leaves you. A woman like you does not deserve a man like this."

"We have an arrangement," Elspeth says.

"That's right," Teddy says.

Raphael ignores him. "I am wondering why you have come here, Dr. Elspeth Faber. After Darlajane B. talked to me, I had you looked up. I find that you are not a gene hacker, but a respectable scientist—a palaeontologist. That is, if you are who you claim to be."

"A palaeoanthropologist," Elspeth says.

"In any case, you are not someone who is in the business

of selling exotic animals, and I am not someone who is interested in old bones."

"I came here to talk to you about Pleistocene Park."

"Really? You want to talk with me, see my lovely creatures, see my labs, perhaps. And what do I get from this?"

"It was your idea," Elspeth says, "to show me your famous saber-toothed cat."

"And what can you show me?"

"I haven't come here to trade secrets with you, Monsieur Raphael."

"Raphael. I am Raphael," the man says, looking at her from under the brim of his Stetson. "And if you are Elspeth Faber, perhaps you can tell me something about your father. Something about his work that no one else would know."

He has the body of the white devil, Elspeth thinks. He knows what it is, and he's playing with me. She says, "I really don't know all that much about his work. I mean, I can tell you what I do know, but I think you know it already."

"You are his daughter. You are, like him, a scientist. And you say that he did not discuss his work with you?"

"Actually, I was hoping I could discuss it with *you*. I would very much like to talk about Pleistocene Park, and Danny Lovegrave."

Raphael stares at her. She sees something harden in his gaze and realizes at once that she's said the wrong thing. She's been honest and direct with a man who isn't used to honesty and directness. He's judged her and found her wanting. He turns to Teddy, shakes his head. "She wants to talk to me. Of course she does. And snoop around my labs too, no doubt, and try and charm a few secrets out of the charmless Dr. Królicki. Teddy, Teddy. You have obviously fallen on hard times, my old friend. You have obviously lost your edge. I very much think that this woman is not Dr. Elspeth Faber: I think that you have been taken in by a confidence trickster."

"If you 'looked me up,'" Elspeth says, "you'll have seen my photograph on my homepage at the Museum Web site. I have my passport right here—"

Raphael ignores her. "Do you know how many eager little cunts come here, Teddy, pretending to be someone or something they are not, trying to get close to me so that they can steal my secrets? Do you know what I usually do to them? But don't worry, because just this once, because of our old friendship, I will be kind. You can take her away, and you can tell Darlajane B. that she should be ashamed, taking part in something like this."

Elspeth says, "Which of Danny Lovegrave's sabertooths is it? Huey, Dewey, or Louie?"

"His name is Mobutu," Raphael says. " 'All-Powerful Soldier.' "

Elspeth says, "Danny Lovegrave made three of them—three that survived to full term, anyway. He named them after Donald Duck's nephews. But I don't suppose you know that, because you didn't buy this one from Danny himself, did you?"

Raphael tells Teddy, "I think you had better leave. And take this little schemer with you, before I change my mind."

"Wait," Elspeth says. "I'll give you some hard proof."

She steps out of her sandals and swarms up the sagging mesh fence, Raphael reaching for her a moment too late as she drops down to the hard dirt on the other side, breathless and dizzy.

"You will come out at once," Raphael says, and gestures impatiently to the tall, cadaverous driver of the jeep, who pulls a rifle from the back seat and starts to walk towards them.

Elspeth smiles at Raphael through the fence's mesh. "I just want to say hello to an old friend. I know this animal, and it knows me. It won't hurt me."

"Come out now," Raphael says, "or Wamos will shoot you. Not fatally. That would be no entertainment. In the belly, maybe also in one knee. After that, even in his condition, I think Mobutu will be able to catch you and make a meal of you."

"I think we should all calm down," Teddy says. "Raphael, I know you're worried about your cat, but Elspeth isn't going to hurt him. She's going to climb out of there right now. Isn't that right, Elspeth?"

"If you want me, come and get me," Elspeth says, her heart beating quickly and lightly as she turns away and walks barefoot across hot, hard, red earth, making sure that she keeps between Wamos and the sabertooth. Something crunches underfoot, an old bone. The big cat raises its head, its nostrils flaring as it takes in her scent. Elspeth lets it sniff her hand, then squats beside it and scratches vigorously behind one of its ears, her fingertips digging into coarse hair and tough hide, the ear, big as her palm and tufted with black hair, starting to twitch as she finds the sweet spot.

"You poor thing," she says. "What happened to your brothers?"

The big cat yawns, pushes its head against the rub of her fingers. Its breath is foul. The black gum around its left incisor is pulpy and pulled all the way back to the root.

"You poor thing," Elspeth says again, tears pricking her eyes. For the sabertooth's stoic suffering, for the memory of the last time she saw her father whole and well, the bad way that visit ended.

Raphael is calling to her. When she looks at him, he says, "Come back, and we will talk!"

"I'm fine where I am," Elspeth says, "except you might have Wamos put up his rifle."

Raphael gestures impatiently. Wamos slings his rifle over his shoulder and steps back from the fence. Raphael takes off his Stetson and mops his brow with a white handkerchief. "Mobutu knows you. But I am not sure what it means."

"When Danny Lovegrave designed the sabertooths," Elspeth says, still scratching around the sabertooth's ear, leaning against the muscular heat of its flank, "he hardwired them to recognize his scent, and my father's scent, too. A little trick—Danny Lovegrave was very fond of tricks. Anyway, half the genes that code for my immune system came from my father, so to the saber-toothed cat I smell very much like him."

"This is very interesting," Raphael says, "but if you really are Dr. Elspeth Faber, I do not think you came here to talk about saber-toothed cats."

"I saw the video of Nicholas Hyde and the white devil," Elspeth says. "And Teddy recognized a couple of the men in it."

Teddy says, "We're not here to cause any trouble. That's the furthest thing from my mind. In fact, we can probably help you."

Raphael ignores him. "And why are you interested in Nicholas Hyde, Dr. Faber?" There is something sly and playful in his voice now. "Is it because of the white devils, or because of what he was?"

"Of what he was? What do you mean?"

"What he was to me was a very great disappointment," Raphael says, holding his Stetson flat against his pink silk shirt for a moment, then fixing it on his head.

"I think we've been out here in the heat and dust and the goddamned flies for long enough," Teddy says. "Elspeth, why don't you come back, shimmy over the fence? We can talk over a long, cool drink—"

That's when the lab building explodes.

Cody thinks that four hundred grams of Semtex, stuffed into a couple of lengths of plastic pipe and placed just right, does a pretty good job, blowing out a wall of the laboratory block and shattering every window, a ball of red flame and black smoke punching through the roof of the solvent store as the big drums of toluene and acetone and methyl and ethyl and propyl alcohols ignite. He's lying in the shade of big, close-growing bushes on a little knoll above the dirt road that runs past the laboratory building to the airstrip, the position he took up after he planted his packages early that morning, lying still as a snake in the growing heat. Watching through his yellow field glasses as the fat fuck who owns the place drove up and started talking with the blond man and Elspeth Faber. Who actually, can you believe it, climbed the fence of the enclosure and walked over to pet the cat-thing. Cody thinking then that enough is enough, thinking that Jean Badiledi has chickened out, and phoning the first of his little packages.

As fire takes hold in the lab building and black smoke climbs into the sky, Cody sets down the field glasses and fits the stock of the M-23 rifle against his shoulder and sights through its scope. It's a four-hundred-metre shot, no big deal. He has an erection, throbbing between his belly and the hard earth. He feels that he has the whole world in his power, feels that he has all the time in the world. He says a little prayer and takes a breath and as he lets it out squeezes the trigger, seeing a spurt of black oil jump above the jeep's hood as the copper-jacketed NATO round smashes into its engine block. He takes another breath and sights on the driver and fires, sees the man's head come apart in a puff of pink mist, turns the rifle a fraction and fires again, clipping the white-suited fat man as he scrambles away on hands and knees, the glancing impact of the high-velocity round knocking him into the ditch. The blond man must have had some combat training, because he's done a fast crawl on his elbows behind the jeep. Elspeth Faber is hunched by the cat-thing, and Cody holds off from putting it out of its misery because he doesn't want to risk hitting her. People are stumbling away from the burning lab building now, and he takes out three of them before the others get the idea that they're being shot at, shoots one more as they scatter out of sight. It's just forty-five seconds since the first pair of bombs went off, and now Cody phones the rest.

The roundhouse barn disintegrates, shards of aluminium siding flying out in a near-perfect circle as the roof drops straight down; a moment later, the fuel tanks at the end of the airstrip blow. A mushroom of flame and smoke boils into the sky; the helicopter parked nearby is knocked onto its side; animals near and far start bawling and screeching and roaring. A cow wanders out of the burning wreckage of the barn, its back on fire, a stream of blood pouring from its muzzle. Cody fires at and misses someone scrambling out of one of the windows of the lab building, sees a zebra-striped Range

Rover come barrelling along the road. He thinks for a moment that it's Jean Badiledi, then sees that some big black buck he doesn't recognize is at the wheel, a white man beside him. Cody gets up on one knee, switching the M-23 to burst mode and with a single twitch of the trigger raking the vehicle as it goes past.

Michel pushes the Range Rover hard as he heads back towards the house, swerving past a battered red 4×4 heading in the other direction. Nick feels the rear end of the Range Rover swing out and thinks for a moment that Michel has lost it, but then its front tires bite into the ground and it straightens out and slams and rattles down the dirt road, hurtling past the house and its gardens as two more explosions send up mushrooms of smoke.

Buildings are on fire along the right-hand side of the road, and there's a huge fire beyond, orange flames whipping forty or fifty metres into the air and reefs of black smoke billowing across the road. People run past. A cow ambles along, seemingly unaware that it's on fire. A sudden blizzard of paper flattens against the windshield like giant snowflakes. Michel flicks on the wipers to try and clear them, and there are three distinct bangs, as if they've run over rocks on the road. Something sings through the cabin and punches a crazed hole in the windshield. Michel grunts and grabs at his thigh; Nick reaches for the steering wheel as the Range Rover slews, plunging through thick smoke and banging hard over a ditch, just missing a zebra-striped jeep. The top of Nick's head slams against the roof as a section of wire-mesh fence goes down under the Range Rover's wheels; he's punched back against his seat as air bags blossom, and discovers that somehow the Range Rover has come to a halt.

Michel is clutching his thigh with both hands. Bright red blood wells between his fingers. Nick pushes the deflating air bags away, unclips his seat belt, kicks open the door. "It went right through," Michel says as Nick starts to haul him out.

Glass shatters around them and something cracks by Nick's ear, and he realizes that someone is shooting at them and pulls Michel the rest of the way in a hurry, the man howling as his bloody leg bumps over the door sill.

Beyond a brief space of bare red earth a slim woman crouches under a thorn tree, her face framed by short black braids, one arm on the shoulder of the big tawny cat beside her as she stares boldly at Nick, like an illustration of one of those Old Testament stories about tested faith.

The long drift of smoke parts for a moment and Cody glimpses motion on the far side of the Range Rover, the white guy dragging out the black buck, and he stands up and stitches another burst across it before charging out of the bushes towards the road. A red 4×4 barrels past the burning lab building, Jean Badiledi at the wheel—the man has more backbone than he thought. Cody waves, but instead of slowing, the 4×4 swerves right at him. He throws himself to the side, but something smacks against his hip and sends him flying. He rolls over and over in a cloud of dust, picks himself up half-stunned, pain all down his left side, as the 4×4 speeds past the airstrip and vanishes into the smoke boiling out of the burning fuel tanks. Cody starts to limp after it, realizing that Badiledi has a play of his own.

"You hit him!" Magne Leroy says, turning in his seat, trying to see what happened to Cody Corbin.

"Of course I hit him!" Jean Badiledi's blood is singing in his head. It's like being in combat again. He brakes hard and cracks the door and swings down from the 4×4 into the smell of smoke and burning fuel oil.

One man lies dead on the road, and another lies in a dry ditch, blood all over the front of his white suit. A blond man crouching behind the jeep ducks out of sight when Jean aims his pistol at him for a moment.

Thick billows of black smoke from the burning fuel tanks
blow across the road. Jean can't see Cody Corbin. The man
went down, he has to be badly hurt, but he might not be dead.
He shouts at Magne Leroy, tells him to make sure of Corbin,
and walks around the zebra-striped Range Rover, his pistol
extended in front of him. There is Nicholas Hyde, kneeling
beside another wounded man, putting pressure on his leg, and
a little way beyond, squatting under a tree beside some kind
of big cat, is a young woman who must be Elspeth Faber, the
stepdaughter of Teryl Meade.

Nicholas Hyde looks at Jean and says, "Give me a hand."

"Of course," Jean says, and shoots the wounded man in the
chest, shoots him again as Nicholas Hyde kicks backwards and
sprawls in the dirt, says in the ringing silence that follows the
shots, "I want you to stand up, put your hands on your head."

Nicholas Hyde gets up slowly, keeping his eyes on Jean.
He tilts his head towards the burning fuel tanks and says,
"You did all this?"

"I am here to save you from the man who did all this. You
too, mademoiselle!" Jean says, pointing his pistol (his rapid
pulse is making it tremble slightly, but he feels amazingly
calm) at the young woman.

Nicholas Hyde stands there with his hands up by his shoulders, says, "Are you still working for Teryl Meade?"

"I am here to help you. Both of you into my vehicle.
Quickly, if you please!"

"I don't think so," someone else says, and Jean turns just as
the blond man raises the rifle (Jean realizes with dismay that it
was lying by the dead man) and fires three rapid shots, two
kicking up dirt, the third punching into Jean's belly. He drops
his pistol and sits down, breathless and amazed. And sees
something break into a lopsided run, running past the woman,
running straight towards him—the huge cat, its mouth full of
knives.

Cody raises the M-23 as someone comes running out of the
thick smoke towards him, but it's only Jean Badiledi's driver,

Magne Leroy. The big man slows, says, "Captain Badiledi wants to kill you!" and keeps running.

Cody hears shots up ahead and starts running too, pain spearing his hip at every other stride. He sees through a veil of smoke three people scrambling into the red 4×4. One of them is definitely Elspeth Faber, and he's pretty sure that one of the men is Nicholas Hyde. He lifts the M-23 and squeezes off a burst, but the 4×4 bounces over the ditch and speeds away, heading towards the airstrip and the little zebra-striped Beechcraft, disappearing into the smoke. Cody slows to a walk, skirting the fat man who sits in the ditch holding his blood-soaked belly, warily approaching the big tawny cat that's crouched over Jean Badiledi, its jaws clamped around his neck. The man gargles blood as the cat worries at him, tries to reach a black cylinder lying just out of reach. Or maybe his hand is just clenching in reflex, maybe he sees Cody watching him die, maybe not.

When he's sure Badiledi is dead, Cody switches the M-23 to single-shot mode and shoots the cat right between its milky eyes. He steps up and prods it with the rifle's barrel, and something smacks into the dirt a couple of metres away—an arrow, dug deep at an angle. He turns, sees through a curtain of smoke and dust a man trying to fit another arrow to his weird-looking bow, and switches the M-23 to full auto and gives the scudder everything left in the magazine.

Cody listens to his harsh breath in the ringing silence, then slings the rifle over his shoulder and pulls his Colt Python from his waistband and walks back to the man in the ditch, lying there with blood all over his nice clothes, looking up at him dully.

"I guess you must be Raphael," Cody says. "You want to try and stand up now, see if you can walk over to that Range Rover? We need to find a nice quiet place where we can talk about these white devils."

Chapter 36

After Teddy Yssel gets the zebra-striped Beechcraft into the air, he and Elspeth Faber consult a map, trying to work out how far they can get on tanks that are less than half-full. While they plot a course north and east of Kinshasa, Nick, in the cramped seat behind them, examines the packages in the canvas carryall that was in the back of the Isuzu Trooper. The automatic he took off the man Teddy shot, stuck in the waistband of his trousers, digs into his belly, so he puts it on the seat beside him. At last, Teddy leans his head back and says, speaking loudly to be heard over the buzz of the little plane's engine, "What do you have there?"

"Pipe bombs."

"You're kidding!"

"Semtex, with phone-chip detonators."

Elspeth turns to look at Nick. She says, "I don't think he's kidding, Teddy."

Teddy says, "What do you mean, phone-chip detonators?"

"You make a call to the phone chip, and the bomb goes off."

"Then for Christ's sake throw them out," Teddy says, "before someone does just that!"

"It's okay. I switched them off."

"Yah? How can you be sure?"

"I learned about stuff like this in the army."

"Throw them out," Teddy says. "What do we want with pipe bombs?"

"Maybe I'll think of something," Nick says.

"You see my bag back there?" Teddy says. "Look inside, you'll find a bottle of Mr. Walker's finest."

There's less than an inch of whisky left in it. Nick unscrews the cap and hands it to Teddy, who takes a long sip (the plane briefly dipping when he takes one hand off the yoke) before offering it to Elspeth. She refuses it with a shake of her head and says, "Should you be drinking and flying, Teddy?"

"I've been shot at, I had to shoot someone, I need a little something to steady my nerves," Teddy says, taking another sip and offering the bottle to Nick, who takes it and puts it away.

Elspeth turns around in her seat and says to Nick that they haven't been introduced yet, and sticks out her hand.

"Nicholas, this is Elspeth Faber," Teddy says. "Elspeth, this tough guy is Nicholas Hyde."

Nick and Elspeth shake hands, smiling at each other. Elspeth's smile lights up her face. It's framed by a kind of cap of small, tight braids, some with coloured beads woven into them. She says, "What were you doing at the ranch, Nicholas? Were you working for Raphael?"

"Raphael told me I was his guest, but the truth was, I was his prisoner."

"He forced you to make that video?"

Her eyes are very dark, almost black; her gaze is serious and direct. Her fine brown skin reminds him of the bloom on sweet chestnuts freshly sprung from their spiky casings.

"Not exactly," Nick says. "And it was sort of my idea to put it onto the Web."

"You caused a big stir."

"That was the plan."

Teddy says, "I hate to break up your conversation, but how about a little help with the navigation?"

They follow the Uamba River as far as they can, and land on fumes in parched scrub near a road a couple of kilometres south of the little city of Bandundu. After they've pushed the plane under a clump of thorn trees, Teddy uses his satellite phone to find the number of a local taxi company, finishes off the whisky, smokes half a dozen cigarettes, and tells Nick how he met up with Elspeth, explains how he knew that Nick was involved with Raphael.

The taxi is a battered Nissan people-carrier covered with

pious slogans, driven by a tall young guy in a red denim jacket and red jeans. Teddy tells him that their car broke down in the bush, and Elspeth spins a story about researching baboon behaviour, keeps up a conversation about the social structure of baboon troops, the bush-meat trade, and the damage baboons do to crops.

As the taxi speeds through the outskirts of Bandundu towards what the driver promises is the best hotel in the city, Nick borrows Teddy's phone, makes a five-second call, and hands the phone back.

"I hope that wasn't to Raphael," Teddy says, only half kidding.

"I'll explain later," Nick says, nodding towards the driver, who's telling Elspeth that baboons are very dangerous now; they ate so many dead bodies after the Black Flu, they have lost their fear of men.

On the pavement outside the hotel, after Nick has paid the taxi driver, Teddy says, "So, who did you call? You know someone here?"

"I phoned a pipe bomb that I left on the plane."

"You're kidding."

"I don't think he's the kind of guy who kids a great deal," Elspeth says.

"You blew up the plane? I don't believe you."

"We could waste time and go back and take a look," Nick says, "or you can just take my word. They'll be looking for three people in a plane with zebra-stripe livery, so we're better off without it."

"They?"

"The army, the police. Maybe Raphael, if he's still alive."

"Cody Corbin," Elspeth says.

"You blew it up." Teddy clutches his head and turns in a circle and says, "Jesus Christ. We could have flown all the way to Pleistocene Park."

Passersby are openly staring at them. Nick says, "We can't talk about it here. Let's check in and find a place to eat. We have a lot to discuss."

* * *

The International Friendship Hotel is the tallest and newest
building in Bandundu, but the fountain in its grandiose lobby is
cracked and dry, the elevators are no longer working, and
there's only cold water in the bathrooms. Nick showers quickly,
seeing different moments from the day whenever he closes his
eyes. As he's dressing in his sweat-stained clothes, the single
bulb in the room's overhead fixture turns orange, flickers, and
goes out. Downstairs, the desk clerk explains, without looking
up from the book he's reading by the light of an oil lamp, that
the city's electricity is turned off at six o'clock every evening
and the hotel's generator broke down three months ago—they
are still waiting for the crucial spare part to be delivered.

Nick says, "So where can my friends and I get something
to eat?"

The hotel's dining room, with its marble floor, crystal
chandeliers, and murals of river scenes, is open despite the
lack of power, but service is slow because the kitchen has to
use camping stoves and only one waiter is on duty. Nick, Elspeth, and Teddy have plenty of time to exchange their stories over a dinner of barely warmed-over tinned asparagus
soup and greasy pork chops and mashed potatoes. Teddy
mostly listens, smoking cigarette after cigarette and drinking
shot after shot of Johnnie Walker Black Label from the bottle
he bought in the hotel's bar, while Nick tells his story about
the massacre at the oil palm plantation and Teryl Meade's attempt to cover it up. He explains how he and Harmony Boniface were betrayed to Raphael when they went into the
rainforest to look for a white devil that had been captured by
villagers, and describes the disastrous hunt with Raphael's
men; Elspeth tells him how Cody Corbin murdered her father
and massacred and burnt the bodies of the Gentle People,
backtracking to explain how her father came to be living on
the little island off Kenya's coast with a small tribe of reconstructed australopithecines.

By this time, they've finished eating and have folded their

napkins—expensive creamy linen spotted with old food stains—and pushed away their plates.

Nick says, "So Cody Corbin and the guy Teddy shot, Jean Badiledi, are both working for Teryl Meade. She paid Cody Corbin to kill Elspeth's father, and Jean Badiledi was heavily involved in her attempts to cover up the truth about the massacre. He threatened me, I think he was responsible for the murders of the baby and the government observer, William Ndinga, and I'm fairly certain he killed a colleague of mine, too."

"A nasty fellow," Teddy says. "Now I don't feel so bad I shot him."

Trying to say it casually. Teddy Yssel, action hero, with his sloppy smile and a slight tremor in his hands, the neck of the bottle knocking against the rim of his glass as he pours himself another shot.

Elspeth says, "Cody Corbin will still be looking for us."

Nick says, "I have the silly idea that I should have stood up to him when he came at us, had a Western-style showdown. Michel would have liked that."

Teddy says, "The fellow had an assault rifle."

"I did notice," Nick says, seeing the man in khaki combat pants and a camo flak jacket walking steadily towards them out of thick smoke like one of those old-fashioned unkillable cyborg villains.

Elspeth smiles at him and says, "Getting out of there was definitely the right thing to do."

Her dark, serious eyes reflect the flame of the candle that burns in the centre of the table. She is wearing blue jeans and a yellow scoop-necked T-shirt that clings to her slim body.

Teddy says, "Man, I was still only halfway inside the car when you floored it. It was lucky I fell on top of Elspeth. Otherwise, I would have broken my arm, instead of just bruising it."

"And I fell on the bag of pipe bombs," Elspeth says.

Teddy knocks back his whisky and looks at Nick across the table and says, "I still think you made a mistake when you blew up the plane."

Nick says, trying to be patient, "Everyone who's looking

for us—the police, Raphael's people, Cody Corbin—will be looking for three people in a plane painted with black-and-white stripes. Getting rid of it, or at least making it look like it crashed, has bought us a little time."

"If you were worried about the zebra stripes, we could have had it repainted. In two or three hours it could have been any colour you wanted."

"And we'd still be three people in a stolen plane," Nick says.

"You blew up the plane, and now we're sitting here because you say it's a good idea to talk. Remind me when we put you in charge," Teddy says, "because I seem to have forgotten."

Nick says, "You can always go home, Teddy. I understand there's a plane back to Kinshasa in two or three days, or a riverboat next week."

"You want to get rid of me, is that it?"

The man staring at him, doing the thing with his eyes, half-closing one and then the other as he tries to focus.

Nick says, "I'm going all the way on this. I absolutely understand that you might not be prepared to follow me."

"Follow you? I don't think you have any idea where to go."

The two men are staring at each other across the white linen tablecloth and litter of dirty plates. Elspeth says, feeling that she has to stop their silly argument before it gets out of hand, "The key to all this is Daniel Lovegrave. That is, if he's still alive."

After a moment, Nick smiles at Teddy and says, "She's right."

"She is?" The poor guy, more than half-drunk, is having trouble keeping up.

Nick says to Elspeth, "The saber-toothed cat was definitely from Pleistocene Park?"

"Sure. Otherwise I couldn't have got near it."

"Right. And Raphael knew that the white devils had a deliberately gengineered metabolic defect, exactly like the saber-toothed cat," Nick says. Putting it together, getting it straight. "So either someone told him about it, or he knew that the white devils were from Pleistocene Park, knew they would need the same special dietary supplement as his prized sabertooth. In any case, it links him directly to the place. Elspeth, you said that your father and Teryl Meade and Daniel Lovegrave successfully recreated a species of extinct hominid for Pleistocene Park, but that Teryl Meade quit."

"She turned up in the States," Elspeth says, "and made her big statement renouncing gengineering. She was on all the chat shows. She even made the op-ed page of the *New York Times*. And then she joined Obligate."

"And meanwhile something happened to your father. A laboratory accident, or an attempt to silence him."

"I don't know all the details," Elspeth says, "because the one time I visited Pleistocene Park, I had a big argument with my father over what he was doing, and it was only after Teryl had left that I tried to get back in contact. But he didn't seem to want to talk, except to say that he was fine and that I shouldn't worry. And whenever I suggested he come visit me, or that I should visit him, he stonewalled or got mad. I thought at the time he was still upset because of what I'd said about his work, but now I know it was probably because of what he called his 'laboratory accident.'"

Remembering with a chill his frightening, uncharacteristic rages, the ravings that would leave her upset for days afterwards, that she knows now were manifestations of his dark half. Of Dr. Dave.

"But he managed to escape," Nick says, "with the hominids he and Teryl Meade and Daniel Lovegrave had created."

"Four years ago," Elspeth say, "two years after Teryl left. It was right in the middle of the Black Flu pandemic, and Pleistocene Park was one of the targets in the war against bioterrorism. It was hit by at least two cruise missiles, and I suppose that's when Daddy escaped with the Gentle People. He had to travel across hundreds of kilometres of dying forest, right across what would become the Dead Zone, but he got out."

Teddy is watching them owl-eyed, a cigarette drooping from one corner of his mouth.

Nick says, "So it's possible that your father and Daniel Lovegrave were still working together after they made the Gentle People, after Teryl Meade left. Or perhaps she left because she didn't like where they were taking the research."

"Or perhaps neither my father nor Teryl liked it, but she got out and he didn't. I tried to talk to her," Elspeth says, "after I found out about what had happened to my father. But I couldn't get through the PR people she'd hired, and my father wouldn't ever talk about it. Wouldn't, or couldn't. Anyway, I let it go. All that mattered to me, before this, was that he was somewhere safe."

Nick says, "Your father didn't ever talk about the white devils?"

"Jesus," Teddy says. "Her father was murdered, and the guy who killed him just now nearly killed us. Why don't you ease up?"

"Because it's important, Teddy. Because we need to decide what to do now, before Cody Corbin or someone just like him comes after us."

Elspeth picks her words carefully. "I don't know if my father had anything to do with making the white devils, but I do think that they were made in the same way as the Gentle People."

She has to fortify herself with a shot of whisky before she can tell Nick and Teddy that her father had liberated the Gentle People from Pleistocene Park and had been living with them for the past four years, but she can't bring herself to reveal what they really are, why Teryl is so determined to destroy all traces of her complicity. She hopes that she won't have to. She hopes that there are no more white devils, or that Danny Lovegrave disneyed them up from chimp stock after all, solved all the problems that had stalled the creation of the keystone species of the Pleistocene Park project.

Nick says, "Could Lovegrave have done it on his own?"

"Lovegrave was in charge of the gengineering. Qualia, which was mostly Teryl and my father, worked on neuronal enhancement, editing engrams, and instinct reinforcement."

"Mind-sculpting," Teddy says.

"That's a crude way of putting it, but yes. Lovegrave made the Gentle People, but my father and Teryl made them what they were."

Nick says, "Did you ever meet Lovegrave? Do you know anything about him?"

"Sure. He was a friend of my father long before Pleistocene Park. He was your average science geek. Clever but somehow childish, not quite grown up. He wasn't married, always had some kind of inappropriate girlfriend, the kind who wears too little and drinks too much at a party, and usually causes some kind of trouble. He liked to do card tricks at parties whenever he got bored, but mostly he liked to watch. He'd whisper to me out of the side of his mouth, tell me who was having trouble getting funding, who was sleeping with who . . . This was while he and my father and Teryl were working at Harvard, before Qualia and Pleistocene Park, before I moved back to Kenya. I haven't seen him since then. The one time I visited my father after he moved to the Congo, Danny Lovegrave was away on business."

Remembering the thrift-store checked shirts he'd always worn over faded black T-shirts, the way he folded back his sleeves like a plumber or a carpenter, his scuffed Timberlands and trodden-down Converse All Stars. A stocky man beginning to run to fat, with an indoor pallor and thinning blond hair brushed straight back, sometimes tied in a ponytail, sometimes not, his intense blue eyes watchful and secretly amused. He drove an immaculately restored MG in British Racing Green; once, when she was just twelve, he let Elspeth "take it for a spin." Her father was furious, but Uncle Danny laughed it off. He was brilliant, impulsive, selfish, absolutely indifferent to the feelings of other people.

Teddy Yssel pours what's left of his last glass of whisky into his coffee, half-melted ice cubes and all. He says, "So all we have to do is find this fellow. Who has been missing in action ever since the Dead Zone was created. Who everyone thinks is dead."

"Actually, I have a lead," Nick says. "Michel, the guy

Badiledi shot dead, told me where Raphael bought his saber-toothed cat."

Teddy sips his coffee, makes a face. "And?"

"He bought it from some kind of mission in the Dead Zone. That's why I quite understand if both of you don't want to come along with me."

Elspeth says, "Where exactly in the Dead Zone?"

"That's the problem. Michel didn't say."

"The Dead Zone is a big place."

"I know."

"About the size of the American Southwest."

"One and a half million square kilometres," Nick says. "But there can't be too many missions left. We can visit the church here tomorrow, maybe someone there can help us."

"Père Mike," Teddy says, and takes another slurp of coffee as Nick and Elspeth stare at him. "He's not exactly a priest, but he used to help run this mission near the Pleistocene Park facility. I met him once. He started out working for some Canadian charity in one of the big permanent refugee camps at the Rwandan border and stayed on to help a couple of Catholic brothers who were running a mission in the forest. They were killed in the civil war, ten, fifteen years ago, and he took charge of the place, turned it into an orphanage and a food-distribution centre."

Nick says, "And you just happened to meet him? Or was he something to do with Raphael's smuggling business?"

"No, nothing like that. I was working for Raphael when I met Père Mike, it's true, but we met by accident. This was just before the Black Flu and the Dead Zone and all the rest of the madness. Raphael bought a lot of his stuff from Uganda, and I was coming back with a load when one of the flaps jammed. I had to put down to fix it—it was at the Pleis-tocene Park facility, as a matter of fact."

Elspeth says, "You were at Pleistocene Park?"

"The airstrip, not the place itself. Père Mike was listening in to the radio traffic, called me up and drove a hundred klicks of forest road with this kid who had the plastic disease very bad, persuaded me to fly the kid to Kinshasa. And that's what I did. He was a very persuasive man, very stubborn."

"This was back when you were helping Raphael smuggle antibiotics and guns and fake magic bullets," Nick says, and smiles when Teddy stares at him. "Michel told me all about that when I mentioned your name. Our friend Theodore Yssel, Elspeth, was one of Raphael's pilots, once upon a time. But then he crashed a plane, and Raphael fired him."

"Right into the river," Teddy says with a smile that doesn't quite work. "I was drinking pretty heavily back then. It was one of those things."

Elspeth has a sudden bad feeling, the same sense of bottomless dismay she'd felt when she'd thought that Teddy and Darlajane B. were about to take her for everything she had. She says, "You told me that you knew the men in Nick's video clip. You didn't tell me that you met them when you were a drug smuggler."

Teddy says, "Not drugs—antibiotics. It was a very big business. There were street sellers in every city, sheaves of shrink-wrapped pills over their arms. People bought them by colour. Red or blue for different kinds of fevers, white for what they called diseases of the heart and mind, red and yellow for the plastic disease, yellow for venereal diseases . . . I was working for the relief agencies, ferrying workers to the big camps on the Rwandan and Ugandan borders. I flew maybe one trip a month on the side. A lot of people were doing it. I know this will sound like the worst kind of excuse, but it's the truth. It's what happened. A man would find you in a bar, suggest that your plane needed insurance. We were flying in war zones, we couldn't *get* insurance, but that wasn't the point. If we didn't do these side trips . . ."

Teddy raises his right hand, palm flat, makes a sharp whistle as he brings it down on the table.

Elspeth says, "They'd shoot you down?"

Teddy says, "They'd do something to your plane. A blocked fuel line, a leak in the hydraulics, what a shame, it happens all the time. Or maybe you would be walking down the street, get a bullet in the head from some passing car."

"Everyone was doing it," Nick says, "and everyone was making money out of it, too."

Teddy says, "Believe me, I didn't do it for the money. When Raphael's man told me I was buying insurance from him, I knew it was one of those offers you couldn't refuse."

He looks at Nick, looks at Elspeth, wretched and defiant. Elspeth feels a prick of pity, thinking that his squalid little secret isn't one-tenth as bad as hers.

Teddy says, "The first trip I did free. That's how it was. It was only after they were sure you wouldn't talk that you got paid. Anyway, I did not work for Raphael for very long. I crashed my plane, lost a load of antibiotics, and had to swim for my life. Had to get out of the DRC pretty damned fast after that. Johnny Grundlingh got me another job, the same company we were still working for when we ran into the white devils. Raphael's agent found me a month later. He had a couple of thugs with him. He asked for payment for the lost cargo, I asked him about the insurance on the plane, and he had the two thugs hold me while he broke my nose. He was a skinny little fucker, took him three tries . . . So anyway, they kicked me unconscious, took the money I had on me, and that was the end of it."

Teddy stubs out his cigarette, pushes his chair back from the table, and grabs his whisky bottle as he stands. "It is late, and I am drunk. Tomorrow, I will fix us a ride to Père Mike's place. And don't worry, no planes," he says, and gives Nick and Elspeth a sloppy salute and walks away, only once bumping into another table on his way down the long, dimly lit dining room.

Nick watches him go, then looks at Elspeth and says, "We should leave him here."

"Are you serious?"

"Why not? He's a drunk, he used to work for Raphael . . . I don't think he can be trusted."

"What are we going to do, sneak out of here in the small hours of the morning? Teddy saved your life when he shot Badiledi, and he's involved in this thing for the same reason as you—the white devils killed his friend. Maybe he's done some bad things in the past, but I think he wants to make up for that now. Besides, he knows where we're going, and if we do sneak out on him, he'll only catch up with us. Exactly what kind of place are we going to, anyway? And what are we going to do when we get there?"

"We haven't really talked about that, have we?"

"I guess we have a lot to talk about." She hasn't yet asked him about the business of him having been cloned from his dead brother. How he feels about that, how he feels about the world knowing . . . She says, "I don't even know your real name."

"Is that important right now?"

"You're this mysterious guy, full of secrets, and Teddy, on the other hand, has worked here, he knows about Père Mike and his mission. If it came to it, if I had to make a choice between you two guys, maybe I should go with him rather than with you."

"Then I guess I'll have to put up with Teddy."

Nick smiles when he says it; after a moment, Elspeth smiles, too.

Nick says, "That moment when I saw you, with that big cat . . ."

"It was a pretty crazy moment . . ."

Both of them looking at each other across the table in the candlelight.

Nick turns, signals to the waiter. As the old man begins to walk very slowly down the length of the dining room towards them, Nick says, "There's a bar just across the road. What do you say to a nightcap?"

The bar is little more than a scattering of tables and chairs on a strip of threadbare grass between the river embankment and the unlit road. At one end, a pick-up band is playing intricate, guitar-heavy jazz-funk; at the other, vendors are selling cold beer, cooking shrimp and fish and plantain on charcoal-fuelled griddles. It's a popular place, and most of the tables are taken; Elspeth finds a free one while Nick queues for beer. It's pleasant to sit in the buttery evening warmth, in the middle of the chatter and laughter of the easygoing crowd, the musicians chugging along in a groove, yellow and green biolumes stuck here and there in the sandy grass, a fat African half-moon laying fugitive silvery streaks on the long, low waves that break around the boulders at the foot of the embankment, a few lights glimmering in the darkness beyond the broad black sweep of the river. An old man sits cross-legged, watching a little TV in his lap. Two boys in spex grab shapes in the humid air as they spar in some shared virtuality. Three men pass a fat reefer back and forth, watching a teenage couple making out and commenting on the action. And someone comes up behind Elspeth, someone not Nick; a distinguished man in a blue business suit who says something when she looks up at him, switches to English after she tells him that she doesn't speak French.

"When you are done with your friend, I will be happy to talk with you."

"You've made an assumption about me," Elspeth says, "and it's wrong."

The man's smile is nicely calculated. He's forty-five, fifty, the orange silk shirt under his blue jacket buttoned at the neck. He says, "I have been here five days on business. But now my business is done, and I am in the mood to celebrate. And if I may make an observation, mademoiselle, you deserve better than your friend."

An expensive cologne, an expensive old-fashioned watch with a gold and steel band. A worldly manner, at ease with approaching a strange woman. Damn right he has made the wrong assumption.

"Imagine that I'm not interested," Elspeth says, "and then disappear."

The man's smile remains sincere. "My friends and I will be here for a while. Think about it."

Elspeth watches him swagger back to the table that he shares with two younger men, watches him tell them something that makes them laugh. She thinks of all the times she has been alone in bars like this, of all the men who have come on to her. Men with their easy assumptions, men who have already made up their minds about her, men who don't listen to what she has to say, or listen just enough while waiting for an opening, a way of steering the talk in the direction they want it to go. If she had told him that she was a palaeoanthropologist, he would no doubt have shifted his ground, apologized, pretended to be interested in her work. They might even have had a semblance of a civilized conversation, but there would have still been the inevitable question in the air. And if she had told him, today, just a few hours ago, I let a tiger kill a man . . .

"Hey," Nick says. He carries two beer bottles in one hand, and a paper bowl of shrimp in the other.

"Hey," she says.

"I don't know what these are," Nick says, handing her one of the sweating long-necked bottles, "but the woman who sold them to me said she makes the best beer in Bandundu. The shrimp are from a local farm. I thought, after trying the hotel's attempt at international cuisine, we might want some real food."

Elspeth sniffs the top of her uncapped bottle, wrinkles her nose at the strong, sweet, musty odour. "Sorghum beer. Yum."

"We could go back to the hotel, wake up that waiter, try the dubious house white or the questionable house red."

The shrimps, fat and gleaming, black stripes burnt into their pink shells from the griddle, speckled with finely chopped chillies, nestle amongst chunks of fresh pineapple. Elspeth shucks one and takes a bite, says, "Let's stay here. I like this place."

"So do I."

They clink bottles, and both smile at the same moment, embarrassed by the gesture. Elspeth eats the rest of her shrimp. It's sweet and delicious, and the fresh pineapple goes surprisingly well with it. She starts to peel another, says, "You don't mind the people staring at you?"

"Because I'm the only white man here? Let them. I worked with quite a few Kenyans in Witness. I'd swear your accent was more American."

"Is this the catching-up-with-our-pasts part of the date?"

"Let's say it's trying to make idle conversation with a colleague over a nightcap, after a very difficult day."

There's a pause. They drink beer and eat shrimp. Nick eats them New Orleans style, heads and all. His eyes are bright blue in his tanned face. He has very English features, Elspeth thinks, the kind you think of as refined. Good cheekbones, a narrow blade of a nose, a long upper lip. A quiet, self-contained man. Not trying to be cool but managing it anyway.

Nick says, "We're finding this difficult for some reason."

"Why don't you ask me how come I have an American accent, when I was born in Nairobi?"

"Okay. How come?"

"Because I was born in Nairobi," Elspeth says, "but my father and I went to live in Boston when I was very young."

"Just you and your father? He was—what? Divorced?"

"A widower."

"I'm sorry."

"It was a car accident, sort of. A truck driver ran into the back of my mother's car, and when she got out to look at the damage he stabbed her and ran off. I was just four years old, and I don't remember any of it, thank God. He'd been hired by the transport company just two days before, he'd used a false name . . . To make a long story short, he was never caught. There were rumours that it was a political assassination, that my mother was killed as a warning to my father. At the time he was involved in protecting the National Parks from exploitation, a very hot issue. It made my father very angry, very bitter with Kenya. So when he got a job offer at the Harvard Medical School, we moved from Nairobi to Boston."

"And how did you like Boston?"

"The first winter, I thought the world had come to an end. I had never seen snow before, and there was so much of it. Have you ever been to the States?"

"Not yet. We had a holiday place in Italy, I was posted to Albania once, when I was in the army, I did some biodiversity survey work in France and Portugal, and now I'm here.

But I've discovered that I like to travel, and who knows? Maybe I'll end up in Boston one day. Or Nairobi."

"If you're ever in Nairobi, I know some good restaurants. Family places off the tourist trail. Not that there are many tourists, these days."

"You don't have a boyfriend in Nairobi, anyone like that?"

Nick asking this very casually, smiling at her before popping a chunk of pineapple into his mouth.

Elspeth says, "I had a couple of boyfriends before Daddy came back from the dead. University things, nothing serious. And then I had Daddy to look after, I had my work . . . Does this still count as idle conversation?"

"Why not? So, you grew up in America, and moved back to Kenya with your father."

"It's a bit more complicated. I came back to Nairobi to study palaeoanthropology . . . and I guess, if I'm honest, because I was pissed off at my father for marrying Teryl. Teryl and I didn't get along. The classic stepdaughter-stepmom rivalry. After she and my father got married, I hated the way my life had changed, and I moved out as soon as I could. They had set up Qualia by then; it was still a going concern when I moved out. But then the government money they relied on dried up, and that's when they became involved with the Pleistocene Park project."

Elspeth is suddenly wary. She has strayed too close to the thing that she isn't ready to talk about.

Nick says, "I was wondering about that name. Qualia."

"My father used to say that it's the reason why telepathy is impossible. One reason, anyway."

"It's a mind thing."

"It's a consciousness thing. In fact, it's at the seat of the problem of consciousness—of why our experience of seeing the world is different from that of, say, a video camera. Qualia is the plural of quale, and a quale is a specific quantity of subjective experience. At its most basic, it's the banananess of the taste of bananas, the redness of red, the yellowness of yellow. It's why every person experiences the world in a different way."

"And is that why I can't read your mind? Because your yellow would be my red or green?"

"My father used to say that it's because the map is not the territory. You can map every neuron in someone's brain, every connection between every neuron, and the state of every connection from moment to moment. It would be fantastically difficult, but with enough computing power it could be done. But although consciousness is generated by the activity of neurons, the quality of consciousness is independent of that activity."

"Because of these qualia."

"Exactly. My father showed me my own mind a couple of times. It's a pretty simple procedure. You lie down on a couch in a quiet, darkened room, with your head on a deeply dished plastic block. The block is densely packed with superconducting quantum monopoles that measure the electrical activity generated by your brain at a very fine resolution, and you watch false-colour topographic maps of that activity on a screen. The least active parts in blue, shading through red to the most active parts in yellow."

Remembering the glow of the screen in the dusty dark, the way the disposable plastic cover of the couch stuck to her bare legs, her father's quiet, patient voice explaining what she was seeing.

Elspeth says, "Usually, there are two bright yellow ovals, one in each hemisphere of your brain. Those are the areas of high neural activity, and there are green lines, reentrant pathways, zigzagging between them. As you watch, the boundaries of the yellow ovals shift, some green lines brighten, and others fade. That's the dynamic core, the seat of consciousness, and it's always shifting and changing because from moment to moment different subsets of neurons are responding to sensory input and contributing to the conscious experience. The taste of beer, the sound of the band, the feel of the chair you're sitting on—"

"The face of the woman opposite."

"Everything changes from moment to moment, and if you were able to freeze each moment of ongoing consciousness, you'd get a series of qualia, each one a single subjective state out of billions upon billions of possible states."

"One of which would be the beer-music-chair-woman quale."

"Exactly."

"It's a pretty nice one."

"Each quale defines a subjective experience. The dynamic core has billions of possible states, and each state is subjectively different in every person, which is why mind-reading is fundamentally impossible. Every map is different, and each map can only give you the quantitative definition of a particular quale, not the subjective conscious experience. You can tell that someone is thinking about something red, and that it's making them happy, for instance. But not *why* it's making them happy."

"And that's what your father and Teryl were working on. Mapping consciousness."

"Qualia were only part of it. My father was very interested in engrams generated by groups of neurons that lie outside the dynamic core. He discovered more than fifty of them. Some are generated by the activity of only a few closely linked neurons; others by clusters of tens of thousands of neurons distributed throughout the cortex. Some engrams encode primitive or learned reflexes; others are like subroutines or partial personae. Kind of like ghosts in the machine."

Thinking for a moment of the way her father's face would change when Dr. Dave came out.

Nick says, "I met someone on a blind date who wanted me to try Emotional Reorientation. She told me all about engrams."

"And did you? Try it, I mean."

"I suppose that for better or worse I prefer to think my own thoughts. How about you? Didn't your father help invent Emotional Reorientation?"

"That was Teryl, using research she stole from my father. His opinion was that it was about as much use as stirring your brains with a spoon. Erasing minor engrams certainly affects the emotional climate of the mind, but it's as crude and as po-

tentially damaging as old-fashioned lobotomy or elec-
troshock treatment."

"You never wanted to follow in your father's footsteps."

"He was a genius, a hard act to follow. And I was a pretty
stubborn kid; I wanted to do my own thing . . ."

There's a silence. Nick takes a sip of beer and says, "You
seem to be taking our adventure a lot more calmly than me, if
you don't mind me saying so."

"It doesn't seem very real yet. Perhaps I'll stage a nervous
breakdown when it finally sinks in. How about you?"

"Today was the third time in a week that I've been in some
kind of firefight. I hope I'm not getting used to it."

"You didn't see any action while you were in the army?"

"I had basic training, and then I was assigned to work in
an ordnance depot as a kind of glorified clerk. That was
about it."

"This was after you quit medical school."

"Medical school was my mother's idea, and I was unhappy
about it, but what really changed my mind was the Black Flu
pandemic. The university closed for the duration, and I volunteered for emergency work, ended up in this triage centre
outside Oxford. It was an army hospital that had been built to
treat casualties of limited nuclear war in Europe, a huge place
that had been mothballed since the end of the Cold War. Very
weird, like working in a time capsule. I remember that there
were Bakelite telephones on every ward, and we had to
change the plugs on every piece of equipment because of the
antique sockets. We had mobile phones, but they didn't work
half the time because the place was built like a castle, reinforced concrete walls a metre thick. There were more than a
hundred wards, each with thirty beds, but we weren't short of
patients. We were treating people whose magic bullets had
been overwhelmed, and refugees and visitors to the country
who didn't have magic bullets. There were people on trol-
leys, on mattresses laid between beds . . ."

"It must have been tough," Elspeth says. Remembering the
smoke of the great burning that had tainted Nairobi's air for
three months, the power cuts and food shortages, tanks rum-

bling down deserted streets, soldiers in biohazard suits herding people who had been in contact with victims of Black Flu into isolation camps . . . And in the middle of all that, she and David Oloitip had been trying to find a hiding place for her father and the Gentle People.

Nick says, "I guess it should have been harrowing, but we were so busy that we didn't have time to think. We were shut in with the patients, with soldiers maintaining the perimeter. There were rigorous isolation procedures, but despite that, and despite our magic bullets, about ten percent of the staff got sick, and most of the people who got sick died. And more than three-quarters of the patients died, too. Someone with full-blown haemorrhagic influenza turns into, basically, a man-sized blister. There's nothing you can do but put them on a drip and give them morphine. I worked there for six months, and after the emergency was over and the place was shut down, I knew that I didn't want to go back to university. Even then, I felt I was in a kind of competition with my dead brother. I had to be good at everything he was good at. I had to match up to him in every respect. The Black Flu crisis gave me the chance to drop out of the race, and I took it gladly, and joined the army. I served two years, spent some time in Albania, but otherwise I was working, as I said, in this big ordnance depot. I was studying electronics, hoping to make the grade as a radio operator and get transferred to an active unit, when I had my heart attack. I was never shot at, never had to shoot at anyone, either, until now."

"I've been working at Lake Turkana for five seasons now," Elspeth says, "and we always carry guns, but we've never needed to use them, thank God. Mostly, it's in case we're attacked by leopards or hippos—more people are killed in Africa by hippos than by lions—but there are plenty of bandits about, too."

"I guess there are bandits all over Africa."

"These were *shifta*, mostly from across the Somalian border. You passed them on the roads, they came into Loyangalani for medical treatment at the Catholic clinic, mostly they didn't cause any trouble. A group of them came to visit the camp last year. They were curious about what we were doing there. Ragged, wild-looking men riding horses, camels . . . We talked to them, showed them some of our finds, tried to explain what we were doing, fed them and gave them some medicines, and they thanked us and rode off. All of them were carrying rifles, of course, and several had rocket-propelled grenades, too, so we thought it would be prudent to stay friendly with them."

"So you're a rough, tough, gun-toting archaeologist."

"Palaeoanthropologist."

"Right. And you've been in some tight spots. You know how to handle yourself."

A woman comes up to their table with two fresh bottles of beer, says with a grin that a friend has bought these; he wonders if they would like to join him and his friends. Nick looks at Elspeth, who says, "Not my idea. If you like, you can thank the gentleman three tables over. The one in the blue suit, the older guy?" Saying, "Wait—"

Because Nick is pushing back his chair, standing up. He walks over to the man in the blue suit and talks to him, leaning close, one hand on the man's shoulder, the other two men at the table watching. Blue Suit smiles and shakes hands with Nick, and Nick walks back, casual but neat in his short-sleeved white shirt and dark pants.

Elspeth says, "What did you tell him?"

"I said that I understood how you get to feeling a little lonely in a town like this, that I understood that gentlemen like him and his two friends wouldn't want anything to do with those girls in hotpants dancing over by the band. I said that if he needed to find a woman, one of the desk clerks at the hotel could probably help him out. I also thanked him for the beers, and offered to buy him one, so he needn't think we owed him anything. He assured me that it wasn't necessary."

"I already told him I wasn't interested."

"But I bet he didn't listen," Nick says. "Frankly, I don't blame him."

"Are you trying out a line on me?"

"Actually, I don't know where we're going with this."

His smile makes him look incredibly young.

"You asked me out for a nightcap." Elspeth thinks she sees a way of moving towards what she wants to talk about, and raises her fresh bottle of sorghum beer and says, "Why don't we drink to extended kinship?"

"Extended kinship," Nick says, and they clink bottles. "Now we've toasted it, you'll have to explain what it is."

"It's what makes us human," Elspeth says. "Every primate species that lives in groups or troops—extended families—exhibits kinship behaviour. If the group is threatened by a predator, for instance, all the adult males will risk their lives by distracting the predator with threat displays while the females carry the young to safety. Even young males without any children will join in."

Pausing to let Nick think about it.

He says, "Even if they don't have direct relatives to protect, they'll certainly have indirect relatives who'll share some of their genes."

"That's how it is in primates, but we take it further. We have extended kinship. The firefighter who runs into a burning building to save a stranger, people who donate blood to help strangers they never meet . . . It's more than duty, or morality, or ordinary kinship behaviour. We even try and save other species. One time in the States, I was twelve or thirteen, my father and I drove down to the coast with one of his zoologist colleagues to try to save a pod of porpoises that had beached themselves. There were fifty or sixty people there, strangers to each other, digging channels, keeping the porpoises wet with towels and buckets of seawater until the tide came back in . . . That's what makes us so unique. We risk our lives for strangers. We extend kinship to the whole wide world, or—this is the other side of the coin—we make war on strangers. We exhibit extended kinship, but we are also able to objectify whole classes of human beings."

Elspeth takes a drink of beer. Nick is watching her, quiet and thoughtful, but she can't tell what he's thinking.

She says, getting to it at last, "I told you about engrams, that my father defined more than fifty of them? He believed that one particular engram, cd2, controlled hostility against those perceived to be outside the kinship group. He excised cd2 from the Gentle People, and just before he was murdered, he told me that whoever made the white devils could have designed their behaviour around it."

"So that's what we're in the middle of. The war of the coin's two sides. The Gentle People versus the white devils."

"I don't think it's that simple," Elspeth says. "The Gentle People lacked cd2, but they were still capable of displaying aggression toward each other. And we know that the white devils are capable of kinship behaviour."

"They're pure hate," Nick says, something unforgiving in his voice, his face. "Walking atrocities. They attack on sight, and when they do, it's kill or be killed. There's no mercy in them, Elspeth."

"They came back to rescue the one that had been caught by those hunters. They stuck together. They attacked people, but they didn't attack each other."

"So you think, what? There's some sliver of goodness in them? You think that they could be redeemed?"

"Perhaps I don't see things in black and white. What would you do? Wipe them off the face of the Earth?"

"Why not? If you'd seen what they did, you wouldn't stop to think about it."

Nick is giving her a hard, flat look, as if he's daring her to argue with him. The nice mood that they so carefully built has gone.

She says, "What do you want, Nick? Revenge? Is it as simple as that?"

"I want to speak for the people who died. I want the world to know the truth about what killed them. What about you, Elspeth? If we do find the person who made the white devils, if we find more of them, what will you do?"

She should tell him what she thinks the white devils really are, but his sudden anger has surprised and unnerved her, and she finds that she isn't ready to take that step, not yet. She says, "I want to find out the truth, just like you do. I want to find Danny Lovegrave and talk to him. I want to prove that

Teryl Meade had my father and the Gentle People killed. But
we don't know what we're going to find, do we? We don't
even know that Lovegrave is alive. Until we do . . ."

Nick's anger has passed; now he just looks tired. He
yawns, massages the back of his head with the flat of his
hand. His cropped black hair makes a crisp sound under his
palm. "I promise I won't do anything rash, Elspeth. We'll
find out what's happening at this mission, and then we'll decide what to do. Okay?"

"Okay."

"One thing Teddy Yssel had right, we should get some rest.
We have a lot to do tomorrow."

Chapter 37

The speedboat that Teryl Meade sends to bring Cody Corbin
across the Malebo Pool to Brazzaville has a knife-shaped
hull of black composite and two oversized reaction motors.
Moonlight lays shivering lines of light in its wake as it idles
past the long curve of a sandbar towards the mouth of a little
inlet, almost exactly an hour before the agreed rendezvous.

Cody, in his combat pants and a black T-shirt, tiger stripes
of camo paint across his cheeks and forehead, is lying under
a loose covering of dead fronds between the crotch of a split-
trunked palm tree that leans over the water. He's been lying
there for several hours, trying to ignore the clouds of insects
that swirl along the edge of the water, trying to think like the
lizard he once read about, a little scudder lives under stones
somewhere in the Himalayas, or maybe it was New Zealand,
moves just once or twice a year to catch a bug but otherwise
hunkers down, motionless, in a realm far beyond patience.

Now, when he hears the muffled throb of the boat's reaction motors, Cody's heart quickens. He pulls down his night-

vision goggles and the moonlit scene becomes as bright as an overcast afternoon. He can clearly see the men in the well of the boat: two unarmed men in civilian clothes, as agreed, plus two extra bodies in black coveralls and flak vests, balaclavas and goggles masking their faces, sniper rifles slung over their shoulders.

"You're so sneaky," he whispers, reaching for the M-23, "but I'm sneakier."

The boat's motors cut off; Cody waits until the two snipers are climbing over the side before he stands up and skips down the steep bank. One of the snipers is fast, swinging his long-barrelled rifle around just as Cody shoots him, a double tap that knocks the man back into the well of the boat, the other sniper turning to look at his fallen comrade when Cody's next shot clips him in the head.

Cody trots through the shallow reach of water to the sandbar, fires into the air. The two men still in the boat raise their hands above their heads. "Either of you gentlemen have any English?" Cody says. The two men look at each other and Cody levels the M-23 at them and asks his question again. One volunteers that he speaks a little, and Cody says, "Good for you," and shoots the other guy. The survivor falls to his knees and starts to babble in a mix of French and English; after he's checked that both of the snipers are dead, Cody has to climb into the boat and haul the man up by the collar of his shirt and pull him bodily over the side onto the sandbar. Standing over him, saying, "Are you left-handed or right-handed?"

The man lies on his back, shivering as he stares up at Cody. He's pissed his pants; Cody can smell it.

"Left or right?" Cody says again, and when the man raises his right hand puts his boot on his wrist and shoves the muzzle of the M-23 against the upturned palm. Says, "As long as you help me out, brother, everything will be fine. First thing I need to know, you no doubt have some message you were going to send after your friends caught me. You tell me what it is, right now, and I won't have to shoot off your fuckin' hand."

* * *

"**N**ow I'm here," Sherman Cates tells Teryl as he climbs out of the Seraph, "perhaps you'll tell me *why* I'm here." His white suit is freshly pressed, but otherwise he has the rumpled look of someone recently woken from deep sleep. He has wet-combed his blond hair, and a cowlick sticks up above his left eye.

"My men have acquired Cody Corbin," Teryl says. She's cranked up, in no mood to pussyfoot around. "He's going to make a statement right here, and you're going to be a witness to it."

Sherman looks around at the weedy lot, the dark buildings of the abandoned sugar refinery, the two military jeeps parked at the foot of the long concrete jetty. He looks at Teryl and raises an eyebrow and says, "If you coerce him, it won't be admissible."

"I'm not going to *coerce* him, Sherman; I'm going to *torture* him. Don't look at me like that. This isn't the States. Cody Corbin contacted me directly. Not through the cut-out, but on my own private phone. Badiledi must have talked; I never should have trusted him."

Sherman puts his hands together as if in prayer, touches the tips of his fingers to his lips. He says, "I suppose this man has something to do with the job you gave to Captain Badiledi. The job you don't want me to know anything about."

"He said that he wanted to meet me, to talk face to face. He said that he wanted to discuss the matter of the white devils. He said that he has proof that Daniel Lovegrave is still alive. He said that he wanted to renegotiate the terms of his contract."

"And?"

Teryl has a small pistol in the inside pocket of her red leather jacket. She has a sudden strong urge to take it out and put a bullet into Sherman's bovine face. "*And,* I know that he must know about my involvement with the Gentle People.

Think about it. The man eliminated Raphael, and now he wants to blackmail me."

"I recall, Teryl, that I warned you at the time—"

"Stop fussing, Sherman. Listen to me. Cody Corbin wanted to talk face to face, asked for a boat to bring him across from the other side of the Malebo Pool. I did what he asked, but I also arranged a little surprise. My men sent the signal that they captured and disarmed him half an hour ago. They're on their way back right now."

"You're under all kinds of pressure, Teryl. I understand that, and that's why I'm asking you to consider very carefully the step you're about to take. You're about to cross a line—"

"I've already crossed that line, Sherman. Listen. Cody Corbin is going to confess to the murder of Matthew Faber. He's going to confess to the massacre of the Gentle People. I'm going to tape it all, and we'll take it to Freddy Layne. You'll verify that Cody Corbin was shot when he tried to kill me, that it was a dying man's confession."

Sherman thinks about this. He says, "And this man, Cody Corbin, wants to kill you because?"

"He's a Radical Green terrorist, wanted for murder and mayhem in half a dozen countries. He killed Matthew because of his involvement with Pleistocene Park, and that's why he wants to kill me. Are you following this? He tries to break into my home, and my bodyguard shoots him. You're with me at the time, a social visit, and we obtain a dying man's confession."

"And this is what you'll tell Freddy Layne? Jesus, Teryl, he won't buy it for a second."

"He doesn't have to *buy* it, Sherman. All he has to do is realize that I've handed him a PR coup."

"And if Mr. Corbin does not cooperate?"

"We'll still have the body of an extremist who tried to assassinate me after he murdered my ex-husband. We can let Freddy draw his own conclusions."

"Let me talk to the man. Perhaps he's simply looking for a better deal, now that he has some leverage."

"Bullshit."

"I can't be a party to murder, Teryl. You must realize that."

"You don't have any choice," Teryl says, and walks a little way down the jetty, leaving the man to think it through.

Kinshasa is a little heap of lights far across the black void of the Malebo Pool. She leans at the rusty iron railing, listening to the slow slap of waves, breathing in the fresh, clean smell of air blown across vast volumes of open water. She tries to tell herself that she has come this far, that this is just one last job, a final bit of tidiness, but there's a hot tarry ball in her stomach, an intensification of the anxiety that's filled her ever since she returned to Africa. It's the feeling she gets when data she's trying to riddle for sense refuses to yield an answer, remains no more than an intricate, stubbornly unforgiving knot of meaningless numbers; it's the feeling she had when it became clear that Qualia would lose the sweet, fat government contract that was its only means of support. Matthew was blithely unconcerned about their plight, saying it wasn't so bad, the worst that could happen was that they'd have to find jobs in academia again, and she was utterly unable to make him see why she couldn't do it. All he cared about was finding some little niche where he could get on with his research, piss away his time playing with engrams, building arcane theories; he didn't understand how impossibly humiliating it would be for her to go back, to knuckle under, to admit failure.

That was why, when Daniel Lovegrave made the offer, she swallowed her pride and against her better judgement agreed to work for the Pleistocene Park project. Matthew was in his element, surprisingly. Moving to Africa and collaborating with Danny Lovegrave reenergized him. She couldn't tell him that she didn't understand as much of his work as he thought she did. She couldn't tell him that she was skimping on her own work, relying on a couple of bright postdocs. Pride stopped her: pride, and the fear of looking foolish, of being found out. She more or less stopped talking to Matthew, but he was so engaged with designing the neurological maps for what would become the Gentle People that he didn't notice. But Danny Lovegrave noticed, of course. Danny Lovegrave noticed everything. That was why she had to leave, because she knew that Lovegrave saw through her, saw that she was no more than merely competent, an ordinary, run-of-the-mill scientist without a spark of originality, the Big Ideas that made reputations forever beyond her reach. After she left, she was able to convince herself that she'd quit out of principle, because of her disgust at what she and Matthew and Danny Lovegrave had been forced to do to create the Gentle People and satisfy the terms of their contract. And she began to hate Matthew because he'd been so selfishly absorbed in his work that he'd done nothing to stop her leaving; she blamed him for allowing herself to be seduced by Danny Lovegrave, for her involvement in the crime that now threatens everything she has won for herself, that threatens to leave her naked, exposed, ridiculed, ruined, disgraced. Even thinking about it disgusts and frightens her, intensifies the burning of the tarry ball in her stomach, like a bolus of poison she can't quite bring herself to throw up.

One of the soldiers at the end of the jetty whistles sharply. A spotlight ignites, sweeps its beam across the black water. Sherman Cates says, right behind her, making her jump, "Is that it?"

The boat is driving steadily towards them, a tiny black shape caught in the unforgiving glare of the spotlight, casting a sharp shadow against the fan of its white wake.

Teryl feels a piercing pang of relief. She's been strangling the railing; rust flakes sting the palms of her hands, grittily adhere to her sweaty skin. She says, "If you aren't going to help me, Sherman, now's the time for you to go. But if you go, I don't ever want to see you again."

Sherman has taken off his jacket and carefully draped it over the crook of his left arm. Saddles of sweat are turning his white shirt translucent under his arms; he dabs at his brow with his handkerchief. The burnt-orange scent of his cologne is heavy in the hot, dark air. He says, "If there's any other way—"

"There isn't," Teryl says, and starts towards the cluster of soldiers at the end of the jetty, her heels tip-tapping on concrete as she picks her way over coils and knots of rusting steel cable. The soldiers are Badiledi's men, each of them paid a thousand dollars for this work. She would have preferred to use Brazilians—she doesn't think that the Congolese soldiers are professional enough to keep quiet—but she has to work with what she has.

She's halfway down the jetty when, with a snarling noise, the boat suddenly surges forward. The oval eye of the spotlight chases it across the black water, the soldiers rush to the edge of the jetty, shouting into the darkness, and a tremendous flash bursts in the night, silhouetting the men in a moment of white glare.

Teryl tries to blink away afterimages that multiply and swarm in her sight, realizes that the boat's reaction motors have stopped. A soldier clambers down a ladder in the steep side of the jetty and leans out, reaching with a hooked pole towards the boat as the spotlight plays over it. Teryl, her heart suddenly tripping, sees bodies slumped in the well, and then the boat bumps against the jetty and there's a shocking flash of red flame and the air body-slams her and she's sitting down, her ears ringing, stuff falling out of the air all around, rattling against the jetty, splashing in the water. The beam of the spotlight shines at a drunken angle through a thick pall of yellow-white smoke. The boat has vanished. One of the soldiers is picking himself up when someone appears at the edge of the jetty not twenty metres from where Teryl sits, a shadowy figure whose extended arm spits a lick of flame. The soldier collapses, and the figure hauls itself to the top of the jetty and slowly walks towards Teryl, silhouetted against the smoky glare of the searchlight.

He's half-naked, shaven-headed. His jeans are soaking wet and cling to his thighs. A rifle wrapped in plastic is slung over his shoulder. In the distance, there's the sound of the Seraph starting, a long, slithering squeal of tires—Sherman Cates making his getaway. Headlights stroke across the jetty, briefly lighting the tiger-striped face of the man as he looks at Teryl and says, "Professor Meade. My fairy godmother."

Teryl's fear is like a great wing beating in her head. She swallows, manages to say, "Mr. Corbin. What's all this?"

Cody Corbin squats down so that they're face to face, stares at her with a quizzical, almost kindly expression. Water drips off him onto dusty concrete. His elbows resting on his knees, his wrists crossed. Teryl tries very hard not to look at the big pistol that dangles from his right hand.

"I believe your men wanted to kill me," he says. "I'm very disappointed in you, Professor Meade. You misled me. Seems that every job I did for you was to cover up your crime."

"You said that you know where the white devils are. You want to put an end to them. So do I."

"I bet you do. Yeah, I know where they are, and I also know *what* they are." Tilting his head one way, then the other. "You know what I mean, don't you? Those atrocities you sent me to kill, they're the same deal, ain't they? Kissin' cousins, you might say."

"We can make a deal, Mr. Corbin. Whatever you need to finish this job. Money. Men. Resources."

"I haven't seen any of your money yet, and I don't believe I care to. No, from now on, I'm happy to have nothin' more than God on my side."

"It was Matthew Faber. He made them. Him and Daniel Lovegrave. You need me, Mr. Corbin. Please—"

"I don't think so," Cody says, seeing the worm writhing behind the crack in the woman's cold mask, and brings up his Colt Python and shoots her point-blank between the eyes.

He squats there for a minute, head cocked, staring past the dead woman at the dark, ruined factory but seeing nothing. It's been a hectic few minutes. Cutting the man's throat when they were in sight of the shore; using the flashbang grenade as cover to slip over the side; swimming to the jetty; triggering the pipe bomb he left behind in the boat. He feels a kind of hollowness now that it's over.

At last, he straightens up and walks towards the jeeps at the end of the jetty. He needs to find a boat so that he can cross back to the other side of the Malebo Pool, pick up his stuff and the motorcycle he bought in Kinshasa. He still has a long way to go, but with God on his side and his angel at his back, how can he lose?

Chapter 38

While Teddy Yssel goes off to arrange the ride to Père Mike's mission, Elspeth and Nick trek around the shops and the covered market in the centre of Bandundu. They don't talk about last night, about the white devils and Danny Lovegrave, about what might or might not have happened between them. Nick does say, "We really don't know what we're getting into, do we?" and Elspeth tells him, "Teddy knows about the mission, I know about Danny Lovegrave, and you know about the white devils. Together we'll figure it all out."

They buy long-sleeved T-shirts and hiking trousers, baseball caps, light running shoes, a dozen pairs of knee-high socks, a sewing kit, knives and machetes and short-handled shovels, flashlights, field glasses, a collapsible plastic water bag and water bottles and micropore filters, packs of freeze-dried food and freeze-dried orange juice and coffee, toilet tissues, biolumes, a camping stove that can run off solar power or gas or kerosene, cooking gear, matches, duct tape, iodine paint and antibiotics and aspirin, hammocks, groundsheets, mosquito netting and lightweight sleeping bags, and rucksacks with aluminium-tubing frames to carry all this booty. Elspeth tells Nick about working on the desert shore of Lake Turkana, and Nick tells her about his biosurvey work, how he loved walking long transects through the swamp-forest, throwing quadrats, counting species.

"I wore spex at first, with a pattern-recognition program

that flashed up the name of every common plant in the field of view; it had keys I could use to identify the more obscure species. The mosses were the worst, you had to zoom right in on these tiny features, leaf-margin shape, details about perianth and capsule morphology . . ." He has that nice smile again, the one that makes him look about eighteen, all innocence and enthusiasm. He says, "It drove me crazy at first, but I learned to work the keys, and pretty soon I mostly didn't need the spex. It was the kind of work that didn't give you time to think about anything else. We would work from dawn until dusk, find a place to camp, build a fire, eat, go to sleep. I never before slept so well," Nick says. "It was like we were the last people left on Earth."

They buy cameras, little things that fit in the palm of the hand, with quantum-bubble memories capable of storing hundreds of movie clips and thousands of photographs. Nick spends ten minutes in close conference with the lugubrious Indian owner of an electronics emporium, emerging with an epaper map and the biggest satellite phone Elspeth has ever seen, with space for enough batteries to power it for a month.

"I fixed it so we get driven all the way," Teddy says, when he meets up with them in Nick's hotel room. "We're not going on some kind of camping expedition, we won't need half this stuff."

Nick asks about the ride, and Teddy says that it's some fellow Darlajane B. found for him; he's already on his way from Kinshasa and should be here in two or three hours. "He has plenty of experience, he knows the Dead Zone, we'll be in good hands," he says, and touches something on the floor with the toe of his shoe. "What's this? Duct tape?"

"You use it to cover up blisters," Nick says.

"What's wrong with sticking plasters?"

"Duct tape doesn't sweat off so easily. You haven't spent much time in the forest, have you, Teddy?"

Teddy hooks down his sunglasses and looks over the top of them at Nick and says, "Have you ever been in the Dead Zone?"

"You have?"

"I've flown around the edges of it. I've seen enough to know that it isn't anything like the forest. This Boy Scout stuff isn't going to do you any good out there, take my word."

"I know what I'm doing, Teddy."

"If you don't stop quarrelling, boys," Elspeth says, "I won't let you go with me."

They order sandwiches from room service, and Nick spreads the map across the bed. The Dead Zone is a roughly oval white blotch bordered with richly indented bays and fractally recomplicated curls and spits and archipelagos. A vast amoeba shape, bigger than the combined areas of Texas, New Mexico, Arizona, and Nevada, that occupies most of the northern half of the Democratic Republic of the Congo and straddles the borders of the Central African Republic, Sudan, and Uganda.

Teddy drags his thumb across the map's zoom icon, points to the spot deep inside the Dead Zone where he says Père Mike has his mission. It's beside a river that runs north into the great arc of the Congo River, to the west of the abandoned city of Kisangani.

"That used to be the big city in the region," Teddy says. "It was where the riverboats terminated, because there are falls and rapids in the river above it. It was where Kurtz, in that novel, was supposed to have his station."

Elspeth says, "How do you know that Père Mike's still there?"

"I don't. All I know is that this is where he had his mission in the good old days, before the Black Flu and the Dead Zone."

"I found a news clip about him," Nick says. "There was a big fuss because he didn't move out when the Dead Zone started to spread, and he refused to move to one of the refugee camps afterwards. He disobeyed a direct order from his bishop, although since he wasn't really a priest, the bishop didn't have all that much authority over him. Anyway, he said that he was going to reclaim the land. Heal it, was how he put it."

Teddy does his thing with the sunglasses again. "You did some research on him, uh?"

"This morning, as soon as the electricity came on. There

are a couple of public-access computers in the coffee shop in the lobby, and I had the manager open up the place for me."

"You had to check up on my story," Teddy says. "Well, now you know I was telling the truth, maybe you can share with me what else it was you found."

"About Père Mike? That's it. Apart from a phone number and a Web site, but both of them are dead."

Elspeth has been studying the map. She says, "This place really is pretty close to the Pleistocene Park facility. It's possible, if Danny Lovegrave is still alive, that he didn't move too far. Maybe he and Père Mike have gone into partnership."

"Perhaps Lovegrave is helping Père Mike 'heal the land,'" Nick says.

"Or perhaps he's selling those animals to keep the place running," Teddy says.

"It isn't much," Nick says, "but I guess we don't have anything else."

Teddy says, "My idea is, if Père Mike is at home to visitors, we can say we're journalists chasing a story. Perhaps we are lucky, and he will give us an interview, he will want to boast about what he does and who he knows. We take a look, we find out what we need to know, and we get out. And if there is any gunplay, if even a *knife* comes out, I'm gone."

His look is defiant and serious.

Nick says, "You don't have to come along if you don't want to. It's not an obligation."

"I fixed up our ride, didn't I?" Teddy says. "Of course I'm coming. I just want you to know that I've had enough of being shot at."

The driver that Teddy has found, Kanana Mubibya, is a cheerful, skinny man in his fifties, with a shock of grey hair and cheeks pitted by a childhood attack of chickenpox. Nick pays half his fee in advance and asks him what he knows about Père Mike and the mission; Kanana shrugs and says he knows the Dead Zone as well as anyone. "As long as you know where to go," he says, "I can take you there."

He drives his matt-black Land Rover at a good speed along the rutted roads, making liberal use of his horn, saluting every vehicle that passes in the other direction, greeting women trudging along the verge with plastic buckets or huge cloth-wrapped bundles balanced on their heads, a boy herding half a dozen scrawny goats. He smokes skinny, hand-rolled cigarettes that he manufactures as he drives, steering with his knees or asking Teddy Yssel, who rides shotgun, to help him out.

"We will find a place to rest tonight, and cross over into the Dead Zone tomorrow, God willing," he says. "There has been little activity in the area for many weeks, and the road is dry. Getting there, it should not be a problem."

"By activity he means soldiers," Teddy tells Elspeth and Nick, who sit side by side on the rear seat.

"The army, and also helicopter patrols," Kanana says, twirling one hand over his head. "Of course, not many people cross into the Dead Zone from this side. Jackals, mostly."

"They strip out stuff from abandoned villages and towns," Teddy says.

"There is nothing much left within a day's drive inside the Dead Zone," Kanana says, "and further in it is too dangerous. But do not worry, I am the best. I will take you where you want to go, and I will bring you back."

"Amen," Teddy says, and produces a quarter-bottle of whisky from the inside pocket of his silvery jacket and takes a sip.

"Let me," Nick says, leaning forward and holding out his hand.

"Why not?"

Teddy smiling when he hands the bottle to Nick, then losing his smile because Nick flips it out of the window and says, deadpan, "You have any more?"

"Why the fuck did you do that? All I need is a savoury sip now and then. What's the problem?"

"We're on the clock now," Nick says, giving Teddy a hard look.

Teddy appeals to Elspeth. "Can you believe this?"

"You two work it out between yourselves," Elspeth says. "I'm not part of this dick-measuring contest."

"Man, that was all I had."

"I hope so," Nick says.

They drive through low hills terraced with green fields. They drive through farmland eroded into deep gullies or reverting to scrub—there are no longer enough people to keep nature in check. The road narrows to a single track hemmed by giant trees. They drive past huts standing amongst strip fields hacked from the forest, one every couple of kilometres. Sometimes small animals—half-dead porcupines, despondent monkeys—are staked by the road. Live meat for sale, Kanana says, bush meat, very good for the immune system, as good as magic bullets. They drive through several abandoned villages, through a village where children run out to meet them, pied dogs chasing alongside. The forest is open at first, trees set well apart from each other, with tall grasses and stands of giant ferns and shiny-leaved bushes growing amongst them, but then the road begins to climb in switchbacks that each rise a little higher than the one before, and the forest closes in on either side. The canopies of the big trees mesh overhead, enveloping the road in a heavy green gloom that deepens as the light begins to die out of the sky.

At sunset, Kanana pulls the Land Rover off the road and drives in low gear through a belt of tall elephant grass. A half-collapsed mud hut is smothered under a blanket of vines, and the rusting hulk of a small truck sits on its axles with bushes grown through its engine block, these relics of human habitation dwarfed by the ramparts of the forest.

Nick and Teddy get into an argument about the hammocks. Teddy says that he doesn't have to help put them up, he's sleeping in the back of the Land Rover like a civilized man, and Nick says, "Why don't you take off your sunglasses when you talk to me, Teddy? It's dark enough now; you won't make your hangover any worse."

"I don't get hangovers."

"Now that you've stopped drinking," Nick says, "you might find out what one is."

Later, while Nick is showing her how to make camp in the forest, Elspeth says, "We're all in this together, so why don't you try and ease up on Teddy?"

"He's a drunk, Elspeth. He may seem like a stand-up guy to you, but he let himself be run off in Brazzaville, and only came back when he had second thoughts. And then there's his murky past . . . He can't be trusted."

"We're back to that again. Teddy told us about Père Mike and showed us where the mission is. And he got us the ride, so he has as much right to be here as you or me." Elspeth sits in the middle of her hammock, swings up her legs, and lies down. "Hey, this isn't so bad."

The hammock is slung between two young trees at the edge of the forest. Following Nick's instructions, Elspeth cleared the weeds and grass under the trees and cut away branches as high as she could reach, in case any snakes or spiders were hiding there, tied a rope a metre above the hammock and slung mosquito netting and a groundsheet over it to provide shelter.

Nick says, as he checks her knots, "I used the Web to find out where the mission is. It wasn't hard." He hesitates, then says, "I did have the thought that we could have left Teddy behind, bought some kind of vehicle, and driven there ourselves. But in the end I figured it would be safer if we had someone along who knows about the Dead Zone."

"You would have left Teddy behind, but taken me."

He smiles at her and says, "Of course. You're the girl who can tame tigers."

Teddy and Kanana have broken out the biolumes and the camping stove and cooked up a mess of freeze-dried rice and shrimp. The shrimp tastes like fish-flavoured cardboard, but the hot food is welcome. While they eat, Kanana tells the story of how he became caught up in the spread of the Dead Zone. He says that he was working as a truck driver, operating one of the big ore-carriers that ferried coltan into Uganda, when he heard on the radio that the USA had declared war on bioterrorism. The next day, the trees began to die, their leaves turning yellow and falling, the fallen leaves breaking down into sticky puddles and pools and slow, viscid streams, the cellulose that made up much of their bulk converted by a virus-borne enzyme into a new form, cellulose-9, with a room-temperature melting point.

"You heard all the time the noise of branches falling, and then whole trees falling," Kanana says. "Because the wood was softening, you understand, and could no longer hold up its own weight."

Kanana had been driving his empty truck towards the coltan mines, but turned back as the forest died and dissolved. "Everyone had only one thought—to escape from this terrible thing. No one knew what it was. No one knew then that it was caused by a virus that had escaped from one of the laboratories the Americans had bombed. People saw the trees melting and their first thought was that it would happen to people also. There were many stories of people falling asleep and waking to find that they were stuck in a puddle of their own liquid flesh and bone, just their head and perhaps an arm left. Animals were fleeing too. One time I saw hundreds of elephants cross the road, so many that the road was blocked for three hours."

Nick says, "This was in the middle of the Black Flu pandemic."

"Of course," Kanana says. He is sitting cross-legged, in a threadbare tweed jacket two or three sizes too big, its greasy collar up around his ears, the cuffs of the sleeves turned back to the elbows. "America said that the Black Flu was a biowar disease, it did not know then that it was natural, that it came from the forest. So it declared war on bioterrorism, attacked laboratories in the Congo, in Cuba, Colombia . . . Many of them owned by American companies, which moved because they could not any longer work in America. The missile that blew up the laboratory and released the virus which melted the forest, it was American too."

Nick says, "What I don't understand is why you were driving around the forest when everyone was dying of the Black Flu."

"Let the fellow tell his story," Teddy says.

"It is easy to explain," Kanana says. "Coltan is a very valuable mineral. Europe and Asia and America are very hungry for it. This is the only place where it is found, and it has caused much trouble, much war."

"It's used in mobile phones, spex, all kinds of electronic goods," Teddy says.

"I know what coltan is," Nick says. "I didn't realize that it was still being mined in the middle of the Black Flu pandemic."

"Of course, of course," Kanana says. "It was dangerous, and not just because of the Black Flu. Many desperate people who would try and hijack a truck, so they could escape, you understand? But the work was well paid," he says, rubbing the tips of his thumb and forefinger together, "and I had a family to feed. That's why I was there."

"Tell them the rest," Teddy says. "Tell them how you saved those people."

Kanana says, "My truck was empty, so I took many people in the hopper. They were packed in there and they were banging on the roof of my cab, telling me to drive as quickly as I could, that they were being roasted by the sun. But it was not possible to drive fast. There was much traffic, and many people on foot, and by now the stuff from the trees was flowing across the road. It filled the potholes like mud in the rainy season. Many trucks got stuck in it. People on foot got stuck in it too. It was like molasses. It did not flow fast, but there was so much of it. In one place, it had flowed down a stream bed and carried away the bridge there. We drivers laid down two steel beams that we took from a truck loaded with construction material, and we crossed one by one. The best way was to line up your wheels and drive as fast as possible. We cheered each other on. Then one fellow, following two or three trucks behind mine, lost his nerve and stopped halfway, and when he started again, his wheels slipped and the truck went over. It landed upside down, and the people in it were stuck like ants in honey. We could not get to them—it was too dangerous. The stuff was liquid at first, you see, but then it began to harden. So we had to leave them.

"By this time, the edge of the Dead Zone had moved far ahead, and all around us the last of the big trees were beginning to melt like so many candles. We could not stop because the stuff would flow around the wheels of our trucks, it would harden, and in an hour we would be stuck. We passed many people who had become exhausted and had laid down to rest and had become stuck. Animals which came to eat them were stuck too. I suppose their bones are still there.

"So, I kept driving. I drove for two days and nights, following the truck in front of me. I ate pills to stay awake. Tiny black ones: all the truck drivers used them so that we could keep to our schedules. I had a little water, nothing else. The people in the hopper, most of them had no water at all. Some died, but most of them survived—I carried twenty-eight living people out of the Dead Zone. Of course, we were all immediately put in a camp, because people thought we were carrying the virus that made the Dead Zone. That was a bad time. Many died of the Black Flu and other diseases in the camps, and then there were the floods, because when it rained, the water flowed straight off the Dead Zone. And after the floods there were plagues of locusts, and then a drought that lasted a year, and the famines and the wars," Kanana says, "but nothing was as bad as driving through the forest while it melted."

Chapter 39

The first thing that Elspeth sees when she wakes is Nick's empty hammock. It's just before six. The sky is grey, and the air is cold and still. Thin scarves of mist wind through the forest canopy, hang above the stands of elephant grass and the vine-smothered hut and the wrecked truck. The windows of the black Land Rover are fogged with condensation. Weeds and grass are silvered with dew, printed with a trail of dark footprints that leads away along the edge of the forest.

Elspeth pulls on her jeans and a dry pair of socks, shakes her boots to dislodge any unwelcome visitors and laces them up, and follows the trail of footprints to where Nick stands at the edge of the forest, staring into the shadows beneath the giant trees. As she walks up to him, he says, "I thought I'd come out here and think things through. Or not exactly think; let the wheels spin."

She supposes that it's meant to be an apology. She says, "You were pretty pissed off at everyone yesterday."

He shrugs.

"You don't have to take charge, Nick. We're all in this together."

"I was thinking about Kanana's story. I'm fairly sure that he was telling the truth about being caught up in the spread of the Dead Zone, but I don't think he was transporting coltan. The whole area was in a state of chaos. Hundreds of thousands of people were trying to escape from the Congo. Rwanda and Uganda had closed their borders to try and stop the Black Flu spreading, the UNHCR was trying to cope with the flood of new refugees . . ."

"You think Kanana was smuggling people across the border?"

"I'm wondering what he's been smuggling lately. Also, I'm wondering how Teddy knows him."

"Teddy said through Darlajane B."

"Yeah, but did you notice how, when Kanana was telling his story, Teddy prompted him? He said, 'Tell them how you saved those people.' As if he'd heard it before, and knew what the good part was. But how could that be, if they only met yesterday?"

"Teddy took me to Darlajane B.'s place. All kinds of people pass through it. Maybe Teddy and Kanana met there one time and shared a bottle of whisky."

"Or perhaps they met when they were both working for

Raphael. Perhaps they're still both working for Raphael, despite Teddy's colourful story."

"Teddy and Raphael certainly weren't on the best of terms. The reason I was in the enclosure with the saber-toothed cat was that it seemed to be the only way of proving who I was. Teddy introduced me, but Raphael flat-out refused to believe him. Anyway, Raphael's almost certainly dead. I don't think Cody Corbin would have spared him."

There's a pause, and then Nick says, "I guess not."

"The white devils killed Teddy's best friend, Nick. That's why he's here."

"So why did he tell us Darlajane B. fixed up the ride with Kanana if he knew the guy all along?"

"If you think he's hiding something, has some kind of separate agenda, you could always ask him straight out."

"I'll think about it," Nick says.

"I always find it's better to get these things in the open. Especially as we're on the clock."

"Touché."

Elspeth says, "Is there anything else I should know?"

Nick looks off into the trees. "I think we should be careful around those two, that's all."

There it is again, a little hesitation like a catch sticking.

Elspeth says, "I had the feeling yesterday, when you told us what you'd found out about Père Mike on the Web, that you were hiding something. That you'd found out something else, something you don't want Teddy to know about."

There's a pause while Nick looks at something in his head. He says, "When this all began, I asked my Wizard to find out about Teryl Meade and your father and Qualia. I looked it up yesterday, and it had some new information about Teryl Meade. She's dead, Elspeth. Someone killed her early yesterday morning. Obligate claims that she was assassinated by Loyalist guerrillas, but I think—"

Elspeth has the sensation of falling through space while standing still. She says, "Cody Corbin."

"He was deeply involved with the Radical Green movement. Perhaps Badiledi told him who he was working for, and it pissed him off. Or perhaps he went over to Brazzaville to make a new deal with Teryl Meade, and things got out of hand. Anyway, there it is. I'm sorry."

"Are you sorry because she's dead, or because you didn't tell me right away?"

"Mostly because I didn't tell you," Nick says. "You wanted to prove that Teryl Meade had your father killed. I guess I was worried that if you knew that she was dead, you might give up the chase."

"That's not all I want," Elspeth says. "What did you think? That I planned to confront Teryl, force her to confess?"

"Or stand outside her office building, make a statement to the media."

"As if I would even be allowed into the country."

"You'd be infiltrated across the river by a good friend of Darlajane B.'s. You'd make your statement, Teryl would get so angry she'd come out, try and claw your face off with her fingernails, but you'd wrestle her to the ground and she'd be led away in handcuffs . . ."

"Teryl's style isn't—wasn't—confrontational. She'd store her anger, wait and wait, and then stab you in the back when you weren't expecting it."

They're both smiling.

Elspeth says, "Even if she's dead, it doesn't bring back my father and the Gentle People. I don't want her to get away with what she did. I don't want Cody Corbin to get away with it, either. I want the world to know the truth, Nick. And I want to make amends for what my father did."

"You seem to be taking this very calmly."

"I haven't seen Teryl for more than six years. Then one day she phones me and starts ranting about white devils, tells me it's all my father's fault. And in less than a week, my father's dead, she's dead . . ." Elspeth tries and fails to picture Teryl murdered in her own blood. She says, "I should feel relieved that she's dead, but it's as if she's somehow escaped. If I gave up now, I'd let her get away with what she did."

"Absolutely."

"Why were you worried that I wouldn't come with you? Because you need me to get close to Danny Lovegrave?"

Nick says, "That isn't it at all. Will you let me show you something?"

A narrow path winds between the trunks of the giant trees. Weak red light slants through gaps in the canopy. A bird some way off is calling hesitantly, a noise like a cracked bell that emphasizes the rapt, heavy stillness.

Elspeth says, "I thought it wouldn't be as open as this. I thought it would be, I don't know, more jungly."

"There are different kinds of forest. Don't you have anything like this in Kenya?"

"I've never been in a *bona fide* rainforest. When I visited my father at the Pleistocene Park facility, I flew in, flew right out . . . I didn't see much of the country."

"It's like a machine," Nick says. "A green machine for processing light and water and air into life. It's been here for millions of years, and there's a high input of solar energy and a stable climate, ideal conditions for a very rich biodiversity. There are big trees competing for sunlight high above, and plants which can survive in their shade on the forest floor, and in between there are vines and creepers, epiphytes growing at different heights on tree trunks, in the crooks of branches, liverworts and mosses that only grow on the epiphytes . . . Niches within niches within niches, and every niche, no matter how small, is occupied by a species that's precisely adapted to exploit it. A forest in England might have just four species of tree growing in any given two hectares. Out here, you can find as many as eighty species growing in the same area. Along a single six-kilometre transect, you can count a thousand species of flowering plants, five hundred species of trees, maybe a hundred of butterflies. And then there's the macrofauna. Hundreds of species of birds, monkeys, elephants, pygmy hippos, leopards, lizards, snakes . . . There's even a species of crocodile, the Congo dwarf crocodile, that lives in burrows that it hollows out amongst tree roots. It hides during the day in its burrow, comes out at night to hunt birds and frogs and insects."

"We had problems with crocodiles at Lake Turkana. The site where we were working wasn't far from the edge of the lake."

"These are a lot smaller than your regular crocodile. Fierce, though. You push a branch into the burrow, they'll clamp their teeth around it, and because they are too dumb to let go, you can haul them right out. They make pretty good eating."

"They taste, what, like chicken?"

"The default flavour for exotic animals," Nick says. "Actually, it's more like greasy lobster."

"During the border war with Ethiopia, a lot of bodies ended up in Lake Turkana, so no one eats the crocodiles." Elspeth looks around at the great trees that in every direction rise above the thin scrub of bushes and saplings. The mist has evaporated. The slanting shafts of sunlight are growing hot and brassy. She says, "Don't you think we should head back? We have a long day ahead of us."

"I know. Cooped up in the Land Rover with Teddy bitching all the way. But you're right, we've gone far enough," Nick says, and turns his back to her and unzips his fly and urinates against one of the lichen-encrusted buttress roots.

Elspeth laughs. "This is an unasked-for level of intimacy."

Nick shakes off the last drops, tucks himself in, zips himself up. Already, seeming to materialize around him out of the hot, humid, green air, tiny sweat bees and half a dozen species of butterfly are settling on the wet ground, avidly sucking up urea-rich mud.

"A butterfly bar," Elspeth says.

"Nitrogen is in short supply," Nick says, "and nothing is wasted in the forest."

White butterflies with black swooshes on their forewings, bright scarlet butterflies, large black-and-white butterflies with splashes of orange on their hindwings, orange butterflies marked in black with the biohazard trefoil. Some land on Nick's shirt to suck at rings of dried salt-sweat. A large specimen of the brown-and-orange biohazard species alights on Elspeth's elbow. She lifts her arm to look at it, says, "Don't tell me that's natural."

"It's a very simple hack, just a few genes that affect the patterns on the wings, and a couple more that affect mating behaviour—so males and females will recognize one another."

Elspeth watches butterflies crowd the wet ground, their wings opening and closing or shivering as if in ecstasy. "The logos are for soft drinks or candy. American products."

"Most of the gene hackers were American, and I guess they mostly lived off soft drinks and junk food when they were working. The whole ads-on-butterfly-wings thing actually started as a publicity stunt for a soft drink, in Korea. There was so much public outrage that it was quickly withdrawn, but gene hackers quickly picked up on it. The first ad butterflies were irradiated, so they couldn't breed after they were released. But these are all fertile, and they're all infected with the retroviruses that spread the various hacks. They not only reproduce, they infect other butterflies of the same species, so they displace the native forms very quickly. Obligate pays schoolchildren to collect them, ten cents for every hundred butterflies, but it's just a gesture. The point is not to eliminate the infected butterflies, I think, but to show that Obligate is doing all it can to rid the forest of gengineered organisms. And of course it helps indoctrinate—"

"It's a wonderful surprise," Elspeth says, and steps up to him and kisses him there in the solemn cathedral quiet of the forest, with butterflies swooping through the air around them like bright fragments of stained glass.

Something sounds far off in the green distance—the Land Rover's horn. Nick and Elspeth reluctantly break their embrace.

"I guess it's time to go," Nick says.

While Nick and Kanana are loading up the Land Rover, Teddy sidles over to Elspeth and says, "Your man has a lean and hungry look, doesn't he?"

"He's been through a lot, Teddy."

Teddy takes his time lighting a cigarette. He has a faint tremor in his fingers. His cap of blond hair is matted with sweat, and sweat has darkened the front of his blue shirt. He says, "Let's see, my best friend was shot dead right beside me, and I lost my job because of it. I've been shot at by a crazy guy, and now I'm in the middle of the fucking jungle, heading for the worst place in the world . . . But despite all that, I don't believe I look like a wannabe suicide bomber."

"He's had all that, too, Teddy, *and* had his personal life dragged through the media."

"Did he happen to say anything about that, during one of your little heart-to-hearts? Is that why he's tooled up for a one-way ride?"

"About being a clone? No, he didn't. I guess it's like being anyone else. None of us remember being born, so what do the circumstances matter?"

"It seems to matter to Obligate, or why would they smear it across the media?"

"It's illegal to make a clone of a human being, but it isn't illegal to *be* a clone. Why Obligate did it, it's distraction. Nick has a good story to tell, so Obligate puts out another to get the media's attention. It's pure black propaganda."

"I understand. How he came into the world, it's illegal, but it's against the law to determine the sex of your child, and plenty of people do it, and anyway, no one would blame their kids for what they did. That's not the point," Teddy says. "What matters is how he feels about it. You know, I bet he wants to destroy these white devils because they are like him. Made things, unnatural. He hates himself, so he hates them even more."

"That's pretty simplistic, Teddy."

Teddy sucks on his cigarette. "People aren't so very complicated, in my experience. I was just wondering, by the way, if you saw him pack his rucksack."

"As a matter of fact, I didn't. Why?"

"I'm certain he still has that pistol he took off that guy I shot. What I'm wondering is, has he also brought along the rest of the pipe bombs?"

The rainforest presses close on either side of the red clay road, giant trees rearing out of tall, tangled banks of bushes and creepers, the Land Rover crawling like a beetle at their feet. Nick rides shotgun, friendly and relaxed, cadging one of Kanana's skinny, hand-rolled cigarettes, asking him who is responsible for maintaining the road.

"The army rounds up villagers, tell them that they must keep the road clear or there will be trouble. Soldiers are very bad," Kanana says, and turns his head and spits out of the open window.

Teddy, slouched on the back seat behind Kanana, arms folded over his chest and a baseball cap pulled down to shade his face, says, "They don't much bother with people going into the Dead Zone, luckily for us. They are more worried about what might come out."

"The UN is supposed to pay them to patrol the edges of the Dead Zone," Kanana says, "but politicians steal much of the UN money and the soldiers are not paid, so instead of doing their job, they oppress the people. No one outside this country cares about the Dead Zone any more. America has other concerns. There are no air patrols now, because America has withdrawn its planes, and our own air force, it has no fuel. So people are moving back into the Dead Zone. They mine coltan, cobalt, germanium, gold. Ten thousand *creuseurs* are digging for diamonds south of Mbuji-Mayi. The Dead Zone has become very permeable, luckily for you."

Nick asks how people manage to live in the Dead Zone, and Kanana shakes his head and says they manage very badly, it is a desolation. "You'll see for yourself how bad it is in there, but don't worry, I know it well. Isn't that so, Teddy?"

"You're the best," Teddy says.

Nick turns to look at him, says, "Hey, Teddy, I was wondering about something. When did you crash your plane? Was it before or after the Black Flu?"

"Before. Then, like I told you, Johnny found me a job. Johnny and me, we stuck together."

"Yeah, I remember you telling me that the first time we met. You always stuck together, I think you said."

"More or less, sure." Teddy doesn't move, but Elspeth, sitting beside him, sees that he's suddenly wide awake, his eyes sharp under the bill of his baseball cap.

"So was your friend Johnny working for Raphael too? Because if he was, how could he help you find a new job?"

"Well, he wasn't working for Raphael."

Nick is watching Teddy, quiet and intent. He says, "How come? You were both working in Kinshasa, doing the same kind of job . . ."

Teddy stares at Nick from beneath the shade of his baseball cap, says at last, "What's your problem, Nicholas? Why do I get the feeling you don't believe anything I say?"

"I'm just trying to get it straight in my head, that's all."

"Johnny was working for a Kenyan company, the same one we were both working for until a week ago. He was flying in and out of the refugee camps along the DRC border just like me, but in the other direction. So after I lost my plane, that's what I did, too."

"And then Raphael's men came out all the way to the camps to find out what happened to your load of antibiotics. It must have been a pretty lucrative business," Nick says, "for them to go to all that trouble."

Teddy takes off his cap, runs a finger over the bump on the bridge of his nose. "You see that? That's what they did to me. Broke a couple of ribs too, and knocked out a couple of teeth. Yes, it was in one of those refugee camps, but I don't know why they were there; you'd have to ask them."

Nick winks at Elspeth, says, "With a little more work it'll make a great story, Teddy. The kind that people make into movies."

Teddy says, "No one makes movies about true stories any more, they're all too sad," and fixes his baseball cap on his head, settles down again.

"Hey, Kanana," Nick says, and Elspeth thinks he's going to ask when Teddy met him, but instead Nick bums another cigarette, holding the wheel while Kanana rolls it, settling back to smoke it with apparent relish.

The Land Rover struggles up a long slope, the rainforest

withdrawing on either side, hot sunlight pouring down on meadows of tall yellow grass studded with the pinnacles of termite mounds, and suddenly people step out onto the road ahead, half a dozen men with assault rifles, a personnel carrier parked off the road to one side, a freshly burnt-out truck squatting in a wide circle of charred grass on the other.

Kanana shakes his head when Nick asks if they are soldiers. "Sometimes they are soldiers, sometimes they work for themselves. You let me talk, okay?"

"Yeah," Teddy says. "Don't ask them what they're doing here, can they prove it. Be polite."

A lean young man in an unbuttoned camo jacket steps up to the Land Rover. He wears a black beret at a jaunty angle, his eyes are masked by sunglasses, and there are officer's pips on the shoulder tab of his jacket. Kanana winds down the window and tries to speak to him, but the officer shakes his head impatiently and orders them to get out.

"Stay close to me," Nick tells Elspeth.

"I've been through more than enough roadblocks," Elspeth says. "Teddy, why don't you hand the man here some of your cigarettes, get us on a friendly footing?"

The soldiers open the back door of the Land Rover and begin to paw through the rucksacks while the officer pockets without comment the pack of cigarettes that Teddy presents to him and takes his time inspecting their passports. Kanana keeps up a constant supplicating chatter to which the officer pays as much attention as the flies that buzz around them. Heat simmers over the narrow sea of yellow grass. The heavy air presses close as a headache.

One of the soldiers finds something in one of the rucksacks and whoops with delight and lifts it high: a bottle of whisky. Nick gives Teddy Yssel a hard look, and Teddy widens his eyes innocently and says, "It's a better bribe than a few cigarettes."

A very tall soldier in a sleeveless mesh T-shirt and blue jeans, an ammunition belt draped around his neck and more than a dozen ID tags jingling on his chest, snatches the bottle from the man who found it, takes a long drink, and hands it to another man, this one in a tattered wedding dress worn over camo trousers, the ruffles of its skirt bunched around his waist. As he tilts the bottle to his lips, the others crowd around him, laughing and jostling like children anxious to get their share of an unexpected treat.

Elspeth stands behind Nick and Teddy, trying not to make eye contact with the officer, trying to be as inconspicuous as possible. She knows how quickly this could turn bad. A scuffle, a burst of automatic fire, soldiers bundling her into the long grass. Every soldier takes a drink and the last one hands the half-empty bottle to the officer, who drains it in three long swallows, as if the whisky is no stronger than lemonade.

"Jesus Christ," Teddy says, with reverent awe.

The officer makes a speech in French; Kanana says that the soldiers need food, that they have been living off the bush for a long time. Nick says it's no problem, and politely asks the soldiers to step aside and digs into his rucksack and hands out silvery food packs. He presents half a dozen to the officer and says that it must be difficult working out here.

The officer, sorting through the food packs, reading their labels, says that it's not so bad.

Nick says, "No problems we need to know about?"

The officer gives him a serious look, and says in English, "The road, we improve it. Then, no problems."

"That's shrimp and wild rice, there," Teddy says. "That one, it's banana and chicken curry. They're all pretty good—better than army rations, I bet."

This has to be translated. The officer makes a speech to Kanana, who says, "He thanks you for your contributions and wants to know if you have any more whisky."

"Tell him that's the last of it," Teddy says.

The officer says that's good; his men are hard to control when they have too much to drink. He gives an order, and two soldiers walk over to the personnel carrier, come back with a cardboard tray of Pepsi-Cola cartons.

The officer smiles, says in English to Nick, "Ten American dollar each. You need, yes?"

Nick says, "It goes towards improving the road?"

"Think of it as a toll," Teddy says.

After Nick has paid for the Pepsi-Cola, keeping his back to the soldiers as he peels bills from his slender roll, the officer hands back their passports and asks in a friendly, casual manner where they are going. Nick tells him that they are journalists, that they want to take a look at the Dead Zone so they can write about it. The officer shrugs, says there's nothing to see, no stories to tell. Nick says that if that's true, they'll come right back, and the man laughs.

Five minutes later, they're on their way again, bouncing over ruts and lurching through deep potholes. Nick leans his arm on the back of his seat and tells Teddy Yssel, "Lucky they found the whisky."

"Yah, before they looked in your rucksack, maybe found that gun you stole."

"No," Nick says. "I'm carrying that, just in case."

"Or the pipe bombs."

"I got rid of the pipe bombs, Teddy."

"Yah? I'm surprised, because you seem to like to use them." Teddy takes off his baseball cap, wipes sweat from his forehead, puts it back on. "I don't know what I'm going to do about my edge now," he says.

Kanana is pointing at something, a cluster of trees standing by the road. Things that look like huge weaver-bird nests hang from their lower branches, attended by a murder of crows. The birds flap into the air as the Land Rover goes past, complaining harshly to each other. Elspeth looks away, but can't escape the smell that blows in through the open windows.

Teddy turns in his seat to watch the gallow trees recede, says, "I make it eight."

"That's how they do it," Kanana says. "That's how they improve the road."

Chapter 40

The rainforest closes in again and the road gets worse, all swales and humps and dips. The Land Rover grinds down into and up out of big holes that even in this dry season are floored with sticky yellow mud. Twice, Kanana has to drive into the margin of the forest to pass the rusted hulks of abandoned trucks. It takes them five hours to travel a hundred kilometres. Close heat, the bench seat sticky under Elspeth's thighs, the acrid smell of cigarette smoke, the roar of the Land Rover's engine, its seasick sway. The big trees knit a thick green roof high above the road. Elspeth imagines that the trees are like an army, manoeuvring behind them, closing off their line of retreat. Kanana hunches over the wheel, peering through the cracked windscreen and its fringe of talismans into the forest's underwater gloom. Nick slumps beside him, his knees bent against his chest and his feet on the dash; Teddy Yssel seems to sleep most of the time, stirring every hour or so, looking around as if puzzled to find himself still in the Land Rover, lighting a cigarette, dozing off again.

An hour before sunset, the forest falls away and the road widens, a cracked, corrugated two-lane blacktop laid straight through the ruins of a small town in a cradle of tree-covered hills, the buildings half-buried by creepers and bushes, a tank rusting on its unravelled treads at a crossroads. The blacktop gives out at the far end of the ruined town and the road narrows again, climbs a small hill. And there, spread before them, is the Dead Zone.

Elspeth has seen hundreds of pictures of the vast and famous desolation—pictures as iconic as the napalm-blasted landscapes of the Vietnam war, Hiroshima after the Bomb, the cratered moonscape of Flanders in the First World War.

But nothing has prepared her for the sheer scale of the Dead Zone, the chains of glassy lakes that simmer between crests and pinnacles of naked rock, the ranges of deeply gullied hills spiked with thousands of dead, half-melted trees: a post-apocalyptic wasteland that, with the sun setting through blood-red layers of cloud beyond it, looks like a slice of Hell risen to the surface of the world.

Teddy stirs and says, "I can tell you that it definitely looks better from the air."

Kanana hauls on the steering wheel and the Land Rover bumps across an apron of low, scrubby bushes and stops. They all climb out into blood-warm air, squinting at the vast sunset. Nick and Elspeth walk to the edge of a steep drop above a little river that rushes towards the Dead Zone over and around broken sheets of hardened cellulose-9. On the other side of the river, a belt of scrub, green and vibrant in the last of the light, has grown up around the white poles of dead trees.

"Wait there," Nick says, and scrambles down to the edge of the swift brown river.

Teddy joins Elspeth, watching as Nick potters around for a few minutes before climbing back with a rough, pitted shard that gleams like a giant flake of ancient varnish. He turns it around and around, inspecting its edges and the dark veins threaded through it, suddenly makes as if to toss it to Teddy, who raises his hands to ward it off and says, "You must be careful with that stuff. It's worse than plutonium."

Nick grins and says, "It's only a novel form of cellulose. I'm amazed there's so much of it still around, but I guess it's like plastic, nothing can eat it."

He hands the shard to Elspeth. It is surprisingly light. Its surface is grainy and slightly tacky, like freshly cured resin.

"You catch something from that," Teddy says, "you're going to have to walk out of here on your own."

"The virus that did this could only infect tropical hardwood trees," Nick says. "It took over their cells and forced them to produce the enzyme that turned ordinary cellulose into this stuff, and then it died out, stopped by the suicide genes designed into it. An amazing piece of gengineering."

Elspeth pitches the shard towards the river. "So amazing that it could have destroyed every plant in the world. We were lucky it didn't mutate, or some stupid gene hacker didn't start playing with it."

Teddy squints into the setting sun, the light burning up from the glassy lakes. "The government says the Dead Zone does not grow any more," he says. "but anyone who flies over the forests knows there are always new places appearing. I reckon that one day it will come back, and the whole world will be like this."

Once again, Elspeth and Nick choose to sleep outside, Elspeth on one side of the Land Rover, Nick on the other. Elspeth lies awake a long time, curled like a question mark in her sleeping-bag liner to accommodate the various humps and troughs and stones that have made themselves apparent under her groundsheet after she lay down. Listening to the frying-fat sizzle of insects in the luminous brush, the chuckling rush of the swift little river. Thinking about the kiss she stole in the cloud of butterflies, the way Nick leaned into it. If he really didn't want to tell her about Teryl's death because he was worried she wouldn't come with him, then that must mean something. And the way he leaned into that kiss, the way he looks at her when he thinks she doesn't notice him looking at her: that all means something, too. But here they are now, Nick saying goodnight and turning over and going to sleep as if nothing had happened. That cool, deadpan way he has, impossible to read. He said to her in the open-air bar back in Bandundu that he didn't know where they were going with this, and she thinks now that she doesn't know either.

She wakes with a start. Nick's face leans close to hers. His forefinger touches her lips, presses lightly when she starts to ask him what he's doing. All around the Land Rover, the scrubby vegetation glows a cold blue-green under the starry sky, every leaf burning with a different intensity, merging like the stars of the Milky Way into a bank of foggy light. Another simple hack, Nick told her, when it started to get dark and the luminescence became apparent—a jellyfish gene. Saying, as they wandered through it, away from the Land Rover, "Teddy is slick, isn't he? He has an answer for everything."

Elspeth said, "He spends a lot of time telling all kinds of unlikely stories to likely looking women in bars, hoping to impress them. Embroidering the truth is second nature to him. I thought you were going to start in on Kanana, too, ask him what he really was doing in the forest when it started to melt."

"Do you remember Teddy telling me that I shouldn't have blown up the plane, because he could have got it repainted? What I should ask Kanana," Nick said, "is why he's just had his Land Rover resprayed. I noticed this morning, when we were loading up, that there are spatters of black paint on the tail-lights where someone didn't mask them properly. I should ask, are there black-and-white stripes under the fresh paint?"

"But Raphael's dead."

"We think that Cody Corbin must have killed him, but we don't actually know. Maybe Raphael made a deal. We'll wait," Nick said, "see where this is going, but sooner or later, we're going to have to deal with it."

Now, with Nick leaning over her, Elspeth hears something moving stealthily through the brush somewhere close by. Nick takes his finger away from her lips and says very quietly, his breath warm on her ear, "What do you think it is?"

"Maybe one of your dwarf crocodiles," Elspeth says, thinking of his white devil, brought back to life and armed with a human thigh bone and a dreadful grin, thinking of the American mercenary, Cody Corbin, creeping towards them, his face blackened, a big knife in his teeth.

Nick says, "Maybe one of the ordinary kind. If anything is left alive in the river, it would be crocodiles."

"We should wake Teddy and Kanana."

"Let's not. Do you want to take a look with me?"

She takes a machete, stays right behind him. They circle the Land Rover, tiptoe through glowing bushes. The Moon is setting behind long, thin clouds at the horizon, a half-lidded sleepless eye. Streaks of cold white light gleam on the ravaged land beyond the rushing river.

Nick freezes, holding the pistol up by his face; Elspeth can't hear anything, but he suddenly angles away through the bushes, moving quickly and surely. She chases after him. The ground slopes down, plates of cellulose-9 crunch underfoot, slick as ice, and Nick's feet suddenly slide out from under him. Elspeth drops the machete and grabs his arm as he falls, and they're suddenly sliding down a smooth steep chute in a rattling avalanche of stones and shards, fetching up at the bottom breathless and bruised and shaking with laughter.

"I haven't done anything like that," Nick says, "since I was a kid. Are you okay?"

"I think so. Nothing broken, anyway. Do you really think it was a crocodile?"

"Whatever it was, I think we made enough noise to scare it away."

"Just as well. All we had was your gun and my machete, and I dropped the machete . . ."

"You can kill a crocodile with a handgun. You aim for the base of the skull, one shot through the brain."

"You've actually done that?"

"I read about it once. I was hoping to show off."

They lie side by side, not quite touching.

Nick says, "Did you ever go sledding, in Boston?"

"Sure."

"It hardly ever snows in the south of England, but it snowed once when I was a kid. Not just the usual dusting, but a real blizzard. I was seven, and I thought it was the most wonderful thing in the world. There was a river at the end of our garden, with steep fields rising beyond. My mother took me up to the top of the fields, sat me on an old wooden sled she'd dug out of the junk in the stables, and I rode it all the way down. Over and over, all afternoon. I was wet and cold and happier than I'd ever been in my life. Just now, that was exactly the same rush."

There's a silence. When she's certain he isn't going to say any more, Elspeth says, "Look at the stars."

Their rigid patterns span the black sky from horizon to horizon, bright and sharp and remote.

Elspeth says, "Some nights, at Lake Turkana, I used to lie out like this."

"Summer, when I was a kid, that's what I used to do, too. Lie on a blanket on the lawn . . . I had this old pair of binoculars, they had just enough resolution to make out the components of double stars, galaxies. But mostly I just lay there, looking up. If you do that long enough you feel as if you're falling into the sky. I used to camp out in the grounds, too. I guess even then, even though I didn't know what I was doing, I was practising for my great escape."

"The grounds? You make it sound like a stately home."

"It wasn't nearly as grand as that, although it was the biggest house in the village. The manor house. Elizabethan, half-timbered, seven bedrooms, six bathrooms, set in four acres out in the country south of London. We had our own orchards, a wood, a lake . . . Do you really want to hear about this?"

"If you want to talk about it."

"My mother managed to find me after the news of the massacre got out. Her lawyer hired a data miner who traced me. She phoned me, and I hung up on her. Hung up, ripped the line out of the wall, smashed my mobile . . ."

There's a silence. They look up at the starry sky. Elspeth can feel the heat of his body, a scant centimetre from hers.

Nick says, "She fucked me up, Elspeth. Maybe she didn't mean to, but she did. What she wanted, you see, what she wanted more than anything else in the whole wide world, was to bring my brother back."

He speaks with a dry, clinical precision. Elspeth supposes that he's spent a lot of time thinking about this, whittling it down to the stark essentials.

He says, "Any ordinary parent would give their life for their child—it goes without saying. My mother would have killed herself and harrowed Hell if that would have brought Christopher back. She had him late in life, and he was everything to her. Her marriage had more or less broken up; she only stayed with my father, pretending to play happy families, for Christopher's sake. After the accident that killed Christopher and my father, she was mad with grief, but it was a cold, calculating madness. She wanted Christopher back, and because she had the contacts from my father's business, she knew that there was a way to do it. It was illegal, it was expensive, it was highly experimental, but she was desperate. Mad with desperation. So mad, that after I was born it wasn't enough to have a son genetically identical to the son she'd lost. That would have been no better than saving just one of a pair of identical twins, and for my mother that wasn't good enough, not by a long chalk. You could clone Einstein, you understand, and instead of getting a world-class genius in physics you might get someone who's happy playing second violin in some provincial orchestra—"

"It's nurture as well as nature."

"Exactly. My mother isn't a stupid woman. Crazy, almost certainly, but not stupid. After she brought me home, she tried to make sure that my childhood was as close as possible to Christopher's. So that I would grow up to be like him, you see. I played with the same toys, was encouraged to have the same hobbies, wore the same clothes, watched the same TV programmes, went on the same holidays, went to the same prep school, the same public school . . . It was an enormous and exhausting exercise in futility. Even identical twins, raised in exactly the same environment at the same time, develop distinct personalities. And I was growing up years after Christopher's childhood; my father was dead, his friends had grown up, and my mother wouldn't allow me to have any friends at all . . . I spent my entire childhood treading a tightrope. Half the time I was being smothered, protected, hidden from the world; the other half I was being punished because I had unwittingly broken unwritten rules or deviated from an ideal that only existed in my mother's head.

"When policing my life got too much for her, she'd lock me for days at a time in my room—Christopher's room. I'd look out at the church and the graveyard where he and my father are buried and watch the swallows and house martins and dream of escaping. But I was so under her spell that it took a worldwide disaster to make me do something about it. I went to the same university, started the same medical degree that my brother had been taking before the accident. And then there was the Black Flu, and everything changed. Even my mother couldn't stop history in its tracks. That was when I volunteered to work in the isolation hospital I told you about, and after that I joined the army.

"My mother went along with it. I suppose she thought that in the same circumstances Christopher might have done the same thing. But when I had my heart problem, when I went home after the operation that fixed it, she tried one last time to hang on to me. After I got better, she didn't want me to leave, and we had a knock-down, awful row. That's when she told me what I was, what she had done. And, well, I ran. And I guess I'm still running."

"Do you think you'll ever forgive her?"

"She's crazy, Elspeth. She never got over Christopher's death. She refuses to believe that I'm not him. When she looks at me, she doesn't see me at all. She only sees what she wants to see; she sees her dead son. I didn't walk out on her because I found out that I was a clone. I knew all along that there was something strange about the circumstances of my birth—after all, my father died almost a year to the day before I was born. No, I walked out on her because I couldn't find any way of telling her who I really was. I went to London, and got a job as a hospital porter. My mother found me three weeks later. Turned up at work, caused a scene . . . So then I made a proper job of disappearing, and that's how I eventually ended up here, in Africa."

He looks at Elspeth in the bright starlight, and she looks back, feels herself falling into his deep, drowning gaze. They're holding hands. When did they start holding hands?

Elspeth says, "Just about every science meeting I go to, someone will come up to me and say they once knew my father. In a sympathetic way, but with a hopeful look in their eyes. Scientists are gossips in the worst way. Knowledge is power, and a lot of what goes on at science meetings isn't about the research that's being presented, but who's talking to who, who isn't talking to who, the problems someone has getting funding, the demotions and promotions ... People want to know what happened to my father, why he went to the Congo, why he left the mainstream. They wonder what he did, wonder if I might know anything about it. They hint about the possibility of collaborative work, about their influence on this or that grant-awarding body. They suggest that they could do me a favour by salvaging something from the ruins of my father's career. It isn't even that I'm the daughter of someone famous; I'm the daughter of someone *notorious*. A dangerous eccentric. A crazy genius . . ."

There's a pause. At last, Nick says, "The first time I saw you, standing under the tree with that big cat? I was pulling Michel out of the car, I was being shot at, but for a moment it was like . . . Have you ever been walking down a street and looked at someone at the same time they looked at you?"

"And your eyes meet, just for a second? Sure."

"That's what I felt. It wasn't the ideal circumstance for an introduction. We should have seen each other across some crowded room—"

"A casino. You'd be wearing a white tux, sipping a martini—"

"You'd be in a strapless number. Tight-fitting, glittering."

"I think you should know that I'm mostly a jeans and T-shirt kind of girl."

"You'd look good in anything," Nick says, and they reach for each other and kiss. After a while he says, muffled against her throat, "What are we getting into?" and she says, "Don't worry," and finds his mouth again with hers.

Maybe she sleeps for a minute or two afterwards, going off somewhere, coming back to find Nick propped up on one elbow, looking down at her, his face a shadow against the starlight, brushing her cheek with his fingertips.

"Hey," he says.

"Hey."

He says, "I don't know if that was the right thing to do, but it felt right."

Elspeth smiles up at him. "You're trying to be, what's the word? Gallant. Like a true English gentleman."

"We're very polite, we English."

"Just don't say thank you."

"It's what I feel like saying."

The Moon has set. The stars seem brighter and much closer. Elspeth feels the heat of her blood radiating from her bare skin. Her jeans and panties are bunched around her knees. She should really pull them up, but she doesn't want to move, and when Nick eases down to hold her, she lets herself be held.

He says, "We still don't have the faintest idea what we're getting into, do we?"

Elspeth realizes that he isn't talking about them. She says, "Have you figured out what you're going to do about Teddy and Kanana?"

"We could wake them at gunpoint, tie them up, leave them here and drive off. We know where the mission used to be, and that phone I bought is enabled for satellite navigation."

"We just drive up to this mission and ask about white devils?"

"That's the problem. Maybe we should torture Teddy and Kanana before we set off, get them to spit out everything they know."

He's lying on his side against her, his arm under her breasts, his fingertips stroking the top of her arm. She looks at him and he smiles, and she smiles too. They're having fun.

She says, "Hold an open bottle of whisky in front of Teddy's face. That should do it."

"Kanana would be tougher."

"Do you really think that Raphael is still alive? That Kanana is working for him?"

"I'm fairly certain that he was alive when we left. He'd been shot, but he was alive."

Elspeth nods, seeing Raphael for a moment, the fat man

curled up on his side in the shallow ditch, both hands pressed to the place on his hip where blood made a growing wet spot on his white trousers.

Nick says, "Of course, he would have had to convince that guy, Cody Corbin, to let him live."

Elspeth says, "Right. And I don't think someone like Cody Corbin would let someone like Raphael live."

"Raphael is good at talking. But I think you're right. If Raphael was still alive, he would have sent someone to bring us back. Or kill us. But if Raphael's dead," Nick says, "why is one of Raphael's men driving us to the mission?"

"Teddy arranged it. Maybe we should just ask him."

"It's an idea."

"But you'd rather see where this is going."

Nick is no longer smiling. "If we ask Teddy about Kanana, he'll just give us one of his stories. I want to find out the truth."

Chapter 41

The next morning, as the Land Rover drives deeper into the Dead Zone, Elspeth dozes, on and off, in the backseat. Remembering how she and Nick talked with the stars spread above them, how they made love. Remembering how they walked back through the softly glowing bushes, not looking at each other, hardly speaking; and as soon as they lay down under her mosquito net, on her sleeping-bag liner, they started to make love again, slow, languid, as helpless as drowning swimmers. In the middle of it, she said, "What will Teddy think?" and Nick said, muffled against her neck, "I don't care what Teddy thinks."

And now whenever she opens her eyes she sees him scrunched all the way over on the other side of the Land

Rover's backseat, staring out of the window, lost in his own thoughts.

Kanana follows the course of the river as it flows north and east, driving over bare rock, over humps and basins of dried, deeply cracked mud, over stretches of pitted cellulose-9 that crackle like cellophane under the Land Rover's tires. The land shimmering, burning. Mirages tremble above chains of pools and lakes like hardened varnish that are half-buried by fans of eroded clay and rock and that have flooded wherever the river is dammed or blocked; Kanana has to make long detours around basins of muddy water in which rafts of half-melted tree trunks float and vast clouds of blackflies breed. Rain has deeply gullied the hills or stripped them back to bedrock, leaving a landscape something like the desert along the eastern shore of Lake Turkana. The river runs through belts of dense bush and young trees, but very little grows elsewhere: sere grass, spindly bushes, seedling trees that bear no more than a handful of yellowing leaves.

Teddy says that the cellulose-9 poisoned the land, but Nick says that it's more like the result of some huge slash-and-burn campaign. He says that thousands of square kilometres of laterite soil have been washed away, that the Congo is stained red at Brazzaville, a thousand kilometres downstream. He says that despite their diversity and productivity, rainforests exist on a knife-edge; essential nutrients like nitrogen and phosphorus are scarce, locked in wood and living tissue, and tightly recycled through thousands of closely connected species. In the Dead Zone, that cycle has been broken. The river fertilizes the land along its length every time it floods, but everywhere else nutrients have been washed away with the soil or are trapped in undecaying slabs and sheets of cellulose-9.

A few people have returned to reclaim the land. Now and then Elspeth glimpses flashes of green amidst the shimmering mirages, and in the middle of the day they stop at a hut set amongst narrow strip fields of maize and sugarcane and cassava, the hut's gappy lattice walls woven from canes and stuffed with lumps of cellulose-9, its roof made of overlapping sheets of cellulose-9 weighted with stones.

Kanana pours two jerrycans of gasohol into the Land Rover's tank and talks with the farmer, a tall, grave, skinny man wearing only a pair of ragged shorts. A baby is fretting inside the hut, and a woman stands in the doorway with two toddlers clutching at her long skirt, refusing with a smile the carton of Pepsi-Cola that Elspeth offers her.

Kanana says that the farmer hasn't seen any soldiers for many weeks. "He has given us this," he says, holding up what looks like a dried worm swaying at the end of a loop of twine. "You will pay him five dollars, and give him cigarettes."

Nick catches the scrap of dry tissue between thumb and forefinger. "It's a nice souvenir, Kanana, but what exactly is it?"

"It is the navel cord of his last child. It will protect us."

"It's an African thing," Teddy says. "You wouldn't understand."

"What I can't understand," Nick says, as he counts out five one-dollar bills, "is what they want with money around here."

Before they drive off, Kanana loops the scrap of tissue around the rearview mirror of the Land Rover. "That man is proud," he says. "He needs money to bribe soldiers, but he will not beg. So I tell him that you want to buy the charm."

"If it'll protect us from white devils," Teddy says, "I'm all for it."

Kanana says, "I was brought up as a Catholic—I was an altar boy in the cathedral, in Kinshasa. I do not believe in magic, but there are many people who do. So when they see the charm, perhaps they leave us alone."

Elspeth laughs, and explains to Nick that it's a perfect example of African pragmatism. He smiles, the first time he's really looked at her since they set off.

"There's nothing funny about it," Teddy says. "We need all the protection we can get. We need *your* navel cord, Nicholas. Think what rare magics that could work."

"Fuck off, Teddy," Nick says, but with no more force than if he's brushing away a fly.

The Land Rover climbs a long, rough slope above the river

and bumps onto a track winding away along a ridge of exposed rock. Kanana speeds up. Raw sunlight pours through the dusty windscreen, and the air inside the Land Rover grows hot and stuffy. After a couple of hours, Teddy stirs and says to no one in particular, "You know, because of the story we're caught up in, Daniel Lovegrave is really a magician."

"He's really a scientist," Elspeth says. "If he's still alive, that is."

"Of course he is. But he's also a magician."

Nick says, "What story are you talking about, Teddy?"

Teddy says, half-turning, leaning an arm on the back of his seat, "Our quest. You didn't notice this was a quest story?"

"I don't have your active imagination," Nick says.

"Well, I do read a lot," Teddy says, seeming to take no notice of Nick's hard look. "Back in Riebeecksland, there wasn't any fiction. We had the Bible. We had history, but that was taught to us not as a story, you understand, but as propaganda, as justification for our existence. We had agricultural textbooks, engineering manuals. A few people had radios or TVs hidden away, although it meant ten years of community service if they were caught or denounced. That was it. When Johnny Grundlingh and I escaped into the real world, we discovered all this incredible made-up stuff. It was amazing. It blew us away. The first time we went to a movie, it was just too much. After five minutes we had to leave, walk around outside, get up our nerve to go back inside. We stood at the back of the cinema, in the dark, looking at those larger-than-life images and punching each other on the arm, saying, can you believe this? Because, you understand, we *couldn't* believe it. The first time I walked into a library—I tell you, I felt like sitting down on the floor and crying, I was so happy."

Elspeth says, "What kind of stuff do you like?" She can't imagine Teddy Yssel reading anything longer than a 'zine article, the kind with lots of pictures.

"Novels," Teddy says. "The weirder the better. Reality, man, how I want to forget reality. All my childhood my nose was rubbed raw against reality. What I read—you know those old heroic fantasies, three fat volumes, or six, or ten? Big sto-

ries full of magical heroes and unrelentingly evil villains.
That's what I like to read."

Nick says, in that deadpan way of his, "You're a romantic,
Teddy."

Teddy lights another cigarette. Taking his time, saying, "It
is a considerable part of my charm."

Nick says that he doesn't understand what those old fantasies have to do with Daniel Lovegrave being a magician,
and Teddy smiles and blows a riffle of smoke and says, "They
all tell the same kind of story, which is why you either love
them or hate them. There's a wounded land, damaged by
some great evil, and you get a band of heroes gathering up
the rings or swords or crystals they need to confront or extin-
guish it as they travel across the land towards its fortress or
mountain or whatever. And here we are, three different people come together, travelling across a wasteland towards the
redoubt of the evil magician. All we're missing is the magic
crystals."

"Maybe that dried bit of navel cord counts," Nick says.

Elspeth says, "I don't remember Danny Lovegrave being
evil. Silly, sometimes. Smart, it goes without saying. He was
my father's friend from way back—one of the first my father
made when he moved to the States. They were very different,
but they were also very close. Teryl hated that—hated the
way Danny Lovegrave would turn up at the house unan-
nounced, would keep my father up to two or three in the
morning. The funny thing is, Teddy, Danny Lovegrave liked
to do magic tricks, card tricks. My father loved having parties, and I seem to remember that at every one Danny Lovegrave would gather a few people around him, break out his
cards. Teryl said he was showing off—she hated that he was
disrupting the social flow, doing something she couldn't understand. And I guess he *was* showing off. He loved being at
the centre of some intimate little circle, a little cabal where
he had absolute control. I was pretty young then, easily impressed, but he really was very good. It was the one thing he
took seriously."

She remembers how he'd ask someone to think of a card,

remembers the way he'd narrow his eyes as he studied the person for a whole minute before producing it from the top of the deck. She remembers how he would maybe raise one eyebrow when they expressed their amazement, that he'd ask them to shuffle it back into the deck, and it would reappear in a pocket or inside someone's shoe, one time in the glove compartment of a locked car. He'd get someone to write their name on a dollar bill and tear it in half across the signature, get someone to put one half in an envelope and burn the other in an ashtray. They'd open the envelope and find nothing there, and he'd tell them to look in their wallet or purse, and there it was, whole and unharmed. Danny Lovegrave giving a little shrug when people asked him how it was done, amused by the stir he caused but careful not to show it. He told Elspeth that the real secret of magic was to read your audience, build up their expectations, and then divert their attention from what you were really doing, but even after he taught her a few basic tricks, enough to fool her friends at school, she never once caught him out.

Nick says, "If Teryl Meade hated Lovegrave so much, why did she agree to come out here and work on the Pleistocene Park project?"

Elspeth says, "My father and Teryl needed the work after they lost the government contract. And the Pleistocene Park project, when it began, was enormously prestigious. Teryl wasn't in my father's or Danny Lovegrave's league, but she was tremendously ambitious, so she swallowed her pride and went along."

Teddy says, "He definitely sounds like the kind of fellow who could have created something like the white devils."

"If he did," Elspeth says, "I don't think it was because he wanted to make the world a worse place. He was selfish, he was mercurial, restless, irresponsible, but I don't think he was evil."

Teddy says, "You know what I think? I think that someone who makes something evil, even if it's by accident, has to be evil too."

Elspeth says, "You think the white devils are evil? That they deserve to be destroyed, it's as simple as that?"

Teddy's cigarette crackles when he draws on it. "It's like when you get some animal that attacks people, Elspeth. You can't reason with it. You have to deal with it."

Elspeth says, "If the white devils are no more than animals, killing them would be like killing a lion because it's a lion."

"I don't know about you, Nicholas," Teddy says, "but you don't try to forgive or redeem a lion that gets into the habit of eating people."

Nick says, "He has a point, Elspeth. The white devils were made as weapons. Maybe they can't help what they are, but that doesn't excuse the bad stuff they've done."

Elspeth says, "People do 'bad stuff,' too. We're the white devils, the Gentle People . . ."

She's said too much. Nick is looking at her, looks as if he's about to ask the question she's been dreading. Her heart quickens in anticipation, and Teddy Yssel says, "Heads up, my friends. Here's where we stop for the night."

The Land Rover speeds down the rough track into a wide valley. There's a huddle of huts inside a rough wall built of mud and plates and lumps of cellulose-9, and a string of square, bright green ponds and neat green fields stretches beside the slow, muddy river.

Nick leans forward and says, "You know this place, Teddy?"

"Kanana told me about it."

"Is okay," Kanana says. "I been here six, seven times. I do business with these people, no problem."

Nick settles back, glances at Elspeth, says, "Well, if you know them . . ."

Half a dozen naked girl-children run up to the Land Rover when it stops. Elspeth hands out cartons of Pepsi-Cola and the girls drink thirstily, amazing each other with gassy burps. Their skins are tinted by a mantling of ochre dust. Dust dries Elspeth's mouth and nose. It has settled in the folds of her clothes and on the matt-black paint of the Land Rover; it hazes the air and blurs the glare of the setting sun. Everything has taken on the hue of an old-fashioned photograph, the colour of the land blowing away into thin air.

While Kanana talks with a couple of village elders, Nick and Elspeth walk through the fields to the river. They have told Teddy that they want to fill their water bottles, but really they want a chance to talk privately.

Elspeth says, "I took a look at the tail-light this morning."

"So I saw."

"And I thought I was being so careful."

"It's okay. I'm fairly certain neither Teddy nor Kanana noticed."

"There's a place under a corner of the rear window where the paint has run, too." She looks at Nick. "Teddy didn't ask Kanana if we were going to stop here. He knew. As if they'd already arranged it."

"I saw how you picked up on that. We're less than fifty kilometres from the mission, and we have at least another hour of daylight, but instead of pushing on, we stop for the night. I think Teddy and Kanana are planning to do something," Nick says, "and I think it's going to happen here, tonight."

"So we have to do something first."

"Absolutely. My suggestion is that we take the Land Rover, strike out on our own." Nick raises the hem of his shirt, shows Elspeth the automatic pistol tucked into the waistband of his tan trousers, and says that when he pulls it on Teddy and Kanana, she'll get the card for the Land Rover and start it up.

"As long as you promise you won't shoot them."

"We take the Land Rover and their phones, and leave them here. What kind of guy do you think I am?"

It's a good question. Elspeth says, "If we're going to do it, let's do it, get it over with."

"I thought as soon as it gets dark," Nick says. "We can drive in the dark, but Teddy and Kanana will have a hard time following us on foot. Are you sure you're up for this?"

"I shot a man with a spear gun, when I had to. So we drive to the mission and introduce ourselves to this guy, Père Mike. We could say that we're journalists . . ."

Nick is shaking his head. "We should take a look around first. Stop a few kilometres away, leave the Land Rover someplace out of sight, do some scouting, find out what's going on before we decide whether to drive in. And if we do drive in, I don't think we should pretend to be anything other than ourselves. You know Lovegrave, Elspeth, and he knows you. I think we should tell the truth, don't you?" Saying it with that quiet seriousness, holding her gaze. Saying, "Think about it. It'll be easier if we keep it simple."

"We don't even know that Danny Lovegrave is alive."

"Maybe I can find out right now," Nick says.

Women are working knee-deep in the green water of one of the square ponds, scooping black mud into panniers made from curved pieces of cellulose-9, balancing the panniers on top of their heads, and carrying them into the fields. They stop and stare as Nick walks towards them, call to each other in high voices like nervous birds. He points at the turbid water, asks a question in French. The women look at each other, look away, either too frightened or too shy to talk to this stranger. Nick asks his question again, patient and courteous, and a skinny grey-haired woman in a ragged yellow wrap-around that leaves her breasts and arms bare says something, points at a pile of shards of cellulose-9 stacked along the edge of the shallow green water. Nick picks up a flat translucent piece of cellulose-9, points with it at the pond and asks the woman another question, the two of them talking while Elspeth and the other women watch. Elspeth hears Lovegrave's name mentioned a couple of times. Nick points to the goats that are grazing on the other side of the shallow river, tended by a couple of young girls, listens to the woman's long, halting reply, and thanks her.

"I thought the ponds were some kind of irrigation system," he tells Elspeth, "but it turns out they use them to turn cellulose-9 into fertilizer. They bury the stuff in the mud at the bottom of the ponds, and some kind of process rots it down, dissolves it. See how thick with algae the water is? I thought it was something to do with that, but the women say it is important the stuff is covered by the mud at the bottom. And the goats, listen to this, can eat cellulose-9."

"Goats will eat anything," Elspeth says, remembering with a heartsick pang Sergeant Mbau's War Against The Goats, "but they can't digest everything they eat. What did you find out about Danny Lovegrave?"

"I'm getting to it," Nick says. "It turns out these are special goats—they not only eat cellulose-9, they digest it."

"You're kidding."

Nick is smiling. "It gets even better. The woman told me that the goats were given to them by a white man called Daniel Lovegrave."

"So he's alive."

"There's something else. Have you noticed that apart from the old guys who came out to talk with Kanana, there are no men about, and no boy-children either? I asked the woman about it, and she said that soldiers took them away."

"Lovegrave gave them the goats in exchange for their labour?"

"He gave them the goats a while back, but the soldiers came recently. I think there's something deeply bad going on, and Lovegrave's in the middle of it."

They look at each other in the deepening ochre light.

Elspeth says, "There's something you should know. About the Gentle People and the white devils." She says, "They weren't gengineered from chimpanzee stock."

"I know."

"You do?"

"Well, I guessed. If I've got it right, the plan was to create australopithecines by rewinding the genome of chimpanzee ova back to some kind of common ancestor, and then playing it forward in a different direction. Add genes, suppress others . . ." He smiles at Elspeth and says, "I read about it in *Scientific American*. Lovegrave was going to do the gengineering, and your father and Teryl Meade were going to do the mind-sculpting, so that the australopithecines would behave like australopithecines, not like chimpanzees."

"Lovegrave planned to use chimpanzee ova to create the australopithecines," Elspeth says, "but I guess he couldn't get it to work. He had to regress the chimpanzee genome, then splice in appropriate human genes . . . It was too complicated. So he and my father and Teryl decided to try a simpler route rather than lose face."

"They used human eggs instead," Nick says.

"And it worked," Elspeth says. "The ancestral species of all hominids diverged from the ancestral species of chimpanzees and other great apes more than seven million years ago, but our ancestors diverged from australopithecines much later, only two to three million years ago. There's less difference between us and the australopithecines than between the australopithecines and chimpanzees, so it would have been much easier for Lovegrave to use human ova as a starting point. All he would have had to do was suppress or modify the activity of a half-dozen developmental genes, and activate a few others that are no longer usually expressed."

Nick thinks about that, says, "Your father and Lovegrave used human ova to make the Gentle People. Later on, Lovegrave used the same techniques to make the white devils. He just added a few extra genes into the mix."

"I think so."

"When did you find out that the Gentle People weren't as advertised?"

"More or less as soon as I'd taken charge of them. I arranged for some basic medical tests, screening for parasites and disease and so on. Human DNA showed up in the blood samples."

Nick says, "It's funny, isn't it? It all comes down to blood. I asked a friend of mine to test dried blood that got on the belt I was wearing when I shot and killed a white devil at the oil palm plantation. That guy Teddy shot, Jean Badiledi, had my friend disappeared—he must have found out that she'd discovered what the white devils were. Ironically, I was hoping the blood would prove that they were gengineered chimpanzees. I thought Teryl Meade and Obligate were involved with some kind of clandestine project that had developed them as terror weapons against the Loyalist guerrillas. But then you told me about your father's murder, and said that the Gentle People were killed and burned to ashes, and I realized that Teryl Meade wouldn't have gone to such extremes just to cover up the truth about some gengineered chimpanzees."

"I should have told you at once, but I've kept this secret for a long time. I didn't even tell my father that I knew the truth about the Gentle People until all this trouble with the white devils started."

"I appreciate that you were able to tell me. I really do."

Elspeth says, "If anyone had found out, my father would probably have been put on trial for violating every international treaty on the use of human material in gengineering. He was already a broken man; a trial would have served no purpose but to kill him. And the Gentle People would probably have been killed too." She says, "I suppose that I was half-hoping that I'd find out that Danny Lovegrave had died. That there aren't any more white devils."

"He's alive," Nick says, "and it sounds like he's still in business."

There's a hardness in his face now. Elspeth says, "The white devils are human, Nick. Human children. If we do find more of them at the mission—"

Nick shakes his head. "I'm sorry for what was done to them, for the ordinary kids they could have been, but I don't regret for one second that I had to shoot two of them. They're monsters, Elspeth. Killing is all they know. If we do find Lovegrave . . ."

He's looking at the road that runs above the gently inclined slope of strip fields. Elspeth sees the Land Rover speeding away in one direction and another vehicle heading towards the village from the other, several kilometres away but coming on fast, trailing a plume of dust that glows red as blood in the last of the sunlight.

And then Nick is running and Elspeth drops her water bottle and chases after him as he races at a slant through fields of beans and maize, drawing ahead of her, disappearing around a corner of the wall that encloses the village compound.

She's sweating hard and out of breath, half-walking, half-jogging, when she reaches the road. Where Nick is sitting with his hands clasped on top of his head, looking up at Teddy and the pistol that Teddy is pointing at his face.

Chapter 42

"I know Kanana," Teddy says, "Kanana knows these fellows, and that's how I was able to contact them and pretend to sell you out. *Pretend*, Nicholas: that's the key word. To get on their side for just a little while, so I can find out about this fellow Lovegrave, and the white devils. And as soon as I've done that, I'll get you and Elspeth out of this, you have my word of honour on that. So what you have to do now, my friend, is lighten up, admit it's a good plan, and go along with it."

Nick says, "Teddy, I don't know what's dumber. That you're going to get us all killed, or that you can't see it."

They're wedged in opposite corners of a cage welded to the load-bed of a small truck that's speeding through the night across a gently undulating plain of patchily glowing scrub and lakes of cellulose-9 that shine like ice in the moonlight. Nick's right wrist is handcuffed to one of the crossbars and his back is against the cab where Elspeth is riding, wedged in there with their rucksacks and the three men who came to take them to the mission, muscular soldiers bristling with body mods and armed with assault rifles and machine pistols.

Teddy says, raising his voice above the growl and rattle of the truck, "You're pissed off because I didn't tell you about it. I understand. But you know why I didn't tell you? It is simple: because you would not have listened. Because you think like a soldier, and your only idea was to go in with all guns blazing. *That* would have got us killed. This way, we get them to take us right where we want to go. And because these fellows think I'm on their side, I'll be able to ask questions and look around. And when the time comes, I'll be able to get us out."

"If you're on their side," Nick says, "why did they take away your gun?"

"Hey, you're the one they handcuffed, not me. Listen, my friend, one more time. They trust me because Kanana told them I was an okay guy, and they know him because he worked for Raphael—he came here to collect the saber-toothed cat, amongst other things. He told me that they don't want people finding out their secrets; they always did the exchange at that village. Exotic animals for equipment and biochemicals and cash. It was a regular little business, Nicholas, and that's what they think this is."

"Kanana might still be working for Raphael," Nick says. "He might have sold us all out; did you think of that?"

"No, I told you, Raphael's dead. His wife and his mother are right now fighting over who gets the ranch and his money. Both of them in the house, shouting and screaming at each other, throwing things, their bodyguards armed to the teeth and getting ready to shoot it out . . . That's why, you see, Kanana was so happy to get out when I asked him," Teddy says, getting into his story, not yet tired of telling Nick how clever he's been. "That night after we got away, when you thought I was drunk? When you were having your heart-to-heart talk with Elspeth that you thought I didn't know about, in the bar over the road. What I did was phone Raphael's ranch, ask to speak to a couple of guys I knew back when. One of them was Kanana. I told him how he could earn some money, and like I said, he was only too happy to get out. The only glitch was, instead of bringing an unmarked vehicle, he resprayed one of Raphael's Land Rovers. They have a full-scale workshop at the ranch, and he did a pretty good job, but my one worry was that you'd spot it."

"I did," Nick says. "And now I wish I'd done something about it right away."

"It's a good thing you didn't," Teddy says, "because I might have had to shoot you, put an end to our friendship."

He feeds a cigarette to his lips, but drops his lighter when the truck bounces over a ridge, lunges for it a moment too late as it slides across the ribbed metal deck towards the cab. Nick catches it left-handed and flicks it to show Teddy the flame, says, "Give me a cigarette, and I'll give this back."

"Yah," Teddy says, "I get near you and maybe you try something funny, because you're still angry at me. You stay angry, Nick, I won't set you free after I've found out about the white devils."

Nick realizes that it's a waste of time trying to convince Teddy that it's unlikely any of them will survive the night. The man is invincibly stupid, and has convinced himself of his own cunning.

"If you won't come over here," Nick says, "throw me the pack of cigarettes. I'll take one, put the lighter in the pack, throw it back."

"I give you my cigarettes, how do I know you won't keep them?"

"You have to trust me, Teddy. The way you want me to trust you."

Watching Teddy think about that, the man's face a pale blur in the moonlight. Teddy grinning and saying, "Well, that's true."

They do the swap. Teddy lights his cigarette and says, "What you have to do now, to show your trust in me, is tell me where you hid the explosive."

"You saw the soldiers search my rucksack, Teddy." Nick draws on his cigarette. His mouth is very dry, and the smoke has a chemical taste that burns the back of his throat. "You know they didn't find anything."

"Where did you hide it, Nick? In one of the food packs, maybe? One of the water bottles?"

Nick's next drag on the cigarette tastes even worse; he flicks it through the close-set bars, a comet-tail of sparks scattering as it falls into the dark behind the speeding truck. He wonders what Teddy would say if he told him that this morning, while the others were breaking up camp, he armed the phone-chip detonators in the two devices he made from the Semtex in Captain Badiledi's pipe bombs.

Teddy draws on his own cigarette. The reflection of its glow puts twin sparks in his eyes. "Nicholas, I know you brought the explosive along, so why don't you tell me where it is? Suppose we need to get out in a hurry? It will provide a diversion."

Teddy Yssel wants to get his revenge and be able to walk away. But ever since Nick saw the news clip, saw his mother talking about the circumstances of his birth, he's known that he would have to ride this all the way to the end because there is no longer any place in the world where he can hide from her. He thinks of Elspeth, and it is a good thought to hold on to, there in the cage, in the rushing dark. Will she think that what he wants to do is a betrayal? And if she does, will she forgive him?

Teddy is saying now that if Nick doesn't trust him, he can't trust Nick, maybe he'll have to leave him behind, and Nick says, "Hey, Teddy, why don't you give it a rest? You sold me out, you sold Elspeth out, so do you seriously think I give a fuck about your opinion?"

Which shuts Teddy up for a while. He sits in his corner of the cage, chain-smoking, aggrieved, and also, Nick believes, beginning to worry that his plan isn't such a good idea after all. The truck climbs a long slope between what look like thousands of giant chess pieces that loom out of the darkness—termite castles, bigger than any Nick has ever seen. A scrub of bushes and spindly trees closes around the road, glowing like clouds of backlit fog, cut through at one point by a long strip of packed dirt that stretches away right and left. An airstrip, Teddy says, suddenly excited, pointing to a plane glimmering far off in the moonlight.

"I'll have to get a closer look at it," he says, "see if it is operational. It could be our way out of here."

Nick says, "If the mission has an airstrip, why did Père

Mike drive all the way over to the Pleistocene Park facility with that sick kid he wanted you to fly to Kinshasa, when you could have flown right to his front door?"

"I suppose it could be the airstrip is new."

"Or it could be that you never were at Pleistocene Park. It could be you never met Père Mike, it's just another of your colourful stories."

"You have to trust me, Nicholas. Why don't you trust me?" An anxious edge in the man's voice now.

Nick says, "Maybe, Teddy, it's because I'm the guy wearing the handcuffs."

The truck passes two long sheds sunk so deeply in the earth that only their roofs show, camouflage netting stretched above them. Nick sees a long slope cleared of vegetation and rising to a kind of camp—tents and sandbagged bunkers and a white-walled, single-storey building—behind coils of trophic wire, and then the truck makes a sharp turn away from it, climbing towards a big, swayback tent fringed with dangling strings of fairy lights and clusters of biolumes, a picket fence of poles topped by ornamental carvings ranged in front. Music booms into the night, throbbing bass and drums overlaid by skittering runs of cockroach guitar and looped and spliced sorcerous incantations.

Heavily armed soldiers dressed in a pick-and-mix motley of military gear surround the truck as soon as it stops. The door to the cage is flung back. Someone reaches through the bars to unlock Nick's handcuffs, and he follows Teddy out of the cage, trying to ignore the half-dozen guns pointed in his direction, looking over the heads of the soldiers, looking for Elspeth. As soon as he jumps to the ground, someone whacks him in the back of the knees with a shock stick. Fiery pain shoots up his legs, he sits down hard, and two men step in and wrench his arms back and fasten the handcuffs back around his wrists.

It's done quickly and competently, the men who handle him unarmed, the men with guns standing well out of reach. Someone shines a torch over him and says, "Pit bait," and someone else, a small, neat man in a clean white lab coat, dwarfed by the soldiers around him, says, "No, no, this is the clone. He's a valuable specimen. He's money in the bank." Smiling at Nick, saying, "Yes, I know about your strange story, Mr. Hyde. Don't look so surprised. We may be isolated, but we have a good satellite link."

Nick squints up at him. "Are you in charge?"

"I'm Tony Todd." The man amps up his smile when Nick doesn't respond. Black hair is slicked back from his pale face. "*Dr.* Tony Todd. I'm English, like you, an English scientist. You don't yet know it, but I'm your last, best hope. Where did your mother have you made?"

Tony Todd asks this casually, but his gaze is grabby, skittering over Nick's face.

Nick says, "What am I, your lab specimen?"

"If you tell me all about yourself, it will help me convince Captain Nsanzuwera that you are valuable."

"Then it isn't just to satisfy your prurient interest?"

"I am a scientist, Mr. Hyde, my interest is purely scientific." Watching Nick, saying, "Also, I can perhaps help Elspeth Faber."

"Where is she?"

"You are twenty-four, twenty-five years old? So you are one of the first. Was it the Italians or the Cubans?"

"I was born in Palermo."

"Giulio Pompeiano's team?"

Nick doesn't say anything, but Tony Todd, perhaps seeing something in his face, nods.

"You were lucky to survive. I believe that even by the standards of the early days of human cloning, Professor Pompeiano's success rate was very low. Have you had any problems? Weight gain? Early onset of arthritis? Metabolic defects, severe allergies? Remember my offer, Mr. Hyde. Help in exchange for candour."

"I had a heart attack."

"Really? How old were you when your heart attacked you?"

"It was a couple of years ago," Nick says, trying to keep

his tone light, "and I'm all fixed up now. If you are in charge here, Dr. Todd, you'll let me see Elspeth Faber, let me make sure she's okay."

"These are Captain Nsanzuwera's men, Mr. Hyde, not mine. But Captain Nsanzuwera and I, we're business partners. If you cooperate with me, I can keep you and Elspeth Faber out of his pit. If not . . ." Tony Todd gives Nick a long, hard look, then says, "Hold him tightly, please. I need to take a sample."

Two soldiers grip Nick's arms and haul him to his feet; Tony Todd flourishes a tiny transparent plastic cylinder with a spring-loaded needle inside it and presses it against Nick's neck. When Nick jerks away from the sting of the needle, one of the soldiers, a brawny man with bleached hair, cuffs the side of his head as if chastising a naughty child.

Tony Todd pockets the cylinder and says, "I believe your mother's solicitor is Anthony Ryder of Rutledge and Ryder, in London."

Nick says, feeling as if he's falling through space, "She has no money. She spent it all on me."

"Ah, but according to the news clips she is very anxious to get you back." Tony Todd points his phone at Nick, takes a picture, the flash dazzling, takes another. "Her solicitor has posted a reward for news of your whereabouts. You didn't know that? Well, it's very lucky for you that he did. If it all works out, you get to go home. I think these pictures plus your DNA will be enough proof, don't you?"

"And Elspeth Faber? You'll let her go too?"

"Oh, we have plans for Dr. Faber. Bring these two along," Tony Todd tells the soldiers. "Captain Nsanzuwera is waiting."

Nick calls out when Tony Todd walks away, but the man doesn't look back. The soldiers laugh, pat Nick on the back, on his cheeks, on the top of his head, and push him towards the tent.

Teddy Yssel edges between the soldiers and says quietly, "What did the fellow in the white coat want?"

"Who is Captain Nsanzuwera, Teddy? What does he have to do with Daniel Lovegrave or Père Mike?"

"He's second-generation *interahamwe*," Teddy says. "His father was in the militia that was driven out of Rwanda after they massacred the Tutsis."

"So this guy is like Samuel Nyibizo. Some kind of warlord who muscled in and took over."

"He own this place," a soldier says. His words are slurred because of the short, stout tusks that poke out on either side of his mouth. "Now he own you too."

Nick says to Teddy, his mind racing, "Has he been selling animals to Raphael? How about white devils? Has he been selling those too? Or maybe Nyibizo's Loyalists—"

Stopping suddenly, trying to wrench free from the soldiers who hold his arms, because he sees that what tops the posts in front of the tent are not ornamental carvings at all but the skulls of men and white devils, blackened skin shrunk to bone, dry flesh pulled back from mouths to expose ordinary teeth or crooked palisades of fangs.

"Jesus Christ," Teddy says.

"They fight in the pit and lose," the soldier with the tusks says. "Now it your turn."

The soldiers drag Nick and Teddy past the posts into the small crowd beneath the canvas roof. The men and women, standing around a low wall of roughly mortared cinder blocks that encloses a hole or pit sunken into the ground, cheer and clap the new arrivals, making as much noise as the amplified music. All of the women are African, but at least half the men are white. Most wear fatigues and camo gear, but there's a sprinkling of white coats too. They are drinking from bottles and plastic cups, gnawing on half-burnt corncobs and skewers of greasy grey meat. Pressure lanterns hung from the stout bamboo poles that support the canvas roof throw fans of harsh light across faces turned into Halloween masks by tusks and horns, fangs and feathers and cartilaginous ridges. On the other side of the pit, a lean young man in neatly pressed jungle-camo jacket and trousers stands on a low platform, light sliding over the lenses of his big sun-glasses as he watches two soldiers push Elspeth towards him.

The young man leans down, catches hold of Elspeth's wrist, and effortlessly hauls her up. Plastic stacking chairs are produced, and with elaborate courtesy the young man sits Elspeth in one of them, leaning close to her, saying, "Look grateful, Dr. Faber. I just save your life."

A slightly built man in an immaculate white lab coat scrambles onto the platform and says breathlessly, "Dr. Faber? Dr. Faber, I am Dr. Tony Todd. I'm very pleased to meet you—I once had the pleasure of working with your father. This is my business partner, Captain Felix Nsanzuwera."

The young man bows slightly, and Elspeth says to him, "Where is Père Mike?"

"The priest? He die, a long time ago."

"But this is his mission."

"I told you: a long time ago."

"And Professor Lovegrave, he's here."

"You don't worry about him," Captain Nsanzuwera says, sitting down next to her. His wide, friendly smile shows teeth as white and even as tombstones. His hair is razor-cut close to the bumpy contours of his skull. His cheeks are nicked with many tiny triangular scars. Heavy brass and steel rings weigh down his earlobes. He's younger than Elspeth, no more than twenty-three, twenty-four, but has an aura of calm, absolute power, acknowledging with a regal wave the soldiers who dump the rucksacks at his feet like tribute. He says, "You don't worry about anyone but me, Dr. Faber. You my guest. I make you welcome here. You want anything, beer, coffee, something to eat, you just ask, I have it brought."

"My two friends—"

"You worry for them—is only natural."

"Why don't you bring them up here? I'm sure they'd like to meet you."

"Maybe later," Captain Nsanzuwera says.

"Don't worry," Tony Todd says. "Thanks to me, Captain

Nsanzuwera knows who you are and knows who your father was, too, and what he did here. You'll be safe as long as you cooperate with us, and your friends will be safe too."

Tony Todd has thinning black hair plastered to his scalp, a monkey's clever, dark, sad eyes, and an untrustworthy smile. Elspeth thinks that although he may have been a scientist once upon a time, his pristine lab coat, with its collar turned up at the back and a neat row of pens in its breast pocket, is now no more than a symbol, something to distinguish him from the mob.

She says, "Is Danny Lovegrave still alive?"

"Listen to me, Dr. Faber," Captain Nsanzuwera says. "It is very simple. You help me, I let you live. You and this man work together, like he tell me, or else . . ." He points at the pit. It's five or six metres across, more than two metres deep. Barbed wire is strung around the top of the low wall that encloses it. A skinny, bare-chested man is picking bits of bloody meat from the white sand floor and dropping them into a plastic sack.

"Bread and circuses," Tony Todd says. "Don't judge us by this barbarism, Dr. Faber. It certainly isn't my idea."

Captain Nsanzuwera says, "This scoundrel say we are savages, but trust me, he is much worse."

"Of course you're savages," Tony Todd says. "Only savages would spike heads on poles."

"*Pour encouragez les autres*," Captain Nsanzuwera says, and winks at Elspeth over the top of his sunglasses. "You help me, Dr. Faber, and maybe you don't fight in the pit. Maybe you don't end up like them."

"Bring my friends up here," Elspeth says, "and then we can talk."

But Captain Nsanzuwera ignores her, turning away to watch as a man in leather trousers, ammunition belts crossed over his bare chest in Mexican-bandit style, jumps on top of the pit's low wall and struts around it. The crowd shouts at him; the man shouts back and lifts a stout bamboo pole and shakes it above his head. Barbed wire is wound around both ends; the man holds it in the middle, like a ceremonial mace.

It's very hot under the canvas roof, a close, sticky, animal heat, and there's a strong smell of drink and smoke and sweat. Elspeth's shirt is pasted to her back by sweat. She sees soldiers push Nick and Teddy forward. Nick's arms are bound behind his back. He looks straight at Elspeth for a moment, and then a soldier jerks him around and points at men dragging two cages towards notches in the low wall. The cages, made from crudely welded steel bars, are not much bigger than the half-naked birds stuffed inside them.

Captain Nsanzuwera says to Elspeth, "I am sorry we have only chickens. These scoundrels are lazy. After we sell the good animals, they don't make any more."

Elspeth wants to call out to Nick, to jump down and run to him. Perhaps Captain Nsanzuwera sees this; he lays a hand over hers.

"Considering the conditions we have to work in," Tony Todd says, "we work miracles."

"I'd like to talk to my friends," Elspeth says. "I want to be sure that they're all right."

"Maybe later," Captain Nsanzuwera says, patting her hand. "After the show."

The clean-up man is climbing a crude ladder out of the pit. The black plastic sack slung over his shoulder sags with wet weight. The pitman makes another circuit, stops beside one of the cages and rattles the barbed-wire crown of his pole across the bars. Men and women cheer as the bird strikes at the pole, and the pitman pulls it away, makes a pantomime of pretending to lick the black blood that drips from it.

The men standing on top of the cages haul up the barred doors and stamp their feet, and two birds lunge out and fall to the white sand. If they are chickens, they have been seriously hacked. They are the size of vultures. There are matted black feathers on their breasts and overlapping scales on their backs, with tufts of hair at the joints. Their wings are leathery nubs. Their beaks are cruelly hooked.

The people around the pit lean at the wall, cheering and laughing, as the birds square up to each other before engag-

ing in a sudden flurry, striking with beaks and long, sharp ankle spurs, wing-stubs flapping as they climb into the air, fall
apart. Black feathers float down; there's blood spray on the
white sand. Captain Nsanzuwera watches intently, elbow on
knee and chin on fist, as the birds engage and separate, engage again. One digs a spur deep into the breast of the other
in mid-leap, twists on top of it as they fall to the sand, its
hooked beak striking at its opponent's head with mechanical
frenzy.

A noise goes up around the pit, half groan, half cheer. The
bare-chested pitman leans against a post and carefully aims
what looks like a blunderbuss into the pit. The muffled explosion of the shot is barely audible above the noise of the people and the music; a weighted net wraps around the
victorious bird, and the pitman vaults down and drags it away
from the bloody remains of its victim.

Captain Nsanzuwera takes a long pull from a bottle, offers
it to Elspeth. She takes it and sips, gags on a mouthful of
thick, sweet banana beer. Captain Nsanzuwera tells her to
keep it, asks her if she thinks it was a good fight, and seems
satisfied when she smiles at him and toasts him with the beer
bottle. This isn't so bad, she thinks. It's no worse, really, than
the cockfight she once saw in Loyahgalani. But now Captain
Nsanzuwera leans close to her, saying, "Is the main event.
Who you choose?"

"What do you mean?" Elspeth says, and Captain Nsanzuwera gestures, and Nick and Teddy are shoved forward. Nick
looks up at Elspeth as Captain Nsanzuwera points first at him
and then at Teddy Yssel, back and forth, back and forth, like
a child trying to choose between two different but equally delicious candies. Smiling at Elspeth, his eyebrows raised, enjoying her reaction.

Elspeth says, "You need them both. If you want me to
work for you, you need them both."

"I don't think so," Captain Nsanzuwera says.

Teddy is shouting something, but she can't hear him over
the thumping music.

Tony Todd says, "The clone."

"Yes, yes," Captain Nsanzuwera says, and makes an irritable gesture.

For a horrible moment, Elspeth thinks that he has chosen
Nick, but it's Teddy who is seized by half a dozen soldiers,
spun around, and pushed towards one of the gaps in the wall
of the pit.

Nick lunges after Teddy, but someone grabs the handcuffs
that pin his arms behind his back and he almost falls down.
Blond-haired, red-faced Teddy is struggling in the middle of
a knot of soldiers, his shirt half ripped off, shouting to be
heard above the music, his voice high and hoarse. "I saw the
plane! You need someone to fly it, I'm your man! I can fly
anything! I can fly *helicopters*—"

The soldiers steady him at the gap in the low wall around
the pit. The pitman waggles the knot of barbed wire at the
end of his pole in Teddy's face, points it at the pit's white
sand floor, points it at Teddy. People cheer and whoop and
stomp. Teddy, realizing what is about to happen, is suddenly
calm, stands straight-backed and bare-chested amongst the
soldiers, the rags of his shirt hanging around his waist, his
face pale and composed as he stares at something light years
beyond the tent. Then one of the soldiers kicks his legs out
from under him, and he falls awkwardly to the white sand,
struggling to his feet as people jeer at him, ducking away
from the beer bottles that fly out of the darkness.

Nick wrenches free and lunges towards the pit, his pulse
thumping red and black in his head. He shouts to Teddy, but
everyone around him is shouting too, and Teddy doesn't hear
him. Someone strokes the back of his head, as if trying to
calm him, and he jerks away from the touch.

Two soldiers jump down into the pit. One knocks Teddy to
the ground and plants a boot on the small of his back; the
other takes a long knife and makes a slashing cut across the
back of Teddy's ankle. Teddy rolls over and tries to stand up
as the soldiers climb out of the pit, but his injured foot twists

under his weight when he tries to take a step, and he cries out and falls to one knee.

The young man in the big sunglasses is standing on his chair, making a mostly inaudible speech. A few people cheer, but most are watching the two men who are manoeuvring a cage into a slot in the wall. A soldier jumps on top of the cage and pulls up the door. Nick expects some monstrosity to flop out, but instead it's a leopard, lithe and quick as it leaps down and runs past Teddy and tries to climb the canted wall of the pit, snarling and dropping back when the pitman jabs at it with his pole.

Teddy picks up one of the beer bottles that litters the sand and smashes it against the wall and kneels awkwardly, his face set with pain, keeping the broken bottle between himself and the prowling leopard, sparks of light glittering on the crown of jagged glass as he swings it in wide arcs. Nick closes his eyes when the leopard makes its charge, knows from the howl around him that Teddy is down.

Two soldiers grab his arms and drag him backwards. He sees Elspeth on her feet, shouting at the officer, sees a soldier jump onto the platform and swing his rifle in a short arc that connects with the back of her head. Nick shouts her name, but the soldiers pull him in the other direction.

Chapter 43

Nick is lifted up and swung face down into the back of an open-topped jeep, lies there with his arms cuffed behind his back, his heart hammering, as two soldiers climb in front. The jeep speeds away downhill and swerves to a sudden stop; the two soldiers drag Nick out, set him on his feet, hustle him down a flight of concrete steps. There's a strong zoo smell. Cages line both sides of a long aisle, dimly lit by a few widely spaced red lights. Most are empty, but things stir here and there as the soldiers push Nick down the aisle and shove him through the open door of a cage at the far end. The door slams behind him, and one of the soldiers says in French, "Turn around, walk backwards until you hit the bars. Now sit down, okay, and stay still."

Nick does what he's told. The soldier tells him quickly and quietly that tomorrow he'll be in the pit, food for the beasts, then unlocks the handcuffs and steps back as Nick pushes to his feet.

The man is white, with a broad, flushed face shiny with sweat, a cap of yellow and black leopard fur instead of hair. A pale animal is moving back and forth inside the cage behind him. The soldier smiles and holds up Nick's watch, swinging it to and fro, and his companion, an older man, also white, with a grey buzz cut and eyes that are completely red except for the black dots of his pupils, tells him not to be a fool.

Nick rubs his bruised wrists, says in French, "You fellows aren't from around here, are you? Where are you from? What are your names?"

The soldier grins at his comrade, strikes a pose. "My name is Paul-Jon. And you, my friend, you are a dead man."

"I'm Nicholas, Paul-Jon," Nick says, and sticks his right hand through the bars. "Pleased to meet you."

The soldier laughs. "You want to pull me close, try to get my gun. But listen," he says, raising his left hand, showing Nick the five sharp, curved black blades that crown the knuckles of his fingers and thumb, "if I get close to you, you will know it."

"I'd like you to try," Nick says, with a pleasant smile, "because you look like the kind of stupid son of a bitch who thinks a few mods are enough to make him some kind of tough guy."

The insult so much more satisfying in French, round and hard in the mouth.

Paul-Jon takes a step forward, his face hardening, says sharply that he'll show Nick what kind of man he is.

"The kind of man," Nick says, "who thinks he's smart because he can steal a watch from a man in handcuffs."

"The Englishman has a point about the watch," Red-Eye says, and in one quick move grabs Paul-Jon's wrist and twists his arm straight up behind his back. Paul-Jon yells and drops the watch; Red-Eye picks it up from the floor and smiles at Nick and says, "Now that's how you take a watch from a man."

Nick says, "Are you going to give that back?"

Red-Eye holds it up and looks at it, looks at Nick, says, "I don't think so. It's a nice watch. Expensive."

"I guess your Captain Nsanzuwera doesn't pay you so well. If you let me out of here, I'll let you keep the watch, and tell you where I've hidden my money, too."

Paul-Jon massages his wrist, stares hard at Nick. "You try and make a fool of us."

"In your case, I don't have to try very hard," Nick says.

"Maybe you like to try your tricks against this," Paul-Jon says, and turns around and kicks at the bars of the cage on the other side of the aisle.

Something moves out of the shadows, moves very fast, reaching through the bars and snatching at Paul-Jon as he steps back. Something pale and naked and smaller than a man. A white devil.

"This is what you fight," Paul-Jon says. "Maybe you'll think of a way to kill it with your bare hands, but I don't think so."

Nick does not get any sleep in the bare cage, in the long, red-lit shed. Across the aisle, the white devil watches him with an eager, tireless fascination, climbing over the bars of its cage to try different vantage points, moving with uncanny ease despite the hump across its shoulders that pushes its head to one side. Nick tries and fails to see the small boy that it should be. Half a dozen times during the night, it's possessed by a violent rage, dashing around and around the confines of its cage, slamming noisily against the bars, biting at them or gripping them with taloned fingers and shaking its head violently back and forth, its little eyes clamped tightly shut, its wide mouth gaping in a silent scream, its black tongue writhing like a snake amongst the snaggly forest of its fangs. Its musky stink grows stronger during these seizures, and the other animals in the cages down the length of the long shed stir and begin to shriek and howl too. There's a troop of hairless monkeys that restlessly parades over and around the inside of its cage, moving with the singleminded unity of a flock of birds or a school of fish. There's a vulture at least three times the size of any vulture Nick has ever seen in nature, a huge sack of dusty black feathers brooding on the concrete floor of its cage. There's a red and yellow parrot with a wrinkled tumorous growth that might be a naked cerebral cortex covering its head like a badly fitting hat, muttering random strings of numbers to itself. There's an alert two-headed dog, the ugliest pig Nick has ever seen, with spade-shaped tusks projecting from its snout and leathery black skin, a couple of perfectly ordinary leopards.

After the seizures leave it, the white devil slumps against the bars of its cage, breathing shallowly and staring at Nick, who can talk to it then without rousing it into a fresh fury. He calls it Dogboy, the nickname of a particularly crazed and reckless squaddie he knew from his first few months in the army, a young kid from Liverpool whose favourite trick was to eat a beer glass, snapping off big shards with his teeth, chewing them with relish, spitting the bloody fragments into an ashtray. When he got drunk enough on a Saturday night in the mess, Dogboy would jump on a table, howl like a wolf, and announce that he was ready to fight anyone in the place. When no one rose to his challenge, he would head for the biggest man he could see, fists swinging in a wildly uncoordinated full-frontal assault that usually left him on the floor, bleeding and stunned, inside sixty seconds. He was utterly without fear or malice; half an hour after being knocked down, he'd be laughing in a corner with his mates, claiming that he could have had the fucker if he really wanted to, taking a gulp from his pint of lager and then holding it up to display the blood unspooling in the amber liquid.

"This is the difference between you and me, Dogboy," Nick tells the white devil, as he laboriously sharpens to a point the metal tags at the ends of his bootlaces by rubbing them on the concrete floor. "You're fully equipped for mayhem, but I have to make my own weapons. A woman I know would tell you how that makes me human, how I come from a long line of generalists who weren't much good at any one particular thing except abstract thinking. But you, you poor little monster, you've been turned into a specialist. The only thing you can be is a weapon; the only thing you're good at is killing. And that's why I'm going to get out of my cage while you stay locked up in yours."

When he's done all he can with the bootlaces, Nick squats in a corner of his cage and waits, his back pressed against the bars. Light brightens beyond the ventilation louvres set along the walls, just under the roof. The air is hot and stale, and Nick grows so thirsty that at last he risks drinking from the soupy water in the shallow tin pan that's bolted to the bars of his cage, hoping that his magic bullet will deal with any bugs.

At last, the door at the far end of the shed opens to admit a long finger of dazzling light that drives the white devil into a frenzy. A man pushing a tall cart begins to work his way down the long aisle of cages, dropping food into them, filling troughs and pans with water he scoops from a big plastic container with a long-handled ladle. His shaven head is crisscrossed with thick scars, like a smashed vase put back together by a clumsy child. He wears loose orange coveralls. His sandals, made from old tires and string, make a slapping sound on the concrete. While he's using a long stick to push a mess of ground meat into the white devil's cage, Nick bangs his palms on the bars until the man turns to look at him, blinking slowly, his eyes dull and his face impassive.

"You have keys?" Nick says, rattling the door of the cage, miming turning a key, miming pulling the door open. He has the bootlace coiled in the palm of his right hand, one end knotted around his forefinger. "I shouldn't be here. You let me out, I'll certainly recommend you for promotion."

The man yawns, showing toothless purple gums and the scarred stump of a tongue, ladles water into the tin pans of the two cages, then slowly and stolidly pushes the cart back down the aisle and out through the door.

The white devil squats in a corner of its cage, cramming handfuls of meat into its mouth, swallowing without chewing.

A few minutes later, the door opens again. Paul-Jon steps through and closes it and walks down the aisle, tapping the barrel of his assault rifle against the bars of the cages, stirring up a flurry of shrieks and grunts. The parrot gabbles a long string of numbers; the two heads of the two-headed dog bark in counterpoint. The white devil looks up, staring through the bars in its cage and licking its fingers with surprising daintiness as Paul-Jon slings his assault rifle over his shoulder, shows Nick a bowl woven from bamboo leaves.

"Look what I bring you. A piece of sausage, mmm, made of fish and maize"—holding it under his nose before dropping it on the floor and grinding it under his heel—"and manioc and a piece of pineapple. The breakfast of a king," the soldier says, inverting the bowl, the food falling to the floor. He drops the bowl on top of the mess and mashes it down with the heel of his combat boot, smiling all the while at Nick.

The white devil starts rattling at the bars of its cage.

Nick says, "I think it likes you."

"He'll like *you* this evening," Paul-Jon says. "He'll drink your blood and break open your head to get at your brains. The white-coat tries to convince Captain Nsanzuwera that you are important, you are worth money, but I think the captain sees through his lies. You fight tonight, and you die. The white devil will get your brains, and Captain Nsanzuwera's people will cut out your heart and eat it, to give themselves protection. But before you fight, you are in my care."

"And you don't want me to eat, because you hope that hunger will weaken me. Well, it won't. It'll keep me sharp, it'll give me an edge. All I need is water, and your friend with the cart gave me plenty," Nick says, scooping a palmful from the pan and drinking it noisily, smiling at Paul-Jon. "Water is all I need."

"I could shoot you," Paul-Jon says. "In your ankle or your knee, maybe in your belly."

"If he wants me to fight a good fight, I don't think that would make your captain very happy."

"I say you tried to escape."

"Why would I want to do that? I have my friend over the way, and this delicious water," drinking another palmful and smiling at Paul-Jon. "I have everything I need."

"You like that water? I'll make it taste even better," Paul-Jon says. He steps forward and spits into the pan, and Nick flicks the bootlace into his face, hard and fast. The sharpened end strikes Paul-Jon's eye, the soldier shrieks and claps a hand over it, and Nick grabs the back of his head with both hands, the leopard fur hot and bristly under his palms, and slams it against the bars, once, twice, snatches at the assault rifle as Paul-Jon drops to his knees.

The banana clip catches as Nick drags the rifle through the bars. Then he has it, levelling it at Paul-Jon as the soldier gropes for the pistol shoved in his webbing belt. "Wait," Nick says, "don't do it." But Paul-Jon is either too dazed or too stupid to obey; he brings up the pistol, weaving like a punch-drunk boxer as he tries to take aim, and Nick shoots him in the chest and shoots him again, the noise very loud under the low roof, the impact knocking Paul-Jon across the aisle into the bars of the white devil's cage, his legs folding under him as he sits down dead.

A single shot smashes open the plate of the big lock of the cage door. Nick pulls back the tongue of the lock, stumbles out. The space between the cages is full of acrid smoke. Every animal in the place has gone crazy. The white devil looks up when Nick aims the rifle at it, bares its rack of spiky teeth. Nick thinks of the horrible moment when the white devil dropped onto Harmony Boniface's back, thinks of Isabel Fonesca lying in the dirt with her throat ripped out, the white devil that killed her glaring at him with a mouthful of her flesh caught in its mouth, and still he can't shoot, not in cold blood, and then the door at the far end of the long aisle slams back.

Nick is smashing the wooden louvres of a ventilation grill with the butt of the rifle when the soldiers catch him and wrestle him to the ground. No one notices when the white devil reaches through the bars of its cage and snaps the keyring from Paul-Jon's belt.

Chapter 44

"The mods are our bread and butter," Tony Todd tells Elspeth. "The mods—and, of course, the heroin."

Elspeth says, "That's what you do now? Grow poppies? Sell drugs?"

She's sitting in a plastic chair, in the same smelly denim shirt and khaki jeans she's been wearing for more than twenty-four hours, nursing a cup of weak instant coffee. She woke just a few minutes ago, on a squalid bed in a small, hot room in the old bungalow, to find Tony Todd leaning over her. He told her then that she didn't have a concussion, but she isn't so sure. She has a goose egg behind one ear and is pretty sure that she was drugged to keep her quiet—there's a tender spot on her neck like a fresh bee sting, and she feels spacey, disconnected, as if she's a step behind the world.

"Actually, we grow yeast," Tony Todd says. He's standing at the rail of the veranda of the old mission bungalow, his back to Elspeth, his hands locked behind his white lab coat like mating crabs. "It's a straightforward hack, yields very pure product. We also have strains that produce crystal methamphetamine, the soldier's choice of drug in combat, and LSD. But the mods are our unique selling point. Tweaked skin-cell cultures, implants . . . Nsanzuwera's people love them. They think a mod gives them the attributes of the animal it's derived from. They think it gives them power. They think it makes them fierce. They think it makes their enemies fear them."

The veranda is cantilevered above a steep slope that drops to a wide bend in the river. It's the middle of the morning, hot and sultry. Tall ranges of purple-black clouds edging in from the west have not yet covered the sun. The sluggish river, thick with silt, shines like molten gold; beyond it, light's alchemy turns the plain of cellulose-9 and scrub into a magical kingdom, a djinn-haunted desert where rainbows chase each other across crystalline dunes and spectral halos burn over the bejewelled shards of shattered tree stumps.

Tony Todd says, "Leopard mods are particularly popular. We have to insert or modify about twenty genes into epithelial cells to grow the fur; the fangs we fake up with tooth buds that have had a couple of key developmental genes tweaked. Between you and me, Elspeth, that's about all there is to most of the mods. Exaggeration and modification of existing structures, activation of sleeping genes, all very much easier than inserting animal genes and getting them to express properly. That requires real research, and we're not equipped for it, not any more. We can download hacks of existing genes from the clandestine sites, of course, but you wouldn't believe the trouble we have with something as basic as getting jellyfish genes to express properly . . ."

Droning on until Elspeth realizes that he's stopped talking, has turned to look at her. She says, picking up on one of the things he mentioned, "Jellyfish genes?"

"For luminous tattoos. It's the same sequence that hackers used to turn the forests such pretty colours at night. They used a modified tobacco mosaic virus to get it inside plant cells; we use a modified herpes virus . . ."

Elspeth goes away for a few moments, wondering where Nick is and if he's all right, if he's thinking about her, while Tony Todd tells her about skin bleaching, one of the very first mods developed after what was left of the Pleistocene Park

crew moved here, a retrovirus applied in a topical cream that
inserts a gene in the cells of the dermal layer, switching off
melanin production.

"It's still very popular. They believe it turns them into
ghosts, makes them immune to bullets."

He's looking at her again, this small, slender man in his
white coat and worn jeans and sandals, his black hair slicked
back, his face shiny with sweat. A greedy, anxious look, as if
she's a great but dangerous prize on which he's bet his life.

Elspeth says, "By 'they,' I assume you mean Africans. People like me."

"Not at all like you, Elspeth," Tony Todd says, managing to
sound both conciliatory and condescending. "These are not
primitive people, they are not stupid people, but they are not
educated. They don't have the advantages that you and I enjoy. They've been at war for generations. War is all they
know. It's their natural habitat, and that's what we've had to
adapt to—it was Lovegrave's genius to recognize that. He
saved all of us, Elspeth. He kept us together, organized the
evacuation of the research facility after the missile strike, led
us across a hundred kilometres of dying forest, and persuaded Père Mike to take us in."

Elspeth feels that she is being led somewhere too, step by
step. She says, "How did Père Mike die? Did you kill him, or
was it Captain Nsanzuwera?"

"Oh, he killed himself, poor fellow. He was a good man, in
his way, but he was weak, he was indecisive, and I suppose it
all became too much for him . . ." Tony Todd dismisses Père
Mike with a flick of his fingers. "It was Lovegrave who discovered a trade for us, a way of making ourselves useful to
the soldiers. You've seen oxpeckers, the little birds on the
backs of buffalo and elephants? That's us. Oxpeckers are tolerated because they remove insect pests; we're tolerated because we provide a service. Lovegrave is a great man,
Elspeth, but lately . . . Well, frankly, he's ill. His work isn't
all it could be. That's why we need you."

Tony Todd folding his arms across the buttoned-up front of
his white coat, watching her, waiting for her to catch up, un-

able to disguise his impatience. Saying, "We need you because you're your father's daughter."

"Danny Lovegrave stole my father's equipment and his techniques. He's been using them . . ."

"Your father ran away, Elspeth. He left his equipment behind and, if you want to swap accusations, stole the australopithicines."

"We called them the Gentle People."

Tony Todd nods. "Because they lacked the cd2 engram, I suppose. Well, they were as much Lovegrave's as your father's, Elspeth—you have to look at it from our point of view. Your father abandoned us in our hour of need, stole valuable specimens, left us to fend for ourselves. Everything we've done since has been for the sake of survival, and to save our research."

Elspeth feels herself floating off again, as if she's expanding into the immense light-filled landscape beyond the river, the bruised sky . . .

Tony Todd steps closer, claps his hands. "Elspeth! Please, Elspeth. You have to pay attention. This is important."

She manages to focus on his face. "You injected me with something."

"Last night, yes, to help you sleep, keep you calm. Drink that coffee, walk around a little, get your blood moving, and in no time you'll be as right as rain."

"Why don't you cut to the chase, explain what you want from me."

"You have a very direct manner, just like your father."

"You want me to do something for you. And you said we didn't have much time . . ."

Remembering the young officer, Captain Nsanzuwera, his sunglasses and his stupid smile. Remembering the noise and the close heat of the crowd under the canvas roof. Remembering Teddy Yssel in the pit, armed with only a broken bottle as he faced the lithe spotted cat . . .

Tony Todd is bending over her, pinching her cheeks. When she pushes him away, he says, "You were out of it for a minute."

"You killed Teddy."

"Not me. The pit, that's Nsanzuwera's thing." Tony Todd folds her hands around the cup of coffee. "Drink this. You'll feel better."

"You want me to do something, and if I don't . . ."

Seeing for an instant herself naked and helpless in the pit, a ring of people screaming above her.

Tony Todd takes a breath, says, "All you have to do is agree to teach me your father's techniques."

Elspeth looks at him.

Tony Todd says, "When Lovegrave heard that we had brought you here, he told me that you were your father's daughter, that everything he knew, you know."

"Danny Lovegrave told you that," Elspeth says.

"If you teach me, you see, we won't need Lovegrave. You can take him away with you, have him stand trial for his crimes against humanity. He is a great man, there's no question, but he has made many mistakes. Your father, for instance. He and Lovegrave had a falling-out, and Lovegrave tried to change your father's mind. And, well, he went too far."

Elspeth is suddenly wide awake. "It was Lovegrave who shattered my father's mind? What about Teryl? Was she in on it too?"

"Dr. Meade? She left before it happened; it was nothing to do with her. No, it was Lovegrave," Tony Todd says, his gaze aimed somewhere above her face.

Elspeth says, "How did it happen? Was it because my father refused to help Lovegrave with the white devils?"

"We call them spooks," Tony Todd says.

"You brought them with you when you left Pleistocene Park. You kept them here, I believe, until very recently."

"And that's why you came here." Tony Todd smiles, obviously thinking that he's achieving some kind of rapport. "I quite understand. You want to find out the truth. You don't want to think that your father was a bad man. I wasn't working on that part of the project, you understand, I was working on the mastodons, but it's my understanding that Lovegrave designed and created the spooks, and he destroyed your father's mind because he wouldn't sculpt *their* minds. Your father is blameless, Elspeth; it was Lovegrave all along. And if you want the world to know that your father is innocent, well, perhaps I can help you."

Elspeth takes a sip of vile cold coffee. Her head is still pounding, but her thoughts are clear now. "You want to make more white devils, don't you? Anything to get by. And Lovegrave has refused to help you."

Tony Todd turns his back on her again, stares out across the magical kingdom of light. "Do you know what it's been like here? Do you really know? As soon as we began to rebuild this place, bandits came, looking for loot, wanting to kill everyone. They *did* kill people, too, until Lovegrave convinced them that we could be useful to them, and changed their minds, and made them love him. The problem was that it made them no good for fighting; and then another little group of bandits would come along, and then another. We fed them heroin, gave them the mods they demanded . . . Did I tell you about eye colour? That's almost as popular as skin bleaching. Red eyes, black eyes, leopard eyes, snake eyes, *glowing* eyes . . ."

His narrow shoulders go back as he takes a deep breath. "Lovegrave worked tremendously hard to keep us together in the early years. He was an inspiration. But now? He's ill, Elspeth. He can't deliver the goods any more. He makes too many mistakes, he's careless, he isn't reliable. *He's not a well man.* And we still have to do the work, struggle on . . . He keeps saying that he wants to die," Tony Todd says, strangling the rail of the veranda. "But if he did, what about the rest of us? We're supposed to gladly leap on his funeral pyre? I don't think so."

"So that's why you're helping Captain Nsanzuwera. Where does he come from? He doesn't look the bandit type."

Tony Todd turns around. "Help me, Elspeth, and I'll help you. I've told you the truth about your father, and I've taken steps to help your friend, too. I've convinced Nsanzuwera that he's valuable, that we can ransom him. If you help me, you can both go free."

"You think you can get money from Nick's mother."

"I see you know the story."

"You could just walk away from all this," Elspeth says.

"I sometimes dream of escaping. Of getting back to the real world. But it isn't possible," Tony Todd says with a bitter look. "We're all one big happy family here. We're all wanted for the same crimes, even though some are more guilty than others."

"Lovegrave hypnotize everyone," Captain Nsanzuwera says as he steps through the French windows onto the veranda. "He mess up their minds. They do anything for him, which is why they make such good slaves. Isn't that right, Dr. Todd?"

"What do you want, Nsanzuwera? I haven't finished here."

"Dr. Todd, he talk too much." Captain Nsanzuwera favours Elspeth with a big smile. His camo jacket and trousers are freshly laundered and neatly pressed. A quirt of black, braided leather is tucked under his left arm. The chunky satellite phone that Nick bought in the electronics emporium in Bandundu is clipped to his webbing belt, and Elspeth is certain that the red shirt under his jacket is one of Teddy's. He says, "Being direct, it is not in Dr. Todd's nature. And his mind, it wanders, because of his habit. Because of his self-medication."

"It's necessary," Tony Todd says. "You know it is."

"Dr. Todd has himself a little habit," Captain Nsanzuwera says. "He give himself something he love more than Lovegrave. It's good pure stuff, eh, Dr. Todd? Straight from the culture to your blood. But it does make your mind wander. You talk and talk and talk, you never get to the point. Well, *I* am a direct man. *My* mind is clear. So I tell you, Dr. Faber, that Dr. Lovegrave has never told anyone the secret of his mind-changing apparatus. He does not trust anyone—not even Dr. Todd. Especially Dr. Todd. He keep it all in his head. It would not be a problem if he would do what I tell him to do, but he doesn't. Over some things Dr. Lovegrave is very stubborn. And he's dying, too."

"He's not a well man," Tony Todd says, "but I wouldn't say he's dying."

"He's dying," Captain Nsanzuwera says. "None of his people want to admit it, Dr. Faber, because, you see, they love him so very dearly. But it is the truth, as anyone with an unclouded mind can see. And that is why . . ." He looks at Elspeth expectantly.

"That's why you need me," she says, understanding now that Danny Lovegrave lied to save her when he said that she knew her father's techniques, and wondering how she can turn it to her advantage.

Captain Nsanzuwera steps up and grips her chin in his fingers, turns her head this way and that. "How are you this morning? Did this butcher treat you properly?"

The young soldier's breath smells of banana beer; his gaze, behind the dark lenses of his sunglasses, is wandering and unfocused. He's drunk, Elspeth thinks, drunk in the middle of the morning.

Tony Todd says, "She'll live."

Captain Nsanzuwera winks at Elspeth. "You a fierce woman, very brave. You want to kill me last night because of what happen to your friend. To show I hold no grudge, I make sure that the man who knock you out is punished. Maybe I give him to you, you use as your first patient, eh? You can change his mind in a very bad way."

"There's no need," Elspeth says. "But perhaps, if you want to grant me a favour, my friend—"

"As a matter of fact, I am very angry with your friend," Captain Nsanzuwera says, although he sounds more amused than angry. "He just now kill one of my men. He try to escape, and shoot the poor fellow dead. Somehow, in the confusion, the spook is set free too, and now I must waste time looking for it. It is a great nuisance."

"You can still save your friend, Elspeth," Tony Todd says. "All you have to do is agree to work with me."

"Perhaps if you let Nick go right now, I'll consider it."

Nsanzuwera puts an arm around Tony Todd's shoulders and gives him a playful hug and says, "She is very stubborn. But that doesn't matter, does it? We change her mind."

Tony Todd, unhappy and uncomfortable in the young soldier's embrace, is staring at the ground. "I told you that it isn't the ideal course of action. Lovegrave is unreliable. There's a risk that he'll damage her higher functions, and then she'll be about as much use as the zombies."

"You do not trust Lovegrave. But I have less trust of you, and that's the important thing." Captain Nsanzuwera pushes Tony Todd away and tells Elspeth, "You teach this fellow the mind-sculpting techniques, he will have power over me, worse than Lovegrave. He know that, which is why he is nice to you, why he make all kinds of promise he cannot keep. Don't look so miserable, Dr. Todd! You try your best. I respect you for it. But, you see, my idea is better. The knock on her head, it will not affect the treatment, will it?"

Tony Todd gives a sulky shrug. "I suppose not."

"Excellent. We go and wake Dr. Lovegrave. He help us change her mind. And on the way, we show her what happen to people who cause trouble."

Elspeth, with two soldiers at her back, follows Tony Todd and Captain Nsanzuwera down a narrow path of hard-packed red clay that cuts through an abandoned encampment—rickety huts and collapsing trenches half-hidden by dense thickets of giant bamboos and ferns and bushes and a dozen species of palm tree. Captain Nsanzuwera tells her that this is where Lovegrave's followers lived after the forest died and the cruise missiles destroyed most of the Pleistocene Park facility.

"When I find them, they live like animals, hide from planes and spy satellites, high on heroin . . . I change all that, of course. Now they work for their living, like everyone else."

Elspeth says, "Hey, Dr. Todd? I was wondering where you got your nice white coat. You've been here four years; I doubt you brought along a big bale of them when you abandoned Pleistocene Park."

"From a medical supply company in Kinshasa," Tony Todd says, without bothering to look around at her. He's been sulking ever since Captain Nsanzuwera mentioned his habit.

"We make money from the animals," Captain Nsanzuwera says. "That's how you find us, eh? Trace us through the tiger we sell to that scoundrel Raphael."

"I always said it was a mistake," Tony Todd says, "getting involved in petty deals like that."

"You get your supplies, your enzymes and gene sequences, your nice white coats and the rest of that scientific shit, I get money," Captain Nsanzuwera says, grinning, rubbing his thumb and forefinger together. "Was a good deal."

Elspeth says, "Who did you sell the white devils to?"

"When you help us, then maybe you find out," Captain Nsanzuwera says. "But by then, your mind will be changed. You love me so much, you don't care about anything else."

The path passes through a stand of tall ferns into a little clearing where two soldiers guard half a dozen cages built of close-set bamboo poles, each cage smaller than a phone booth. Two of the cages are occupied. One of the prisoners calls to her—it's Nick—and she pushes past the soldiers.

"Hey," he says.

"Hey."

He smiles at her through a gap in the stout poles. His face is bruised, and one side of his mouth is swollen. There's dried blood in his hair, dried blood caked under his nostrils. Mosquitoes whine and sing; he keeps brushing at the small black flies crawling over his skin. He says, "How's your head? That was quite a whack you took."

She touches the tender goose egg, tells him she's fine, but that he looks like hell.

"They knocked me around a little bit. Nothing serious."

"Nsanzuwera said you killed a man . . ."

"He stole my watch, wouldn't give it back." Nick looks away, looks back. "It was in one of those sheds, where they

keep their animals. There was a white devil in the cage across
the aisle, Elspeth. We were right. This is where they came
from."

"I know."

"I shot a man to death. I took his rifle away and the stupid
bastard drew his pistol on me. I shot him, shot my way out of
my cage, and put the rifle right in the white devil's face. And
it looked at me, and I couldn't shoot it."

"You were going to shoot it, after what I told you?"

"But I couldn't."

They look at each other. Elspeth says, "I was told it escaped."

"While the soldiers were dealing with me. It was smart
enough to take the keys from the man I shot."

"Nick, I'm so relieved that you couldn't shoot it."

Captain Nsanzuwera steps up to the cage and tells Nick,
"Tonight we will see how you do in the pit. If you win, perhaps I'll let you go."

"If you let me go now," Nick says, "I'll let you keep the
phone. It's a good one. Full Web access from anywhere in the
world, a nice screen, a keyboard that folds out . . ."

Captain Nsanzuwera grins. "It is very good, much better
than the ones my soldiers use, so it is only right I keep it. I bet
it cost you much money. I have your cameras and your pistol,
and I have your friend here, too. Say good-bye to her now.
Perhaps I let you see her again, eh? Before you go into the
pit."

Nick pushes his arm between the bamboo poles. Elspeth
reaches out and the tips of their fingers brush for an instant,
and then Captain Nsanzuwera pulls her away. She doesn't
look back as she's led away; she won't give Captain
Nsanzuwera or Tony Todd the pleasure.

A path hacked through the dense secondary growth along
the riverbank leads past a flat-topped barge moored under a
sagging sweep of camouflage netting to the foot of a slope of
raw earth and rock. Half-naked men are working in hot sunlight hazed with red dust, levelling a space near the top of the
slope, toiling downhill on a series of rickety bamboo ladders
laid between palm trees, carrying baskets of spoil which they

dump in the river. The place smells of smoke and dry, hot earth and sewage. Near the swampy edge of the river, two men are digging out a little yellow bulldozer sunk up to its axles in red clay, working slowly and clumsily. Captain Nsanzuwera stamps over and tells them to put their backs into it, whipping at their shoulders with his quirt, then snatching up a shovel and digging furiously for a couple of minutes.

"That's how it's done," he says breathlessly, his face shiny with sweat. The men stare at him, slack-mouthed, not even bothering to brush at the flies clustering around their eyes, and he slashes at them with his quirt again. One man wraps his arms around his head; the other tries to dodge away and trips and falls to his hands and knees. Captain Nsanzuwera kicks at him and shouts, "Work hard! No work, no shots!" Aiming a final kick at the man as he crawls away, then stalking back to Elspeth and Tony Todd and the soldiers.

"You think I am cruel," he says to Elspeth, "but those, they are zombies, not men. Too stupid to feel pain, almost too stupid to work." He's quite calm now, wiping blood from his quirt with a handkerchief before holding it out so that Elspeth can inspect it. "It's made of hippopotamus hide, like a sjambok. But you see how it shine? The leather is fixed up with industrial diamond. It sting like a hornet. You have to beat these zombies hard to get any work out of them—their brains are scrambled, and they take Dr. Todd's heroin for so long that they don't feel pain like ordinary men." He makes a sweeping gesture with the quirt. "What do you think of my little kingdom?"

Elspeth thinks that it looks like a scene from a low-rent Biblical epic. She says, "I'm amazed that no one has tried to stop you."

"No one care about the Dead Zone any more," the young soldier says. "The UN pay a few local soldiers to patrol the perimeter, but the rest of the world, it pretend this doesn't exist. No one care what happen here any more. Perhaps some American technician see it on a satellite picture, but so what? He thinks people are mining something, coltan or diamonds

or gold. Still, it make sense to hide the new laboratory underground, just like the old one, and that's what we do."

They climb a dirt path to a square doorway set in a mound
of red dirt covered with big shards of polymer. Off to one
side, a soldier sits in a plastic chair in the shade of a raffia
palm, tensed in a kind of whole-body flinch, his rifle laid
across his knees, knots of flies crawling over the bloody
swabs dropped around his feet, while a man in a white lab
coat uses a kind of stapler to punch implants into his scalp,
and a ragged man with a withered arm deftly dabs at the
blood running down his face.

"You take her to him," Captain Nsanzuwera tells Tony
Todd. "And he does what he agrees to do."

"He knows the woman, Nsanzuwera. What if he doesn't
cooperate, or tries one of his tricks?"

"He agree to do it. He is very keen. I think because he want
to die, because he know I kill him when I have someone else
who do the work." Captain Nsanzuwera unscrews the top of a
silvery flask and takes a long swallow. "Besides," he says, "I
tell him if he try any trick, I torture him."

"Oh yes, that worked very well last time. He doesn't have
any nerve endings left on his skin; that's why he just laughed
at you."

"This time I dig down and find some nerves," Captain
Nsanzuwera says. He takes another swallow, wipes his mouth
with the back of his hand, and recaps the flask. "Remember
to tell him that, and watch what he does carefully. By the end
of the day, I want her to be on our side. I want her to be loving me more than anything else in the world. The way you
love your habit. The way, I believe, you still love him."

Tony Todd says, "You want this so much, why don't you
watch him work?"

"You know why. I have my work, and you have yours."

"My dear captain, I do believe you're afraid."

"This place stink of his devilry," Captain Nsanzuwera says,
"and the sight of him make me sick. It make any reasonable
human being sick. You are upset because you don't get to
learn the secrets of mind-sculpting, but that is too bad. You do

what I say, Dr. Todd, or maybe I put a couple of your people in the pit, eh? And meanwhile I am busy. That spook is still loose. I want it back, so my men have some sport tonight."

As Captain Nsanzuwera walks away, Tony Todd glares at Elspeth and says, "This is all your fault. You should have agreed to help me."

"We could still help each other," Elspeth says, but Tony Todd makes an impatient gesture, and the soldiers grab Elspeth's arms and legs and lift her up and carry her through the square entrance into a rectangular metal-walled cave—a freight container buried in the slope, with plastic crates and racks of glassware stacked in the back around a big chest freezer.

The soldiers duck through a doorway roughly hacked out of one of the walls into another container, this one smelling strongly of earth and rot, a single biolume doing very little to light it, and drop Elspeth on an iron-framed bed. One man holds her down while the other two fasten heavy straps over her shoulders and waist, tighten buckles around her wrists and ankles.

As Tony Todd leans over her and adjusts a strap across her forehead, bracing her head against a deeply dished block of plastic, Elspeth hears a slow, heavy tread, and wet, laboured breathing as someone comes into the room. The soldiers back away; Tony Todd looks around.

"Elspeth," Daniel Lovegrave says, right behind her. "How nice of you to stop by."

Chapter **45**

Nick leans inside the narrow punishment cage, the sun hot on his head and shoulders, as he watches the soldier with the grey buzz cut and red eyes, Paul-Jon's comrade, come down the path. The man compact and muscular in a white sleeveless T-shirt and jungle-camo cargo pants and high-top combat boots, talking briefly with the two guards before coming over and standing in front of Nick, saying in English, "I have to admit, you got big balls."

Nick looks at him. "Did they find the white devil yet?"

"The spook? It prob'ly hasn't gone far. Needs its special salt to stay alive. When the Rwandans stop and think, they'll bait up some traps. Meanwhile they run around, have themselves some fun hunting for it."

"Perhaps the white devil will have itself some fun, too."

"You better hope it's grateful for what you did. Soon as they find it, they going to put it with you, my friend, in the pit."

Red-Eye slings his matt-black assault rifle over his shoulder, pulls a soft pack of cigarettes from one of the pockets of his cargo pants, lights two cigarettes and passes one through the bamboo bars of Nick's cage. Looking at him with those blood-red eyes, the little black dots in their centres like flyspecks, saying, "They beat up on you some, uh?"

Nick sucks in cool smoke. His watch hangs loosely on Red-Eye's left wrist, but he knows better than to mention it. He says, "I'm fine. Fighting fit."

Red-Eye leans close, says quietly, "How it is, in the pit, you kill the spook, they put in a leopard. You kill that, they put in another, or maybe that big pig they save for a special occasion. Point is, once you're in, that's it. The trick to surviving the pit, my friend, isn't how good you can fight. It's making sure you stay out of it."

"Maybe you can put in a good word for me."

"Maybe." Red-Eye says. He looks around as the other prisoner asks for a cigarette, tells him in French to shut his mouth, says to Nick in English, "These fucking Rwandans. That one, he's in there for killing one of the scientists. Actually, he raped her first; then he shot her in the eyes."

"And he's going in the pit too?"

"He should. He's been in there a week to think things over, prob'ly be let out in a couple of days. Maybe tonight, if they catch the spook, and Nsanzuwera decides to make you part of an all-star spectacular." Red-Eye smiles around his cigarette. "Don't seem fair, does it?"

"Well, I did kill your friend."

"That shithead Paul-Jon was no friend of mine. I'm a professional soldier," Red-Eye says. "Like you, uh? You were in the British Army?"

"For a little while."

"You see a lot of action, I bet. After the Black Flu, the Americans and the Brits were looking to fight anyone ever bought a petri dish."

"I was in Albania," Nick says.

"Yeah? How many you kill?"

"We mostly sat around, drinking beer, watching football on TV, movies . . ."

"I bet," Red-Eye says, clearly not believing him. "Me, I'm Quebecois, served with the Canadian Army. I came here as part of the UNAMIR force supposed to be keeping the peace in Ethiopia. We were pretty heavily equipped, had armoured personnel carriers and tanks, but the nearest we got to any action was watching people kill each other. We were monitoring this refugee camp one time, government soldiers came in, looking for rebels, looking for arms. They rounded up all the men and marched them out, killed them all a couple of kilometres down the road. Came back the next day and mostly trashed the place, killed women and children they said were terrorists, took away others for what they called questioning. And we couldn't do nothing about it, because the politicians told our general not to interfere . . ." Red-Eye spits on the ground between his boots. "That was UNAMIR."

Nick smokes his cigarette, waiting for the man to get to the point. He wants to ask about Elspeth, seeing again her look as she was led away by Nsanzuwera and Tony Todd. But it's like the watch: if you ask for something, it gives the other guy the advantage, and then you can't negotiate. All you can do is beg.

Red-Eye says, "I left the army soon after that, came back to work as a professional security adviser for a mining company in the east, near Goma. This was before the Black Flu, before things went bad. When they did, I fell in with a couple of guys I used to know in UNAMIR, we did some real for-hire soldiering. I signed up with Nsanzuwera because he ran a nice, tight outfit, one of the best. Ever since he came here, though . . ." Red-Eye touches his temple with his forefinger, shakes his head, one experienced soldier bitching about an officer to another.

Nick says, "He's gone native."

"He's settled in. You seen all the mods. And most of the guys, they get themselves a habit, use heroin they grow here in the yeast."

"But you aren't settling in. Despite your eyes."

"You know how it is. You get drunk, wake up with a tattoo," Red-Eye says, smiling, touching the corner of his right eye. "This, it's my only lapse, and besides, it's not just for looking fierce. They gave me two viruses, one to change the colour, the other to change the cells at the back, the rods or cones or whatever. Now I can see a little way into the infrared, see warm bodies in the dark. Gives me an edge in night fighting."

"So you've been here awhile, and now you're restless."

Nick has been trying to get it straight in his head. First there was the mission, run by Père Mike. Then Lovegrave and his crew came here after they fled the Pleistocene Park facility. They took over, probably killed Père Mike. And now Nsanzuwera and his crew have taken over in turn.

Red-Eye says, "You bet I'm restless. We been here four months now, for what should have been an in-and-out job. Nsanzuwera heard about it from one of the jackals who strip out stuff from the abandoned towns. We came here to make some quick money, sell the exotic animals they have, take their drug cultures, clean the place out and move on. But somehow, we're still here. Those two, Tony Todd and Daniel Lovegrave, have been whispering poison in Nsanzuwera's ear. It's a bad scene. And getting worse."

Nick says, "You sold a saber-toothed cat to a man named Raphael. That's how I found out about this place."

"We sold one to this Ugandan general too, but yeah, Raphael got some of the animals."

"But he didn't get the white devils."

"What we call them is spooks, but white devils is just as good. They why you're here, uh? To find out about them after they killed your buddies."

"You know about that?"

"We keep up. How did they do?"

"They ambushed and killed five Brazilian soldiers."

"Took their weapons?"

"Took them and shot at me."

"We taught them about guns. The little fuckers aren't as dumb as they seem, got the idea pretty quick. They fast too, and absolutely no fear in them. You were lucky to get out."

"I shot one of them," Nick says. "And when I went looking for them with Raphael's men, I shot another."

Red-Eye feeds Nick another cigarette, says that he wants to hear all about it. When Nick has finished his story, he says, "The thing I can't work out is why they were sent down the river, to Green Congo."

Red-Eye shrugs. "They were supposed to be sold to the Loyalists there. But I guess they got free."

"Nsanzuwera is trading with Samuel Nyibizo's Loyalists?"

"Sure. Nsanzuwera's father and Nyibizo, they go way back. Both of them were high-ranking *interahamwe* who fled Rwanda after the genocide, got involved with the civil war in East Congo. Nsanzuwera grew up in one of those camps around Goma, was seeing action before he got hair on his balls. I don't think he ever wear civilian clothes. Anyway, that fat guy, Raphael, wanted the white devils bad; we should have sold them to him, moved on. But Nsanzuwera saw an opportunity to make more money by getting Raphael and the Loyalists to bid against each other, and the Loyalists won. Then that little shit Tony Todd whispered in Nsanzuwera's ear, saying he could make more of them, get a regular trade going. White devils, the flies, I don't know what else. So now we're building the place up, settling in . . . Next thing you know, we'll be advertising for gene hackers. It's a bad scene, my friend, very bad."

"You could just walk away," Nick says.

"I thought about it. But it's a two-day, three-day drive to civilization in any direction, and there's no guarantee Nsanzuwera wouldn't send someone after me. He already put a couple of people tried to desert in the pit." Red-Eye looks around again, says, "You want to get out, I can help you."

"You help me, and I help you, right?"

"You're a tough guy. I bet you can be some help."

Nick has smoked his second cigarette down to the filter. He stubs it out on one of the bamboo bars, says, "Let me out, we can talk about it."

Red-Eye stares at him. "I think you know what needs to be done. What's to talk about? None of the Rwandans know shit, and I have a couple of good guys on my side. We take what we want, we get out. Maybe I even let you take out the scientists, what do you say?"

"I'll be happy to talk about it," Nick says, "after you let me out."

Red-Eye smiles and shakes his head, takes a final drag on his cigarette and flicks the butt away. The other prisoner starts talking again, begging for water, for cigarettes. Red-Eye kicks at the bamboo poles of the cage and tells the man that as far as he's concerned he can rot there, turns back to Nick. "That woman you came with, the one I know you want to ask me about, I saw her being carried into Lovegrave's so-called laboratory, hole in the ground at the top of the rise there. We don't do anything about it, he and his pals will fuck with her head, maybe give her a few mods, make her a lot less pretty." He looks up at the sky, where black clouds are beginning to edge across the sun. "It's gonna rain pretty soon. Rains a couple of hours every day around noon. I'll be back when it stops, and you better be ready to tell me what you want to do."

After Red-Eye has gone, Nick squats in his cage and tries to think it through. Not that there's much to think about. It's pretty clear what Red-Eye wants. He wants Nick to kill

Nsanzuwera, and then he'll either kill Nick or let him be killed by Nsanzuwera's men. It's a better option than facing the white devil in the pit, but not by much. If he agrees to it, Nick thinks, all he can hope for, once he's out of the cage, is a chance to get away from Red-Eye. Don't think about it, just do it. He has a picture of himself making some karate move, grabbing Red-Eye's rifle, putting it in the man's face, but it's pretty fuzzy, there and gone. Maybe he can at least get Red-Eye to agree to take Elspeth with him . . .

He remembers the look that he and Elspeth exchanged when they first saw each other, the way the air seemed to crackle between them. Elspeth standing under the tree with the big cat, that picture so clear and strong he knows he'll never lose it. He remembers the sudden hungry desperation of the first time they made love, the sweet slowness of the second. So very different from the other women he's made love to, their abandon that somehow seemed forced, the dirty words they used, the tricks they wanted him to try on them, that they wanted to try on him. He remembers how, in the middle of it all, Elspeth looked down at him in the cold glow of the bush filtering through the mosquito net, her braids hanging around her face, her expression serious and intent. Saying, *I know you.* And that was it—it was like they already knew each other; that second time, it was as if they both missed each other so much that they couldn't wait, as if they'd been missing each other all their lives.

He's been trying to forget ever since the way Elspeth looked down at him and what she said. He's tried to put it at the back of his mind, tried to tell himself it was only mutual fear and desperation that brought them together. After Michel showed him that news clip of his mother, and he realized that he would never be allowed to tell the truth about what happened to Tre Thompson and the others at the oil palm plantation, he knew that the only thing left for him was to make sure he destroyed Lovegrave and everyone and everything involved with making the white devils, no matter what the cost. He set out on a one-way ride, no compromise, no way back, no regrets for what might have been. But he failed at the first hurdle, when he didn't move quickly enough to avoid getting caught up in Teddy's dumb plan, and then he failed again, when he had the white devil in his sights and couldn't shoot it, and now everything is mixed up; he can't help hoping that somehow he and Elspeth will both get out of this . . .

Black clouds cut across the sun. Thunder rolls between the sky and the earth. A hot, leaden breeze stirs the fronds of the palm trees that stand in the green scrub around the little clearing. Fat drops of water randomly pock the hard-packed earth, and then, with a sudden release of pressure and drop in temperature, rain sweeps in like a curtain, solid and unrelenting. In only a few seconds, Nick is soaked to the skin. Water runs over his face, under his sodden shirt and trousers. He wipes water from his face with a hand, snorts water from his nostrils, wonders if it is possible to drown like this.

The prisoner in the cage next to his is squatting too, his arms wrapped over his head. The two soldiers shelter under a palm tree, holding a plastic sheet over their heads and sharing a cigarette, barely visible through the pounding rain. The ground turns into a slick red morass with small streams running everywhere. Red-stained water rises around Nick's boots. He's watching soil being washed away around the bases of the bamboo poles of the cage, thinking dully that perhaps he'll be able to pull one loose, when two quick muzzle flashes blink in the corner of his eye. He turns and sees through the downpour a bare-chested man squatting over the bodies of the guards—a white man, but not Red-Eye.

The other prisoner watches silently as the man stalks towards Nick, a long-barrelled handgun in one hand and a wicked-looking knife in the other. He stares at Nick through the bamboo poles, rain running over his shaven scalp, rain dripping from his eyebrows and nose and chin and ears, then says, "You're the clone."

"Who are you?" Shouting to make himself heard over the tremendous noise of the rain.

The man smiles, touches the tip of his tongue to the wide blade of his knife, and Nick knows: the man who ran towards them through the smoky aftermath of the explosions at Raphael's safari park, the man who murdered Elspeth's father.

"I should show mercy and kill you," Cody Corbin says. "What do you say?"

"I'd say there are worse monstrosities than me to worry about. Also, I brought along the Semtex from Captain Badiledi's pipe bombs."

"Yeah? But those soldiers have it now."

"They have my stuff, but they don't know about the Semtex. I hid it pretty well."

The American mercenary kisses the knife again, thinking about this, then says, "We should get out of this rain," and starts sawing at one of the rope knots that bind the bamboo poles together. Nick braces himself against the back of the cage, kicks at a loosened pole while Cody Corbin pulls at another, until there's enough space for him to squeeze through.

The other prisoner immediately begins to shout and plead, stretching his arms through the bamboo poles of his cage. Cody Corbin sticks his handgun in the waist of his trousers and turns away, showing Nick the angel on his back, its wings spread across his shoulders as it tramples a writhing serpent, and walks over to the pair of dead soldiers and picks up one of the assault rifles. Nick realizes what he's about to do and screams, his voice lost in the noise of the rain and the rifle firing on full auto, the mercenary shooting from the hip, the arc of fire cutting across the other prisoner's cage and blowing a spray of blood and bamboo splinters into the pouring rain. Cody Corbin tosses the rifle to one side and walks back to Nick, takes out his handgun and gestures with it, says, "Let's go."

The path that climbs the slope has become a fast, muscular stream. Rain smashes through palm fronds, rattles against clumps of bamboo; twigs and leaves torn from bushes rush by on foam-flecked red water. Nick scrambles through this flood ahead of Cody Corbin, bent double, rain lashing his back, gritty water running over the tops of his boots. His shirt and trousers are plastered to his skin. Whenever he loses his footing and falls to one knee or has to grab at clumps of coarse grass to keep his balance, the mercenary jabs the handgun in the small of his back, forcing him to climb on, breathless and half-drowned.

When he reaches the top of the slope, a great wing of rain beats over him, more water than air, and nearly knocks him down. He claws water from his face and yells that they should find some shelter until the storm is past, but Cody Corbin shakes his shoulder, points to the right, and pushes him forward. They walk downhill through beating rain and drenched grey scrub. Rain falls out of the dark air and hits the ground with a tremendous roar and leaps back knee-high. Nick can't see more than a dozen metres in any direction. They pass several termite castles, huge things two or three times the height of a man, and then a shadow looms through the rain, resolving into the tail of the plane that Teddy Yssel pointed out last night.

It's a Boeing 767, thirty or forty years old and painted white, VIPER stencilled in faded black paint across its fuselage. Rain blurs its fuselage and wings. The big tires of its undercarriage are flat, peeling away from the rusting drums of the wheels in huge flakes and shreds. Deflated orange emergency chutes hang down on either side of the fuselage like the pockets of a looted corpse, wet and shining in the rain.

Nick shelters beneath one of the wings while Cody Corbin scoots up an aluminium ladder propped under one of the emergency-exit doors. Rain beats loudly on metal overhead; the back edge of the wing sheds a shimmering waterfall. It doesn't occur to Nick to try to run, he wants to see what the man plans to do, and when Cody Corbin appears at the open door and beckons urgently, he dodges through the rain and climbs the ladder into the plane.

The passenger cabin has been stripped down to the ribs and rivets of the airframe. The floor is scaled with empty nylon grain sacks lettered A GIFT FROM THE PEOPLE OF THE UNITED STATES OF AMERICA. There's a wide circle of char where, long ago, someone lit a fire. Rain drums on the fuse-lage, but it's a lot quieter inside than out. Cody Corbin stalks away down the length of the plane; when Nick follows him into the cockpit, the mercenary is using a T-shirt to mop water from his shaved head and bare chest. He looks at Nick for a moment, then pulls another T-shirt from a day bag and tosses it to him.

Nick dries his hair and face. Water drips from his clothes, forms a huge puddle around his sodden boots. The other man settles in the flight engineer's chair and sets, of all things, a flat-board slide guitar in his lap. He pulls a scattershot of eerie wails from it, moving the barrel of the big handgun up and down the steel strings, all the while watching Nick, his eyes dark and judgemental, no particular expression on his face. Rain lashes at the thick glass of the cockpit's wrap-around windshield, makes a sound like falling gravel over-head. The control yokes and the throttle levers, the banks of dials and gauges and switches, the hooded computer screens: all are dusty and dead. Nick thinks that nothing looks deader than dead electronics; this plane isn't going anywhere.

"What's it like," Cody Corbin says at last, "bein' a monster?"

"Nothing special. I suppose like being anyone else."

"That's not what they say on the news. They say you're crazy. They say you're brain-damaged. They say you made up the story about the white devils."

"When we first ran into each other, at Raphael's place, you were working for Teryl Meade. Who are you working for now?"

The mercenary makes a lonesome sound on the slide guitar and says, "You like my pistol?"

"It's a Colt Python, isn't it?"

"It's my daddy's. From the last production run of 1996, matt stainless steel, with the six-inch combat barrel and a Hogue MonoGrip. I have it loaded with .38 jacketed hollowpoints. Hot loads. Just one will kill a man by hydraulic shock if he's hit anywhere in the torso. You mentioned Teryl Meade? I used this pistol to terminate my contract with her. If I kill you, it won't be because she paid me to, but because I figure you aren't cooperating, you aren't telling me the truth. You understand?"

"Do you mind if I sit down? I'm still feeling a little shaky."

"Take a load off."

Nick sits on the arm of the co-pilot's chair. Moving slowly, keeping his hands visible. There's an assault rifle propped near the day bag, he can see it out of the corner of his eye, but he knows that the mercenary will blow off his head if he makes a move towards it.

"So, now we understand each other," Cody Corbin says, "maybe you can tell me—who was that woman you arrived here with?"

"Elspeth Faber."

"What I thought. You met up with her at that monster factory, you decided you had a mutual interest, you found your way here."

"Do you know where she is now?"

"There was another man with you. Blond, about your size. Saw him with Elspeth Faber at the monster factory, saw him again last night, when you were all brought in. What happened? They find you sneakin' around the perimeter?"

"Something like that."

"So where's your blond friend now?"

"They killed him." There's something in Nick's throat. He swallows, says, "They put him in a pit, with a leopard."

"Were fixing to kill you too, I bet, until I came along."

"Don't think I'm not grateful. Can I ask, if you terminated your contract with Teryl Meade, why did you come here?"

"The white devils—you weren't lyin' about them?"

"No."

Cody Corbin plucks stray notes from the guitar in his lap. "What I thought. I saw that video clip of yours, and I knew straight away that thing wasn't a fake. I knew it was something to do with the monstrosities Elspeth Faber's father made. That was before Raphael got around to telling me that you brought back a dead one—if I'd known that, I would have taken a proper look around before I blew up his labs."

"Raphael told you about the white devils?"

"He didn't want to tell me anything at first, but toward the end I could hardly stop him talkin'. He told me what they were, he told me where they came from. So then I went to have me a little talk with Teryl Meade, and when I was finished with her, I got hold of a motorcycle, and here I am."

"You rode all the way here on a motorcycle?"

"And I'll ride out, when I'm done. Where do they keep their white devils? I took a look in those half-buried sheds, saw monsters in one and slaves in the other, but didn't see anything like the thing in your video."

"There was a white devil in there," Nick says. "They had an idea that I was going to fight it. A sort of grudge match. Last night they put me in a cage, and the white devil was in the cage opposite mine. It's sick—it suffers fits, and it had some kind of hump on its back. Perhaps that's why it didn't go down the river with the others. Anyway, one of the guards got careless, and I managed to get out of my cage. There were other soldiers nearby, and I didn't get very far, but the white devil managed to escape in the confusion. As far as I know, it's still running around somewhere."

"That's what the soldiers are lookin' for, uh? It's keepin' 'em busy, which made it a lot easier to get to you. How did you find out about this place? Elspeth Faber told you, is that it?"

"As a matter of fact it was Teddy Yssel. The man who was killed last night. He was a pilot, and he worked for Raphael, back before the Black Flu. He tracked me down after he saw the video clip and recognized one of the men in it. He was in Nairobi at the time, and hooked up with Elspeth Faber. They came all the way to Kinshasa to confront Raphael, and that's where I met them. I'd already found out that Raphael was getting his exotic animals from a mission that used to be run by someone called Père Mike. Teddy knew who that was, and that's how we ended up here."

"A useful man, this friend of yours."

"His best friend was killed by the white devils, in Green Congo. He wanted to do good by him."

"And he came looking for revenge, uh? That why you came all this way?"

"I had friends killed by the white devils too. And when I tried to tell the truth about it, Obligate and Teryl Meade tried to silence me."

"And they let the world know just what you are, when you wouldn't keep quiet. I bet you resent the hell out of that." Cody Corbin smiles when Nick doesn't say anything. "There's no one here but you and me and God. We can speak freely, I reckon. You want revenge, like your dead friend. Nothin' wrong with that far as I'm concerned."

"What about you?"

The mercenary sets the slide guitar on the floor and sits back, the handgun in his lap, hands laced behind his shaven head. "Why am I here when there's no money in it, is that what you mean? Well, sir, I'll tell you. I work for other people when I have to, but this is my real work—God's work. I'm here to remove from the face of the Earth the atrocities made by men who think they know better than Him, who think they can meddle with His creation. It says in Ecclesiastes, chapter one, verse eighteen, 'He that increaseth knowledge increaseth sorrow.' I'm here to do some diminishing in that respect," Cody Corbin says with a hard look that chills Nick's blood. "You and me, I reckon we pretty much want the same thing, so why don't you tell me what you've seen here?"

"I haven't seen much. There are around two dozen soldiers, some women who might be camp followers, those guys in the white coats . . . There's a pit where they let animals fight each other, under that big circus-tent affair—"

"Where your friend was killed last night."

"And there's the shed where they keep their animals. That's about it."

"I've seen a little more. The other shed is where they lock up their slaves at night. And the soldiers are dug in up above the river, around what I guess used to be the mission."

Nick nods. "I only caught a glimpse of it."

"They have their slaves diggin' out something in the slope above the river. That's where the laboratories are, I reckon.

Buried under a big pile of dirt, some kind of cut-and-cover job. I didn't get to look inside, but that's where they took your girlfriend just before the rain started. That has to be the primary target, but maybe I let you provide some diversion. You sure these soldiers haven't found that Semtex?"

Captain Nsanzuwera was wearing one of Teddy's shirts. And he was carrying the satellite phone.

"I'm sure," Nick says.

"Then let's go get it, while the rain gives us cover and the soldiers are busy looking for their white devil. Then we'll lay waste to everyone and everything in this unholy place—how does that sound?"

Nick knows that he won't survive any partnership with Cody Corbin. He says, "Before we do anything, I need to find Elspeth Faber. I need to make sure she's safe."

The mercenary smiles and says, "I can see you're thinking, why should I trust this man? You think that once we get that Semtex, I'll shoot you in the back. But where I come from, a man's word is as good as any written contract. You shake on a deal, you don't back out of it. So we'll shake, and then we'll get it on."

Cody Corbin holds out his hand, but when Nick doesn't take it, his smile begins to fade. "The way I see it, you're either with me or against me," he says, then cocks his head. "Hear that? Someone's coming."

Chapter 46

"I need it now," Lovegrave says. "Just a little taste to get rid of my little aches and pains. To get rid of this goddamned tremor . . ."

Danny Lovegrave's voice is as thick as a ten-handkerchief head cold, with only a trace of the nasal Boston accent Elspeth remembers so well. She's strapped to the plastic-covered mattress, unable to see him, unable to move her head, staring up at a patch of white paint on the ceiling of the buried freight container while she listens to him bicker with Tony Todd.

"Look at my hands," Lovegrave says. "How am I supposed to work like this? This man enjoys torturing me, Elspeth. He hooked me on heroin several years ago. He doles it out like a parent rewarding a child every time it does a good poop."

"You know that it's to help you with the pain," Tony Todd says.

"And when he wants me to do something I don't want to do, Elspeth, he withholds it. Of course, he can't do that for too long, because the cold turkey would kill me. Maintaining my habit has become a fine test of our wills."

"If I didn't make you work," Tony Todd says, "we would all be dead by now."

"Nonsense. You and the charming Captain Nsanzuwera are as thick as thieves. Did he tell you about his blackfly project, Elspeth? And then there's his new business, which is where you come in; he isn't quite bright enough to manage the mind-sculpting, and I refuse to have anything to do with it. Even I have my standards."

Tony Todd says, "Bullshit you have standards. You won't tell me your secrets, despite all I've done for you, but you're happy to fix her up so she can work for Nsanzuwera; you'll do it whether or not I give you a shot."

"If you don't want me to do this, there's an obvious way out." Lovegrave lowers his voice. "A little miscalculation, Dr. Todd, an accidental overdose, and you won't have to worry about me any more."

"Don't you see that you'll ruin the balance of power? Once *she's* fixed up, as soon as Nsanzuwera's certain that she'll do whatever he wants, he won't need *you* any more."

"It's interesting, isn't it?" Lovegrave says. "The only way you can stop me doing this is to kill me, and if you don't kill me, Nsanzuwera will do me the honour after I've 'fixed her up.' She'll be my replacement, and I'll get the rest I deserve. A quick dispatch, no more pain. That's the deal I made with the good captain, and I believe he's a man of his word. Either way I get what I want. Blessed relief from this vale of tears . . . Spare me the heartbroken look. You're like a puppy that can't understand why it's being punished."

"You made me what I am."

"And as I know very well, the heroin is no substitute, is it?"

Elspeth remembers how Danny Lovegrave liked to tease, remembers how he enjoyed his little cruelties.

"You think you're so clever," Tony Todd says, "but you don't know Nsanzuwera like I do. Perhaps he won't kill you, have you thought of that? Perhaps he'll sell you to some private zoo."

"Anything," Lovegrave says, "to get away from your babbling. I hope, Elspeth, that you haven't told this scoundrel any of your father's secrets."

"Not a one." Elspeth is waiting to see where he's going with this. She doesn't believe his talk about wanting to die, doesn't doubt that he wants to involve her in one of his clever little schemes. Perhaps he wants her to help him escape, which is why he told Tony Todd and Captain Nsanzuwera that she knew all about mind-sculpting, so that she would be brought here . . . She says, "This new business you mentioned—Dr. Todd wants to make more white devils, doesn't he?"

"White devils?"

Tony Todd says, "It's what the outside world calls the spooks."

Lovegrave says, "Both appellations are equally insulting, don't you think, Elspeth? I prefer to think of them as my children."

Elspeth says, "Does he want to make more of them?"

Lovegrave says, "He likes to think that he's already done it. But if I'm Frankenstein, he's Moreau."

Tony Todd says, "Let's get this over with. Do it right, and I'll give you a shot. And no silly tricks. I'll be watching you every second."

"Of course you will. Hungry for any scraps that fall from my table . . ." Something big and slow moves in the shadows at the edge of Elspeth's vision, settles behind her. "Try and relax," Lovegrave says. "This will soon be over."

"And then you'll be part of the family," Tony Todd says, and leans over her and presses a patch to the side of her neck. His breath touches her face. It smells like stale bread. "Don't worry. It's only a mild hypnagogic, mixed up with a little muscle-relaxant."

"Something to make you nice and sleepy and receptive," Lovegrave says. "We can't have superfluous activity messing up the mapping process, can we? I was so sorry, by the way, to hear about your father . . . Was he happy, in his last years?"

Elspeth can feel a not-unpleasant tingling in her blood. "I suppose so. In his own way."

Going along with Lovegrave's game, because she doesn't have any choice.

"And the australopithecines? Were they happy?"

"In their own way."

"Are they still alive, by the way? The news reports didn't mention them."

"The man who killed my father killed them, too. And burned up their bodies."

"This man, would he have been working for Teryl, by any chance?"

"He tried to kill me as well."

"Teryl always was a terror for neatness. Didn't we have fun together, back in Boston? I remember how brave you were when I let you drive my car that time. And the way you stood up to Teryl . . . Be brave now, Elspeth. Favour me with the truth."

"Truth for truth."

"Why not? How are you feeling, by the way? Nice and sleepy, I bet."

"I'm fine," she says, but her muscles are as weak as water, and her tongue is a dead weight in her mouth.

Tony Todd says, snappy with impatience and barely repressed anger, "Let's get it done. I have your shot right here. See?"

"She's not quite ready. This poor sap snoops on the data flowing through my laptop, Elspeth, but after all this time he still hasn't figured it all out. It's easy enough to find a particular engram and delete it. Any corner-shop charlatan can do that. Even Teryl could manage it. The tricky part, the part that Dr. Todd has trouble with, is the intuitive corrections you have to make while amplifying an engram. Every dynamic core responds in a fractionally different way, and small mismatches in the initial stages of integration can quickly amplify into gross errors and complete failure of the conditioning process. It needs a certain talent to get it right, and Dr. Todd just doesn't have it."

Tony Todd says, "Maybe she'll show me, when you've fixed her up."

"She'll do whatever Captain Nsanzuwera wants her to do, no more, no less. What I'm going to do now, Elspeth, is turn you into one of Nsanzuwera's good little soldiers. It isn't so bad, not really. The process induces a very direct euphoria, more powerful than anything pharmaceutically induced. You'll feel good when you're doing what Captain Nsanzuwera wants you to do, and you'll feel bad when you're not."

"What you did. To Todd."

"He hates me, but he can't help loving me too, despite the heroin. How did the australopithecines grow up, by the way? Were they fractious at all? Were they quarrelsome?"

"Sometimes."

"I knew it. Your father erased cd2 in them, but I bet their brains grew new pathways, new engrams."

"Nothing black or white." Elspeth thinks that she sounds horribly drunk. Not that it really matters. Not that anything matters . . .

Lovegrave says, "Hold still now, I'm not as deft as I used to be."

Cold fingers lift her eyelids, tape them back. A light comes on, illuminating the rust-spotted patch of white paint on the ceiling.

Lovegrave says, "I'm sure you know that the plastic block on which your head is cradled once belonged to your father. I'm going to use it to measure electrical activity generated by your brain when it is presented with visual stimuli. I'll watch your mind while Dr. Todd watches us both, trying to steal my secrets . . . No, don't try to move. Lie still, enjoy the show."

Perhaps Elspeth passes out for a moment. Faces, landscapes, and single words are flowing over the ceiling. She feels only lightly attached to her body, floating into a vague vastening something like sleep, coming back to the dim green light of the biolumes, plastic slick with her own sweat wrinkled beneath her, hot air sour with the smell of sickness, the pictures on the ceiling, the click of a laptop's keyboard, the murmur of the projector's fan, Lovegrave's thickened voice spinning an endless monologue for the benefit of Elspeth or Tony Todd, it isn't clear. Perhaps it's a story he's telling himself.

"We've evolved from apes who learned to stand upright and venture out of the close horizons of the forest onto the limitless plains, and sight is our primary sense; we can't help processing what we see. Each pattern and picture you see now, Elspeth, forces your consciousness into a new state. Subsets of neurons firing for tens of milliseconds contribute to a single integrated neural process that persists for hundreds of milliseconds—in other words, transitory associative states lead to a final state of recognition. By measuring patterns of neuronal activity during repetition of visual stimuli, and running those patterns through your father's dynamical system and perturbation models, I can plot pathways of neural integration and differentiation. What I'm mapping here on my laptop, for the benefit of the ever-attentive audience at my elbow, are the patterns of connectivity and activity that underpin your consciousness . . ."

This soft monologue a soothing background, washing through Elspeth, fading away as she feels herself float out of her body, returning when something cold slides into a vein in her neck.

"The magic potion needed to complete the ritual," Lovegrave says. "Sodium glutamate, mostly, enriched with oxygen fifteen. Traceable brain food to help me see what you are thinking."

A picture of a laughing child is displaced by the snarling

mask of a white devil. Elspeth tries to sit up, but it's like one of those bad dreams where you can't run from your worst fear.

Lovegrave says, "Did Dr. Todd happen to say anything about your father's so-called accident, Elspeth? He threatened that he would."

"I was only trying to motivate her," Tony Todd says.

"Of course you were. By putting the blame on me, no doubt, hoping that she'd agree to help you undermine my authority . . . Let me tell you the truth, Elspeth. I didn't hurt your father; neither did Teryl. She'd already left, right after our major funder pulled out. It was a smart career move, so I guess I can't blame her for it, but I know it wasn't because, as she later claimed, she suddenly saw the light and repented. She ratted us out, she left your father in sole charge of the kids . . ."

The green-lit darkness, the bright pictures above. Neutral scenes now. A red balloon in a blue sky. A field of golden wheat stretching to the horizon under a blue sky. A blue sea breaking in white waves on a white beach. A red balloon in a blue sky. Half-remembered images that used to play as a screen saver on her father's computer . . .

Lovegrave says, his voice a low, intimate rumble just behind her head, "The truth, Elspeth, is that your dear departed father did it to himself. He told me that he wanted to think better—do you remember his silly motto? He wanted to erase his cd2 engram. He wanted to get rid of all the primal fear and anger that makes us do bad things. I suppose he was a little crazy by then. Teryl had left, our work was being repudiated, we were abandoned, reviled . . . I suppose we were all a little crazy. Your father talked about doing it for a long time, and when everything started to fall apart around us, he decided to take the plunge. And it went wrong. He got rid of cd2 all right, but the procedure shattered his dynamic core into a dozen independent subprocesses, each unable to properly integrate with the others. He gave himself the same kind of dissociation syndrome, so-called multiple personality disorder, that one sees in patients who have suffered massive psychological trauma. But you know all about that, I'm sure."

The light dies, leaving an enlarged afterimage (the colours inverted, a yellow balloon floating in a green sky) of the last picture.

"Listen carefully, Elspeth," Lovegrave says. "This is the next step of the process. I've used functional magnetic resonance imaging and magnetoencephalography to map your neuronal activity while you watched those pictures, and now I'm going to use tightly focused magnetic fields to enhance reentrant pathways in particular parts of the brain. The potion you drank will help me to monitor the process—glutamate is a neurotransmitter, and the paramagnetic signal from the oxygen isotope changes when the glutamate molecules bind to the appropriate receptor in the synapses of activated neurons."

Elspeth glimpses movement from the corners of her eyes, a bulky shadow suddenly blurred when saline solution floods her eyes. A hand shakes a black handkerchief with a clumsy imitation of a conjuror's gesture. Its fingers are fused into a buckled flipper, leaving only the clever thumb free.

"Let me help you with that," Tony Todd says. Impatience gives an edge to his voice.

"I'm not quite completely crippled," Lovegrave says. "This was your father's, too, Elspeth. Do you remember it? It's packed with superconducting threads that focus the magnetic field at nanometre scales—a very elegant piece of kit, as Matthew used to say. Given enough time, I could use it to change the connections of every neuron in your brain. But all I'm going to do today is a simple stimulation of your pleasure centre, little better than twiddling electrodes in your cortex. Still, they have all learned to love me like this. Loyalty is nothing more than anticipation of happiness, as Dr. Todd knows very well."

The flipper clumsily smooths the handkerchief over Elspeth's head. She rolls back her eyes and glimpses the swollen, lopsided face leaning above her, struggles feebly against the straps.

Lovegrave makes a hushing noise, strokes her hairline. "Lie still," he says. "Think of nothing."

His flipper presses something, another drug patch, onto the

soft skin behind her ear. Her blood slows; she feels that she's sinking away from the room. The white light that brilliantly illuminates every pock and rust flake in the patch of white paint sprayed on the ceiling shrinks smaller than a man's hand and keeps shrinking, a dot, a point, nothing at all.

Nick and Cody Corbin lean side by side, staring out of the streaming windshield of the cockpit as an open-topped jeep carrying three soldiers in green slickers drives slowly up to the plane and disappears under its wing.

The mercenary says, "Maybe they're just sheltering from the rain. Their search line went straight past a couple of hours ago; they didn't stop to look inside. Lucky for them."

"They think the white devil is an animal," Nick says. "So they were looking for it in the bush, they wouldn't think to look—"

Voices echo inside the stripped passenger cabin beyond the half-closed door of the cockpit. Cody Corbin steps quietly to the door, holding his Colt Python up by his face in a two-handed grip. He gestures to Nick to move out of the line of fire, then kicks the door open and steps through, firing two quick shots, after a few seconds two more, the noise flat and loud in the plane's stripped metal tube. Nick is thinking about making a move towards the assault rifle when the mercenary steps back into the cockpit, saying, "Like fish in a barrel—"

Outside, the jeep's motor starts, a discreet cough barely audible through the noise of the rain. Cody Corbin grabs the rifle and bolts into the passenger cabin. Nick follows, sees him swing through the open door into the rain and swarm down the ladder. The two soldiers he shot lie close to each other in a spreading puddle of dark red blood, one on his back, the other on his stomach. It looks like the mercenary got them both with chest shots, finished them off with a shot in the head apiece.

Nick grabs a Kalashnikov with a spare clip taped to its metal stock and runs to the door, then has an idea and runs back and quickly searches the soldiers, getting sticky blood all over his hands before he finds the satellite phone clipped to the belt of the one sprawled on his back.

He slides down the ladder to the ground, soaked to the skin all over again, sees Cody Corbin chasing after the jeep, smashing through sodden brush and firing from the hip like some stupid action hero, the sound of gunfire muted by the noise of the rain. He should stop and take careful aim, Nick thinks, perhaps use the rifle's rocket-propelled grenade. And a moment later, that's just what the man does. The explosion throws up a geyser of red mud; the jeep swerves, straightens, and speeds away, vanishing into the downpour. Cody Corbin fires another long burst after it, and as he turns and begins to walk back towards the plane, Nick goes the other way, running straight out under the wing into the waist-high brush.

The rain makes a tremendous noise, pounding down all around, thrashing through the bushes, hissing into the red mud, but the crack of a round snapping past his head is unmistakable. Nick drops to the ground, rolls over, wipes mud from his eyes, and rises to one knee and stays still, kneeling amongst spindly bushes that provide no cover at all, rain pounding on his head and shoulders as he sights along the Kalashnikov's barrel towards the solid shadow of the plane, no more than two hundred metres off yet barely visible in the gloom and the rain.

The way the mercenary ran after the jeep showed that he doesn't have any combat training. He's a good fearless shot, at least at close range, but he has no discipline. Nick is sure that he'll come after him, maybe at the most try some kind of dumb flanking move; all he has to do is wait for one clear shot. He is pretty sure that he can shoot without hesitation. He has never killed a man before today, but he shot Paul-Jon when he had to, and he killed two white devils too, tells himself now that he would have shot Dogboy if he'd had a moment more.

He keeps the Kalashnikov moving in a tight arc centred on the plane, kneeling high so that he can sight across the tops of the grey bushes, paying particular attention to termite castles the mercenary might use as cover. A breeze picks up, blowing huge billows of rain, bending the tops of the grey bushes, and then a seam opens in the sagging black clouds and the sun shines through for a moment. The sun is near the horizon now, and a long wedge of golden light sweeps across the plateau like God's own finger, burns through vast curtains of falling rain, puts a shine along the top of the plane's fuselage, and silhouettes half a dozen termite castles and Cody Corbin, off to the right. As the man drops out of sight, Nick swings the Kalashnikov around and snaps off four quick shots, then takes a breath and rises to his feet and fires twice more. He sees bits of brush kick up, nothing else, and kneels down and resumes his stance and waits, rain still falling around him but more quietly now, the shaft of light fading as the break in the clouds closes. Nick is aiming to the left of the spot where the mercenary vanished. If he wasn't hit, he'll either keep moving in the same direction or try and double back; Nick thinks that he's the kind of sneaky son of a bitch who'd favour the second option.

He counts out a minute in his head, seeing nothing, counts out another. His sodden shirt and trousers cling tightly to his skin. His legs are beginning to stiffen, and he can feel his pulse in the tender place where one of the soldiers socked him above his right kidney with a rifle butt, can feel the bruises of his beating hot and tight on his face. The rain is growing lighter, dying away with a regretful hiss.

He's counting out his fifth minute when he hears the sound of motors, sees two jeeps loaded with soldiers swing around the nose of the plane. The man standing up beside the driver of the lead jeep, pointing at the plane, pointing into the bush and shouting orders, is Captain Nsanzuwera.

Nick crouches low, starts to move as quickly as he can away from the plane, fixing on a clump of rocks that stands like a broken monument amongst the scrub, halfway to the line of green secondary growth that marks the edge of the steep drop down to the river. He wonders if Cody Corbin is also retreating, wonders if the mercenary is crazy enough to take on the soldiers. He's only about a hundred metres from the rocks now. He can lie low behind them, wait until the soldiers lose interest. The soldier who escaped in the jeep only saw Cody Corbin; they won't be looking for two men . . .

Someone shouts. A moment later, bullets crack and whine around Nick, and he throws himself full-length into the mud. A round shreds the top of a bush a couple of metres to his left, makes a weird whooping noise as it tumbles away. Nick risks raising his head to take a quick peek, sees a soldier standing on the wing of the plane, pointing directly at him, sees one of the jeeps begin to move slowly through the bush in his direction.

He finds the satellite phone he took off the dead soldier, snaps it open, starts punching in one of the two numbers he carefully memorized in the hotel room in Bandundu. He can hear the jeep getting closer. His fingers are wet and cold; he's shaking with the rush of adrenalin. He forces himself to go slowly and carefully as the long string of black numbers grows from left to right on the little screen. He can hear the whine of the jeep's engine and the wet crackle of vegetation crunching under its tires, hears someone shouting at him in French to drop his weapon and stand up, hands out. He botches one of the numbers, wastes precious seconds finding the delete key, punches in the last three and places his thumb on the *call* button and stands, a tight coldness spreading over every centimetre of his body. He might have botched his hasty bit of rewiring, or perhaps Captain Nsanzuwera discovered the little booby trap—no, if he had, he would have made sure Nick knew about it. Or perhaps the satellite phone Captain Nsanzuwera took from him isn't switched on . . .

The jeep is less than fifty metres away now, coming towards him slowly, bumping through the soaked brush. Captain Nsanzuwera stands next to the driver, holding on to the top of the windshield; a soldier stands behind them both, leaning against the roll bar and aiming a fat assault rifle at Nick.

Captain Nsanzuwera says loudly, "Nicholas Hyde! I see something in your hand! Drop it now, or you get shot!"

Nick presses the *call* button.

There's a brief flurry of bleeps as the phone finds a connection and dials. And then the phone chip Nick patched into the aerial and power pack of the big satellite phone responds and kicks a fractional current to the detonator inside the Semtex charge packed into the space that formerly housed the phone's secondary power pack.

One moment, Captain Nsanzuwera is smiling at Nick; the next, he comes apart from the waist up in a flash of flame and flesh and blood and bone fragments and superheated air that kills the driver and the soldier behind him. The jeep piddles past Nick, its upholstery and the clothes of the dead men on fire, ammunition in the assault rifle and various small arms beginning to cook off with small sharp bangs as it comes to a halt. By then Nick is already up and running, sprinting past the rocks, running towards the belt of vegetation. He reaches its shelter just as the soldiers by the plane recover from their shock at seeing their commander blown to bits, and start a ragged, impotent fusillade.

Chapter 47

Tony Todd undoes the strap across Elspeth's forehead, flips open the buckles that hold down her wrists and ankles, the straps over her shoulders and waist. A spike of woozy pain punches through her head as he helps her sit up, asking her how she feels.

"I've had better days." She remembers Lovegrave pressing the drug patch behind her ear, the pictures glowing on the ceiling . . . And what? What happened after that? What did he do? What did he do to her?

"The first rush soon fades," Tony Todd says, "but the good feeling never quite goes away, and you'll always want to try and win it back. It will become an induced behaviour as deep as any habit. You won't be aware of it until something triggers it, but it will be there all the same. And when it's triggered, it's like nothing else . . ."

Elspeth is remembering other things now. The flipperlike hand. The awful face. She says, "How long has he had the plastic disease?"

Tony Todd, coming back from something in his mind, gives her a sharp look. His white lab coat seems to ripple in the green underwater glow like a flag of kelp in a deep sea current. Behind him, half a dozen men and women are crowded into the doorway, some in white coats, some not. Lovegrave's disciples, Elspeth realizes, come to watch their master at work.

She says, "He's dying of it, isn't he? That's why you need someone else to do the work."

"I believe," Tony Todd says, choosing his words carefully, "that he contracted it soon after we reached the mission. The first couple of months, we helped Père Mike treat the sick, and many of them were dying from the plastic disease. He hid it from us for a long time. For too long. We tried antibiotics, we tried surgery, but the disease had already reached into his bones, and it kept returning. It's all through him now."

"His magic bullet didn't protect him?"

"I never had one," Lovegrave says, and by degrees emerges from the shadows beyond the foot of the hospital bed, bent and swollen in a robe of stained black cloth that's cinched at his waist with a broad leather belt. In the green light of the biolume, he looks like a rotting jack-o'-lantern, like a monk ruined by gluttony and unspeakable vice. He takes tiny, uncertain steps, leaning on a short aluminium cane, breathing heavily and wetly. The people in the doorway stir and murmur.

Tony Todd says, "You've worked hard today. Now you've had your shot, you should rest. Get some sleep."

His tone sweet and false, the way someone who hates children or knows nothing about them talks to a child.

"But I want to talk to my guest," Lovegrave says, and slowly and with great care settles himself on the bed next to Elspeth. The metal frame squeals as it takes his weight. He lays the cane across his thighs and looks sideways at her. Smooth white protuberances break through the scaly red skin of his scalp and brow; his smile is lopsided, half-buried by the goitrous swellings of jowls and chin. "Do you believe in karma, Elspeth? I, personally, do not, but to those who do, I suppose I must be a living lesson in its efficacy. I never had a magic bullet fitted, because I was using psychoactive viruses that gave me lovely little localized fevers and inflammations of the brain, helped to alleviate my terminal boredom. A magic bullet would have protected me from the plastic disease, but it would also have put a stop to my only source of pleasure. So you see, I'm suffering for my past indulgences. I am half-blind, half-deaf, and everything tastes of burnt rubber. My digestive system is in a constant state of rebellion, and then there are the maggots. The woman who looks after me is unable to keep away all the flies, so every day my pretty little nurse uses cactus thorns to pick maggots from the folds in what was once my flesh. Still, I've lived a life that's full, travelled each and every highway, all the rest of that crap. No regrets, eh?"

"You really should rest," Tony Todd says.

"Do be quiet. Now that Dr. Faber is herself again, I want to have a little heart-to-heart with her." Lovegrave touches the side of his neck with a flipperlike hand and winks at Elspeth with his good eye. "If she isn't feeling too woozy after our little session, that is."

Elspeth realizes then what he's done. Or rather, what he hasn't done. He hasn't changed her mind at all; he put her to sleep instead, with the patch he surreptitiously stuck on her neck. Uncle Danny and his little tricks.

She says, "Is that why you saved me from Captain Nsanzuwera's pit? To talk?"

Lovegrave smiles, his good eye glittering with mischievous intelligence. "Why not? You're all grown up now, Elspeth, a real scientist, a credit to the profession. It's been a long time since I had a chance to talk with one of my peers. And who knows? Perhaps it'll teach Dr. Todd a thing or two."

"You see how he is?" Tony Todd says. His hands, thrust into the pockets of his white coat, are making and unmaking fists. "Spiteful. Ungrateful."

Elspeth says to Lovegrave, "You promised that if I told the truth, so would you."

"Truth for truth. I haven't forgotten."

"Why don't you start by telling me how the white devils escaped?"

"Oh, you know how it is," Lovegrave says carelessly. "Maybe it's spring, or maybe your children have grown up and moved away, or maybe you learn you're dying. In any case, you get the urge to tidy up, to get rid of unnecessary encumbrances. Perhaps I was out of sorts, I wanted to simplify what was left of my life. Or perhaps, as they were my only children, it was time I gave them a chance to make their own place in the world."

"It was a stupid trick that could have killed all of us," Tony Todd says.

"That was rather the idea."

"You don't mean that."

"Do you really think I want to spend the rest of my life like this? With only you for company?"

They're like a couple trapped in a worn-out marriage, Elspeth thinks, rehearsing old grievances in front of every new acquaintance. She says, "What really happened?"

Lovegrave says, "Captain Nsanzuwera sold my children and some other goodies to his friends in Green Congo. He put them on a barge, sent them off down the river. But I had a man on the barge. The man, in fact, who was supposed to look after my children on their little trip. He knew that I was very unhappy about the whole thing, and I suppose he must have let them go."

Tony Todd says, "You told him what to do, and you knew he'd do it. Don't pretend that you weren't responsible for what happened."

Lovegrave tells Elspeth, "Perhaps I suggested it to him,

but really, he didn't need much encouragement. He had been their keeper from the very first. He fed them, cleaned them, cared for them . . . And in the end, he sacrificed himself so that they could go free rather than be used as some kind of terror weapon. After he found out that my children had escaped, Nsanzuwera tried to torture me, and when I laughed in his face, he withheld my heroin. I nearly died, but unfortunately Dr. Todd decided to interfere, and he and the others nursed me back to a semblance of health. That's the problem, you see," he says, jabbing his cane in the direction of the people in the doorway. "They love me too much to let me die."

Elspeth makes herself look at him. She says, "I know what the white devils really are."

Lovegrave's smile is a dreadful thing. "Oh, I doubt that very much."

"If you strip away the gengineering, they're human. Just like the Gentle People."

"I never doubted that you knew about the Gentle People," Lovegrave says. "As for my children, I suppose it started as a joke—perhaps the only joke I ever regret. I turned what Matthew had done when we made the Gentle People through a hundred eighty degrees. I induced low serotonin production, amped up activity in the ventromedial prefrontal cortex—"

"You reinforced the reentrant pathways of the cd2 engram."

"I made them fierce, strong, quick to anger, quite without fear. Who knows what they might have become, if they had been allowed to grow up properly? But the bandits came, and treated my children like freaks, and then Nsanzuwera took over, and established a systematic programme of brutalization. He gave them prisoners to kill, allowed them to feed on the corpses . . ."

"They were already brutalized," Elspeth says.

"I'm not ashamed of what I did. And in the end, when I could, I gave them their freedom."

"My father paid a high price for your gesture," Elspeth says. "Teryl had him murdered because of it."

She thinks that she should feel more than she's feeling at the moment.

"Is that why you're here? Revenge for your father's murder?" Lovegrave is amused. "Or perhaps something nobler. Perhaps you thought you could save me."

Why is she here? She came to Kinshasa to talk to Nicholas Hyde and get enough evidence to ruin Teryl, and instead found herself on the run with him, Teryl dead, and Lovegrave dying in squalor, a prisoner of his own creations. The truth she hoped to uncover isn't simple after all—it's sordid, messy, and ignoble, and she's become intractably tangled up in it.

She says, "Teryl had my father murdered because of what you did. Yes, I wanted to see her brought to justice for that, and even though she's dead—"

Lovegrave says, "Wait a minute. Teryl is dead?"

"She was murdered a couple of days ago. Obligate claims that she was assassinated by Loyalist guerrillas. I think that she was killed by the man she hired to murder my father and the Gentle People."

"How wonderfully, ironically neat that would be. So the bitch is dead. I'm surprised that you didn't tell me about this, Dr. Todd. After all, you took a great deal of delight in telling me about the death of poor Matthew. How he gloated, Elspeth, over my tears."

Tony Todd says, "That's why I didn't tell you about Teryl Meade. I didn't want to upset you again."

"Listen to his honeyed words, Elspeth. All lies. The one thing he's good at."

Elspeth says, "Even though Teryl is dead, I still want the world to know what she did, and why."

"The truth could hurt your father, Elspeth."

"Nothing can hurt him now. And it could help your children. Some of them are still alive. They're being hunted down, but if people know what they really are, perhaps they can be saved."

Lovegrave makes a humming sound as he thinks about this. He says, "I didn't mean for Matthew to be harmed, Elspeth. I had a profound respect for him. He had a unique and very special mind. He was my colleague and my friend. You know, we had such high hopes when we came here. It was a new start. We had the best equipment, the best people, and such ideas, such ambition. Matthew's plans to create new ways of thinking, my plans to recreate an entire lost ecology . . . We had such plans, and what did we get instead? Hubris clobbered by nemesis."

Elspeth says, "All you did was make bad science from bad ideas. You never did any good—you never even tried."

"There are the goats," Lovegrave says, "and the termites."

Tony Todd makes a noise of disgust.

Elspeth says, "I saw the goats, in the village where I was taken prisoner."

Lovegrave says, "The villagers discovered that cellulose-9 rots in oxygen-free water, and built ponds to speed the process. Back in the early days, when I wasn't quite as ill as I am now, when most of the equipment we rescued was still working, I discovered that bacteria in the mud possess an enzyme that digests cellulose-9. I cloned up the gene for the enzyme and transferred it to strains of bacteria that live in the rumens of goats, and other strains of bacteria that are symbiotic with termites. Because they can eat the cellulose-9, the goats and the termites could clean up the Dead Zone and speed up the return of the forests. Perhaps I'm nothing but a monster, but I like to think that I have tried to do some good in my long and latterly unfortunate career."

"If you really want to do good, tell the world what you've done."

Lovegrave pats her on the hip and says lightly, "Oh, I don't think Captain Nsanzuwera would allow that, do you?"

Tony Todd says, "After a couple of sessions, you'll see things differently, Dr. Faber. You come with me now, I think you've done enough talking." He reaches for her arm, pulls her to her feet.

Lovegrave says, "Was Matthew happy, in the end?"

Elspeth shakes off Tony Todd's grip. "I think so. Yes. He

had his island, his children. Sometimes, I think he was happier than anyone else in the world."

"When Teryl left Pleistocene Park, after she made those silly, so very public denouncements, Matthew's heart was broken. That was when he started experimenting on himself. Perhaps he was looking for happiness, in his own peculiar way. Anyway, I'm glad he found it. We have come back to karma. Matthew had his island, his happy little family, and since the spread of the Dead Zone, I've had nothing but degeneration, savagery, horror . . . And if Captain Nsanzuwera and Dr. Todd get their way, it will go on and on, horror upon horror."

Tony Todd rounds on him. "I do all I can to keep you alive, and in return I get nothing but malice and spite."

"You keep me going," Lovegrave says, "because you can't quite get rid of what I put in your mind, despite all the heroin you take. You keep me going because if your dirty little scheme with Captain Nsanzuwera is going to succeed, you need to know how to remake minds. When they write my obituary, they'll say I was a Frankenstein, that I made monsters. But I'm no plague bearer, am I, Dr. Todd? And I'm no vivisectionist, either."

"That's enough!"

Lovegrave says, "If Dr. Faber is going to work for Nsanzuwera, she'll need to know what she'll be dealing with. Where shall we start? With the flies, or with your new adventures in surgery? With those poor boys—"

"I'm doing it to keep you alive!"

Tony Todd's voice is shrill and loud, out of control. The people in the doorway shrink back like children frightened by quarrelling parents. One woman, her brow lumpily swollen by keloid growths, is crying.

"You're doing it to save yourself from Captain Nsanzuwera's pit," Lovegrave says. "You used to be my creature; now you want to make yourself his. Take a look next door, Elspeth, at the cages of flies. Ask Dr. Todd what he's growing—"

Tony Todd makes a high-pitched sound and snatches up Lovegrave's aluminium cane and starts beating him about the head and shoulders. Lovegrave slumps over by degrees, making a snoring noise that might be distress, might be laughter. Elspeth catches hold of the cane on an upstroke, but Tony Todd knocks her to the floor, and is about to strike at her when two soldiers push through the men and women in the doorway.

Tony Todd glares at them, breathing hard, and says, "Can't you see we're busy?"

One of the soldiers, a beefy, red-faced man with a crest of blond hair, grabs Elspeth's wrists and hauls her to her feet. His companion, made grotesque by convoluted bat-ears and vampire incisors, tells Tony Todd, "We need to talk with this bitch right now. Do you have a problem with that?"

Nick lies amongst tall weeds and grass in a field of unmarked graves, near a bend in the track that curves up the long slope to the old mission building and the soldiers' camp. The darkening air is hot and wet, and the rainstorm has brought out a deafening chorus of tiny frogs that tirelessly sing two-note whistles each to each. Nick's trousers and T-shirt are soaked through; he has smeared mud on his face and hands to try and protect himself from the mosquitoes that swirl around him.

He watches as the slaves shuffle down the track in a long file, some twenty men shackled at the ankles, their heads bowed with exhaustion, picks and shovels slung over their shoulders, their shadows thrown a long way behind them by the setting sun. He watches as they are locked into the smaller of the two low sheds that squat beside the track a few hundred metres behind his position, watches the four soldiers who escorted them climb into a jeep and speed away towards the camp, where people are hurrying to and fro beyond the perimeter of tangled trophic wire. A truck is parked in front of the bungalow, people coming and going around it, and he wonders briefly if they're packing up, getting ready to make a run for it, but then soldiers walk out through a gap in the wire, walking in single file, almost certainly following an unmarked path through a minefield. There are eight of them, four moving towards the airstrip and the plane, the others heading for his position. One wears night-vision goggles; another holds the leashes of two big lion-coloured dogs with spike collars, the dogs casting about eagerly as they lope along.

Nick remembers the way he used to feel when he realized that his mother had spied him in one or another of his hiding places in the garden. The soldiers cross the road. In five minutes they'll be on him. He pulls out the satellite phone he took off the dead soldier in the plane, dials the second of the two numbers he memorized, says a quick prayer that Red-Eye and Cody Corbin weren't lying—that Elspeth isn't anywhere in the camp—and presses the *call* button.

It's growing dark outside. The warm air smells very fresh, smells of wet earth and green, growing vegetation. Elspeth takes in great cleansing gulps, purging herself of the stink of Lovegrave's burrow, while the two soldiers bind her wrists with wire. When they turn her around and march her up the steep, muddy path between thick stands of wet bamboo, Tony Todd scurries after them, saying that this woman is too valuable for the pit, saying that this isn't what Captain Nsanzuwera would have wanted.

"We had a plan," he says, and the blond soldier swings around and knocks him down with the stock of his assault rifle. Stands over him and says, "Someone helped this bitch's friend escape. Nsanzuwera is dead, there are at least two unfriendlies running around, we're going to question her. That a good enough plan for you, Dr. Todd?"

Tony Todd, sprawled in the mud, his white coat spread beneath him, hands half-raised to ward off another blow, says nothing.

"You aren't so fucking clever now," the blond soldier says, and spits on him and tells Elspeth, "We're going to fix your friends, and then I'm going to fix you. Been a long time since I had any educated pussy."

The vampire soldier pulls Elspeth close to him and makes a

ucking noise next to her ear, and the blond soldier starts to say
something that's suddenly drowned by a tremendous clap of
thunder. A ball of red flame rolls into the sky beyond the top of
the slope. For a moment, every leaf and stick of bamboo stands
out clear and distinct from its shadow, and Elspeth sees someone step out of the bushes onto the path, his arm extended.

She ducks instinctively the moment the man fires. The
back of the blond soldier's head blows apart in a sleet of red
matter and he crashes backwards into a stand of bamboo. The
vampire soldier pushes Elspeth away, saying, *"Merde,
merde,"* starting to bring up his assault rifle, and the man
shoots him in the chest. The soldier spins around and drops to
his knees, and the man shoots him in the head and steps over
the body and walks past Elspeth, who sees with a clean shock
that it's the man who killed her father, the man who came
running through thick smoke down the middle of the road at
Raphael's safari park, shooting at the 4×4 as he ran, like
something out of a Wild West movie.

Cody Corbin, his face and shaven scalp smeared with
tiger-stripes of mud, a pistol in his hand and an assault rifle
slung over his shoulder, his eyes wide and white, looks down
at Tony Todd. The scientist has been crawling backwards towards the undergrowth, and now raises his hands and says,
"Wait," as the mercenary brings up the big pistol and shoots
him twice in the chest.

Elspeth stands amongst the dead men, struck dumb by
shock. Cody Corbin shoves the pistol in the waist of his
trousers, grabs her bound wrists, and pulls her down the path,
towards the entrance to the buried laboratories. Saying,
"Show me the atrocities, Dr. Faber, and maybe I'll let you
live."

Nick packed most of the Semtex into the hollow aluminium
tubing of the rucksack's frame, topping it out with a phone
chip and detonator taken from one of the pipe bombs. He
switched on the phone chip early yesterday morning, and
more than twenty-four hours later its battery is still good: as

soon as the satellite phone makes the connection, the front of the mission building blows out in a billowing cloud of dust and yellow smoke. A hard, sudden noise rolls across the scrub and the airstrip, and the four soldiers who were advancing on his position turn around just as a secondary explosion, probably a fuel store, lofts a ball of red flame that nicely silhouettes them. Nick raises the Kalashnikov and drops all four with a single burst. It isn't planned; he simply reacts when they present a clean target. He shoots them and they fall down. A moment later, two big dogs come running towards him through the scrub, trailing their chain leashes. He shoots one, misses the second as it swerves around the rough pillar of a termite castle, takes careful aim as it springs at him, and shoots it in the chest, rolling aside as it ploughs past him and quivers and lies still.

Yellow flames dance along the length of the mission building's roof. The truck parked in front is on fire too. A woman begins to scream, far and small in the distance. One of the soldiers from the other search party runs back up the slope, but in his panic must have forgotten about the safe path through the minefield—a lightning crack of smoke and dirt tosses his body to one side. The other three soldiers are standing back to back, shooting at random into the gathering darkness.

Nick hunkers down until the gunfire dies away. As the surviving soldiers retreat towards the burning wreckage of their camp, he makes a decision and gets up and runs in the other direction. The door of the smaller of the two sheds is fastened by a padlocked iron bar. He shoots off the padlock, lifts the bar, and drags the door open. It's very hot inside, barely lit by the green glow of a couple of dying biolumes that hang like rotten fruit from the cross-braces of the roof. The stink of sweat and sickness and human waste is incredible; Nick starts to breathe through his mouth as soon as he steps inside.

Most of the men who are sitting or sprawling in a line on the rammed-earth floor stare at him dully or seem to be asleep with their eyes open, but the three men at the front stand up as soon as they see Nick. One of them, a scrawny man in faded and frayed red shorts, his left arm withered and bent up like a chicken wing, says in English, "Are you United Nations? United Nations soldier?"

"I'll set you free," Nick says. "After that, it's up to you."

The ankles of the men are shackled together by long plastic cords, and the cords are looped around a steel chain that runs the length of the shed, welded at either end to lengths of steel girder driven deep into the hard earth floor. It takes the last two shots in the Kalashnikov's magazine to blow a link open. The three men at the front of the line immediately pull the broken chain through the loops of their shackles, but the rest stay on the floor or slowly stand up, looking around as if bewildered by their sudden freedom. They're as skinny and ragged as scarecrows, and many have the characteristic plaques and nodules and swollen joints of the early stages of the plastic disease.

The man with the withered left arm solemnly shakes Nick's hand, says that he is Louis de Dieu Nzirati. Starvation has burned away his flesh and pale hard plaques disfigure his face, but he carries himself with an irreducible dignity. He introduces the greybeard, Pascal, and the younger man, Thomas, explains that they were working for Père Mike before Lovegrave and his scientists arrived, that they're the only surviving mission workers.

"Very bad things are done here," Thomas says. He wears only a pair of filthy jogging pants, grey with a red stripe. He is shivering and hugging his bare chest, and his wide smile has nothing to do with happiness. A deep white scar cuts down the left side of his face, closing the eye. "They murdered Père Mike when he protested—they said he died of a disease, but I know they poisoned him. And now, the white-coats take children. They have taken poor Pascal's son."

Nick says, "I came with a woman. About so high, hair in braids, khaki-coloured jeans and a denim shirt. Have you seen her?"

The three men look at each other.

Grey-bearded Pascal says, "They take my son, they take boys from the village. They butcher them."

Thomas says, "Six weeks ago they do this. They work on them secretly. We don't see them, but I speak to the soldiers, I know they are still alive."

Louis says, "I work as a medical orderly. You help us save the children, I promise I show you where they take your woman for treatment."

Nick says, "What do you mean, treatment?"

Pascal says, "First you help me find my son."

Louis says, "It will take no time, I promise. You help us save the children, we help you find your woman, we all escape. Are we agreed?"

"If it takes no time," Nick says, thinking that he doesn't have much choice.

As the three men drag the broken chain through the shackles of their dull-eyed fellow prisoners and start pulling them to their feet and pushing them towards the door, the satellite phone rings, playing the famous phrase from *La Marseillaise* twice before Nick answers it.

A voice says, "Is that the Englishman?"

"Who is this?"

"The man who still has your watch."

Nick sees the grey-haired, red-eyed soldier, says, "Are you ready to give it back?"

"Why not? Just come and get it."

"Maybe I will," Nick says, shaking his head when Louis looks at him and points at the door.

Red-Eye laughs. "Man, I believe you would. But I have someone I think you would like more than any watch."

Nick has a cold, falling sensation. He says, "Let me speak to her."

"Soon. I have two men who are bringing her to me right now."

"I don't believe you," Nick says, and breaks the connection. He rips the tape that binds the spare magazine to the stock of the Kalashnikov, slams the magazine into the re-

:eiver and works the bolt, and says to Louis, "We can't bring
hese guys."

"We must," Louis says. "Dr. Todd scrambled their brains,
and they are dosed up with heroin to keep them calm, so they
:an work. They can't look after themselves—they are like
zombies. And without heroin, in a day, two days, they will
become very ill."

Pascal says, "They are our brothers. We do not leave them."

"We are responsible for them," Thomas says.

The three men standing in front of the others, looking at
Nick with nervy defiance and bravado.

"There is a barge," Louis says. "We will get them aboard
hat after we find the children. And of course, your woman."

Nick has a picture of himself leading a conga line of brain-
damaged men through the twilight and says, "No way." Louis
starts to speak, but the phone rings again, and Nick holds up
a hand, presses the phone's *yes* button, says, "You don't have
Dr. Faber, do you?"

Red-Eye says in his ear, "What is it you want? Why you
come here?"

"You know why."

"The spooks? Man, you can have them. Kill them all, I
don't care. Them, and the original one that's prob'ly still
wandering around somewhere."

"You couldn't find him, huh?"

Nick risks taking a look around the edge of the doorway
of the shed. The mission building is still burning vigorously at the top of the rise. Only a little light lingers in the
west, but the moon is rising, its half-disc big and soft and
bright.

Red-Eye says, "That was a good trick, with the phone. And
you had explosives hidden in something else, too. Or was that
your friend, blew up the house?"

"Where are we going with this?"

"I keep you talking long enough, I can pinpoint your position."

"But not my friend. Or Dogboy, come to that."

"Dogboy?"

"You don't know who I have working for me," Nick says "and you've lost a lot of men."

Cody Corbin killed four that he knows of, plus the guy in the cage, and he has killed eight himself. And then there's the guy who trod on the mine . . .

Red-Eye says, "You killed two women when you took out the mission building, motherfucker, and there's another I don't think will live. That make you happy?"

Nick says, "I also killed Captain Nsanzuwera. That's what you wanted me to do, wasn't it? So on the whole, I'd say you owe me."

"You think so, eh?"

"All I want is the white devils."

"And your woman, but I think you already have her. The two men I sent to get her aren't answering their phones."

Nick thinks of Cody Corbin, and doesn't say anything.

Red-Eye says, "You still there? I make a deal with you."

"I'm listening."

"What it is, we're pulling out. One truck, one jeep. The Rwandans, they wanted to stick around and hunt you down. They were very badly pissed off that you killed Nsanzuwera, but I fix them, you understand? You don't have to worry about them any more. So overall I would say we are quits."

"Okay," Nick says.

"You shoot at us, we'll shoot back," Red-Eye says. "Otherwise that's it."

The phone goes dead. A few moments later, a jeep and a truck drive out through the perimeter of the camp, headlights glaring as they come around the curve of the track and speed away into the darkness beyond the airstrip. Pascal and Thomas run a little way after them, dancing and whooping and hugging each other. Louis says to Nick, "Can you be sure they have all gone?"

"You can take that risk," Nick says, thinking of Cody Corbin, "or you can stay here. I know what I'm going to do."

Chapter 48

The men make a lot of noise as they move through the brush. They're silhouetted against the cloudy green glow of the bushes, stumbling it seems at every other step when the long loops of their shackles catch on tufts of grass or thorny branches, the line bunching up when one or another of them stops, Louis and Pascal and Thomas encouraging them on with urgent whispers and little slaps. Nick brings up the rear of this shambling procession, fear and impatience knotting his bowels. Half of him wants to crawl under a rock; half wants to clout every one of the zombies around the head, get them moving, get them across the stretch of scrub as quickly as possible. He imagines a sniper left behind in the soldiers' camp, equipped with night-vision goggles. He imagines Elspeth, strapped down, helpless, Tony Todd's sleek head bent over her, a circle of raggedy people in white coats holding hypodermics, trays of surgical instruments . . .

The zombies are herded past the tent over the fighting pit, down a steep path through thick vegetation, bushes and bamboos and grasses softly burning red and yellow and orange as well as the usual green, a fairyland garden of giant soft flowers. A clear flat space makes a stark shadow in the multicoloured glow, and Pascal and Thomas run down the path towards it.

When Nick and Louis catch up with them, they're struggling to pull down the big stiff bolts of the door of what looks like a freight container half-buried in the side of the slope. Ventilation holes have been crudely cut into its metal sides, and steel mesh welded over them. Nick helps Pascal and Thomas drag open the heavy door, half-choking on the thick, greasy stink that rolls out. A wedge of moonlight strikes into the metal box and Nick sees pale shapes huddled together, eyes glinting as they look up at him. He sees claw-tipped hands shielding eyes. He sees needle-filled mouths, chests and backs ridged with hard plates, scabbed wounds, fresh scars. He sees several slim, pale figures scramble to their feet and jerks up the Kalashnikov, and then he's struggling with Louis, who says loudly, "No! Do not shoot! These are the children!"

Pascal pushes past and steps inside, moving amongst the pale figures, looking closely at every face, asking the same question over and over again. One of them touches Pascal's arm and speaks softly to him, and he walks stiff-legged out into the moonlight and sits down and begins to beat his head with his fists, his grief raw and immediate and inconsolable.

The zombies stir uneasily as the pale figures creep out of the freight container like small, nervous ghosts. There are eight of them, all boys, all made over into approximations of white devils. Sharp new teeth have lacerated gums and lips, spiked through cheeks. The mouth of one boy is so full of ivory needles that he gapes like a lamprey.

Thomas lifts up the smallest child and cradles him in his arms. Tears shine on his cheeks. He says, "This is the worst place in the world."

The oldest boy steps forward and says, "The white men said they would change our minds. They said they would make us fierce. They said they would make us into soldiers. They said we were going to be sent down the river to kill many men."

He speaks formal, schoolroom French, but it's hard to understand him because a rack of spikes pushes out his upper lip and gives him a bad lisp. He's so thin that every little ridge and suture of the gristly plates of cartilage growing under the skin of his chest stands out clearly, like the bark of an ancient tree. He is trying very hard not to cry. He says that the white men tried out their techniques on the youngest boys first, that many boys died of infection or because the things the white men put in their mouths and under their skins grew too quickly. He says that some of the older boys killed themselves when they saw what they were becóming.

"We take you downriver," Louis says, "but only to make you well." Beside him, Thomas joggles the solemn little monster he cradles in his arms and kisses him and tells him that he will be made well too.

Nick steps between them and looks at Louis and says, "I asked you about the woman, and you told me she was taken to a laboratory. Where is it?"

Louis turns to point along the slope, and at the same moment, there's a clap of thunder and a tongue of smoky red flame spits out into the night, and Nick realizes at once that Cody Corbin is still alive.

The woman, Elspeth Faber, refuses to tell Cody what's inside the buried laboratory. "They had you as prisoner," he says, 'and this is your chance to get even," but she just looks at him with a thinly veiled contempt. It's the kind of look that Cody's so fucking tired of seeing, the look he's gotten all his life from people who think they know better than him. Most anybody back in the States, soon as he opened his mouth and they heard his backwoods accent; many of the so-called enlightened liberationist fighters he hung around with in Mexico; the braver of his kidnap victims; most lately the kid, Rusty, although Rusty lost it and never got it back after Cody tossed the snake at him to show him who was who and what was what. It's the look of people who think they're better than him because they've been to college and read a few books, who think knowledge is more important than belief. Man, is he ever tired of it.

He shakes her by the shoulders, says right into her face, 'What's wrong with you? I rescue you, I save your life, and you won't help me? What kind of deal is that?"

He's tempted to kill her, but he knows that Nicholas Hyde is still around, because who else would have blown up the soldiers' camp? And while that scudder's still running around, this woman could be useful. So Cody tells her that if she tries anything dumb he'll shoot her in the gut and leave her to die slowly, and drags her into the freight container.

Doors to the left and right, scientific crap piled in back, the air thick with a graveyard stink of rot and wet earth. And there, someone moving in the shadows in the right-hand doorway, an immensely fat man, big as a bear. Cody pushes Elspeth Faber aside, brings up his assault rifle. For a moment he and the man look at each other, the man's face red and white and horribly swollen like something out of a medical textbook, and then the man raises something slender and metallic and Cody shoots him, two in the chest and one in the head, and the man drops like a sack of shit. Cody steps through the smoke, steps over the body, sees in dim green light a man and two women crouching by a bed, the women screaming and hugging each other as Cody swings his rifle around, the quick burst that ends their screams loud in the metal-walled room.

Elspeth Faber is shouting at him, her voice small and flat in the echo of the gunfire, doesn't stop shouting until he slaps her so hard a comma of blood squirts from her nose.

"You should thank me," Cody says, poking at the fat man's body with his rifle, "for riddin' the world of a monster like that."

The thing the man pointed at him isn't a gun at all, he sees, but a metal cane.

"That's Lovegrave," Elspeth Faber says. She's crying, both hands lifted to her face as she presses the knuckle of her thumb to her bleeding nose. "Daniel Lovegrave. Now you've killed him, can you please stop this?"

Cody slings his rifle over his shoulder and takes out his camera and snaps a quick shot of the fat man's body, another of his swollen face. "This is the guy made the white devils? Sweet Lord Jesus, what happened to him?"

The woman starts to say something about disease, but Cody glimpses a man in a white coat dodge through the doorway behind her and grabs up his rifle and shoots and misses, sees someone else in the doorway and shoots again, this time seeing his target thrown backwards hard—a woman, the breast of her white coat quickly turning wet and red.

Cody grabs hold of Elspeth Faber's wrists, drags her with him, past the dead woman into the other room. It smells sharply of chemicals, and is full of equipment. A couple of glass-fronted incubators that according to their digital read-outs are set at blood temperature, their shelves crowded with stacks of petri dishes and flat-sided bottles half-filled with cloudy liquid. A bench with a microwave oven and a couple of pressure cookers. The steel drum of a big centrifuge. Plastic crates crowded with brown-glass solvent bottles. After Cody has checked that no one is hiding behind any of this stuff, he pulls out the little camera and starts taking pictures, telling Elspeth Faber, "I got this idea from my last client. Figure it'll be good publicity if people can see what I put away. That rig is for sequencing DNA, but it doesn't look as if it's been workin' for a while, does it? And those three things, like hot-water cylinders, with the pipes comin' out of them? They're culture vessels."

"For yeast," Elspeth Faber says.

"Mutant yeast, uh? What about these?" Cody says, framing a shot of dozens of glass aquarium tanks racked along one wall, each full of tiny flies swirling like smoke over what looks like a finger's breadth of blood, the blood under a kind of skin or membrane crawling with more flies.

"Blackflies," Elspeth Faber says. "I think they're one of Tony Todd's little projects—I think they might be carrying the plastic disease."

"We're going to find ourselves somewhere safe," Cody says, "so you can sit down and tell me all about everything, on camera."

He sets his rucksack amongst the solvent bottles, pushes her outside. The fire in the house at the top of the slope is dying back. The half-moon hangs a hand's span above the desolation across the river, dimming the patchwork colours of the scrub. Cody walks Elspeth Faber up the path to where the three dead men lie, shows her the little radio switch, says, "You want the honour? No?" and presses it.

The muffled explosion of the kilo of Semtex is not very loud, but it blows a long tongue of red flame out of the open door of the freight container. The ground shudders under Cody's boots and a great slide of dirt and rocks rattles down, running out past either side of the container.

Cody waits a few minutes, but nothing comes out of the freight container, and no one comes down the path. No, wait. Something is moving down the slope way off in the distance, a line of people it looks like, shadows against the multi-coloured clouds of vegetation. Cody lifts his field glasses to his eyes, focuses on the line of men, sees small, pale, naked figures moving with them.

"Look at that," he says. But the woman is running away down the slope, crashing through bushes glowing blue and red and yellow, stumbling and going down on her knees and getting up and running on, running pretty well for someone with her wrists bound together. Cody trots after her, thinking why is it that they always have to try and make a run for it? He catches up with her the third time she falls down, just past a couple of freight containers that sit at the edge of a kind of big step cut into the slope. He gets a good grip on a handful of her braids, pulls up her head, and says, "I helped your friend escape, you dumb cunt. *I'm on your side.*"

"I saw someone," she says.

"I saw 'em too," Cody says. "Men and monsters, headin' down to that barge down on the river, I reckon. Looks like we still got a little work to do."

He's pulling her to her feet when he hears voices, sees two shadows moving through the skimpy green-and-yellow light of the bush on the far side of the wide apron of cleared and levelled earth. He clamps a hand over Elspeth Faber's mouth and pulls her back into the shadows between the freight containers as the two men start across the clearing. One of them—thank You, Lord—is Nicholas Hyde.

The hard, bright light of the rising half-moon bleaches colour from the glow of the bamboos and tall grasses; Nick thinks that it's like walking through an underexposed black-and-white photograph. Across the river, the Dead Zone shines like a field of ice. Ahead, a thinning finger of black smoke drifts from the top of the slope. Cody Corbin is out there somewhere, looking for monsters to kill. And Elspeth . . .

Don't let her be dead, Nick thinks as he skirts the edge of a pond. Let her be okay. Let me find her. Pale islands of scum revolve on black water, giving off a strong, sharp, sweet smell like windfall apples rotting down to mulch. He forces himself to go slow, to creep from shadow to shadow, to stop, check the way ahead, move on. Thinking, let me find her, let her be safe, let us get out of this. These words running around and around in his head like the childish prayers he'd offer up in moments of extremity, to appease one of his mother's sudden rages, before an exam, the one time he'd boxed in an interschool tournament. Maybe she wasn't in the laboratory, he thinks. Maybe they took her somewhere else. Not to the mission building, because Red-Eye would have used her to bargain with me, because I would have killed her when I blew it up, but somewhere safe.

A narrow path leads through brush towards a stretch of flat ground cut into the slope. Two freight containers squat side by side, edges gleaming in the moonlight. Nick is creeping towards the edge of the brush when he hears someone smashing through vegetation behind him. He turns and raises the Kalashnikov just as Pascal steps into a patch of moonlight, thin and ragged as a ghoul.

"I come with you," Pascal says. He is breathing hard through his mouth, his naked chest rising and falling with each breath. He is clutching a long-handled shovel. He gives Nick a fierce, desperate look and says, "We find the people who killed my son."

Nick keeps his gaze on the man's face and says that they have to be super-careful. "We can't be sure that all the soldiers have gone. And there's another man, a very bad guy—"

Pascal says, "I kill him. And kill the white-coats who kill my son. I kill them all," and pushes past Nick and starts across the stretch of open ground, walking quickly and then seeming to trip, going down to one knee and dropping the shovel, reaching for it when the second shot, fired into the echo of the first, knocks him onto his back.

Nick rolls behind a heap of earth, hears someone say his name as he brings the Kalashnikov to bear, and there's Elspeth, standing in the gap between two freight containers at the far edge of the flat space, her head tipped back because Cody Corbin, standing right behind her, is pulling on a handful of her braids. Moonlight slides on the long barrel of the Colt Python; its muzzle rests under Elspeth's chin, in the hollow behind the hinge of her jaw.

Nick can't get a clear shot.

The mercenary says loudly, looking this way and that, "I believe that was you blew up those soldiers. Not a bad job." He pulls hard on Elspeth's braids, hard enough to make her gasp. He says, "I don't want to mess up your girlfriend's fine looks. Why don't you step out where I can see you, so we can have a civilized talk?"

Nick stands up, the metal stock of the Kalashnikov socketed firmly in his shoulder, its muzzle pointing at Elspeth.

"Hey," Elspeth says.

"Hey."

Cody Corbin says, "What I can't figure out is, if you blew up the soldiers, and I blew up the scientists, who are those people with the monsters?"

Nick says, "They're not any part of this."

"I saw the monsters," the mercenary says.

"They're children," Nick says. "Innocent children. Tony Todd mutilated them. He wanted to make more white devils, and the best he could do was disfigure children with implants."

"He's telling the truth," Elspeth says. "Lovegrave told me all about it."

Cody Corbin says to Nick, "Are you fixin' to take them away? I thought you want them as dead as I do."

He's standing right behind Elspeth. Nick can't see much more of him than a sliver of his face, the hand holding the gun to her head.

"I was fixing to find Dr. Faber," Nick says, "but you've saved me the trouble."

His voice sounding to him flat and unconvincing as it carries across the wide moonlit space.

Elspeth says, "He killed Tony Todd, Nick. And Danny Lovegrave, too."

"He did? Between us," Nick says to Cody Corbin, "I think we did a pretty good job."

Trying to get the man on his side. Smiling at him, trying to swallow the sick feeling he has, seeing Elspeth helpless with the gun pressed under her jaw.

The mercenary says, "You got any Semtex left?"

Nick sees movement in the tall, moon-whitened grass to the left of the two freight containers. He says, "The mission building and the satellite phone that killed Captain Nsanzuwera took everything I had."

"The bomb in the phone was a neat trick," Cody Corbin says. "I'll have to remember that one. I see you have the rifle you shot at me with, I believe a Kalashnikov. Reliable guns, Kalashnikovs, but none too accurate, uh?"

There's definitely someone moving through the grass. Just one person, Nick thinks. Maybe one of the soldiers was left behind, or perhaps it's one of the white-coats. He says, "If you think you still have business here, why don't you let Dr. Faber go?"

Cody Corbin jabs Elspeth hard with the Colt Python, pushing its muzzle into her jaw so that she has to stand on tiptoe. He says, "What you're goin' to do is raise the rifle over your head, then throw it away far as you can. After that, we can walk down to where your friends are gettin' ready to make off in that barge, and we'll see what's what. Otherwise I blow your girlfriend's motherfuckin' head off and deal with you afterward. Your choice."

Nick says, "Let's leave her out of this. How about just you and me? Your father's Colt against my Kalashnikov. What do you say?"

"I say you're pretty desperate."

Nick can hear the smile in the man's voice. He says, "I'm

as much a monster as anything here, remember? Let Elspeth go, and we'll square off. Lay our guns on the ground and give a count and go for them."

"Or how about I shoot your girlfriend if you don't give up the rifle?"

"You know that if you shoot her, I'll shoot you. We can take position at either end of this clearing. Like, if you remember the movie, Clint Eastwood and Lee Van Cleef."

Cody Corbin points his big handgun at Nick, says, "Then how about I just shoot you?"

"I'll put down the rifle," Nick says, "and we can talk, okay?"

He takes a breath, then raises the Kalashnikov above his head and sets it down. Stands still, every square centimetre of his skin tingling. The mercenary pushes Elspeth forward, out of the shadows between the two freight containers, and she suddenly bucks away from him and starts to run. Cody Corbin fires a single shot that cracks past Nick, no more than a metre from his head, and Elspeth stops at once, standing with her head down and her bound wrists crossed in front of her.

"You think she hoped to get away while you and I had it out," the mercenary says, "or did she maybe think you'd grab up the rifle and shoot me when I shot her?"

Nick lets out the breath he has been holding. His heart is loud in his head. He says, "No one has to shoot anyone."

"No, sir," Cody Corbin says, still pointing the big handgun at Nick, "we have some monsters to get rid of. Like I said, you can help me, or I shoot you, and then I shoot your girlfriend. You stand up now, walk yourself over here."

Right in front of Elspeth, a pale misshapen person parts the tall grass like a curtain and steps through. It's the white devil. It's Dogboy. Dogboy rises up on the balls of its feet, its gargoyle face level with Elspeth's waist, its nostrils flaring. Elspeth stands absolutely still. Cody Corbin twitches his head to see what Nick is staring at, and Dogboy runs straight at him.

The mercenary gets off one shot before the white devil knocks him down. He tries to get his hand under its chin, but it snaps sideways, quick as a snake, and bites off several of his fingers. The Colt Python goes off again, muffled, firing into the ground, and then the white devil is worrying at the man's throat, and he's kicking and shuddering under its weight.

Elspeth runs towards Nick, gets in front of him, her arms spread wide, and he says it's okay, he isn't going to shoot anyone. She lowers her arms and steps towards him. He gets a glimpse of Cody Corbin and the white devil, and looks away. Dogboy is feeding now.

"We can't leave him here," Elspeth says as she comes into Nick's embrace. "We're going to have to bring him with us."

Chapter 49

The barge is twenty metres from stem to stern, broad-beamed and low in the water. Every seam of its steel hull weeps rust and the red paint of the little tin-roofed wheelhouse at the stern is shabby and faded, but the beat of its twin diesel engines is strong and steady. Nicholas Hyde, perched on a coil of oily rope at the blunt point of the bow, can feel it throbbing through the deck. He's been keeping watch there for the past three hours, shining a flashlight into misty darkness and looking out for snags and shoals and sandbanks. His eyes sting, and his throat aches from shouting advice to Thomas, who has taken over the wheel from Elspeth. Now, half-past five in the morning, the sky is rapidly brightening, and the river is growing broader, its currents stronger. Curtains of mist blow apart, and for a moment Nick glimpses a long reach of water flashing far ahead.

The barge has been creeping along at not much more than walking pace, but now the big diesels make a throaty roar as Thomas throttles them up. A fat cloud of blue smoke puffs from the stovepipe exhaust that juts over the stern, and the barge drives with increasing speed through coils and drifts of mist smoking off the water.

Nick stands and stretches, limps towards the wheelhouse. The passenger in the forward hold starts making a lot of noise, beating on the steel plates of the floor, slamming to and fro against the steel walls. Perhaps it hears or smells him as he goes past, or perhaps it is disturbed by the increased vibration of the diesels. By contrast, the men crowded together in the narrow space between the two cargo holds are asleep or nodding out; only one is on his feet, his arms wrapped around his bare chest, his head tucked to one side, a silver strand of drool connecting his chin to his shoulder. Like the others, he's shackled to the rope that's stretched between bolts in the covers of the cargo wells, and can only shuffle a few paces towards Nick before he's brought up short, the poor guy holding out his hands, pale palms up, saying, "Muh muh. Muh muh."

"Wants his shot," Thomas says. He stands inside the wheelhouse, looking at Nick through the window he has slid open to catch any breeze. Although it's not quite dawn, the air is already hot and close.

Nick leans on the sill and says, "You can slow down, Thomas. It would be a shame to hit something and sink this fine boat."

"I saw the big river."

"We'll get there."

"It is more than five hundred kilometres to Kinshasa. Even though we travel with the current, it will take two or three days. The zombies will be all right without their heroin for a few more hours, perhaps until the evening. But then they will get a fever, they will sweat and shiver and shake. After that . . ." Thomas makes a shrugging movement with his head.

"If we burn up all the fuel, or hit a snag or a sandbank, we'll be laid up a lot longer than a couple of days," Nick says.

Thomas stares at him. His one good eye is bloodshot and open too wide.

"Think about it," Nick says. "Even if we double our speed, those poor guys are going to be hurting long before we get anywhere we can find help."

"Maybe so," Thomas says after a few moments, and takes one hand off the wheel and racks back the throttle, catches the wheel again as the barge, slowing, slews a little in the current.

Nick says, "How are you holding up?"

Thomas's smile twists the long scar down the side of his face. "I'm good. I'm strong. You don't have to worry about me."

The man telling himself as much as Nick.

Nick grins and says, "We got away, didn't we?"

Thomas's smile broadens. "I take us all the way."

Elspeth climbs out of the hatch in the deck to the side of the wheelhouse, stepping off the ladder that slants down to the windowless crew space, with its big table and filthy kitchen nook and tiers of narrow bunk beds. She is carrying half a dozen ration packs stacked against her denim shirt, the topmost caught under her chin. She says, "The kids are mostly asleep. Louis was sleeping too, and then the phone rang. Your English friend, wanting to talk to him again."

Last night, Nick asked his Wizard to find the number of Lucy Stewart, the PR guru. He phoned her and left a message; when she phoned back less than ten minutes later he handed the phone to Louis and told him to tell the woman his story.

"She works hard to stay at the top of the PR business," Nick says now to Elspeth, and switches to French, tells Thomas about the call.

"I don't mind it," Thomas says, "if she gets us the money she promises."

"You sound doubtful," Nick says.

"I know you want to help us," Thomas says. "But unless this woman can do magic, what good are her promises?"

"She makes money from thin air," Nick says, "so I guess she *is* a kind of magician."

Thomas says, "Right now we need medicine for the children. The zombies need heroin. But it is no good wishing for them."

Nick says, "You're a practical man."

Thomas says, "After Nsanzuwera and his soldiers came, after things got very bad for us, my friend Simon built a little aeroplane from sticks. He said that in the night it would change into a real aeroplane. He said that he would fly all of us to Paris. Of course, it did not happen. It was only an idea of an aeroplane; it was only sticks and string." Thomas goes away for a moment, looking at something inside his head, then says, "Two weeks later, Simon went into the pit, and the white devils killed and ate him. You really think that's the kind of story this woman can sell?"

Elspeth sets the stack of ration packs on the deck, leans against the rail, and stares out at the river. She feels dull and stupid with lack of sleep and unspent fear, is only vaguely aware of Nick and Thomas's conversation. The barge's twin screws make a smooth double hump that spews out long streamers of creamy bubbles, these lines of foam diminishing as they float away on black water under layers of mist. Mist winds through the tops of the young trees that stand up to their knees in water on either side of the wide river, the trees swaying when the wash of the barge hits them, trees and river dwindling away into thickening mist, mist and darkness swallowing up everything that has happened since poor, foolish Teddy Yssel betrayed them to Captain Nsanzuwera.

She has the same breathless sense of suspension that she felt just before she arrived at the refugee camp and found out what had happened to her father, saw what he had brought with him out of the heart of the Dead Zone. She has already decided what she has to do, she borrowed the satellite phone and discussed it with David Oloitip, but she isn't sure how to begin to tell Nick about her plans, or how to tell him about Danny Lovegrave's last little surprise.

She doesn't turn around when she hears him step up behind her. He says, "I think I caught sight of the confluence just now, so I guess we made about sixty kilometres in the night."

Trying to sound reassuring, but mostly sounding tired.

Elspeth says, "We've got a long journey ahead of us. Maybe we should find some place to pull in, rest up for a few hours."

"Once we reach the big river," Nick says, "there will be islands. We could stop at one, sleep out the heat of the day."

"In hammocks," Elspeth says, looking at him.

His eyes are red-rimmed and his short black hair is matted with dirt. He's unshaven, and the left side of his face is swollen and tender from the beating he got when he tried to escape from the animal shed. The legs of his jeans are raggedly cut off at mid-thigh. The bandage wrapped around his left leg, above the knee, is spotted with dried brown blood. As far as Elspeth is concerned, he still looks pretty terrific.

He smiles and says, "Definitely in hammocks. In some shady spot where we can reach out to pluck fruit from the vine."

Thomas makes a short, forceful speech in French, and Nick tells Elspeth that he wants them to know that he won't stop unless they decide to bury Pascal's body. "He wants to keep going," Nick says. "He wants to put a good distance between ourselves and that place, and never look back."

"He has the right idea," Elspeth says, and nudges the stack of ration packs with a foot. "I brought you guys breakfast, if you want it."

"I don't think I can eat anything just yet," Nick says, "but our guest is awake and making a lot of noise. Maybe food will shut it up."

Elspeth kneels and shuffles through the packs, holds one up and says, "Why don't we see if he likes beef Stroganoff?"

"Muh," the man says, holding out his hands to Elspeth, to Nick, as they go past. "Muh muh."

"This wasn't what I pictured," Nick says. "Rescuing a bunch of brain-burned heroin addicts."

Elspeth says, "And the children."

Nick says, "I guess that's something."

Letting his tiredness show in his voice now, in his face.

Elspeth says, "What did you expect? A megalomaniac with a secret headquarters and a private army and a plan to hold the world to ransom?"

"And a white cat. Or maybe a mutant cat, with two heads and no hair. Instead I got Captain Nsanzuwera and that weird little guy, Tony Todd. I didn't even see Lovegrave."

"He was there all right."

"I didn't get to see the blackflies, either."

Elspeth remembers the glass tanks, each containing thousands of tiny flies swirling like smoke over a finger's breadth of blood. She says, "Cody Corbin took pictures with that little camera. You're welcome to check them out."

"I met a doctor back in Brazzaville who said that there was a new strain of plastic disease spreading along the river. You really think this is where it came from?"

"That's what Danny Lovegrave wanted me to think."

"With all the key players dead and the laboratory destroyed, it's going to be hard to prove."

Elspeth points at the zombies, says, "Half those poor guys are infected with it. We can isolate the bacteria from them, sequence the DNA, compare it with the DNA of this new strain in Green Congo . . . Of course, proving that the Loyalists are breaking international law by using biological weapons will only help Obligate."

Nick looks at her, serious and cool and determined, and says, "I think Obligate will have plenty of problems of their own after the media gets hold of the story of how Teryl Meade tried to cover up the existence of the white devils."

They pull away the square of buckled plywood that covers the hole in the platform over the forward hold. The white devil, Dogboy, stops beating on the wall and squints shyly up at them, like a schoolboy caught in the middle of some minor bit of naughtiness. Frayed fragments of bitten-through rope are strewn all around him. Elspeth drops in the ration pack and he sidles towards it, his head cocked, nostrils flaring, suddenly peaceful.

"If you can spare a piece of clothing," Nick says, "we can drop it in, keep him quiet that way."

"That's not a bad idea."

Like the saber-toothed cats, the original white devils were hardwired to recognize the scent of Danny Lovegrave and Elspeth's father. Last night, she walked right up to Dogboy, and he turned from the bloody mess he was making of Cody Corbin and meekly submitted when she lowered the loop of rope over him. He only began to panic when Nick and Elspeth started to drag him towards the barge. He pulled back, squalling and thrashing, and when they proved stronger suddenly ran forward and slashed Nick's leg with his claws before Nick managed to knock him out with the metal stock of the Kalashnikov.

On the barge, while Louis cleaned and bandaged Nick's wound, Elspeth found the courage to start to tell them about her conversation with Danny Lovegrave, the story he'd told her about how he'd arranged the escape of the white devils.

"Uncle Danny and his little tricks," Elspeth said. "I think he really did love them, in his own way. He set them free rather than let them be used by the Loyalists. They were his children, his lost boys."

Hesitating then, wondering if she should show Nick what Danny Lovegrave had passed to her with his very last bit of sleight of hand.

Louis asked her to put her finger on the knot as he tied the bandage around Nick's leg, and said, "It was different with the children. Dr. Todd could not repeat Dr. Lovegrave's work, so he used surgery instead. He didn't think we knew, it was supposed to be secret, but the other white-coats talked about it in front of me and Thomas and Pascal because they did not think we understood."

Nick and Louis started talking about Tony Todd's plan to butcher children into *kidogo* versions of the white devils, the moment passed, and then they were too busy—finding out how to start up the barge's big diesel engines, getting the children and the zombies settled, anxious to get away in case the soldiers came back—to talk any more.

Now, looking down into the hold, watching as the white devil strips back the foil covering of the ration pack with his rack of spiky teeth and starts lapping up the cold stew, Elspeth thinks that there's a way of working around to telling Nick about what Danny Lovegrave gave her and what she plans to do. She says, "Tony Todd's butchery of those poor boys can be fixed, but Dogboy is what he is. The claws and the teeth, the hardwired behaviour and accelerated maturity and all the rest, they're in his genes, they can't be erased. But they don't make him any less human. My father said that the Gentle People were important because they were intermediates between modern humans and the common ancestor of hominids and primates. The white devils—essentially, they're no different from the Gentle People. They're intermediates too."

"Two sides of the same coin," Nick says.

Elspeth says, "We were talking about islands . . . I want to find an island for Dogboy where he can live in peace."

As soon as they were safely under way last night, she borrowed the satellite phone and called David Oloitip and told him what had happened, what she was bringing back with her. David listened patiently, and told her that he couldn't promise anything, but he would do his best. Now she feels immediate relief when Nick understands and tells her he thinks it's a good idea.

"And if any of the other white devils are still alive," he says, "perhaps they could live there too. Like the Gentle People."

"I have money coming to me, from my father's patents. It seems somehow appropriate to use it to look after this poor little guy, maybe even try to find out how to help him." Elspeth digs with two fingers into the breast pocket of her denim shirt, lifts out a little rectangle of blue plastic, a memory card, says, "I found this in my jeans pocket—another of Uncle Danny's conjuring tricks. I used your phone to take a look at what was on it. Dozens of sound files, it turns out, and every one I sampled is Danny Lovegrave talking about his research. About the Gentle People and the white devils." She pauses, then says, "One file, a short one, was labelled with my name. It's a kind of confession, telling me what the white devils really are."

"They aren't gengineered children?"

"They're that, all right, but a very particular kind."

She watches Nick think about this. At last, he says, "They're clones of Lovegrave, aren't they?"

"Of Lovegrave and my father. In the message he left for me, Lovegrave says that he used up his stock of *in vitro* fertilized human embryos when he made the Gentle People, but he had a stock of unfertilized eggs stored in liquid nitrogen. He created the white devils using a variation on the standard Roslin technique. He took epithelial cells from himself and my father, and gengineered them to shut off certain developmental genes and add others. One of the added genes coded for antibiotic resistance, so he could isolate and grow up successfully treated cells in culture. He fused the cells with enucleated eggs, shocked the eggs to trigger development, and implanted the viable embryos in refugee women who carried them to term. So I guess Dogboy is either my father or Lovegrave. Not that I want to find out."

"He's neither," Nick says. "Trust me on that, I do know a little bit about clones. What do you want to do with this?"

"Danny Lovegrave was supposed to change my mind, condition me so that I would be loyal to Nsanzuwera. But instead he secretly stuck a drug patch on my neck and put me to sleep. I think he hoped that because Nsanzuwera would believe that I'd been conditioned, I'd no longer be treated like a prisoner, and I'd get a chance to escape. We came here to find out the truth, to speak for our dead. Danny Lovegrave gave the truth to us."

"The blackflies, the white devils . . . We'll have to get our stories straight before we reach Kinshasa."

They smile at each other, and Elspeth wonders if Nick feels as shy and uncertain as she does. This is the first time they've been alone since . . . when? Since the time they plotted against Teddy and Kanana, and she told him how Danny Lovegrave and her father and Teryl had made the Gentle People from human stock. She wasn't sure what he wanted to do then; she isn't now.

"I have some news, as well," Nick says. "Apparently, my mother is in Kinshasa. With her lawyer and an ex-SAS guy who said, at the one news conference they held, he has every confidence that he'll be able to find me. I suppose they tracked the release of the video clip to Raphael's web server, like you. Or perhaps one of Raphael's men found out about the reward that my mother's lawyer is offering for my safe return."

"I wondered why you went so quiet after you talked with your Wizard last night. What are you going to do?"

"It told me something else, the answer to a question I asked what seems like a hundred years ago, in Brazzaville. It's found someone in Cape Town who can provide me with a completely new, clean identity. All I have to do is make a call, fly to South Africa and pay the woman ten thousand dollars, and within twenty-four hours I'll be someone else, free to go anywhere in the world."

"Is that what you want?" Elspeth says, and at the same moment Louis scrambles out of the hatch beside the wheelhouse and calls to them. He holds the satellite phone over his head and does a little dance, his bare feet slapping the planking of the deck. Thomas talks to him in French, speaking too quickly for Elspeth to follow, and Louis shakes his head, sets down the satellite phone, and goes to the stern and picks up a blue plastic bucket. The bucket's handle is tied to a length of rope. Louis lowers it over the side and hauls it back up, using his knees and his one good hand, gets a grip on the edge and swiftly inverts it over his head, spluttering and blowing and blinking in the quick downpour. He grins at Nick and Elspeth as they walk towards him, says, "We are going to be rich, Thomas and me."

"Lucy Stewart came through," Nick says.

Louis says, "She sells our story. She says for tens of thousands of dollars. She says, get a lawyer."

"It's good advice," Nick says.

Thomas is watching them through the open door of the

wheelhouse. He and Louis talk in French, and then Louis says in English, "Better than the money, she arrange for us to be picked up. There is an abandoned town, fifty, sixty kilometres downstream from where we are now. When we get there, a helicopter will be waiting. A Chinook. Paid for by CNN. It will take all of us to Kinshasa."

Elspeth looks at Nick, who smiles back and shrugs.

"Thomas and me," Louis says, "we want to start a new mission. A place run by Congolese, for Congolese. We talk about it all the time we are held prisoner. How I came to work at the mission, it was after I was shot by bandits. I was a truck driver, and they hijack my truck, shoot me when I run away. I was shot in my shoulder, which is why my arm is useless. Père Mike treated me and saved my life, and I felt it was my duty to repay the debt. So I stayed at the mission, and Père Mike taught me some medicine. Pascal and Thomas too—that's why we weren't made into zombies when Lovegrave's people took over. So now, Thomas and me, we build a new mission. We look after the zombies there, maybe other people if we can. But first, we tell our story. We tell everyone what was done there."

Something moves in the hatch beside the wheelhouse. Elspeth sees a crooked white starfish tipped by black thorns reach out of the darkness within the square opening and grope blindly at the raised edge. Another starfish climbs beside it, and they grip the edge of the hatch and a head rises out of the darkness: brown, human eyes in a face as white as death, a mouth that's trying to shape a smile around a snaggled crowd of little ivory knives and blades. It's the youngest of the boys. He gets a leg over the edge of the hatch and hangs there awkwardly for a moment, his hands trapped by the ridged keg of his chest, a frown creasing his forehead as he tries to work out the mechanics of his position.

Thomas whistles to get everyone's attention, points ahead. The young trees crowding along the edges of the river have peeled back on either side, revealing a wide expanse of dark water that stretches away under a bank of mist. It's the Congo River. There's a distinct boundary, a roiling, braided mass of

currents, where the smaller river runs into it. Tree-clad islands loom out of the mist like ghostly ships wrecked at the
edge of the world.

The little boy throws his arms forward and hooks his claws
into a joint of the splintered planking and hauls himself up,
feet awkwardly splayed on either side of the hatch's rim, his
pale behind arched up and his head tucked down. Elspeth and
Nick smile at each other. Just as the little boy gets to his feet,
the barge rocks over clashing currents at the confluence of
the Congo River and its tributary. The boy staggers, and Nick
scoots forward and scoops him up before he can fall. The
child frowns at Nick, as if trying to decide whether to laugh
or cry, and then relaxes against his chest.

Thomas hauls on the wheel and the barge turns east, into
the rising sun. A blaze of white light fills the long reaches of
mist above the river's dark, muscular flow with evanescent
rainbows. Across two kilometres of water, the line of the forest along the far bank flares like a vivid green fuse.

Elspeth says to Nick, "Are you serious, about running
away, changing your identity?"

"I asked my Wizard to arrange it after all that fuss about
the massacre, after my mother found out that I was in Brazzaville. It seemed a sensible precaution at the time."

"And now?"

She has that breathless feeling again, a dizzy yawn in the
pit of her stomach.

Nick gives her one of his calm, deadpan looks. "Now the
whole world knows about the peculiar circumstances of my
birth, I think it would take a little more than a new passport to
find a new hiding place, don't you?"

"I had the idea that you were going to walk away, like one
of those old movie heroes."

"I hear there's some interesting palaeontological work being done at Lake Turkana. Maybe I can help out."

"Not for a while. The season's over, we have a lot of technical work to do on this year's finds, we have to find new
funding . . ." For the first time in days, she thinks of Harry
Brenner's media conference; the story about the white devils

is going to blow it out of the water. "Besides, I'm not even sure if I'll have a career after this. Louis and Thomas want to tell the world what happened to them, and you want to tell the truth about what killed your friends. The best I can do is try to shelter Dogboy from the fallout."

The little boy in Nick's lap yawns, showing far too many sharp teeth. Nick joggles him, says, "Why don't I help you? After all, I probably know more about the white devils than anyone else in the world, and Dogboy and me, we're both in need of a hiding place. I might have to borrow one of your T-shirts, though, so he'll think I'm part of the family."

"I'm sure we can work something out."

They smile at each other.

Nick says, "We'll take it easy, see what happens."

"Right."

"But the first thing I have to do," Nick says, "is find my mother. It's time I made her understand exactly who I am."